I0592301

Trübner and Co

The Westminster Review

New series. Vol. XLIII.

Trübner and Co

The Westminster Review
New series. Vol. XLIII.

ISBN/EAN: 9783742827555

Manufactured in Europe, USA, Canada, Australia, Japa

Cover: Foto ©Andreas Hilbeck / pixelio.de

Manufactured and distributed by brebook publishing software
(www.brebook.com)

Trübner and Co

The Westminster Review

THE

WESTMINSTER

REVIEW.

JANUARY AND APRIL,
1873.

"Truth can never be confirm'd enough,
Though doubts did ever sleep."
SHAKSPEARE.

Wahrheitsliebe zeigt sich darin, daß man überall das Gute zu finden und zu schätzen weiß.
GOETHE.

NEW SERIES.
VOL. XLIII.

LONDON:
TRÜBNER & CO, 57 & 59, LUDGATE HILL.
MDCCCLXXIII.

LONDON :

SAVILL, EDWARDS AND CO., PRINTERS, CHANDOS STREET,

COVENT GARDEN.

CONTENTS.

ART.   PAGE

I. *Sophokles.*

    1. Sophokles, erklärt von F. W. Schneidewin. Sechste Auflage, besorgt von A. Nauck. Berlin. 1871.

    2. The Tragedies of Sophocles, with a Biographical Essay. By E. H. Plumptre, M.A. London. 1867.

    3. Die Religiösen und Sittlichen Vorstellungen des Aeschylos und Sophokles. Von Gustav Dronke. Leipzig. 1861.

    4. Sophokles und seine Tragödien. Von O. Ribbeck. Heft 83 in der Sammlung gemeinverständlicher wissenschaftlicher Vorträge. Berlin. 1869   1

II. *Parliamentary Eloquence.*

    1. A Book of Parliamentary Anecdote. Compiled from Authentic Sources. By G. H. Jennings and W. S. Johnstone. Cassell, Petter, and Galpin : London, Paris, and New York. 1872.

    2. The Orator : a Treasury of English Eloquence, containing Selections from the most Celebrated Speeches of the Past and Present. Edited, with Short Explanatory Notes and References, by a Barrister. London : S. O. Beeton.

    3. Select British Eloquence, embracing the best Speeches entire of the most Eminent Orators of Great Britain for the last Two Centuries ; with Sketches of their Lives, an estimate of their Genius, and Notes Critical and Explanatory. By Chauncey A. Goodrich, D.D., Professor in Yale College, New Haven, Conn., U.S. London : Sampson Low and Co.

    4. Parliamentary Logic : to which are subjoined two Speeches delivered in the House of Commons of Ireland, and other pieces. By the Right Hon. William Gerard Hamilton. London. 1798.

    5. Hansard. New Series   38

ART.   PAGE

III. *The Decline of the Old French Monarchy.*

     1. Histoire de France au Dix-huitième Siècle. Par J. MICHELET. Paris. 1867.

     2. Mémoires du Duc de Luynes sur la Cour de Louis Quinze (1735-1758). Publiés sous le Patronage de M. le Duc de Luynes, par MM. Dussieux et E. Soulié. Paris.

     3. Journal et Mémoires du Marquis d'Argenson. Publiés pour la première fois d'après les Manuscrits Autographes de la Bibliothèque du Louvre, &c., par M. Rathery. Paris .   70

IV. *Religion as a Subject of National Education* .   . 111

V. *The Republicans of the Commonwealth.*   Part II.

     1. Essays on Historical Truth. By Andrew Bisset. London. 1871.

     2. The Lives of William Cavendish, Duke of Newcastle, and of his wife Margaret, Duchess of Newcastle. Written by the thrice noble and illustrious Princess, Margaret, Duchess of Newcastle. Edited by Mark Antony Lower, M.A. London. 1872 146

VI. *The Christian Evidence Society.*

     Modern Scepticism. Sixth Edition. Faith and Free Thought. Hodder and Stoughton. 1872 186

VII. *The Gladstone Administration* 208

Contemporary Literature.

     Theology and Philosophy 242
     Politics, Sociology, Voyages and Travels 263
     Science 292
     History and Biography 301
     Belles Lettres 318
     Art 336

THE

WESTMINSTER

AND

FOREIGN QUARTERLY

REVIEW.

JANUARY 1, 1873.

ART. I.—SOPHOKLES.

1. *Sophokles, erklärt von* F. W. SCHNEIDEWIN. *Sechste Auflage,
   besorgt von* A. NAUCK. Berlin. 1871.
2. *The Tragedies of Sophocles, with a Biographical Essay.*
   By E. H. PLUMPTRE, M.A. London. 1867.
3. *Die Religösen und Sittlichen Vorstellungen des Aeschylos
   und Sophokles.* Von GUSTAV DRONKE. Leipzig. 1861.
4. *Sophokles und seine Tragödien.* Von O. RIBBECK. *Heft
   63 in der Sammlung gemeinverständlicher wissenschaftlicher Vorträge.* Berlin. 1869.

ENGLISH scholarship has not done much for the better
understanding of Sophokles. He is not a poet who has
taken close hold of the English mind. His works are studied of
course in the general university curriculum ; but he has not become
a poet often read and oftener quoted as have some of the classic
writers. Those who really find in him a source of intellectual
delight read his works in a German edition. But of what classical
writer may not this be said ? It is very seldom that an English
editor has the patience to make a complete presentation of a
classical author—to do for him what Professor Munro has done for
Lucretius—with that loving study and exhaustive research which
characterize the labours of the German editor. So far the case
of Sophokles is not single. But perhaps there is no instance of
an author of such renown as Sophokles, with so general a con-
sensus of people willing to admit his claims, who has made so
little impression upon the majority of cultivated minds. The

reason is that the majority of cultivated people never bring themselves under his influence. The English scholar is for the
most part satisfied with a textual or critical knowledge: the
whole field of classical literature must be hurried through rather
than any part explored. And the result of this is scholarship
rather than knowledge.

Now with many authors this may be sufficient; it cannot be
so with all. Homer, for instance, will give up his beauties in
broad and easily taken bands of continuous narrative. Apart
from the necessities of philological studies, which are beside the
present question, Homer, like Chaucer, is easy reading. Those
that run may read the *alto rilievo* of the Iliad or Odyssey. But
before a group of statuary you must *stand.* And the difficulty
is that the intellectual life of the present day does not admit of
long standing. The progress of science and the march of new
ideas are continually urging on the student mind. And to almost
all the doubt must occasionally present itself, Is it worth while
to spend this time before these works of ancient art? Now,
whatever the answer to this question may be, it is certain that
the secret of Sophokles cannot be won without loving and
leisurely study. For in his works exists the highest form of one
species of art; and that an art which will yield its essence to no
hurried student. It is a significant circumstance that few English
translations of the works of Sophokles have been attempted.
The version of Mr. Plumptre is the fourth of its kind. Those
that have preceded it are of little importance. It is true that no
author suffers more from translation than Sophokles: but that
is the least element in the unpopularity of his dramas amongst
English readers. The reader unacquainted with the Greek
language may yet be fascinated by the "tale of Troy divine"
in the musical and monotonous lines of Pope, or the inadequate
interpretations of Cowper and Lord Derby: he may even, if he
be a Keats, find his vision dazzled by the misty prospect which
he catches of the vast Homeric continent; but he is not at all
likely to be charmed with Sophokles. To understand Sophokles
one must place oneself in the intellectual position of an average
Athenian of the time of Perikles. Mr. Galton says[*]: "The
average ability of the Athenian race is, on the lowest possible
estimate, very nearly two grades higher than our own—that is,
about as much as our race is above that of the African negro."
The average English reader, therefore, whose knowledge of
Sophokles is derived from Mr. Plumptre's very creditable version,
will probably lay down the book without any extraordinary
interest in the subject. He will miss the plaintive clink and

[*] "Hereditary Genius," p. 342.

jingle of subjective sentimentality which he has been accustomed to associate with poetry, and he will probably wonder at the renown of the poet. But the earnest student of Sophokles will find in the original enough to reward him. His mind will be strengthened by the contemplation of perfect types of character, bold, severe, and beautiful. He will pass into a gallery of statuary where he will see sights that can never leave his inner eye. Serene faces, familiar, yet unusual in their lofty humanity, will look down upon him; voices, more divine than human, though rising from the depths of the human heart, will speak to him, and his ears will be filled with a holy and awful music.

The best guides to the higher knowledge of Sophokles are the German works whose titles are given at the head of the present paper.* Schneidewin's edition is known to students of Sophokles ; so ought also to be the essay by G. Dronke, snatched from his friends and from literature by an all too early death. Dr. Ribbeck's paper, though short, is a concise estimate of the extant dramas, and is written in a genial and scholarly style. The present essay is an attempt to connect the works of Sophokles with the periods of the poet's life, and to point out the chief dramatic characteristics of the several plays.

It was in the year 469 before our era, at the spring festival of the greater Dionysia, that' Athens saw the first trilogy of Sophokles. The city was then full of new life ; it was the charmed period when future greatness lay in bud, and not yet in blossom. The terror of the Persian had been changed into an immortal memory, and Athens was winning for herself the hegemony of more than the Grecian race. This spring festival had drawn many strangers to the city. The islands had not yet learned to dread her power or doubt her justice, and sent their loyal visitors to join in her rejoicing.

Two days of the festival had already passed, and a trilogy or rather tetralogy had been presented each day. One was the work of Æschylus, for fourteen years the master of the Athenian stage. Upon the third day a trilogy by a new poet was presented. What this work really was is uncertain; it has, however, been inferred from a passage in Pliny, that one drama was the *Triptolemus*. It was a subject that had never before been chosen for the stage, but it was well adapted to win favour at Athens at the present time. Already the city had conceived the design of

---

* No writer upon the life of Sophokles can forget the obligation which he is under to Gottbold Ephraim Lessing—Mr. Plumptre most unaccountably (p. xxii.) calls him Gottfried Lessing—whose splendid fragment of a " Life of Sophokles " remains to show later writers what the great German critic might have done in this direction.

uniting under a central power the scattered members of the Ionian race, and the confederacy of Delos was in part a realization of her desire. In the subject which he chose, Sophokles would have an opportunity of idealizing the national aspiration.

Triptolemus was the youthful hero of Eleusis, the herald of agriculture and peace, the friend and host of Demeter. He was a traveller too, and where he lighted from his winged car, he left a blessing of corn and wheat behind him. Thus Sophokles was enabled to depict, as we know from Pliny he did depict, far lands and foreign places, gladdened by the gifts that came from Attica.

Whether he fully indicated such a mission for the new Attica we cannot know; he was certainly too wise to miss the opportunity altogether. It may well be that this power of representing the national feeling, formed the distinctive characteristic of the first trilogy of Sophokles; it is at least easier to believe this, than that he surpassed the veteran Æschylus in technical excellence. There was, however, a large section of the audience, who preferred the Æschylean trilogy. Never, perhaps, in such a cause, had party-feeling run so high. Æschylus was himself from Eleusis; the new writer had won the suffrages of the elder poet's own townsmen. But the victory was not to be adjudged by popular acclamation. The custom was that ten judges should be elected by lot, one from each tribe. Why the ordinary mode of decision was not retained, it is not easy to ascertain. At any rate the presiding archon Aphepsion did not venture, in the excited state of popular feeling, to follow the ordinary practice, and this accident inaugurated a change in the method of electing the tragic judges.

Kimon and his nine colleagues representing the Attic tribes were at this moment the popular heroes. They had but newly returned from their victorious contest with the Persians at Eurymedon, and they had brought back from Skyros the bones of Theseus to be laid in Attic soil. Moreover, they had been absent during the preparation of the competing choruses, and, if any, they were free from bias and prejudice. Whatever their decision might be, it would be accepted by the Athenians. With happy tact, Aphepsion chose them as judges, and they were at once sworn into the office. Their verdict was for Sophokles. From the fact that henceforth only those who had seen service were allowed to adjudge the tragic prizes, we may infer that the decision was both memorable and satisfactory. Such at least seems to be the sentiment with which Plutarch speaks of it : "ἔθεντο δ' εἰς μνήμην αὐτοῦ καὶ τὴν τῶν τραγῳδῶν κρίσιν ὀνομαστὴν γενομένην."

Whether it was the subject, the poetical handling, or the grace and beauty of the principal actor, Sophokles himself, that turned the scale in favour of the *Triptolemus*, we miss the play with regret. The result of the decision was that for many years Sophokles became the favourite actor of the Athenian stage. There is greater importance to be attached to this fact than at first sight appears. It means not only that the successful dramatist was able to present his views of art and ethics to the Athenian people ; but that he was able to mould and perfect the form of presentation. Nor must we forget the rival interests of the several tribes as an element of success. The Choragus who had assisted in the production of a successful trilogy was rewarded even more than the author. The actors were chosen for the same places in the representations of the ensuing year, and we know that Sophokles not only established a society of the best actors, but also wrote his plays with special reference to their powers and capacities. One success, therefore, was earnest of farther renown, and a stepping-stone to it. The Choragus naturally granted to his successful author more liberty than would be conceded to an untried competitor, and it was this feeling of confidence in the poet, which enabled Sophokles, as it had already enabled Æschylus, to achieve his ideal of dramatic art upon the stage. But before we pass on to relate the gradual growth of the drama in the hands of Sophokles, it will be well to speak of the young poet in his personal relations to the Athenian people, who had just crowned him with the ivy-chaplet.

If tradition is to be believed, he was not unknown to them. He was not born of low or ignoble parents, for in this case the comic stage would have rung with jesting allusions to his parentage. His father, Sophillus, was undoubtedly a man of respectable rank, a knight it may be. Plutarch speaks of Sophokles as a person of good birth, and other writers attribute to him an excellent and complete education. Probably with truth, for it is undoubted that he possessed in a high degree those elegant personal accomplishments which were deemed necessary accessories to an Athenian gentleman. As the promising son of a well-known citizen, he would be a youth who claimed attention ; and the story of Athenæus, which speaks of his surpassing beauty, is a record of the influence of his boyish grace upon his contemporaries. It declares that he of all the Athenian youths, was chosen to lead the choir of boys who danced round the trophies in Salamis, after the defeat of the Persians. Aftertimes gladly recalled the happy coincidence which linked the three great names of Attic tragedy around the memorable victory of Salamis, for Æschylus fought in the battle, Sophokles led the pæan, and Euripides was born on the day of victory, within the fortunate isle. The years which immediately followed the victory formed a bright era in the history of the Athenians. They feared no more for the barbarian invader, nor, by the prudence of Themistokles, for the treachery of the selfish Spartana. At home there was room in every sphere for the development of genius, and genius was not absent. Under the hands of Æschylus the drama was growing towards perfection, and the people built the great stone theatre of Dionysus. A tradition says that Æschylus was the teacher of Sophokles in the dramatic art: it is most likely he was his teacher only as he was the teacher of every Athenian who had the right to hear his dramas. In this sense, each one of his audience was his pupil, and not with regard to art alone. It was his province to bring the minds of men from the dim religious darkness of old theogonies into a fuller light, though a light by no means so full as it was hereafter to be. Great questions had been asked, and there was none to answer them ; men's minds were troubled with the inconsequence of virtue and sorrow, and the polytheistic heaven of Homer was dark and silent above them. The leading ideas of the tragedies of Æschylus were the supremacy of Zeus, and the moral order of the Universe. By chains, not always of gold, the world is bound about the throne of Zeus. Vice leads to punishment in this generation, and the next, and the third. Yet no voluntarily pure man can come to ruin :

ἰκὼν δ' ἀνάγκας ἄτερ
δίκαιος ὢν οὐκ ἄνολβος ἔσται.   Εὐμ. 550.

The contest of Destiny and Free-will is a mystery which finds its solution only in this moral order. Σωφροσύνη or moderation is a conscious voluntary submission to the moral order. Any transgression of the line between Right and Wrong is ὕβρις, and leads to ruin. It is a disorder of the mind, a disease, a distemper, without expiation and without cure. Æschylus does not represent the gods as leading man into the commission of guilt. In the choice between good and evil, man is free. A good deed must be, as an evil one is, ἀνάγκας ἄτερ. No one is punished by the Divine hand without fault of his own. But sin once committed is followed by a judicial blindness which leads to other and greater guilt. This dangerous downfall is accelerated by means of a divine power known simply as "Daimon," or as "Alastor," or sometimes "Ate," whose influence may extend to a whole race. This brings us to the subject of "family guilt," which is frequently a motive in the Greek dramas. The idea that guilt was hereditary sprung from the notion that it was inexpiable. Hence a house fell from one crime to another, until the anger of the gods swept it away root and branch. It is an extension of the primitive "lex talionis ;" murder brings murder, ῥύμμα ῥύμματι τίσαι, and guilt gives birth to guilt. And

what Ate or Alastor is to the individual, that Erinnys is to the
family, working it madness and blindness, and involving it
deeper and deeper in the slough of crime.

βοᾷ γὰρ λοιγὸς Ἐρινὺν
παρὰ τῶν πρότερον φθιμένων ἄτην
ἑτέραν ἐπάγουσαν ἐπ᾽ ἄτη.—Cho. 402.

Yet the individual is free. If he belongs to a doomed race,
then it is true there is in him an hereditary tendency which
shall lead him to guilt and ruin, but the decision rests with himself. He is not given over to Ate until he has himself been
guilty of sin (ὕβρις). In much of this ethical system Æschylus
has taken and arranged prevailing popular beliefs. By his
monotheism, which made Zeus supreme, he attained to the idea
of order in the universe. His conception of sin is one which
is not alien from some forms of modern thought, and his belief
in free-will and individual responsibility, exercised considerable
influence upon later philosophy.

Sophokles did not remain unaffected by the teaching of his
contemporary, though his nature was essentially different. His
works are to the works of Æschylus, as the clear light succeeding
to a thunderstorm. He took the gain and added to it. We
shall see in what way.

Whatever had been the progress made by Æschylus, Sophokles
at once perceived that the mechanical and technical appliances
of the art, of which he now held supreme command, were by no
means perfect. It would be strange if they had been, while the
art itself was so young. The old monologue with the chorus as
interlocutor, gave place to the drama, when the earlier poet
introduced a second actor, and made dialogue possible. But
this, it is clear, left room for farther changes. Sophokles
availed himself of the opportunity. His first change was the
separation of the functions of author and actor. It is said that
he took this course for a personal reason, the weakness of his
own voice, which could not fill the vast space occupied by his
audience. But there was probably another reason also, the feeling
namely, that each character would more readily attain to its adequate excellence if separated from the other. He himself did
not take any leading character after the appearance of the
Triptolemus, but the care with which he trained his actors,
testifies to the importance which he attached to this branch of
the art. A more significant change was the introduction of a
third actor upon the stage. That this improvement was made
by Sophokles we have the testimony of Aristotle. It is possible
that even earlier, Æschylus may have used three actors, and it is
difficult to understand how some of the scenes of his earlier plays

8 *Sophokles.*

could have been represented by two actors only, but the adoption
of this number as a permanent feature of each play, is due to
Sophokles. Besides these greater changes, no matter of detail
escaped him; we learn from the same source that he carefully
directed the arrangement of the scenery and the stage. The
palace of Æschylus, with doors central, right and left, gave place
to a more elaborate stage, and much art must have been required
in fitting the theatre for the scenery of the *Œdipus at Kolonus*.
Yet the greatest innovation was the mode which Sophokles
adopted in treating a subject itself. Æschylus wrote his dramas,
and treated the subject in the form of a trilogy. When Sophokles
abandoned this form of composition, and chose to develop his
subject in a single play, it is certain he risked much. But his
artistic sense could not err. What the poetical material lost in
breadth and depth, it gained in concentration and intensity. It
followed, that in the plays of Sophokles first was seen the real
spirit of Greek dramatic art, the perfect statuesque poise of form
and expression which we have learnt to look upon as the chief
characteristic of the Athenian drama.

We return to the year of the first victory of Sophokles, from
which these improvements have led us. It was a year marked
by an event of more importance for mankind than the supremacy
of Sophokles, the birth of Sokrates. Herodotus was then a boy
of sixteen years, Thukydides an infant of three, and Euripides a
child of twelve. Seven years later Perikles rose to the height
of his power, and Athens of her glory. This is the date of the
appearance of the Oresteian trilogy, a trilogy worthy of Æschylus
and of Athens, and the only one we possess. But it unquestionably exhibits marks of the influence of Sophokles. A third actor
appears in every play. Three years later Æschylus died in Sicily,
and for the next fifteen years we know nothing of the personal
history of Sophokles. History has not much to say even about
the silent growth and development of the city under the governing hands of Perikles, nor is it necessary that much should be
said when the memorials are imperishable. At the end of this
period, by some caprice of popular taste Euripides was allowed to
gain the first prize.

The next year Sophokles exhibited his *Antigone.*

It is almost as fatal to an author's reputation to write too
much as it is to write too little. We learn that Sophokles had
written one-and-thirty dramas before he composed the *Antigone*;
yet if any of these lost dramas approached at all in majesty or
power the thirty-second, which remains to us, we may well
lament the irreparable theft of time. Perhaps they, as well as
the *Antigone*, aided in securing the election of Sophokles to a
general's rank. The time at which it was exhibited has not

been fully illustrated by the luminous pen of Thukydides, but some rays of historical light allow us to see the internal political activity of the city. The establishment of a complete democracy by Perikles and Ephialtes was not accomplished without much resistance, and it was difficult to keep aloof from party strife. The conservative or stationary faction, under the leadership of Kimon, drew around them the wealthy Athenians, who saw their oligarchical power passing away with the old order of things. The centre of their union was the Council of the Areopagus, and any change in that institution appeared to them as sacrilege and profanity. But the victorious cause was with their opponents. The Areopagites were stripped of their time-hallowed privileges, which were certainly not in accordance with the spirit of a pure democracy. Æschylus had been a vigorous partisan of the conservative party, and took occasion in his Oresteian trilogy to inculcate popular respect for that court and the other decaying institutions whose power Perikles and Ephialtes sought to banish or curtail. And the artistic effect of the poem is lessened by the zeal of the partisan. Müller says with truth, that Æschylus seems almost to forget Orestes in the establishment of the Areopagus and the religion of the Eriunys. Sophokles never forgot that his first duty was to his art. And so far is the *Antigone* above the atmosphere of controversy and dispute which blurred the *Eumenides* of Æschylus, that it was actually claimed by both parties as a witness to their views, and was received by both with unmixed applause. We cannot wonder at it. No play of Sophokles seizes with such over-mastering power the human heart, no play is so full of noble thought, and in no play is the lyric element so harmoniously blended with the march of events, accompanying it as with the sound of serene and divine music.

The plot is as follows:—Eteokles and Polyneikes have fallen at the gates of Thebes in contest: Eteokles fighting for the Thebans, Polyneikes, with seven great princes, against them. Both brothers perish, and Kreon is made king in the place of Eteokles. At once he issues a decree that Eteokles shall be buried with due honours, and that the body of Polyneikes shall be left unburied and exposed. When the drama opens, Antigone has just heard of the proclamation of the decree. She therefore suggests to her sister, Ismene, that they should bury the body of their brother. Ismene shrinks from the attempt, and is met by the full scorn of Antigone, who goes forth, daring "a holy crime." Shortly the news is brought to Kreon that his authority has been defied, and that rites of sepulture have been performed upon the body. As yet the offender is unknown. But this is soon revealed, and Antigone appears, led in by the guard. A

great scene follows, when Antigone appeals to the divine
unwritten laws against human ordinances. Kreon pronounces
her doom; she is to be buried in a living sepulchre—a bloodless
but horrible fate, not unknown of old. The action is, however,
delayed by the entrance of Hæmon, Kreon's son and Antigone's
affianced husband, who pleads for her. Yet it is not to Kreon's
paternal affection that he appeals, but to the principle which
the new king has set before himself—the safety and unanimity
of the state. There are already murmurs, indistinct but deep,
heard in the city against the severity of the king's decree.
Kreon's passion and blindness grow more intense as he listens to
his son, and before the king's fiery words Hæmon is driven away,
crying that his father shall see his face no more. From the
depths of this darkness the audience are lifted by the strains of
the Chorus, who sing, " *Love, ever victor in war* ;" and as their
music dies away, Antigone is led across the stage to her lingering
doom. Again the Chorus waken to music, but it is music in the
minor key, and can no longer lighten or delay the growing
terror. Teiresias, the blind but infallible prophet, appears, and
describes the imminence of the divine anger for Kreon's crime.
His prophetic utterances terrify the king, who hurries to undo
the wrong be has committed. In vain. Upon reaching the tomb
of Antigone, he finds her hanging dead by her girdle to the
vaulted roof, and is in time only to receive the passionate curse
of his son, and to witness his self-inflicted death. When Kreon
reaches home, bearing the corpse of Hæmon, he finds that
Rumour, swifter than his laden steps, has already told all to the
ears of his wife, and that she has slain herself in anguish and
despair. So all the fountains of feeling, young love and parental
affection, which can never be long pent up, have broken loose,
and are all the more terrible for the unholy obstructions which
they have swept away.

The character of the chief person, Antigone, stands forth
in just and magnificent proportions. All that is beautiful
in womanly nature—nay, rather in human nature—shine
forth from that supreme ideal, a mind that sees the right,
and a soul that dares to do it in the face of death. Never had
love and strength been so combined upon the Athenian stage,
and the Athenian spectators must have experienced the same
feeling in gazing upon that representation as pilgrims did when
they were ushered into the presence of the Olympian Zeus of
Phidias. We have lost the one, we can still be taught by the
other. The heart of man has not ceased to be shaken by the
contest which is waged between temporary expediency and selfish
interests on the one side, and on the other the unchanging
laws of higher duty, for these laws " are not of to-day, nor of

yesterday, but they live always, and their footsteps are not known."

The secondary characters throw the figure of Antigone into bolder relief. Ismene, who knows what is right, follows the way which leads to personal security. The grandeur of Antigone dwarfs even the natural nobility of her sister when she seeks to share the death she has not earned. Kreon errs through insolence. He is wanting in the vision which has made the path of Antigone clear; he has forgotten the rights of the gods, and his own way leads to ruin. Only when this ruin is full in view does he perceive that he has gone astray, and discover that there is something higher than love to the state and to his country—loyalty to the great unwritten laws. Nor does the character of Hæmon, noble as it is, disturb the unity of the impression which we receive from Antigone. She stands the central commanding figure of the group. And as she thus stands alone, so in her the one prominent feature is her heroic allegiance to duty. Other traits there are, but they serve to bring out this one characteristic. She is no unwomanly person, portrayed in rough masculine lines. Her language to Ismene, if it seems harsh, is forgotten when she says to Kreon :

ὅυ τοι συνέχθειν ἀλλὰ συμφιλεῖν ἔφυν,

for we know that these words come from the depth of her nature. Then, when the work which she has set herself has been accomplished, when the expression of her natural feelings can no longer mar or render equivocal her devotion to the dead, she breaks into lamentations like those of the Hebrew daughter, which show how tender and womanly a life is about to be sacrificed. Once only before has she shown any indication of the mental struggle through which she has passed, and that is when strung by Kreon's unconcern she breathes forth the sighing complaint, "O dearest Hæmon, how thy sire dishonours thee !"* The delicacy with which Sophokles has treated the love of Hæmon and Antigone secures still farther the predominant effect. It is hard to imagine such restraint in modern art.

The Chorus, of whose surpassing melody mention has already been made, had certain peculiarities in this play. It did not, like most choruses, consist of persons of the same age and sex as the principal actor, but of Theban elders. Nor did it at once take part with Antigone. Even here she is left alone. But by its submission to Kreon it serves to deepen the impression of the

* The MSS. gives this line (572) to Ismene. Schneidewin has rightly, and for unanswerable reasons, assigned it to Antigone. Dindorf and Hibbeck agree with him.

monarch's irresistible power ; and by not participating at once in the action, it is enabled to rise to a higher atmosphere of wisdom, which culminates in the choric song,

πολλὰ τὰ δεινὰ κ.τ.λ.

So, too, in its last songs, the painful instances of suffering which are recalled added to the darkness of Antigone's fate.

The effect of this perfect drama upon the Athenians was great, and as has been said, universal. Although Sophokles had hitherto taken only that share in public life which was the duty of every Athenian citizen, they now elected him as one of the college of generals, at whose head was Perikles. It happened to be the time of the war with Samos, which had revolted from Athens, and the ten generals with sixty triremes sailed for that island. Sophokles took sixteen of these ships and proceeded to Chios and Lesbos, to procure a further contingent. At the former island we hear of him through Athenæus, who records the opinion of Ion, that he was not able nor energetic in political affairs, but behaved as any other virtuous Athenian might have done. (Ath. xiii. 81.) This assertion probably had its origin in the playful self-depreciation with which Sophokles spoke of his own strategic power ; and it is quite possible that Perikles treated his poet-colleague with a good humoured irony, which he accepted in the same spirit. This view is borne out by the story which Athenæus tells of Sophokles : that, having snatched a kiss from a fair face at Chios, he exclaimed amidst the laughter of the company, "Perikles says that I know how to compose poetry, but have no strategic power ; now, my friends, did not my stratagem succeed ?" It is certain, however, that, whatever his power as a general, he did not lose the confidence and affection of his fellow citizens ; for, five years later, he was treasurer of the common fund of the Greek Confederacy. Afterwards for nearly thirty years we do not hear of his taking any part in public life. But it was no time to him of intellectual inactivity. During this period he wrote eighty-one plays, which is almost at the rate of a trilogy a year. If we remember all that this includes—the composition and the instruction of actors for so many and so frequently successful dramas—we shall cease to wonder that Sophokles did not seek to meddle with statesmanship. And once more we shall regret that so little has come down to us of that abundant intellectual wealth.

The commencement of the Peloponnesian war, and the death of Perikles, turned one page of Athenian history ; but Sophokles to the end of his long life continued to live in the spirit of the Periklean age. Ten years after the appearance of the *Antigone* he published the *Œdipus Rex.* The general outlines of the story are easily told. Laius, King of Thebes, and Jokasta his wife, were told by the God at Delphi, that should they have a son, Laius would be slain by his hand, and Jokasta would become his wife. Therefore, when their son Œdipus was born, they determined to destroy him, and gave him to a herdsman that he might be cast out upon Mount Kithœron. This herdsman, however, smitten with pity, gave the child to a comrade shepherd, who carried him to Corinth, where the boy was adopted as son by the king of that city. Many years afterwards, Œdipus at Corinth heard the oracle which had been delivered concerning him ; but he was still in ignorance as to his parentage. Thinking, however, that he was the son of the king of Corinth, he left Corinth lest the oracle should come true, and travelled towards Thebes. Upon his way he met his real father, and a quarrel having arisen, a contest ensued in which his father fell and all those who accompanied him save one. Œdipus then arrived at the kingless city of Thebes, which was ravaged by the murderous Sphinx. He freed the city from the Sphinx and accepted the proffered throne, and with it the hand of the widowed queen, little dreaming that she was his own mother. For years the city was prosperous, and four children were born to him. Then a plague fell upon the people. All this was before the action of the play begins. An oracle now declares that the pestilence is sent because Laius has been forgotten. His murderer must be ejected. Œdipus pronounces a curse upon the unknown assassin, and sends for Teiresias the blind seer, if peradventure he may be able to declare the man. Teiresias, enlightened by his art, scarce dares to tell what he knows, and is evilly treated by Œdipus. Then Jokasta complicates the confusion. She openly asserts her disbelief in oracles ; for her own son had been destined by these lying witnesses to marry her ; whereas he was slain, and she was wedded to Œdipus. Yet out of this security

" Surgit amari aliquid,"

Laius was slain at a "triple way;" terrible words that set sounding a sullen chord in the breast of Œdipus, for long ago *he* slew a man upon a triple way. One witness there was, and he is now summoned. Meanwhile a messenger arrives to say that the king of Thebes, the reputed father of Œdipus, is dead. This is a gleam of light upon the eyes of Œdipus, for the oracle has been proved false. The messenger has still farther comfort. Œdipus need not dread the fulfilment of the oracle at all, since he is not the son of the king and queen of Corinth, a fact dimly hinted before, but now for the first time clearly told. Then whose son is he ? A new passion seizes the king, and he is determined to unravel the mystery of his birth. The messenger is able to aid him in this, for he received the king as a foundling at the hands of a servant of

Laius. All is now ready for the catastrophe, which Jokasta, more quickwitted than her son, at once foresees. The witness of his murder of Laius, who at this moment comes up, is no other than the herdsman who had given him as an infant to the Corinthians. The electric circle is completed, the spark shatters the divine edifice of royal prosperity and the hearts of the audience, and the oracles of the gods are evidently true. Jokasta has already ended her existence; and Œdipus, unable to endure the sight of his own misery and that of his family, puts out his eyes.

There are several reasons why this drama should be assigned to this period, notwithstanding the absence of authoritative data. The vivid description of a pestilence was probably written by one who had witnessed the virulence of the Athenian scourge. Some commentators have believed the chorus ἅ μοι ξυνίῃ κ.τ.λ. to have reference to the mutilation of the Hermæ. If this be true, the play must necessarily be of later date than that supposed above. It probably refers to the reckless spirit of licence which exhibited itself in Athens as a reaction against the popular superstitions of the earlier period, and which eventually led to the profanation. The drama is in fact a protest against the disregard of religion, and a magnificent exhibition of the vanity of human attempts to cross the decrees of fate. In this respect it stands alone amongst the plays of Sophokles. It depicts the contest of an honourable and noble character with a foregone destiny. To add to the interest of the picture, the man who is unable to solve the riddle of his own history, is the one who alone was able to unravel the enigma of human life proposed by the Sphinx, and it is only when the eyes of his corporal vision are darkened for ever that the organs of his spiritual sight are unclosed. At first his house is the only one spared in the pestilence, and all eyes are directed to him as the saviour of the state ; yet it is his house which is the cause of the plague. Then his own blind eagerness to discover the regicide, the curse which he unwittingly imprecates upon himself, the gradual lifting of the curtain fold by fold till he breaks into the exclamation,

ἰού, ἰού, τὰ πάντ' ἂν ἐξήκοι σαφῆ,

are terrible instances of the irony which Sophokles is accustomed to ascribe to destiny, but nowhere so powerfully as in this play. Surely but slowly the end approaches. Now the progress of events is delayed by some joyous choric song like the ἵππερ ἐγὼ μάντις εἰμί, κ.τ.λ.; now there falls upon the play some beam of hope which makes us believe that the gathering thunderstorm will be dispersed or break up into sunny tears and the dewy delight of averted calamity. But the vain hopes and the vanishing glory serve only as preludes to the complete darkness of the catastrophe, which, at last, suddenly envelopes the whole heaven.

It is not only modern admiration which the play has won.
Aristotle has taken it as the model of a drama, and its effect
upon contemporary minds must have been great. It is equally
admirable as a whole and in single passages. The choruses are
generally like the atmosphere of the play, of a lurid and broken
colour, so that we know not whether light or darkness will
prevail. The earlier choruses approach in thought and expression
to the language of Milton, or of modern poetry. Thus the description of the rapid deaths in time of pestilence, so different as
it is from the picture given by Homer (Il. 1) has that touch
about it which belonged later to Dante.

ἄλλον δ' ἂν ἄλλῳ προσίδοις ἅπερ
ἐνπτερον ὄρνιν,
κρεῖσσον ἀμαιμακέτου πυρὸς ὅρμενον
ἀκτὰν πρὸς ἑσπέρου θεοῦ.

"And one soul after another might be discerned flitting like
strong-winged bird with greater force than invincible fire, to the
shore of the Western God."

It recalls, too, the half-mediæval, wholly beautiful lines of Mr.
Rossetti in his poem of the " Blessed Damozel."

> "Heard hardly, some of her new friends
> Amid their loving games
> Spake evermore among themselves
> Their virginal chaste names;
> *And the souls mounting up to God,
> Went by her like thin flames.*"

Another passage (lines 476 *et seq.*) is more Hebrew than
Greek in its description of the Cain-like homicide.

φοιτᾶ γὰρ ὑπ' ἀγρίαν
ὕλαν, ἀνά τ' ἄντρα καὶ
πέτρας ἅτε ταῦρος,
μέλεος μελέῳ ποδὶ χηρεύων,
τὰ μεσόμφαλα γᾶς ἀπονοσφίζων
μαντεῖα· τὰ δ' ἀεὶ
ζῶντα περιποτᾶται.

"For sullenly turning his sullen step, he wanders moodily
under the wildwood, or amid caves and rocks, like a bull, and
avoids the divine voices that rise from the central oracle of the
land. *But they live, and are whispered around him.*"

Yet this incomparable poem won only the second prize; the
first was gained by the work of Philokles. Time, in preserving
this alone, has reversed the decision of the judges. The reason
of that decision may lie in the nature of the play itself. To the
Athenians, who after the taking of Miletus could not endure

the scenic shadow of their loss, the unsoftened representation of
their sufferings in the Theban plague, and the direct promulgation
of the doctrine of irresistible destiny may have seemed unwelcome
and ill-timed. And the conclusion of the play is less relieved
than that of any other. It is not broken up into those short
cries and natural lamentations, with which many tragedies
close, but solemnly and sadly to the beat of throbbing trochaics
the figures pass from the stage like the muffled pomp of a
funeral procession, and the curtain rises upon a silent and awe-
struck audience.

It is far otherwise with the *Œdipus at Kolonus.* Like the
Philokteles, it has a plot which depends upon divine intervention, and one in which the sequence of the episodes is not
absolutely perfect in connexion, though each episode is perfect in
its own characteristic beauty. After the events depicted in
Œdipus Rex, the blind king with his daughters remained at
Thebes, until he and Antigone were thrust forth by Kreon. For
many long months they wandered through Greece, whilst Eteokles,
the younger son of Œdipus, drove out from Thebes Polyneikes
the elder, who betook himself to Argos and gathered an army to
make him king again. At last Œdipus and Antigone came to
the plain of Kolonus, near Athens. Here, beneath the shade of
an olive-grove, the aged king sits down to rest, and here an inward
confidence tells him that he is approaching the term of his sufferings. This olive-grove is sacred to the Furies, and it is sacrilege
for ordinary men to approach it. The news reaches Theseus that
a stranger has set foot within the holy precincts, and he hastens
to the place. Before his arrival Ismene comes in haste to tell
her father of the fratricidal war upon which her brothers have
entered, and that Kreon is hurrying to carry back Œdipus, since
an oracle has declared that his presence will bring victory on
either side. Œdipus pronounces a curse upon his son, and reveals
his intention of blessing Athens by remaining within her territory.
Theseus now arrives, and not ignorant of the responsibility he is
incurring, assures Œdipus of a courteous and secure hospitality.
Œdipus in return acquaints him with the benefits which his
presence will confer upon Athens, and the calamity which will
ensue to Thebes. Theseus accepts with confidence the divine
privilege which Œdipus offers, and once more assures him of his
protection. If ever a situation made a supreme demand upon
an Athenian chorus, it is the present. We have come to the
middle point between the beginning and the end of the action.
The Acropolis of Athens, though as yet unblessed by the works
of Phidias, rises within sight of the beholder. Kephissus draws
her silvery threads through the foreground, and the hero-prince
of Athens, in accepting the charge of Œdipus, unites the new and

the old, and links historic to heroic times. The music which shall not mar the harmonious suspense of this situation must be subtle indeed. But the music of Sophokles is never of a negative kind. It increases and enhances the dramatic feeling. Accordingly it is here that we find the greatest choric ode of the Greek drama. The undying chords of the poem which follows raise the mind of the hearer to a level with the exaltation of Œdipus himself.

Εὐίππου, ξίνε, τᾶσδε χώρας.

"Guest, thou art come to the noblest spot
Of all this chivalrous land."

But this lofty tranquillity is broken by the entrance of Kreon, who endeavours to persuade Œdipus to return to Thebes. Upon his refusal, Kreon has recourse to violence, and carries off Antigone, Ismene having been previously secured. Theseus however restores his daughters to the blind king. The next scene brings upon the stage Polyneikes, who seeks reconciliation with his father. This he does not succeed in obtaining, and he leaves the stage begging for the kind offices of Antigone in his burial. The play now draws to a close. The euthanasia of Œdipus is all that remains. The hour of destiny has come, and the Passing of Œdipus—no man knows where or whither—completes the purpose of the gods.

A question so debated as the date of this play can scarcely be answered satisfactorily here. Critics both ancient and modern have connected it with the latest period of the author's life; but there are portions of the drama which seem to belong to an earlier date, and to have reference to that period of reactionary licence which was marked by the mutilation of the Hermæ. By its subject it is closely connected with the *Œdipus Rex*, and there is nothing improbable in the supposition that even if it were first produced after the author's death, it was begun whilst the subject of Œdipus was fresh in his mind. And if any parallelism is to be drawn between Sophokles and the great German poet, this work may well be compared with the "Faust," from which the *summa manus* was so long withheld. The allusions in the poem itself do not fix it to any definite date. All that can be said with certainty is that it is subsequent to the *Antigone;* for while both plays that have Œdipus for their subject contain references to the *Antigone*, that drama has not a single allusion to the action of the other two. Whether, however, we are to credit it with an earlier or later origin, we should be doing an injustice to the spirit of Sophoklean poetry if we were to suppose that political allusions brought down the drama into a realistic atmosphere. It is idle to attempt to connect the Theban and Athenian struggle which the poet mentions, with any special date.* It is more profitable to win the freedom of that ideal land in which are brought together the blind old king and the hero of Athens.

In some respects the *Œdipus at Kolonus* differs from the other dramas. There is in it a perplexing mixture of manner which suggests both a return to the style of Æschylus and a concession to the growing influence of Euripides. The self-completion and perfection of outline, which marked the *Antigone* and the *Œdipus Rex* are wanting here. The drama is the fragment of a trilogy of Æschylean breadth; it is rhetorical and lyric in the style of Euripides. The real Sophoklean characteristics are not, however, absent, sweetness and power of expression, lofty and graceful sentiment, and a perfection of rhythm and vivid delineation. But it is a series of linked scenes rather than a drama proper. Of scenes that begin with the peaceful olive grove, and end in the euthanasia of the world-worn Œdipus. Nothing could be finer or more effective than that touch of the pen of Sophokles which paints, not indeed the death of Œdipus, but Theseus, who alone saw it, with his face shaded by his hand, as though to shut out some stupendous revelation. To this history of Œdipus Sophokles has given the only satisfactory and worthy conclusion which was possible. In his life he was a contradiction to the laws that regulate human affairs; he remained a contradiction in his death. Others passed by the grove of the Eumenides with bated breath and averted faces—he found there rest and a conclusion of his toils. The grove trodden by Bacchus, nymph-traversed and nightingale-haunted, was to him, upon whom all tempestuous airs had broken, a haven "windless of all storms." And here the troubled life at length ceases, and peace is found at last. In the choruses of this play the poet's love of Athens finds expression. Many poets had spoken with enthusiasm of the "violet-crowned city," but never with such beauty and exalted passion as does Sophokles in the ode, εὐίππου, ξίνι, κ.τ.λ. The legends connected with it are probably false, but they bear witness to the opinion of the ancients concerning it. Sophokles, unlike his rivals in the dramatic art, remained true to his native city. No offer of foreign patronage could tempt him to leave Athens. Æschylus died in Sicily, Euripides in Macedonia. There were many princes who would gladly have welcomed Sophokles to their courts—indeed, there were many who invited him thither; but he remained unmoved by their offers, and never left his city except to do her service and to further

* Schneidewin suggests the ἱππομαχία τις Θραχεία ἐν Φρυγίοις, mentioned Thukyd. ii. 22, as a possible occasion.

ser interests. The anonymous biographer says that he was φιλαθηναιότατος, "most enamoured of Athens." And the city repaid his affection. The same biographer says, "In a word, such was the grace of his nature that he was beloved by all."

It is unfortunate—it is more than unfortunate—that of the personal history of the poet we know so little. Few and far between are the dates that we can assign to the events of his life. The seventeenth year after the supposed date of the *Œdipus Rex* saw the calamitous termination of the Sicilian expedition. Amongst the names of the ten elderly men elected *Probuli* to meet the emergency of the crisis, we find that of Sophokles. If this be indeed our poet, we have here another instance of the confidence and love which the city felt towards the tragedian, who was now eighty years old. The seventeen years to which reference has been made are important in the history of Greek literature. They include the birth of Plato, the exhibition by Aristophanes of the *Knights*, the *Clouds*, and the *Peace*, but they cannot definitely be connected with any play of Sophokles. Possibly the *Elektra* falls within this period. It is at any rate marked by the best characteristics of the poet. It dispenses with the breadth of treatment which a trilogy allows, and concentrates the interest upon the action of a single play. In the trilogy upon the same subject which Æschylus exhibited, probably thirty years earlier, the death of Klytemnestra forms an episode of the middle drama, and the ethical problem of filial duty in antagonism to divinely-directed justice is sketched only in outlines which leave much to be filled in.

Sophokles treated the subject as follows :—During the absence of Agamemnon in the Trojan campaign, his wife Klytemnestra formed an adulterous union with Ægisthus, and upon the return of Agamemnon, slew her husband and wedded with Ægisthus. Elektra, daughter of Agamemnon, fearing foul treatment for her brother Orestes, then a child, sent him out of the country, whilst she herself remained, together with her sister Chrysothemis, at Argos, waiting for the manhood and return of Orestes to claim his hereditary throne. When due time arrives, Orestes, under the direction of Apollo, comes back to Argos unheralded and unknown. He is accompanied by his faithful attendant the Pædagogus, who brings to Klytemnestra an account of the death of Orestes at the Pythean chariot contest. The play opens with the arrival of Orestes and his attendant at Argos. Elektra comes forth to bewail the death of her father and the delay of Orestes, and is comforted by such consolation as the chorus can offer her. Next, Klytemnestra, who has been terrified by a dream, appears, and an angry altercation takes place between her and Elektra. When this is concluded, the Pædagogus enters and announces the

c 2

death of Orestes. The grief of Elektra occupies the attention of
the spectators until the entrance of the disguised Orestes and
Pylades his friend, bearing an urn which contains the pretended
ashes of Orestes. In the interview between Orestes and Elektra
which follows, a recognition takes place, and nothing remains
to be done but to effect the revenge. Orestes therefore enters
the house and slays his mother, and Ægisthus, upon his arrival,
shares the same fate.

The work of Sophokles is finer and fuller of artistic power
than the work of Æschylus. The character of Elektra is un-
borrowed, and forms a contrast to that of the Æschylean Elektra.
She, and not Orestes, is the centre of the action, and though
not the actual avenger, is really the prompter and promoter of
the deed. In the *Choephoræ* we are perpetually reminded that
the death of Klytemnestra was the work of the gods; Elektra
falls into the background, a weak, suffering woman, whose
strongest trait is love for her brother, and he, a mere tool in the
hands of the deity, after numerous hesitations and delays in
accomplishing the divine purpose, becomes a victim of madness
and terror. The Sophoklean drama is more valuable than the
Æschylean trilogy. In the *Elektra* we have, as in the *Antigone*,
a distinct and noble type of character set in full light and drawn
in clear lines of power. Elektra is the personification of justice
and fidelity, as Antigone is of love and strength. Like justice,
she never wavers from her purpose. When all hope of the
return of Orestes has ceased and his death seems certain, she
herself undertakes the work which should have been his, for
vengeance must be done, and the house of Agamemnon must
be freed from the accursed and abiding crime. And when
Orestes reveals himself as her brother, she does not leave the
central position of the group. One short burst of natural joy,
and she is ready to take any measures which may bring about
the punishment of the murderess. Nay, she stands on guard
while the deed is being done, and to the prayers of Klytemnestra
her answers are stern and inexorable as destiny. With subtle
words of double meaning she leads Ægisthus into the prepared
snare, and then forbids parley or delay—ἀλλ' ὡς τάχιστα κτεῖνε,
she says—and the house of Athens is freed from its long and
intolerable servitude.

The character of Elektra, as we see it in its final manifestion, is
as terrible as it is grand. Klytemnestra endeavours to justify her
own conduct, and to represent it as righteous; but Elektra strikes
the key-note in her long nightingale lament, when she says,

ὁολὸς ἦν ὁ φράσας, ἴρος ὁ κτείνας.

Chrysothemis, weak and vacillating, ready to condone the past and enjoy the present, serves as a foil to the stronger character of her sister. The same may be said of the Chorus, which although sympathetic, does not rise to the same heights of sublimity or lyric sweetness as in the other plays of Sophokles. Dr. Ribbeck sees here a reason for believing the *Elektra* to be an early work. Yet it is not the lyric element which we should expect to see failing in a younger work, and the conception and delineation of character in the *Elektra* is of the highest kind. The balance of proportion between the brother and sister is admirably kept. Orestes is not the instrument of the gods, though under their protection, but of Elektra. By her side he must not waver, he must proceed at once to vengeance. That portion of the ethical question which Æschylus has indicated in the *Eumenides* does not come into the drama of Sophokles.

The description of the chariot race has always been regarded with justice as a masterpiece of art, and there is scarcely anything more touching in literature than the scene which describes the recognition of brother and sister, and the rapid change of mood, which, in broken iambics, passes from hopeless sorrow into overpowering joy.

In the *Elektra*, Sophokles presents before us a character, which, as it were, wrestles with destiny, and conquers; in the *Ajax* we have a character ennobled by its very defeat. Ajax was the most distinguished of the Greek generals in the Trojan war, next to Achilles, and upon the death of Achilles a dispute arose for the arms of that hero. The claimants were Ajax and Ulysses, and the arms were adjudged to the latter. Full of anger at this decision, Ajax determined to slay both Ulysses and the Atridæ, who had acted as arbitrators; but as he was going by night to accomplish his revenge, he was inspired with madness by Athene, whose aid he had previously rejected. In this madness he fell upon the flocks of cattle around the camp, and slew some and carried others to his tent, thinking he had captured in them his rival and his enemies. When day dawns his right mind returns, and he is overwhelmed with the ignominy of his position and resolves to put an end to his life. This he accomplishes by falling upon his sword. The Atridæ command that his body should be left unburied, but Teucer resists them, and he is honourably buried. This drama is placed here, not because it certainly belongs to this period, but because its date is undetermined and undeterminable. Schneidewin and others assign it to an earlier period, make it indeed nearly contemporary with the *Antigone*, both on account of its resemblance in lyric measures to the Æschylean dramas, and on account of the rarity with which a third actor is brought

forward.   But the *Antigone* sufficiently shows that Sophokles
had passed this stage.   Others see in the speeches which follow
the suicide of Ajax an approximation to the rhetorical style of
Euripides.   Those who adopt a middle course, will place it rather
in the long undated period, when the literary activity of
Sophokles was at its height.   It is a poem in which the national
feeling of Athens was likely to find especial gratification.   Of all the
heroes celebrated in the Iliad, Ajax was the only one that Athens
could claim as connected with herself.   Salamis had been in
close union with Athens from immemorial time, and one Athenian
tribe took its name from Ajax.   Herodotus tells us (viii. 64), that
before the battle of Salamis, the Athenians prayed to all the
gods, and to Ajax and Telamon.   This connexion gives rise to
the beautiful ode

                 ὦ κλεινὰ Σαλαμίς κ.τ.λ.

   The drama opens with a scene which breathes the frenzy of fierce
hatred and lust for murder that mark Northern poetry rather
than Greek.   Yet it serves to set a stamp upon the character of
Ajax, and to indicate his disposition, not without a warning note
of admonition.   The degradation into which Ajax has fallen is a
punishment for the excess of that self-reliance which forms a
heroic character, the first sin which he commits is insolence
(ὕβρις).   When setting out to battle, he rejected the pious prayer
of his father, that he might wish to be victorious by the help of
the gods, and added the vaunt, "With a god's help, even a
man of nought may win the victory; but I, I trust, without
God's help shall be victorious."   And in the battle itself, when
Athena proffered aid, he bade her go elsewhere, for he would
none of it.   Such is the disposition of the man who finds too late
that he is powerless against the gods.   But against disgrace his
unyielding mind still contends.   The real interest of the drama
lies in the moral conflict between heroic independence and the
necessity of submission to higher authority.   The motives for
submission are forcibly brought out, the agony of disgrace, and
the strength of domestic affection.   The turning point is reached
when Ajax says—"I, once as strong as steel, have now been
softened by the words of this woman as steel is softened by the
bath, and I shrink from leaving amongst my enemies, her a
widow, and my son fatherless."   Yet from the shame there is
now but one escape, and from that he does not shrink—death.
But ere he goes to the baths of ocean and the sea-marge, where
he may appease the wrath of the goddess by his death, he freely
acknowledges his error.   Honour and authority are worthy of
submission.   Snowfooted winter yields to blooming spring, and
dark-tiarned night gives place to bright-crowned day.   Life is full
of change, so he too bends to authority, fears God and honours

the Atridæ. Another scene reveals Ajax about to put an end to the life he can no longer honourably cherish. His last prayer is earnest and simple—That Teucer may first raise his body, and give it rites of sepulture; that Hermes may grant him funeral escort; and that Helios may rein in his golden car, and tell the sad news to his aged father and mother. Then follows the farewell of the Greek to the bright sun, a long adieu to Salamis and illustrious Athens, and all the plains and crystal founts of Troy.

It is perhaps worth pointing out that this drama has several Shaksperian peculiarities. As in the works of our own drama-tist, overflowing sorrow finds relief in a play upon words.

αἰᾶι, τίς ἂν ποτ' ὤιθ' ὧδ' ἐπώνυμον
τοὐμὸν ξυνοίσειν ὄνομα τοῖς ἐμοῖς κακοῖς ;

The speech already referred to (line 646), which describes in the form of a soliloquy a moral crisis, is in the manner of the English writer, and the final monologue of Ajax recalls the meditation of Hamlet.

Minuter resemblances might be noted. The cry of the sailors in their search for their lost chief—πόνος πόνῳ πόνον φέρει—may almost be translated by the " Double, double toil and trouble ' of the Witches in Macbeth.

But a more characteristic peculiarity of the drama is the sea air which blows through it, and the number of nautical allusions which must have been grateful to a seafaring people. Sophokles never forgets the mariners of Athens in his eulogies of the city. In the great choric song of the *Œdipus at Kolonus*, the crowning glory of the land is " the well-used oar fitted to skilful hands, that leaps through the sea in the train of the hundred-footed Nereids," and here from the first we are thrown into sailor company. It is to the "shipmates of Ajax, from over the sea," that Tecmessa turns in her trouble, and it is they who search for their lost leader at the last, though Sophokles with poetic propriety reserves the discovery of his body for Tecmessa herself. And to the sea the thoughts of Ajax turn in his despair:

> " O ye paths of the watery reach,
> O ye caves of the sea,
> O ye groves of the Ocean beach,
> Where my steps were wont to be."

By the death of the hero atonement for all his sins is made, and his body is honourably buried by the sea he loved.

It is a real satisfaction to arrive at a period when we can attach a date to a play of Sophokles. In B.C. 409 appeared the *Philoktetes.* Before this time Athens had passed through the conspiracy of the Four Hundred, and had seen the recall of Alkibiades. In the measures of the oligarchical body we are told Sophokles concurred, not because they were good, but because they were expedient. "οὐ γὰρ ἦν ἄλλα βελτίω," are the words attributed to him. The anecdote, however, may possibly refer to another Sophokles. It is possible also that Sophokles had little sympathy with the later democracy, which may have alienated amongst others the mind of the poet. But his poetry retained the astonishing energy and freshness of his younger days. The *Philoktetes* shows no sign of the decay of intellectual power. It is worthy of the first prize which it received. The subject was not a new one upon the Attic stage. Æschylus and Euripides had handled it before, and other tragedians had aided in making it familiar to an Athenian audience. Sophokles, while adopting the well known mythical outlines as the groundwork, succeeded in lending the drama a new and powerful motive. These outlines are to be found in Homer. (Il. 2. 716). Philoktetes, carrying the arrows of Hercules, joined the expedition against Troy, but being wounded in the foot by a serpent, he was left in the island of Lemnos. In the tenth year of the war it was predicted by a Trojan prophet that Troy could only be taken by the arrows of Hercules, then in the possession of Philoktetes. Accordingly Ulysses and Neoptolemus, son of Achilles, were sent to Lemnos to bring Philoktetes with his arrows to Troy. The play opens with the landing of these messengers upon the island of Lemnos. Ulysses tutors Neoptolemus in deceit, and urges him to gain possession of the arrows by falsehood. Neoptolemus obeys, and having persuaded the suffering Philoktetes that he is about to take him home is entrusted with the arrows. When Philoktetes discovers the treachery that has been practised upon him, he endeavours to commit suicide, but is prevented. Feelings of pity and compassion now come upon Neoptolemus, and he restores the arrows in spite of the angry remonstrances of Ulysses. The mission has thus nearly failed of its object, when Hercules descends from heaven, and bids Philoktetes proceed to Troy, where he shall win renown and be healed of his sore disease. The interest of the play does not centre in the person whose name it bears, but in the person of Neoptolemus. It is *his* character that Sophokles has brought out from the massive block of tradition in proportions of exceeding beauty. Between Philoktetes hardened by suffering, and Ulysses wily and wise, the open-hearted son of Achilles stands forth a contrast to both. This contrast of character, together with the dramatic development of natural nobility in the person of Neoptolemus, is the work of Sophokles alone, and bears his stamp. The minor characters are powerfully drawn. Philoktetes is immovable in his love to his friends and in his hatred to his enemies. The extreme agonies of physical suffering which wring from him cries and groans, leave him still tears for the misfortunes of his friends and imprecations for his foes. He is, in the words of Lessing, "a rock of a man,"* a hero still, though life has lost all that is worth living for, except constancy and submission to the gods.

The Ulysses of this drama is differently portrayed from the Ulysses of the *Ajax*, and the Ulysses of Homer. He is brought forward in an ungracious part, and one more in accordance with the *rôle* he takes in the plays of Euripides. He counsels deceit and is willing to attain his end by means honourable or dishonourable. We must not however forget that this end is the well-being of the Greeks, and that the means are poetically justified by his knowledge that neither persuasion nor violence will avail to shake the firmness of Philoktetes. The psychological interest lies then in the struggle through which the mind of Neoptolemus has to pass. On the one hand, with the bow of Philoktetes he may win undying renown by the taking of Troy, but he must desert and deceive his father's friend, leaving him doubly desolate and deprived of the means of supporting his piteous existence. On the other hand he must bear the bitter reproaches of Ulysses, the loss of the promised glory, and the failure of the Achæan arms, but he will have respected the rights of a suppliant and his plighted word. How will the struggle end? The sincerity of a noble nature prevails. Already the treachery inspired by Ulysses has been successful; the bow of Philoktetes is in his hand, but he can no longer endure the part he has been compelled to play: he leaves the path of deceit into which he has been misled, and assumes the character which he has already shown to be his. The intervention of the "*deus ex machina*" serves only to justify what has happened, it neither diminishes the interest nor interferes with the action of the play. The psychological question has been already answered.

The *Trachiniæ* is to be considered a later work than the *Philoktetes.* Otherwise it is probable that Sophokles would have used the connexion that lies in their subjects. For the bow of Philoktetes was none other than that bequeathed him by Hercules at his death. The *Trachiniæ* tells the story how the death of Hercules was unwittingly brought about by his wife Deianeira. Many years before the opening of the play, Hercules had slain the Centaur Nessus by means of his unerring and poisoned arrows. As he was dying, the Centaur bade Deianeira take of the blood of his wound and the poison of the arrow, and

---

* "Laokoon," ch. iv. p. 31.

preserve it, for it would prove an unfailing philtre to recover her
husband's affection if he ever forsook her for another woman.
When the play opens, Hercules has been long absent, but is now
returning with captives, the reward of his victorious arms.
Amongst these captives, who arrive at Trachis before Hercules,
is the beautiful Iole, and Deianeira is not long in learning that
she it is who now possesses the affections of her husband. Therefore she imbues a garment with the philtre she had received
from Nessus, and sends it to Hercules, bidding him wear it whilst
transacting the sacred rites of Zeus. The venom of the mixture
does not fail in its efficacy. It seizes at once upon the body of
Hercules, who is consumed with intolerable burnings. In the
agony of death he orders himself to be borne home, but the news
flies before, and Deianeira ends her life with her own hand. Upon
his arrival, Hercules bids his son Hyllus erect a funeral pile for
him on Mount Oeta, and after his father's death marry Iole.
The drama concludes with the promise of Hyllus to obey his
father.

The opinions as to the value of the drama have been
various. A. W. Schlegel deemed it of far inferior merit to that
of the other plays, and many modern readers have agreed with
him. Schneidewin, a critic of weightier authority, places it exceedingly high amongst the works of ancient art. In looking at
it, however, we must regard it as a diptych rather than a single
picture. From this circumstance it suffers perhaps when compared
with the other works by the same author. Nevertheless each
part has its own merit. In the first part the figure of Deianeira
forms the centre; in the second, the half-divine half-savage character of Hercules exercises a strange imperious fascination upon
the spectator. Nothing can be more delicately and finely
represented than the amiable character of Deianeira, the faithful
and forgiving wife. It is in the true colour of Sophoklean irony
that the sympathy of a tender nature which leads her to express
pity for the captive woman, draws her most closely to Iole, who
is the cause of her misfortune. And it is the very strength of her
love for Hercules which brings about his ruin and her own. The
first part of the *Trachiniæ* may indeed be ranked with the best
dramatic exhibitions of character. Nor is it deficient in those
cross lights and special excellences in which the best abound. The
self-devotion and feminine dignity of Deianeira reaches its climax
when she implores Lichas to tell her the whole truth :—

τὸ μὴ τίθεσθαι τοῦτό μ' ἀλγύνειαν ἄν·
τὸ δ' εἰδέναι τί δεινόν ; οὐχὶ χἀτέρας
πλείστας ἀνὴρ εἷς Ἡρακλῆς ἔγημε δή;
κοὔπω τις αὐτῶν ἐκ γ' ἐμοῦ λόγον κακὸν
ἠνέγκατ' οὐδ' ὄνειδος.

This is in the very spirit of mediæval devotion, and almost in the words of the " Nut-browne Mayde :"

> " Though in the wode I understode
> Ye had a paramour,
> All this may nought remove my thought
> But that I will be your.
> And she shall find me soft and kynde,
> And courteys every hour."

For vigorous word-painting, the passage which describes the virulent corruption of the poisoned wool rotting away into nothingness, is unsurpassed. (Lines 695 *et seq.*)

The second portion of the diptych is less agreeable to modern feeling, since the character of Hercules seems little fitted for the tragic stage. By his semi-divinity he is above humanity, by his semi-brutality he is below it. Hercules suffering is most likely to gain our sympathy ; for the picture of excessive suffering is redeemed from the peril of awaking horror or disgust by the consistency and firmness of Hercules. He meets death with his spiritual strength still unbroken, and his self-possession when he recognises his real position changes the grief of the spectator into admiration of his undaunted fortitude.

The marriage which he is represented as proposing between Hyllus and Iole, however repugnant to modern feeling, was too firmly an article of popular belief rooted in popular tradition to be neglected in the drama.

Nor does Herodotus (vi. 52) deem the tradition unworthy of notice, since it was from Hyllus that he traced the descent of the Dorian invaders of the Peloponnese.

The link which binds together the two portions of the drama and preserves the unity of the action is the magic poison of the Centaur. In the first part we have the motives which lead up to its use ; in the second we see its effects. The same protagonist took the parts both of Deianeira and of Hercules.

The long and illustrious life of Sophokles was now drawing to a close—a life more enviable, perhaps, than that of any man who has lived so long. He had seen the growth of the Athenian state ; he was spared the sight of her last declining days. He was the contemporary of all the great men who had made Athens glorious ; and he was the personal friend of many of them. Ten years older than Euripides, he yet survived him, and lived to see his own son Iophon wearing the ivy crown. One pleasing anecdote is told of the last year of the poet's life. When the news of the death of Euripides in Macedonia reached Athens, Sophokles was preparing a tragedy for exhibition. As a last tribute of respect to the memory of his rival, he himself appeared in mourning at the head of his chorus, and the choral company

were without the wreaths which they were accustomed to
wear.

The wife of Sophokles was a native of Athens and was named
Nikostrate. By her he had one son, Iophon, already mentioned.
By Theoris of Sikyon he was the father of Ariston, whose son,
Sophokles, reproduced the *Œdipus at Kolonus* two years after
the death of his grandfather. A story related by Cicero, and
often repeated, asserts that Iophon brought his father before the
Phratores on the ground of mental incapacity to manage his own
affairs. There is much improbability in the story and we may
well discredit any tradition of dissension in the family of
Sophokles. Hardly, if the story be true, could the comic writer
Phrynikus have written, as he did, a few months after the poet's
death, a lament with the concluding words—

καλῶς δ' ἐτελεύτησ' οὐδὲν ὑπομείνας κακόν.

The immediate occasion of his death is unknown, and various
accounts are extant. One tradition asserts that it was joyous
excitement at again winning the tragic prize. Be it so. καλῶς
δ' ἐτελεύτησεν. In the year B.C. 406, the year of the battle of
Arginusæ, Athens lost her two great tragic writers, Sophokles
and Euripides.

Our consideration of the plays will be more than imperfect
unless we examine briefly the religious views with which they
are interpenetrated and coloured. What was the religious
position of the mind that conceived and brought them forth?
Art and religion have often been combined, but never more
intimately than in the dramas of Sophokles. Γέγονε δὲ καὶ
θεοφιλὴς ὁ Σοφοκλῆς ὡς οὐκ ἄλλος, says the anonymous
biographer: "Sophokles was beloved of the gods as no other."
And the attitude of the poet's mind was one of reverent, almost
superstitious, adoration of the gods. Æschylus, no less than
Sophokles, believed in the nothingness of human nature and the
omnipotence of Zeus. For man he marked out a narrow path
beyond which he could not go without offending those unsleeping
powers which punish the insolence of men to the third and fourth
generation of them that transgress. This narrow path he named
σωφροσύνη; Sophokles called it εὐσέβεια, reverence.

In the *Elektra* the chorus says to Elektra (1093)

> "Thus have I found thee not in prosperous case
> Advancing, but of all the highest laws
> Wearing the crown by reverence (εὐσέβεια) of Zeus."

And in the same play, commending her language, the chorus
says (464)

> "The maiden speaks with reverence."

In the chorus of the *Œdipus Rex* (863) the doctrine of
εὐσέβεια is laid down at length. And in the praise which Œdipus
gives to Athens (Œd. Kol. 1125) the highest is that she is the city
where Reverence dwells:—

ἐπεὶ τό γ' εὐσεβὲς
μόνοις παρ' ὑμῖν ηὗρον ἀνθρώπων ἐγώ.

How comes it then, if this be a chief article in the religion of
Sophokles, that so many of his characters are found speaking
against the gods? The number of characters who so speak is
not very great. Tecmessa accuses Pallas of working the bane of
Ajax (Ag. 652). Philoktetes doubts the justice of the gods
(Phil. 447), and again (1035). Hyllus (Trach. 1266) speaks
still more harshly of their unkindness, and reproaches (1272)
Zeus himself. But it is to be remembered that Sophokles himself does not always speak by the mouth of his characters. Their
verisimilitude lends a force and warmth to the personification
which is absent from the poems of Æschylus. It is quite in keeping with the Sophoklean stage that his *dramatis personæ* should
not be without a tinge of popular superstition. Instances may be
selected. Thus, Teucer is persuaded that the sword of Hector
was fabricated by the Erinnys; Hercules calls the fatal robe
which takes away his life a web of the Erinnys; Deianeira is
the victim of a popular superstition when she sets her hopes upon
a love-charm; and the guardians of the corpse of Polyneikes are
instances of a similar delusion, when they believe that the unseen
burial was supernatural.

But Sophokles, as he had received from the hands of Æschylus
the drama already formed, so, too, he accepted from him a body
of religious doctrines already in advance of popular belief. Nor
was the progress which he inaugurated in this line of thought
less striking than his development of the dramatic art—as far
as the liberation of human thought is concerned it was more
important. Æschylus, as we have seen, attributed the misfortunes
of mortals to a judicial blindness, the consequence of previous
guilt whereby a man falls into greater sin and supreme destruction. His teaching is the teaching of Eliphaz the Temanite;
" Remember, I pray thee, who ever perished being innocent? or
when were the righteous cut off?" (Job iv. 7.) Sophokles distinguished between the guilty blindness and involuntary crime.
With regard to the former he held the same position as did
Æschylus. When a mortal willingly, and with full intent, commits a crime, the Deity punishes him with moral madness; he
is delivered over to Alastor. Yet for all the actions committed
in this madness, he, and none other, is responsible. It is so with
Ajax. He deliberately rejects the aid of Athene, and falls into
a madness from which there is no escape. It is so with Kreon.

He designedly neglects the honour due to the gods below, and pursues a course which is the result of madness. The chorus recognise the chastisement of a divine hand when they speak Kreon as—

> ἀνὴμ ἐπίσημον διὰ χειρὸς ἔχων
> ιθεμις εἰπεῖν, οὐκ ἀλλοτρίαν
> ἄτην ἀλλ' ἀντος ἁμαρτών.

and he himse acknowledges it (1272),

> ἐγὼ μαθὼν δείλαιος. ἐν δ' ἐμῷ κάρᾳ
> θιὸς τοτ' ἄρα τότε μέγα βάρος μ' ἔχων
> ἔπαισεν.

But from this frenzy, involuntary guilt is separated by a wide interval. As Ajax is a striking instance of the one condition, so Œdipus is of the other. The contrast between the two is sharp and complete. Œdipus is presented to us as a righteous prince, wise above the common standard of humanity, for he alone could solve the riddle of the Sphinx—as god-fearing, for he never doubts the oracles of the gods. When he hears of the death of his supposed father, Polybus, there is mingled with his first cry of wonder a note of distress for the credit of the oracle.

> φεῦ φεῦ, τί δῆτ' ἄν ὦ γύναι. σκυποῖτό τις
> τὴν Πυθομαντιν ἑστίαν; (Œd. R. 000.)

The sins which he committed were all involuntary, and he repeatedly asserts it.

> τά γ' ἔργα μου
> πεπονθότ' ἐστὶ μᾶλλον ἤ δεδρακότα.

Yet upon him descend the heaviest misfortunes. What is the conception which Sophokles designs to express by this? There is no answer in the *Œdipus Rex;* it is found in the *Œdipus at Kolonus.* It is this answer withheld that so closely unites the former and the latter dramas. In the latter, Œdipus comes before us under the guidance and protection of the gods. They have used him for their purpose, a divine one, an unknown and mysterious one, but a just one; and now, having drunk the cup of sorrow to the dregs, he is their sacred and especial care. He himself says (287)

> ἥκω γὰρ ἵρος εὐσεβής τε καὶ φέρων
> ὄνησιν ἀστοῖς τοῖσδε.

And therefore his passage from life is gentle and kindly. He is not, for God takes him. As his life has been beyond all others wretched though morally guiltless, so his death has beyond all others a fuller promise of happiness.

If we gather up the teaching of Sophokles upon this point, we find :—That the gods have a great progressive plan of the

Universe, which they carry out in spite of, or sometimes by means of individual suffering. That every man who seeks to do right is, notwithstanding his misfortunes, under their protection, and will finally be rewarded according to his merit. That voluntary guilt tends to worse, and lastly to ruin. This advance from the religious position of Æschylus is great, but it leads to results no less important. It leads, firstly, to the possibility of making a consciousness of right and justice an acting moral power. Thus Œdipus sets before his daughters (Œd. K. 1613) as a recompense for their labours and sufferings on his behalf, the consciousness that they had done their duty and won his love. Elektra and Antigone are penetrated with this feeling. Elektra says (352) " Be it my only reward that I am conscious of doing my hard duty." The sentiment of Antigone is the same (460) :

> " That I shall die I know without thy words,
> And if before my time 'tis gain to me."

This teaching of Sophokles is a herald of the truth declared by Plato, that the moral consciousness of right in a man's own heart is the measure of his happiness.

Secondly, and here we must touch upon the mystic side of the religion of Sophokles, it imbues his dramas with a lofty spiritualism. It stands in opposition to the religion of rite and profession. It calls for the spirit and not the letter. Œdipus (Œd. K. 498) declares that the sacrifice of one pure soul rightly offered, avails more than ten thousand which are not so given. It adds a significance to the sincere unspoken prayer, for the god hears it before it is said. Klytemnestra will not utter her prayer (El. 637) for the god knows her desire, though she may not put it into words. And the voice of the god speaks within the breast of man to guide and direct him. This inward voice brought Œdipus to the grove of the Eumenides, as he himself says (Œd. K. 96) and led him—ἄθικτον. ἡγητῆρος—to his last resting-place.

And thirdly, it finds a place in the religion of Sophokles for the doctrine of the immortality of the soul.

This doctrine was only dimly present to the popular mind ; it was no active moral power. The motive to justice and righteousness lay in the fear of punishment in this life—of punishment at the hands of the civil magistrate or the offended deity. True, in Hades the unholy were unholy still, and suffered a shadowy retribution for their crimes, but the real punishment was in this life. Sophokles recognised a purer motive for human action, the love of right for its own sake, and for the sake of the divine approval. Antigone can look forward to a long and joyous existence with the dead (Ant. 73-76), for with them she will dwell for ever. And so the highest duty is the duty of living in accordance with the will of the gods, careless of praise or blame, reward or punishment, from any but Their hands, and with eyes directed to that other life, where wrongs are righted and where justice is done.

ἐπεὶ πλείων χρόνος,
ὃν δεῖ μ' ἀρέσκειν τοῖς κάτω τῶν ἐνθάδε,
ἐκεῖ γὰρ ἀεὶ κείσομαι.

The monologue of Ajax sets this point of view still farther in contrast with that of Æschylus. Æschylus has exemplified the terrors of conscience with appalling power in the persons of Klytemnestra and Orestes, but the passion which he represents is rather that of remorse than that of penitence. The fear of punishment is the moving cause of terror. In the ethics of Sophokles, conscience leads to a penitent recognition of personal guilt and a desire of amendment—

ἡμεῖς δὲ πῶς οὐ γνωσόμεσθα σωφρονεῖν;

is the cry of Ajax when he seeks to atone for his crimes by a voluntary death. And the same moral revolution is exhibited in the case of Kreon. (Ant. 1319.)

Thus in the hands of Sophokles, religion passed from a negative to a positive phase. It was no longer sufficient as in the time of Æschylus to live a quiet life with no overweening self-exaltation or insolent rivalry of the gods, but heart and hand must be alike pure, and both devoted to the service of the gods.

Gotthold Ephraim Lessing, in his essay upon the "Education of Humanity," has traced the process by which a single nation rose stage by stage to fuller knowledge. The nation which he selected was the Hebrew nation, but it is not the only one which submitted to the divine education. In the works of Sophokles we see the Greek mind passing to a higher stage. It is not a final stage; that can never be reached as long as humanity endures, but it is one that could give strength and confidence to minds that loved the truth. That it did so to the mind of Sophokles himself we may learn from his works. The perfection of restraint and repose which reigns like a summer atmosphere in his compositions, is the result not only of a mastery of diction and a supreme command of art. The knowledge of the sorrows of humanity and a co-existing capacity of beholding above all a ruling order, which recompenses and atones for all, are the characteristics which give an immortal interest to the dramas of Sophokles. They reveal to us a man who was indeed θεοφιλής "beloved of God."

And however dimly his contemporaries may have understood the humane theology which pervaded his works, they understood time of his death the Lacedæmonians were threatening Athens from Deceleia. The family burial-place of Sophokles lay eleven stades from Athens, upon the road to Deceleia. When Lysander the Spartan heard that Sophokles was dead, he granted a free pass to the funeral procession, and the body of the great tragedian was laid to rest under the protection of the Lacedæmonians. Nor were there wanting due tokens of respect at the hands of his fellow-citizens. As a hero they honoured him with a yearly sacrifice. A siren was sculptured upon his tomb, to indicate the entrancing sweetness of his strains, and Simmias the pupil of Sokrates wrote his epitaph. Forty years after his death, his bust was placed in the Athenian theatre, and the state took in charge the text of his works.

And yet against the life of Sophokles there are those who bring the charge of impurity and immorality. Such a charge we can but dismiss with indignation. A few anecdotes retailed by that prurient collector of slander, Athenæus, form the body of the charge. They are not worth the time that would be spent in contradicting them. There is nothing in Plato, there is nothing in Plutarch that can sully the pure lustre of the name of Sophokles. Plutarch indeed relates (Perikles, viii.) that upon one occasion Perikles bade Sophokles remember that a man must not only keep his hands pure, but his eyes from beholding evil. If there is in this anything more than a commonplace application of a moral maxim, it is a testimony that at least the hands of the poet were pure. Of his thoughts as mirrored in his writings we can ourselves judge. Aristophanes amidst all his baseless attacks upon his contemporaries, never brought this charge against Sophokles; modern writers with less knowledge, have had greater audacity. This, however, matters but little to him or to us.

In looking back upon the life of Sophokles as a whole, perfect and radiant, it is difficult to find in the range of literature another like it. From his boyhood to his death, there seems to be nothing to mar the beauty of his career. Germans find an analogous instance in the life of Göthe, but the analogy does not go far. Both Sophokles and Göthe lived long, and won that favour from their countrymen which is generally given to the illustrious dead alone. Each of them possessed the highest culture of his time, and aided the diffusion of that culture. The comparison cannot in reality go much farther. The life of Göthe is open to us in its minutest details: we are compelled to be satisfied with the merest outline of the life of Sophokles. Göthe has dissected for us (not without vanity) his own sentiments, emotions, and passions. Only behind the works of Sophokles can we discern the calm and majestic figure of the

Greek poet. Yet the dimmer personality is not the less impressive. To something of the calm which belongs to the works of Sophokles, Göthe could, and did attain; but it is the same with a difference. Göthe by a sublime selfishness, and his progress marked with the sorrows which he caused, rose into a clear intellectual ether. Sophokles brought down the wisdom of another sphere to brighten the ways of men. The one was a child of earth who made a path for himself to the serene heights; the other was a son of Olympus, about whom the inextinguishable glory of his birthplace shone for the delight and instruction of the world.

P.S.—Two editions of Sophokles, at present only published in part, will go some way towards familiarizing English students with the spirit of Sophokles. The one is by Mr. Jebb, Public Orator of Cambridge, the other is by Professor Campbell of St. Andrews. As a portion only of each edition is before the public, it has been deemed better to exclude them from comment in the body of this paper, but this much may be said, that we can hope everything from the complete edition by Professor Campbell. His essay on "the Language of Sophokles" is admirable and exhaustive, and the notes and introductions to the plays already published are full of refined and suggestive enthusiasm.

Mr. Jebb has set forth his views upon the genius of Sophokles in a lecture recently delivered at Dublin, and since published in *Macmillan's Magazine* (Nov. 1872). This lecture is clear, scholarly, and critical, but both the points selected and the views expressed seem scarcely adequate to the subject. The four manifestations of the genius of Sophokles which he chooses are: First, the blending of a divine with a human characteristic in the heroes of Sophokles. Secondly, the effort to reconcile progress with tradition. Thirdly, dramatic irony; and lastly, the portrayal of character. The first of these manifestations is illustrated by the cases of Ajax, of Œdipus, and of Herakles. Ajax, we are told, is human by his natural anguish on his return to sanity; he is divine by his remorse and the sense that dishonour must be effaced by death. But surely his remorse and repentance are human too. His mere cries of distress, apart from the higher feelings, are ludicrous, and insufficient to link Ajax to human nature. Nor does his nearness to Athene, as one who had spoken with her face to face, suffice to give him a divine character. The heroes of Euripides also speak with the gods face to face. The lecturer has not here brought out a real manifestation of the genius of Sophokles; he has united accidents and imagined them to be the essence. The intense suffering of Œdipus the King, and the marvellous death of Œdipus at Colonus are two conditions through which the character of Œdipus passes, and are not more especially characteristic than are the sufferings of Medea, who is finally carried away by the dragon-chariot of the sun. The genius of Sophokles is certainly not revealed in the union of the superhuman and the commonplace; it is manifested by its power of *idealizing* humanity. The superhuman element which Sophokles introduces, forms no part of the essence of any character, it belongs to the cycle of popular beliefs, which as we have seen, he used for the purpose of verisimilitude.

Secondly.—The idea that Sophokles preserved the balance between superstition and free thought, that he endeavoured to graff progress upon tradition is misleading. In religious matters we have seen that the advance which he made was both definite and important; in politics he was the disciple, as he was the colleague, of Perikles. If he shrank from the extreme measures of a later democracy, it was because he clung to a system which had raised Athens to her highest political efficiency, and because he distrusted a variation which exaggerated and distorted the true democratic principles. Moreover, he was justified by the results.

Thirdly.—The lecturer's canon upon dramatic irony is only partially true. "The practical irony of drama depends on the principle that the dramatic poet stands aloof from the world which he has created." In fact the question of dramatic irony cannot be so summarily dealt with. The manner of Professor Campbell in treating of this characteristic (pp. 112-118) is far more diffident and satisfactory. Irony, as he says, is always accompanied with the consciousness of superiority. But the exhibition of this consciousness must be destructive of artistic effect. It is better to refer the irony to fate than to ascribe it to the author; it may, perhaps, be best not to use the word at all, but to refer the effect which every one feels, to an artistic and legitimate application of dramatic elements such as contrast and pathos, which reach their highest power only when used by the most skilful hands. Mr. Jebb thinks that Sophokles delineates broadly, and with a "deliberate avoidance of fine shading," the characters of his primary persons, and seeks for the more delicate touches of portraiture in the subordinate persons. The persons, however, to whom he refers as illustrations must be spoken of as secondary with caution. Thus Deianeira is of equal importance with Hercules in the *Trachiniæ;* the same protagonist took both characters. The real interest of the *Philoktetes* centres in Neoptolemus. But perhaps the chief inadequacy of Mr. Jebb's view of Sophokles, a view which, as has been said before, is set forth with the charm of a scholarly and balanced style, results from his notion of the religion of Sophokles. In his opinion, Sophokles is the highest type of a votary of Greek polytheism, and no more.

D 2

He does not see in his hand that torch which was to be passed on to Plato, and through him to other times. His religion had, he says, shed upon it the greatest strength of intellectual light which it could bear without fading. His art was indeed the highest of its kind, and remained his own ; but the impulse which he gave to a freer and more enlightened reverence may be traced in the best of Greek literature, the works of Plato. It is probable, therefore, that the edition by Professor Campbell will be a truer guide to the appreciation of Sophokles, for the editor has already acknowledged his obligation to Professor Jowett.

Art. II.—Parliamentary Eloquence.

1. *A Book of Parliamentary Anecdote.* Compiled from Authentic Sources. By G. H. JENNINGS and W. S. JOHNSTONE. Cassell, Petter, and Galpin: London, Paris, and New York. 1872.

2. *The Orator : a Treasury of English Eloquence, containing Selections from the most Celebrated Speeches of the Past and Present.* Edited, with Short Explanatory Notes and References, by a Barrister. London : S. O. Beeton.

3. *Select British Eloquence, embracing the best Speeches entire of the most Eminent Orators of Great Britain for the last Two Centuries : with Sketches of their Lives, an estimate of their Genius, and Notes Critical and Explanatory.* By CHAUNCEY A. GOODRICH, D.D., Professor in Yale College, New Haven, Conn., U.S. London : Sampson Low and Co.

4. *Parliamentary Logic : to which are subjoined Two Speeches delivered in the House of Commons of Ireland, and other pieces.* By the Right Hon. WILLIAM GERARD HAMILTON. London. 1798.

5. *Hansard.* New Series.

MANY have been the writers on the theory of Government, and the framers of model governments and paper constitutions. None of these, however, devised Parliamentary Government as it actually exists amongst us, or foresaw its rise. Yet to all appearances it is the form of government which will universally prevail. The English tongue bids fair to become the speech of the greater part of the globe, and wherever an English-speaking race is to be found, English parliamentary institutions, more or less completely developed, are to be found also, and wherever despotic governments are overthrown or modified, parliamentary government on the English model takes their place. Nothing can be more true than Mr. Bright's description of England as "the home of freedom and mother of parliaments."

It is interesting to compare the present position of the House of Commons—"the centre of gravity of the British constitution,", as Lord Russell calls it—with the humility of its origin. The rise and progress of the House of Commons is due to that which is the source of most of the evils which afflict and many of the blessings which enrich humanity—viz. the want of money. Our constitution is the result of the necessities of our kings. Their wars were expensive and could not be carried on without money: they sacrificed power to this necessity. This is the true origin of the House of Commons. Mr. Carlyle states pretty accurately what occurred :—

"Borough members and knights of the shire were summoned up to answer whether they could stand such and such an impost? and took upon them to answer, ' Yes, your Majesty, but we have such and such grievances greatly in need of redress first.' Nothing could be more natural and human than such a Parliament still was; and so, granting subsidies, stating grievances and notably widening its field in that latter direction, accumulating new modes and practices of Parliament, greatly important in world history—the old Parliament continued an eminently human veracious and indispensable entity, achieving real work in the centuries."[*]

Here we part company with Mr. Carlyle, who of course disparages modern parliaments, which—*pace* Mr. Carlyle—we assert are as indispensable entities and achieve as real work as did ever their predecessors in the times of Plantagenets, Tudors, or Stuarts.

In this manner, and by these means, the House of Commons has gathered into its hands a very large proportion of the political power of the country. It has outlived the influence of the Crown; it has shaken off the dictation of the aristocracy; in taxation and finance it is supreme; it has a very large share in legislation; it can control and unmake, and sometimes nearly make, the executive government. A seat in it is eagerly sought after by every man of culture and ambition, and also by many who, having neither one nor the other, yet possess wealth, and find the easiest road to social standing is through the House of Commons. With what feelings foreigners regard it is well illustrated by a passage in Bunsen's Life :—"I saw before me the

---

[*] "Latter-day Pamphlets :" Parliaments.

empire of the world governed, and the rest of the world controlled and judged by this assembly. I had the feeling that,' had I been born in England, I would rather be dead than not sit among them and speak among them."[*]

Lord Macaulay has correctly defined parliamentary government as "*government by speaking.*" We need make no apology for recalling to the reader's memory the passage in which this definition occurs:—

"Parliamentary government, like every other contrivance of man, has its advantages and its disadvantages; on the advantages there is no need to dilate. The History of England during the hundred and seventy years which have elapsed since the House of Commons became the most powerful body in the state, her immense and still growing prosperity, her freedom, her tranquillity, her greatness in arts, in sciences, and in arms, her maritime ascendancy, the marvels of her public credit, her American, her African, her Australian, her Asiatic Empires, sufficiently prove the excellence of her institutions. But these institutions though excellent are assuredly not perfect. *Parliamentary government is government by speaking.* In such a government the power of speaking, is the most highly prized of all the qualities which a politician can possess; and that power may exist in the highest degree without judgment, without fortitude, without skill in reading the characters of men or the signs of the times, without any knowledge of the principles of legislation or of political economy, and without any skill in diplomacy, or in the administration of war. Nay, it may well happen that those very intellectual qualities which give a peculiar charm to the speeches of a public man may be incompatible with the qualities which would fit him to meet a pressing emergency with promptitude and firmness. It was thus with Charles Townshend. It was thus with Windham. It was a privilege to listen to those accomplished and ingenious orators. But in a perilous crisis they would have been found far inferior in all the qualities of rulers to such a man as Oliver Cromwell, who talked nonsense, or William the Silent, who did not talk at all. When Parliamentary Government is established, a Charles Townshend, or a Windham, will almost always exercise much greater influence, than such men as the great Protector of England, or as the Founder of the Batavian Commonwealth. In such a government, parliamentary talent, though quite distinct from the talents of a good executive or judicial officer, will be a chief qualification for executive or judicial office. From the book of dignities, a curious list might be made out of Chancellors ignorant of the principles of equity, and First Lords of the Admiralty ignorant of the principles of navigation; of Colonial Ministers who could not repeat the names of the colonies, of Lords of the Treasury who did not know the difference between funded and unfunded debt, and of Secretaries of the Indian Board who did not know whether the Mahrattas were Mahometans or Hindoos. On these grounds some persons incapable of seeing more

---

[*] "Bunsen's Life," vol. i. pp. 499, 500.

than one side of the question, have pronounced parliamentary government a positive 'evil, and have maintained that the administration would be greatly improved if the power now exercised by a large assembly were transferred to a single person. Men of sense will probably think tho remedy very much worse than the disease, and will be of opinion that there would be small gain in exchanging Charles Townshend and Windham for the Prince of Peace, or the poor slave and dog Steenie."*

This is illustrated by Lord Macaulay's own case. His Reform speeches, not any special qualification for the offices he held, made him Secretary to the India Board, Legislative Councillor in India, and Secretary at War. Perhaps in the case of the Indian Secretary who was ignorant as to the Mahrattas he refers to his own experience.

Parliamentary government is not only government by speaking, but by *parliamentary* speaking. Parliamentary eloquence is a species wholly distinct from the eloquence of the bar, the pulpit, or the public meeting. With few exceptions—Lords Brougham and Selborne being tho most noteworthy—lawyers have rarely taken the highest place among parliamentary speakers. The same holds good of the long series of bishops who have sat in the Lords; of later prelates we can call to mind only three eminent as speakers, the late Bishop of Exeter and the present Bishops of Winchester and Peterborough. When lawyers have attained the first rank, it has been more often—as in Lord Lyndhurst's case—in the Lords than in the Commons.

With the exception of Mr. Cobden and Mr. Bright, the orators of the public meeting have not taken high rank in the House. Cobbett entered Parliament only five years before his death, and from the first his demeanour prejudiced the House against him, and, except perhaps in Committee on matters of detail, he never gained its ear. The late William Johnson Fox was another instance. Many remember how he swayed his audiences at the great meetings of the Anti-Corn-Law League. Those speeches showed that in diction and delivery he was far more of an orator than Mr. Cobden, and even than Mr. Bright; but his early training for the Nonconformist pulpit left its traces on him, and contributed to spoil his efficiency in the House. The beauty of his style may be judged by the following passage on Athens, taken from one of his sermons:—

"There arose the social spirit to soften and refine her chosen race, and shelter as in a nest her gentleness from the rushing storm of barbarism; there liberty first built her mountain throne, first called the waves her own, and shouted across them a proud defiance to des-

* "Miscellaneous Works," vol. ii. pp. 330-1. Art. William Pitt.

potism's banded myriads; there the arts and graces danced around humanity, and stored man's home with comforts, and strewed his path with roses, and bound his brows with myrtle, and fashioned for him the breathing statue, and summoned him to temples of snowy marble, and charmed his senses with all forms of elegance, and threw over his final sleep their veil of loveliness; there sprang poetry, like their own fabled goddess, mature at once, from the teeming intellect, girt with the arms and armour that defy the assaults of time and subdue the heart of man; there matchless orators gave the world a model of perfect eloquence, the soul the instrument on which they played, and every passion of our nature but a tune which the master's touch called forth at pleasure; there lived and taught the philosophers of bower and porch, of pride and pleasure, of deep speculation and of useful action; who developed all the acuteness and refinement and excursiveness and energy of mind, and were the glory of their country when their country was the glory of the world."[*]

This is poetizing in prose. It is beautiful, though too ornate; but such a style is quite unsuited for Parliament. Great writers, with the exception of Lords Macaulay and Lytton, have not ranked high as parliamentary speakers; who, in their turn, Mr. Gladstone excepted, are seldom great writers. "Sir James Mackintosh," says Lord Macaulay, "spoke essays, Mr. Fox wrote debates, his history reads like a powerful reply thundered from the front opposition bench at three in the morning." On the other hand, the greatest parliamentary speakers, when they speak out of the House, often fail. According to Mr. Disraeli, "The greatest member of Parliament that ever lived" was Sir Robert Peel; "he played on the House of Commons as on an old fiddle;" but Peel, he says, "could not address a public meeting, or make an after-dinner speech, without being ill at ease, and generally saying something stilted or even a little ridiculous."[†]

What, then, is the *differentia* of Parliamentary eloquence, that which makes it what it is? Mr. Rush, once American minister to this country, records a conversation in which Sir James Mackintosh said the true light in which to consider parliamentary speaking was as animated conversation on public business, and that it was rare for any speech to succeed in the House which was raised on any other basis. Mr. Canning acceded to this remark, and said it was true as a general rule that speaking must take conversation as its basis rather than anything studied or stately. The House was a business-doing body, and the speaking must conform to its character. It was jealous of ornament in debate, which, if it came at all, must come as without consciousness. There must be method also; but this should be felt

---

* "Memorial Edition of Collected Works of W. J. Fox," vol. iii. p. 194.
† "Life of Lord George Bentinck," pp. 48, 231.

in the effect rather than seen in the manner—no formal divisions, set exordiums, or perorations, as the old rhetoricians taught, would do. First and last and everywhere you must aim at reasoning, and if you could be eloquent you might at any time, but not at an appointed time.*

Parliamentary eloquence, therefore, according to these authorities, is conversation on public business based on reasoning. This was so, judging from the meagre records which have come down to us, from the earliest times, and is more than ever the case in the reformed and re-reformed House. Mr. Disraeli attributes to Sir R. Peel the gradual introduction of a new style into the House of Commons—of the didactic—suited to the age and to the novel elements of the Assembly which he had to guide.

" He had to deal with greater details than his predecessors, and he had in many instances to address those who were deficient in previous knowledge. Something of the lecture, therefore, entered into his displays."†

" The exigencies of modern criticism," says another writer, " have called into being a class of public speakers, whose effusions fall as far short of the professional orator in permanent beauty as they excel them in immediate utility. As the character of the House of Commons, remodelled under the Reform Bill, has become more business-like; so the most popular and powerful speakers there are those who, rejecting the beautiful, apply themselves to the practical."‡

The House of Commons, said the clever writer of " The Stranger in Parliament," admires Mr. Macaulay delivering an essay; but it more admires, because it is business, Mr. Walpole explaining a bill. This was in a great degree true long before the first Reform Act. The case of Burke is an illustration so apt as to be almost hackneyed. His speeches, as they are now printed, are nobly instructive to the young writer; but as models they would be fatally injurious to the young orator. Burke was no popular speaker in Parliament, except upon those rare occasions when all considerations give way to the desire to hear what a first-rate intellect has to say upon matters vitally affecting the State. His sobriquet of the dinner-bell is well known, as is also Goldsmith's couplet—

" Too deep for his hearers, he went on refining, ·
And thought of convincing while they thought of dining."

Mr. Rush relates that Erskine said to him, " I was in the House when Burke made his great speech on American concilia-tion—the greatest he ever made—he drove everybody away.

---

* " Second Residence at the Court of London," pp. 44, 300.
† " Life of Lord George Bentinck," p. 229.
‡ " Critical Biographies—The Late Sir Robert Peel." By George Henry Francis.

When I read it, I read it over and over again ; I could hardly think of anything else."* In fact, it is more than doubtful whether Burke ever spoke his speeches as they are now printed. They were carefully revised for publication, and revised in order to be perfect literary compositions, and it is as such that they deserve our praise and require our study.†

The mention of Burke reminds us of a greater philosopher and writer, who in his day adorned the House of Commons— Lord Bacon. We possess three of his speeches, " Published by the author's copy." Two of them were made in the Commons. Comparing them with his best-known work, it is as true of him as of Mackintosh, that he "spoke essays." Here is a specimen of the parliamentary speaking of the Reformer of Philosophy :—

"Mr. Speaker,—I have, I take it, gone through the parts which I propounded to myself; wherein if any man shall think I have sung a *placebo*, for mine own particular, I would have him know that I am not so unseen in the world but that I discern it were much alike for my private fortune a *tacebo* as to sing a *placebo* in this business. But I have spoken out of the fountain of my heart. *Credidi propter quod locutus sum :* I believed, therefore I spake, so as my duty is performed. The judgment is yours ; God direct it for the best."

If Ben Jonson's well-known description of Bacon's oratory refers to him as a parliamentary speaker, what pleased the Commons of Elizabeth would disgust the Commons of Victoria. The taste and feeling of the House has of course varied from age to age, and many things well received at the time they were uttered, would not be tolerated now. Every one knows the legends as to the elder Pitt's supremacy in the House of Commons—his overbearing demeanour—his reply to Morton, " Who laughs at sugar now ?" "Gentle shepherd, tell me where,"‡ and knowing what an assembly of English gentlemen in any or every age would bear with, one may, without undue scepticism, consider the historical character of these legends at least doubtful, but there are authentic passages in his speeches which no position or reputation in the House could render tolerable now. Take by way of illustration the following oft-quoted passage :—

"I speak not now with respect to parties. I stand up in this place single and independent. As to the late ministry (turning himself to Mr. Grenville, who sat within one of him) every capital measure they have taken has been entirely wrong ! As to the present gentlemen,

---

* " First Residence at the Court of London," p. 237.
† See Lord Lytton's " Miscellaneous Works," vol. iii. pp. 103-5.
‡ They will be found in the memoir prefixed to the selection of his speeches in " Select British Eloquence," p. 52.

to those at least whom I have in my eye (looking at the bench where
General Conway sat with the Lords of the Treasury), I have no
objection; I have never been made a sacrifice by any of them. Their
characters are fair, and I am always glad when men of fair character engage in His Majesty's service. Some of them did me the honour to ask
my opinion before they would engage. These will now do me the justice
to own I advised them to do it; but notwithstanding (for I love to be
explicit) *I cannot give them any confidence.* Pardon me, gentlemen
(bowing to the Ministers—the reader will observe the flagrant breach
of order), confidence is a plant of slow growth in an aged bosom.
Youth is the season of credulity. By comparing events with each
other, reasoning from effects to causes, methinks I plainly discover the
traces of an overruling influence."*

Charles Butler says in his "Reminiscences"—"Those who ·
remember the air of condescending protection with which the
bow was made and the look given, will recollect how much they
themselves at the moment were both delighted and awed, and
what they themselves conceived of the immeasurable superiority
of the speaker over every other human being that surrounded him."

We suspect Butler, writing as an old man, coloured this too
highly, as when he likens Sir W. Grant delivering a judgment
in the Rolls Court to Adam naming the beasts in Paradise.
Certainly of late years no man, however eminent, not even Sir
R. Peel in the zenith of his power, would have dared to attempt
anything approaching this in matter or manner. Pitt, moreover,
was essentially an actor, and now anything approaching to the
theatrical in elocution, manner, or attitude is fatal to a speaker's
success. Parliamentary speaking exhibits abundance of the hesitating, humming, and drawling, which according to Lord Lytton, are
" the three graces of English conversation." Sir R. Peel's favourite
attitude was to cross one leg over the other, and put one arm
under the tails of his coat, while the elbow of the other rested
on the table, "a very pleasant chatty way"—as Mr. Francis
remarks—but not quite in keeping with high oratory.

Pitt's reputation is greater as an orator than a statesman.
On one question, however, he exhibited that foresight which,
when followed by general agreement, is the surest test of statesmanship. In the speech we have quoted, referring to the
borough representation, he said:—

"This is what is called the rotten part of the constitution. It
cannot continue a century. If it does not drop it must be am-
putated."‡

* "Select British Eloquence," p. 103.
† *Ibid.* p. 103, note.
‡ *Ibid.* p. 105 and note. Spoken in 1766. Within the century Parliament
was twice reformed.

" We have here," says the learned editor of the very valuable work
whence our quotation is taken, " the first mention by any English
statesman of a reform in the borough system. A great truth once
uttered never dies. The Reform Bill of Earl Grey had its origin in the
mind of the elder Pitt."

The interest and importance of the subject, for the redistri-
bution of seats is evidently coming to the front, induces us to
give another illustration of his opinions on reform. In his great
speech on the state of the nation (1770) he said:—

" The boroughs of this country have properly enough been called
the rotten parts of the constitution. I have lived in Cornwall, and
without entering into any invidious particularity, have seen enough to
justify the appellation. . . . The representation of the counties is
still, I think, preserved pure and uncorrupted. That of the greatest
cities is upon a footing equally respectable, and there are many of the
larger trading towns which still preserve their independence. The
infusion of health which I now allude to would be to permit every
county to elect one member more in addition to their present representation. The knights of the shire approach nearest to the constitutional
representation of the country, because they represent the soil. It is
not in the little dependent boroughs, it is in the great cities and counties
that the strength and vigour of the constitution resides; and by them
alone, if an unhappy question should ever arise, will the constitution
be honestly and firmly defended. I would increase that strength,
because I think it is the only security we have against the profligacy
of the times—the corruption of the people and the ambition of the
Crown."*

This is the first distinct proposal for a reform in Parliament.
The style of the younger Pitt would hardly be acceptable to
the altered constitution and temper of the House. His clearness,
which, when he chose, was remarkable, and his powers of
reasoning and sarcasm, would of course have always given him
a high place among debaters, but his long succession of round
and stately periods, " a couple of powdered lacqueys of epithets
(as Plunket said) waiting on every substantive," would not suit
the more business-like tone and temper of the present day.

Fox, whose eloquence answers David Hume's description of
that of the Greek orators, "disdain, anger, boldness, freedom
involved in a continual stream of argument," and who, like
Cobden, had all the unpretending plainness which belongs to the

---

* " Select British Eloquence," p. 117. In " The Workman and the Franchise," by the lamented Frederick Denison Maurice, it is stated that " the
younger Pitt said in his first speech on the Reform of the Representation of
the House of Commons, that his father had believed it to be the great
necessity of the time. This opinion must have been expressed privately in
his declining years: it had never been announced to either branch of the
Legislature." This is disproved by the quotations above given.

perfect style of eloquence, would in every age and in any popular assembly, have held the highest place. It is doubtful whether the House would now tolerate some of his strong passages. Mr. Bright has been howled at for saying milder things than the following, taken from Fox's speech on Secret Influence :—

"Sir, it is a public and crying grievance that we are not the first who have felt this secret influence. It seems to be a habit which no change of men or measures can operate with success. It has overturned a more able and popular minister [Lord Chatham] than the present, and bribed him with a peerage, for which his best friends never cordially forgave him. The scenes, the times, the politics, and the system of the Court may shift with the party that predominates ; but this dark, mysterious engine is not only formed to control every ministry, but to enslave the constitution. To this infernal spirit of intrigue we owe that incessant fluctuation in His Majesty's councils by which the spirit of government is so much relaxed, and all its minutest objects so fatally deranged. During the strange and ridiculous interregnum of last year [between the resignation of Lord Shelburne and the appointment of his successors] I had not a doubt in my mind with whom it originated, and I looked to an honourable gentleman opposite to me [Mr. Jenkinson] the moment the grounds of objection to the East India Bill were stated. The same illiberal and plotting cabal which then invested the throne and darkened the royal mind with ignorance and misconception has once more been employed to act the same part. But how will the genius of Englishmen brook the insult ? Is this enlightened and free country, which has often and successfully struggled against every species of undue influence, to revert to those Gothic ages when princes were tyrants, ministers minions, and governments intriguing ? Much and gloriously did this House fight and overcome the influence of the Crown by purging itself of ministerial dependents ; but what was the Contractors Bill, the Board of Trade, or a vote of the revenue officers, compared to a power equal to one-third of the legislature, unanswerable for and unlimited in its acting ? Against those we had always to contend ; but we knew their strength, we saw their disposition ; they fought under no covert ; they were a powerful not a sudden enemy. To compromise the matter, therefore, Sir, it would become this House to say, Rather than yield to a stretch of prerogative thus unprecedented and alarming, withdraw your secret influence and whatever intrenchments have been made on the crown we are ready to repair ; take back those numerous and tried dependents who so often secured you a majority in Parliament ; we submit to all the mischief which even this succession of strength is likely to produce ; but, for God's sake, strangle us not in the very moment we look for success and triumph by an infamous string of bedchamber Janizaries."[*]

During the Corn Law debates, Lord George Bentick denounced

---

[*] "Select British Eloquence," pp. 479, 80.

Sir R. Peel's supporters "as paid Janizaries and renegades." Sir Robert censured "the exercise of such language as injurious to the cause of legitimate debate, and as calculated to create unmitigated disgust." Mr. Disraeli afterwards justified his friend by the example of Mr. Fox, and quoted this passage.

We doubt also whether the House now would tolerate this, from the opening of Fox's speech on the Westminster Scrutiny, remarkable in itself, still more as that of a fallen minister whom the late election showed was equally in a minority in the country and in the House.

"Sir, I have no reason to expect indulgence, nor do I know that I shall meet with bare justice in this House [expressions of disapprobation from the ministerial benches]. Sir, I say that I have no reason to expect *indulgence*, nor do I know that I shall meet with *bare justice* in this House [expressions of disapprobation renewed]. Mr. Speaker, there is a regular mode of checking any member in this House for using improper words in a debate, and that is to move to have the improper words taken down by the clerk for the purpose of censuring the person who has spoken them. If I have said anything unfit for this House to hear or for me to utter—if any gentleman is offended by anything that fell from me, and has sense enough to point out and spirit to correct that offence, he will adopt that parliamentary and *gentlemanlike* mode of conduct: and that he may have an opportunity of doing so, I again repeat, that I have no reason to expect *indulgence*, nor do I know that I shall meet with bare justice in this House."[*]

Twice afterwards he returned to the attack, and repeated the same words.

One other extract we must make from this speech for the sake of the terse and forcible statement of what is in fact a truism, though not so regarded in parliamentary debate.

"Sir, it is exerting the worst tyranny upon the understanding of men if they are to be for ever condemned for having entertained doubts upon a subject purely theoretical. Extinct is every idea of freedom, and lost is the boasted liberty of debate and the spirit of free thinking in this country, if men are to be debarred from profiting by practice, and changing opinion upon the conviction of experiment."[†]

Notwithstanding that the great innovator Time may have rendered some passages in Fox's speeches unsuitable to the present House, any one who would acquire the art of public speaking, whether in Parliament or elsewhere, should *study* at least the six great speeches collected in the volume from which we have taken our extracts. Lord Brougham, in his letter of advice to Zachary Macaulay on the training of his son as a speaker, said of Fox's speech on the Westminster Scrutiny, "The first part of

---

[*] "Select British Eloquence," p. 482.   [†] *Ibid.* p. 495.

it he should pore over till he has it by heart." In the homeli-
ness of Fox's diction we are reminded of Mr. Cobden, "Give me,"
said Fox, "an elegant Latin and a homely Saxon word, and I will
always choose the latter." Fox and Cobden were alike in another
respect. Curran said of Fox, "he was the most honest and
candid of speakers, and spoke only to convince fairly. It seemed
to me as if he were addressing himself to me personally."[*] This
is equally descriptive of the great Free-Trader.

We have often heard it said that Parliamentary eloquence is
not what it was; that there were giants in old days with whom
no man of late times can compare. Charles Butler, in his
"Reminiscences," laid down the arbitrary rule "that no member
of either House can be ranked among the orators of this country
whom Lord North did not see, or who did not see Lord North."
Let us test this by facts. Lord North saw or was seen by the
two Pitts, the first Lord Holland, Fox, Burke, Mansfield, Sheridan,
Dunning, Barré, Charles Townshend, Windham. The roll of
orators would close here, and the great speakers of the period
from 1820 to 1827, which, according to Lord Russell, was the
most brilliant for oratory in the House of Commons,[†] would be
excluded. We should therefore lose the great men of that
period, viz. Grattan, Plunket—in the opinion of the best judges,
the most perfect orator of that time—Earls Grey and Grenville,
Canning, Peel, Brougham, Lyndhurst, and also all those who
have arisen since, including Lords Derby, Russell, Ellenborough,
Macaulay, and Lytton, Sheil, O'Connell, Gladstone, Disraeli,
Cobden, and Bright. The truth is, as stated by a recent writer
on this subject, "Whenever speaking was possible, there have
been able, forcible, and fine speakers."[‡]

While referring to the period 1820 to '27, we may remark that
Lord Russell records that, notwithstanding Mr. Canning's theory
of House of Commons speaking, in his practice, "the *purpurei
panni* of his speeches did not sometimes well combine with the
plain broadcloth of a business argument."[§] One of Canning's
happiest efforts was his reply to Sir James Mackintosh's defence of
the adjuration "by the *hate* you bear to Orangemen," contained
in an address to the Irish people by the Catholic Association.
Our quotation will illustrate the fate of those who, like Mackintosh, speak essays, or introduce metaphysical subtleties into debates.

"I will not follow every gentleman who has strained his faculties to
explain away this unfortunate expression; but will come at once to my

---

[*] "H. Crabb Robinson's Diary," vol. i. p. 421.
[†] "Speeches: Introduction," vol. i. p. 42.
[‡] *Quarterly Review*, No. 264, April, 1872, p. 463.
[§] "Speeches," vol. i. p. 42.

honourable and learned friend the member for Knaresborough [Sir James Mackintosh]. to whom the palm in this contest of ingenuity must be conceded by all his competitors. My honourable friend has expended abundant research and subtilty upon this inquiry, and having resolved that phrase into its elements in the crucible of his philosophical mind, has produced it to us purified and refined to a degree that must command the admiration of all who take delight in metaphysical alchemy. My honourable and learned friend began by telling us that *hatred* is no bad thing in itself. ‘ I hate a Tory,’ says my honourable friend, ‘ and another man hates a cat; but it does not follow that he would hunt down the cat, or I the Tory.’ Nay, so far from it— hatred, if it be properly managed, is, according to my honourable friend’s theory, no bad preface to a rational esteem and affection. It prepares its votaries for a reconciliation of differences—for lying down with their most inveterate enemies, like the leopard and the kid in the vision of the prophet.

“ This dogma is a little startling, but it is not altogether without precedent. It is borrowed from a character in a play which is, I daresay, as great a favourite with my learned friend as it is with me—I mean the comedy of *The Rivals*, in which Mrs. Malaprop, giving a lecture on the subject of marriage to her niece (who is unreasonable enough to talk of liking as a necessary preliminary to such a union) says, ‘ What have you to do with your likings and your preferences, child ? Depend upon it, it is safest to begin with a little aversion. I am sure I hated your poor dear uncle like a blackamoor before we were married ; and yet you know, my dear, what a good wife I made him.’ Such is my learned friend’s argument, to a hair.

“ But finding that this doctrine did not appear to go down with the House as glibly as he had expected, my honourable and learned friend presently changed his tack, and put forward a theory, which, whether for novelty or for beauty, I pronounce to be incomparable ; and, in short, as wanting nothing to recommend it but a slight foundation in truth. ‘ True philosophy,’ says my honourable friend, ‘ will always contrive to lead men to virtue by the instrumentality of their conflicting vices. The virtues, where more than one exist, may live harmoniously together ; but the vices bear mortal antipathy to one another, and therefore furnish to the moral engineer the power by which he can make each keep the other under control.’ Admirable ! but upon this doctrine, the poor man who has but one single vice must be in a very bad way. No fulcrum, no moral power for effecting his cure. Whereas his more fortunate neighbour, who has two or more vices in his composition, is in a fair way of becoming a very virtuous member of society. I wonder how my learned friend would like to have this doctrine introduced into his domestic establishment. For instance, suppose that I discharge a servant because he is addicted to liquor, I could not venture to recommend him to my honourable and learned friend ; it might be the poor man’s *only* fault, and therefore clearly incorrigible. But if I had the good fortune to find out that he was also addicted to stealing, might I not, with a safe conscience, send him to my learned friend with a very strong recommendation, saying, I send you a man whom I know to be a drunkard; but I am happy to assure you he is also a thief: you cannot do better than employ him; you will make his drunkenness counteract his thieving, and no doubt you will bring him out of the conflict a very moral personage—my honourable and learned friend, however, not content with laying down these rules for reformation, thought it right to exemplify them in his own person, and, like Pope's Longinus ' to be himself the great sublime he drew.' My learned friend tells us that Dr. Johnson was what he [Dr. Johnson himself] called *a good hater ;* and that among the qualities which he hated most, were those which my honourable friend unites in his own person —that of Whig, and that of Scotchman. ' So that,' says my honourable friend, ' if Dr. Johnson were alive, and were to meet me at the Club of which he was a founder, and of which I am now an unworthy member, he would probably break up the meeting rather than sit it out in such society.' No, sir, not so. My honourable and learned friend forgets his own theory. If he had been *only* a Whig, or *only* a Scotchman, Dr. Johnson might have treated him as he apprehends ; but being both, the great moralist would have said to my honourable friend, 'Sir, you are too much of a Whig to be a good Scotchman ; and sir, you are too much of a Scotchman to be a good Whig.' It is no doubt from the collision of these two vices in my learned friend's person, that he has become what I, and all who have the happiness of meeting him at the club, find him—an entirely faultless character."[*]

It was of course impossible for the House of Commons to be twice reformed without the results thus described by De Tocqueville :

" All laws which tend to make the representative still more dependent upon the elector, not only affect the conduct of the Legislature, but also their language. They exercise a simultaneous influence on affairs themselves and on the manner in which they are discussed."[†]

This is illustrated by the greater length of our debates. In the unreformed Parliament, until its later days, few but the party chiefs spoke. In the singular and now little known book mentioned at the head of this paper, one of "Single-speech Hamilton's " dicta shows the estimation in which speeches by the rank and file of party were then held. "Let government always state its argument upon some clear principle : their followers must have something to say, and it is no great matter what."[‡]

In the time of Walpole and the elder Pitt an adjourned debate was, we believe, unknown. According to Lord Brougham

---

* "Select British Eloquence," p. 694, 5.
† " Democracy in America," part ii. vol. iii. p. 189. English Translation.
‡ "Parliamentary Logic," p. 37. A new and methodically arranged edition of this book would be a great boon to all training for public speaking of any kind.

Pitt first introduced long speeches. In the days of Lord North and the younger Pitt adjournments were certainly rare, and so far as we can learn were never for more than one night. A week or fortnight's debate was unknown. De Tocqueville's proposition is further illustrated by the useful but modern practice of "calling attention" to subjects at the time of moving adjournments or on going into committee of supply—the Friday evening *conversazione*, as it has been called. It is further illustrated by the great number of questions put to ministers nearly every evening; in Pitt's time never more than three or four were put at a sitting.

There is some truth in the following remarks of Sir Arthur Helps; but against them should be set the fact that they are written by one who never has been in Parliament, and as his writings show, is thoroughly imbued with the spirit of bureaucracy, and therefore jealous and impatient of Parliamentary control :—

"The vanity or diseased activity, or the desire for prominence induces members of the Legislature to busy themselves needlessly in interference with the Executive. The action caused by these motives should be steadily resisted, or otherwise great mischief may ensue, and indeed does take place at the present time. Needless returns are called for, occupying the time and attention of public offices which ought to be otherwise employed; needless questions are asked in Parliament which sadly waste the time of the Ministers who have to answer them ; and what is a far more serious evil, the public officers are hampered, worried, and weakened by a sense of their double responsibility ; to their chiefs and the country on the one hand, and to Parliament on the other."[*]

The distinction drawn, or rather the opposition suggested, between the country and Parliament, its representative, is amusing and significant.

Another result of the greater dependence of the members upon the electors is that speeches are often made less to the House than to the constituencies. This was the case with Mr. Bright's earlier Parliamentary speeches; he has now abandoned the practice, and his influence in the House has immensely increased. In former times this habit did not prevail. "Consider" (is Hamilton's advice) "not only whether the argument is for or against you, but whether the House of Commons topics are for or against you."[†] Mr. Canning, acting on a maxim attributed to the younger Pitt, that "eloquence is in the assembly,

---

[*] "Thoughts upon Government," p. 36, 169. Comp. Mr. Lowe's "Letters and Speeches on Reform," p. 89, 92.
[†] "Parliamentary Logic," p. 45.

not in the speaker,"*—meaning that the speaker is effective in proportion as he gives utterance to the thought or feeling which prevails in the assembly—used during a debate to move about the House and converse freely with all sections of members. In his speech he expressed in his own striking language the opinions he found prevalent in the House, and the speech of its leader formed a sort of *precis* of the reasons which guided the vote of the majority. The modern custom of speaking in Parliament to the public requires dexterous management, as the House is jealous of it, and its avowed or frequent practice would be fatal to the success or position in the House of any member.

Bearing in mind these changes in the tone and habits of the House, produced by the changes in its constitution, and acting on the canon of David Hume that "criticism is nearly useless unless the critic quotes innumerable examples," let us devote the remainder of our space to an examination of House of Commons eloquence, as illustrated by some of those who since 1832 have been its chief speakers.

Earl Russell is now a dweller in what has been happily described as "the political middle state in which the disembodied spirits of men who once lived in the House of Commons await upon red benches the final judgment of history;" but since, as Lord John Russell, he introduced the first Reform Act, and was for so many years leader of the reformed House, of which, as Mr. Disraeli well said, "his character and career are precious possessions which the members of that House will always cherish,"† he may well claim our first attention. Mr. Disraeli, in "Coningsby," describes the Whig leader's speaking in terms on which we cannot hope to improve, and which we therefore venture to transcribe.

"Lord John Russell . . . . is not a natural orator, and labours under physical deficiencies which even a Demosthenic impulse could scarcely overcome. But he is experienced in debate, quick in reply, fertile in resource, takes large views, and frequently compensates for a dry and hesitating manner, by the expression of those noble truths that flash across the fancy of men of poetic temperament when addressing popular assemblies. If we add to this a private life of dignified repute, the accidents of his birth and rank, which never can be severed from the man, the scion of a great historic family, and born, as it were, to the hereditary service of the state, it is difficult to ascertain at what period or under what circumstances the Whig party have ever possessed, or could obtain a more efficient leader."‡

---

* *Vide* Lord Lytton's "Miscellaneous Works," vol. iii. p. 100. Comp. "Realmah," by Sir A. Helps, vol. i. p. 273.

† Hansard, ii., April, 1851.   ‡ "Coningsby," ed. 1853, p. 201.

"What an array," said Samuel Rogers to the Duke of Wellington, "there is in the House of Commons against Lord John Russell—Peel, Stanley, Graham, etc."—"Lord John," replied the Duke, "is a host in himself."* Lord Brougham also has left on record his opinion that "Lord Russell's errors are insignificant compared with his great merits as a judicious leader of his party, his perfect honesty, and his inestimable services . . . . As a speaker he is very good, clear, and distinct, if not always forcible; as a debater he is quite first-rate."†

The Quarterly Reviewer whom we have before quoted says "he particularly excelled in a comprehensive reply at the end of an important debate." This is true, and he bore in mind, or at least acted on, Hamilton's dictum, "Consider of your conclusion, that you may be ready to finish whenever you find it convenient."‡ When his party was ready to vote, and the whipper-in pulled his coat-tail, or otherwise gave him notice, Lord John would at once come to the "Well, then, I say, sir," which was the usual beginning of his perorations. Mr. Gladstone, and even Lord Palmerston, would run the risk of losing the division rather than not say all he wished to say. Spite of the deficiencies to which Mr. Disraeli refers, and of another to which he does not allude—viz., the poverty of the diction of Lord Russell's speeches—we never heard among Parliamentary speakers one more successful or impressive. It was our fortune to hear one of his ablest House of Commons efforts of later years. At the general election in 1857, Lord John found it necessary to conciliate an active section of his city supporters by promising to reconsider the question of the ballot with reference to its successful working in the Australian colonies. Shortly after the new Parliament met, Mr. Berkeley brought forward the subject. The House was indisposed to debate it, or even to listen to its supporters. A new member, an Irish barrister, insisted on addressing the House, and spoke with much of that physical force oratory' which is a mark of the *perfervidum ingenium Hibernorum tam Scotorum.* The effort, let us hope, relieved the speaker himself, for the House resembled the "bursting forth of Bedlams," and the shrieks of 'vide, 'vide, and other Parliamentary forms of inarticulate interruption prevented any of the speaker's words reaching the ears of strangers, or alas! of those who might otherwise have recorded them for the benefit of admiring constituents. At length the Irishman, satisfied or exhausted, sat down, and Lord Russell,

---

* It is amusing to compare this estimate of Lord Russell with that of William IV. *Vide* recently published "Memoirs of Baron Stockmar," vol. i. p. 329.

† "Life and Times," vol. iii. p. 469. ‡ "Parliamentary Logic," p. 37.

then out of office, rose from a back bench. The House immediately quieted down, and he proceeded—as regarded his engage-
ment with his constituents—

> "To keep the word of promise to the ear
> And break it to the sense."

As a fulfilment of his pledge it was a mere evasion. Not
one word of fresh argument was adduced. The speech was a
verification of Sydney Smith's saying, "The Russells never alter
their opinions; they are an excellent race, but they must be
trepanned in order to be convinced." The old fallacies against
the ballot, uttered in introducing the first Reform act, were repeated, as they were in the very last debate on the question in
the Lords, the speaker ever seeming superbly unconscious that
they had been as oft refuted as repeated. In fact their repetition became, to quote Carlyle, "enough to make not only the
angels but the jackasses weep." The Australian evidence was
got rid of by a not very apt quotation from the old comedy of
The Rover; nevertheless the House delightedly listened, and
cheered at the repetition of each well-known fallacy and plati-
tude, as the admirers of Mario or Patti applaud their execution
of a favourite air. At length the speaker by way of peroration
rose to an unusual pitch of dignity and impressiveness, calling
to our mind Lord Lytton's description of him in the "New
Timon":—

> "But see our statesman when the steam is on,
> And languid Johnny glows to glorious John"—

and declared "So long as I have a vote to give I will give it
against the ballot, and in favour of the more ancient, the more
English, the more manly way of open voting."

Mr. Disraeli, in the scene in "Coningsby" when he describes
Lucian Gay as treating the members of the Grumpy Club to an
imitation of a debate, writes of the mimic:—"After having endured for hours in sarcastic silence the menacing finger of Sir
Robert, shaking over the green table, and appealing to his misdeeds
in the irrevocable pages of Hansard, Lord John himself could
not have afforded a more perfect representation of pluck."[*]

This imaginary scene was recalled to our mind by a real one,
the occasion, namely, when the late Earl of Derby made his
memorable attack on Lord Russell, while Foreign Minister,
likening him to "Bottom the weaver," and describing his policy
by "the two homely words meddle and muddle." It was nearly
the last occasion on which Lord Derby—with much diminished
fire and force, it is true—poured out on the head of an opponent

---

[*] P. 169, ed. 1853.

one of those vials of mingled fire and bitterness which of old he used to empty on the heads of O'Connell and the Whigs. In describing one of these attacks, which took place thirty years before that to which we refer, a writer of that day said—

"The impenetrable coldness, we might almost say the apathetic insensibility, of Lord John Russell, was proof against it all; and while the tones of his great opponent's burning oratory yet lingered in the ear amidst the thunders of the enthusiasm they had kindled, the noble Lord, with his usual quiet coolness of manner, proceeded to be sarcastic about it."

So, on the occasion of which we write, there could not be a more perfect representation of pluck, of impenetrable coldness, than Lord Russell, when with his usual quiet coolness of manner, he retorted on his opponent—"The noble Earl reminds me of what was said of the late Mr. Sheridan, that he resorted to his memory for his jokes, and to his imagination for his facts."—To borrow again from the same writer, "This was chilling."

In "The New Timon," Lord Lytton says of Lord Russell—

> "Next cool, and all unconscious of reproach
> Comes the calm Johnny who upset the coach;
> How formed to lead, if not too proud to please,
> His fame would fire you, but his manners freeze;
> Like or dislike, he does not care a jot,
> He wants your vote, but your affection not."

"The British Constitution preserved in ice," was the description of his oratory given by a very competent judge. "On the boards of the House of Commons," Mr. Cobden once said to us, "Johnny is one of the most subtle and dangerous of opponents; take him off those boards and I care nothing for him." After considerable experience of Lord Russell's extra-Parliamentary speeches, we rate his versatility as a speaker far higher than did Mr. Cobden. A memorable instance was in 1857, when an attempt was made by the Palmerston Government to exile from the House of Commons every man who had been sufficiently independent of party to vote for Mr. Cobden's resolution in reference to the affair of the Lorcha *Arrow.* The Association which managed the electioneering affairs of the Liberal party in the city, lent themselves to the conspiracy at head quarters. Lord Russell was erased from the ticket recommended by the Association, and there was substituted for his name that of a highly respectable city banker, who had for some years sat in Parliament, and whose career was modelled upon that of the member who has left the following record of his experiences:—"I was never present at any debate I could avoid. I never voted but once according to my own opinion. I found that the only way to be quiet in Parliament was always to vote with the Ministers." Lord Russell would not tamely submit to the indignity put upon him, and threw himself on the people. He called a meeting, at which his former supporters, the chief of the city Whigs, were "conspicuous by their absence," and announced that he came to appeal to the electors from the decision of the so-called and self-appointed Liberal Association, and proceeded with his usual quiet sarcasm to deal with his betrayers and their catspaw.

"What would be thought (said the noble Lord) of any gentleman who should so treat his old servant, who should say to him, Why, John, you're getting old, you have made two or three mistakes lately; I have made up my mind to get rid of you, and I have sent for a young man from Northampton to fill your place."

Never was appeal more successful. Lord Russell was triumphantly returned, and the young man from Northampton experienced the fate of Codrus :—

> "Nil habuit Codrus, attamen infelix ille,
> Perdidit totum nil,—"

he disappeared from Parliament for ever. From Lord Russell let us turn to his great opponent.

Superior to Lord Russell in diction, in delivery, in fluency, in power and tone of voice, and unrivalled, at least amongst living speakers, in sarcasm and invective, Mr. Disraeli is in point of moral force inferior as a speaker to the great Whig leader. However Lord Russell may disappoint or irritate his hearers (and he has frequently caused us to experience both these sensations) he always produces in their minds a conviction of his thorough sincerity. Mr. Disraeli on the contrary never seems to us more than a very clever and gentlemanly actor, the accidents of whose career cause him to make the particular speech he is making, as they might in different circumstances have caused him to make one on the other side. We heard him in 1859 make his début in Parliament as a Reformer, and propose the first Tory Reform Bill; it seemed to us then, and we retain unaltered the impression, that, as regards any feeling of conviction or interest shown by the speaker, he might as well have been proposing not the extension but the extinction of the suffrage. The same effect was produced by his speech when his party determined to defend Church rates as one of the outworks of the Establishment. It was then that he first appeared as leader of the Parliamentary Churchmen, a character which he maintained for some years with indifferent success and then laid aside, but which lately he has shown signs of reassuming. Spite of his high-sounding phrases about "our parochial system" and "the Church of England," it was clear that he could as easily have thrown the cold glitter of his rhetoric into a speech in favour of the total and immediate abolition, not only of Church rates, but of the Establishment itself.

In Mr. Disraeli's delivery there is a peculiarity which on our first hearing him, struck us arose from his acting on this advice of Hamilton :—

"Preconsider what you mean should be the finest part of your speech, and in speaking connect it with what has incidentally fallen in debate ; and when you come to that premeditated and finest part, hesitate and appear to boggle ; catch at some expression that shall fall short of your idea, and then seem to hit at last upon the true thing. This has always an extraordinary effect, and gives the air of extempore genius to what you say."*

We showed this passage to a friend who sat in the House with Mr. Disraeli for more than thirty years, and he agreed with us.† Mr. Disraeli's diction in speaking and in writing is not drawn from that "well of English undefiled," to which our greatest speakers and writers have ever resorted His style often nearly approaches, not seldom actually attains to, the bombastic. Sometimes he ludicrously misuses words, as when writing of the accession of Dr. Newman, he says "That extraordinary event has been *apologized* for but never explained,"‡ evidently thinking the *Apologia pro vita sua* was intended to be an apology in the popular sense. Dr. Newman thus characteristically disposes of this taunt :—

"I should also venture to offer the same passage [in his "Catholicity of the English Church"] to the notice of an eminent Statesman and brilliant writer, who has lately gone out of his way to observe that 'the secession of Dr. Newman is an extraordinary event, which has been apologized for but has never been explained,' except that I doul t whether a genuine politician could possibly enter into any motives of action not political, and was not likely, even in the province of physics, t) demand reasons of state or party interest in explanation of a chimpanzee being confined of a human baby, or a Caucasian man developing into an Archangel."§

It was Mr. Disraeli's bombastic diction, and his too confident and presumptuous manner, which offended the House and caused

* "Parliamentary Logic," p. 43.
† "Brougham," said Lord Granville, " used to introduce his most elaborately prepared passages by a slight hesitation. When he seemed to pause in search of thoughts or of words we knew that he had a sentence ready cut and dried." —"Senior's Conversations of De Tocqueville," vol. ii. p. 63.
‡ General Preface to Collected Edition of Novels. 1870.
§ "Essays : Historical and Critical." By J. H. Newman. The allusion is to a Speech of Mr. Disraeli, in which he said—"The question is this—Is man an ape or an angel ? My Lord, I am on the side of the angels."

his melancholy failure when he first spoke in it. It was a striking contrast to the graceful, harmonious, modest, and almost timid maiden speech of Mr. Gladstone, which made an impression as favourable as that made by Mr. Disraeli was unfavourable.* The House (it has been well said) will have *kotou* from new men. Now that the House and the public are used to Mr. Disraeli, there appears nothing in the speech, when read, to have deserved the storm of hostile feeling which the report shows it provoked.

Before we part from Mr. Disraeli, we must in justice observe, that his speech in 1855 against the Borough Franchise Extension Bill contains this passage, which Lord Russell—a very competent judge—pronounces to be " equal to any speech of our greatest parliamentary speakers."

" I doubt very much whether a democracy is a government that would suit this country ; and it is just as well that the House, when coming to a vote on this question, should really consider if that be the real issue, between retaining the present constitution—not the present constituent-body, but between the present constitution and a democracy. It is just as well for the House to recollect that what is at issue is of some price. You must remember, not to use the word profanely, that we are dealing really with a peculiar people. There is no country at the present moment that exists under the circumstances and under the same conditions as the people of this realm. You have, for example, an ancient, powerful, richly endowed church, and perfect religious liberty. You have unbroken order and complete freedom. You have estates as large as the Romans; you have a commercial system of enterprise such as Carthage and Venice united never equalled. And you must remember that this peculiar country, with these strong contrasts, is governed not by force ; it is not governed by standing armies, it is governed by a most singular series of traditionary influences, which generation after generation cherishes and preserves because they know that they embalm customs and represent the law. And with this, what have you done ? You have created the greatest empire that ever existed in modern times. You have amassed a capital of fabulous amount. You have devised and sustained a system of credit still more marvellous, and, above all, you have established and maintained a scheme, so vast and complicated, of labour and industry, that the history of the world offers no parallel to it. And all these mighty creations are out of all proportion to the essential and indigenous elements and resources of the country. If you destroy that state of society, remember this—England cannot begin again. There are countries which have been in great peril and gone through great suffering ; there are the United States, who in our own immediate day have had great trials ; you have had—perhaps even now in the States of America you have—a protracted and fratricidal war which has lasted for four years ; but if it lasted for four years more, vast as would be the disaster and desolation, when ended,

* " Autobiographical Recollections of George Pryme, M.P.," p. 523.

the United States might begin again, because the United States would only be in the same condition that England was at the end of the war of the Roses (and probably she had not even three millions of population), with vast tracts of virgin soil and mineral treasures, not only undeveloped but undiscovered. Then you have France. France had a real revolution in our days and those of our predecessors—a real revolution, not merely a political and social revolution. You have had the institutions of the country uprooted, the orders of society abolished—you had even the landmarks and local names erased. But France could begin again. France had the greatest spread of the most exuberant soil in Europe; she had, and always had, a very limited population, living in a most simple manner. France, therefore could begin again. But England—the England we know, the England we live in, the England of which we are proud—could not begin again. I don't mean to say that after great troubles England would become a howling wilderness. No doubt the good sense of the people would to some degree prevail, and some fragments of the national character would survive; but it would not be the old England—the England of power and tradition, of credit and capital, that now exists. That is not in the nature of things, and, under these circumstances, I hope the House will, when the question before us is one impeaching the character of our constitution, sanction no step that has a preference for democracy, but that they will maintain the ordered state of Free England in which we live."*

With these words the Conservative leader led his followers against the proposal to reduce the borough franchise from 10*l.* to 6*l.* Within two years he proposed household suffrage, and the "superlative Hebrew conjuror" again carried his party with him.

Lord Lyndhurst, who had heard Pitt and Fox, and whose own high place amongst speakers stamps his opinion with authority, assigned the first place among modern parliamentary orators to the late Earl of Derby. Lord Brougham, who more than any man of his own day or who is now living, studied oratory as a science and practised it as an art, when asked whom do you consider the greatest orator in England? used to give the evasive and enigmatic reply, "Lord Derby no doubt is the second," implying of course that he himself was the first. The general verdict, we apprehend, will place Lord Derby in the first place. A reminiscent whom we have before quoted thus records his impression.

" I have heard Pitt and Fox and other great speakers, but never any to equal Lord Derby, when Mr. Stanley, for eloquence and sweetness of expression; his manner was most graceful, and his voice harmonious.

---

* Hansard, May 5th, 1865. *Vide* also "The Oratorical Year Book for 1865," pp. 192-4.

I never missed a debate, and observed his speeches and his conduct on every occasion, and I could not help thinking his object was to become Prime Minister, than that he was actuated by any definite political principle."[*]

Two of Lord Derby's colleagues in the Grey Administration have recorded their opinions of his speaking and his services to the first Reform Act; it is interesting to compare them with one another and with that of the outsider whom we have just quoted.

"Stanley's talents (says Lord Brougham) were of a very high, though not of the highest, order. He was a perfectly ready and a very able debater, with great powers of clear and distinct statement, with a high pitched voice, far from musical, but clearly heard in every part of the House. He argued closely, but he required much backing and cheering, and never could fight an uphill battle."

What follows is scarcely credible, and requires confirmation.

"In debate, he, like Canning, stuck at nothing in order to snatch an advantage. With the gravest face he would invent what he assumed his adversary to have said, but what he notoriously never did say. His judgment was *nil*, or nearly so. He would make a statement, well aware that it would be answered; and committed the most unpardonable of all errors, that of suppressing a fact or ignoring a paper which he knew must be produced against him. . . . . This all proceeded from the desire to gain a momentary triumph."

His services to Reform are thus estimated: "He was quite Reformer enough naturally to take to the Reform Bill, having on that subject nothing to unsay; but he helped it very little, being fully engaged in his own, the Irish, department."[†]

On the other hand, Earl Russell, who sat in the Commons with Lord Derby, and was therefore a better judge than the Chancellor, who, it is known never entered the Commons as a visitor until thirty years after he ceased to be a member, gives a more generous, and we believe a more correct judgment of his once colleague and afterwards opponent.

"Throughout the debates which took place upon the Reform Bill, while Lord Althorp and I had the greater portion of the labour, and a still larger portion of the responsibility, the palm of eloquence in debate belonged undoubtedly to Lord Stanley. . . . . . By his animated appeals to the Liberal majority, by his readiness in answering

---

[*] "Autobiographical Recollections of George Pryme, M.P.," p. 253. On the other hand Earl Russell says—"Lord Derby, a man noble by character as well as by rank, was always ready to sacrifice office for the sake of maintaining his opinions.—"Speeches," vol. i. Introduction, p. 170.

[†] "Life and Times," vol. iii. pp. 375, 6.

the sophisms of his opponents, by the precision and boldness of his language, by his display of all the great qualities of a parliamentary orator and an able statesman, he successfully vindicated the authority of the Government and satisfied their supporters in the House of Commons."*

Lord Derby's greatest speech was the one which in 1833 as Irish Secretary he made on the celebrated Coercion Bill. Lord Althorp, as leader of the House, introduced the bill in a speech showing he had no heart for the task. The liberal majority were disappointed and sullen, and there was every prospect of the loss of the bill and the defeat of the Government. Earl Russell relates† that Mr. Stanley (as he then was) said to him, " I meant not to have spoken until to-morrow night, but I find I must speak to-night;" he then took his official box of papers to a private room, and two or three hours afterwards rose, and explained with admirable clearness the insecure and alarming state of Ireland. The House became appalled and agitated at the dreadful picture which he placed before their eyes. He then turned upon O'Connell ; he recalled to the memory of the House that O'Connell had spoken of them as " 658 scoundrels," and thus excited the anger of the men so designated against their slanderer.

"Sir, I do not advert to expressions said to have been used by the honourable and learned gentleman at a meeting of the humbler classes in this metropolis ; I do not advert to expressions which I will not believe, till I hear them avowed, could have proceeded from the lips of, shall I say, any member of this assembly ? No, but from the lips of a man who had any pretensions, the very remotest pretensions, to the name and character of a gentleman."

He then went on to accuse O'Connell of seeking to trammel and control the speeches and votes of members. He read part of a letter from O'Connell to the Irish Volunteers calling their attention to the votes of certain members, and proceeded :

"Sir, does the honourable and learned gentleman admit that interference with the powers of Parliament ?"

"Mr. O'Connell.—Certainly."

"Mr. Stanley.—Then I put it to this House, whether in the abused and prostituted name of liberty, any frothy declaimer for popular rights ever put forward so flimsy a veil over a most unconstitutional and tyrannical interference with the privileges of the Legislature, by a self-constituted and arbitrary tribunal, by this outrageous appeal— not to the people to whom the honourable gentleman is responsible for his conduct in Parliament, but to the volunteer society, which is to spread its mighty arms throughout Ireland until it brings every-

---

* "Speeches and Introduction," vol. i. p. 69.   † *Ibid.* pp. 35, 6.

thing within its grasp, and subjects everything to its uncontrolled and uncontrollable dominion."*

The House, which two hours before seemed about to yield to the great agitator, was now (says Earl Russell) almost ready to tear him in pieces. In the midst of the storm which his eloquence had raised, Mr. Stanley sat down, having achieved one of the greatest triumphs of eloquence ever won in a popular assembly by the powers of oratory. It was, perhaps (says another eye-witness), the most complete and sudden reanimation of a whole party with his own spirit by one man not recognised as, or claiming to be, its leader, that has been witnessed in our time.

Even in Lord Derby's latest days, when time had impaired his voice, it was a great intellectual treat to hear him address the House of Lords. In that House, the most striking characteristic of his speaking, having regard to the arrogance which lay deep in his character, was the deference, almost humility, with which while in fact leading the House, he offered his advice to his peers. The last time it was our good fortune to hear him, about three years before his death, he forcibly brought back to our minds Lord Lytton's description of him in "St. Stephen's."

> "Yet who not listens with delighted smile,
> To the pure Saxon of that silver style;
> In the clear style a heart as clear is seen,
> Prompt to the rash, revolting from the mean."

Prompt to the rash he ever was, and that evening showed that age had lessened neither his promptitude nor his rashness. The occasion was the Roman Catholic Oath Bill; in speaking against it he referred to an expression more forcible than elegant of its supporters, who called the bill "one to unmuzzle the Dissenters," and thus characteristically dealt with it.

"Unmuzzle us, says an honourable gentleman who has lately been returned for an Irish county by the influence of the Roman Catholic priesthood. Unmuzzle us! and why? Because we are harmless? No! because we want to bite. If a man comes to me with a dog with a muzzle on, and says, Take the muzzle off this poor creature; he will do no harm, he is quite harmless, and besides, the muzzle is half-rotten and affords no great protection—I understand him; but if he says, This is a most vicious animal, and nothing prevents his pulling you and me to pieces except the muzzle which is put round his neck, and therefore I want you to take it off, I am inclined to say, 'I am very much obliged to you, but I had rather keep the muzzle on.'"†

---

* See the Speech in Hansard, Feb. 27th, 1833; and in "The Orator." S. O. Beeton, 248 Strand. 1866.
† Hansard, July, 1865. "Oratorical Year Book," 1865.

This, like his rash admission "Tell me the names of the great landowners of a county, and I will tell you the politics of the county members," served as a weapon to his opponents. It was taken as a declaration of Conservative policy, and at the general election which immediately followed, the cry of " muzzling the Dissenters " was raised against the party, and materially contributed to their defeat.

Mr. Gladstone fills so prominent a position, and the beauties and defects of his speeches are so familiar to everybody, that we must dismiss him with few words. The reminiscent whom we have before quoted, says that from the first his speaking was like that of Lord Derby, " like a stream pouring forth," and he records the remark of a foreigner, that until he had heard Mr. Gladstone speak, he never believed that ours was a musical language ; but that after hearing him he was convinced that it was one of the most melodious of all living tongues.* The most striking difference between Mr. Gladstone and his contemporaries is the greater amount of earnestness, even passion, he throws into his speeches. " When (says a shrewd observer) he is bent upon replying, he will evidence in an unmistakable manner his impatience for the opportunity ; when it comes he will spring to his feet with the animation of an athlete, and supposing his wrath to have been really roused, he will seek no means to limit or moderate the intensity of its expression."†

In connexion with this, it is interesting to note a remark of Mr. Gladstone's to Bunsen, who asked him why he did not speak oftener. He replied that he was withheld by restraint upon himself lest he should find too much difficulty in keeping within Christian bounds of moderation in endeavouring to utter faithfully the truth, and yet avoid all that might be construed into personality.‡

Mr. Gladstone has been truly called the most polished speaker in the House of Commons, his defect is that he has no appreciation of the charm or value of terseness. Some of his late speeches exhibit a marked improvement in this respect, notably that on introducing his Irish Church Bill, in which, as Mr. Disraeli remarked, there was not a word wasted.

Mr. Bright holds by general consent so high a place among the great speakers of the House of Commons, that we need not refer more particularly to him, and we turn to his great coadjutor Mr. Cobden.

Some remarks depreciatory of Mr. Cobden's rank as a

* " Pryme's Autobiographical Recollections," p. 253.
† " The Gladstone Government." Cabinet Pictures, by a Templar.
‡ " Bunsen's Memoirs, &c.," vol. ii. p. 306.

parliamentary speaker appear in the *Quarterly Review* article to which we have before referred. We dissent from our contemporary's estimate. What Sir Robert Peel said of Mr. Cobden's eloquence, that it was "all the more effective because it was simple and unadorned," is as true of his parliamentary, as of his extra-parliamentary speeches. It is impossible to find in popular oratory any example of finer taste in the arrangement of what the speaker had to say, and the manner of saying it. His greatest parliamentary effort was his speech in 1849— to which recent events give additional interest—when he first brought before the House the question of International Arbitration. Though the subject was novel, and thought by some a fit one for ridicule, the motion was nevertheless received by the House with great seriousness and respect. It was opposed on the part of the Russell Government, by Lord Palmerston, in a spirit of moderation and deference, and though rejected it was evidently with regret. We can give only one extract.

"I feel regret that there should be so much misapprehension in the House, in reference to the motion I am about to make. What has just fallen from the hon. member for Bucks (Mr. Disraeli) is a proof of this misconception; for he would not have presumed to sneer at a motion before it was made, unless he had conceived that there was something so unreasonable and preposterous about it, that it ought to be condemned before it was heard. I have heard that learned gentleman indulge in a sneer before on many occasions; but they have been *ex post facto* sneers. I have never until now heard him sneer at a matter by anticipation. He has grounded that sneer on an observation drawn forth by a subject which was calculated, above all others, to move the milk of human kindness in our bosoms. How it was possible for an honourable member, in reference to the answer returned by the American President to Lady Franklin's letter, to indulge in a sneer of that kind I cannot understand; unless it be that the honourable gentleman is incapable of anything but sneering. I accept those acts of the American and Russian governments as proofs that we live in altered times. As the right honourable member for the University of Oxford (Mr. Gladstone) has well observed, at no former period of the world's history has there been an instance of foreign governments sending out, at their expense, to seek for scientific adventurers unconnected with their own community. Accepting this as a proof that we live in different times from those that are past, I think there is nothing unreasonable in our seeking to take another step towards consolidating the peace of nations, and securing us against the recurrence of the greatest calamity that can afflict mankind."*

The secret of Mr. Cobden's influence as a speaker lay in this,

---

* "Speeches of Richard Cobden, Esq., M.P., delivered in 1849, revised by himself," p. 95-6. See also the Speech in "Bright and Rogers's Collection."

that he was filled with one aim, and one only, to convince his audience how their interests lay ; and he absolutely identified himself with them for the moment, in order to bring these interests home to them. Simple and unadorned as were his speeches—" My speeches," he said, " never have any perorations " —they contain indications that, had he pleased, he might, like Mr. Bright, without impairing his efficiency have adopted a more ornate style. In his memorable correspondence with Mr. Delane he gives an interesting account of his method of preparation.

" I am not in the habit of writing a word beforehand of what I speak in public. Like other speakers, practice has given me as perfect self-possession in the presence of an audience as if I was writing in my closet. Now my constant and overruling thought, while addressing a public meeting, the one necessity which long experience of the arts of controversialists has impressed on my mind, is to avoid the possibility of being misrepresented, and prevent my opponents from raising a false issue—a trick of logic as old as the time of Aristotle. If I have, as some favourable critics are pleased to think, sometimes spoken with clearness, it is more owing to this ever-present fear of misrepresentation than any other cause : it is thus that the most noxious things in life may have their uses."[*]

Mr. Lowe resembles Mr. Cobden in the simplicity of his delivery, and their speeches are similar in their lucid arrangement, in the terseness of their diction, in the sequentially linked chain of their argument and their ingenious logic ; but Mr. Lowe's speeches show a subtle irony, an elegant scholarship and rhetorical artifices of every kind, the result of an education which Mr. Cobden never had. We extract from a speech of Mr. Lowe's, made immediately after taking the Chancellorship of the Exchequer, a passage which, both for its thought and diction, might have proceeded from Mr. Cobden.

" This House of Commons comes in pledged, as every other House of Commons has been, to rigid economy ; and here we have to encounter a difficulty. Because, although I remark no man objects to economy in the abstract, it is only in the abstract they do not object to it. And for very simple reasons, because there is no such thing as practising abstract economy in the world. As soon as it ceases to be abstract, and descends into the region of concrete economy, it becomes one of the most distasteful matters in the world. If it be economy in the public stores and munitions—shall I say pens ?—it is said to be un-worthy a great nation. Every man mends his own pen when it will not write ; but it is considered intolerable that public clerks should mend their pens. If it is public buildings upon which millions after millions have been thrown away with very doubtful results, we are

---

[*] " Correspondence between Mr. Cobden, M.P., and Mr. J. T. Delane, Editor of the *Times*," pp. 12, 13.

told that ' a thing of beauty is a joy for ever,' and that is considered satisfaction for the millions that are lost. If it is economy in that most painful of all directions, the reduction of the staff of public offices which are over-manned—the sympathy of all—and I fear of the House of Commons—goes with the small minority who suffer for the public good, and not with the public on whose behalf the economy is exercised."

On the other hand we shall search Mr. Cobden's speeches in vain for anything approaching to this, the peroration of Mr. Lowe's speech on the third reading of the Tory Reform Bill.

"Sir, I was looking to-day at the head of the lion, which was sculptured in Greece during her last agony after the battle of Chæronea, to commemorate that event, and I admired the power and the spirit which portrayed in the face of that noble beast the rage, the disappointment, and the scorn of a perishing nation and of a down-trodden civilization ; and I said to myself, ' Oh for an orator, oh for an historian, oh for a poet, who would do the same thing for us.' We also have had our battle of Chæronea ; we have had our dishonest victory. That England, that was wont to conquer other nations, has gained a shameful victory over herself. And oh that a man would rise in order that he might set forth in words that could not die the shame, the rage, the scorn, the indignation and the despair with which this measure is viewed by every Englishman who is not a slave to the trammels of party, or who is not dazzled by the glare of a temporary and ignoble success."

Mr. Lowe has reprinted his Anti-Reform Speeches of 1865-6,* and no better models of Parliamentary eloquence can anywhere be found. However much we may dissent from his views, no one capable of appreciating them can regard these speeches otherwise than with admiration. Between the peroration of his speech on the first reading of the bill of 1866, and that of Mr. Canning against Lord Russell's proposal for Reform in 1822, there is so close a resemblance both in idea and words, that we cannot but suspect Mr. Lowe of plagiarism.

"I cannot help conjuring the noble lord himself to pause before he again presses it upon the country. If, however, he shall persevere—and if his perseverance shall be successful, and if the result of that success be such as I cannot help apprehending, *his be the triumph to have precipitated these results, be mine the consolation that to the utmost and*

"It may be that we are destined to avoid this enormous danger with which we are confronted, and not—to use the language of my right hon. friend —be fated to compound with danger and misfortune. But, Sir, it may be otherwise ; and all I can say is, that if my right hon. friend does succeed in carrying this measure through Parliament,

* " Speeches and Letters on Reform." With a Preface. By the Right Hon. R. Lowe, M.P. R. J. Bush, Charing Cross.

latest of my power I have opposed them."—Mr. CANNING, 1822.

when the passions of the day are gone by, I do not envy him his retrospect. *I court not a single leaf of the laurels that may encircle his brow. I do not envy him his triumph. His be the glory of carrying it; mine of having to the utmost of my poor ability resisted it."*—Mr. LOWE, 1866.

One element, or more accurately an inseparable accident, of Parliamentary eloquence is knowledge of the forms and usages of the House, and a tactful application of it in the conduct of business. These have often secured for men of inferior abilities as speakers the highest Parliamentary position. Harley was a tedious, hesitating, and confused speaker, who would not have been listened to patiently for five minutes anywhere but in the House of Commons, yet he was the most influential man in the House of his day, and he owed that position not to eloquence or statesmanship, but to House of Commons tact. Lord Castlereagh's tact, good humour, and courage, made him on the whole rather a favourite with the House, though he mercilessly taxed their patience, and not unfrequently severely tried their gravity, as when he spoke of "the herculean labour of the honourable and learned member, who will find himself quite disappointed when at last he brings forth his Hercules,"—confounding his mother's labour, which produced that hero, with his own exploits. Of the combination of this tact with ability as a speaker, we will give two modern instances.

To Mr. Milner Gibson, whose exclusion from the present Parliament, and therefore probably from the present Cabinet, is a loss to his country and to his party, we owe the Repeal of the Taxes on Knowledge—*i.e.,* the advertisement duty, the paper duty, and the newspaper stamp. The movement against them originated with Mr. Cobden, who induced Mr. Gibson to undertake its Parliamentary management. "He," we quote Mr. Cobden, "by his dexterity and ability in debate, by his exquisite tactics, by his knowledge of the forms of the House, and by accepting the assistance of honourable gentlemen on the other side of the House,"* carried almost single-handed the necessary measures. The way in which he carried the repeal of the advertisement duty is an illustration of his Parliamentary knowledge and dexterity. In Mr. Gladstone's first budget he proposed to reduce, not repeal, this duty. Mr. Gibson's amendment for its repeal was defeated by three votes. The Committee

---

* "Speeches," Bright and Rogers' Edition, vol. ii. p. 76.

then proceeded to consider the original motion, to the effect, "That for every advertisement there shall be payable the duty of 6*d*." Perceiving that five more of his supporters had come in since the division, Mr. Gibson moved another amendment, "that the duty be 0*l*. 0*s*. 0*d*.," which was carried by a majority of two, and the duty thus practically repealed. Mr. Gibson is remarkably adroit in framing resolutions, so as to permit the co-operation in their support of parties generally opposed to each other. "I find (he once said to the writer) truisms the best things for the House of Commons." Instances of this adroitness are the resolution in the case of the lorcha *Arrow*, which though moved by Mr. Cobden, was drawn up by Mr. Gibson, and the resolution moved by himself as an amendment to the second reading of the Conspiracy to Murder Bill, on reading which, one of the shrewdest members of the opposition, Mr. Henley, said, "Why, it's as true as gospel," and by his advice his party combined with the Radicals in its support, and ousted the Palmerston Government.

Mr. Gibson is not a mere tactician. His abilities as a speaker are of a high order, and he had the ear of the House. His speeches on the Corn Law question are fit to rank with those of Cobden and Bright. Several of them were thought worthy by the great French economist Frédéric Bastint to be translated into French, and are published in his "Cobden et La Ligue ; ou l'agitation Anglaise pour la liberté des échanges."[*] In the Reform debates of 1866, Mr. Gibson's reply to the alarmist speeches of Mr. Lowe and others, was one of the best on the Liberal side.

Amongst the *Dii minores* of the House of Commons, one of the best known was the late Mr. Henry Berkeley, for so many years the leader of what appeared to be the forlorn hope of the Ballot. In spite of the ridicule of *The Times* and its followers in the press, the indifference of the Parliamentary supporters of the measure, the opposition and personal alienation of the leaders of his own party, and the languor and depression caused by ill-health and the increase of years and infirmities, Mr. Berkeley persisted in his annual motions, supporting them by speeches which showed him to be a master of the art *ridentem dicere verum*, the style best suited for a popular assembly, especially when the speaker, as in his case, has to address them on a subject repugnant to the majority, and the argument on which was worn threadbare. Nothing could be happier than his reply to Lord Palmerston, who had spoken of him as annually mounting his hobby-horse. "The noble lord calls it my hobby-horse. Take care the day does not come when

---

[*] "Œuvres Complètes de Frédéric Bastiat." Tome iii. Paris: Guillaume & Cie.

he and all of you (addressing the Treasury Bench, where Mr.
Gladstone, Mr. Lowe, and others were sitting) will be glad to
get up behind me." The whole House cheered to the echo this
pointed, and as events have shown, prophetic retort.

Mr. Berkeley's speeches frequently displayed a logic and power
of argument which showed that he would have done well at the
bar, for which he was originally intended. His genial good
humour, and his position as a son and brother of Earls, procured,
as we well know, a hearing for him as the advocate of the ballot,
which would not have been given to one of a more democratic
stamp. He was also a very good tactician. Of his dexterity in
parliamentary warfare, this is an instance. On one occasion his
motion for the ballot came on unexpectedly during the dinner
hour ; enough friends were present to keep a House, but the Tory
benches were deserted, and the whippers-in were the only
occupants of the Treasury bench. Mr. Berkeley saw his
opportunity, he merely said that the arguments he had formerly
used appeared unanswerable, and he therefore would only move
for leave to bring in his bill. Lord Palmerston could only say,
"The member for Bristol had given an example in his own person
that silent voting was better than audible argument." The
House divided, and the motion was carried by a majority of 33.
The triumph, though temporary, was substantial. Of course the
bill was rejected on the second reading, but the dexterous tactics
of their leader gave the friends of the ballot the opportunity of
introducing their plan of secret voting to parliament and the
country. The bill then brought in by Mr. Berkeley, founded on
the Electoral Acts of Australia, is in substance "The Ballot Act,
1872." His labours made the carrying of the ballot, not only
possible, but inevitable. He is gone without seeing the success
of his persistence. For his friends, who were many—

Flere et meminisse relictum est.

We must end our reminiscences here, but before closing this
paper, we will allude to the objection often made, and lately
renewed by writers in the *Daily Telegraph*, and other thoughtless
persons, that parliament wastes too much time in talking, that
members should forego their right of discussion, and pass the
measures which Government puts before them. This is the
popular application of Carlyle's fantastic notion, that "silence is
the eternal duty of man," and his cynical saying "that England
and America are going to nothing but wind and tongue." If
members acted on this suggestion, it would degrade our great
and famous House of Commons to the level of the French Corps
Législatif under the second empire. The life-blood of parliamentary government is full and free debate. It is a very superficial

view of the functions of the House of Commons to judge its
work by the bills it passes, without reference to its debates. It
was well said lately—"It is one of the functions of Parliament
to be the great debating society of the nation, in which all the
great questions of politics are theoretically discussed in long and
tedious preparation for their actual settlement."[*]   A generation
which does everything in a hurry, of course wishes its legislation
to be done in haste ; but we trust the sober, reflective, and in the
best sense of the word Conservative spirit which is the chief
characteristic of Englishmen, will prevent any interference with
the right and custom of thorough and exhaustive debate.

"Though not one vote is gained (said Burke) a good speech has its
effect. Though an Act of Parliament which has been ably opposed,
pass into law, yet in its progress, it is modelled and softened in such a
manner that we see plainly the minister has been told that the
members attached to him are so sensible of its injustice or absurdity
from what they have heard that it must be altered."

To the same effect is a more recent authority :—

"The forms of the House of Commons (says one who has been
its leader), are the result of accumulated experience, and have rarely
been tampered with successfully, while on the other hand a
Parliamentary Government is by name and nature essentially a
government of discussion. It is not at all difficult to conceive a mode
of governing a country more expeditious than by a Parliament ; but
where truth as well as strength is held to be an essential element of
Legislation, opinion must be secured an unrestricted organ. Superfluity of debate may often be inconvenient to a minister, and sometimes
distasteful to the community ; but criticising such a security for justice
and liberty as a free-spoken Parliament is like quarrelling with the
weather because there is too much rain or too much sunshine. The
casual inconvenience should be forgotten in the permanent blessing."[*]

This testimony is true. The long and thorough sifting which
every proposal undergoes before it takes its place on the Statute
Book, is the security for the stability and permanence of our
legislation. If, as in a recent instance, one measure takes forty
years of discussion before it becomes law, in compensation for the
time spent we have the satisfaction of knowing that all adverse
argument is exhausted and refuted, and that willing obedience
by all to the new law is secured because even its opponents feel
that the action of the majority within Parliament faithfully
represents the conviction of the overwhelming majority in the
constituent body.

---

[*] The *Daily News* on Mr. Miall's Motion, 1872.
† Mr. Disraeli's "Life of Lord George Bentinck," pp. 410, 411. 8th edition.

ART. III.—THE DECLINE OF THE OLD FRENCH MONARCHY.

1. *Histoire de France au Dix-huitième Siècle.* Par J. MICHELET. Paris. 1867.

2. *Mémoires du Duc de Luynes sur la Cour de Louis Quinze* (1735-1758). Publiés sous le Patronage de M. le Duc de Luynes, par MM. DUSSIEUX et E. SOULIE. Paris.

3. *Journal et Mémoires du Marquis d'Argenson.* Publiés pour la première fois d'après les Manuscrits Autographes de la Bibliothèque du Louvre, &c., par M. RATHERY. Paris.

IN the history of no European kingdom do we perceive so early or so rapid a development of the royal authority as in that of France. We may trace the assumption of supreme legislative power by the Crown even to the reign of Saint Louis. By the establishment of a standing army, Charles VII. first pointed out to European royalty a prompt way to arrive at arbitrary power. He it was also who, to the already exceptionally ample regal prerogatives, added the power of levying general subsidies by royal edict alone. But though royalty in France thus garnered betimes the means for foreign aggression and for internal repression, and though, in the latter phase, it ultimately reached the highest point of its ambition, the duration of autocratic ascendancy which may fairly be assigned to it is comprised within a period of little more than half a century. And even this ephemeral triumph of monarchical unity was obtained at the expense of a struggle which, from an early epoch of French history, presents few intermissions of tranquillity, and which had taxed to the utmost the vigilance and resources of the combatants. In forcing his laborious way towards the crowning of the edifice of royalty, the monarch had often been obliged to halt, had often been enticed aside by competing ambitions, or had, not unfrequently, been forced to bend before adverse fortune, and constrained for a time to recede. So equally poised, indeed, were the elements of strife, that for centuries it would have been difficult to detect where resided the spirit of that substantial future power which, by its overwhelming weight, should bring to a close the protracted oscillation, and present unquestioned preponderancy. The appearance of royalty in the full-blown dimensions of its autocratic purple was confined to the reign of a single monarch. With one hand, Louis the Fourteenth committed the suicidal folly of irremediably destroying the support which the monarchy derived from feudalism, severing the chief mainstay by which the past afforded it stability; whilst, with the other,—superbly indifferent to the defence of isolated royalty,—he might have traced some portion of the shadow, cast even into that time, of the coming Revolution.

The first years of the eighteenth century afforded many palpable indications that the spirit of decline had entered with an abiding presence into the old monarchy. Louis XIV. had not merely squandered upon his ambition the material resources of France, but had so contemptuously abused the universal devotion to royalty, that the heart of the nation was rapidly sinking into despair, whilst its mind, loosening itself most. reluctantly from its long reliance upon the sufficiency of existing institutions, was beginning to drift about uneasily in a thousand channels of dangerous speculation.

Although by the upper classes of society Louis XIV. was followed to the grave with indifference, perhaps with complacency, and by the populace with clamorous insult, so powerful and deeply rooted in the heart of the French people was the inclination to lavish its love upon the chief representative of royalty, that the accession of the infant monarch, Louis XV., to the throne was not only hailed with enthusiasm, but fully restored unbounded hope. This strongly-entrenched national affection for royalty maintained itself against a host of adverse facts, and gave, after years of forbearance and sore trial, unequivocal proofs that its ardour had suffered no diminution. No faults or even crimes committed by the King were pronounced inexcusable until they included the degradation of the monarchy itself; then, indeed, it may be said that the heart of loyalty was broken; then was finally extinguished the persistent glow of popular regard, not only towards the unworthy occupant of the throne, but towards the venerable, and hitherto venerated, institution of royalty itself.

Louis XIV. had identified the state with royalty; without the pale of that identity his prejudices, and, yet more, his narrow mind, could perceive no stable political combination. There were but few, however, who participated in this egotistical and cramped conviction. Reaction was close at hand. In the palace, and even from the mouth of his grandson, the Duc de Bourgogne, were heard the first lispings of the new-born political philosophy which enunciated the dogma that "kings exist for the good of the people, and not the people for the good of kings." In 1709, Féuélon, who is designated by Lamartine as the first Radical of the century, was the soul of this political reaction, which had then barely entered upon its initial stage, and predicted that the "old machine would break up at the first shock." The conjecture proved true; but we question whether,

from the special point of view inferred, the old King was far
wrong when, after one of his interviews with the political seer,
he declared that he had been "conversing with the most
excellent and most chimerical mind in his kingdom." The
principles of Fénélon's political morality, though at the present
time accepted as axioms, or as mere trite propositions, were
regarded by Frenchmen just stepping over the threshold of the
eighteenth century either as the elaborate enunciations of a
novel, profound, and startling philosophy, or as wild and incomprehensible delusions. The benevolent Archbishop had, in fact,
anticipated a degree of political enlightenment which implies at
least an initial political training: "Télémaque," now a mere
school-book, was, to the contemporaries of Fénélon, an amazing
repertory of recondite political maxims. A vast mass of obstruc-
tion to intellectual and material development had to be cleared
away before even the foundations of liberal political knowledge
could be easily or safely laid in the mind of the French people.
This fact should be ever present whilst following, step by step,
the downward course of the French monarchy; it should be
borne in mind that we are not in presence of certain maladies
incident to a strong political organization, but contemplating
chronic diseases which had for many centuries been eating into,
and rotting, every limb of the feeble despotism that ruled the
French nation.

There appears to have existed no reason or impediment of
sufficient gravity to outweigh the assumption that if Louis XIV.
had not determinedly and systematically interdicted all political
action on the part of the aristocracy and of the parliaments,—if
the most capable members of any substantial working political
institution had stood beside the cradle of his successor,—the
downward tendency of the monarchy might have been arrested.
But royalty had collected and heaped upon herself all the
multitudinous burthens of power : she had assumed every phase
of authority. She alone, therefore, was regarded as clothed
with responsibility : she alone, in her self-sought absolutism, was
answerable to opinion. Having sedulously sown incapacity
amongst her friends, she was destined in the inevitable hour of
her weakness to reap a harvest of troubles and of dangerous
conflicts. The chief members of those classes that exercised
the most powerful social influence were not only totally deficient
in political education, but were so inveterately disunited, that
no effectual or disinterested attempt to supply the glaring in-
competencies of royalty appeared possible. "Il y a en France,"
wrote Montesquieu at this time, "trois sortes d'états, l'église,
l'épée, et la robe. Chacun a un mépris souverain pour les deux
autres."

In the year 1673, the Parliament, which, since the thirteenth century, had been advancing in the estimation of the public, was despoiled by Louis XIV. of its right of remonstrance—the sole means by which it could legally attempt to modify the acts of power, or presume to offer suggestions touching current political questions. Yet, unlike the noblesse, who were not only deficient in political aptitudes, but in whom there existed no unity of will, or even the mere sentiment of organization, it had not lost its instinct of cohesion, or some few narrow sympathies connecting it with the great body of the nation. At the death of Louis XIV. a deferential appeal to its authority became imperative. The late King had in his will violated both private rights and the laws and traditions of the monarchy. There existed but one agent legally competent to deal with this iniquitous attempt to extend the influence of passion and the lust of power beyond the grave. The Parliament seized with avidity the opportune moment, and, by annulling the testament of Louis XIV. as, seventy-two years before, it had annulled that of Louis XIII., obtained, as the reward of its justice and sub-serviency, the resumption and even extension of privileges which had been in abeyance for more than a generation. Thus the unity of government contemplated by Richelieu and realized by Louis XIV. was overthrown, and the Parliament became, as heretofore during feeble reigns, a power in the State. But that power was ill-defined and often obtrusive. It neither ministered to the strength of the monarchy nor to the well-being of the nation. Glaring, however, as were its short-comings and inopportune obstructions, the Parliament is assuredly worthy of high commendation for the frequency with which it presented itself as a barrier to the enactment of much evil.

From the death of Louis XIV., the footsteps of the old monarchy begin to affect the mind with distinct impressions of their growing feebleness. Not that Royalty had passed into the tutelage of less competent hands than had lately guided it, but that the awe-inspiring mantle of omnipotence with which it had been popularly invested dropped from its shoulders, and disclosed many of its deformities and inevitable deficiencies. It was again obliged to recognise the existence of consultative assemblies to which at times it paid a decorous, though generally a constrained, deference. It had to deal with reactions, parliamentary and aristocratic, that, in presence of its infant weakness and the excited state of the public mind, it could not hope to overbear. To the Parliament were restored its ancient privileges; whilst an incongruous and undisciplined number of the aristocracy were distributed into councils corresponding to, and replacing, the customary ministerial departments.

Surrounded by ill-defined powers and by crowds of jealousies, Royalty needed prudence and conciliation if it hoped to maintain a vantage ground of supremacy more or less modified, and to preserve the State from drifting through a crisis of anarchy. Happily for the prostrate and feverish condition of France, the Duc d'Orleans possessed these qualities, especially the latter, in an eminent degree. Confided to his charge, the interests of the infant monarch were his chief solicitude. He could not hope, however, in face of an all-pervading opposition to the political policy, in its principal aspects, which the late King had obstinately persisted in maintaining, to preserve intact the autocratic power of the Crown ; but he certainly had recourse to the most effectual means of maintaining his own influence, and of husbanding for royalty as great an amount of authority as the temper of the times would permit. He made as effectual use of his enemies as of his friends. Power was reaped by sowing amicable division. His chief method of conciliation consisted in bringing into juxtaposition, and investing with the appearance of power, the representatives of all parties—filling the ministerial councils with an elastic number of men of irreconcilable views, and reserving for the Council of the Regency that unanimity and consequent decision which enabled it, as the supreme appellate assembly, to determine all measures of national importance.

We are by no means disposed to acquiesce in the unfavourable opinion which commonly prevails as to the character of the French Government during the minority of Louis XV. The decay of the monarchy was at that time, we think, far less attributable to the individuals or policy of the Regency than to the accidental weakness of Royalty and, eminently, to its immediate antecedents.

Though no complete dissociation of the political from the moral qualities presented by statesmen would be justifiable, even if it were possible, it must be admitted that great injustice may result from giving undue prominency to the private phase in the character of men who stand before the world mainly in their public capacity. This injustice has been done in a marked manner both to the Regent and to his chief adviser, Cardinal Dubois.

We have no wish to excuse or shelter from reprobation the degrading excesses of the Duc d'Orleans, by referring to his early education and environments; but it should not be forgotten that Louis XIV. had sedulously interdicted political knowledge under any form from approaching his nephew—the destined husband

of his favourite daughter!—and had looked with raised eyebrows
and approving censure upon a course of conduct which was irre-
trievably enmeshing an active and irrepressible spirit in the
toils of folly and debauchery.   This narrow and envious policy
threw a pernicious shadow over the marvellously brilliant
qualities which had illuminated the youth of the Prince, and
corrupted a mind too weak to support the weight of enforced
leisure. Scepticism and voluptuousness, which had been introduced
to the Duc de Chartres in the train of an imperious probibition
to employ eminent abilities in a legitimate and honourable
course, became, from long habit, abiding companions of the Duc
d'Orleans   In spite, however, of a long career of boastful irregularities, the Regent still retained much of his youthful ardour,
and even many of his early generous and lofty aspirations. But
he was careless of his present reputation, and yet more indifferent
to his future fame.   Once only was Philippe d'Orleans known to
be seriously affected at the atrocious imputations of his calum-
niators. The "Philippiques" of La Grange Chancel, in which the
Prince is accused of desiring the death of the young King, overbalanced, though but for a brief season, that cynical indifference
to the hideous form with which his private character was, and is
even now, popularly invested.   This indifference to opinion has
aggravated the severity of history ; but it must at least be admitted
that the foulest stain which malevolence essayed to cast upon
the Regent was effectually obliterated by one who certainly cannot
be suspected of ever having displayed a generous recognition of
benefits received, or, indeed, be credited with possessing the
feeling of gratitude in any of its higher or more refined elements.
" My kingdom," exclaimed Louis XV., whilst acknowledging the
tender care which he had received from the Duc d'Orleans, " was
left by the Regent at peace with the world, internally tranquil,
and in a state of prosperity striking to the eyes of Europe."

How often, moreover, has the name of the Duc d'Orleans been
associated with those *petits soupers* which hold so prominent a
place in the scandalous chronicles of the time, as if some close
and mysterious affinity subsisted between them ! The *petit souper*
was an established institution of the period.   It was to the despotism and hypocrisy which dominated during the latter part of
the preceding reign that is chiefly amenable the peculiarly
depraved character of society under the Regency.   Morality had,
indeed, varied but little.   Publicity was the key to the apparent
change : the veil was raised, or rather thrown aside altogether,
which had hitherto concealed the penetralia of vice.   Let the
degree, however, of credibility due to the criminal excesses
attributed to the Duc d'Orleans be what it may, never, at all
events, has it been objected to the Prince that he ever permitted

any one of his mistresses, however influential, to determine, or even to discuss in his presence, the acts or policy of his government. Malevolence herself could find no opportunity to cast this stone at him. Yet this pestilential influence seemed to infest the political atmosphere of the period. It had swayed and often determined the "Great King," and contributed in the future, more than any other element of destruction, to hasten the decline of the monarchy.

In their estimate of Cardinal Dubois, historians have surpassed in degree the injustice they have meted to the Regent. No epithets are considered too gross to heap upon the indefatigable and over-successful diplomatist. They are piled up with all the persevering zeal of malignity. We have, for example, the Marquis d'Argenson—a man who considered marriage to be an irksome restraint, and religion to be unworthy of a thought—branding the feeble-bodied and sickly little Abbé, who was often constrained to confine himself to herbs as his chief if not sole nourishment, as "one of the most depraved of men." The Comte de Tocqueville speaks of him in terms equally disparaging. "Debauched," "perfidious," "impious," and similar accusatory epithets, are repeatedly applied to Dubois by Saint Simon, who also, with characteristic pettiness and impertinence, likens his face to that of a weasel, and the entire man to a "vilain satyre de mauvais lieux." The contemporary supercilious ultra-aristocrat is outdone, however, by the modern ultra-liberal M. Michelet. "Vraie figure de damné" is an expression which represents the customary language in which the illustrious historian indulges when speaking of Dubois; though to descend to a lower "figure" than the one we have quoted would puzzle, we apprehend, the most acrimonious adept in abuse. In the case of Saint-Simon, imputations against Dubois are obviously based far less upon conviction than upon wounded vanity. The Duke and Peer considered it intolerable that a man whose father had been a physician—an apothecary, the vulgar detractors of Dubois are pleased to say—should be allowed to take precedence of the *haute noblesse* in the Ministry of the Regent. Dubois has not been less foully bemired by English historians. "The wretched Dubois," "the Iscariot Dubois," are designations used by Macaulay, and illustrate with broad accuracy the outrageous tendency of opinion towards the Cardinal. Seldom does vice modify her grossness when she is made to figure in the character of Dubois. Incapable of substantiating any just claim to an exceptionally conspicuous aspect, she is maliciously made to assume her most repulsive appearance. Was, then, Dubois a model of propriety because his enemies were unable to establish by commensurate proofs the monstrous vices they imputed to him? Very far from it. True,

there was little in his morality which afforded sufficiently noticeable appearances to render it distinguishable from that of the
mass of his colleagues, or, indeed, from that of his most virtuous
detractors; but assuredly such morality occupies no very high
position in the estimation of the world. His manners and
language were gross,—the latter often offensively so,—and frequently led to unfavourable constructions; but that his character
as a whole may pass muster with that of the then existing
courtier-world appears fairly presumable. Would Fénélon have
advised his nephew to cultivate the acquaintance of a man
notorious, even in that age of loose morals, for the wantonness
of his profligacy? Would Massillon have compromised his courageous and severely virtuous character by promoting the election
of an old debauchee— viewing Dubois in the most favourable
light selected by his maligners—as Archbishop of Cambrai, and
assisting personally at his installation? "With your spirit and
virtue,"—it is thus that the mother of the Regent writes to the
Abbé Dubois,—"you have little need to dread calumny: rest
assured that the world will eventually do you justice." In spite
of a contrary opinion subsequently expressed by the Princess,
such a deliberate judgment cannot be gainsaid. In the funeral
oration he pronounced over the remains of this lady, Massillon
speaks in the highest terms of the Cardinal. If reference be
made to the voluminous correspondence of Dubois with Stanhope
and Walpole, no eye, however microscopically powerful, can trace
any resemblance between the indications there exhibited of many
features which must have contributed to constitute the moral
character of the accomplished French diplomatist, and the repulsive satyr-like lineaments that may be found bedaubed on all
the defamatory sheets of the time, lineaments which have been
copied without examination, and not unfrequently with placid
satisfaction, into accredited and lasting historical productions.
Dubois has exposed himself to censure chiefly on that phase of
his career which presents him struggling for the Cardinalate.
But the unscrupulous pertinacity of his efforts in that direction
loses much of its unseemliness when it is considered how frequently
he was made to feel that the maintenance of his political position
depended, in very great measure, upon his speedy promotion to
a Princedom of the Church.

How, then, is all this lively virulence to be accounted for?
No doubt its action upon the Duc d'Orleans may be largely
referred to personal animosity. From the little hotbed of defa-
mation at Sceaux, the discomfited Duc du Maine, and the implacable Princess, his wife, scattered profusely over France
libellous pamphlets and satires against the Regent and the
members of his ministry. Dubois, from the very obvious

influence which he exercised over the chief of the government, was specially singled out to serve as a target for slander.

But no interested or personal incitements to hatred and calumny can be numbered among the causes of that unabated malignity shown towards Dubois by those who, at a later period, were capable of laying bare the truth, and who aspired to rank as historians. We may safely assume that most of the aspersions which have been cast by French historians upon the leading members of the Regency have derived their inspiration not from a virtuous abhorrence to profligacy, at a time when profligacy was fashionable, but from a hatred of that close alliance contracted with England which formed the basis whereon the foreign policy of the Regency was constructed.

"Dubois sacrificed the honour of France and every elevated principle to his personal interests." So we are assured by Sismondi.[*] The same scandalous influences, we are told, biassed the Duc d'Orleans in his dealings with neighbouring states. If, however, it be assumed that the foreign policy of the Regency was motived almost solely by such base considerations, it would nevertheless be difficult to show that any other policy would have contributed so substantially towards the well-being of France, or have affected her honour less injuriously. If the young King had died—an occurrence which the very delicate health of Louis XV. at that time rendered by no means improbable—the French Crown would have been exposed to the formidable pretensions of the Spanish monarch, Philip V. What course could more naturally present itself to the Regent than to seek the friendship and alliance of the English King, who happened himself to be menaced by dynastic pretensions. Did the Spanish alliance present sufficiently hopeful advantages to render an unreasoning adhesion to it a wise or even justifiable course? Was France prepared, in her then exhausted condition, to burthen herself with the monster schemes which Alberoni contemplated for changing dynasties and redistributing territories? To have moved in such directions would have been to encounter a European coalition whose formidable dimensions and power—especially since the victories of Belgrade and Peterwaradin had

* "It has been often affirmed, on the authority of Saint-Simon, that Dubois sold himself to England. But what need had England to buy a man who sought her alliance? France and England were not on an equal footing: to use the expression of Dubois, 'on ne jouait pas à bille égale avec les Anglais.' However susceptible of venality, the Abbé was not then in a position to sell himself. So far from being the corrupted, it was he—according to official documents—who attempted to corrupt. Convinced of the advantages of the English Alliance, the Regent ordered Dubois to offer Stanhope a bribe of 600,000 livres."—*Revue des Deux Mondes, Mai,* 1679.

left disposable the great military resources of Austria—afforded little scope for favourable anticipations. An alliance with England was no doubt at that time more than usually distasteful to the French people, because it involved the disruption of what had come to be regarded as, of all foreign relationships, the most eligible and natural. But this alliance was no novelty. In recent times Henry IV., Mazarin, and even Louis XIV., had often disposed it as a key-stone in constructing the edifice of their foreign policy: in truth, the chief object of the Quadruple Alliance was to compel a fulfilment of the arrangements and conditions set forth in the Treaty of Utrecht.

The English alliance and the rupture with Spain were very materially influenced by the Cellamare conspiracy. In that unsuccessful attempt to revive the forms and general political tendencies which had irrevocably disappeared with Louis XIV., we are struck by encountering for the first noticeable time a man flying from the overthrown camp of the malcontents, and, whilst stepping upon the threshold of the new *régime*, expressing in adulatory strains the praises of the Regent: a man who was destined to stand out later as arch-plotter in a conspiracy which even then gave indications of form and consistency; and which, looking in a diametrically opposite direction from that which had just been trodden out, was fated to achieve colossal proportions and colossal success. That man, we need hardly say, was the young Arouet de Voltaire. His apparition on the scene marks significantly the moment when the old society, casting aside further hesitation, entered with determined levity on a course leading inevitably to its own immolation.

The reality of this coincidence is sufficiently attested. The internal policy of the Regency, though presenting here and there among the myriad existing abuses and injustices a wholesome spirit of reform, affords upon the whole a by no means favourable aspect. We are disposed to think, however, that at least one phase of the home administration which this period presents has been generally regarded too severely. The legacy of debt and financial disorder which had been bequeathed by Louis XIV. to his successor ought surely to mitigate the harshness of criticism towards many of the daring and baseless schemes which were hazarded by the government of the Regency. Appearances were desperate, and a desperate appeal to empiricism appeared to be the only possible escape from the dastardly impolitic refuge of bankruptcy urged by the shallow-souled Saint-Simon, and the only means by which an exhausted exchequer could hope for replenishment. Let us not overlook, moreover, amidst a thousand projects, more or less impracticable, the premature attempt to impose a general tax—*l'impôt proportionnel*—so per-

fect and simple in the equity of its adjustment that it overtops
even the highest flight of transcendental justice essayed at the
Revolution. With the exception, perhaps, of the Duc de
Noailles, France was unable at this time to boast of any politician
who could claim more than a very shallow insight into the
specialities of finance. The Regent, abandoning himself in this
case, as in too many others, to superficial recommendations, was
struck by the brilliant and certainly shrewd schemes of an
adventurer who was not insensible to the glory of staking the
monetary resources of a great nation upon certain daring though
specious speculations. Law was installed Contrôleur-Général
with much éclat: and it must be conceded that he displayed as
much capacity and ability on the side of profound suggestions
and wise initiations, as he showed unbounded audacity and
recklessness in setting afloat speculations the success of which
depended upon the wildest chance. When the temporary outcry and hubbub, proceeding chiefly from disappointed gamblers
and over-eager fortune-hunters at the disparition of too confidently anticipated wealth, had subsided, there was discovered a
residuum of substantial and permanent good which more than
compensated a score of bubble projects.

By fostering a spirit of gambling speculation among the aristocracy and the middle classes, the Regent hastened the already
rapid progress of immorality. He connived not less recklessly at
the stealthy advance of religious scepticism. From Vendôme
and Conti, from the literary coterie presided over by Ninon de
L'Enclos, from Jean Baptiste Rousseau, to whom was attributed
the "Mosclade" which rendered him illustrious among the irreligious, impiety began to spread and settle downwards. It must,
indeed, be unhesitatingly conceded that the cardinal fault of the
Regent was the commingling of corruption—embracing a prodigal
licence of opinions that stretched to the ridicule of tradition, and
that scrupled not to treat with levity and a questioning tone
even the most serious elements of established authority—as an
all-saturating ingredient in his home policy, an ingredient which
quickened, and in great measure created, the most formidable
enemies that royalty had ever encountered. Thus progressed the smoothing process for the more rapid decline of the
old monarchy.

The Regency—so far at least as its internal policy is concerned—may not inaptly be regarded as a worthy prologue to
the reign of Louis XV.; and—with more latitude still—the
short ministry of the Duc de Bourbon may be looked upon as a
very characteristic beginning. Immeasurably inferior to the
Regent in all that constitutes capacity for government, and yet
more immediately and offensively contrasting with him in those

brilliant qualities of mind and manner which are often capable of surrounding with a halo of fascination many even of the most condemnable faults, the Duc de Bourbon exhibits a character stained with the foulest profligacy. Unlike his predecessor, he presented no conflict of extremes: no startling intermissions of brightness broke in upon the darkness of his character. He was base, sordid, and licentious, without any noticeable counterbalancing qualities. Anxious to retain power as the most copious means of ministering to the gratification of his all-engrossing low propensities, he was yet so deficient in penetration—his low cunning so blinded his low intelligence—that no glimpse of near disaster to his interests disclosed the impolicy of intrusting his mistress, Madame de Prie, with the supreme direction of public affairs. Here we are presented with a specimen of that species of direct agency by which Royalty was led, through national disaster and disgrace, into utter and irremediable contempt. This is indeed the beginning of the end. On the petty caprices and vanity of a member of the demi-monde—to use a pertinent modern French phrase for which we have happily no sufficient equivalent—is tossed about, and twisted into every form of degradation, the foreign policy of the country. Wantonly insulted, Spain breaks up the Congress of Cambrai, and assumes an attitude of hostility. At home, Páris-Duverney, the minister of Madame de Prie, anticipating the temerity of the Revolutionary Government, launches into a wide field of fiscal and even political speculation. But such disorder was premature. The nation was alarmed, and the downward progress of the Monarchy was checked for awhile by the wise counsels of the venerable Bishop of Fréjus.

If the selfish alloy discernible in Fleury's wisdom had produced a less deteriorative effect upon the character of Louis XV., we will not go so far as to say that France would have been spared the ordeal of a revolution, but assuredly we may be permitted to infer that her inevitable passage into a new social and political state would not have been through so much wanton destruction, or through such a series of calamitous failures. In disinterestedness of character, as well as in most of the other brilliant qualities possessed by the Regent, Fleury was singularly deficient. No magnanimous impulse ever prompted him to deviate from the rut of decorous usage, or from the path of his own interest. Yet it must be admitted that even before his accession to power—whilst principally occupied as preceptor to the young King—he appeared little solicitous as to the progress made by his royal pupil in the most essential parts of a kingly education. He had neither aptitude nor taste for politics. Accident thrust him suddenly, at an advanced age, into the uncoveted

position of Minister of State with absolute control; and he
seems gradually to have become tempted by reasons derived
from the sophistry of ambition,—by a self-flattering persuasion
of the necessity of his presence in the Ministry for the welfare
of the nation,—to hold on to that dizzy height. With the
intoxicating taste of unlimited power he imbibed the poison of
jealousy towards any instruction which might impart political
competency to the youthful monarch. This jealousy increased
with time and the habit of authority. It prolonged indefinitely the tutelage of Louis XV., encouraged his natural indifference to the duties of his position, and, if it did not openly
counsel profligacy, it yet smoothed the paths to sensual indulgence. The immediate and visible consequences of this morbid
anxiety on the part of Fleury to prolong an illegitimate ascendancy were certainly beneficial to France; but it may justly be
doubted whether the good resulting from the tenacious clinging
to power of the octogenarian Minister was not counterbalanced a
thousandfold by the injury which such selfish obstinacy inflicted
on the future of the nation.

No event, indeed, could have tended more directly to serve
the pressing wants of the nation than the inauguration of a
Ministry proclaiming a policy of "peace abroad, economy at
home." For seventeen years did Fleury consistently endeavour
to follow the course dictated by this prudential political declaration. He hastened to appease the just anger of Spain, and to
consolidate the alliance with England. But a new generation
had sprung up since the disastrous warlike operations of the last
reign, to whom the monotony of peace was becoming irksome;
and this incipient disaffection was sedulously fomented by the
old generals Villars and Berwick—the conspicuous centre figures
in the party of opposition to the pacific policy of the Minister.
It was also evident that, however great the aversion entertained
by the nation for financial adventurers, little admiration was
shown for the obtrusive parsimony of the new Administration.
The neglect and curtailment of the navy, for example, presumptive—truly to some extent—of subserviency to England, incited
a perpetual commotion amongst a host of sensitive national
prejudices. In this instance the blind jealousy of the people
stumbled upon a prescient particle of wisdom, and justly
branded as improvident, economical calculations which were
based mainly upon the shallow assumption of a durable
European tranquillity. There was indeed little chance that
such a *politique bourgeoise*—as the Cardinal's system of government was aptly designated by D'Argenson—could be rendered
palatable to a nation not as yet gifted with that peculiar wisdom,
so highly appreciated in our own times, which places the imme-

diate and obvious demands of substantial self-interest before the less palpable dictates of seemingly barren honour.

The aristocracy opposed with ever-increasing energy the pacific counsels of the Minister: nor was their opposition altogether unjustifiable, for war was the only outlet that an over-centralizing government vouchsafed to them by which they could directly participate in public affairs—a limited scope of action which affected most disastrously the fortunes of the old Monarchy. In spite, then, of the very powerful influence which Fleury—who emphatically disclaimed any desire to rank among *ministères historiques*—could bring to bear towards the maintenance of peace, France drifted with much enthusiasm into a war beginning with a mere empty flourish of chivalrous intentions, and ending with a most substantial material acquisition. If no part of the doubtful honour of initiating the war can be claimed by Fleury, surely to him must be awarded the chief merit due for that triumph of French diplomacy—the Treaty of Vienna.

By the part which she took in the war of the Austrian Succession, France cast an indelible stain upon her honour, and compromised the high position which she had long enjoyed in the scale of nations. The pacific Cardinal vainly struggled to arrest the torrent of disgrace. But the King had become weary of the monotonous rule of his old preceptor, and had begun to lean towards less temperate and sage advice. "Unfortunately for his glory," says Voltaire, "Fleury was unwilling to relinquish a power rapidly slipping from his grasp, and, though arrived at the verge of the grave, was still reluctant to resign himself to the tranquillity of private life."

It is by no means surprising that Fleury's contemporaries should have directed their chief attention to the foreign policy of his administration: but in these days, the world is far more interested in tracing the course which the Cardinal pursued in reference to the internal affairs of France. We are struck with the calm which prevailed on all sides. Religious dissensions, if not entirely extinguished, were for the most part decorously hidden from public view. The Jansenists and Molinists were induced, from a feeling of respect and personal regard entertained for the Cardinal by the great body of the French clergy, to assume an appearance of conciliation, and in this the beneficent action of the Minister's authority was conspicuous. But his extreme jealousy of all influence not emanating, at least indirectly, from himself, urged Fleury not only to interdict all vehement controversies upon such inflammatory topics as religion and politics, but to extend a repressive action over the discussion of subjects which never ventured to trespass beyond the ample

G 2

boundaries of science and literature. Nothing could have been more impolitic, nothing could have tended to produce more serious disaffection, not merely towards the temporary administrators of the old Monarchy, but towards its form and principles, —the titles to its very existence,—than the discountenancing, and even the enforced dissolution, of such harmless, nay meritorious, associations as, for example, that which met in the *entresol* occupied by the Abbé Alary. What excuse could there be for the most captious timidity to regard with suspicion such men as the Abbé de Braggelone and the Abbé de Saint-Pierre, the Marquis de Saint-Contest and the Marquis d'Argenson, men who stood among the foremost promoters of political and social order? But Fleury presented in his selfishness a proneness to over-caution. Though in power a king, his political anxieties as well as his financial economics were mostly intent upon subordinate and even trifling matters. Justly distinguished and honoured as a member of the Clergy, he was yet an accomplished courtier, and fixed his attention less upon France than upon Versailles. Ranking among the most minutely practical and shortsighted of statesmen, he contrived to picture danger to his position from the continued existence of the society of the *Entre-sol*, and failed to perceive that an undiscriminating imprisonment of thought tended to multiply the real perils which menaced the by no means impregnable fabric of the existing Church and State. Whilst the colossal foe was besetting the very gates of the citadel, he was keeping watch in a remote quarter at an almost imperceptible crevice by which danger had little chance of ingress. The peace he laboured to spread over France was the peace, if not of absolute intellectual stagnation, at least of an external acquiescence in those dogmas which he had recognised in politics and theology. But peace, with supervisors such as the then Ultramontane Clergy, could possess no germs of permanent vitality. It sowed, in the midst of a sullen conformity, the seeds of intemperate discussion and of wild subversive theories ; and the reapers were already preparing for an early harvest. Voltaire was studying the free institutions of England ; Montesquieu was diligently occupied upon his great work, the "Esprit des Lois ;" Diderot, D'Alembert, Jean Jacques Rousseau, were at hand, secretly qualifying themselves to take advantage of the first opportune moment to begin the work of indiscriminate destruction.

But Fleury outlived the novelty of tranquillity which had been transiently accepted by the mass of Frenchmen. The exclamation of D'Argenson, "The Cardinal is dead at last," merely expresses the national impatience.* And yet with the disappearance of that venerable figure we seem to lose sight of the last conspicuous worthy representative of France under the veritable ancient régime. We sink at once into a political chaos. We see the old Monarchy assailed—indirectly, it is true, but most effectively—on all sides. Its defenders are lukewarm, and its guides, impatient of the trammels of a settled policy,—utterly incapable, indeed, of elaborating the simplest political combinations,—subject it, with all the recklessness of ignorant depravity, to the ever-varying fantasies of passion and caprice, the object one moment of derision, the next of contempt.

From the death of Fleury to the accession of Louis XVI. to the throne, no French statesman acquired sufficient influence over the King—or rather, it should be said, over the King's mistress—to confer upon his actions such an amount of freedom as to justify us in referring to him much of the responsibility attached to the policy of the government. Louis XV. declined to name a successor to the late Cardinal, and, in imitation of his great-grandfather, proclaimed that he himself intended to perform the duties of prime minister. No announcement could have shaped itself more ominously : it seemed virtually to syllable the death-warrant of the old Monarchy. Not that Louis XV. was deficient in capacity. The absence of acquired ability was partly compensated by a natural incisive intelligence which, but for an incurable apathy, might have enabled him to escape the chief disasters of his reign and the opprobrium of the world.

In reviewing the character of Louis XV., we are led, by an almost irresistible impulse of association, to compare it with the character of our Charles II. ; for, how widely soever the two kings may differ from each other in many special phases, their characters, when comprehensively compared, present broad and striking similarities. And yet how dissimilar were the auspices under which they were matured! How incomparably more favourable to the English monarch, both in variety and value,

---

* The light in which Fleury's death was popularly regarded is perhaps reflected pretty fairly in the following epitaph current at the time, and which appears in the " Mémoires du Duc de Luynes :"—

> "Ci-gît un cardinal antique,
> Mentor rusé, ministre sans éclat,
> Qui sut pousser la politique,
> Jusqu' à mourir pour le bien de l'État.
>   Fleury est mort, vive le Roi !
>
> Sans richesses et sans éclat,
> Se bornant au pouvoir suprême,
> Il n'a vécu que pour lui-même,
> Et meurt pour le bien de l'État."

were the opportunities derived from apt instruction and experience. For many years before his accession to the throne, Charles had had misfortune in many of its aspects thrust upon him, and had been initiated into the principal mysteries of the human character. On the other hand, no vicissitude ever broke the monotony of slavish adulation and obsequious compliance which waited upon Louis XV. from the cradle to the grave. Charles had visited many parts of Europe: Louis rarely caught a glimpse of the world save from the windows of Versailles. The French King was nurtured in the most corrupt and vitiated epoch which occurs in the annals of French society: Charles came to the throne at one of the most austere periods of English history. Louis had exhausted the novelty and charms of authority long before he arrived at maturity: Charles accepted the invitation of his country to assume supreme power long after the age at which the human faculties have attained their full develop-ment. Most of the external influences which had been brought to bear upon Charles favoured the presumption that he would stand forth in the future a model of kingly perfection: the unmitigated depravity of most of the influences which were cease-lessly thrust upon the unfortunate French monarch could surely presage no ray of wisdom, scarcely even a gleam of common sense. Yet Charles turned out to be one of the grossest of sensualists, one of the most sluggish of rulers, and one of the meanest of kings. Louis XV. was profligate in the worst sense of that term: he had an invincible repugnance—amounting even to disgust —for State affairs; but the meanness which he displayed was rather a taint derived from the pernicious atmosphere in which he had his being than a natural blemish of his mind. It can hardly be deemed probable that, under any circumstances, the French King would have sold the independence of his country, or huckstered the birthright of his nearest relative for the purpose of silencing the demands of debauchery. Whether, towards the close of his life, when the assaults of profligacy— unremitted for half a century—had begun to weaken the last faint resistances of honour, he was personally implicated in what was termed the *Pacte de Famine*, there appears hardly suf-ficient evidence to prove; but that he connived at the existence of such a nefarious and cruel compact, and was fully aware that it derived its chief inspiration and activity from his Minister of Finance, Terray, seems to be undeniable. The obsession of Madame du Barry and her creatures was gradually reducing the old French monarch to a depth of degradation where he would be fitly associated with the naturally low-minded Charles.

At no former period had France demanded more active govern-ing energy from her sovereign: never had the special interests of Royalty, no less than the general welfare of the nation, needed so urgently a watchful guardian and a wise administrator. Never, on the contrary, was France more destitute of such guidance than in the middle of the eighteenth century. That Louis XV. should have been constrained to disguise his profound unwillingness to exercise authority in a becoming kingly fashion, and induced to assume even the appearance of directing the administration of public affairs, are sufficient proofs of the utter absence of accredited governing ability in the nation. The princes who stood near the throne had been tried and found wanting. The jealousy of the late Cardinal had banished every promising statesman—notably Chauvelin, who had ably performed the duties of Minister of Foreign Affairs—from the chief offices in the government. At the death of Fleury, therefore, Louis XV., to his great surprise and discomfort, perceived that he was the only notable functionary in the central administration. " D'où vient," he exclaimed, "qu'il n'y a plus d'hommes en France?" But though assuming the title, he had no intention of performing the duties, of Prime Minister. To his mind business presented more terrors than abdication itself. The merest whisper of State matters disconcerted and annoyed him. A single word concerning the Church or the Parliament was sure to elicit the exclamation "*Cela m'ennuie*—speak to me no more upon the subject. The house is on fire and the master says don't talk to me about it, *Cela m'ennuie!*" True, he was the deviser of what was termed the "Secret Ministry"—an instrument manœuvred with perfect ignominious elaboration mainly for controlling and often thwarting the ostensible action of French diplomacy. But to the King this was a perfectly congenial occupation, affording the enjoyments of power unhampered by the annoyances of responsibility ; and he sought to palliate the creation of such an occult influence, on the ground that its chief object was "to support the Poles, and enable them to elect a king of their own choosing!"

This mere nominal assumption of the functions of Prime Minister by the King resulted, as a matter of course, in the isolation and independent action of each section of the Administration. Jealousies, wranglings, and general insubordination, were rarely absent from the Cabinet Council. Occasionally meddling endeavours were made to give an aspect of unity to the most important measures of the government. Cardinal Tencin sought for a time to exercise an indirect influence over the official proceedings of each minister : but the interdiction of the King— "plus de prêtre"—rendered him powerless. It was notably the Maréchal de Noailles who attempted to act as a kind of deputy Prime Minister, though with "less real authority or influence than many a mere courtier, and with less power of inspiring fear

than many a court valet."   Thus the way was gradually prepared
for the supreme influence of the King's chief mistress.

The earliest and least politically unworthy of the personages
who practically constituted what may be designated as a female
dynasty of Prime Ministers, the Duchesse de Châteauroux,
managed, by some supremely potent feminine artifice, to rouse
the lethargic Monarch into a temporary active consciousness of at
least one part of his duty.   The King, suddenly shaking himself
free from the trammels of his early education, presented himself
to his troops not only as their leader, but in such a manner as to
afford very flattering hopes that he would become their conside-
rate companion.   Then it was that by general acclamation the
military chief was saluted as Louis the " Well-beloved."   Then
it was that there flashed forth a spark from that naturally kingly
disposition which had been overlaid and nearly extinguished by
an early commenced systematic surcharging of sensuous allurements—" What have I done," exclaimed the King, " to be so
loved ?"   What, indeed !   With equal astonishment he might
have demanded, ten years later, when, in order to avoid traversing
Paris amidst the execrations of the people, he passed aside by a
newly-formed road bearing the ominous designation Chemin de
la Révolte, " What have I done to be so hated ?"   His agreeable astonishment in the one case was as natural as his indignation
in the other was justifiable.   He had done little indeed to be
either loved or hated.   His criminality consisted infinitely less
in what he did than in what he left undone.   His own personal
misgovernment, though it should have descended lower in the
scale of iniquity than had been reached by that of any of his
ancestors, would most probably have caused a much smaller
amount of disastrous consequences, at least to the future of the
nation, than that lowest of all unkingly states of abasement and
ineptitude—self-effacement by the ineffably humiliating intrusion
of an incapable, a capricious, and an abandoned woman.   Each
successive mistress of the King flaunts a lower type of infamy,
and at every change the Government, or rather Misgovernment, of
France contrives to present darker and yet darker phases of incapacity, a more wanton caprice, and an ever-lessening aspect
even of a semblance of regard for the national interests.   Again,
and yet again, the old Monarchy descends a more pronounced
angle in its decline.   This increase in the velocity of its sinking
becomes startling when two distant epochs in the period of its
declension are compared.   Look at it, for instance, when arrived
at the last stage of degradation—literally falling—in 1774, and
then cast a backward glance to the year 1744, when it may be
seen still firmly supported by the affection of the people, yet
bewilderedly stumbling into contempt from the clashing of

crotchety, incapable ministers, and from its subjection to the
guidance of women as devoid of political aptitude as of feminine
purity.   Yet how light, how transparent, appears the stain of
imbecility and guilt which overshadows Madame de Châteauroux
when it is contrasted with the black infamy which covers Madame
Du Barry !   There was at least a feeling of pride, to all appearance
little less than chivalrous, in the former which prompted her to
urge the King upon the path of glory.   True, the successes
achieved in Flanders, crowned though they were by the immeasurably prized victory gained at Fontenoy,—the last brilliant
ray shed upon the old Dynasty,—"might," as Frederick II.
declared, " have redounded as much to the glory and profit of the
cause for which hostilities were undertaken if they had been
achieved on the banks of the Scamander."   But the natural and
substantial point of view whence such victories were regarded by
the Prussian Monarch was far beneath the lofty pinnacle, from
which they were complacently viewed by the French people. To
France, the glory of her King commended itself far more agreeably
than would any amount of profit accruing to herself.   Louis XV.
made three campaigns: victory attended him : he was idolized.
The prayers of the people had at last been heard : the long and
obstinate hope of the nation was realized : France had found her
King !   Yet a few months and the pleasing illusion vanished.
The warlike inspiration which had armed the King disappeared
at the death of the Duchesse de Châteauroux.   It did not consist with the corrupting and intensely selfish schemes of Madame
de Pompadour to connive at the permanent establishment of
any feeling or occupation in the King's mind which might eventually presume to throw a shade upon her own immediate
supremacy.   Little persuasion was needed to induce Louis XV.
to shut himself up in Versailles.   The war languished into
disaster.   It had been based at the outset upon injustice : it was
dragged on at last without object ; and led finally to the treaty
of Aix-la-Chapelle, a treaty so humiliating to France that the
expression " Bête comme la Paix"—originating in the *halles*—
became proverbial throughout the country.   At this period there
steals into view the first wide-spread indication of the rapidly
approaching disenchantment and alienation of the French people
from their King and—though yet but vaguely—from Royalty itself.

Feebleness and inconsistency circulated unchecked throughout
every department of the government.   To-day, France is seen
aiding, in a most costly and inefficient manner, Frederick II. to
carry out his nefarious aggression against Maria Theresa :
to-morrow, she will be descried contributing assistance, in a tenfold more costly and inefficient manner, to humour Maria
Theresa's implacable feelings of revenge towards the Prussian

King. At home, patronage and persecution alight in alternate gusts upon every party and faction: at one time magistrates, at another time bishops,—two bodies of men in a chronic state of antagonism,—are lectured, and many even banished, as may happen to accord with the passing moods of court caprice, or avarice, or fear.

From the death of Louis XIV., the Parliaments of France had affected functions which virtually transformed them into quasi-political bodies—thirteen *Étuls-généraux au petit pied.* Such assumptions were based upon glaringly untenable grounds, and were a perpetual source of irritation to Louis XV. "The Parliament and the Clergy," remarked the King to Madame de Pompadour, "are always at daggers-drawn: their quarrels distract me. As to the Parliament, it is an assembly of republicans; I detest it." But Royalty lacked the will and the energy to trace for itself any definite position and power; whilst most of the subordinate departments of the government presented a similar deficiency of determinate authority. Ever at variance amongst themselves, and retaining power not on the basis of capacity and fitness, but subject to the wayward fancies of a vain and an incapable woman, the members of the Ministry sought to make the most of their very precarious tenure of office, and pursued crotchets or aggrandizement without concert and with little opposition. Occasionally an able man may be found among them, such as the Marquis d'Argenson, the Cardinal de Bernis, the Duc de Choiseul; but they were generally in mind, if not in body, dwarfs such as Puysieux, Saint-Florentin, and Rouillé, who in 1749 occupied the foremost places in the Cabinet.* Few men of ability would condescend to accept office under such derogatory auspices, or to enter upon a position so precarious in its nature as not unfrequently to belie the promise even of a few months. From 1756 to 1763, at least twenty-five changes occurred in the composition of the Council of State.

Amidst this chaos of pettinesses and contrarieties in the elements of the administration,—with the King, the Parliament, and the Clergy, in perpetual disaccord,—the people, though willing enough to obey, were bewildered, and their respect for authority weakened, by the ever-recurring uncertainty as to what authority obedience was strictly due. In vain they looked around for guidance: weakness, prodigality, and shameless inconsistency

---

* The epitaph suggested for the Comte de Saint-Florentin—

"Ci-git un petit homme à l'air assez commun,
Ayant porté trois noms et n'en laissant aucun "—

affords a sample of the contemptuous estimation in which the *personnel* of the Government was regarded by the public.

met them on all sides. They were crushed by fiscal burthens, and humiliated by the continued insult of defeat heaped upon the diplomacy and warlike operations of the Government. During the Seven Years War, France saw herself dishonoured, defeated, insulted and impoverished : she saw her colonies torn from her, and their brave defenders, such as Dupleix, Vaudreuil, Montcalm, wantonly neglected and suffered to perish in order that no fraction of the national resources might be diverted from ministering to the petty personal predilections of Madame de Pompadour. This woman had been addressed by the very virtuous Empress Maria Theresa as *ma cousine!* How could she, who had been from her very infancy prepared for the calling of a courtesan,—whose mother is said to have died from excess of joy when she was told of the brilliant shame which her daughter had achieved,—forbear exaggerating the gratitude of her vanity by placing France without reserve or limitation at the disposal of Austria ? The powerful urgings of policy and revenge, seconded by the skilful and delicate manœuvrings of Kaunitz, must be held responsible, in great measure, for the condescension of the Empress, as the tempting bait of imperial friendship must be charged with over-inflating the vanity of the courtesan. To prolong the interchange of the appellations *ma cousine* and *mon amie* between the mistress and bawd of Louis XV., and a princess whose pride and purity had been considered impregnable, France sacrificed 200,000 men, and was driven at last, from utter incapacity and exhaustion, to take refuge in a peace justly termed "shameful !"

"The Government," says Lacretelle, "has become so feeble that in fact it is not it which impresses a movement on the nation, which is agitated, amused, divided by cabals, studies systems, seeks to discover a new destiny, obeys badly, and has not yet revolted." The nation, it is true, had "not yet revolted;" but it was fast hurrying towards the confines which separate contemptuous acquiescence in the existing order of things from overt acts of opposition to authority. For some time it had felt troubled and indignant; but when, at length, authority appeared to be irreclaimably despicable, its mood changed, and it began to stifle a useless indignation, and to laugh at abuses and vices which it despaired of seeing remedied.[*] The permanency of this unnatural relationship between Government and people was impossible. Even then uneasy presentiments existed, and prophecies were hazarded, of coming commotions.

---

[*] Take, as an instance, the motley crowd of sarcastic epigrams which the people inscribed upon the pedestal of a triumphal statue erected to Louis XV. *after* the defeat at Rosbach, and a multitude of other humiliations.

Disorganization had begun : Reconstruction was yet in embryo, though cursed with an unnatural vigour. "The seeds of an inevitable revolution," wrote Voltaire, "are thickly scattered abroad : I shall not be present at the harvest of change, but the young are indeed fortunate, for they shall see admirable things." "Discontent," observes M. d'Argenson, "pervades every class of society. . . . Inflammatory materials are found on all sides. An *émeute* may spread into a revolt, which, in its turn, may kindle a *total revolution*." The King himself was not altogether free from some unpleasant forebodings of approaching political convulsion ; but he imagined that he had calculated its distance sufficiently accurately to warrant the assurance of his own safety, and as to his successor, why he might meet it " as best he could."

Within a society thus constituted—rotten to the very core —there was generated, almost inevitably, a motley swarm of innovators. In it the Philosophers became a power. Ministers of State, magistrates, and courtiers, such as D'Argenson, Malesherbes, and Richelieu, not only gave them flattering proofs of sympathy, but blunted in their behalf the legitimate shafts of the law. In 1751, Diderot and D'Alembert dedicated the Encyclopédie to the Minister of War, the Comte d'Argenson ; whilst Choiseul and Malesherbes granted them the *privilége* of that remarkable work—"a Babel," exclaims M. Michelet, " alphabetically arranged ; a monstrous dictionary in thirty folio volumes ! The Encyclopédie was far more than a book : it was a faction."

Such patronage—not, in effect, very far removed from treason to the State—was by no means a very surprising result of the inveterate feebleness which presided over every department of the Government. In 1757, appeared a Declaration of the King, registered by the Parliament, which denounced the penalty of death "against the writer of any work in which religion is attacked, in which any doubt as to the royal authority is hazarded, or which should tend in any way to trouble the tranquillity of the kingdom." In face of this Declaration, Malesherbes, who had been Directeur-général de la Librairie since 1750, might have been observed very pleasantly occupied, as he himself acknowledges, in correcting the proof sheets of Rousseau's " Emile "—a work which eloquently impugned many of the most familiar and long-established results of experience, and which, in spirit at least, ran counter to every clause of the Declaration ! The Parliament caused to be burnt on the same day by the hands of the public executioner the " Dictionnaire Philosophique," of Voltaire, and an " Instruction Pastorale" of the Archbishop of Paris. Its *arrêt* against Rousseau's " Emile" was issued in June, 1762, and its *arrêt* against the Society of Jesus in the following August !

Inconsistency was no less conspicuous among the Clergy. Religion was abandoned to the assaults of her most insidious enemies, whilst a fierce and an aimless internecine war was raging within the precincts of the Church. Though continually and authoritatively urged by the King, conciliation in no form was permitted to gain a footing between the fierce belligerents. The chief firebrand, Christophe de Beaumont, Archbishop of Paris, was inexorable; and though he suffered for his obstinacy, he brought incalculable mischief upon the Church. The inflexible language of the Jesuits, issuing from Ricci, the General of their Order,—"Sint ut sunt, aut non sint,"—ensured their own destruction and increased the dangers that thickened around Royalty. The principle of authority, which was the most characteristic dogma of the Company of Jesus, received, by the suppression of that Company, a severe shock in all its varied manifestations. The blow which struck it from the hands of the Church made it shake in the grasp of the civil power.

Thus, on all sides, were decadent influences preying upon the Monarchy. Neither of their existence, however, nor of their sinister action upon the tottering edifice of Royalty, was the King altogether unconscious. He tracked, with a sequential sagacity all his own, the drift of the New Philosophy to its ultimate destructive consequences. In his unkingly squabbles with the Parliament, he made spasmodic attempts to assert the absoluteness of the royal authority. But the intermittent energy and the feeble perseverance with which he sought to stem the torrent of innovation were not merely futile, but visibly tended to increase the violence of the innovating influences. It may, indeed, be confidently presumed that far greater and more sustained resistance on the part of the King would have led to equally unsuccessful issues, seeing that the very instruments and parasites of power were coquetting with the representatives of the beleaguering forces.

But though Louis XV. and his ministers had undermined the strong love of Royalty—even as the Clergy had weakened the sentiment of Religion—in the people, no coherent conception had yet presented itself by which the existing monarchical government could be either superseded or improved. No institution existed that could foster a spirit of liberty, or even suggest the elements of political knowledge. True, the folly and arrogance of the controlling orders in the State had for some time spurred public attention towards whatever happened to present itself, with more or less distinctness, in a political form; but then such appearances were invariably seen to emerge from indirect quarters. If Voltaire had not been cudgelled into energy and philosophy by the lackeys of the Chevalier de Rohan, it is very probable that the greatest spirit-stirrer since Luther would have slumbered through life as a court poet. His cherished home was in the palaces of princes. His worship of power was excessive and often servile. For some adulatory verses addressed to Madame de Pompadour, he was recompensed by rich presents, and ranked for a time as a Court official. Nor was he less obsequious to Madame Du Barry, as evidenced by his " Histoire du Parlement de Paris," and by many fulsome personal flatteries lavished upon the favourite. But his vanity and irritability counterpoised his servility. It was not the existing organization of power that he opposed, but certain special acts of authority. The unjustifiable seizure of his " Lettres sur les Anglais " served rather to sharpen his wit and to inflame his caustic humour, than to estrange him from arbitrary power. He had little love, or indeed comprehension, of political liberty. There existed in his mind no pet theory of government importunately seeking to thrust itself into practice. It was indirectly, and for the most part inadvertently, that he stirred into more coherent expression the festering irritation of the people towards their rulers, and urged the reduction of vague political generalities into something approaching definable forms. So far, indeed, was he from harbouring democratic sympathies that, in a letter to M. Bordes, he says : " The people will always be stupid and barbarous. . . . . . They resemble beasts of burthen for which a yoke, a goad, and daily provender are necessary." It was mainly through the Church that he wounded the Monarchy. His religious scepticism, unlimited as it appears to have been, derived little support from any chivalrous devotion to the interests of an enlightened intellectual freedom. It entered his mind mainly through the many wounds inflicted upon his vanity. The Church possessed at that time few capable defenders. Authority usurped the place of discussion, and seldom troubled itself to verify the justice or prudence of its decisions. Among a mass of unwise suppressions and interdictions of works, either published or intended for the press, may be observed many referring to certain productions of Voltaire, works which produced pernicious consequences mainly *because* surreptitiously circulated. Is it surprising, then, that Voltaire, dominated by a vain and exquisitely sensitive mind, should have revolted from the Church ; and, breaking impetuously through all the restraints of decorum, should have assailed her with unmeasured sarcasm and invective, calling her, in the bitterness of his wrath, *l'infâme !*

The impetus that Voltaire and his powerful auxiliaries of the Encyclopédie imparted to religious scepticism cleared the way for the irruption of political inquiries. Hostility, however, continued to be chiefly directed against the Church. Attacks upon the Clergy happened at the time to be regarded with indifference by the people, and to meet with the connivance, if not the direct encouragement, of Madame de Pompadour, because they ministered to the gratification of her malice,—for from among the Clergy stepped forward her chief opponents,—and because they suited the moods of certain disreputable court intrigues. Political speculation in the crude and impracticable forms usually imparted to them in France during the latter half of the eighteenth century may, indeed, be detected, though in very modified and timid forms, showing themselves at a much earlier period. As Corruption, though newly tricked out by Philosophy, could point, not with any show of palliation, but merely with a sign of continuity, from Duclos to Brantôme ; as Scepticism with a sneer might point from Voltaire to Bayle ; in like manner shallow political theorists might, with some specious airs of extenuation, if not of authority, point from Rousseau to Massillon and Fénélon.

For many years speculative thought had been ceaselessly on the watch to entrap any stray power which, under so weak a Government, was sure to escape occasionally, even from the chief strongholds of authority; and now the propitious moment was eagerly seized by the philosophers, and, with hardly less avidity, by nearly the entire complement of educated society. In 1753, Rousseau dragged into the arena of discussion the very foundations of human society in his "Discours sur l'Origine de l'inégalité parmi les hommes." The "Contrat Social" appeared in 1762, and "Emile" shortly after. The publication by the Marquis de Mirabeau, in 1755, of the "Ami des hommes" gave importance to the Economists, who pushed on vigorously their assaults upon the outposts of the ancient régime, and assiduously wrought into prominent and detailed relief the heavy abuses which crushed the people. Though inveighing against the iniquitous privileges enjoyed by certain classes of the community, and against most parts of the existing system of taxation, these financial reformers advocated the centralization and unity of power. The most serious injury which they inflicted upon the old Monarchy resulted from hasty, unreasoned, and violent attempts to restore its vigour. Yet one of the least vigorous of monarchs regarded them with favour. Quesnay, their chief, was, by very special appointment, as well "thinker" as physician to Louis XV. The lavish expenditure of the court rendered ever-recurring the presence of financial difficulties. The wildest schemes therefore promising to augment the public revenue elicited attention and often applause. But the agitation of such interesting inquiries could not fail to quicken the prying investigations which were rapidly increasing round the more strictly political constitution and attributes of the Monarchy.

The wonderful progress in the power and influence of the

agencies that were consciously or unconsciously undermining the old régime is vividly exemplified by such works as the "Esprit des Lois" and the "Contrat Social." How wide the difference between the political characteristics of the two publications, yet how short the time between the first appearance of the one and that of the other! In that brief interval the adoration formerly paid to royalty throughout the country had given place to feelings of contempt, if not of abhorrence. The "Well-beloved" of yesterday was by the populace of to-day execrated. Reports, not devoid of substantial appearances, pointed out the King, who had rarely ceased to heap upon himself the most grossly palpable follies and shortcomings, as the perpetrator of certain foul atrocities—atrocities, it is true, utterly fictitious, yet producing effects upon the ;multitude—hitherto fanatically loyal—little less damaging to royalty than if they had been realities. It may, indeed, be affirmed that a monstrous fiction, wantonly invited by the King, became one of the most effective destroyers of the monarchy. Apart from the multitude, however, the bulwarks of the monarchical institution were assailed far more than the monarch himself. It could not, indeed, without gross inconsistency, have been otherwise. In the infinitely varied attacks upon the old fabric of society, corruption presented itself as a very accommodating weapon. Welcome and efficient, then, must have been the aid which the King, as the most influential devotee of the prevailing fashion of debauchery, afforded to the philosophers in their intemperate undermining of all those institutions and customs which constituted the vitality and main substance of the ancient régime.

It may seem that Diderot—who, though he may not have been, in the exaggerated language of M. Michelet, "a revolutionary torrent, the Revolution itself," expresses with notable fidelity the most turbulent developments of French thought at this period—anticipated the bloodthirsty future in the oft-quoted lines:

> "Et mes mains ourdiraient les entrailles du prêtre,
> A défaut d'un cordon pour étrangler les rois."

However baleful may have been their indirect influence, these verses are little more than mere "sound and fury." Not a whisper of conspiracy against the Government could be heard even among the arch-initiators of radical theories who frequented the salons of Saint Lambert, Morellet, Suard, Helvétius, or even of the so-called "maître d'hôtel de la Philosophie," Baron d'Holbach. It would be most unjust to charge the distinguished writers who flourished at this time with any direct intention of planting the seeds of political anarchy.

They were utterly unaware of the consummate skill with which
they were elaborating the weapons that, in other hands, would
be fatally used against the ruling powers. With rare exceptions,
they sowed the wind of change unmoved by any anticipations of
even remote political tempests, far less suspecting that the very
next generation would reap the whirlwind of Revolution. Even
on other points they were often amazed and troubled at many an act
or opinion fairly deducible from their writings. An instance presents
itself in the answer elicited from Rousseau to certain questions
submitted to him by a would-be emancipator of his enslaved
country who had begun by abandoning his wife and children.
" Dare any one," exclaims Rousseau, " who prescribes as a law
unto himself to break the social ties of son, husband, and father,
usurp the name of citizen ? dare he usurp the name of man ?"
In spite of Rousseau's antecedents, we feel no hesitation in believing that the indignation expressed on this occasion was
genuine. The pertinacious warfare which Voltaire waged upon
the Clergy, the Church, and apparently upon Christianity itself,
was popularly construed into a crusade against all religion whatever, and spawned a motley tribe of blasphemers. Yet it is but
fair to doubt hostility of feeling towards at least the main precepts of the Christian faith in the man who could speak in the
following manner of the Founder of Christianity :—" Celui qui
savait tout a daigné tout nous dire en nous disant d'aimer."
There is little foundation for believing that even Diderot sought
deliberately to tempt the existing morality and religious sentiment to find a "lower deep ;" for at that time both morality and
religion among the upper classes in France had reached such a
low stage of degradation that below it the last faint traces of the
former must have disappeared and given place to absolute licence,
whilst the remains of the latter would probably have presented
themselves under the form of some bastard species of Fetichism.
Then again, D'Alembert, without fear of subjecting himself to the
charge of noticeable exaggeration, is able to say in a letter to Voltaire : " My writings and my conduct speak for me to those who are
willing to hear ; I defy calumny, and dare her to do her worst."
Most of the conspicuous writers of the time might with equal
confidence have submitted their character to general criticism.
Who could surpass Helvétius or D'Holbach in beneficence and
generosity ? Even those who ostentatiously professed Atheism,
such as Naigeon and Sylvain Maréchal, were not exceptionally
dissolute or unscrupulous. Most of the unpropitious light in
which the conspicuous pioneers of the Revolution have generally
been regarded must be attributed to the extravagances—verbal,
written, or acted—perpetrated by the vast crowd of their immediate soi-disant disciples. It must be admitted, however, that,

considering the general tenor of their masters' teaching, these men cannot be deemed illogical when they formulated deductions which outraged common sense, or be regarded as inconsistent when committing acts which shocked the feelings of the world.

It was chiefly from the prevailing epidemic of licentiousness —from the reckless patronage of novelty for the indefinite amount of excitement it promised—among the ruling and prominent classes of society that inspiration flowed upon the directing mind of France. Feeling how incompetent it was to guide its anger in a safe direction, the nation sought to alleviate, if not revenge, its immediate wrongs, and the degraded position which it held in the eyes of Europe, by fastening contempt and derision upon the administrators of the Government, and upon the most conspicuous firebrands of the Church. What a jostling and ever-increasing multitude of songs, epigrams, satires, were directed against the Jansenists, the Jesuits, the Petticoat Dynasty, the erewhile "well-beloved" King himself!

Did this contemptuous defection of the mind of the nation from its natural rulers, both lay and clerical, afford no premonition to the Government of some more or less imminent danger to the old monarchy? With the exception, strange to say, of the King, no member of the ever-varying ministry appears to have betrayed any distinct foreboding of the kind. "Far sooner," exclaimed Louis, in a moment of petulant anger, "would I hear again the thunder of artillery than all this scratching of pens." But he calmed his fears and his obsequious conscience by the delegation of repressive power and responsibility to Choiseul and Malesherbes, whom he esteemed—surely with many reassuring appearances—as both competent and loyal. With all his sagacious forebodings, however, Louis XV. had not, and, from the character of his environments, could not have, the faintest inkling of the extreme depth to which the mind of the nation was saturated with the prevalent philosophical eccentricities; nor could he picture the possibility of disloyalty in the most distinguished servants of the Crown. Yet we perceive that the ablest minister of his reign, and the most devoted and self-sacrificing royalist of whom his race can boast, suffered their judgment to be overpowered and led captive by the charms of the new philosophy. It is said that on one occasion M. de Malesherbes, in his official capacity, as Directeur de la Librairie, gave Diderot notice that on the following day he should send officers to seize his papers. "Your announcement," answered the great encyclopædist, "annoys me horribly; how can I manage in so short a time to remove all my manuscripts? Besides, it is not so easy in twenty-four hours to find any one who will take charge of them." "Send them to me," wrote Malesherbes; "no one

will come here in search of them." When we are confronted by
such startling complicity between one of the firmest adherents
of royalty, and one of the master-underminers of the monarchy,
much of our astonishment at the rapid crumbling away of the
crazy fabric composing the ancient régime must disappear.
There was, indeed, at this time, a vast parade of persecution,
but, truly, no persecutors.

The Duc de Choiseul connived hardly less directly at the
advance of the invading host of new opinions. But being far
less deficient in penetration, and less prone to a credulous belief
in the facility of human perfectibility than his amiable colleague,
his connivance can claim far less extenuation. The sincerity of
his loyalty was assuredly beyond suspicion; but he cherished
still more ardently his vanity and popularity. Though the most
prominent and punctilious of grands seigneurs, he succumbed,
with subtly-calculated levity, to the blandishments of the religious
and political heresiarchs. " It is characteristic of this *siècle de
l'esprit*," says M. Michelet, " that Choiseul, who rarely humoured
the King, accommodated himself with unwearied attention to
the humours of the salons." Choiseul was the first French
statesman who deciphered the declining value of the royal
favour, and the rapidly increasing importance with which popular opinion was inflating itself. Having supplanted Cardinal
de Bernis in the favour of Madame de Pompadour,—who, urged
by many experiences of her own weakness, had for some time
felt the absolute necessity of delegating part of her authority
into abler keeping than that of mediocrity,—he soon brought
within his control nearly the entire action of the Government.
At the beginning of the year 1761 he was made Minister of
War, and when, towards the close of the same year, he became
Minister of Marine, he adroitly consigned the portfolio of
Foreign Affairs, which Bernis had been constrained to resign
into his hands, to the obsequious keeping of his cousin, the Duc
de Praslin; thus holding or controlling the three chief elements
of power. But he was not the man to rehabilitate the dege-
nerate monarchy, or even appreciably to check its decline. His
duty, under most of its aspects, was made to twist itself towards,
and bow before, that brilliant Parisian society of which he may
be regarded as a notable specimen, a society which, with perverse
self-complacency, seemed charmed at its successful endeavours
to stamp upon itself the reputation of being pre-eminently
frivolous and Utopian.

Many of the mental lineaments of Maurepas—who, as minister
and courtier, exercised throughout the greater portion of the
period under consideration a many-visaged influence over the
King and Government of France—which Marmontel sketches with

H 2

lively fidelity, bear a marked resemblance to those of Choiseul. "A lynx eye to detect the failings of his fellows: a mind fertile in expedients for attack, admirable in address for defence." These qualifications were regarded by French statesmen as the chief, if not the sole, requisites for the conduct of public affairs. Choiseul and Maurepas represent—somewhat flatteringly no doubt—not only the *personnel* of the French Government, but the élite of French society, during the reign of Louis XV. Sceptical and scoffing, they fraternized with the giant pioneers of destruction, and but rarely gave evidence of possessing even a mediocre degree of the creative faculty. Their policy seldom changed its direction, setting—in spite of the grossest and most calamitous inconsistencies—steadily towards an immediate gratification of the unreasoning passions, or the petty vanities, of the feeble dispensers of power. This policy, though it sometimes weighed upon them with an uncomfortable pressure, seldom met with much resistance. Such men, however, notwithstanding their general compliancy, were merely tolerated in the ministry to give it an appearance of cohesion, and to impart a necessary weight of official authority for the due carrying out of the routine business of the Government. Naturally jealous of its independence, distinguished ability was not invariably found sufficiently pliant to bend implicitly before the polluted idol that royalty had set up. Subserviency to the King's mistress, and political ignorance, were, therefore, the most distinctive features of each successive Ministry that attempted to govern France from 1744 to 1774.

The subversive spirit of the times, emboldened by a widespread disregard in the regions both of thought and action for the religious or political future of the nation, showed itself especially rampant and contagious in its onslaught upon the Jesuits. The overthrow of those vigilant guardians of the Church was the first great triumph won by the philosophers over the established forces of society. It was hardly an exaggeration on the part of Frederick II. to proclaim Voltaire the most redoubtable "King" in Europe. To the despotic ruler of the then most energetic representatives of French thought is chiefly referrible the discomfiture of the great champions of unity in the Church. Yet he regarded the brilliant victory he had achieved merely as a first step towards more radical encroachments upon the domain of ecclesiastical authority. "What does it avail me," he asks in a letter to La Chalotais, "to be delivered from the fox (the Jesuit), if I am handed over to the wolf?" (the Jansenist). Important, however, as was that success, and materially as it influenced the issue of the momentous struggle between the destructive and the conservative forces of

French society, it cannot be regarded as affording many grounds of exultation to the victors; for the defenders of Catholicism were at that time feeble in the extreme, and yet more blind than feeble. They could descry no very formidable danger menacing the Church until the near approach of the day on which Christianity itself was banished by decree from the soil of France!

It cannot be said that so complete a dimness of perception clouded the mind either of Louis XV. or of Choiseul. But the clamours of the present drowned the whispers of the future. The King was nearly as much a slave to superstition as to licentiousness. He was fully aware, too, of the great value which should be accorded to the existing alliance between Church and State: but his extreme though groundless jealousy of the Dauphin, to whom the Jesuits were especially devoted, quickened his acquiescence in the Edict of 1764. Then, again, the Parliament worked upon his fears, and arrested any effective resistance which his reluctance to the measure might occasion, by threatening to demand a statement of his secret expenses (*acquits au comptant*), a statement which would expose to public opprobrium the monstrous items of his vile extravagance; whilst Choiseul still further paralysed his opposition by placing before him the alternative of suppressing the Jesuits or the parliaments, presenting thus the questions:—Would he hazard a revolution? would he risk a recurrence of scenes of which the Chemin de la Révolte was a consequence? was he prepared to witness again a series of bloody conflicts in the streets, and to hear repeated the ominous cry, "Allons brûler Versailles?" As to Choiseul, opposition to the Jesuits afforded no symptom whatever of religious significance. But the minister perceived its admirable utility as an instrument of expediency. He used it with much adroitness as a shield to ward off the blows aimed at many parts of his policy. By it he conciliated the favour both of the Parliament and of the philosophers: by it he calmed the irritation of the nation at the Treaty which closed the Seven Years War, a war which, from numerous Austrian associations and influences, and still more from personal ambition, he had been mainly instrumental in bringing about and prolonging. The ability, the confidence, the incomparable tact and ease with which he contrived to carry on that disastrous conflict without compromising his popularity are proofs, no doubt, of his wonderful diplomatic and conciliatory powers. Rousseau declares, indeed, "that but for the ability displayed by Choiseul, the Seven Years War would have proved fatal to the French monarchy." Such praise, however, applied to one of the chief instigators and supporters of a ruinous contest seems to wear a rather ambiguous, if not an ironical, air. Be that as it may, the disasters and desolation which the protracted hostilities produced were not the less conspicuous. The exaggerated language in which M. Michelet too often indulges is, in reference to this deplorable war, so profoundly imbued with a mixture of reality that it seems shorn of its generally startling incongruity, and merely serves to deepen an otherwise inevitable impression. "What," exclaims M. Michelet, "had Austria gained? Nothing at all. Frederick remained the same. What had France lost? The world, no more."

The close alliance between the Princes of the House of Bourbon, cemented by the *Pacte de famille*,—made public by Choiseul in 1761,—which met with such loud applause in France, and such astonishment abroad, contributed as much to soothe the national irritation occasioned by the Peace of Paris in 1763, as the expulsion of the Jesuits tended to conciliate the forbearance of various embarrassing influences after the actual ratification of that peace. We are far more disposed, however, to congratulate Choiseul on the tact which he displayed, and on the good fortune which attended him, than on the possession of very exceptional capacity. He had fallen upon weak times. The avenues to power had long been filled by a motley refuse of courtiers and politicians. Royalty had lost its dignity and prestige. Even a minister of ordinary ability and independence would have been hailed with applause. It is by no means surprising, then, that Choiseul—who possessed many of the characteristics of a statesman, who was endowed with a subtlety of shallow penetration that almost raised him above the necessity of ordinary political study, whose mind though devoid of any profound conviction, perhaps seldom entertaining a more plausible persuasion, never quailed in presence of difficulty, but grasped vast projects with a confidence so easy in its action that temerity seemed absent, and even chances of failure insignificant —captivated the French people, and was surrounded in exile, as he had been besieged during the time of his power and prosperity, by a host of distinguished admirers and partisans. Versailles itself was depopulated, for there was an instinctive feeling even among courtiers, that with Choiseul had departed the last remnants of French honour.

The "Cocher de l'Europe," as the Empress Catherine was wont to designate the fascinating and skilfully-impelling French Minister, influenced by the prevailing spirit of the times as much as by the natural levity of his mind, had become so accustomed to square his policy in deference to the demands of the present, that he rarely vouchsafed a glance beyond the probable duration of his official life. This shutting out of view all but the appearances and present necessities of to-day gradually contracted within so narrow a range his naturally short, though marvellously clear, vision, that the politic flatterer of Madame de Pompadour stumbled at last on the very threshold of his own erewhile exquisitely accurate appreciation of whoever or whatever might sensibly influence his fortunes. By ministering to the revengeful spirit of one woman, and pandering to the contemptible vanity of another, he maintained an influential though inherently precarious position in the government, little heedful of the present, and still less of the future, interests of his country. Thus he made but insignificant efforts to arrest the hand which was erasing the French colonies from the map of Asia and America, whilst he looked on with a scarcely ruffled equanimity at the costly and bloody campaigns in Europe which were sapping the resources of France, and casting a dark stain upon her military reputation. By assuming hardly the bare possibility of a cordial alliance between Russia, Austria, and Prussia, having the dismemberment of Poland as the cementing object, he pooh-poohed for some time all assurances of the first actual stealthy steps of the crowned conspirators towards their prey: thus contributing still further to impair the honour and interests of his country. By the expulsion of the Jesuits from the kingdom he scattered conciliation around him and tightened his hold on the reins of power; but, however salutary this measure might have been under less dangerously perturbed aspects of social opinion, at this unfavourable conjuncture such an act tended to strengthen the growing disrespect for authority, and thus increased the instability of the tottering monarchy. By the injudicious nomination of Laverdy as Contrôleur-général in 1764, and by the still grosser error of conferring the office of Chancellor upon Maupeou in 1768, he paved the way to the final and fatal quarrel between the Crown and the Parliament; thus again, and more radically, contributing to shake the old political construction: and, finally, by an overweening self-conceit which pictured his indispensability in the conduct of public affairs, and by a consequent over-confidence in the stability of his position,—to the extent even of believing that neither the King nor the King's mistress "dare" dismiss him,— his habitually quick discernment and sense of danger became hoodwinked, and he fell; thus depriving France at a most critical moment of the only statesman who, however conspicuous his shortcomings, possessed a quality of conciliation peculiarly well suited to break the shock of her approaching calamities.

The contemptuous disregard for established institutions which had been wantonly making its way for half a century among the upper classes, and that of late had begun to spread with ominous rapidity over the whole nation, but which had been hitherto decorously veiled by the members of the Government, was now proclaimed with marked emphasis by those who had succeeded in snatching the reins of power from the Duc de Choiseul. The late policy of conciliation, frequently censurable, no doubt, for its lack of discrimination, was swept away by a rigid predetermined spirit which hastened to override all opposition. The decrepit old monarchy, obviously demanding the gentlest means and appliances to strengthen its dilapidated constitution, was incontinently seduced to assume braggart airs of vigour. The nation looked on apathetically, smiled at the assumption, shrugged its shoulders, and passed on its own speculative way. Not only had its sympathies, in every mood and manifestation, become detached from royalty and its environments, but a distrust of even a possible reformation in such quarters—a distrust distempered, no doubt, and destined to run a mischievous and fatal course, yet surely not without considerable justification—was substantially growing up in company with motley groups of systems, theories, and aspirations, often charming in many of their aspects, but in reality possessing hardly a grain of solid truth or practical utility.

The Comtesse du Barry hurried as far beyond her predecessor in the path of reckless vigour and audacity as she lagged behind her in the direction of much that is regarded as intellectual culture and refinement. The assertion, "elle était des nôtres," which, in a letter to D'Alembert, Voltaire affirms of Madame de Pompadour, surely cannot be viewed, at least in many of its superficial aspects, as an exaggeration. To point out a difference of some few degrees of vanity and laxity of morals which, at the cost of an unpleasant investigation, might be detected in the character of the two women, would be a bootless labour, seeing that at this time the Court had reached a depth of depravity where any change in its moral aspect, if not very considerable, was difficult of detection, and could therefore present little social, and still less political, significance. Though nearly twenty years interference in State affairs had imparted little political wisdom to Madame de Pompadour, they had at all events familiarized her with a few political outlines. This acquaintance with the general features presented by the principal institutions of the country, and a morbid dread of danger to her influence by subjecting the King to unwonted political excitement, would have restrained the Marquise from adventuring any radical change in the framework of the monarchy, however enticing the present advantages which it might promise. Unshackled by a scruple, and with the temerity of utter ignorance, the Comtesse sought to gratify her revengeful passions and her cupidity by hazarding a *coup d'état* before which even Richelieu or Louis XIV. would have stood appalled. She was jealous of Choiseul because his influence over the King approached too near an equality with her own, and she hated him because he dared to doubt the stability of her position, and presumed to curtail his homage towards her of its most soothing incense: she hated the Parliament because it embarrassed the action of the royal authority, and therefore the freedom of her own will; and she chafed at the shadow of honesty which yet lingered timidly about the financial transactions of the Government, because it sometimes whispered moderation to her cupidity. To Choiseul she opposed the Duc d'Aiguillon; to the Parliament, its erewhile president, Maupeou; and to the wavering influence of honesty in financial matters, the Abbé Terray.

Of these principal instruments and advisers of Madame du Barry, the Duc d'Aiguillon, Minister of Foreign Affairs, though not ostensibly the chief of the new Administration, exercised the most general influence over the policy and acts of the Government. He had been Governor of Brittany, a position for which he was peculiarly unqualified. Proud and incapable of conciliation, he soon forced opposition to his authority upon the provincial Parliament, and finally found himself exposed to serious accusations of maladministration. Transferred to the central authorities, his trial was eagerly entered upon by the Parliament of Paris, and proceeded without encountering any opposition from the Duc de Choiseul. Hence the implacable hatred of D'Aiguillon both towards the Minister and the Parliament.[1] Many causes of a very interested and, it need hardly be said, disreputable nature induced the King and his mistress to favour the accused. The Parliament, urged by its usual injudicious anxiety to parade a little political importance, and by the supercilious demeanour of the man whom it was but too willing to condemn, entered upon a series of intemperate proceedings which rendered it easily accessible to the attacks of its enemies.

Audacity, freed from every check of justice or morality, formed the mainspring which gave motion to the internal policy of the Government. The Contrôleur-Général, Terray, showed a vigour in dealing with the apparently hopeless embarrassments of the treasury so effective and unscrupulous that Madame du Barry herself was satisfied, even to the extent of her avidity. " Cynical as a satyr, to whose supposed countenance and manners his own bore much resemblance," he treated all interests, except those of Du Barry and her clique, with a perfect equality of disregard and injustice. An example of this unqualified cynicism is afforded by the Archbishop of Narbonne, who, remonstrating with the Contrôleur des Finances against the injustice of certain requisitions upon the clergy, observed, " Why, surely, sir, this is helping yourself to money directly from our pockets with a vengeance !"   " Where, then," inquired Terray, with cool surprise, " would you have me search for it ?"   A partial national bankruptcy was also regarded as a ready means of gratifying the rapacity of the Court ; for immorality had reached a stage where no feint was made to repudiate the companionship of dishonesty.

That boldness of spirit, nourished chiefly by levity and the lowest passions, which wantoned in a continual defiance of opposition and danger, evidenced so conspicuously by D'Aiguillon and Terray, pervaded still more engrossingly the mind of the Chancellor Maupeou.   Never more at ease than in the midst of strife, never more fitly and agreeably occupied than when heading the forces of destruction, Maupeou deservedly enjoys tho unenviable distinction of having imparted the greatest, if not the very last, downward impulse to the rapidly sinking monarchy. Truly Madame du Deffand may be excused for writing, in a moment of astonishment and alarm, that the Chancellor was " not a man but a devil."

Maupeou had been accused of many shortcomings, and even of dishonesty, by the Parliament which he sought to destroy. Hence he was urged by a spirit of revenge, no less than by a natural predilection for violent changes, to second with unscrupulous energy the pestilent ambition of Madame du Barry, who sought to disembarrass herself of that assembly, and thus become enabled to abuse at discretion the resources of unlimited power. A conflict between the Parliament and the Crown, eminently personal in its character, afforded admirable facilities for alluring the disputants into a course of reckless imprudence, and was therefore regarded by Madame du Barry and the Chancellor as a propitious opportunity for adventuring their *coup d'état.*

The Parliaments had not escaped the deteriorative influences of the times.   During the preceding century these assemblies had often exercised considerable power.   Whether suffering persecution, or in a state of revolt, they seldom failed to command respect.   Even under the repressive rule of Louis XIV. they maintained a dignified and an irreproachable demeanour.   A long monotony of despotism, followed suddenly by tolerated liberty of action and unbounded licence of manners, affected most perniciously the character of the Magistrature.   From the commencement of the reign of Louis XV., the Parliaments began to diverge into petty and questionable courses, regardless alike of the legitimate limits of their own jurisdiction, and of the rights which belonged to others.   Ever failing to consolidate any accidental increase in their power, they succeeded most effectually in irritating the King, and in giving permanence to his hostility.   Agitating mainly and often obtrusively for the defence and furtherance of their own prerogatives, and for their own material interests, they gradually forfeited all pretensions to public spirit, lost the strengthening reliance which the people had been wont to repose in them, and stood before their enemies in all the weakness of isolation. "The Parliaments have a disastrous termination in store for them," predicted D'Alembert in 1766, "a termination which is nearer at hand than is generally supposed. They are too fanatical, too doltish, and too tyrannical." This censure, though too general and unqualified, was occasionally amply justified, as, for example, in the well-known cases of Calas, Sirven, the Chevalier de la Barre, and Lally. Numerous, however, as were the reprehensible points in the character of the Magistrature at this time, its general aspect must be admitted to contrast favourably with that presented by the character of any other prominent class of French society. The chief and ruinous error which had long marked the career of the principal Parliaments—notably the Parliament of Paris—was an inopportune intermeddlement with political or quasi-political matters. This propensity grew apace during the latter years of Louis XV.'s reign. The parliamentary bodies, unwittingly or imprudently overlooked the fact that royalty had abdicated its chief power into the hands of unscrupulous minions, who had little knowledge of, and no respect for, any constituent element of the monarchy save that from which they immediately derived their importance and their emoluments.

The oft-recurring conflicts between the Parliament and the regal power varied but little in the manner of their development : " refusal of the Parliament to register a royal edict—*lit-de-justice*—persistence of the Parliament—exile or imprisonment of the magistrates—reciprocal concessions—submission or victory of the Parliament—seeming reconciliation of the disputants." Through such a course, in reference to the powers in question, were the acrimonious religious contests of 1753 and 1756 reduced to apparent tranquillity. On no occasion could either of the disputants boast of achieving more than a very shadowy advantage ; the substantial result being invariably to hurry both of them another stage towards destruction. Thus toilsomely we advance, until, in 1769, we are startled by an invocation which reminds us that we are entering upon the last years of the monarchy. The Cour des Aides, in behalf of the Parliament, supplicated the King "to listen to the nation itself by the mouth of the States-General." We are by no means surprised to encounter at nearly every step of these quarrels as much inconsistency as weakness. "The Parliament in 1766 declared that the King was accountable to God alone, and then declared its own right to resist the King, in the name of the King, and in the interest of the King!" But the inconsistency and weakness so conspicuous in the Parliament were, in 1770, opposed, not as heretofore, to similar inconsistency and weakness, but to a decision without limits, and to an unscrupulousness which had no counterpart in the character of the Magistrature.

The Parliament persisted in prosecuting the trial of the Duc d'Aiguillon, notwithstanding a formal injunction from the King to stay any further proceedings. To this indiscretion—this bearding of despotism—it added with passionate eagerness the crime of prejudication, incriminating the ex-Governor of Brittany, and inflicting upon him certain penalties, with no justificatory plea beyond that afforded by extra-judicial and *ex parte* evidence. Blindly anticipating results similar to those which had usually attended the adventuring upon particular acts of opposition to the Crown, the Parliament determined to subject both King and people to mischievous embarrassments by temporarily arresting the accustomed current of its duties. At this juncture the Duc de Choiseul ceased to form part of the government, and with him departed concession, even to its mere appearance, from the Ministry. The attitude assumed by the Parliament had been expected and desired by Maupeou. In January, 1771, the Chancellor exiled the magistrates, confiscated their appointments, and installed a new Parliament, composed chiefly of men who were also members of the Grand Conseil. Before the end of the year every provincial Parliament had been reorganized and rigorously shorn of all but judicial functions.

Was the summary destruction of these distinguished assemblies by so despicable an instrument effected without resistance? Was no hand or voice raised to prevent the fall of bodies that for ages had fought the battles of the people against the encroachments of Feudalism, of Ultramontanism, and of Royalty itself? Truly there appeared opposition in all quarters; but its total efficacy fell far short of the individual energy of the Chancellor: it was all but universal, and all but lifeless. We must not, however, forget to do justice to the Avocat-Général, Seguier, who, with prophetic fervour, courageously declared to the King that "the dissolution of the Parliaments must inevitably tend to shake the foundations of many of the most ancient institutions and customs of the country; that violent or abrupt changes in fundamental laws or established usages are often the cause or the pretext of revolutions."

The selfish and foul temerity which ignorantly thought to invigorate the regal authority by freeing it from all restraint, had, in reality, withdrawn the only remaining prop which possessed any inherent strength to keep it from falling. A vital principle of royalty was imperilled, and rudely deprived of its importance in the public mind, when the magistratic position was made precarious. Was not the spirit of change, then so rife in the public mind, hurried by the destructive measure of the Ministry impetuously to display itself before the people clothed and armed with the highest official authority? May not that act, in effect, be regarded as the last step of the old Monarchy, and the first of the Revolution?

Of all the chief elements which had formerly contributed to make up the governing power of the French monarchy, royalty alone remained. It was now dragged into the immediate presence of the people. No more inauspicious moment could have been chosen for hazarding this, at any time, dangerous juxtaposition. Nothing in the prevailing temper of the nation, or in the character of the King, or in the spirit which animated the ministry, augured propitiously of such a confrontation. Royalty stood confessed in all its obscene debility, and confirmed the universal contempt with which it had long been regarded. The royal will, however,—now without a rival,—was universally acknowledged and obeyed; though rarely was an act of obedience unaccompanied by an impatient sneer, if not by an execration. Opposition, bewildered and lost in a crowd of political contradictions and illusory social theories, was, as yet, too timid, disjointed and doubtful, to assume a threatening aspect. Placing very decidedly apart her literary celebrities, France seemed hopelessly abandoned to the spirit of feebleness. The discontent and irritation of the people at the dishonest and profligate home administration of the Government, and the yet less endurable humiliation felt at its dastardly foreign policy, presented themselves among all classes in an infinite variety of satirical forms, forms well suited to elude the coarse grasp of despotism. Disconcerting as such wide-spread opprobrium must have been to Louis XV., it was insufficient to induce him either to make any sign of self-reformation, or to assume the energy which repressive measures would render necessary. He had lost the support of every influential party in the nation, and was unable to command the services, much less the devotion, of any capable individual possessing either the confidence or the respect of the people. He had been all his life laboriously, though to some extent unconsciously, employed in alienating himself from his subjects, and his long perseverance had at last brought him to the extreme limits of isolation. There was now as much excess in the hatred which France heaped upon royalty, as there had been intemperance in the love which she had formerly lavished upon it.

It seems highly probable that if the life of the old King had been prolonged, the Revolution would have hastened its steps, and been clothed with tenfold terrors. Scarcely an institution—political, religious, or social—existed which was not infected with incurable debility, if not with absolute rottenness : and yet all things wore their accustomed appearance ! The Monarchy with its old forms was still there, though the vitality which faith in the sufficiency of its governing attributes could alone bestow had forsaken it. France was virtually in a state of anarchy. She had withdrawn her last lingering regard from royalty before her feelings or her understanding had arrived at even a shadowy determination as to any promising political course to be pursued. There would have been no émeute, no partial outburst of disaffection, for there appeared no political leader, no political project. The entire nation stood on the brink of unfathomable speculation : the signal for the momentous plunge was trembling on every lip : the pause was inspired solely by a wholesome fear of the political chaos, and the dread social derangement, into which the meditated plunge might sink the nation. It was surely a circumstance of high and salutary importance that the fatal word did not pass into articulate utterance before the people had been partially propitiated, and at least superficially schooled, by witnessing a series of attempts, abortive though they were, at conciliation and reform.

The imminently menacing approach of the Revolution was suddenly checked by the death of Louis XV., in 1774. But the ancient régime had virtually passed away with the old King. The monarchy had reached the extreme limits of decline, and was kept from falling mainly by the amiable disposition and conciliatory policy of Louis XVI. Its own misdeeds, and, yet more, the determined spirit of change which now occupied an all-powerful position in the national mind, rendered the preservation even of its bare existence a task of supreme difficulty. What but ruins had Louis XV. left behind him ? If, then, his unfortunate successor had been endowed with pre-eminent wisdom and energy, no amount of judicious political skill and labour would have enabled him, with so much that was dangerous and rotten scattered around, to reconsolidate the Monarchy upon its ancient basis. But Louis XVI. possessed little wisdom and no energy. Timid in judgment, he was continually seeking refuge in impossible compromises. Anxious to do good, yet ever hesitating as to the means. The ample folds of his philanthropy embraced all. The old and the new were to be reconciled : Maurepas was induced to shake hands with Turgot ! What was this but a constrained and unnatural interchange of civility between incarnate frivolity enshrined in effete prejudices, and the representative of stern political consistency incautiously hurrying upon untried changes :—between the man " who would have written the history of France in a series of songs," and the man who would fain mark out the future of the nation by the rule and square of an impossible, because inflexible, justice.'

By the aid of inherently antagonistic agents such as these did Louis XVI. attempt to restore the declining energies of the expiring Monarchy. The impending dissolution, however, was not thus to be averted. Where, indeed, could the man be found fully qualified to cope with the exigencies of the crisis? It was a complicated and unprecedented political conjuncture, for the management of which there was needed unprecedented human capabilities. It is not surprising, then, that the feeble Monarch had to encounter a series of harassing disappointments, and, though mainly influenced by the most righteous intentions, to suffer the reproach of precipitating a succession of bitter party contests that, ever diverging further and further from the path of conciliation, terminated at last in an appeal to the judgment of the States-General.

Art. IV.—Religion as a Subject of National Education.

IN the controversy as to the nature and extent of the subjects of education to be embraced in the national system, parties seem to have divided themselves into denominationalists and undenominationalists; into advocates for combined secular and religious teaching, and advocates for the separation of secular from religious teaching. The advocates of undenominational teaching, and for the separation of secular from religious teaching, in relation to this question, are also both together classified as secularists. The parties so classified together under the name of secularists, for the most part, maintain that the education to be imparted under the national system should not extend beyond the subjects of secular education, and that there should be no religious teaching by the authority or at the expense of the State. They do not desire that no religious teaching should be given, but they maintain that the proper persons to impart it are the parents or guardians, or the clergy, or any other persons who may be employed for the purpose, without the interference of the State. On the other hand, the denominationalists, and the advocates for the combination of religious with secular teaching, maintain that it is the duty of the State to provide for both. This party is made up almost entirely of persons belonging to Protestant denominations, and, to a great extent, of persons belonging to the Established Churches of England and Scotland. But the persons who compose it are not of any uniform denomination, or of any uniform

set of denominational opinions. There are many of these persons
who hold principles which, in many respects, are hostile to each
other. They cannot unite, except in so far as they have common
ground on which to take their stand. They, therefore, perceive
that while they ask the State for religious teaching to children,
such teaching cannot, in so far as authorized by the State, be
the teaching of any special denomination. On that footing they
profess themselves willing to consent that the religious teaching
shall be limited to the reading and explaining of the Bible,
according to the authorized Protestant translation. Some of
them even profess themselves willing to limit the religious teaching to the mere reading of the Bible without explanation, and
without note or comment. They do not offer any proposal for
the teaching of any religion by the State, other than the Protestant religion, or any provision applicable to children who
cannot, or will not, accept Protestant teaching, except their
being permitted to withdraw during the time of the religious
teaching of the other children. Neither is it known that the
advocates of Protestant religious teaching have made any proposal as to the mode of extending any national system of religious teaching to Ireland, in which it would fall to be administered
among a population mostly Roman Catholic, by local Boards
consisting for the most part of Roman Catholic members.

The terms secular and religious, as used in this controversy,
indicate the direction of the leading tendencies of opinion, but
they are not in themselves correct or accurate definitions, capable of consistent or distinct practical application. In consequence of this want of accuracy they not only fail to set forth
the proper points at issue, but, in putting many departments of
the controversy at cross-purposes, they both cause and add to
much of the confusion which exists.

The terms secular and religious, are both used in popular
significations. In popular signification, secular teaching would
be held to include civil history as a part of it. In popular
signification, the term religion is undoubtedly held to include
morality, and more particularly the whole heads of morality included in the Ten Commandments.

But if these definitions of the popular signification of the
terms secular and religious be correct, the separation, in
practical education, of what corresponds to these terms is in
many respects impracticable. A great part of civil history consists of the history of religious controversy, and of events arising
out of religious controversy, and it is impossible to conceive any
teaching of civil history from which the history of such controversies could be excluded. Such history as the history of our
own country—that of England or Scotland—or any other his-

tory, would be unintelligible without the history of religion and of religious controversies. The religious elements of civil history would be equally unintelligible without some historical instruction as to the tenets of the religions which were the subjects of such controversies. History at large is simply a description of the events and progress of humanity. No influences have had greater bearing on these than the religious beliefs of races and nations at successive epochs of time. In a great measure, religion has been to history what the mind is to the body, and nothing could be more barren and profitless than to teach a mere catalogue of events without any attempt to illustrate or explain the causes which led to them or the consequences which followed them.

In the same way, in the most restricted secular education, it is not supposed that it can be intended to leave the mind and conscience a perfect blank as to the obligations of ordinary moral duty. There could be no education or training of any national or personal value which could fail to inculcate such duties as those of good behaviour, charity, benevolence, decency, honesty, and truthfulness. But there, again, the functions of religion, in the popular signification of the word, are intruded upon. If it be said that moral duty is not necessarily founded on Biblical religion, but may be founded on what may be called natural religion, the answer is the same. Natural religion is still religion, and falls to be equally excluded by the arguments which would seek to separate secular teaching from religious teaching. We may add that, if ever moral duty shall become dissociated from religious beliefs of any kind in the popular mind, the time when it will be so is so far off that a consideration of its probability can scarcely affect our view of the subject now in question. The arguments for secular teaching separately from religious teaching would therefore go to exclude, in the secular department, all proper teaching, either of history or morality, from the national system of education. But could there be anything worth calling education from which all knowledge of civil history and of the duties of ordinary morality and conduct are attempted to be excluded? Would such an education, even if it could be had, be a suitable object of state expenditure, or would it be a suitable training for the citizen or member of society? It seems to be impossible to make any answer but one, and, if so, the theory of secular education separately from religious education falls to pieces by its own insufficiency and inconsistency. The theory of the secularists leads to another anomaly. The only religion of which there is any special jealousy among its various denominations, and the only religion which is the subject of controversy, is the Christian. There is no objection made to the teaching of the ancient mythologies, and probably no special objection to the Brahminical, Buddhist, Mahommedan, and other non-Christian religions being described and explained. But the doctrines of Christianity must not be taught, described, or explained in any way. The absurd result would therefore follow that no religion shall be taught unless it be held to be false, and that the only religion which the state, as a state, professes to hold to be true shall not be taught at all.

Having shown the insufficiency and impracticability of the proposed theory of secular education separately from religious education, it is intended now to examine the views of those who propose that the national system shall embrace what they are pleased to designate religious as well as secular teaching. The advocates of this system are classified as Denominationalists, because, although they advocate religious teaching along with secular teaching, they maintain, for the most part, that such religious teaching cannot be imparted except through the medium of adherents of recognised religious denominations. They also maintain that there should be statutory provision to the effect that religious teaching should be so imparted. Some of the Denominationalists would probably disclaim insisting on carrying out their minor sectarian differences in regard to the selection of teachers, but they would all insist that the teachers must be at least Episcopalian or Presbyterian in some shape or other. They are not of the view of the poet Schiller.

" What my religion? Those thou namest? None.
None, why? Because I have religion !"

They have no idea of a religion without a name, and just as little idea that any person can be truly religious who is not an adherent of a recognised religious denomination.

The views of the Denominationalists might be very suitable if people were all of the same denomination, or if there were no differences of religious opinion. But when, besides smaller subdivisions, the same state contains Roman Catholics, Episcopalians, and Presbyterians, Methodists, Baptists, Independents &c. &c. and when these leading denominations are so fundamentally hostile that, as a rule, the Episcopalians will not accept Presbyterian religious teaching, the Presbyterians will not accept Roman Catholic religious teaching, and the Roman Catholics will not accept any Protestant religious teaching, there can be no common ground for religious teaching by the state on a denominational footing. It may be that denominational Presbyterians in Scotland are so blind to principle that they are willing that Roman Catholics in that country should be taxed for teaching a denominational religion which they abhor; but let them put themselves in the position of Presbyterians in Ireland taxed for propagating Roman Catholicism, and they might see matters in a very different light. The case of the Roman Catholics is put as the largest and most conspicuous instance of the injustice and inconsistency of the application of the denominational principle. But besides the Roman Catholics, there are numerous other denominational bodies in every part of the United Kingdom, and many families and persons not denominational, who would feel it to be flagrant oppression to have denominational religious teaching of which they do not approve authoritatively forced upon them, or to be forced to pay for, or to be parties in any way to, its being imparted to others. If there were more Episcopalians in Scotland or more Presbyterians in England this would be more evident; but the Presbyterians in Scotland and the Episcopalians in England form such a large proportion of the population that each within their own sphere are all but paramount, and, in the strength of each within their own territory, they are apt to overlook the rights and interests of those who differ from them. Artemus Ward describes the ancient Puritans in America as rejoicing "in having come from a land of despotism to a land of freedom, where every man can enjoy his own religion in peace and prevent every other from enjoying his'n." It is thought that more people than the Puritans have similar ideas of freedom in such matters.

It may be said that some Denominationalists are willing to abandon all religious teaching except the teaching of the Bible. But the Protestant translation of the Bible is itself held by Roman Catholics to be a sectarian book. They decline to use it. And the endless varieties of interpretation of many passages of the Bible itself are the foundation of all Christian sectarianism.

Even if there were no objection in principle to the teaching of the Bible being the subject of legal enactment, it is not easy to see how such an enactment could be carried out in practice, how it could be legally regulated, or how any breach of regulation on the subject should be punished. A law is no law if it can be violated with impunity. It is very easy for the state to enact in the abstract that the Bible should be read in schools; and perhaps such a legislative recognition of the Bible might satisfy minds which have no idea of the business of practical legislation; but to minds capable of understanding matters of the kind it must be plain that a mere enactment that the Bible shall be read can have no effective operation unless it also specify what is to be done if it should not be read in the manner which may be so prescribed. The law in such a case must also specify how much is to be read on each occasion, and in what order it is to be read, and whether or not it is to be read continuously or by selection. Those who desire that it shall be read continuously must be prepared to say whether or not they gravely propose that children shall be compelled by law to read and teachers to teach such passages as the nineteenth and thirty-eighth chapters of Genesis, and many others equally objectionable, under pain of fine and imprisonment if they do not read and teach such passages. If, again, it be proposed that only selections shall be read the selections must be defined by law. Who is to define them, or who can define them to the satisfaction of all concerned?

It must also be enacted that what is read must be read with reverence and not with levity.

In order to make each such enactment legally effectual the law must also direct that the violation of the enactment shall be legally punishable by some of its ordinary known punishments of whipping, fine, and imprisonment, which can only be inflicted by the ordinary course of legal prosecution and trial.

If teachers and pupils themselves feel, or are trained to feel, a religious reverence for the Bible, there can be no occasion for legislation on any of these points. If they do not of themselves feel such reverence, any enactment requiring them to affect and display a reverence which they do not feel, under pains and penalties if they fail to do so, would be simply a law for the encouragement and enforcement of hypocrisy.

The next point of consideration in regard to the Bible being taught on a religious footing is whether or not the teaching should be restricted to mere reading without explanation, or whether or not it should be both read and explained. Some Denominationalists contend that it should be both read and explained, meaning by its being explained that it shall mostly be explained in accordance with their own points of view. Other Denominationalists, seeing it to be hopeless, even among themselves, to expect any uniformity in each having it explained according to their own views, propose that it shall be read without note or comment, and that it shall not be explained in any way.

The proposal of reading the Bible without note or comment is open to all the objections which have been already stated on that point. It is open to further practical difficulties, and leads to other palpable absurdities. What would be the meaning of prohibiting a teacher from giving any explanation as to the contents of the Bible, or how could such a prohibition be carried out? Hebrew history and the history of Christianity are part of the history of the world. Could it be made penal to speak of God or Christ, or to speak of Hebrew kings, or prophets, or lawgivers, or of Christian apostles and disciples, or of their doings or sayings, when reading the Bible, and not penal to speak of them on any other occasion or if their names occurred in any other book or history? How could such a proposal be carried into operation? Or what would be the honour or advantage to the cause of religion in having the Bible read under the eye of a master gagged by law, in the face of its own clearest doctrines, from explaining its terms in any way? "Teach these words diligently unto thy children &c."—see Deut. vi. 6, 7. See also to the same effect Deut. xi. 9, and Psalm lxviii. 5, 6, not to speak of the more general precept as to training up children in the way in which they should go. The only excuse, if it be an excuse, for the proposal that the Bible shall not be explained, is that those who make it have not taken the trouble to consider beforehand whether or not the proposal could be carried into effect, or the absurd and monstrous consequences to which it would lead if it were attempted to do so. It means, if it mean anything at all, that any teacher conversing with a pupil on any subject mentioned in the Bible shall be liable to fine, imprisonment, deprivation of office, or whatever other punishment may be awarded for the so-called offence. Such legislation is not to be thought of. A directory enactment which does not go to these results must be wholly ineffectual. But when legislation cannot be made effectual, it is a demonstration that the subject in regard to which it fails is not, in that respect, a proper one for legislative interference.

If, on the other hand, it is to be required by positive legislative enactment that the Bible is to be both read and explained, the explanation must be given either at the pleasure of the teacher, or according to fixed principles to be defined by law. To enact by law that the Bible might be explained in any way, according to the different opinions of each individual teacher, whether orthodox or heterodox, believing or unbelieving, would not, in the eyes of the Denominationalists, who insist on the national teaching of the Bible, be any legislation at all. The other alternative of attempting to define by law the principles on which it should be taught, opens a field of endless controversy, in regard to which it is hopeless to expect that the denominational advocates of Biblical education can ever arrive at uniformity or concord. Is it, for example, to be taught that the Bible is the subject of plenary or of only partial inspiration? Is it to be taught that it is perfectly free from error, or is it to be taught, in the language ascribed to Principal Candlish, that it is in some parts covered with a crust of human error? If so, is it to be taught what parts are supposed to be crust and what parts are supposed not to be so? Is it to be taught that the Biblical account of the Creation is a Divine and authoritative account of the Creation, or is it to be taught, in the language ascribed to the Duke of Argyll, that it is an account which no intelligent person can now receive? Is it to be explained, or is it to be concealed, that the unanimous, or all but unanimous, verdict of men of science is to the same effect? Is it to be taught, according to the anthropomorphous ideas of the writer in Genesis ii. 23, that God rested from His work in the sense of having been fatigued, and that he was thereby refreshed, as stated in Exodus xxxi. 17; or is it to be taught, according to the language of Christ, on being challenged by the Jews for healing the impotent man on the Sabbath-day, "My Father worketh hitherto, and I work"?—see John v. 17. Is it to be taught that an ark containing one window was a suitable or possible structure in which its inmates, as enumerated in Genesis, could have lived? Is it to be taught that the name of God given in our Bibles as Jehovah (now stated by scholars to be more properly Yahve) was not revealed until it was revealed to Moses in Egypt—see Exodus vi. 3—although the same name is mentioned in a previous part of the history in the time of Abraham?—see Genesis xxii. 14. Is it to be taught, as in John i. 18, and elsewhere, that no man hath seen God at any time; or is it to be taught, as in Exodus xxiv. 10, 11, that God appeared unto Moses, and Aaron, and Nadab, and Abihu, and seventy of the elders of Israel and the nobles of Israel, and that they saw the God of Israel? Is it to be taught that the preface to the ten commandments, "I am the Lord thy God, which brought thee out of the land of Egypt" &c.—see Exodus xx. 2—applies to the whole of the rest of the world, who never were in Egypt, as well as to the Hebrews who were in it? Or is it to be taught that the commandments following that preface do not apply to and are not obligatory on Egyptians, who never left Egypt, and that therefore these Egyptians are not within the pale of Biblical application? Is it to be taught whether or not the version of the fourth commandment given in Exodus xx., or the version of the same commandment given in Deut. v., is the true version? They differ very substantially as to the grounds on which the commandment is founded. Or, if one of them be held to be the correct one, what is to be said as to the other? Or is it to be taught, or is it to be concealed, that there are in the Pentateuch different versions of what is said to have been spoken and written on the two tables of stone? Is it to be taught, according to the second commandment, that God will visit the sins of the fathers upon the children unto the third and fourth generation; or is it to be taught, according to Ezekiel xviii. 20, that "the son shall not bear the iniquity of the father, neither shall the father bear the iniquity of the son?" Is it to be taught that God sanctioned human slavery, not only of captives, but of Hebrews by Hebrews, as in Exodus xxi., and that God actually said to Moses such words as these—see 20 and 21—"If a man smite his servant or his maid with a rod and he die under his hand, he shall be surely punished. Notwithstanding, if he continue a day or two, he shall not be punished, *for he is his money?*" Is it to be taught that such an argument could or could not be used by a modern slave-owner? Is it to be taught that the enslaving and outraging of the women of Midian by the Israelites was perpetrated by the immediate direction of God, as related in the 31st chapter of Numbers, and that God, through Eleazar the priest, received thirty and two women as part of the Lord's tribute from the prey? And is it to be explained by the usages of ancient history what is the meaning of the priests' receiving such tribute as this? Is it to be taught that the incident mentioned in Judges xvi. 1 was a proper occasion for the exertion of the supernatural strength of Samson, or even a decent one to be recorded in the manner in which it is? Is it to be taught, because the Amalekites attacked or resisted the Israelites on their way from Egypt, that, about four hundred years afterwards, a God of justice and mercy, the Supreme Ruler of the Universe, could, with reference to the posterity of these Amalekites, have uttered to Samuel such words as these : "I remember what Amalek did to Israel, how he laid wait for him in the way when he came up from Egypt. Now, go and smite Amalek, and utterly destroy all that they have, and spare them not, but slay both man and woman, infant and suckling, ox and sheep, camel and ass,"—see 1 Samuel xv. 2, 3,—or that Samuel, in hewing Agag in pieces before the Lord in Gilgal, " because his sword had made women childless "—that is, because he had defended his country—committed an act deserving of either Divine or human approval? Apart from its Biblical connexion it may be doubtful if there is anything in history more atrocious than the destruction of the Amalekites, or more feeble than the pretext for it. Is it to be taught that the trickeries of Jacob, the treachery of Rachel, and the deathbed animosity of David were proper acts to receive Divine reward and blessing? Is it to be explained whether the passage in 2 Sam. xxiv. 1—" And the anger of the Lord was kindled against Israel, and he moved David against them to say, Go and number Israel and Judah "—or the passage in 1 Chron. xxi. 1, referring to the same event, where it is said, " And Satan stood up against Israel, and provoked David to number Israel," is the proper or higher authority, and if so why so? Is it to be concealed or explained that it is now matter of ordinary historical knowledge, at least among Biblical scholars, that the idea of Satan was acquired by the Hebrews during their captivity in Babylon from the dualistic doctrines of the Zoroastrians, and that these doctrines ultimately prevailed over the monotheistic doctrine of the Hebrews, so emphatically expressed by the prophet

Isaiah?—see Isaiah xlv. 5-7. Is it to be taught, as matter of Divine command, or as matter of edification or example, the condition in which that prophet is said to have walked about for a period of three years?—see Isaiah xx. Is it to be taught whether or not the anthropomorphic ideas of the ancient Hebrews, in speaking of God as resting and being refreshed, as being unable to drive out the inhabitants of the valley—Judges i. 19 —and as "daily rising up early," and the like—see Jeremiah vii. 25,—or the doctrine that God is a spirit, are the views most in accordance with enlightened religion? Is belief in witchcraft to be taught as a doctrine sanctioned by Divine authority, or if not, is it to be explained how it was at one time believed to be so, and why it has now ceased to be believed? Or is it to be taught that the predictions in regard to the children of Israel as to lending money in Deut. xxviii. 44, and other predictions in the same chapter, have been fulfilled by facts? Or is it to be explained how a star could lead to or indicate any particular place?—see Mat. ii. 9,—an idea familiar to ancient poetry, but as an actual fact impossible. Or is it to be taught that the precepts of the Sermon on the Mount—Mat. v.—which every one professes to admire, but which few attempt either to practise themselves or inculcate on others, are precepts which were intended to be so neglected and disregarded? Or is it to be taught that the time from Friday evening till Sunday morning corresponds to the three days and three nights mentioned in Mat. xii. 40? Or is it to be taught that believers can handle serpents and swallow poison with impunity, or heal the sick by laying hands on them? —see Mark xvi. 17, 18. Or is it to be taught that the direction to the disciples in Mat. x. 10, to take no staves with them, or the direction in Mark vi. 8, to take nothing for their journey "save a staff only," are both divinely inspired records of the same address? As matter of mere human history the discrepancy is of very little importance, but even with regard to so small a point as this it seems impossible to maintain that the two narratives are both supernaturally and infallibly correct. The same writings cannot be, in the same sense and at the same time, both divinely correct and humanly incorrect. Or, which of the conflicting accounts of the inscriptions on the cross, and the events at and after the crucifixion is to be taught as the true one? Or is it to be explained, with reference to the predictions in the New Testament of the second coming of Christ in glory before that generation should pass away, and of the end of the world, and of the last time, all during the lifetime of persons alive at the time of these predictions, who, it is said, were not to taste of death till the predictions should be fulfilled; who were not to sleep, but to be changed, and to be caught up in the air; and the like—see Mat. xvi. 27, 28, xxiv. 34; Mark viii. 38, ix. 1, and xiii. 39; 1 Cor. vii. 29, xv. 51, &c.; 1 Thess. iv. 14-17; Heb. ix. 26, x. 37; 1 Pet. iv. 7-17; James v. 8; and 1 John ii. 18 —but which predictions have not been fulfilled in any sense within any ordinary or reasonable meaning of the words,—that they have so failed? Some reply to the non-fulfilment of these predictions is attempted by saying that with the Lord one day is as a thousand years. This only meets half the case. It has no application to the point that the predictions were to be fulfilled within the lifetime of the generation to whom they were uttered, or of some of them. Or is it to be taught that St. Peter was right or wrong when, in defiance of all special rites, ceremonies, doctrines, and creeds, sacrificial or otherwise, he proclaimed in the broadest language, without limit of time or place, that God was no respecter of persons, but that in every nation whoso feareth God and worketh righteousness is accepted of Him?—see Acts x. 34, 35.

These are merely a few of an infinity of points which would have to be definitively settled before it would be possible to direct by positive enactment, on what principle and to what effect the Bible should be explained, as part of a national system of Biblical teaching. Any number of additional examples might have been given; but, probably, without entering into still more sacred points of controversy, a sufficient number have been stated to show that, in the face of the advanced intelligence of the age, it is not possible to make the nature of religious teaching the subject of any directory legal enactment. The matter cannot be passed over in silence. If it is to be a subject of specific legislation the whole of the points which have been mentioned, and a great many more, must be confronted, and specific direction must be given as to the manner in which each is to be dealt with, with specific punishments or penalties in case any point shall be treated in any respect differently from what the law may prescribe. It is not enough to answer to this, as might be done in regard to Scotland, that religious teaching was formerly required by law to be given in the parochial schools, and that it was so given without any such precision of enactment as is now maintained to be necessary. This is true, but these parochial schools were then under the control and jurisdiction of the Established Church of Scotland, which had power to enforce religious teaching according to its own doctrines and confessions, and which had also power to try and to dismiss schoolmasters who failed to do so. This jurisdiction on the part of the Church of Scotland is now at an end, and the civil law has no standard, either there or elsewhere, by which to try questions of doctrine, except such as may be prescribed to it by the Legislature.

Another set of principles have to be considered. The advocates of
denominational religious teaching to a great extent make it a part
of their own principles that the Bible is the sole foundation of
human morality, that without the Bible there is no such thing as
human morality, and that if morality were not founded on the
Bible it would cease to exist. They regard the so-called morality
of the heathen, and of all past and present nations who have not
founded upon the Bible, not only as being no true morality, but
as being rather sinful than otherwise. They would, no doubt,
desire to enforce the teaching of the same principles to the young.
Facts, both historical and contemporary may be at variance with
them, but the prepossessions of those who profess these principles
are such that they have no particular regard for facts adverse to
their own views. They look upon them as dangerous snares and
ambuscades to be avoided, rather than as manifestations of
Divine government, not limited, either in the past or in the
present, to any one race or creed. They even dread to have
their minds enlarged beyond the petrified standards of their
churches, by the teaching of nature and history. The
Westminster Confession of Faith, being the confession of the
Church of Scotland, lays down on this point as positive dogma
that

"Persons not elected, although they may be called by the ministry
of the word, and may have some common operations of the Spirit, yet
they never truly came to Christ, and therefore cannot be saved ; much
less can men not professing the Christian religion be saved in any
other way whatsoever, be they ever so diligent to frame their lives
according to the light of nature and the law of that religion they do
profess ; and to assert and maintain that they may is very pernicious
and to be detested."—See chap. x. sec. 4.

It is further laid down that, "by the decree of God for the manifestation of His glory, some men are predestinated unto everlasting life, and others" (of course including those not professing
the Christian religion) are "fore-ordained to everlasting death"
(see ch. iii. sec. 3), and that the number of men so fore-ordained
"is so certain and definite that it cannot be increased or diminished"
(see ch. iii. sec. 4). It is further laid down that the fate of those
so fore-ordained to death, who are called "the wicked," is to be
"cast into eternal torments, and to be punished with everlasting
destruction from the presence of the Lord and the glory of His
power" (see ch. xxxiii. sec. 2). And the articles of the Church of
England in the same manner, as to good works done otherwise
than in the light of the Christian faith, lays down that they are
not pleasant to God, but have the nature of sin (see Art. XIII).
It must be considered whether or not it shall be imperative that

these views are to be followed, or whether or not it shall be permissible on the part of those who hold different opinions, to explain that human morality, more or less advanced, is in all nations as old as human civilization, and that there can be no doubt that long before the Decalogue, and in nations which never heard of Moses or of the Israelites, murder and adultery and theft and falsehood were recognised as crimes or vices, and that generosity, charity, reverence towards parents, and piety towards the Supreme Being were regarded and extolled as virtues. We know that all these views prevailed in the refined civilizations of Egypt, India, and China, long before the time of the Israelites, and that the religious codes and records of these nations, which are in these respects the wonder and admiration of scholars, aim not only at rectitude and courtesy of outward behaviour, but at the highest degree of inward purity and virtue. Ancient Chinese records tell us that centuries before the Christian -era some of their philosophers inculcated "rectitude of heart and loving our neighbour as ourselves."* The doctrines of Zoroaster among the Persians in the same way were directed fundamentally to the distinction between right and wrong and good and evil. In the Bible itself, in the Book of Job, which has come into the Hebrew literature evidently from a foreign source, we find, especially in the discourse ascribed to Job in chapter xxvi. and those which follow, much higher sentiments of morality and practice than in anything of its time with which it is associated. Greek civilization was later. Like the others, it was entirely unconnected with Hebrew influences. In practical worship the Greeks were polytheists. But, beyond and above the minor and more familiar deities, they reverenced, sometimes under the name of Zeus and sometimes without any name, a supreme and overruling power that was in all and over all. They mentally wrought out for themselves and embodied for ever in their philosophy a very high ideal of the attributes of au overruling providence, of right and wrong, and of virtue and vice, in all their senses divine and human, as well as of a future state. Some of the writings even of the earliest of the Greek dramatists on this subject are singularly grand and beautiful. The following extracts are from the writings of Æschylus (born 525 B.C.) as translated by Professor Blackie :—

> " For Jove doth teach men wisdom—sternly wins ·
> To virtue by the tutoring of their sins.
> Yea! drops of torturing recollection chill

---

* See "Maurice's Mental and Metaphysical Philosophy." Second edition, p. 57.

The sleeper's heart; 'gainst man's rebellious will
Jove works the wise remorse.
Dread powers, on awful seats enthroned, compel
Our hearts with gracious force."

" 'Twas said of old, and 'tis said to-day,
That wealth to propitious stature grown
Begets a birth of its own;
That a surfeit of evil by good is prepared,
And must bear what allotment of woe
Their sins were spared.
But this I rebel to believe: I know
That impious deeds conspire
To beget an offspring of impious deeds
Too like their ugly sire;
But whoso is just, tho' his wealth like a river
Flow down, shall be skaithless—his home shall rejoice
In an offspring of beauty for ever."

" Lordless life or despot-ridden,
Be they both from me forbidden.
To the wise man strength is given;
Thus the gods have ruled in Heaven—
Gods that, gently or severely,
Judge, discerning all things clearly."

" Oh! would that Jove might show to men
His counsel, how he planned it;
But ah! he darkly weaves the scheme,
No mortal eye hath scanned it.
It burns through darkness brightly clear
To whom the god shall show it;
But mortal man thro' cloudy fear
Shall search in vain to know it.
From their high-towering hopes the proud
In wretched rout he casteth;
No force he wields, his simple will
His quiet sentence blasteth.
All godlike power is calm and high,
On thrones of glory seated;
Jove looks from heaven with tranquil eye
And sees his will completed."

The following extracts are from the writings of Sophokles
(born B.C. 497) as translated by Professor D'Arcy W.
Thompson :—

" Oh God! what pride of man can hold in check thy might? The
years roll by for ever and for ever, but thou sleepest not nor waxest
faint."—*Antigone*, 604.

" No ordinance of man shall override
The settled laws of nature and of God.

> Not written these in pages of a book,
> Nor were they formed to-day or yesterday.
> We know not whence they are; but this we know,
> That they from all eternity have been,
> And shall to all eternity endure."—*Antigone*, 453.

> "Speak thou no word of pride, nor raise
> A swelling thought against the Gods on high,
> If thou in wealth thy neighbour shall surpass,
> Or that thy hand be mightier than his.
> For time uplifteth and time layeth low
> All human things; and the great Gods above
> Abhor the wicked as the good they love."—*Ajax*, 127.

The following extracts are from the writings of Euripides (born B.C. 480), also as translated by Professor Thompson:—

> "The Gods are slow to anger, but their anger moveth very surely;
> They correct with chastisement the proud in heart and the vain
> ones that despise holiness;
> Time goeth on apace, and the wicked saith the Gods see not,
> But they, unseen, behold all his doings, and in due time will follow
> on his track."—*Bacchæ*, 882.

> "Oh thou whose footstool is the great round world,
> Mysterious Being, whatsoe'er thy name,
> God, Fate, or Nature, or Intelligence,
> I cry to thee in prayer; for tho' thou mov'st
> Noiseless, unseen, yet I acknowledge thee
> In all thy dealings usward just and good."—*Bacchæ*, 200.

Socrates was put to death in the year 400 B.C. He died for the sake of right and truth. He could have saved his life, if he had chosen, by stooping in the least to flattery or falsehood, or even to asking for it. He taught of divine things and of justice, and of right and wrong. Some passages from the Memorabilia of Xenophon illustrate his doctrines.

"The great God," he says, "who has formed the universe, and supports the stupendous work whose every part is finished with the utmost goodness and harmony; he who preserves them perpetually in immortal vigour, and causes them to obey him with a never-failing punctuality, and a rapidity not to be followed by our imagination; this God makes himself sufficiently visible by the endless wonders of which he is the author, but continues always invisible himself."

He cites from a poet whose name has not come down to us the following prayer: "Great God! give us, we beseech thee, those things of which we stand in need, whether we crave them or not; and remove from us all those which may be hurtful to us, even though we may implore them of thee." And he tells his followers that "it has always been a maxim with him that it is never allowable to commit injustice, not even in regard to those who injure us, nor to return evil for evil."

Isocrates, a later philosopher, who died B.C. 338, in a discourse to Nicocles, King of Salamis, teaches equally high doctrine. "Be assured," said he, "that the most grateful adoration and sacrifice that you can offer to the Divinity is that of the heart in rendering yourself good and just."

Plutarch, in vindicating even the so-called brute worship of the Egyptians, places, or attempts to place, their sentiments on a higher basis.

"Philosophers," he says, "honour the image of God wherever they find it, even in inanimate beings, and consequently more in those which have life. We are therefore to approve, not the worshippers of these animals, but those who by their means ascend to the Deity. They are to be considered as so many mirrors which nature holds forth, and in which the Supreme Being displays himself in a wonderful manner."

But further he says that

"As the sun and moon, heaven, earth, and sea, are common to all men, but have different names according to the difference of nations and languages, in like manner, though there is but one Deity and one Providence which governs the universe, and which has several subaltern ministers under it, men give to this Deity, which is the same, different names, and pay it different honours according to the laws and customs of every country."

The laws of Sparta, under which theft is said to have been held to be a virtue, will no doubt be quoted on the other side. But it was only in a military point of view. At one period, or rather at several periods of its history, Sparta was little better than a belligerent encampment. Its whole male youth were trained for military predominance by strength, discipline, and subtlety. To steal without being discovered was merely one of the details of military training. In a civil point of view theft was theft in Sparta as much as anywhere else. It was no more a permanent characteristic of Spartans to be thieves than it is of Welshmen. They were not organized as robbers, but as a military tribe carrying on warfare, as often defensive as aggressive, according to the most rigid and severe military discipline of the time. Even if some of them were thieves by profession, and even if they were to attempt to justify their being so, which they never did, it is not by any example so singularly exceptional and peculiar that the inductions of experience otherwise all but universal can be met or contradicted. The Italian and German freebooters in the middle ages and the Scotch Borderers, who did not profess to be Pagans, but very much the reverse, plundered their neighbours as a means of ordinary livelihood, and even of proud gallantry, but it was never said that they advocated theft as theft, or that they did not, as far as possible, maintain a sort of integrity among each other. It is not at all clear, however, in regard to some of their raids that they did not justify themselves to some extent by the example of the spoiling of the Egyptians and other not unsimilar precedents. The proverbial allusion to "honour even among thieves" is a testimony, to the general instincts of mankind being in favour of rectitude.

Among the Romans the whole of the sins forbidden in the second table of the Decalogue, except perhaps the last, were forbidden by their ancient laws, and we also know that reverence for the Supreme Gods and for parents was among their most sacred duties. All this was established among them without the least connexion with Hebrew influences.

We know, on the other hand, that the doctrine of the "Logos," corresponding in some respects to the manner in which the word "logos" and the doctrine of the Logos are introduced into the gospel of John, belong to the speculations of Plato several centuries before; that some of these doctrines of Plato were taught among the Alexandrian Jews, that they appear in the writings of Philo-Judæus, and that it is not clear that some parts of the gospel do not belong to the same school. Is this to be taught as an historical fact, or is it to be concealed?

We also know that many passages in the writings of Seneca and in those of St. Paul have a singular similarity to each other, and that those similarities are too numerous and too exact to be the result of accident. They must, therefore, have either been copied by Seneca from St. Paul or by St. Paul from Seneca; or they must have come from a common source accessible to both, such as the literature, the scholasticism, or the conversation of the time. There is nothing to give the least ground for the idea, and it is not a probable one, that St. Paul copied them from Seneca. There is equally little ground for supposing that Seneca copied them from St. Paul. Seneca was not a Christian. On the contrary, he lived and died as a philosophic pagan of his time. There is no hint anywhere that he had any contact with Christianity as a matter of serious attention, much less that he had borrowed or was likely to borrow any of its precepts or maxims. Commanded by Nero to put himself to death, and having selected bleeding in a warm bath as the mode of his death, we have a description of him to the last moment of consciousness, and we know that he made not the least mention in any way of the doctrines of Christianity. The passages which have been referred to must, therefore, have come from sources common to both. St. Paul appears to have made free use of such sources. The well-known quotation by him, "Evil communications corrupt good manners," is a familiar example. The exclamation ascribed to Christ on the occasion of his appearance to Paul at the time of his conversion, "It is hard for thee to kick against the pricks," or "against the goads," a phrase which occurs several times in the ancient Greek and Latin drama, is a still more singular instance of the use of popular Greek phraseology. St. Paul goes further. In his sermon at Athens he sets forth the full brotherhood of all nations of men, and he expressly recognises the Deity of whom the Greek poets say "For we also are his offspring," as the same Deity in whom we live and move and have our being, and who is not far from every one of us. (See Acts xvii.)

If religious teaching under that name is to be provided 'and enjoined by law the attitude to be taken on every one of the points which have been noticed must be considered and defined and made the subject of positive rules, with suitable punishments for their infringement. But if the remarks which have been made as to the impracticability of doing so be well founded, it would seem to show that there is no mode by which the teaching of the Bible, on a special theological or religious footing, can be the subject of specific or efficient practical directions by any legislative enactment, prescribing, as would require to be done, in exact or statutory language, the nature, extent, and tendency of such teaching, or by which their observance could be compelled or their violation prevented.

It appears, then, that the views of the Secularists and those of the Denominationalists both fail to afford any consistent principles of action for general adoption. The religious element cannot be separated from the secular elements of education according to the former, nor combined with them according to the latter. It is not merely that it cannot be separated according to the views of the Secularists. It cannot be separated at all, any more than the mind or the moral nature can be separated from the animated body.

But, if the elements of religion cannot be separated from secular or general education, and if it cannot be imparted according to the views of the Denominationalists, it follows either that there can be no such thing as general national education, or that a mode of imparting its religious elements must be devised which shall be sound in principle and acceptable in practice.

It is thought that there is such a mode, and that its principle should consist in teaching the elements of religion and of religious history as matter of fact, instruction, and behaviour, on precisely the same footing as all other subjects of ordinary teaching.

Let children, for example, be taught as matter of fact that, according to observation and experience, order and law exist in nature, that we are endowed with reason capable of appreciating such order and law, and that, as a rule, most men, or at least most civilized men, have inferred by the exercise of their reason that there is a great invisible Author of such order and of such intelligence. Let them be taught that we have consciences informed by our reason, and that, from our experience of ourselves and intercourse with others, it has been found that self-restraint as regards ourselves, and the exercise of duty as regards others, is most satisfying to the reason and most grateful to the conscience, and that the reason and conscience have within themselves a sentiment of aspiration towards and communion with the Invisible. Let them be taught that we have remains, traditions, and histories of past races. Let them be taught, as matter of fact, that there is a book called the Old Testament which is recognised by the Jews and by Christian nations as a sacred book; that this book is made up of a number of ancient books or writings written from time to time by men of the Hebrew nation, the latest of them being the writings of Malachi, who lived during the fifth century before the Christian era; that these writers are believed by Jews, and by many Christians, to have written their works under the inspiration, guidance, or dictation of God; that there is another book called the New Testament, which is recognised by Christians as being also a sacred book; that this book is also made up of several minor books or writings; that these books or writings are believed to have been written by the apostles and disciples of Christ; that these apostles and disciples are believed by many Christians to have written under similar divine inspiration; and that the contents and doctrines of this book are received and believed, in whole or in part, by Christians, but are not received or believed by Jews.

It will also fall to be taught that the Bible, which is made up of these Old and New Testaments, is the only book which is recognised as sacred and authoritative, according to the creeds and doctrines of Christian churches. But it will fall to be taught at the same time that the Jews were and are a very small part of the population of the world, and that Christian nations, even now, do not embrace more than about a fourth part of it. Indeed, except the compulsory proselytization of the American Indians by the Spaniards, and the occupation of previously uninhabited territories, Christianity has made no extension on a national scale since the fall of the Roman Empire. It has lost the ground which it once held in Asia Minor, Egypt, and Northern Africa.

Part of this mode of teaching will consist of informing the young, as a portion of ordinary history, that at such and such ages of the world such and such nations and races have professed such and such religions, that such and such religions have been abandoned, and that such and such other religions have taken their place. The Bible itself continually indicates the differences between the religion of the Hebrews and of the surrounding nations; not, however, so much in a descriptive as on an antagonistic footing, with this distinction, that nowhere in the books of Moses is any disrespect expressed for any of the religious tenets of the Egyptians.

It will also fall to be taught that other nations and races who do not accept the Bible as a sacred book, have books of their own which they regard as sacred; that some of these books are of equal, if not of greater, antiquity than some of the books of the Bible; and that they contain many doctrines and precepts of goodness, virtue, and benevolence which cannot possibly be excelled or surpassed. At the same time, in the light of modern intelligence, some of them abound with errors, absurdities, and peculiarities.

Facts must not be confounded with opinions. It is a fact of history that, at any particular time since the Christian era, so many millions of people professed or now profess Christianity, or that since the introduction of Mahommedanism so many millions of people, at any particular time, have professed or now profess to be Mahommedans, or that so many millions profess Buddhism, or the like. All these are facts forming matter of visible evidence which no person would deny or seek to deny. They are, moreover, facts of which no educated person should be ignorant, and are therefore facts which every person in course of receiving any sort of superior or even ordinary education should be taught. But they are quite different from the sort of allegations, not susceptible of visible evidence, which the adherents of these religions assert to be facts, but which in reality are not substantiated facts, but mere doctrines or opinions peculiar to their respective creeds. For example, the doctrine of the Trinity is maintained to be a fact by some Christians, and the doctrine of the exclusive unity of God is maintained to be a fact by Mahommedans. They are mere opinions. None of them can be taught as fact in the same sense that it is fact that there are so many professing Christians or so many professing Mahommedans. No man, whether Christian or Mahommedan, whether of any creed or of no creed, would deny the numerical statements, while all would deny the doctrinal statements except their own professed adherents.

Keeping this in view, the teaching of the knowledge of religious doctrines as the opinions of those who professed them would fall into the same order and nature as any other subject of education, according to the discretion of the teachers and those under whose supervision they may be placed. Keeping away from obvious indecencies and immoralities, there can be no ground why, within reasonable limits, and in regard to any doctrines whatever, it may not be taught as matter of fact that such and such doctrines were or are professed by such and such people. It is not this that is in any way objectionable. What is objectionable is the teaching, by the authority of the legislature, of certain theological doctrines or opinions as being approved of and authorized by the State as true and orthodox, to the exclusion of other doctrines or opinions pronounced by the State to be untrue or heterodox; or that such and such doctrines are right, and that all others are wrong.

It will be objected against this system that it proposes to place Christianity, as a theology, on the same footing as the ancient mythologies of Greece and Rome, or of any other nations. It does so as matter of principle, but as matter of fact the situation and results are very different. In teaching the ancient mythologies of Greece and Rome it would fall to be taught at the same time, as matter of fact in regard to them, that they have been superseded and driven out of the field by Christianity, and that they have for ages ceased to have any adherents either national or individual. In regard to Christianity, on the other hand, it would have to be taught that it had not only taken the place of these mythologies in their ancient seats, but was now professed by the leading nations of civilization. It is not thought that such a condition of circumstances should entitle any one to say that Christianity should suffer any disadvantage in being presented on such a footing, or that it should thereby be rendered less able in any way to hold the ground which it has acquired. In comparison with other religions still professed in the world it will in the same way hold all the advantages to which the facts entitle it.

It may be objected both by Secularists and Denominationalists, that the system proposed may be made subservient to the personal opinions of the teachers, and that it contains no provision against their imparting bias to their instructions to their pupils. It does not in the meantime. It is almost impossible to do so effectively. A teacher of strong personal opinions determined to propagate them, might find means of inculcating or insinuating them which it would be difficult, even if it were justifiable, to deal with by legislation. It is to be hoped that under a system so discouraging to denominational partisanship as that which is advocated, it will not be frequently found that teachers will attempt to abuse their position in that direction.

K 2

But let it be made quite understood that any attempts of the
kind should be held to be beyond his authority as a teacher, and
they would soon cease to have any weight in so far as not
founded on sound reasoning. This might be accomplished by
expressly declaring by law that no teacher, by virtue of his office,
should have any authority to inculcate, other than as matter of
individual opinion, any theological creed, confession, or catechism,
or any other theological doctrines, tenets, or views. This would
leave him his full individual rights in such matters, but nothing
more. It would make it at once manifest and notorious to all
that he had no superadded official right or authority to require
from any one any assent or submission at variance with the views
of themselves or their parents or guardians in such matters. It
would be a very strong hint to teachers that they would
be expected to abstain as much as possible from inculcating, as
by superior authority, any special or sectarian views on theological subjects, and it would not prevent such further legislation
as might be necessary if, in some rare cases, occasion should
arise for it.

The religious question in regard to education has been thus
fully discussed, because the question whether or not there should
be national religious teaching, and, if so, what kind or kinds of
religion should be so taught, lies at the threshold of every
national measure which has been or can be proposed. In the
English Education Act the Government, with a cry of "Peace,
peace, when there is no peace," have, in the meantime, transferred the difficulties to the local boards. In the Scotch Act the
same course seems to be intended. But it is easy to predict
that such a mode of legislation, after plunging the country for
years into the waste, extravagance, discord, and confusion
which any measures applicable so universally, and not settling but unsettling the relations of almost every parochial community in the kingdom, must ultimately bring back all concerned
to the same legislative authority which ought to have kept
them right from the first, and which might have done so if
sounder principles of legislation on this point had been originally
sought for and acted on.

Human history in regard to religion has been to a great extent a series of errors. In illustration of this it is not necessary
to look back beyond the Christian era, or outside of the pale of
Christian history. In the first ages of Christianity we had the
constant expectation of the immediate end of the world, and
hence to some extent the doctrine of taking no thought for the
morrow, of the rich selling their goods and distributing to the
poor,—this, again, accompanied and followed by societies having all
things in common and carrying to extremes the doctrines of
celibacy, asceticism, and monasticism,—this, again, by the incor-

poration of the Romish Church, the ascendancy of the ecclesiastical over the temporal powers, the mental enslavement of Christendom, the extinction of all freedom of intellectual speculation otherwise than in accordance with the views of the Church, the establishing of monasteries and convents, the encouragement of credulity, pilgrimage, and mendicity, and all this accompanied by every kind of vice, profligacy, and corruption, as well within the Church as outside of it. Ecclesiasticism has ever fostered mendicity and credulity more than industry and independence. The heart of Europe became sick of fraud, imposture, and corruption, always increasing in shamelessness and absurdity, which reached its culminating point in the sale of indulgences. Audacity could scarcely be carried further. But the Divine can never be wholly extinguished in humanity. The grand, honest, truth-loving soul of Luther refused to recognise the impious assumptions of the Church. Armed with the might of right and justice, he burst the trammels of its yoke and founded a cause which, under the name of Protestantism, has since been embraced and upheld by all the most advanced and most progressive nations of the world. The rivalry of Protestantism has to a great extent re-established the purity and repressed the tyranny of practical Romanism.

Protestant history has, however, its errors as well as that of Romanism. It was part of the belief of the time at which it took its rise that there could only be one true church, and that all who did not belong to the true church were heretics or infidels, to be suppressed or exterminated. This excluded any proper idea of what is now known as toleration. If, therefore, the Church of Protestantism was the true church, it was the duty of Protestants, in so far as they could not convert Romanists, to suppress and eradicate them, or at all events to prevent the public worship and practices of Romanism, just as much as the Romanists held it to be their duty to treat Protestants and Protestantism and other heresies in the same manner. Possibly some of these opinions still prevail in such regions as Belfast, Londonderry, and the like. Hence wars and counter-wars, and persecution, torture, and putting to death, not only by Roman Catholics against Protestants, and Protestants against Roman Catholics, but among Protestants themselves, as in the same kingdom between Episcopalians and Covenanters, and also against Independents, Quakers, and others holding opinions different from those of the majority of the time. Almost every established sect of Protestants has made similar claims to be the only true church, and as incorporated bodies they have never withdrawn these claims. In the exercise of their claims, where circumstances have permitted, Protestant churches have in some directions gone quite as far, and in some instances farther, than even the Romish Church. The Puritans for a time had their own way to a great extent in America, and accordingly we find, among other laws made by them of a similar nature, that the

"early Virginia code prescribed death for blasphemy of the Trinity or the King, and also upon being convicted for the third time of profane swearing. For want of proper respect to a clergyman, one was publicly whipped, and obliged to ask pardon in church for three successive Sundays. The penalty for not attending church and the Sunday cathedral lesson was, for the first offence, the loss of a week's provisions, for the second whipping, and for the third death. If a colonist, on arrival, refused to go to a clergyman to give an account of his faith he was to be daily whipped until he complied." *

Civil society in Great Britain as well as in America has ceased to permit the claims of the churches to be carried to their logical results; but as late as the year 1696 Scottish Protestantism brought to the scaffold, in Edinburgh, Thomas Aikenhead, a lad of eighteen, on account of his theological opinions.† Indirectly, the consequences of resistance to the claims of the churches which have acquired legal predominance may still be very severe. The present age is familiar with the outrages occasioned in Ireland by the levying of tithes on the Roman Catholic peasantry in order to maintain a Protestant church, and the bloody roll of executions by which they were attempted to be kept down previous to the passing of the Irish Tithe Commutation Act in 1838. In obedience to clerical doctrines marriage with a deceased wife's sister in Scotland is still legally punishable by death. It is only the change in public opinion which prevents this law from being enforced.

But if the churches have been deprived of the aid of the criminal law in the punishment of differences of theological opinion, and of advances in the progress of thought and intelligence, they have still reserved to them the alternative, when such movements appear within the churches themselves, of stifling them by the force of ecclesiastical discipline—a discipline which extends in its ultimate effect to deprivation of office, and, so far, to deprivation also of the means of livelihood. This discipline has all along been, and still is, either actually or potentially, in continual operation. Some of the best minds in Scotland continue to feel the horror and shame which was excited by the death of the distinguished divine who may be said to have fallen its victim in 1867; not on any argument as to vital or fundamental principles, but on a point as little incidental to the real questions at issue as if it had been the wearing of a flower in his buttonhole. He had aroused against himself the inexorable

* See "The English Colonization of America." By E. D. Neill. Strahan and Co.

† Macaulay's "History of England," vol. iv. pp. 781-784.

odium theologicum, and he had to be put down. If he could not be beaten by argument on the grounds on which he himself would have preferred to maintain the conflict, he could be beaten by vote on some other ground. But the sacrifice has not been in vain, and it is to be hoped that the ground which he has won by his death as well as by his life from fanaticism and bigotry will never again be lost.

Our established churches have committed themselves to sets of articles and tenets framed more than two centuries ago, and the law has conferred upon them position and privileges on the footing of their constitution under these articles and tenets. Some of them are utterly unsuitable to the present condition of human intelligence. But they are the foundation of the edifice, and the whole spirit of incorporated ecclesiasticism is enlisted in their defence. It is an expressed and professed part of the doctrine of these churches that those articles are not infallible; but woe be to the man who points out any respect or particular in which they are fallible or erroneous, or who calls for their correction !

Churches profess not to be hostile to science in so far as science is not hostile to religion. Science cannot be hostile to true religion. Science is the knowledge of the facts and laws of nature; that is, of the laws of God in nature. The providence of God in his works cannot be known without the study of those works. His works in nature are the shape in which He reveals that part of his providence, and it should be regarded as a part of true religion to receive and appreciate and apply this part of His revelation as much as any other. So far as it goes, and is rightly understood, it is a direct, perfect, and authentic revelation. History may err, tradition may err, men may profess to be inspired prophets who have neither prophecy nor inspiration, writings may err, but nature cannot err. The facts and laws of nature, correctly understood, may be at variance with tradition and history and with statements in writings held to be sacred, or these may be at variance with the facts and laws of nature, but neither nature nor the science of nature can ever be at variance with true religion. If, therefore, the churches mistrust science the mistrust recoils upon themselves. If they had confidence in truth they ought rather to embrace and foster it. How they have treated it is well known. How they might treat it, except for the strong sentiments of an intelligent laity in its favour, can easily be conjectured.

The churches are not wholly answerable for all this. The State has tied them by the letter of their antiquated standards. All attempts at relaxation of these standards have hitherto been in vain. Human nature advances in light and knowledge and experience, but the churches stand still. The day which uttereth

speech unto day speaks to them in vain ; the night which
showeth knowledge unto night shows none to them. God declares himself in the heavens and in the firmament, but they
must neither see nor hear except the language of the remote
past. The law does not allow them. They are bound by oaths
to adhere to articles and opinions compiled in an age of great
mental, and of almost total scientific ignorance, by men emerging
from a struggle of life and death, and to reject the evidence of
their reason and their senses, against all newly-discovered
truth which may appear to vary from these articles and opinions.
They are rewarded by livings and dignities if they act according
to these engagements. They are liable to be punished by deprivation and loss if they open their eyes or their minds to anything else.

Such a condition of things might have been tolerable a generation ago, when, for the most part, neither clerical nor popular
knowledge had greatly, if at all, advanced beyond the lights of
the age when these ecclesiastical fetters were forged. In those
days, for the most part, clergymen believed what they taught
and preached, both as regards fact and doctrine. The people
also mostly believed what they heard, and the results, with precept and example which are always more in accordance with
the sentiments of the time than the doctrines themselves, might
have been more or less beneficial. Men were acting according
to the lights which they had to a considerable extent, and so
far, perhaps, they could do no more. The recent advances in
criticism and science have been so great and so rapid that a new
condition of things has arisen. The most intelligent portion of
the laity do not believe a great deal that they hear from the
clergy ; and, what is worse, there are great doubts, not confined
to any particular class, if the clergy themselves can altogether
believe some things that they are bound to teach.

It is not strange that such a condition of circumstances should
be ultimately arrived at. It was feared by the Church more
than two centuries ago that the scientific demonstrations of
Galileo, at variance with their standards of belief, would have
shaken their authority. In strict logic they should have done so.
But the great power of the Church, its hardihood of pretension
and assertion, the unconditioned nature of its arguments, and
the general ignorance, want of perspicuity, and submissiveness
of the laity, enabled it to fill up the breach in some shape or
other more or less vague—

> " If shape it can be called that shape had none
> Distinguishable in member, joint, or limb;
> Or substance may be called that shadow seemed,
> For each seemed either"—

and claimed her ground as before.

The churches received another shock in regard to the doctrine of witchcraft. It is undoubtedly scriptural, and undoubtedly erroneous. No one of the least intelligence now attempts to maintain that there is or ever was such a power. It no longer finds any recognition, except among savages. Yet throughout Christendom, and even under Protestantism, it has had its victims by thousands. It is estimated that in England three thousand persons perished by legal executions during the sitting of the Long Parliament, besides those who fell at the hands of mobs. In Scotland the clergy were the great witch-finders. This continued till after the middle of the seventeenth century. The total number of victims in Scotland is estimated at upwards of four thousand. The absurdities and cruelties of these persecutions became so shocking to the advancing enlightenment and good sense of the laity that they had to be abandoned. But no church has ever yet, as a church, renounced the doctrines which led to them, or expressed the least contrition for the terrible consequences to which these doctrines led, or relinquished by one jot or tittle the standards which maintain them. They may have ceased to particularize or call attention to them, but in the mass they re-affirm everything as before.

It may be that the majority of mankind will always be slow to attain rational logical consistency in their views. This is matter of progress in reasoning power. Reason is the highest gift of God to man. It is not given in the same degree to all men or to all ages, or even to the same men at all times. It is improved by cultivation and exercise. Its operation is deteriorated and confused by want of exercise, by perversion, or by abnegation of its rights and powers. Reason is the only faculty by which we can judge of evidence. Rational belief is the result of evidence. Belief that is not the result of evidence is not rational or intelligent belief. Reason is also the faculty by which we distinguish between right and wrong. Conscience operates instinctively in the same direction.

The churches assail the functions of reason. They say that man's reason is foolish, vain, proud, carnal, unregenerate, and the like, and that the human reason cannot discern the things of the Spirit, and so on. They address their arguments to this effect to the reason to pronounce this judgment on itself. If the reason be all that they call it, how can it pronounce any sound judgment upon this or anything else? By continual hardihood of assertion on such a footing they have succeeded to a great extent in obscuring the operation of the reason, and in so far displacing reason by unreason as to obtain some assent to their views. Reason is the light which shines in the darkness. There may be more or less light, but the light itself can never be darkness. If we surrender our dependence upon reason, we

fall into unreason, without chart or compass of any kind, and are
at the disposal of those who choose to lead or to drive us as
they please. Unreason has its faiths as well as reason, but they
are faiths made up of heterogeneous fragments, not, perhaps,
excluding all truth or all goodness, but mixing error with truth,
and leading to all manner of inconsistencies and delusions and
their consequences. New shapes are infinite. Some views
prevail for a time and disappear, and are followed by others, and
so on. But every form of unreason is hostile to reason, and its
adherents have so far the majority that they have prevailed in
some degree in converting the terms of Rationalist and Free-
thinker, describing those who act, or try to act, by the light of the
great gift which God has given—from terms of honour and
esteem into those of obloquy and reproach. In the same way,
those who have not only no faith that the laws of God, as revealed
in nature, will accord with their own traditional notions, but are
full of doubt and fear that they will not, have ventured, in the
face of the obvious applicability to themselves of such terms as
infidel and sceptic, to turn them against those who patiently
search for and study the manifestations of God in all His ways
and works, and whose hopes are continually sustained and excited
by ever increasing evidence of harmony, benevolence, and
wisdom.

It may be, that, in the controversies of the Apostle Paul with
the Greeks, that fervid writer may have rhetorically used
language apparently derogatory of human wisdom, and that such
language may imply distrust of human reason. But true wisdom
could no more be a subject of denunciation than true reason.
He must have meant unwisdom and unreason, or what appeared
to him to be so. The same apostle in his sermon at Athens
charges the Greeks with ignorance. Is it, however, to be concealed or explained that some of the grounds of his own arguments are not in accordance with present information and
opinions? Is it to be explained, for example, that it is not in
accordance with present information, that death was introduced
into the world by the so-called fall of Adam, that it is not in
accordance with an enlightened sense of justice, or even with
Scripture (see Ezekiel xviii) that all should be condemned for
one, and that it is not in accordance with claims of supernatural
authority that predictions should not be verified by results?

Some of the leading errors of Protestant churches have been
attempted to be noticed, and it has also been attempted to notice
their continual hostility to new intellectual influences as regards
the general progress of humanity. It is becoming clearer and
clearer that true religion, as involving the knowledge of God
through His works and ways, through the faculties which he has

given us, is not necessarily the religion of so-called churches, and that the tendency of these churches is to apply themselves rather to the suppression of certain forms of vice or so-called error than to the true development of either moral or intellectual virtue or of dutiful self-reliance. Human nature seems to be treated as a weed, to be restrained because it cannot be extirpated, even in the happy manner said to have been suggested by St. Augustine, rather than as a wholesome plant or flower to be cultivated and improved. In the eyes of the churches, generally speaking, all duty may be held to be comprehended in intellectual submissiveness to the church of which one is a member, and in what it calls by the name of charity, and all such charity may be held to be comprehended in giving liberally for the objects of the churches. It is even held meritorious to be what is called a quiet unostentatious Christian, which generally means a person of good emotional feelings and practice, who has either no intellectual opinions on religious subjects or who carefully conceals what they are. The expression of opinions might awaken intellect; the awakening of intellect might dispel ignorance. Ignorance is said to be the mother of devotion—that is, the devotion of credulity and terror, instead of that of intelligent study and veneration.

These remarks apply to almost all the developments of Romish and Protestant churches. None of them have ever confessed or relinquished any single error of their whole career. Not only this, but each and all of them claim the exclusive monopoly of truth without error. All other religions, except their own and those of their Hebrew and Jewish predecessors, are denounced by them as false and diabolical. Even the best and most admirable works and precepts of all other religions are declared, as in the Articles of the Churches of England, to be not pleasant to God and to be of the nature of sin. The Confession of Faith of the Church of Scotland is to the same effect. It is on these grounds, and to endeavour to establish how opposed to every principle of reason and justice these doctrines are, that so many illustrations have been adduced from the other and more ancient religions of the world, to show that even among the darknesses of outward idolatry God was never without a witness, that He never confined his light to one race or to one faith, but that, in the words of St. Peter, He was no respecter of persons, and that in every nation the righteous were accepted of Him. Flashes of similar truth burst out from time to time from Hebrew as from Gentile writers, and are at utter variance with the cobwebs and abominations of beggarly elements which, by taking the letter without the spirit and a part without the whole, have been woven together for our bodily oppression and for our intellectual destruction. The prophet Micah (vi. 8) says, " What doth the Lord require of thee, but to do justly, and love mercy, and walk humbly with thy God?" The prophet Jeremiah, speaking of the Church in his time (vii. 4 &c.) says, "Trust ye not in lying words, saying, The temple of the Lord, the temple of the Lord, the temple of the Lord are these. For if ye thoroughly amend your ways and your doings; if ye thoroughly execute judgment between a man and his neighbour ; if ye oppress not the stranger, the fatherless, and the widow" &c. Hebrew and Gentile accordingly proclaim the same truth, that God reigns over the whole earth in mercy and justice, that He is no respecter of persons, and that he cares no more for vain oblations of bullocks, or rams, or goats, or new moons, or sabbaths (see Isaiah i.) than He can be supposed to care for the modern rites and ceremonies which have come in place of them. It has been necessary to bring this into prominent notice, because the same bodies who have so diligently obscured and miscalled the position of the whole ancient world except one race, and of all existing humanity except those of their own creeds, still claim to be our true and only religious and moral educators.

Individual clergymen and members of Christian churches have done and are always doing great practical good ; but in so far as they have done so on a free, wise, and generous footing, so much the less are they strict adherents of the tenets of those churches. A counterpart to the rather doubtful compliment as to a man being a quiet, unostentatious Christian is sometimes awarded to such men in such terms as that so-and-so is a very good man, very liberal, not at all strict or bigoted in his opinions. What is thought of the opinions themselves can be inferred when it is made a matter of merit not to adhere to them. Some clergymen in the churches of England and Scotland are among the most able and distinguished advocates of intellectual freedom ; but in so far as they are so, so much the less are they liked by the mass of their brethren, so much the more would the body of their brethren seek to silence them or to drive them from their places.

The State and the churches are both in a false position as long as the State requires by law that the churches shall profess as facts in their confessions and standards what are not believed to be facts in reality. What ceases to be believed should cease to be professed. Let there be perfect veracity above all things, more especially in matters of religion. It is not a question of courtesies which deceive no one. To profess what is not believed is immoral. Immorality and untruth can never lead to morality or virtue. All language which conveys untruth, either in substance or in appearance, should be amended, so that words can be understood in their recognised meanings without equivocal explanations of affirmatives into negatives and of negatives into affirmatives. Let historic acts have their true explanations. Let there be no approbation, express or implied, of what is plainly wrong, false, fraudulent, or cruel. Much more let us avoid ascribing to God, on any authority known to us, acts and language which it would be inconsistent with the nature of the God in whom we believe to have done or said. Shall we have less regard for the good name of the Supreme Being than for that of ourselves and of our fellow-creatures? Who can say to what confusion of thought, crime, and misery, education from generation to generation on such a basis as that against which it is feebly attempted to protest may have led? Who can say if an amiably-disposed Charles the First would have been a dissembler and a despot if he had had an education on sounder and less involved precedents and principles? Who can say what a Mary Tudor, or even a Philip of Spain, might have been if their minds had not been steeled against common humanity by ecclesiastical doctrines? Who can say what a Mary Stuart or a Charles the Second might have been if they had been brought up to believe that the same morality is required from kings and queens as from other people? If we continue to exclude the free circulation of light and truth we may expect some time or other perhaps even a worse Nemesis. There is still much to amend. Thomas Carlyle denounced shams. The shams straightway fell down and worshipped him—*and continue as before.*

It has been attempted to show that in the matter of national education, it being impossible to exclude the teaching of religion, or historically to exclude even the teaching of theology, the only footing on which these subjects can be taught is on an open footing in the same manner as any other subject; and it is thought that, if taught on that footing, any tendency on the part of a teacher to give them a denominational bias can be met in the meantime in the manner which has been suggested.

The present observations are not intended to enter into the expression or discussion of views properly theological; but it is impossible to avoid noticing that it will be a subject of important consideration whether or not the great changes which have taken place in the opinions of European scholarship, and which are still in progress, are, as matters of fact, to be made known or to be concealed. The tendency of these observations is that nothing should be concealed otherwise than at the discretion of the teacher, and that, in so far as regards all fair reasoning, he should conceal as little as possible. Religion does not belong exclusively to any special profession; it is the common right and interest of all mankind.

Even in works professedly scientific there are passages which involve consideration, from the same point of view, as to whether or not they should be disclosed or concealed. For example, in Professor Tyndall's work, "Scientific Fragments for Unscientific People," there are many passages which in the view of the churches are certainly unorthodox. Are such works or such passages to be kept back? Is there to be an *Index Expurgatorius* for science as well as for religion?

It may be objected that the proposed system cannot be applied to Roman Catholics, and that the children of Roman Catholic parents will not be allowed to receive religious or historical teaching through the intervention of Protestant teachers, or probably through the intervention of any other than Roman Catholic teachers. That is a matter which can only be left to time and to their own progress or enlightenment. No system can be forced on them. It will be attempted to be shown afterwards that there can be no effective compulsory system of general education in a free constitutional country. The question, in the meantime, as regards Roman Catholics or others who think along with them, is whether or not the system offered is on a rational and sound footing. If it is, it is for themselves to accept it, or not to accept it, as they think proper. The conscientious obstacle is removed as regards religious doctrine. It cannot be removed as regards matters of ordinary fact. Conscientious objectious, or objections supposed to be conscientious, may apply to other matters than religious doctrine. Irish Roman Catholics may, for example, object to any ordinary history of Queen Mary, or to any ordinary history of Ribbonism or of Orangeism or of Fenianism ; but in such matters concession must stop. It is enough not to enforce the teaching of such matters. They must not be falsified in order to make them acceptable. Government cannot officially compile histories of these matters more or less untrue or erroneous, in order to make them suit each variety of taste. In the same way Roman Catholic parents and guardians may object to the teaching of the elements of astronomy or of geology, or anything else not taught according to the principles of the Vatican. Government cannot lend itself to compile or sanction the preparation of books on these subjects at variance with known facts. In the same way, when the history of religion is presented as matter of fact to be judged of according to evidence, without which no history of any kind can be taught, religion is placed on precisely the same footing as other matters, and any advanced education must embrace it ; otherwise there can be no advanced education at all. Like everything which must pass through a medium more or less imperfect it must necessarily and unavoidably derive some influence from the medium through

which it comes; but in so far as the teacher is the medium his
influence, in so far as it might bo injurious or objectionable, is
negatived as far as possible by depriving him of all official
authority to impress any peculiar views upon that part of his
teaching. If the state do all that is now proposed it will do all
that any state can rightfully do. It is for those to whom such
teaching is offered to take it or leave it, in whole or in part, as
they may think proper. It is probable that at first, in cases in
which the teachers do not happen to bo Roman Catholics, many
may not accept more than the elements of reading, writing, and
arithmetic, but these alone are a great deal in the first instance.
It is probable, on the other hand, that where teachers do happen
to be Roman Catholics some of them may indirectly endeavour
to maintain or instil some of the views of that faith. It is impossible by any civil legislation to prevent their doing so; but
it is much to deprive them of all official right or authority to
propagate such views. Increasing enlightenment will probably
more and more tend to check any attempts of the kind, and
make the whole range of education not merely acceptable but
eagerly sought after, as it already is in Scotland and, as is to
be hoped, very soon will be in England also.

It is understood that the new system of education to be
afforded by the State is intended to be limited to elementary
subjects. In this respect it would be at variance with the principles hitherto acted on in the parochial education of Scotland.
The parochial system was intended to embrace all subjects of
liberal education as understood at the time. This included the
Greek and Latin classics up to the stage of preparing young
men for the university, and the teaching of these has ever since
been maintained under it. The remuneration of the teachers
was adjusted on such a footing as to induce them, as far as
possible, to give fair attention to all the subjects taught by them,
and their reputation and success depended to a considerable
extent on their producing well-taught and able scholars. Boys
could not be made proficient in classics and mathematics unless
they were well grounded in the lower branches of education.
Again, boys or lads from all the schools competed, and their
success or otherwise indicated whose teaching was most efficient.
In this manner a healthy and continuous stimulus operated
through the whole system of parochial education. The principle
of the Government, on the other hand, is understood to be to
provide for what they call national education in the shape of
pecuniary grants or allowances made by the State to each
teacher, according to the number of pupils who are taught up to
certain standards of elementary teaching. The Government are
understood to maintain that it is not the duty of the State to

provide for more than elementary education to the poorer classes, and that as regards all other classes they should provide what they want for themselves and at their own expense.   The Privy Council have been in the practice for many years past of subsidizing schools on this footing.   It is said that a pecuniary inducement has been thereby held out to the teachers to devote themselves more to the teaching of elementary education to extended numbers, than to the higher proficiency of the more able and intellectual of their scholars. This may be considered a good or a bad result according to the different views of different persons. Its tendency is to diminish to all classes, including the poorer classes themselves, the facilities afforded under the parochial system for acquiring higher education. This may lead to a diminution of the qualifications of the teachers of schools, in which teaching beyond elementary teaching may cease to be required. The grade of country schools will thereby become seriously lowered, and families residing in such districts who may desire more than elementary teaching for their children, but who may not be able to afford to send their children elsewhere—which means the great bulk of the middle classes —will be exposed to most material prejudice and injury. This is the class which pays substantially nearly the whole rates and taxes from which the remuneration and subsidization of the schools are provided.   The effect of such administration would be in a great measure to draw funds from one class of society to furnish education to another class who make scarcely any contribution to those funds, and at the same time to diminish the educational resources and facilities of all classes, including the class from which the funds are drawn.   It would be prejudicial in another respect. A teacher of higher qualifications is a better teacher, even of elementary subjects, than a teacher of lower qualifications. In Scotland it would be prejudicial socially, in putting an end to the free and equal footing on which the children of all classes, both higher and lower, have hitherto been in the practice of coming together in the schools throughout the country districts.   There may be waste of power otherwise. A man must be very insufficiently qualified for a teacher if he know nothing beyond the subjects of elementary teaching. If he do know more, and if his time admit, which it will generally do, it would be for the advantage of all concerned that his superior knowledge should be utilized in imparting it to others.

It is the opinion of many who have had opportunities of observation that there is not at present any educational destitution in any part of the rural districts of Scotland in which there is sufficient population to occupy a teacher.   Not that the parochial schools by themselves nearly supply what is wanted.

But almost everywhere that there is room to do so schools have been established, by religious and educational or other bodies and by private individuals, to such an extent that there is scarcely any populous district or locality in which education for children is not more or less accessible. The establishment of a national system of education will probably occasion the discontinuance or withdrawal of the support of some of the schools maintained by the liberality of bodies or individuals under no legal liability to maintain them, and in such cases the effect may be to create the destitution it was intended to relieve. In such cases provision is understood to be made for treating with the owners of such schools or for establishing others when required. But beyond this legislative provision for the extension of education in the rural districts of Scotland did not seem to be a matter of present necessity.

The condition of the cities and of large towns and burghs was so totally different from that of the rural districts that they might have been made the subject of a different system of legislation. It is understood that this was originally proposed by the present Lord Advocate.

Compulsory education as regards the rural districts of Scotland is entirely unnecessary. It would not be practicable if attempted. It is unnecessary because, with scarcely an exception, parents, even of the poorest classes, are so convinced of the advantages of education that they not only need no compulsion, but of their own accord make every effort to send their children to school. In England the desire for education may not be the same, but, if parents do not send their children to school, it is not very obvious how the doing so can be forced upon them. Suppose a child not to attend school. A constable is sent to its parents' house to make inquiry as to its absence. The mother says it has a sore head or a sore stomach, or that it habitually ails, or the like. What can be done? Or supposing the mother to say it has no sufficient shoes or stockings or other clothing, or the like? Are these to be forthwith provided by the public? Or would it improve matters to put both or either of the parents into prison? That would be the only alternative, in Scotland at least, because it is most rare in that country to find parents who have any means out of which they could pay a fine, if imposed, indifferent to the education of their children. Besides this, in a free country and under constitutional government, people cannot be sent to prison without trial. What would a trial cost, or how would pleas as to ailments, inability to work or provide clothing, objections (pretended or real) to parts of the teaching, or the like, be dealt with? Compulsory education, or what passes under that name, may be prac-

ticable in countries with despotic or paternal governments; but
in a constitutional country such as this, except with regard
to the children of criminal and vagrant classes, with whom the
law deals on a different footing, it is as impracticable as, fortunately to a large and, it is to be hoped, to an increasing
extent, it appears to be unnecessary.

These remarks are, however, principally intended as a contribution towards the solution of the difficulty as to the position
which religion is to hold in regard to national education. We
are engaged in the inauguration of a new system, which will
raise almost universal controversy on that point, which will
continue more or less until some sound basis of adjustment
be arrived at. In regard to nations as well as individuals it
would appear that, in many cases, wisdom of action is only to
be attained, if it be attained, by experience more or less of the
evils of unwisdom. It takes wise statesmanship to trace evils to
their true causes. It takes still wiser statesmanship to devise
and apply the best remedies.

Art. V.—THE REPUBLICANS OF THE COMMONWEALTH.

PART II.

1. *Essays on Historical Truth.* By ANDREW BISSET. London.
   1871.
2. *The Lives of William Cavendish, Duke of Newcastle, and of
   his wife Margaret, Duchess of Newcastle.* Written by the
   thrice noble and illustrious Princess, MARGARET, Duchess
   of NEWCASTLE. Edited by MARK ANTONY LOWER, M.A.
   London. 1872.

SOME people who have read a little history have so far forgotten the leading events of the time of Charles I. and of
the Commonwealth as to see no difficulty in thinking it right
and proper that those who rose and fought against King Charles
should have been contented to live under the sway of King
Oliver. Englishmen now-a-days may feel some satisfaction at
the victories of Cromwell and at the fear which his name
inspired all over Europe, without feeling the slightest annoyance
at the reflection, if it should have occurred to them at all, that
under his rule the people of England lost the liberties which

they had held with danger and hardship against the Tudors and
the Stuarts, and which they had successfully defended through a
long and bloody civil war. What must have been the feelings
of the generation that had fought and suffered to find in the
military champion of the Parliament a more arbitrary ruler than
the crowned King whom Oliver had done so much to bring to the
scaffold? And how could the generation that had grown up
since the civil wars think Charles Stuart deserving of dethrone-
ment and death without equally condemning Oliver Cromwell?
If Charles had raised money without the consent of Parliament,
Cromwell had done so too. What was the King's ship-money
compared with the exactions of the Protector's major-generals?
If Charles had entered the House of Commons to arrest the five
members, Oliver had brought armed men to thrust the members
out of the House. If Charles had refused to give up the control
of the militia, Cromwell had used the army to subvert the civil
government, had given the names and powers of a parliament to
a ridiculous assembly of his own nomination, had used every
species of violence and corruption to ensure the return of men
sufficiently subservient to uphold his usurpation, and had prevented his opponents from taking their seats. Nevertheless the
King had died the death of a criminal, and the successful soldier
was reigning in Whitehall. The hand and seal of the one man
were on the death-warrant of the other.

These were arguments too evident to escape attention, too true
to be refuted, and too serviceable not to be used by the Royalist
party as well as by the Republicans, who bitterly accused
Cromwell and his partisans of betraying the good old cause.* It
was not at that time easy to insist that Cromwell had subverted a
weak incapable government because most grown-up people could
remember the great deeds of the Long Parliament, and knew
that it had done more than any king that ever reigned in
England; and if the Parliament had proved too weak to defend
itself this was because it had been betrayed by those who ought
to have made it strong.

The dignified and impressive attitude which the King held at
his trial and execution deeply affected those whose views of
public affairs were largely influenced by the feelings of the heart,
while those whose judgment led them to wish an end to the rule
of a single person felt confounded at the violent dissolution of the
Long Parliament. But the passions aroused by the civil wars
were still strong; the desire for liberty and the hopes of a better

---

* See as a specimen, "A Second Narrative of the Late Parliament (so
called)" &c., represented in Selections from the Harleian Miscellany. London,
1793, p. 414.

state of things were not yet forgotten in the desire for security. Many people, too, had their immediate fortunes to consider; they had bought the lands of the Crown, of the Church, or of the Royalists. Oliver was one man; the Stuarts were an hereditary dynasty, who would bring back with them the Lords, the Bishops, and the whole Cavalier faction, eager to hang, confiscate, and proscribe. Republican feeling still continued to be strong in the army, and there was little likelihood of another general gaining the same ascendancy over the soldiers which Oliver had done. Thus while some of the Republican leaders, such as Vane, Bradshaw, Haslerig, and Scot, kept up a resolute opposition to Cromwell's government, a few, such as Blake and Milton, continued to serve the State under him. Cromwell did his utmost to form a party of his own, and succeeded in attracting to him some able civilians like Whitelocke, who, being in favour of monarchy, though disapproving of his usurpation still thought his rule preferable to the return of the Stuarts. In the course of his short reign the Protector quarrelled with a large number of those who had originally assisted him to power, such as Lambert and Harrison, as well as dexterous politicians like Sir Anthony Ashley Cooper, who had once been his supporter, had sat in the Barebones Parliament, and been a member of his council. In the end he came principally to depend upon those connected with him by blood or marriage, such as his son, Henry Cromwell, Lockhart, who had married his niece, Desborough, who had married his sister, General Fleetwood and Lord Faulconbridge who had married his daughters, and Thurloe, his secretary, an able but unscrupulous man.

People who have dwelt all their lives in these quiet isles in prosperous times and under a free government seem to have lost all idea what military force is; how easy it can make all things to the ruler, how hard to the subject. As Hume has finely remarked: "An army is so forcible and at the same time so coarse a weapon that any hand which wields it may, without much dexterity, perform any operation and attain any ascendant in human society."

Amongst the few historians who have had the courage to vindicate the skill and patriotism of the members of the Councils of State which governed England up to the dissolution of the Parliament by Cromwell, Mr. Bisset[*] holds a highly honourable place. The certainty of blame and misrepresentation incurred in attacking rooted errors may excuse the argumentative form

---

[*] "History of the Commonwealth of England from the Death of Charles I. to the Expulsion of the Long Parliament by Cromwell, being OmittedChapters in the History of England." 2 vols. London. 1864 and 1867.

into which he has thrown the results of his historical researches; nor is it surprising that Mr. Bisset should have been treated with an injustice which has induced him to reply to some of his critics. There is no part of his " Essay on the Commonwealth and Cromwell " more convincing than that in which he deals with an indolent reviewer who wishes our view of the character of Cromwell to be decided by a perusal of his letters:—

"Cromwell, like all other men, great and small, is to be judged not by his words but by his deeds. Cromwell, by his expulsion of the Long Parliament, destroyed all chance of good government in England for at least two generations. He trampled down while living—as his modern panegyrists seek to insult when dead—the statesmen who had made England 'famous and terrible over the world;' and this critic says that the 'collection and juxtaposition of his letters' form 'a crucial test'—of what?—of his sincerity—his sincerity in what? in expelling the Long Parliament and putting himself in its place. Parliaments and single rulers are but means to ends, those ends being the prosperity and happiness of the governed. If Cromwell did not advance those ends by his expulsion of the Long Parliament—and it is beyond a doubt that he did not advance them—of what use is it to talk about 'crucial tests' and 'juxtaposition of letters?' The only valid argument which Cromwell had was that the Long Parliament was incapable of carrying on the government. But the inferiority of Cromwell's government to that of the Long Parliament which he superseded is proved quite independently of the 'contemporary memoirs,' which this critic is pleased to characterize as 'idle gossip,' 'tittle-tattle,' and 'rubbish.' "

This is a point which requires being firmly insisted upon, because in order to justify Cromwell his admirers require the whole history of the period to be overruled and mis-stated, and even if all the memoirs and documents on the subject, save the letters and speeches of Cromwell, are entirely misleading, it seems clear that the conclusion they wish us to adopt only goes to strengthen the cause of the Cavaliers; for if the Civil War was destined fatally to end in military despotism, as the admirers of Cromwell insist, then it was a mistake to have commenced it at all, and Hampden and Cromwell are to be blamed as much as Vane and Ludlow.

If he did not succeed in founding a party of his own, the sagacious Protector did much to cripple and weaken the rival parties of his opponents. He had kept the Royalists impoverished by heavy contributions levied by his major-generals upon them alone; he had allowed their conspiracies to come to a head, and then visited their leaders with death, transportation, and forfeiture of their estates. He had done much to destroy the faith and popularity of the Republican party. He had succeeded in corrupting some of their leaders, such as Lenthal and St. John, and had kept the rest in private life, where their influence went to decay. His schemes were interrupted by a death which might be considered early in view of the robustness of his frame and the temperate nature of his habits, but which seems to have been brought on by declining health, owing to continual anxiety and a fear of assassination which does not seem quite consistent with the keen courage he had ever shown in battle. He died on the 3rd of September, 1658, in the fifty-ninth year of his age. He had been allowed, by the Petition and Advice, to nominate his successor, but had neglected to do so in a public manner, although a written document was said to have existed in favour of Fleetwood, Oliver's son-in-law. The night before he died he had named his eldest son, Richard. This was attested upon oath by Goodwin, his chaplain, and by Major-Generals Whalley and Goffe, whose testimony was received by the Privy Council. Fleetwood engaged not to rest any claims upon the missing paper, even should it be found.

Enthusiastic admirers like Mr. Carlyle are naturally impelled to throw doubts upon this nomination, for it was in every way a serious error. The Protector had allowed his desire of founding a dynasty in his own family to deceive his sagacity, and his parental affection to outweigh his sense of public duty. How much nobler the conduct of a great patriot like John de Witt,* who, though he exerted all his influence to prevent the office of stadtholder being restored in the family of Orange, yet took care to give the young Prince William an education which should help him to rule well, should he be, in spite of all, put over the State.

Such a good judge of human nature as Cromwell must have known very well that Richard had no talents either for politics or war. He bore the character of a good-humoured country gentleman, of manners rather too easy for his father's puritanical court, and therefore given to carousing with the Cavalier gentlemen living in the neighbourhood, and skilful only in hunting, hawking, and horse-racing. His father had never given him any training either in political or military affairs. It created general surprise that Richard should quietly succeed to the power of the great Protector, but the explanation was simple enough. The generals had agreed for the time to recognise him, and the nation knew that they could not resist the army. A letter of Henry Cromwell from Dublin to his brother, as well as some written by Thurloe about the same time, proves that they had

---

* See Burnet's "History of his own Times." Oxford. 1833. Vol. i. chap. ccxxi. p. 405.

little expectation that the government of England would remain
long in their hands. Oliver had ruled with the sword ; without
the sword his rule would not have continued for a week.
His successor had never been in the army and had no skill in war.

All the dissonant parties which Oliver Cromwell had held
under now began to scheme and plot as if the existing government counted for nothing. While the Republicans held secret
meetings, the officers of the army met at Wallingford House, the
residence of General Fleetwood, and but six weeks after the
death of Oliver a deputation of two or three hundred officers,
with Fleetwood at their head, appeared to demand that some
experienced person should be made commander-in-chief, and
that no officer should be cashiered without the sentence of a
court-martial. Richard, in his reply, which had been prepared
by Thurloe, his father's able adviser, observes : " You know the
difficulties my father all his time wrestled with, and I believe
no man thinks that his death has lessened them." In truth
he was asked to give up the means by which his father had conquered all his difficulties, and he was asked to give up his power
by the only men who could help him in it. While Richard's
refusal was accepted for the moment, his conciliatory language
showed his weakness.

Oliver had died seven months after dissolving his last Parliament, and, as Richard's advisers did not feel their position strong
enough to enforce his arbitrary method of levying taxes and
contributions, the army began to fall into arrears and they felt
themselves compelled to call a Parliament.

It was determined that the distribution of seats agreed on by
the Long Parliament and practised by Cromwell should be
abandoned, and that the writs of election should be issued
according to what was called the ancient law, principally because,
as Ludlow tells us, " it was well understood that mean and
decayed boroughs might be much more easily corrupted than
the numerous counties and considerable cities." It was determined that thirty members should be returned for Scotland
and as many for Ireland, and the Government arranged that they
should be returned for places where the military garrisons could
influence the course of the elections. All the arts of a corrupt
government were put into play to procure partisans of the Protector to be chosen. All the appointments in the army and civil
list were in his hands. The officers of the Admiralty and navy
had the power of pressing at their pleasure the men of the
seaport towns into their fleet.* The sheriffs, who were men
mostly chosen for their subserviency, made themselves very

---

* Ludlow's Memoirs. Vevey edition, 1698, p. 617.

useful to the Protectorate, disposing of the writs to whom they
pleased and acting as judges of the fitness of voters. As it was
known that the members returned, would be required to take
an oath of fidelity to Richard Cromwell, the opposing parties
had to consider how their scruples could be overcome. The
Cavaliers were expressly directed by Charles Stuart to try to
procure seats, and it was determined, after much deliberation
amongst the Republicans, to contest a number of places and sit
in the House if elected. The influence of the Government seems
to have been principally directed against the Republican party.
Great efforts were made to prevent the election of Sir Henry
Vane, who was believed to have been returned by a majority
both in Bristol and Hull, two of the largest towns in the
kingdom, though the sheriffs refused to return him; but in
spite of the threats of the Court faction, he was elected for the
small borough of Whitchurch, in Hampshire. Ludlow, too, was
elected, and managed to keep his seat without taking any oath.
Sir Arthur Haslerig, Mr. Thomas Scot, President Bradshaw,
Nevil, and some other well-known Republicans, and Sir Anthony
Ashley Cooper, then in league with the Commonwealth men,
and Lord Fairfax, were also elected. Colonel Hutchinson had
been named sheriff to prevent him being able to represent
Nottingham. According to Guizot,[*] out of a House of 564
members, 504 of whom came from England, there were about
50 determined Republicans, from 100 to 140 members who
wavered between the Protector and a Republic, 72 lawyers
or men in the civil employment of Government, and 100 officers
of the army, besides 200 persons of neutral or unknown opinions.
Bordeaux writes to Mazarin on the 20th of February that three
parts of the Parliament were willing to maintain Richard
Cromwell with limitations to his power. Lord Fauconbridge[†] says
the Commonwealth men in the Parliament were very numerous
and beyond measure bold, but more than doubly overbalanced
by the sober party. Dr. Barwick wrote to Hyde that the Republicans were the minority, but all speakers zealous and diligent.

This may be accepted as evidence that the Republicans, in spite
of all that Oliver Cromwell had done to repress them, were still
a strong party in the nation. The number of Cavaliers who

---

* "History of Richard Cromwell and the Restoration of Charles II." By
M. Guizot. Translated by Andrew R. Scoble. 1856. Vol. i. p. 38.

† Quoted by Hallam in his "Constitutional History of England," London,
1832, vol. ii. chap. x. p. 365. Hallam says in a note, according to a letter
from Allen Broderick to Hyde (Clarendon State Papers, iii. 443), "there
were 47 Republicans, from 100 to 140 neuters or moderates (including many
Royalists), and 170 Court lawyers or officers."

found their way into the Parliament was not large, from which
it may be fairly concluded that their party had not yet become
popular. The Upper House—an unfortunate creation of Oliver
Cromwell's, made up of a number of his most obsequious partisans,
and from which the old peers had kept aloof—was also summoned
to assemble. The Parliament was solemnly convoked by Richard
Cromwell the 27th of February, 1659.

Vane, Haslerig, and Ashley Cooper, the leaders of the Opposition, lost no time in directing against the Government of the
new Protector a vigorous criticism, which his friends had neither
the ability to confute nor the power to silence. The title of
Richard Cromwell was disputed, his right to call representatives
from Scotland and Ireland was questioned, and the upstart
House of Lords turned into derision ; while a vote of condemnation
against Major-General Butler, one of the most brutal of the
military satraps whom the late Protector had put over the
counties of England, might be interpreted as a reflection upon
his Government and a threat that his subordinates might yet be
found responsible for what had been done by his orders. It
appears that the House was unsettled in its views, and Ludlow
claims that the Republican orators made some converts among
the younger members.

"All the meetings of the House," writes M. de Bordeaux, "have
been occupied with very free speeches from the Republicans, and
answers to them from those who are well affected towards the
Government. The more moderate among the Republicans assert
that it will be advisable to grant the Protector the same prerogatives
which were accepted by the late King when the Long Parliament treated with him in the Isle of Wight," and it would have
been well, as events proved, if such an arrangement could have
been made and held to. Richard was not personally unpopular.
"I never knew any guile or gall in him," said Haslerig, his father's
bitter and resolute opponent. He was just the sort of man to
make a good constitutional king in quiet times, but was too fond
of an easy life not to wish to escape from being baited by Republican orators and bullied by unruly generals like his uncle,
Desborough, or his brother-in-law, Fleetwood. Though anxious
to retain his power, he was not prepared for all the intrigues
and violence which were necessary to defend it. The officers of
the army gave Richard almost as much inquietude as the
Parliament. Murmurs began to be heard amongst the Republicans
in the army that the good old cause had been too long lulled
asleep, and the military council which met at Fleetwood's
residence at Wallingford House held parleys with the party who
met at Vane's house at Charing-cross, with the common object of
stripping the Protector of a part of his power. The Wallingford

House party requested that a council of war should be held to consider the state of the nation, and from the day on which this was granted the reign of Richard was virtually over. Soon after there came a humble address and petition from a general council of the officers representing that the common cause was likely to be ruined by the subtlety and artifices of those who had never been able to do it by open force, and praying that the command of the army might be given to some one acquainted with military affairs in whom they could all confide. It was understood that General Fleetwood was meant. The friends of Richard Cromwell, seeing that the separation of the military and civil power would leave him helpless, persuaded him to appeal to the Parliament, and a majority of the House of Commons passed a resolution forbidding the general council of officers to meet without the direction and leave of both Houses of Parliament, and declaring that no man should hold a military command who did not take a pledge not to disturb the deliberations of Parliament. This measure met with decided opposition from the leaders of the Commonwealth party. "Be very wary of proceeding suddenly," said Vane. "This diffidence of your friends ought to be avoided. Take heed you take not the thorn out of another's foot and put it into your own. It never can be policy to distrust those we are obliged to trust." The Wallingford party paid no heed to this prohibition, and the son of Oliver Cromwell had the humiliation to find by actual trial that the soldiers no longer obeyed him, and that even his own body-guard could not be trusted.[*]

Bordeaux writes that his friends had scarcely been able to find two hundred men in the whole army who were disposed to back him. Some companies of cavalry and infantry, under the orders of the rebellious generals, entered the courtyard of Whitehall, "and behaved themselves with considerable licence, particularly in the cellars."

Obliged to yield to the military junto, Richard's last act was to dissolve his Parliament—that is, to shut up the doors of the House and place guards to prevent the members reassembling.

For a few days the control of the Government of England remained in the hands of the unruly generals who had now overturned the Protector and his Parliament; but a little consideration showed them the impossibility of military despotism without a commander whom all were prepared to obey. The generals quarrelled with one another; the officers made their terms with their superiors, and were too anxious to have the good will of their men to venture to repress their disorders. They had no skill in managing civil affairs and felt themselves

---

[*] See letter, May, 1659, Guizot, vol. i. p. 371.

the object of universal dislike. The Sectaries, Fifth-monarchy men, and Republicans amongst the soldiery held violent meetings and discussed their own theories of government. The council of Wallingford House was soon obliged to yield to the demands of the Republican parties in the army, and to restore the Long Parliament.

In spite of the opposition of those who had a share in keeping up Cromwell, a meeting was arranged at Sir Henry Vane's house at Charing Cross, where deputies from the army conferred with Vane, Haslerig, Ludlow, and Major Salloway. After considerable discussion it was agreed that an act of indemnity should be passed securing those who had taken part in the government of the Cromwells from future proscription, and that some provision should be made for Richard Cromwell. The third and fourth propositions, that reform should be made in the law and clergy and that the nation should be governed by representative assemblies and by a select synod, caused a great deal of discussion. The officers had to put up with vague answers, rendered still more unsatisfactory by the knowledge that the parties with whom they were treating had no power to carry out what they promised. It was found from a list furnished by Ludlow that a hundred and sixty of those who had sat in the Long Parliament since the year 1648 were yet alive. After some further conferences sixteen of the old members, accompanied by some officers of the army, went to the house of William Lenthal, the old Speaker, and acquainted him with their desire to recall the Long Parliament. Lenthal, who had been created a peer by Cromwell and had become old and feeble, made many excuses, and they were obliged to issue writs without his signature. The Speaker, however, hearing that it was likely a sufficient number would assemble to form a quorum, made his appearance amongst them.

"About twelve o'clock," says Ludlow,[*] "we went to take our places in the House, Mr. Lenthal, our Speaker, leading the way, and the officers of the army lining the room for us as we passed through the Painted Chamber, the Court of Requests, and the lobby itself, the principal officers having placed themselves nearest to the door of the Parliament House, every one seeming to rejoice at our restitution and promising to live and die with us."

They immediately sent summonses to all the members throughout England, and in the course of time about ninety took their seats.

The first care of the restored Parliament was to remove Richard Cromwell from Whitehall; who, being in debt, took with him little more than two trunks full of congratulatory addresses received on his accession from all parts of England.

---

* Ludlow, vol. ii. p. 651.

Mazarin would willingly have done something to maintain Richard, since he hated and feared the Commonwealth, which, to use the words of Oxenstiern, the Swedish Chancellor, was "exemplary with a witness, or rather minatory, to all princes of the world." He willingly listened to the overtures of the Spanish King to aid in its suppression.

"We agreed," wrote Mazarin to M. le Tellier, on the 25th of August, "that it was too dangerous an example to be allowed to go down to posterity unpunished, that subjects should have brought the King to trial and put him to death ; and that if the Commonwealth of England established itself it would be a formidable power to all its neighbours ; because, without exaggeration, it would be a hundred times greater than the power of the kings of England ever was."*

"I find it somewhat difficult," writes M. de Bordeaux to Mazarin, June 2nd, 1659, "to comply with the order reiterated to me in M. de Brienne's letter of the 25th ultimo, that I must thwart the establishment of a Commonwealth, as there is no probability of success in such an undertaking, unless the Protector has a strong party in England or his friends embrace the cause of the King of Scots. It is very probable that England will fall into the King's power again, or that it will be formed into a perfect republic."

In a letter to M. de Brienne, dated 17th July, 1659, M. de Bordeaux remarks :—

"Whatever confidence may be felt in the friendship of France, there is nevertheless a strong apprehension that storms are brewing abroad which may have power to change the government of England, with which every one expresses great discontent ; not that the Commonwealth is generally disapproved of, but people cannot be brought to believe that those who now possess authority will ever consent to resign it ; and those even who are most opposed to a monarchy declare that it would be better to recall the King than to endure such a government as is now projected."

The government of the country was carried on by a Council of State consisting of thirty-one members, twenty of which were also members of the Parliament ; amongst whom appeared the names of Sir Henry Vane, Sir Arthur Haslerig, James Harrington, the author of the "Oceana," Lieutenant-General Fleetwood, Colonel Algernon Sidney, and Mr. Thomas Scot. Amongst those who were not members were the Lord President Bradshaw, Lord Fairfax, Major-General Lambert, Colonel Desborough, Colonel Berry, Sir Anthony Ashley Cooper, and Sir Horatio Townsend, who was secretly in correspondence with Hyde, the agent of Charles Stuart. The military officers, Ludlow tells us, seldom came to the council, and " when they condescended to come carried themselves with all imaginable perverseness and insolence."

Vane was ordered to examine the financial position of the country. He reported a deficit of 1,500,000*l.**

" Our treasury was so low," says Ludlow, " through the maladministration of the late governments, that though our plenipotentiaries to the two northern crowns had received their instructions, yet they were obliged to stay a fortnight longer before they could receive the sum of two thousand pounds which had been ordered for expenses of their voyage, the taxes coming in but slowly, and the city of *London*, terrified with the reports of an expected insurrection, being very backward in advancing money."

Money, however, must be had to carry on the administration of the country and, above all things, to pay up the arrears of the army. They tried to raise it by an income tax, and by increasing the customs; but, from the weakness of the executive government, they met with great difficulty in collecting the money in a country accustomed to the violent exactions of Cromwell's major-generals. No salary was claimed by the commissioners who conducted the government, though they voted themselves a bodyguard; and they had the courage to reduce the salaries of the public servants. Great exertions were made to appoint sheriffs, justices of peace, and magistrates attached to Republican principles, so as to secure their aid at the next election. It was probably the fear of holding an election with the old Cromwellian sheriffs and other magistrates which induced them to continue sitting. On the 6th of June, 1659, they voted that they should cease to sit on the 7th of May, 1660.

No body of men changes its members more rapidly than an army; which, to retain its efficiency, must be composed of young men possessed of the highest bodily vigour. Thus we may be sure that the soldiery of the Protectorate had lost a large number

---

* Slingsby Bethell, in a tract written during the reign of Charles II. "The World's Mistake in Oliver Cromwell" (republished in the Harleian Miscellany), tells us : " When this late tyrant or Protector (as some call him) turned out the Long Parliament the Kingdom was arrived at the highest pitch of trade, wealth, and honour that it in any age ever yet knew. The trade appeared, by the great sums offered them for the customs and excise, nine hundred thousand pounds a year being refused. The wealth of the nation showed itself in the high value that land and all our native commodities bore, which are the certain marks of opulency. Our honour was made known to all the world by a conquering navy, which had brought the proud Hollanders upon their knees to beg peace of us upon our own conditions, keeping all other nations in awe; and, besides these advantages, the public stock was five hundred thousand pounds in stores, and the whole army in advance, some four and none under two months ; so that, though there might be a debt of near five hundred thousand pounds upon the kingdom, he met with about twice the value in lieu of it."

of the yeomanry or citizens who had quitted their freeholds or trades to fight for the cause of the Long Parliament.

Those who had not retired at the close of the civil wars or during the eight years which had passed away between the Battle of Worcester and the death of Cromwell, getting to look upon the army as the means of gaining their bread, had lost much of their civilian modes of thought and become more imbued with the habits of military discipline. Cromwell had used incessant care to remove those officers who, being friends of the Commonwealth, had disapproved of his usurpation.

"He weeded," says Mrs. Hutchinson, "in a few months' time above a hundred and fifty godly officers out of the army, with whom many of the religious soldiers went off; and in their room abundance of the King's dissolute soldiers were entertained, and the army was almost changed from that godly religious army whose valour God had crowned with triumph into the dissolute army they had beaten, bearing yet a better name."

The pay which Cromwell allowed to his soldiers was sufficiently high to attract men of a good class. They were in part recruited from the Independents, Anabaptists, and other sectaries. The inferior officers especially still retained their Republican feelings, blended in many cases with millenarian views; and it would be very unfair to compare them to a prætorian guard, anxious only for pay and plunder and ready to turn their swords against the helpless. Many of them wished well to the Commonwealth, but had, unhappily, learnt the lesson that the public interest must come behind their own private leanings and that they might safely dictate to the civil government. Cromwell's successors in the command of the army, looking to their men as the source of power, treated them with a familiarity which, especially in time of peace, soon becomes fatal to discipline; all the more so that till the passing of the Mutiny Act in the reign of William III. the laws against disobedience to superior orders were not at all strict.

"Examples of this kind of independence," writes M. de Bordeaux,* "are to be seen daily in London, where the corporals assemble together and deliberate on public affairs. The officers, on their side, hold their own councils, and all seem to dread an oligarchy and demand a republic, which would scarcely accord with the present state of public feeling in England.

"The Parliament meanwhile treats their inclinations with great consideration, and began last week to deliberate on the articles proposed by the army; those which regard the form of government, liberty of conscience and the reformation of the laws met with no difficulty."

* M. de Bordeaux to Cardinal Mazarin, June 9, 1659.

It is likely enough that the army was no longer the formidable body of men which had done such astonishing exploits in the time of the Long Parliament. It is true a small body of them under General Morgan had distinguished itself in Flanders; but at St. Domingo they had shamefully turned their backs upon the enemy. Still the reputation of their great victories and their formidable strength (about 50,000 men) kept the three countries in awe.

The Parliament and Republican party, who were not strong enough to propose disbanding this large body of men, sought to secure themselves from their hostility by raising a militia; but this seemed only to have diminished their popularity without increasing their strength, for the people disliked serving in the militia, and the militia never dreamt of coping with the regular army. The Wallingford House party still continued their meetings, and to please them Fleetwood was nominated commander-in-chief, and, as Ludlow tells us,

"that for the future no man might have an opportunity to pack an army to serve his ambition, as had formerly been practised, a Bill was prepared and brought in constituting the seven persons following—viz. Lieutenant-General Fleetwood, Sir Arthur Haslerig, Major-General Lambert, Colonel Desborough, Colonel Berry, Sir Henry Vane, and myself, to be commissioners for the nomination of officers to be presented to the consideration and approbation of the Parliament."*

Much dissatisfaction was exhibited at the proposal for the officers to receive their commissions from the Speaker. Desborough openly said that he accounted the commission he had already to be as good as any the Parliament could give, and that he would not take another. Considerable difficulty was found in restoring some Republican officers, such as Alured, Overton, and Okey, who had been cashiered by Cromwell for their Republican principles. Sir Arthur Haslerig had a regiment; Ludlow was prevailed upon to take one also. He was soon after made commander-in-chief of the army in Ireland.

This force seems to have been somewhat undecided in its views, some favouring the Protector, some the Wallingford House party, and others being attached to the Commonwealth. As many of the officers held large estates in Ireland they were not very anxious to leave that island to dispute with their comrades about supremacy. Lawson got a separate command from Admiral Montague, known to have a leaning to the Royalists. Monk remained at the head of the army, in Scotland, watching every

---

* Ludlow's Memoirs, vol. i. pp. 660-3.

turn of events, but not feeling it for his advantage to interfere in English affairs.

The strength of the Republican party might appear greater in opposition to Richard Cromwell than when it took the charge of affairs, for now all the Royalists who had reinforced it turned to pull it down. Its connexion with the army was of a very different character from what it had been before the Long Parliament had been turned out by Cromwell and Harrison. That prestige of vigour and success so nobly earned by ceaseless watchfulness, able statesmanship, and great victories by land and sea had been treacherously torn from it. Cromwell, who had reaped the fruits of what they had sown and watered, did his best to calumniate them,* while they had now to struggle against the confusion which he had left behind him.

Even those soldiers who openly regretted their fault in turning out the Long Parliament might be expected to repeat it if their resentment should be aroused by any vote which displeased them. The Government was thus weak; and no government will be respected, much less trusted, by the mass of people for wisdom alone. The Long Parliament before its violent dissolution could not claim to represent the whole of England: that it should represent the conquering party was a necessary result of the civil war. The excluded Presbyterian members soon appeared demanding their seats; nor was it easy for those who had been chased out of the House by Cromwell to show that they had a better right to vote than those who had been chased out by Colonel Pride. At best, then, they were a provisional government who engaged to take the direction of affairs until a new Parliament should be called; and, viewed as such, a better government could not at that time be had. Some people cannot get rid of the idea that these statesmen advocated a democracy such as exists in the United States, with universal suffrage and the rule of the majority. No such republic had, however, at that time ever been heard of, nor was such a scheme of government dreamed of by the Long Parliament. Up to the present

---

* With respect to the insinuation or accusation brought by Cromwell against the Long Parliament that the Bill for their Dissolution which he took away and destroyed contained a clause that the sitting members should retain their seats without re-election, and that they should be allowed to render null the election of those disagreeable to them, Mr. Christie, in his "Life of Sir Anthony Ashley Cooper, first Earl of Shaftesbury," published since our article in the WESTMINSTER REVIEW on the "Republicans of the Commonwealth," July, 1871, has remarked (vol. i. p. 93): "I cannot suppose, with Mr. Carlyle, that the Bill contained a clause providing that every member of the Rump should be a member of the New Parliament without election." See the whole question fully examined in Mr. Bisset's "History of the Commonwealth of England," vol. ii. pp. 469–474.

day the power to elect representatives is in the hands of a
minority of the grown-up citizens of our country, nor do we
conceive that a majority has any right to oppress a minority with
an intolerable government. It seems probable that at several
times the majority of the people of Great Britain would have
brought back the Stuarts even after the Revolution of 1688. If
a majority of the present electors of Great Britain were to be
bent on bringing in such a rule as that of Charles I. or Charles
II. we should be ready, if there appeared a chance of success, to
take part with the minority against them.

At any rate the Commonwealth party were not at all disposed
to admit that they should be deprived of the liberties which
they had won through many a battle and siege by a simple
majority of the electors of the old shires and boroughs. They
wished to exclude the government of a single person; they
desired religious toleration and a free press, and that no favour
should be shown to any privileged class, and they knew that this
would not be granted by Charles Stuart. They pointed out in a
very clear manner the evils which would ensue from the return
of the Royalist party—predictions which were literally fulfilled.*

The greatest of all the political writers of the Commonwealth
was undoubtedly James Harrington, born in 1611. He had
been the pupil of Chillingworth at Oxford. He served for a few
months in Lord Craven's regiment in Holland, and attended the
Prince of Orange in a journey he made to the Court of Denmark,
after which he visited Flanders, France, and Italy, making
himself acquainted with the manner in which these different
countries were governed. The constitution of Venice, the oldest
republic in Europe, where he resided some time, attracted his
attention. It was, he said, a government for preservation. He
admired the equality granted to those allowed to take a part in
the government, but blamed its oligarchical tendency. He does
not in the civil wars appear to have taken an active part, though
favouring the popular side. In the year 1646 he was engaged
by the commissioners appointed by the Parliament to take the
captive King from Newcastle and attend Charles, as one already
known to him, and not engaged to any party or faction. Charles
was fond of his conversation about books and foreign countries;
and, as Anthony Wood tells us, "they had often discourses concerning government, but when they happened to talk of a
commonwealth the King seemed not to endure it." Being anxious
to induce both parties to make conciliations he became suspected
by the Parliament and was for some time under arrest, till

---

* The reader will find these considerations confirmed by the tract of Milton,
"The Ready and Easy Way to establish a free Commonwealth."

liberated by Major-General Ireton. He became a member of the Council of State before Cromwell's usurpation, and was again a member when the Long Parliament was recalled. Harrington is known as the author of the "Oceana," a book which, though never popular, has been often studied by philosophical politicians. Upon a tedious structure of political romance Harrington introduces a number of original discourses upon political combinations, and examines with deep philosophical insight the constitution of different governments, from those of the Greeks and Hebrews down to those of the Dutch and Venetians. It is one of the truest signs of the political sagacity of Plato and Aristotle that some of their remarks are still of value even to the present day; and many of Harrington's political speculations apply to our own times as well as to those of the Commonwealth.

The MS. of the "Oceana" was seized by Cromwell's police, but was given up again to the author at the intercession of the Protector's favourite daughter, Lady Claypole. It was inscribed to Oliver Cromwell, who, after reading it, said—

" the Gentleman had like to trepan him out of his power, but that what he got by the Sword he would not quit for a little paper shot ; adding, in his usual cant," says Toland,[*] " that he approved the Government of a single person as little as any of them, but that he was forced to take upon him the office of a High Constable to preserve the Peace among the several Parties in the nation, since he saw that being left to themselves they would never agree to any certain form of Government, and would only spend their whole power in Defeating the Designs or destroying the Persons of one another."

Besides being a member of the government, Harrington was the leading debater at a club called the Rota, of which the Royalist Anthony Wood gives some account. "Amongst the members were Henry Nevil, Major Wildman, and other well-known Republicans. The arguments of the Parliament House were but flat to those of the Rota. This club had a ballot-box which attracted much attention. They were in favour of the proposal of magistrates and senators going out by rotation as in Venice and Switzerland." "The views propounded at this club," says Anthony Wood, " were very taking, the more because as to human foresight there was no probability of the King's return ;" and accordingly we find the opinions of Harrington or those of the Rota reproduced in the political speeches and pamphlets of that time. Harrington had the sagacity to recognise the true

---

[*] " The Oceana of James Harrington and his other works, some whereof are now first published from his own Manuscripts, with an exact account of his life, prefixed by John Toland." London. 1870. P. 17.

historical character of the Great Revolution. To use the words
of Toland—

" he was convinced that no Government is so accidental or arbitrary an
Institution as people are wont to imagine, there being in Societies
natural causes producing their necessary effects, as well as in the Earth
or the Air. Hence he frequently argued that the Troubles of his time
were not to be wholly attributed to wilfulness or faction, neither to
the misgovernment of the Prince, nor the stubbornness of the people,
but to a change in the Balance of Property, which ever since Henry
the Seventh's time was daily falling into the Scale of the Commons
from that of the King and the Lords, as in his Book he evidently
demonstrates and explains. Not that hereby he approved either the
Breaches which the King had made on the Laws, or excused the
severity which some of the subjects exercised on the King, but to
show that as long as the Causes of these Disorders remained, so long
would the like Effects unavoidably follow."

Harrington was the first to give prominence to the view that
empire follows the balance of property—that is, if the possessors
of property be few in number the government is an oligarchy.
If one man hold in his hand the greater part of the property of
a country it is absolute monarchy, but if property be in the hands
of the people the government becomes a commonwealth. In a
country like England as it was then constituted it was natural
that landed property should receive the greater share of his
attention, for at that time its relative value over moveable
property was much greater, and a much larger part of the population was dependent for their subsistence on the cultivation of
the soil. Nevertheless, he remarks, in such cities as subsist
mostly by trade and have little or no land, as Holland and
Genoa, the balance of treasure may be equal to that of land.
Viewing the form of government as the natural adaptation of the
superstructure—that is, the laws and constitution to the foundation, that is, the distribution of property and the social habits
and customs of the people—Harrington considered that a change
in the foundation might be accelerated, if not actually brought
about, by laws affecting the distribution of property ; hence he
proposed an agrarian law by which no one should be allowed to
inherit more than a rental of 2000*l.* a year. We know not whether
any writer before him in England proposed and argued in favour
of the ballot, which he had seen in use at Venice. He advocated liberty of conscience and a complete system of national
education.

Views so enlightened could not perhaps have been carried into
effect all at once ; but the successful establishment of a commonwealth under the guidance of great statesmen would, it seems to
us, have given a milder and more equal spirit to our laws and a

M 2

wiser and nobler course to our national life. It is very likely that those of the present day who judge them so harshly have never reflected how things must have been viewed in those times. At present it is the march of Democracy and Socialism which excites alarm in Europe. At that time the progress of Despotism must have been regarded with fear and anxiety by every lover of freedom. All the old feudal kingdoms were passing or had passed into absolute monarchies. The statesmen of the Commonwealth had no experience of a successful constitutional monarchy such as has existed more or less since 1688. The prerogatives of a king of England were so great, numerous, and far-reaching that they could not coexist with civil liberty if the throne were occupied by a dynasty always putting them into full stretch against the rights of the people. Charles I. had refused to abandon those powers deemed incompatible with constitutional liberty, and they wisely judged it was impossible to trust to the honour of his son and the stupid loyalty of the Cavaliers. On the other hand, they had an encouraging example of the success of republican government in the United States of the Netherlands, who, to use the words of Milton, "to us inferiour in all outward advantages, notwithstanding, in the midst of great difficulties, courageously, wisely, constantly went through with the same work, and are settled in all the happy enjoyments of a potent and flourishing republic to this day."

Holland has in the end lapsed into constitutional monarchy, more owing to the peculiarity of its geographical position than through any incapacity for republican freedom. Continually exposed to the attacks of its powerful neighbours of Spain, France, and Great Britain, the necessity of self-preservation compelled it to support a large army, in great part composed of mercenaries, and it was through their great talents in leading these armies that the princes of the House of Orange rose to power and, in the end, to regal dignity. The cause of the failure of the English Republic seems to us to have been, as indicated by all the Republican statesmen and writers of the time, the establishment of a military despotism through the guilty ambition of Cromwell and the disorders which his example left behind him amongst the generals of his great standing army. Unhappily for their reputation the Republican party in England left no heirs to their politics. They have been judged by historians deeply imbued with monarchical principles. If Holland has been unjust to some of her Republican statesmen succeeding generations repented of that injustice. If through the folly of the times John Barneveldt perished on the scaffold and the De Witts were torn to pieces by a furious mob, the historians of the Netherlands, whether monarchical or not, do justice to their patriotism and

regret their fate. But the historians of England follow one
another in talking contemptuously of the statesmen of the Commonwealth ; they pass over their great services or boldly attribute
them to others. They quote the letters and pamphlets of the
Royalists as if they were real and fair history, in the same way
that a future historian might quote the leader of a county Tory
newspaper against the government of Mr. Gladstone, while
those writers like Mr. Godwin, Mr. Forster, and Mr. Bisset,
who have the courage to question the prevailing delusion, have
only got a small share of the reputation they have merited.

A projected insurrection of the Royalists was made known
to the Parliament through the aid of Thurloe, the secretary
of Cromwell, who gave the Commonwealth the benefit of his
means of obtaining intelligence. The Parliament was thus able
to take such measures that the insurrection was easily put down,
and General Lambert, who had been entrusted with this affair,
returned with the idea that he could imitate Cromwell. The
leaders of the insurrection were punished with a mildness which
had never before been shown in the Civil Wars, but the confiscation of their estates was a great help to the Commonwealth
labouring under financial difficulties.

Lambert persuaded the officers to draw up a petition which,
if the Parliament had acceded to, would have been a virtual
forfeiture of the control of the army. They demanded that
Fleetwood should be made commander-in-chief without any
limitation of time, and that Lambert, Desborough, and Monk
should also have high commands, and that no officer should in
future be dismissed without a court-martial. They blamed the
Parliament for not using greater vigour in suppressing the late
rebellion of Sir George Booth, and complained that the officers
of the army had not been sufficiently rewarded ; the last especially an audacious misstatement. Sir Arthur Haslerig called
the attention of Parliament to this petition before it was delivered, and any further subscriptions to it were forbidden. In a few
days, however, Colonel Desborough himself delivered one of
similar character, coming from the council of Wallingford House.
The Parliament, which had done its best to avoid a conflict,
when fairly forced into it, acted with courage and dignity. Fleetwood, Lambert, Desborough, and six others were dismissed from
their appointments, and the command of the army committed
to the charge of seven persons, Haslerig, Ludlow, Monk, and
Fleetwood, and Colonels Overton, Morley, and Walton. Orders
were given to arrest Lambert, and Sir Arthur Haslerig declared his resolution to have him shot.

Haslerig was one of the leading spirits in the Council of
State. He is described by Ludlow as

"sour and morose of temper, liable to be transported with passion, and to whom liberality seemed to be a vice. Yet, to do him justice, I must acknowledge that I am under no manner of doubt concerning the Rectitude and Sincerity of his Intentions, for he made it his business to prevent Arbitrary Power whensoever he knew it to be affected, and to keep the Sword subservient to the Civil magistrate."

In respect to Haslerig's bearing the apologies of his friends are at one with the accusations of his enemies. Haslerig was a man of good estate; he was one of the five members whom Charles I. had tried to arrest in the House of Commons; he had proved himself a gallant officer in the Civil Wars, had been made governor of Newcastle and the districts around, and was accused of using great rapacity in sequestrating estates for the benefit of the Long Parliament. Cromwell had offered him a seat in his House of Lords, which Haslerig refused. "As to the State," says Clarendon, "he was perfectly Republican, and as to religion perfectly Presbyterian."

The cashiered generals now appeared, with the soldiers who took their part, and endeavoured to gain over those regiments placed round Westminster for the defence of the Parliament. A scene took place which has often had its counterpart in the disorderly republics of South and Central America. It soon became clear that very few of the soldiers were willing to fight against their old commanders, and the Parliament, being the weaker body, had to yield. To use the words of Whitelocke—

"The *Council of State* so managed the business and so persuaded with all parties, that at the last they came to an Accommodation, to *save the effusion of blood;* and the Parliament was not to sit, but the council of Officers undertook to provide for the preservation of the Peace, and to have a form of Government to be drawn up for a *new Parliament* to be shortly summoned, and so to settle all things.

"This being agreed upon (and it could not be obtained otherwise) the Council of State in the Evening sent their Orders, requiring all the Soldiers of each Party to draw off, and to depart to their several quarters, which was obeyed by them."

Thus fell, for the second time, by military violence, the remainder of the Long Parliament, generally called the Rump Parliament, after having been in power about five months, during which the members of the Government ruled the country under very difficult circumstances, without their adversaries being able to reproach them with any lack either of ability, courage, or honesty, though they wanted one thing, which by some people is considered worth all these virtues together, they wanted success. Their foreign policy, though opposed to that of Cromwell, was prudent and dignified, and made them respected abroad, if the violence of faction would not allow them to be justly esteemed at home.

Mr. Lockhart, their ambassador, had been received with great distinction at Madrid, and had concluded the war with Spain, which, begun in such bad faith, had so much helped the ambition of France and been disastrous to English commerce.[*] Algernon Sidney had, with the support of a powerful fleet, acting in accord with the neighbouring Republic of Holland, compelled the King of Sweden to raise the siege of Copenhagen, it being at that time thought of great importance to prevent Sweden gaining nearly the whole coast of the Baltic.

The revolution caused a split both in the Republican and Military parties. Vane became a member of the Committee of Safety, along with Lambert, Desborough, and Fleetwood, not because he approved of their violence, but because he feared that permanent disagreement with the army would prove fatal to the Republican cause. Ludlow, too, consented to have his name put upon the Committee of Safety, hoping, "as they were now under the government of the sword, to procure the best government that could be, got." By his means a correspondence was kept up between Vane and their more unyielding colleagues in the Parliament, such as Scot and Haslerig. Whitelocke accepted the charge of the Great Seal, principally, he assures us, to watch Vane, of whose views he was an opponent. Bradshaw died about this time, "a stout man and learned in his profession. No friend of monarchy."[†]

The Committee of Safety promised to call a Parliament upon the 23rd of January following, and it appears, from Whitelocke's Memorials, that they took some trouble in preparing a constitution. They must very soon have become conscious of the extreme dislike with which they were viewed by the country, which was not a little augmented by the insolence and disorders of the soldiers.

"In all these commotions," writes M. de Bordeaux (London, October 30th, 1659), "the troops of England have avoided divisions, and the minority has always given way to the majority, whatever cause the latter may have embraced; for which both deserve praise, as union is alone capable of securing them against the general hatred of the whole nation, which endures a military government with regret, and yet has not courage to make an effort to free itself from its yoke."

But in a few days it became known that Monk was dissatisfied

---

[*] The author of "The World's Mistake in Oliver Cromwell" (Harleian Miscellany, 390) says that in the war with Spain we lost 1500 English ships, "according as was reported to that assembly called Richard's Parliament."
[†] Whitelocke's "Memorials."

with the proceedings of the Committee of Safety, had declared for the Parliament, and was preparing to march southward with a portion of the army which he commanded.

It appears that Whitelocke clearly saw the nature of the crisis, and foresaw the line of conduct which Monk would take. He advised Fleetwood either to declare at once for a free Parliament or to send some person of trust to Breda and offer the crown to Charles Stuart upon satisfactory terms ; otherwise Monk would deceive Scot and Haslerig and their associates, and bring in the King without making any terms for the country, whereby the lives and fortunes of the Parliamentary party would be at the mercy of the Cavaliers.

Fleetwood was, however, of too undecided a character to take the choice of two such vigorous alternatives.

When Lambert marched to meet Monk it soon became clear that his confederates were not able to hold the country behind them.   The Governor of Portsmouth admitted Sir Arthur Haslerig and Colonel Morley into that fortress, which now became a rendezvous for the friends of the Parliament. Admiral Lawson brought his fleet into the Thames and declared for the Parliament   Sir Henry Vane endeavoured to gain him over, but he preferred to listen to the arguments of Scot and Sir Anthony Ashley Cooper, who were active on the other side.   Sir Charles Coote assured Cooper of six thousand men out of Ireland on the first notice,* and Fairfax, though much enfeebled by the gout, rose in Yorkshire, gathered together a mingled army of Presbyterians, Royalists, and Republicans, joined by some of Lambert's soldiers, so that before he crossed the borders Monk received the news that the Parliament was restored.   The military junto fell to pieces without a blow. Lambert was deserted by his soldiers in the North, as Desborough was in the South. At Wooler, in Northumberland, Monk received a message from the Parliament thanking him for his services, but not asking him to march further southward, without, however, daring to forbid him. After holding a council of his officers, he determined that they should still continue their march. Historians have taken much trouble to inquire into the intentions of Monk, whether from the beginning he really designed to restore the King, as he and his friends gave out after that event was accomplished, or whether, as Clarendon seems to have believed, the conviction was forced upon him on his march through England that the Rump Parliament had not reputation enough to preserve themselves and those who adhered to them. The nation had now

* See a "Life of Sir Anthony Ashley Cooper, first Earl of Shaftesbury." By W. D. Christie. London. 1871. Vol. i. p. 200.

become tired out by continual insecurity, by the succession of upstart generals without the capacity to rule, and parliamentary politicians without the power, by the insolence of military government without its strength, and by the continuous decline of discipline and authority, which seemed to be rapidly converting the army into bands of janissaries. There is no proof that Monk ever seriously designed, like Lambert, to occupy the place of Cromwell; he seems to have been more given to avarice than ambition. He felt himself getting old, and was anxious to retire upon his spoils; but by his march to London he had put himself at the head of the government, in place of Fleetwood and Lambert. He was now the umpire and arbitrator of everything, and at whatever period the intention to restore the King may have entered his mind he possessed the one quality necessary to carry it through, and that was untruthfulness. To make a Republican army bring back the King required a man who laid not the slightest stress upon promises, to whom lying and perjury were ready weapons, and who could desert his friends, lull his opponents to sleep by promises, betray the soldiers who trusted him, and sell the liberties of England for a dukedom and a sum of money. This man has received due praise from the Royalists, who are not very nice in the choice of their heroes. People who are taught to pray that they might follow the example of King Charles, the martyr of the Episcopalian mythology, may consistently admire "honest George Monk," as Hume delights to call him; but certain it is that, after the Restoration, when he became an object of public attention, he appeared so dull and stolid that men were somewhat surprised he could have succeeded in playing his part so successfully. It seems very likely that Monk derived much assistance from the advice of Sir Anthony Ashley Cooper, a man of great political tact, and possessed with a singular power of persuading those who came within his personal influence.

Nevertheless, the immediate leaders of the two opposing parties did not know how near things were to the end. The remains of the old Parliament again met, Scot and Haslerig and others completely deceived by the protestations of Monk in favour of the good old cause and hatred to the rule of a single person. "Sir Arthur Haslerig, Walton, and Morley," as Whitelocke records in his Memorials, "came into the House in their riding-habits, and Haslerig was very jocund and high." On the other hand, Charles Stuart and his advisers felt their hopes fading away.

"The surprising restoration of the Parliament," writes Clarendon,*

---

* "History of the Rebellion." Oxford. 1712. Vol. iii. p. 707.

,, that had been so often exploded, so often dead and buried, and was the only image of power that was most formidable to the King and his party, seemed to pull up all their hopes by the roots. There remained only within the King's own breast some faint hope, and God knows it was very faint, that Monk's march into England might yet produce some alteration."

But Vane was not so easily deceived by outward appearances; he had, for taking a part in the Committee of Safety, been ordered to return to his house at Raby. Before leaving London he said to Ludlow, " Unless I am much mistaken Monk has still several masks to pull off." It would have been impossible in fewer words to indicate the game Monk was playing. Vane added —

" For what concerns myself I have all possible satisfaction of mind as to those actions which God has enabled me to do for the Commonwealth ; and I hope the same God will fortify me in my sufferings, how hard soever they may be, so that I may bear a faithful testimony to His cause."

It happened most unluckily for the Commonwealth, that during these disorders in England the control of the army in Ireland had fallen into the hands of a party acting under the name of the Parliament, who refused to receive Ludlow as their commander-in-chief, on pretence of his having forfeited his command by becoming a member of the Committee of Safety. Ludlow landed at Duncannon, but was recalled by the restored Parliament to answer the charges against him. If he had remained at the head of the army in Ireland he would, no doubt, from his military talents and steady attachment to the Commonwealth, have been a formidable adversary to Monk. As it was, the control of affairs in Ireland fell into the hands of a number of men who joined in all the measures of Monk to restore the King. Monk's first care was to weed the army of all those officers who, he thought, might oppose his designs. This process of weeding had been carried out so often that men of independent spirit must have felt the post of officer to have been a very insecure one. Oliver had weeded the army of the Republican officers ; the Parliament had weeded the army of the Cromwellians ; Lambert had weeded the army of the friends of the Parliament, who on being restored, had weeded out himself and his faction ; and now Monk set to weed the army of the little honesty and honour that could be left in the higher ranks.

The leaders of the Republican party, or at least those who did not save their reputation by turning traitors, still remain the outlaws of history : against them all slanders bear their own evidence, and the historian must suppress what amount of critical sagacity he may have, lest it should work out anything so unpo-

pular as a verdict in their favour. Mr. Christie, in his " Life
the Earl of Shaftesbury," tells us that there is

"no doubt that Haslerig, Scot, and other Republicans offered to support Monk if he would take the crown himself, since it is stated in
the account of events preceding the Restoration appended to later
editions of Sir Richard Baker's Chronicle, which, though ill written
and clumsily put together, has value as being known to have been
written with much assistance from Sir Thomas Clarges, Monk's
brother-in-law; and the statement is confirmed by many passages of
the dispatches of the French Ambassador, M. de Bordeaux."

We do not know why Mr. Christie does not add the testimony
of Clarendon,* which is much more explicit than that of Bordeaux. It is true that M. de Bordeaux speaks of the sovereignty
which he (Monk) enjoys in all but the name, and the sovereignty
which has been offered to him by the Republicans. Whether this
may be construed into an offer from Haslerig and Scot to make
Monk king is scarcely worth discussing, for at that time Bordeaux was not in the confidence of any of these politicians, and
the offer is said to have been a private one, and even denied by
Monk at the time. Mr. Christie does not assert that this grievous
calumny, which he is so ready to believe, can be traced directly
to Clarges, who, according to Bishop Burnet, was an honest man;
but if the story really comes from him, it must rest in the end
on the word of Monk, who was not an honest man. Is Monk,
who betrayed the faithful friends of the Commonwealth to their
destruction by a thousand falsehoods and perjuries, who accused
Argyll to Cromwell as no friend of his government, and at
Argyll's trial sent his private letters to support the accusation
that he was too much attached to Cromwell's government—is
this man to be suffered to blacken the character of his victims
to all posterity? Both Scot and Haslerig, though they might
have had their faults, were men of very different metal from the
eloquent, crafty, and time-serving politician whom Mr. Christie
vainly endeavours to make us believe to have been an honest and
faithful statesman. When the restoration of Charles II. was
known to be unavoidable, and some members of the Parliament
who had made war on King Charles, protested that they had
neither hand nor heart in the King's execution,

"Mr. Thomas Scot," as Ludlow† tells us, "who had been so much
deluded by the Hypocrisy of Monk, as I have already related, in
abhorrence of that base Spirit, said, That tho' he knew not where to

* "History of the Rebellion." Oxford. 1719. Vol. iii. Book xvi., p. 752.
† This bold declaration of Scot was sworn to by three witnesses at his
trial. See " State Trials," vol. ii. p. 331.

hide his Head at that time, yet he durst not refuse to own that not only his Hand, but his heart also was in it; and after he had produced divers Reasons to prove the Justice of it, he concluded that he should desire no greater Honour in this World than that the following Inscription might be engraved on his Tomb: *Here lieth one who had a Hand and a Heart in the execution of Charles Stuart late King of England.* Having said this, he and most of the Members who had a Right to sit in Parliament withdrew from the House."

Obviously this was not the man to put a crown on the head of George Monk.

It was the Cromwellians who proposed, one after another, to betray their cause, and bring back the King for their own individual profit and safety. In the list of traitors we have the two sons of Oliver himself, Richard and Henry Cromwell, then Lambert, finally Monk; but in this list there is not one of the great leaders of the Commonwealth party.

We have been induced to give a narrative of the events between the fall of Richard Cromwell and the interference of Monk as the best justification of the Parliamentary men; but it is neither necessary, nor indeed possible, to prolong the narrative into the further events of the Restoration, which are correctly enough given in most histories. By the introduction of the excluded members into the House of Commons the Presbyterians found themselves in a majority. Without believing, like Colonel Hutchinson, that had the old Independent party not withdrawn they might still have gained a sufficient number of votes from the other party to uphold the cause of the Commonwealth, it seems to us that, if they had consented to stay, they might have had a considerable influence on the deliberations of the assembly. As it was, the control of affairs was left entirely in the hands of Monk and the secluded members.

. The greatest mistake of the Long Parliament was to have neglected the earliest opportunity to call the country to elect a new Parliament and decide upon the form of government it desired. They thus gave themselves the appearance of a party anxious to govern the nation without daring to test the opinion of those whom they affected to represent. It was not inconsistent with the principles of the Cavaliers to hold down the great body of the nation, since they believed that the whole nation was born in subjection to the reigning monarch and his heirs, and this subjection it was a sin either to escape or throw off. In the same manner an aristocracy may consistently hold under those whom they believe born to be ruled by them; but for men calling themselves Republicans to hold under the larger portion of a nation seems a contradiction in terms, for people can be forced to be subject, but cannot be forced to be free. Had the

Long Parliament been allowed to carry out its own dissolution, as it was preparing to do when interrupted by Cromwell, it is possible that a Commonwealth might have been established by the votes of the majority of the electors in England; but the opportunity had passed away. The people now wearied of military despotism, and, losing all trust in a party which had so often been trampled under by the soldiery, were ready to abandon all the fruits of the Civil War for the repose of a government that would save them from military rule. It was in vain for Milton to pour out his eloquent warnings, which, ratified by experience and preserved by the fire of genius, remain like a continual reproach to the nation that allowed them to pass unheeded.

The elections going almost everywhere against the Republicans, brought in a large majority of the Presbyterians and Cavaliers. The King was restored without any conditions save the voluntary declaration which ho addressed to the Parliament from Breda. This was mainly accomplished through the artifices of Monk, who perceived it was for his own personal interest that Charles should come back unembarrassed by any promises or limitation to his power. It has become the custom to represent that it was necessary to hurry through the Restoration for fear that the discontented soldiers should gather to a head and take vengeance upon those who had betrayed them; but historians, in their anxiety to do justice to this line of argument, fail to see, or at least to point out, that the army had a double reason to be discontented; first, that Charles was restored at all, and second, that it was proposed to restore him without any conditions, leaving themselves, their friends, and leaders exposed to the vengeance of the Cavaliers whom they had so often defeated in the field, and leaving the good old cause for which they had risked their lives and which many of them still loved, to be treated as a failure and a crime. It therefore does not appear very clear, if the proposal made by Sir Matthew Hale and supported by Prynne, that conditions should be offered to the King, would have increased the discontent or danger of discontent from the army. The danger of restoring the King without conditions was very much greater than the danger of restoring him with conditions; and, allowing that there was a danger in both, was the danger not worth the risk? It was indeed impossible for such an important transaction as the Restoration to be accomplished with such rapidity as not to allow the army time to think about it. Three months passed away from the time when the secluded members were restored and the Long Parliament was dissolved, and a month passed away after his declaration from Breda was delivered to the Convention Parliament, until he landed at Dover to take possession of the throne.

The whole nation appeared frantic with an outburst of joy
and loyalty, not at all befitting the commencement of the most
shameful period of English history. The account of the Restoration reads like the end of a novel, where everybody is made
happy save those who hindered the working out of the plot. ·
Unfortunately time and experience falsified the expectations of
every one who expected anything but misery and disappointment.
Charles II. receives a magnificent entertainment from the States
of Holland, upon whom he twice made an unjust war; he confirms
the declaration of Breda, which he was so soon to break, to a
trusting committee of Lords and Commons. This well-written
manifesto was composed by Hyde, who was made Lord Chancellor,
but whom, in the course of time and convenience, Charles allowed
to be chased into exile. The King listens graciously to a depu-
tion of the Presbyterians, for whom he has persecution in store.
He receives a sum of money from a deputation of the City of
London, which he afterwards repaid by depriving the City of its
charter; he sets sail from Holland in the *Naseby*, now christened
the *Royal Charles*, the same ship which the Dutch afterwards
burned in the Medway. On landing at Dover this excellent
prince is presented with a Bible—"the thing which he
valued most in the world;" he then reviews the army, which
he soon afterwards disbands; he arrives at Whitehall, where the
two Houses of Parliament "solemnly cast themselves at his feet
with all vows of affection and fidelity to the world's end." Charles
declares his firm attachment to parliaments, which towards the
end of his reign he entirely got rid of, and his fidelity to the
Protestant religion, which he afterwards renounced. The same
evening he commenced a connexion with a married woman,
whom he ennobled with the titles of Lady Castlemaine and
Duchess of Cleveland.

"The restoration of Charles II.," says Guizot, "was not the
consequence but the cause of a passionate outburst of the mo-
narchial spirit." Charles himself, in the very centre of this
frantic loyalty, was heard to remark, "he doubted it had been
his own fault he had been absent so long, for he saw nobody who
did not protest he had ever wished his return." The King had
been brought back by a Parliament in which the Presbyterians
were as strong as the Cavaliers, and in which there were still
some true friends of liberty, like Lord Fairfax and Mr. Pierre-
pont, who thought it was better to regulate events which they
could not control. Charles was restored to the limited prerogatives of a king of England; the bishops were still kept out of
the House of Lords; the great question of the control of the
militia left undecided; and a Bill was introduced to secure at
least for compensation the purchasers of the Church lands.

Those of the crown had been at once seized upon at the Restoration. Clarendon succeeded in frustrating the measure before the Commons, and the purchasers of the chapter lands, who could produce no title which would satisfy the Royalist courts of law, were ejected without any redress; though, according to Ludlow, they had paid a good price to the agents of the Long Parliament. The Duchess of Newcastle, on the other hand, remarks: "had they not sold such lands at easie rates few would have bought them, by reason the purchasers were uncertain how long they would enjoy their purchases."

The Cavaliers who, like the Duke of Newcastle, returned in the confident expectation of recovering all their estates, found the Act of Oblivion a great hindrance to their suits. In some cases they had sold their lands to pay their fines, and for this there was no remedy. Most of them, however, got back at least part of their estates, so that at the Restoration, as during the Civil Wars, a great shifting of property took place. The Life of the Duke of Newcastle, especially after his sad exile from England, is of little historical value. The Duchess was his second wife, maid-in-waiting to Queen Henrietta, married after he left England; we may therefore excuse the lady for confounding the Duke of Hamilton's expedition into England with that of Charles II. The Duchess had as good a right as Montaigne to say, "Je suis moy-mêsme la matière de mon livre;" but there is something very pleasing in her admiration of her husband, one of the worthiest of the Cavalier party. The book is principally noteworthy as giving an idea of the losses which the Cavalier party suffered in the Royal cause. The Duchess is too high and too loyal to say much of the Roundheads. She writes with a mixture of grace and indiscretion, candour and affectation, which is amusing enough.

By the King's declaration from Breda no one was to be punished save those who should be expressly excepted by Parliament. It had been originally advised by Monk there should be an amnesty without any exceptions. Ashley Cooper, now created Earl of Shaftesbury, protested that not a man should be excluded: "for if I should suffer such a thing," said he, "I should be the greatest rogue alive." Shaftesbury, however, is more leniently judged by his biographer than by himself. The members of the Government, Mr. Christie tells us—

"had each and all to make concessions of opinion and sacrifices of feeling. Royalists forgave Presbyterians and Cromwellites; the King placed old adversaries of his father and of himself in high offices around him; and it was required of the Presbyterian leaders to concur in exceptions from pardon, and join in the trial for their

lives of some who had brought Charles the First to the scaffold and
had in arms resisted the Restoration."

In short, the Royalists had to forgive their old enemies, the
Presbyterians to slaughter their old friends. It must be allowed
that the Royalists had a better part to play, though they seemed
to do it with more reluctance. Monk—who had served and
betrayed more parties than any one save Shaftesbury, who was
destined to betray one more, Montague the friend of Cromwell,
Lord Manchester, Denzil Hollis, and others who had fought
against the King had now the honour of sitting as judges upon
some of their old political allies. Charles II. and the more
furious of the Royalist party at first expected that all the late
King's judges should be put to death; but it was determined in
the Convention Parliament that the number of those attainted
for life and estate should be reduced to seven. There were
many debates on this subject, both in the Houses of Lords and
Commons. Names were put in and struck out, and it was
actually carried that the nearest relations of four lords who had
been beheaded for taking part in the Royalist cause should each
choose one of those who were to be executed, and this was done
by three of them. Charles II. had published a proclamation
commanding the late King's judges to give themselves up within
fourteen days, on pain of being made to lose the benefit of any
pardon or indemnity either as to life or estate; but in spite of
this implied promise, those who had trusted to the King's
honour were tried both for their lives and estates,* and one of
them, Scrope, was executed. Some writers have praised the
lenity which was shown at the Restoration, but it is to be
noticed that they do not give a full account of those who were
punished.

Twenty-nine of those concerned in the execution of the King
were tried for their lives and estates; all were condemned.
At the trials the doctrine of the divine right of kings was
assumed as the basis of the accusation; and as they held that
nothing could, under any circumstances, be lawful save with the
concurrence of the King, Lords, and Commons, it was clear that
a king, however guilty, could never be punished unless he himself desired it. The prisoners, on their side, insisted that in case
two of the three estates should be in the wrong and become dis-
possessed, the Commons could act alone.

Though refused counsel, and often interrupted, insulted, and
overruled, the accused defended themselves with courage and
dignity, some of them, especially Scot and Martin, with great

* See "State Trials." London. 1730. Vol. ii. p. 298.

ability. The sentence was, that they should be drawn upon hurdles to the place of execution and there hanged by the neck, and, being alive, cut down, their entrails to be taken out of their bodies (and they living), the same to be burned before their eyes, and their heads cut off, and their bodies to be divided into four quarters, and heads and quarters to be disposed of at the pleasure of the King's majesty.

This sentence was literally executed upon ten of them, six of whom had sat at the King's trial—Harrison, Scot, Scrope, Clements, Carew, Jones, and Cook, who had acted as solicitor. To these were added Colonel Hacker and Axtell, who had commanded the Guards at the execution, and Hugh Peters, an Independent minister, who had in his sermons publicly justified the punishment of Charles.

Harrison, one of the gallantest soldiers that ever lived, preserved to the last that enthusiastic spirit and that exulting faith which had ever made danger seem of no account to him. On the way to execution, he called several times aloud—

"*I go to Suffer upon the Account of the most glorious Cause that ever was in the World. As he was going to Suffer*, one in a Derision call'd to him and Said, *Where is your Good Old Cause?* He with a cheerful Smile clapt his Hand on his Breast, and Said, *Here it is, and I am going to Seal it with my Blood.* And when he came to the Sight of the Gallows, he was transported with Joy, and his Servant ask'd him how he did; he answered, Never better in my Life."

Scot replied to the sheriff, who refused to allow him to address the people, that "it is a very mean and bad cause which will not bear the words of a dying man."

They all died with the greatest fortitude, justifying their cause to the last. It was feared that Hugh Peters,* the preacher, would not have the same courage as the rest; but at the time of execution his fortitude rose. When Mr. Cook was cut down they brought Mr. Peters near

"that he might see it; and by and bye the Hangman came to him, all besmear'd in Blood, and rubbing his bloody Hands together, he tauntingly ask'd, *Come, how do you like this, Mr. Peters*, how do you like this Work?* To whom he reply'd, I am not (I thank God) terrified at it, you may do your worst."

Milton, who had justified the King's punishment as boldly as Peters, was not tried, though he was for some time in confinement. He is believed to have been saved mainly by the interest

---

* The character of Peters, who suffered much from the slanders of the Royalists, has been ably considered by Bancroft, in his "History of the United States," Boston, 1862, vol. ii. chap. xi. p. 32. Peters had once been Minister of Salem, and was the father-in-law of the younger Winthrop.

of Sir William Davenant, whose life he had been instrumental in saving when his own party was in power.

The other nineteen who had been tried were not put to death, as this could not be done without the consent of Parliament. All their property was forfeited, and they were confined in the Tower, where they were very cruelly treated. It being found that the charity of their friends procured them some alleviation of their miseries, they were disposed in remote dungeons, where most of them soon died. Okey, Barkstead, and Cobbet, who had escaped to the continent, were seized at Delft, with the consent of the States, by Downing, the King's resident in Holland, who had held the same post under Cromwell, and had once been a chaplain in Okey's regiment; they were conveyed to London, and put to death with the usual barbarities. Okey was one of the best officers during the Civil Wars, and had remained a faithful friend to the Commonwealth. He always bore the character of a man of honour and integrity. Three of the King's judges, Goffe, Whalley, and Dixwell, escaped to Massachusetts. Dixwell changed his name, married, and lived peacefully and happily amongst the inhabitants of New Haven.

"For nearly a year," says Bancroft, "Goffe and Whalley resided unmolested within the limits of Massachusetts, holding meetings in every house, where they preached and prayed and gained universal applause." When the Royalist warrants arrived for their apprehension they were searched for in all directions, and after hiding for months in the forests they escaped by night "to an appointed place of refuge in Hadley, and the solitudes of the most beautiful valley of New England gave shelter to their wearisome and repining age." When Hadley was surprised by the Indians during King Philip's war, the town was saved by the appearance of Goffe, the old Puritan soldier, now bowed with years, who darted from his hidingplace, rallied the disheartened, and having achieved a safe defence sunk away into his retirement to be no more seen.*

Haslerig and Whitelocke were included in the amnesty, the House of Commons being specially divided on their cases. Whitelocke paid an enormous fine to Charles, in order to secure himself from further molestation; for a vote of the House of Commons was scarcely sufficient to save a man from the Court. Harrington and Colonel Hutchinson were both imprisoned on groundless charges without ever being brought to trial. Harrington was set free after his health was permanently injured; but Hutchinson died at Sandown Castle, in Kent, in 1664, after eleven months' imprisonment. In his Memoirs written by his

----

* "History of the United States," vol. ii. chap. xi. p. 35, and chap. xii. 101.

faithful and high-minded wife, the reader will find an account of the cruelties practised on the King's judges by their gaolers, as well as on her own husband.

In directing judicial vengeance against the judges of Charles I. it might be said that only a section of the nation in whose name the King was accused had approved either of the trial or execution ; but the trial of Sir Henry Vane might be truly said to be the trial of the great party which had conquered in the Civil War, and which once at least had the adherence of a large majority of the people of England. Vane, when a young man, had taken a part in the impeachment of the Earl of Strafford, by delivering some papers against him which he had found in the cabinet of his father, Secretary Vane. He had been one of the Commissioners who had gained a Scottish army to assist the forces of the Parliament, and one of those sent to treat with the King at Uxbridge and at the Isle of Wight. The organizing of that unrivalled navy which had gained such great victories for the Long Parliament and for Cromwell was mainly his work. Writers of our own time have tried to represent him as an unpractical theorist, but his great sagacity was not denied even by his political enemies. Clarendon says that his understanding in all matters without the verge of religion was superior to that of most men. He was indeed unpractical in the same sense that a pure-minded and honest patriot in giddy revolutions and political emergencies is always more unpractical than an unscrupulous man willing to resort to any shift that will serve his purpose. The truth is, Vane was a far-sighted and sagacious statesman, who was not only wiser than his contemporaries but wiser than his party, for if they had listened to his advice they would have avoided the errors which in the end proved their destruction. He disapproved of the violent expulsion of the presbyterian members and of the execution of the King. He was zealous in urging on the Long Parliament to hurry through their dissolution when that assembly was expelled by Cromwell. He had steadily opposed the tyranny of the Protector and had been imprisoned on account of a pamphlet which he wrote against his government. We may be disposed to condemn him for taking a part in the Committee of Safety, though this is a point on which it is clear a good deal can be said on both sides.

Vane had opposed the Restoration to the last, more from a conviction that such was his duty than from any hope of success. His religious opinions attracted attention even amongst the wild enthusiasts of those times, not so much because they were more fantastic, as because they were more original. An absurdity believed in by millions of men does not seem so absurd as one believed in by one small sect. It appears from his work, " A

N 2

Retired Man's Meditations," that he was a millenarian or Fifth Monarchy man, that is, he believed that Christ would descend and that the saints would reign on earth for a thousand years as predicted in the Apocalypse; but there does not appear any proof that his interpretations of prophecy ever erroneously influenced his political conduct, nor do his religious opinions appear to have been much more extravagant than those of Cromwell.

Vane had been excepted out of the amnesty by the Convention Parliament along with Lambert; but at the same time there was a petition from both Houses of Parliament, which was assented to by the King, that their lives should in any case be spared. He had remained two years in close confinement, "unheard, unexamined," and deprived of his estates, when it was determined that he should be condemned to lose his life through the form of a trial. He was allowed no counsel, and his solicitors or others able to confer with him on matters of law, were refused access to him.

On his trial it was necessary to strain the law so as to rule that a Statute enacted under Henry VII., barring all prosecutions for persons acting under a government for the time being, referred to a Monarchy and not to a Commonwealth. Charles II. was held to be King of England *de facto* as well as *de jure* immediately on the death of his father. Vane was accused of keeping him out of his kingdom, before a court which declared he was at that time actually King. Copies of Sir Henry Vane's papers, containing the substance of what he pleaded, are published in the State Trials. Keeling, one of the King's counsel, is said to have observed on the arraignment day, "Though we know not what to say to him, we know what to do with him." He was declared guilty and sentenced to death.

It was impossible to condemn Vane for being member of a government which had existed several years and been recognised by the whole of Europe, without condemning his whole party, but his real crime was the high opinion men still had, both of his wisdom and integrity. The great men of his party had passed away; Pym, Hampden, and Ireton were dead; some had turned traitors to the cause, others had yielded to the tide; Vane had stood alone, courageously defending, at the hazard of his life, the rights of parliaments, the liberties of his country, and the honour of his cause. As the King wrote to Lord Clarendon, "Certainly he is too dangerous a man to let live if we can honestly put him out of the way." Charles could not honestly put him out of the way; but this mattered little. Vane has been represented by Burnet and Clarendon as a very fearful man. Ludlow writes, "that he had a resolution and courage not to be shaken or diverted from the public service."

However this may be, at his trial and execution he showed a dignity, fortitude, and courage which were altogether wanting in Lambert, the adherent and would be imitator of Cromwell. As it had been observed that the dying speeches of the regicides left a deep impression on the hearers, trumpeters were placed round the scaffold, that the last words of the great republican might be drowned whenever the sheriff should think fit. There is an account of his execution in Pepys's Diary.

"He changed not his colour or speech to the last, but died justifying himself and the cause he had stood for, and spoke very confidently of his being presently at the right hand of Christ; and in all things appeared the most resolved man that ever died in that manner, and showed more of heate than cowardice, but yet with all humility and gravity."

There is also an account of his execution and his last words in the State Trials, which is too long to repeat here, though we may give a short passage.

"Death is but a little Word, but 'tis a great Work to die ; it is to be but once done ; and after this cometh the Judgement, even the Judgement of the great God, which it concerns us all to prepare for. And by this Act I do receive a Discharge once for all out of Prison, even the Prison of the mortal Body also, which, to a true Christian, is a burdensome Weight. In all respects wherein I have been concern'd and engag'd, as to the Publick, my Design hath been to accomplish good Things for these Nations. Then (lifting up his Eyes and spreading his Hands) he said, I do here appeal to the Great God of Heaven, and all this Assembly, or any other Persons, to shew wherein I have defiled my Hands with any Man's Blood or Estate, or that I have sought myself in any publick Capacity or Place I have been in. The Cause was three times stated. *First,* In the *Remonstrance of the House of Commons. Secondly,* In the *Covenant, the Solemn League and Covenant."*—"Upon this the Trumpets sounded, the Sheriff catch'd at the Paper in his Hand ; and *Sir John Robinson,* who at first had acknowledg'd that he had nothing to do there, wishing the Sheriff to see to it, yet found himself something to do now, furiously calling for the Writers' Books, and saying, 'he treats of Rebellion, and you write it.' Hereupon six Note-Books were delivered up. The Prisoner was very patient and composed under all these Injuries, and Soundings of the Trumpets several Times in his Face, only saying, ''Twas hard he might not be suffered to speak ; but,' says he, 'my Usage from Man is no harder than was my Lord and Master's, and all that live his Life this Day must expect hard Dealing from the worldly Spirit.' The trumpets sounded again to hinder his being heard."

In the last words he spoke, he declared his confidence that all the clouds which seemed to overshadow his cause would yet disappear.

The worst punishment that men have for one another, is the same fate which hangs over us all.   Death has long ago overtaken the oppressors as well as their victims, and in reading this record of old violences and wrongs, the victim seems to triumph, the oppressors to be put to shame.   Let us leave the judges, the juries, the sheriffs, and the executioners to their base obscurity. The cause of Vane has triumphed, though those who now enjoy the liberty which he claimed, and for which he suffered, are little mindful, and little grateful to one of England's purest and greatest statesmen.

The Convention Parliament was dissolved, after sitting about seven months, and a new House of Commons was elected under the influence of that besotted loyalty which had greeted the return of Charles II. with such outbursts of rejoicing.   In this parliament, which was not renewed for nineteen years, the Cavalier party had a powerful majority, and proceeded to gratify their dislike to liberty, and their hatred to those who had upheld it.   They passed an Act declaring the whole right of controlling the militia to be in the King, thus deciding one of the most important points contested between Charles I. and the Long Parliament in a way which, if it has been fatal to the liberties of England, has at least given us a good many incapable commanders-in-chief, and cost us several humiliating military reverses.   They introduced the Bishops into the House of Lords.   In open violation of the Declaration of Breda, they passed the Corporation Act, by which all existing magistrates could be removed at the pleasure of Commissioners, and none could in future be eligible for office who had not within a year taken the sacrament according to the forms of the Church of England, who did not renounce the Solemn League and Covenant, and declare the unlawfulness of taking up arms against the King on any pretext.   This Act virtually excluded all honest Dissenters from holding any public offices.   By the Act of Uniformity, all beneficed clergymen were ordered to subscribe to a corrected copy of the Book of Common Prayer, in consequence of which two thousand clergymen of the Presbyterian persuasion left their livings on St. Bartholomew's Day.   At the urgent request of the King, those Provisions of the Triennial Bill, unanimously passed by the Long Parliament in 1641, by which if the King did not call a parliament in three years, it could be assembled without his consent, were abolished.   The only wonder is that they did not bring back the Star Chamber.

Indeed the parliament which represented the Cavaliers, vanquished in the field but now victorious at the polling-booths, was anxious to go farther than Charles and his minister Clarendon thought it safe or honourable to allow.   If we consider the overwhelming tide of servility of the nobility and clergy of the Church of England, the favourable reception and circulation given to books more slavish than any ever written under Asiatic despotism, advocating abject submission to the worst tyrants as an inviolable Christian duty, and when we reflect on the flood of vice and licentiousness which overwhelmed this unhappy generation, we may think that the greater part of the nation not only wished to get rid of its freedom, but to make itself unworthy of being free.

It was no doubt the dislike of the royalists to a standing army, founded on their recollections of the soldiers of Cromwell, the worthless character of Charles II., his indolence, and the gross incapacity of his administration at home and abroad, which saved the nation from totally sinking under the yoke of despotism. Though incapable of carrying out a steady plan of attack against the Constitution of the country, Charles had some able advisers who knew where to strike at the roots of popular freedom. After the Restoration it was no longer deemed possible openly to oppose the Parliament. The House of Commons kept the sole right of regulating Money bills; and the King was obliged to agree to the Habeas Corpus Act, brought in by the Parliament of 1679. It was thought more politic to endeavour to change the character of the electors than to withstand their representatives.

At the Restoration the landed aristocracy came back to the country in full power. In the Convention Parliament the feudal rights of wardship and military service, which had fallen into disuse, were finally abolished, and the loss to the Royal revenue was compensated by a tax upon beer and some other liquors falling upon the whole community. The pride of the aristocracy was much inflamed by the Restoration. The laws of entail and primogeniture were put in play with increased vigour, and were in the next reign introduced into Scotland. This in the end had a powerful effect in depressing the yeomanry and increasing the estates and influence of the great landed proprietors, so that at least they were enabled so to overawe their tenants and the dwellers in the smaller towns, that they had little difficulty in nominating those they pleased to parliament.

But perhaps the most formidable blow which was struck at popular liberties was the invasion of the charters. Since the days succeeding the Conquest, the chartered burghs had been the refuge of the oppressed and the steadiest asserters of constitutional liberty. If the City of London had been active in supporting the Restoration, and turning out the Long Parliament, it soon saw reason to abate in its loyalty, and had supported Shaftesbury when he turned against the Court. It was a grand jury of the city which threw out the bill for high treason against him.

Charles had found it a grievance that they should acquit those whom he wished condemned. It was suggested by Jeffreys that the validity of most of those charters might be inquired into by the writ of *quo warranto.* The charter of the City of London was first contested before the King's Bench, and on its being quashed the King gained the right of electing magistrates of the kind he desired. Thus, during the last three years of his reign, and during that of his successor down to the Revolution of 1688, the Crown was enabled to pack those murderous juries which under the direction of Jeffreys sent so many victims to the scaffold. Jeffreys was employed to make the same charge against many of the burghs. "The most trifling deviations from the terms of ancient charters, the most insignificant offences committed by the officers of boroughs, even against the most obsolete laws, were made the pretences of the forfeiting of charters."[*] And these cases were heard before judges named by the King and removable at his pleasure. Many towns were thus deprived of their charters, and many more gave them up without a contest.

"The King new modelled the charters and restored them, but reserved to the Crown the nomination to all power in the boroughs, and filled them with electors agreeable to himself. Measures which, had they not been defeated by the Revolution, could not have failed, by throwing Parliamentary elections into the hands of the Sovereign, to have introduced a tyranny the more painful to the subjects, because the old forms of freedom would have been continually before their eyes."

The agents of despotism did not forget to send a King's messenger across the Atlantic to the Puritan Commonwealth which was rising in the New World. Two hundred copies of the proceedings against the City of London were sent over to be distributed amongst the colonists of Massachusetts, who, after debating the matter, refused to give up their charter, which, notwithstanding, was taken from them by a writ issued in England.

During the last three years of the reign of Charles II., little seemed to remain of the liberties of the country. The republican party had ceased to exist. The last of the great Commonwealth men that appear in English history are Algernon Sidney and Edmund Ludlow.

Sidney[†] found it intolerable to live in England after the return of the Stuarts.

* Sir John Dalrymple's "Memoirs of Great Britain and Ireland." Edinburgh, 1771, p. 16. See also "Hallam's Constitutional History," vol. ii. chap. xii. p. 613.

† Quoted in "Disses's History," vol. ii. p. 137.

" I confess," he writes, " we are naturally inclined to delight in our own country, and I have a particular love to mine; I hope I have given some testimony of it. I think that being exiled from it is a great evil, and would redeem myself from it with the loss of a great deal of my blood. But when that country of mine is now like to be made a stage of injury, the liberty which we hoped to establish oppressed : the Parliament and army corrupted, the people enslaved, all things vendible, no man safe, but by such evil and infamous means as flattery and bribery : what joy can I have in my own country in this condition ? Shall I renounce all my old principles, learn the vile court arts, and make my peace by bribing some of them ? Better is a life among strangers, than in my own country on such conditions. . . . . . Let them please themselves with making the King glorious, who think that a whole people may justly be sacrificed for the interest and pleasure of one, and a few of his followers. Nevertheless perhaps they may find their King's glory is their shame, his plenty the people's misery."

Sidney returned to England after many years voluntary exile, to fall a victim to an unjust trial, and leave a heroic example to his countrymen.

When Ludlow found that resistance to the Restoration was hopeless he took refuge in Switzerland along with John Lisle, the husband of Alice Lisle, the lady who was put to death for harbouring a fugitive after Monmouth's rebellion. Lisle was murdered by royalist assassins, and several attempts were made upon the life of Ludlow, but without success. Though repeatedly asked, he had refused to engage in the desperate plots of the Wildmans and Fergusons against the Stuarts ; but when the news of the Revolution of 1688 reached the shores of the Lake of Geneva, Ludlow regarded it as the triumph of the cause to which he had been so honest and steady a friend.

" James," says Macaulay,[*] " had not indeed, like Charles, died the death of a traitor. Yet the punishment of the son might seem to differ from the punishment of the father rather in degree than in principle. Those who had recently waged war on a tyrant, who had turned him out of his palace, who had frightened him out of his country, who had deprived him of his crown, might perhaps think that the crime of going one step further had been sufficiently expiated by thirty years of banishment."

He was invited by some powerful members of the Whig party to return to England ; but it would appear that the horror with which the regicides were regarded had increased during the twenty-eight years when no man dared say a word in their excuse.

---

[*] " History of England." London, 1855, vol. iii. pp. 506-9.

"The absurd and almost impious service," says Macaulay, "which is still read in our churches on the thirtieth of January, had produced in the minds of the vulgar a strange association of ideas. The sufferings of Charles were confounded with the sufferings of the Redeemer of mankind ; and every regicide was a Judas, a Caiaphas, or a Herod."

It was brought to the notice of Parliament by some Tory member that one of the regicides had appeared openly in London, and whatever the Whigs may have thought on the matter, they had not the courage to defend him. Some days elapsed before a warrant could be issued against him, and the puritan soldier had time to escape from England and to return to the republican State which had sheltered him so long. He died in the seventy-third year of his age. We have seen his grave in the church of St. Martin, overlooking the little town of Vevey, and the quiet blue waters of the Leman lake, surrounded by the mountains on which he must often have gazed. On the church wall there is an inscription in which his widow records his courage in battle, his mercy to the vanquished, his love of liberty and hatred of arbitrary power. Beside him lies Andrew Broughton, who read the sentence of death on Charles I.

———————

Art. VI.—The Christian Evidence Society.

Modern Scepticism. Sixth Edition. *Faith and Free Thought.*
Hodder and Stoughton. 1872.

IF there be one sign of the times more patent than any other to the eye of the dispassionate observer, it is to be found in the gradual decay of the old theological beliefs. The condition of religious thought in Germany is too well known to readers of this *Review* to render any further allusion to it necessary ; and the subject has been brought under the notice of the general reader in a series of able sketches by the correspondent of the leading journal at Berlin. In France, the recent discussions in the Protestant Synod have brought to light the startling fact that a large proportion of French reformers have altogether thrown over a belief in miracles. We are in possession of evidence which would tend to show the immense progress of rationalistic views in America. We are, however, not concerned with these and other foreign countries just now, and must dismiss them with the remark that it would be indeed a strange phenomenon if a great mental movement, which is making itself so sensibly felt in other Protestant communities should have no counterpart in Protestant England. It is of England that we wish to speak ; and we may not only that it might be expected from what is witnessed elsewhere, that scepticism would make some progress here, but also that there is evidence that it is making very great progress. We are aware that in putting forth this statement, we are at issue with some great authorities ; for example, the *Times* newspaper, and apparently Mr. Disraeli. In the opinion of the statesman speaking not long ago at Manchester, the objections of scepticism have been victoriously refuted over and over again by "inexorable logic." If this be so, then the unbelievers, being altogether an unreasoning illogical class of men, can never hope to make progress and may safely be neglected, like the gentleman who laid a wager the other day that the earth was flat. The *Times* newspaper takes very much the same view. In an article on the Duke of Somerset's volume, the reviewer seems to contemplate "fashionable scepticism," (for the existence of an infidel tailor or shoemaker here and there may perhaps be admitted) as the crotchet of a few idle dilettanti, anxious to cut a figure in west-end drawing-rooms by their paradoxes. Probably a good-sized drawing-room would hold them all ; and if by chance, or by a special interposition, the roof should fall in on them so collected together, we presume that no more would be heard of their silly notions in "west-end circles" for a generation at least ! The same sort of language might doubtless have been heard in certain Roman "circles" with regard to Christianity, for centuries after the death of its founder. "A superstition confined to slaves and hair-splitting Greeks, 'wool-weavers, shoemakers, fullers, and rustics,'* with here and there a Tertullian and a Cyprian recruited from the ranks of advocates and teachers of rhetoric, or a philosophic pervert like Justin Martyr or Athenagoras. We do not profess to know exactly what the religion of these people is, but it must have existed a long time and made very little way, for we remember reading about it in our college days in the pages of Tacitus and the younger Pliny. Marcus Aurelius has noticed it, and Lucian too by the bye. And we believe that Celsus has taken the trouble to write against it. But as a general rule, none of our philosophers or historians or poets have thought it worth their while to take the least notice of it. No doubt the thing goes on, and converts are made, but one never hears anything about them in society except now and then, when the Emperors see fit to come down upon these lunatics." Such we may be sure was the sort of language used in fashionable com-

---

* These are the words of Celsus.

pany in the reign of Decius, and in the hearing of children whose old age was destined to witness the worldly triumph of the "deadly superstition," and the head of the State yielding spiritual obedience to the "Galilæan juggler."

If we wanted any confirmation of the truth of our statement, we might refer to witnesses on the orthodox side more competent from their position and the character of their studies to pronounce an opinion than Mr. Disraeli and the writer in the *Times*. What is the language of such men as Archbishop Thomson, Bishop Wilberforce, Dean Mansel, Dean Goulburn, Professor Mozley, Canon Liddon, Mr. Farrar, and a host of others; in fact, of all recent Christian apologists? We read of "a wide-spread movement of the mind indicative of the first stealing over the sky of the lurid lights which shall be shed profusely around the great Antichrist."[*] "The wide-spread movement against miracles."[†] "A wide-spread unsettlement of religious belief... an impression that the age is turning its back on dogmas and creeds."[‡] "The frightful prevalence of sceptical views among all classes of the community."[§] "A wide-spread defection from the faith which our fathers held."[‖] "A time of much doubt and trial."[¶] While a statesman who is at the same time a theologian, has not hesitated to speak of "hosts mustering and fields clearing for the greatest struggle which Christianity has ever had to face."[**] Utterances of this kind might be quoted to any extent; the stray specimens which we have given show that the orthodox are at length awakening to the real character of the peril which threatens them. In Sheridan's comedy of the "Critic," one of the characters in the burlesque is rebuked by Puff (at least it used so to be acted by Mr. Charles Mathews, though whether to be found in the original we do not recollect), for looking out for the advent of an incoming personage on the wrong side of the stage. This is very much what the bulk of the moderate and Low-Church clergy and laity have been doing for some time past. They have been looking out for the advent of Romanism on one side, while Scepticism has been stalking in on the other.

In truth, no person who has looked beneath the surface of society can be in the least doubt as to the correctness of what is here advanced. Scepticism, if not rampant, will be found to be

---

[*] Bishop of Winchester. Preface to "Reply to Essays and Reviews," p. ii.

[†] "Mozley on Miracles." Ch. ii.

[‡] Liddon. Preface to "The Divinity of our Lord," p. xvi.

[§] Goulburn. Preface to Bishop Magee's "Pleadings for Christ," p. 1

[‖] Farrar. "Witness of History to Christ," p. 8.

[¶] Archbishop Thomson. Preface to "Aids to Faith."

[**] Marquis of Salisbury. Speech at Liverpool, April, 1872.

latent in the most unexpected quarters. Even if, at any time and place, we felt ourselves at liberty to mention the names of men eminent in the Senate, at the Bar, in the Pulpit, from whose lips we have heard a practical disclaimer of all dogma, we should refrain from doing so, owing to our recollection of a jocose piece of advice once given to us by Minister (afterwards President) Buchanan. " Young gentleman," said he, "you have just told a story of something you saw in the United States, which I happen to know is true. But don't tell it again, for your own sake. Very few will believe you. *Rather relate something which is not true, and which will be believed.*" Readers of Hawthorne will remember his exquisitely philosophical tale of "Goodman Brown:" how the poor man, on being persuaded to go to a witch's meeting, found his wife, his pastor, his seemingly virtuous old school-mistress, and all the most esteemed of his neighbours there. So, if any one should be brought to conceive doubts, let him go about and enquire, and he will extract similar doubts from the learned College tutor, the orthodox rector, the Tory squire, the Independent or Baptist leader. Every one remembers the story told (if we remember rightly) by Seneca, of the proposal which was made in the Roman Senate to clothe the slaves in a distinctive dress, and of the reasons which were urged successfully against the project. If every sceptic were clothed in a like uniform to-morrow, we are of opinion that the result would be just as striking to all parties.

More than this, to any one who looks, not necessarily beneath the surface, but merely at the surface of things, it must be obvious that there are some strange appearances in the sky, though we do not regard them, with the early Christians and the Bishop of Winchester, as indicating the return of Nero, or of Antichrist in any form. Nothing is more remarkable than the change in educated feeling which has taken place within the last thirty years, that is, within the recollection of men of middle-age. We remember the time when an "infidel," a person who did not believe in the literal inspiration of the Bible, was to us a dark malignant being, capable of every atrocity. We looked upon him as the ignorant pagans looked upon the Christian who refused to worship their gods, or as this same Christian contemplated the pagan demons by whom he believed himself to be surrounded. Now, on the slightest provocation, over the evening cigar, or it may be from fair lips at the dinner-table, free-thinking senti-ments are uttered which would certainly at that time have relegated the speaker to Coventry. We should suppose that at the Athenæum Club, with its body-guard of bishops, a notorious unbe-liever was once as rare a sight as a General smoking a short clay-pipe on the steps of the Senior United. We have lived to witness both these phenomena, which, in the opinion of Dean Close and the Anti-tobacco League, may have some connexion with each other. In those days, infidel books were produced from dark shops and obscure alleys, somewhere in the neighbourhood of Holborn and Temple Bar, whence the works of Tom Paine were occasionally smuggled into their dormitories by sixth-form boys at public schools. Now, the first publishers announce edition after edition of volumes bearing eminent names, and which are as distinctly hostile to what is commonly called Revelation as anything that Tom Paine ever wrote. A similar change has come over the spirit of the periodical press. Not to say anything of this *Review*, which may at any rate claim to have held its present views in days when they were far less popular, able publications have sprung up like our contemporaries the *Fortnightly* and the *Contemporary*, in which it must certainly be admitted that theological subjects receive a "free handling." A much stronger term might be used to designate some bold and spirited, but too contemptuous articles which have appeared in *Fraser*, with the well-known initials "L. S." And the ablest of the London evening papers, the *Pall Mall Gazette*, has long been noted for articles, the tone of which may be judged by the following extracts:—

"A third answer is, Well, the whole subject (of religion) is involved in mystery, and whether the religion to which you have been accustomed is or is not exactly what one would call true, in that coarse and vulgar sense of the word in which we speak of a statement about common things being true, it is eminently respectable and useful, and, on the whole, speaking generally and subject to reasonable exceptions and modifications, it is not altogether improbable that the best course, at all events for the present, would be to take it as being about as true as it can reasonably be expected to be. . . . . . The third answer is that of the great majority of practical persons."—*Pall Mall Gazette*, June 8, 1872.

"The real question is not about the Athanasian creed, or the details of Mr. Bennett's language about the Sacrament; it is whether the whole Christian religion is or is not based on truth, and out of every seven members of the representative body of the French Protestant Church, four think that it is, and three that it is not. If any one supposes that questions which are asked under such circumstances, and which receive such answers at Paris, are not being asked and will not have to be answered in London, he does greatly err."—*Pall Mall Gazette*, July 4, 1872.

"The excessive activity of the clergy about all kinds of practical matters, and petty doctrinal questions, was probably never exceeded, but none or hardly any of them do the one thing that is indispensable. They do not give to the questions proposed to them answers as direct, pointed, and emphatic as the questions themselves. It is as if an invading army were marching upon London, and public meetings were being held all over London, voting against the enemy, considering how people might be got to dislike him, passing resolutions condemning his proceedings, and, in short, doing every sort of thing except meeting and beating him."—*Pall Mall Gazette*, Nov. 1, 1872.

The same change has manifested itself in the case of the provincial press. From the *Scotsman*, at Edinburgh, to the *Western Morning News*, at Plymouth, articles and reviews have of late appeared which completely strike at the root of the old doctrine of Biblical inspiration. After all this, well might Mr. Gladstone say, when speaking at Willis's Rooms in May last on behalf of King's College, " What is so common as to find, in the very best type, and in the best bindings, on the tables of drawing-rooms and of Clubs, works in which Christianity is spoken of as an antiquated superstition ?" And Mr. Farrer tells us that " the vital doctrines of Christianity have to be defended against whole literatures, against whole philosophies !"

More than this. The reader whose attention has been at any time drawn in this direction can scarcely have failed to notice that there is a large and increasing body of educated men in England (we might almost include in their number the bulk of the educated classes) orthodox in name, but whose theological views, if put down upon paper, would be anything but satisfactory to an orthodox examiner. These are men faithful to the offices of religion, who subscribe to churches and chapels and missions, who form the strength of the church and the more educated dissenting sects. The precise character of their religious belief is a mystery to themselves; they hold what a learned professor of our friends once called a kind of *smudgy* Christianity, and, as they are particularly reticent on these points, it is very difficult for an outsider to form an idea of their creed. Yet, like every one else, they have their moments of expansion, and then we learn that, like Coleridge (who on this, as well as on all other subjects, was pre-eminently " smudgy "), they are satisfied with the Bible, "because it finds them, more than all other books put together, finds them at greater depths of their being," without pledging themselves to the dogma that every word in it is necessarily inspired. The attitude of their minds towards the greater number of the Old Testament miracles may be described as one of benevolent haziness. They may be literally true, or true only after some figurative and allegorical fashion ; either way, they are parts of a sublime system, and, even if they were shown to be quite untrue, it would not in the least matter. Supposing all Bishop Colenso's finnikin criticisms to be established, how would they affect the doctrine of the atonement ? Supposing Methuselah did not live nine hundred and odd years,

the Sermon on the Mount will none the less live till the end of
the world. What does it matter whether there be a personal
tempter or not? Surely there is implanted in us all a tendency
to go wrong; and does not that amount to exactly the same
thing? Of course they do not believe in the hell of Mr.
Spurgeon (nor consequently, we must take the liberty of pointing
out to these good people, in the hell of Jesus, for they are
identical) but in the consequences of evil deeds following their
perpetrator in some mysterious way into another world. Some of
them are quite willing to give up the Apocalypse, others the
Book of Daniel, others the Song of Solomon, others to our
knowledge even the accounts of the Nativity, as possibly a legend
that has been tacked on to the sacred narrative. They all of
them repudiate the idea that men may be condemned hereafter
for " honest mistakes " or " errors in belief conscientiously arrived
at," as uncharitable and immoral. The extent to which these
kinds of views are prevalent is not suspected by such of the
clergy as do not share them; and by the way many, especially
of the younger clergy, do share them. We say that there is
scarcely an educated family in the land in which one or more
of its members may not be found holding opinions such as these ;
and whatever judgment we may pass on them, it must at any
rate be admitted that they are not identical with, that they are
indeed diametrically opposed to, the tenets of orthodox Christianity.

Concurrently with this phenomenon of the advance of
sceptical and semi-sceptical views in England, we observe
another one, common to England and all Christian countries,
and which though inseparably connected with the former, we
may be permitted, in our brief limits, to characterize in a rough
way separately, as the decay from *internal* causes of dogmatic
theology. We believe that there is nothing within our cognizance
upon which Time will not operate; that for Kronos, as for the
French sapeur, nothing is sacred. If this be so, the popular
Christianity of the nineteenth century could not possibly be the
same Christianity as that of the first and second centuries. At
any rate, it is not. The early Christian, if recalled to life, would
be utterly bewildered at the loose way in which his creed at
present sits upon its most eminent professors ; at seeing them
burn incense to Gods, whom though not bearing the names
of Heathen Deities, he would none the less stigmatize as Idols
and Demons. To him, it would be altogether astounding and
abnormal that this world should be now-a-days so much to everybody, when the very key-note of his creed is that it should be
next to nothing, *vilius algâ :* that even the so-called "regenerate" should be devoting themselves with so much assiduity to

worldly pursuits and money-making, during the brief interval of time which separates them from an eternity which, for all but a few, must be an eternity of physical torment : that Bishops and Deans should be consorting peacefully with the worldly, and looking out for good matches for their daughters from among them : that the Scriptures should not be consulted in every difficulty to which they apply, but, on the contrary, quietly ignored or if need be set aside : that all reference to them should be tabooed in the legislature and in polite society as "in bad taste :" that subjects of the highest, indeed to him of the only interest should be treated with a languid indifference : that the debates in Convocation about the Athanasian Creed, and the procession of the Holy Ghost, should not awaken infinitely more attention than the debates on the Public Health and Ballot Bills. In short, the "secular spirit," with which the course of time has rusted over the old original creed, would be an inexplicable portent to him. Sometimes even now, a man of this type, a primitive Christian "born out of due time," starts up among us and strikes even his co-religionists as a being, strange and wild and out-of-place, like a Hebrew prophet at the Court of a Jewish King—a Henry Martyn, for instance, who laments that he has been at a dinner-party without saying one word to the company about Jesus ; grieves at having thought so little about God on his way from Cambridge to London on the top of the stage-coach, and in the course of a walk through the city ; is led to attend a Gresham lecture on music, and goes away, " unable to remain longer in such a dissipated, unholy state :" mourns over his having been induced to "look into a Review," and, being led on by " detestable curiosity about the impertinent subjects of literature ;" is thankful that he is not struck dead in church for not being more attentive in prayer. Yet Henry Martyn (a holy and conscientious man, if ever there was one in this world) was perfectly consistent, and the inconsistent people are those who, professing to hold what Henry Martyn held, do not act as Henry Martyn acted. We believe his views to have been in many respects radically unsound, and based on a false view of Divine Providence. Yet they were the views practically enforced by Jesus and still held up theoretically for our acceptance. The founder of Christianity compared his teaching to new wine poured into old bottles, but now the religion itself has become an old wine, from which the original ingredients have largely evaporated. Hell-fire, the cultivation of poverty, blind indifference to the morrow, the practice of celibacy, the anticipation not to be laid aside for a moment of the immediate return of Christ, humble submission to injuries— these and many other ingredients have escaped, and left it a

religion tempered, aud so to speak doctored, by long keeping, to
the altered character of the times.   Whether the world would
be any the better if the precepts of Christianity were everywhere strictly carried out, is a point on which we are not called
upon to enter.   Suffice it that they are not so carried out—that
they are softened down into meaning something which they did
not originally mean.   And this is a point not to be passed over
in a notice of the scepticism of the age.

No wonder that these considerations—except indeed the last-
named, which they either fail to perceive or else shut their eyes
to—have at length frightened the orthodox.   The tendency of
frightened classes everywhere is to form some sort of organization
for their protection, and the tendency of frightened classes in
England is to place these organizations under the patronage of as
many Peers, Millionaires, and Members of Parliament as can be
secured for the purpose.   In some cases, meetings are held
and addresses are delivered by men of reputation, with a Lord, if
possible, or a Bishop in the chair.   "The Society for the protection
of the interests of brewers and licensed victuallers (President, Lord
Grains) will hold the first of a series of meetings to be addressed by
Sir Cocculus Indicus," &c. &c.   We are all of us familiar with this
kind of thing, and it cannot be denied that it may be of some
service to a threatened cause.   Just, to be sure, as a meeting of the
crew of a ship convened for its protection during a storm may be of
service in that it may stimulate the sailors to greater activity.
But the ship, and the interests of the licensed victuallers, and
let us add those of so-called orthodoxy—it may be well to
remind these worthy people—are tossed on the crests of huge waves
in the ocean of human progress, are as the playthings to tides in
the affairs of collective mankind, which will flow on in their
appointed course as ignorant of them as of Canute, and against
which it may be as useless for them to contend with "meetings"
and "lectures," as for savages to shoot up arrows into the sky
to keep off an eclipse.

These reflections have been forced upon us on receiving the
second series of lectures delivered under the auspices of the
"Christian Evidence Society."   This Society was founded nearly
two years ago, "for the purpose of meeting doubts, among the
educated classes."   It numbers among its lecturers an Archbishop, and three or more Bishops, besides Deans, Professors of
Divinity and Hebrew, Canons, a few eminent Nonconformist
preachers, and other notabilities.   Its list of patrons and chairmen
includes such names as those of the Marquis of Salisbury ; Lords
Shaftesbury, Harrowby, and Cairns ; Mr. Samuel Morley, M.P.,
and Mr. Stevenson, M.P.   With such a "cast" as this, success
of a certain sort was assured.   The religious papers inform us

that the meetings have been crowded, and the first series has
gone through no less than six editions. Whether the meetings
have been mainly attended, and the published lectures purchased
by the class of doubters for whose benefit the Association was
devised, or by orthodox persons, anxious to assist at a demonstration of their own wisdom and the ignorance and blindness of
their opponents, is a point on which certainly we cannot, nor
perhaps can the leaders of the movement, form an opinion.
Judging from analogy, we should expect the latter to be the case.
We should expect a series of meetings convened against the
liquor trade to be attended principally by permissive men, and
gatherings convened against the Permissive Bill to be made up,
for the most part, of licensed victuallers and their friends. Or,
to choose an illustration still more apposite, we should suppose,
(what is indeed the fact,) that lectures against Christianity would
be attended for the most part by infidels ; nor should we expect
that, except under some exceptional circumstances, such a course
of lectures would have any very decided effect on the body of
the orthodox. At any rate, the Society may be congratulated on
numbering among its supporters donors of such a munificent
sum as a thousand guineas, and we should not be surprised to
hear of other like sums being given, and of the lectures becoming,
for some time at least, an annual institution. What we think
the promoters may still more strongly be congratulated upon, is
the *tone* adopted in these addresses. They are the productions
of cultivated men, who may perhaps in some instances have felt
the doubts which they seek to combat, who are at any rate aware
that there *are* difficulties in the way of belief quite beyond the
intellectual grasp of such divines as Dr. Cumming and Mr.
Spurgeon, and we may add of the bulk of preachers, Anglican
and Dissenting, and that such difficulties are not to be
immediately solved by an exhibition of hell-fire. " I have some
knowledge," says Dr. Rigg, the President of the Westminster
Training College, and an ornament of the Wesleyan body, " of
the difficulties of thought and belief which may lead honest men
to become pantheists ; I understand the manner of thought of
one who has become entangled in the mazy coil of pantheistic
reasonings ; at all events I know that honest searchers after truth
may reluctantly become intellectual pantheists, while yet their
heart longs to retain faith and worship towards a personal God."
This excellent spirit marks the whole of the two volumes
before us.

It is not our intention to review these lectures. It would be
impossible, in our brief limits, to review twenty-two independent productions. If we were in a situation to notice them in
detail, we think we could show that there is not one of them

which is not open to serious objections from the other side. Take a specimen or two, culled at random on opening the pages of these volumes. Professor Rawlinson, in some six-and-thirty small octavo pages, widely printed, disposes of the "Alleged Historical Difficulties of the Old and New Testaments." Of those, the Story of the Exodus occupies just six and a half. Does the Professor really believe that the elaborate arguments of Bishop Colenso and others are to be met in this way? To be sure, the time at his disposal would not have allowed him to go thoroughly into the matter; but ought not that consideration to have pointed to the advisability of choosing some other subject, or, at least, of selecting some one difficulty, and dealing with that in a manner which should be satisfactory? As it is, the Professor's "short method" with those who believe that the story of the Exodus has a historic foundation, but is not necessarily inspired in all its details, is amusing and characteristic. The numbers of the sacred text, he says, are exactly the part of it which is most liable to corruption and least to be depended upon. Six hundred thousand may mean sixty thousand, and so on. "Cavils as to their exact numbers, or as to *the particular expressions used* in Exodus, do not touch the main fact, but show (if they show anything) either that our ancient manuscripts are here and there defective, or that *an early Oriental historian does not write in the exact and accurate style of a nineteenth century Occidental critic*"! This, we take it, is virtually a concession of all that Bishop Colenso and the "educated sceptic" contend for: for once admit that an historian does not write "in an exact and accurate style," and we are entitled to make any deductions which common sense may require from his narrative. Theologians have certainly the merit which Napoleon assigned to British soldiers: they do not know when they are beaten. In a similar off-hand way, Mr. Gladstone disposes of the scientific difficulties of the Bible, in about the same number of pages. We wish we could notice this curious production, every page of which must excite a smile in any one who has seriously considered the questions thus raised. We will give one example. Mr. Gladstone, like Hugh Miller, Archdeacon Pratt, and others, quietly assumes a *partial* deluge, which, indeed, the discoveries of science have forced upon him, utterly ignoring the fact, that if there be one statement plainly and unmistakeably set forth in Scripture, from the first of Genesis to the last chapter of Revelation, it is that of a *universal* deluge. "Every living substance that I have made will I destroy from off the face of the earth." "All flesh died that moved upon the earth." "I will destroy man whom I have created from the face of the earth, both man and beast, and the creeping thing, and the fowls of the air."

"All the high hills *that were under the whole heaven* were covered." No ingenuity can get over these plain statements. What will the educated sceptic say when he sees them evaded in this lecture for the hundredth time? Again, mark the disingenuity of what follows. We beg pardon, however: we do not believe that there is any conscious disingenuity on the part of the writer—we believe him to be entirely ignorant of any difficulty in his way.

"We are so accustomed," writes the Bishop of Carlisle, "to the first chapter of Genesis, that I think we sometimes scarcely perceive its peculiarities; but suppose that the reverse order of arrangement had been adopted, and that man, in deference to his dignity, had been represented as coming in first, and that other creatures had been represented as being made afterwards for his use and pleasure, would not this have made a radical change, and introduced an enormous scientific difficulty?"

But this order of creation—viz., man first and other creatures afterwards, is precisely that which is given, not indeed in the first, but in the second chapter of Genesis. In verse 7 man is formed; in verse 9 trees are made to grow, pleasant to the sight and good for food; in verse 18 God determines to make an helpmeet for man, and in 19 proceeds to form animals, but as none of these is found to be an helpmeet for him, woman is created in verses 21 and 22. The divergence between these two narratives is accounted for by a discovery as clearly established as any in the whole domain of criticism: they are, as is well known, the productions of two different writers, known as the Elohist and the Jehovist. But that is not the point here; the point is that the Bishop should quietly assume the absence from the Bible of what he admits would be "an enormous difficulty," when precisely this same difficulty in an aggravated form stares him in the face a few verses further on. Here, again, what will the intelligent sceptic say? Or, take the following, by Mr. Row: "All experience proves that mythic and legendary miracles are grotesque. Yet those in the Gospels are all sober ones, and stamped with a high moral tone." What—we may confidently ask Mr. Row—would he have said to the miracle of turning water into wine at Cana, if he had met with it out of the Gospels? Evidently that it was not sober (we mean no pun), that it was grotesque and clearly apocryphal, that it accomplished no moral purpose, except indeed the exhibition of superhuman power, which, if it be admitted as a sufficient moral end, lets in all miracles of whatever kind. We have noted in reading over these volumes a number of passages similar to the above, but, as we have already said, our object not being to review them, we must leave these, together with an estimate of each contribution, taken as a whole, to such as may have the inclination and the power to enter upon the task.

Our object is a different one. It is to point out ground which we think ought to be taken up, and objections which, if possible, ought to be met by lectures in what we may take it for granted will be a fresh series to be delivered in the ensuing season. We shall make no apology for using the plainest language. The aim of the Society is to remove difficulties in the way of belief, and they ought to be thankful to any one who points out to them without subterfuge what those difficulties really are.

We see it very generally stated by orthodox writers in and out of these volumes, that there is no logical resting-place for the mind between a belief in Revelation on the one hand, and Atheism or Pantheism on the other. "Deism," writes Dr. Rigg, "grants too much to the Christian." And what he calls "the via media of Deism," has been ridiculed by an able writer, Mr. Henry Rogers, in his popular work "The Eclipse of Faith." Granting for the sake of argument that this is so, though we by no means admit the fact, the inference sought to be drawn is obvious. There being no other choice open to us but a "heart-withering negation," a system which denies, or at least ignores, the existence of a God and the immortality of the soul, and the glorious and inspiring promises of Revelation, is it not clearly to the interest of everybody that the latter system should prove true?

The philosopher will not be very much struck with an argument in favour of a theological creed, which is founded on people's supposed interests. But, accepting this ground, we unhesitatingly reply—while begging on our own account to repudiate all sympathy with atheistical or pantheistical views—that it would be greatly to the general interests that Atheism should prove to be true, rather than that the theological system preached among us should prove to be true. And we consider this to be not a mere statement of opinion, but one capable of the most rigid demonstration.

For, what does Revelation teach us? That we are lost, degraded, ruined creatures, born into the world and living in the world under a divine curse. As the grave is the ultimate receptacle destined for the human body, so a place of endless and unspeakable torment is the natural receptacle destined for the human soul. We are not disputing the truth of this dogma. What we affirm, however, is that, if it be indeed true, then the wildest imaginings of the most savage creeds are as sunlight compared with the horrors of our actual situation. Yet a gleam of light (it is but a gleam) is suffered to penetrate to this our dreary prison, in which we are penned up like so many cattle waiting for the shambles. In virtue of a mysterious transaction, to which we need not further allude, a certain number of persons will be "saved," that is to say, will not only be rescued from the general fate, but will exchange it for a condition of endless happiness. Scripture, we think, lays it down very clearly that the number of the saved will be small, and to the same effect is the preaching current among ourselves: yet we will waive this point, and concede that it may be very large. Still, the fact remains that a very considerable number of us are destined by the Creator of theologians to a fate at which imagination stands aghast. And then we are quietly told that we have an immense interest in the existence of such a Creator being proved, or, however, rendered highly probable; and that if an opposite conclusion could be arrived at, it should be promulgated only as "the utterance of an agonized heart, unable to suppress the language of its misery!"

We should like then, this subject to be handled by one of the lecturers in the coming series. We should like him to try and show that the balance of advantage to the human race would be in favour of his system, according to which say x persons are to be made endlessly happy and y eternally miserable, as against one which leaves the fate of $x + y$ altogether uncertain, the most probable inference being that they would all fall into the peaceful and painless sleep of death. We should also like him to try and show us that a person who was himself conscious of being selected for future happiness ought not as a philanthropist to hope that the latter system might be the true one. And if any gentleman should condescend to act upon our suggestion, we must really be excused, if after a perusal of these two volumes and some slight acquaintance with the works of theologians, we ask him to be so good as to stick to his point. It will not do to tell us that every one is offered a chance of going to heaven, and that it will be his own fault if he goes to hell. This really does not touch the question. The fact, as we are told, is, that a great number of persons will be sent to hell; and from whatever cause this may arise, whether from their own fault or not, we say we *hope* it is not true—in other words, that a system which teaches it as a fact is not true. We are quite sure that universal oblivion is a much brighter prospect for the race than this. We are inclined to exclaim with Pliny: "Quæ (malum) ista dementia est, iterari vitam morte? . . . . Perdit profecto ista dulcedo, credulitasque præcipuum naturæ bonum, mortem; ac duplicat obitus, si dolero etiam post futuri æstimatione eveniet."[*] Again, we shall not be satisfied by the lecturer pointing out that Christianity has always borne the title of "good tidings." To be sure it has, and rightly too, on the supposition that without

---

[*] Hist. Nat., vii. 55.

it, we were all of us doomed to endless perdition. But then this statement, for which no shadow of foundation can be deduced from any other source, is part of the system of Revelation, and stands or falls with it.

Far in the depths of yonder heavens there may be, there probably are, worlds in existence bearing on their surface intelligent beings. Judging from analogy, we are led to suppose that such beings, if they exist, undergo a process resembling death. Who, if he casts his thoughts in that direction, will not indulge in the hope that with them death means sleep for all, rather than the wakening of some to endless happiness and of others to endless misery? We are not aware that there would be anything impious, even in the view of theologians, in the indulgence of such a hope, provided it were carefully confined to regions many millions of miles away from the earth. Yet who does not see that the expression of it is an immediate *reductio ad absurdum* of the consoling and inspiriting character which they claim for their Revelation?

This consideration does not indeed touch the truth or falsehood of Revelation. It may be very bad news indeed, and yet be perfectly true. Still, we are in favour of things bearing their right names, and we altogether object to the term "good tidings" being applied to this system as a whole. Moreover, that theologians have never chosen to consider, for we will not charge them with wilfully misrepresenting, the character of their creed, is to us a singular and suggestive circumstance. And although, as we said before, people ought not to found their belief on their interests, yet such is the weakness of humanity that they will often do so; and it is at any rate better to base one's belief upon a true than a false view of one's interest. Now, it is not for the advantage of mankind that the Scriptures should turn out to be literally inspired, for they teach that the greater part of mankind will be damned everlastingly. And it is certainly not to the advantage of mankind generally that the greater part of them should be damned everlastingly.

The mention of the "literal inspiration of Scripture" leads us to make another suggestion. We think that the next session of the Society might be much more advantageously employed, if a few of the lectures, or indeed the whole series, were devoted, with some sort of concert, to a grand offensive movement in favour of Inspiration, rather than to desultory and unconnected skirmishes against Atheism, Pantheism, Positivism, and mythical theories of Christianity. It is utterly impossible to do justice to any one of these subjects in an address of three-quarters of an hour, reproduced in thirty or forty pages of large type. As we remarked just now with regard to Bishop Colenso, so we may observe with respect to Mr. Herbert Spencer—that his arguments are not only not demolished, they are not even touched, in one of the lectures (that on Pantheism) in which a mention of his name, as a name typical of those against whom the argument was to be directed, had led us to suppose that his "First Principles" might be noticed. Moreover, we are of opinion—though we must candidly admit that we may be wrong—that Atheism, Pantheism, Positivism, and Mysticism have taken very small hold on the British educated mind. On the other hand, the doctrine of Plenary Inspiration has most assuredly come to be seriously questioned, and it is incumbent on a body of disputants, banded together for the defence of dogmatic theology, to furnish us with some reasons, suitable to the requirements of the present age, for the maintenance of this doctrine—on which, be it observed, the appalling dogma of eternal punishment rests. This is a very large subject, and having intimated our view—surely a reasonable one—that it might fairly form the theme of a succession of lectures, we are not going to be guilty of the inconsistency of discussing it in a few sentences. But we cannot help expressing, by the way, our own personal conviction that adequate reasons for this belief have never been put before the world from the Protestant point of view. That it was held by the early Fathers and the early Church appears to us not to be an argument, but merely a way of accounting for the origin of the belief historically : not to speak of the danger and in some cases the impossibility of yielding our judgment to such authorities, since the most ancient that we could quote as witnesses to the Canon were also believers in the distinctive tenets of Romanism, as well as in magic, dreams, demoniacal possession, the heathen mythology, the early return of Christ. That it can be established on any *à priori* ground—the argument, which, as Mr. Greg in his "Creed of Christendom" remarks, "does the business" for most people—that is to say, that it is inconceivable that God should furnish man with a revelation and should not, at the same time, provide him with an infallible record of it, seems to us a perfectly unjustifiable assertion. This ground has been entirely given up by every divine of reasoning powers from St. Augustine to Bishop Butler (the whole scope of whose great work is opposed to any such assumptions), and from Bishop Butler to Dean Alford. St. Augustine declared that he should not feel himself called upon to believe in the Bible unless the Church had bidden him to do so. Bishop Butler declares that we are wholly ignorant how far, or in what way it were to be expected God would interpose miraculously, to qualify those to whom He made a revelation for communicating it, or to secure its being transmitted to posterity,*

* Analogy, pt. ii. chap. iii.

and Dean Alford tells us that " we must take our views of inspiration, not as is too often done, from *à priori* considerations, but
entirely from the evidence furnished by the Scriptures themselves."* We must therefore turn to the source indicated by the
last-named writer ; and from what passages, or what single passage in the Bible we are to gather that the whole of it, or any
part of it is necessarily inspired or infallible, we are altogether at
a loss to conjecture. We commend this point to the attention
of the Christian Evidence Society, and we really think that we
are rendering them some service, provided they have any new
arguments to offer, for it is certain that no part of the fabric of
orthodoxy is more rapidly crumbling away than this, which has
hitherto been its foundation-stone. We almost think that we
can trace some faint dawn of a presentiment that Inspiration will
one day have to be given up, in the interesting contribution to
this series of the Bishop of Ely, a prelate who has elsewhere recorded his opinion that the New Testament history and doctrines
might be capable of proof and deserving of evidence, if Inspiration were given up altogether.†

There is another point, in this connexion, which merits the
attention of the Society, and as to which the educated sceptic
demands a reply which he has not yet received. " What is the

---

* N. T., i., sect. vi. 22.

† In "Aids to Faith." We have more than once said that it is not our intention to review these lectures, but having alluded in the text to that delivered
by the Bishop of Ely (in our judgment one of the best of the collection), we
cannot help adverting to the carelessness which marks these addresses to the
"educated." *e.g.* at p. 420, we are told in a note, that " the writings of the
Apostolic fathers are clear about the Godhead of Christ," an expression which,
in a certain sense, is true enough : but which taken in conjunction with the
text above, must be held to mean, " Our Lord's supreme co-equal, co-eternal
Deity," *i.e.* with the Father. Now, this is an altogether unfounded statement, and we challenge the Bishop to quote any passage from any Father
before the close of the second century which maintains this view, while we
could give him scores of passages which distinctly assert the inferiority of the
Son to the Father. One more example must suffice. At p. 449, we are told
that " Mohammedanism, Brahminism, and Buddhism, have either stifled, or at
the best stunted science and made stagnant civilization." We were rather
startled at this, and without going into the case of Brahminism and Buddhism,
we will quote a passage from a book of reference accessible to all, " Chambers's
Cyclopædia." " Broadly speaking, the Mohammedans may be said to have
been the enlightened teachers of barbarous Europe, from the 9th to the 13th
century. It is from the glorious days of the Abbaside rulers that the real
renaissance of Greek spirit and Greek culture is to be dated. Classical literature would have been irreclaimably lost, had it not been for the home it found
in the schools of the 'unbelievers' of the 'dark ages.' Arabic philosophy,
medicine, natural history, geography, history, grammar, rhetoric, and 'the
golden art of poetry,' schooled by the old Hellenic masters, brought forth an
abundant harvest of works, many of which will live and teach as long as there
will be generations to be taught."

precise character of the 'inspiration' to which you claim our assent?" We are aware that many volumes have been written on this subject, but we must say, with Cardinal Wiseman, "that, having perused with great attention all that has fallen in my way from Protestant writers on this subject, I have hardly found one single argument advanced by them that is not logically incorrect."* Whatever it does mean, it certainly cannot mean that every statement in the Bible is to be accepted as infallibly true, for it is clear that not even a miracle can be invoked to cut the knot of a palpable contradiction. Now 2 Chron. xxii. 2 contradicts xxi. 20: we read that God tempted David to number Israel, and that Satan tempted him to do it; while from James we learn that God tempts no man. The accounts of the end of Judas are totally inconsistent with each other. An ingenious writer in the series of Mr. Scott of Ramsgate has given one hundred and forty-four specimens of self-contradiction in the Bible. In one sense, we attach no weight whatever to the greater part of these discrepancies; they may be found in every history, from that of Herodotus to that of Mr. Froude. What does it matter whether the apostles on their journey did or did not take staves, or how often the cock crew? The general truth of the narratives is not affected. But from another point of view—when the plea of inspiration is put in—they assume immense importance. They altogether disprove the plea in the only sense in which we are able to understand it. These self-contradictions as to matters of fact, and we may add the variations presented by Scripture to the known truths of science, are as plain a revelation from God to man that whatever else the Bible may be, it is not in all its parts infallibly true, as if He had written a message to that effect on the face of the sun. Accordingly, theologians, fairly driven out of their original plea, have been for a long time attempting to draft another, with that amount of success which invariably attends all attempts to build in the clouds. We cannot refrain from quoting here a remarkable utterance of Dean (now Bishop) Goodwin:—

"Divine inspiration may imply an absence of errors upon physical questions, or it may not: who shall venture to say, à *priori*, whether it does or no? . . . . . Why not endeavour, by looking at the evidence, to see on which side the truth lies? And if it should appear upon examination, that any chapter contains statements not in accordance with science, then, instead of coming to the conclusion that the Scriptures are not inspired, I should rather come to this—viz., that the idea of inspiration does not involve that accuracy concerning physics which many persons have imagined that it does."

We hold this to be one of the most dishonest passages ever

written. Instead of looking to the Bible and seeing whether in all respects it comes up to the idea which we should form of a divinely inspired communication—and it is all very well to talk about *à priori* judgments, but this is after all the only test which man can apply to it or can in reason be called upon to apply to it—the Bishop *assumes* inspiration, and then proceeds to see how far he can make the dogma square with the contents of the book. Supposing a letter were put into our hands purporting to contain an order from our absolute Sovereign. Other people have seen it and pronounced it to be genuine, but then we know that other people have been mistaken before now, and the responsibility is cast upon us of inquiring. Now suppose we were to argue thus:

"A letter from a Sovereign *may* imply inability to write legibly, errors in spelling and in grammar, errors in plain matters of geography, self-contradictions, &c., or it *may not*. Why not endeavour by looking at the letter, to see on which side the truth lies? If it should appear that it contains such errors and mistakes, then instead of concluding that it does not come from the Sovereign, we shall have to infer that a royal communication is not necessarily marked by correct spelling, correct grammar," &c.

If we talked in this ridiculous way, we should be reasoning exactly like Bishop Goodwin. Look at the way in which such an argument as this might be applied to the sacred writings of the Hindoos and Persians. We have generally heard it said that their cosmogonies and wild legends and impossible geography are conclusive against their having been inspired from above. But it might fairly be said that this is not a proper mode of contemplating the matter—that the proper method was to look at the books, and if they contained anything opposed to science, to conclude that inspiration did not extend to such subjects as these, but might be quite consistent with the origin of the world, &c. being wrapped up in allegories, however ridiculous these might at first sound to European ears. The Brahmin who argued thus would not be making a much larger demand upon our credulity than the Bishop. Again, if the *general* inspiration of a book be no guarantee against errors in fact and in science, why should it be a guarantee against errors of another kind—viz., additions to the text? "The three heavenly witnesses" is a notorious interpolation; why are we not entitled to hold that the accounts of the nativity in Matthew and Luke *may* be legends which have been tacked on to the rest of the narrative? The Bishop would, we suppose, reply that this would be impossible; for that inspiration *would* imply the absence of such an error as this: in other words, he *has* formed his own *à priori* theory of inspiration, which we take to be briefly this—"a guarantee for the absolute truth of every word in the Bible which cannot be proved to be absolutely false. Where falsehood or error is proved, there was no guarantee." At a certain grammar-school of our acquaintance, the head-master used to guarantee that he would never flog a sixth-form boy, and we believe that he strictly kept his promise; but the commission of certain offences was held *ipso facto* to degrade a boy into the fifth, upon which he was immediately birched. The dominie lived before the days of Dean Goodwin, or he might have quoted him as an authority. Less disingenuous because apparently talking nonsense, as Monsieur Jourdain talked prose, without knowing it, are Messrs. Webster and Wilkinson in their introduction to the Greek Testament.

"It will be understood that an inspiration which may be truly characterized as direct, personal, independent, *plenary*, is consistent with the use of an inferior or provincial dialect, with ignorance of scientific facts and other secular matters, with *mistakes in historical allusions or references*, and mistakes in conduct, and with *circumstantial discrepancies between inspired persons in relating discourses, conversations, or events.*"

We do not know by whom this "will be understood"—certainly not by ourselves. Well may the writer of the review from which we have taken the above and the preceding extract exclaim, "We draw a long breath, and wonder where we are!"* Yet when he comes to give us his own views on inspiration, he is not one whit less cloudy. "It does not by any means follow," he says, "because a book is inspired by Almighty God, that it should therefore be *faultless.* . . . . In nature herself, where no one can deny the finger of God, imperfection, waste, &c. are consistent with the presence and agency of a Divine wisdom. Why may it not be so with the Bible?" And he goes on to define what he means by the Bible being inspired. It is "replete itself and pregnant without stint for him that rightly uses it, with that spirit of purity, faith, obedience, charity, which forms the essential temper and characteristic of the church and family of God."

We do not suppose that any one in England, except an Atheist, would object to this definition of inspiration, and even an Atheist might in some degree accept it. Every one, we may say, admits that the Old and New Testaments include the most venerable, and at the same time, the most interesting compositions known to humanity. The Divine Spirit, as we conceive it, certainly does seem to breathe through some of its pages in a way in which it breathes through no other work. And indeed we

---

* *Edinburgh Review*, No. 240, April, 1863.

should expect this to be the case with the sacred records of the Jews—a people distinctly charged with the sublime part of keeping alive the light of monotheism; and with the records of early Christianity—a creed which, whatever its imperfections, is evidently destined, in what may be called "the natural struggle of religions," to outlive, in some form or other, all others. But then this view of inspiration is not a basis sufficiently solid to found dogmatic orthodoxy upon. A book which is admitted not to be faultless ceases to be an idol to all of whose utterances we are bound to bow down on pain of damnation. It has been shown to err in some particulars, where we are able to test it. Is there any good reason for supposing that it cannot err in other particulars, where we are unable to apply an exact test?

Here we see an example of the danger of invoking "analogy," as the orthodox are so fond of doing since Butler showed the way. Why should not the Bible be marked by faults and errors, says the Reviewer, since all God's works in nature are similarly marked by what we call imperfections? Very well then; but we are entitled to carry the analogy a step further. Why should not the *creed* set forth in the New Testament be similarly marked by faults and errors and imperfections, as (humanly speaking) is admitted to be the case with everything else from the hand of God? Why should it not be destined to undergo change like all the rest of God's handiwork? Why should not Christ have been mistaken in his ideas of a physical and never-ending hell, just as he was evidently mistaken (not to say a word about demoniacal possession) when he announced to his disciples "Verily I say unto you, there be some standing here which shall not taste of death till they see the Son of Man coming in his kingdom?" Why should not a belief in miracles, essential to the propagation of a new religion in that stage of the world's history, have been used by Providence as a means of advancing certain truths—like the belief in Christ's immediate return, which was perhaps the most powerful of all causes in spreading Christianity, but which is now seen to have been a complete delusion,—why should they not have been like husks protecting fruits, which drop off when the fruits are matured? Why, in short, should not sublime truths have been allowed to make their way in the world mixed up with gross errors; man's appointed task being slowly and laboriously to disengage the truths from the errors? Dreadful as these suppositions may appear to some, they are such as we are fairly landed in by the use of analogy. These are the methods which mark the communication of all other kinds of knowledge by God to man. Why should they not hold good in the domain of religious knowledge?

These considerations might be carried a great deal further, and there are other themes for exercises which we had thought of suggesting to the Christian Evidence Society. But our limits are reached. We do not think that these essays are calculated to have any appreciable effect in restoring the tottering fortunes of orthodoxy. Here and there, no doubt, an outpost imprudently advanced, may be captured. Here and there an attack, injudiciously and even unfairly made, may be triumphantly resisted. These are the local incidents common to every struggle. But of the general advance of science along the whole line, we can entertain not the slightest doubt. We are equally sure that every additional step in this advance must be increasingly fatal to the claims of orthodoxy. The species of compromises which are attempted to be set up in some of these papers, and in other works (notably on the great point of "inspiration") are, to use the expression of a daily journal from which we have already quoted, of the nature of a compromise between the new 600-pound shot and the side of an iron-clad. "Either the shot will be smashed, or the plates will be penetrated. There is no middle term."

Art. VII.—The Gladstone Administration.

MINISTRIES, like men, are mortal. Like men also they pass through various stages in the course of their decline from the fulness of their strength until they vanish away, and the benches that once knew them know them no more. Not long ago Mr. Gladstone extracted pleasant consolation from the consideration that few ministries have been known in recent years to outlive a very moderate period—a period which his own had already outlasted. He appeared to regard the downfall of the most popular government as an inevitable fate against which it was vain and scarcely desirable to struggle. Doubtless, administrations are doomed to decay and die, like all things human, but the cause does not lie in any inexorable destiny, but in their own liability to error, or, as not infrequently happens, their own perverse disregard of the principles they have undertaken to further. It is human to err, as the Latin proverb tells us, and human weakness often leads to such disregard of the higher motives that ought to influence the members of a responsible Government of a constitutional State, as naturally exposes them to obloquy, and finally brings their overthrow. It is impossible to absolve the Gladstone administration from charges of having been alike prone to error, guilty of culpable weakness, and on many occasions of having shown a strange obliquity of judgment. It is not their political opponents alone who have discovered that they no longer occupy the position they once did. They are no longer strong in the assured confidence and support of an enthusiastic country. They are still indeed—because sure of their majority—recognised as the legitimate Government of the empire. But by their wavering and uncertain conduct, by their manifest preference on many occasions of expediency to principle, by ceasing to be leaders of, and content to become waiters upon public opinion, and by the sad lack of resolution, courage, and trust in their own cause which they have exhibited, they have, to a large extent, repelled those who were formerly their most eager and earnest advocates and supporters. It may be that the Government of Mr. Gladstone does not appear outwardly so feeble as it did a year ago. When Parliament met last session it seemed as if Mr. Gladstone might at any moment be compelled to resign. It was deemed most unlikely that his Government should long escape the shoals and quicksands lying before or around it. There are not perhaps so many immediate perils threatening defeat in prospect now : but the old enthusiasm for Mr. Gladstone, both in Parliament and the country, has vanished. Distrust has taken the place of confidence. The process of alienation, by which friends are made lukewarm, has long been at work ; suspicion reigns in many minds where formerly there was unhesitating and devoted partisanship. It is no longer possible to confide, with bold undoubting faith, in ministers who have proved time-serving and timid. Liberal principles are no longer sure of being applied and promoted by them for the sake of the principles themselves. The House of Commons will meet in February with the consciousness that there is much in the past for which the Government needs forgiveness, and with painful but irrepressible doubts as to what it may do and undertake in the future.

When we inquire more minutely and specifically into the causes of this change in the attitude of the public and the Liberal party towards Mr. Gladstone and his colleagues, we find they have themselves to blame for the result. We see that they have thrown away the most magnificent opportunities, because they have proved faithless to the essential principles of their professed creed. What renders their case worse is, that their sins have not been those of ignorance. They have done good and even great service in the past. These services we fully and gladly acknowledge. But just because of them, because they have so well known how to apply Liberal principles in former sessions, their faults since all the more require and deserve to be exposed. If we are able to bring to clear light the causes of their declension, there may be the more reason to hope for the application of a remedy. It is possible that they may yet recover lost ground, though their difficulties in promoting Liberal legislation now—in carrying boldly forward the banner they once proudly bore, but which they have allowed to be trailed in the dust—will be far more formidable than they would have been, had they never swerved from the paths in which the nation expected them to walk.

The first manifestation of Mr. Gladstone's distinctive influence on the general legislation of the country since he became a Liberal leader was in connexion with parliamentary reform. We owe it to the much-decried Ministry that followed upon the death of Lord Palmerston—during whose later years there had been, as by general consent, a veritable truce of parties—that that subject was dealt with seriously and earnestly. Though the "burning of his boats" brought Mr. Gladstone's fall at the time, it rendered the settlement of reform a political necessity. Accordingly, when the Conservatives came into the brief enjoyment of the power they had long looked forward to, their versatile leader set himself to the hard task of "educating" his party by the marvellous series of Bills and manœuvres that resulted at last in household suffrage in the boroughs. The Conservatives might well feel that they had sold themselves and their principles for nought, for the triumph of their leader prepared their own doom. But, in truth, they were hardly their own masters. A new spirit and temper had been introduced into English politics, which even the *laissez-faire* Parliament of Lord Palmerston was forced to feel. The days of political dilettantism and mere dallying with reform were over and gone. During that period Mr. Gladstone had been chiefly known by his budget-speeches, in which he strewed the byeways of finance with the flowers of rhetoric. His mastery over details, his lucidity of exposition, and his powerful eloquence, had long given him a place in the front ranks of contemporary politicians. He was now to have the opportunity of showing himself a statesman as well as a politician. He was not indeed fortunate at his outset, though the fault was not wholly his. Whatever leader had been called upon to guide the Liberal party at that period would have had the same difficulties and might have experienced the same fate. The followers who would not follow resented the introduction into politics of an earnestness and zeal that were strange to them. A tendency to mutiny was inevitable; and so when Mr. Gladstone—who helped to make the occasion by a Reform Bill that was a clumsy compromise at best—had burnt his boats, he was left deserted, and had soon to endure exile from place and power. He benefited by the experience thus gained. During the two years of the Tory reign his great faults of temper and tactics were corrected. By degrees he came to be more firmly settled in his seat as leader of the Liberals, and learned to hold the reins more lightly without necessarily thereby grasping them less firmly. We cannot approve all his doings during the passing of the Tory Reform Bill. He helped, however, to make the measure a reality instead of the sham it was originally. The compound householder was got rid of, and the various little devices for checkmating with the one hand the extensions offered by the other were dropped one by one. The result was household suffrage in the boroughs, and the Conservatives, who fabricated the instrument, were the first to feel and fall by its power.

Mr. Gladstone had now his opportunity. During the general election in the autumn of 1868 he was not negligent. He had a programme, and it did not suffer from want of exposition. The world will not soon forget that Lancashire campaign in which the right honourable gentleman exhausted the English language and the capacities of the daily papers in speeches of portentous length, which however stirred the country as with the sound of a trumpet. Religious equality was proclaimed for Ireland, the axe was to be laid at the root of both Protestant and landlord ascendancy, and the Irish people would be gratified, it was hinted, in regard to education. The enthusiasm kindled throughout Great Britain on behalf of Mr. Gladstone because of his Irish policy cannot but be considered honourable in every way to the United Kingdom. The newly enfranchised constituencies turned a deaf ear to the appeal of him to whom they owed their enfranchisement, because their hearts and consciences responded to the call of the leader of the Liberal party. A great and generous impulse was doubtless stirred in the national breast. There was no intense desire felt to make an end of the inequalities that for centuries had been imposed upon Ireland. Popular feeling, when strongly excited, is rarely discriminating ; and if, in the fervour of new-born conviction, enthusiasm ran high, and larger results came to be expected from the healing measures than could be fulfilled, we need feel no surprise. Mr. Gladstone himself, with his fervid temperament and impatience of practical obstacles to the attainment of high ends, under-estimated — not the difficulties in the way, for he was ready to encounter and the nation was prepared to sustain him in meeting all these, but—the tenacity of the feelings created by a long course of injustice, which could not be assuaged or allayed in a moment. The memory of centuries of misrule and inequality was not to be expunged at a day's notice by the legislative action of the British Parliament, however generously designed. The disappointment, sure sooner or later to arrive, of such expectations, would naturally tend to produce impatience and dissatisfaction. But for the time the nation and its statesmen were thoroughly in unison in the desire to do justice to Ireland, and Mr. Gladstone therefore came into office at the head of a majority of from a hundred to a hundred and twenty.

The possession of such a majority threw great responsibilities upon the leaders of the Liberal party. It was soon evident that the temper of the new Parliament was very different from that of its dilettante predecessors. Although the new constituencies were still sufficiently under the influence of the traditions of the old to send to St. Stephens a far too abundant proportion of millionaires and representatives of the social respectabilities, there was a real passion for work in the new House of Commons. Attendance by members was considered a matter of duty to the constituencies, and there could be no doubt of the eagerness of the majority to accomplish the work they were sent to Westminster to do. The Conservative benches showed what sad havoc had been made in the ranks of the party, and though their leader, with the courage that rarely fails him under the most adverse circumstances, tried hard to cheer their drooping spirits, it was plain their power, even as the drag-chain upon the wheel of progress, was hopelessly crippled. Mr. Gladstone stood in proud possession of the unwavering confidence of the Liberal party. He had gained possession of the instrument by which he was fitted and made able to do the work he had proclaimed with so much passion and power it was necessary to do. Accordingly, when Parliament assembled in 1869, the Liberals were jubilant while their opponents were disheartened and almost impotent. We have to inquire what use Mr. Gladstone has made of his position and majority, and what have been the results, whether for good or evil, that have followed to the nation.

Four years have passed since he entered office on the crest of the popular wave. Entered office, not to hold it as his predecessors had done, as a mere tool and instrument for registering the policy suggested by others, but to wield substantial power, to be able to carry out his own policy, sure that in doing so he had the nation at his back. Associated with him in bearing the responsibilities of office were men of distinction and reputation, whose capacity had been proved in many a field of parliamentary warfare, though in some cases their ability as practical administrators and legislators remained to be tested. Mr. Bright's presence in the Cabinet gave the Government a large accession of popular strength, being taken as a guarantee for the somewhat doubtful Liberalism of other members. The position of Mr. Lowe was anomalous, for he had gained his main notoriety by a series of brilliant speeches against the democracy, and it was the democracy that wafted him into power and called upon him and his colleagues to legislate against privilege with all its inequalities. Mr. Lowe had also spoken strongly against any departure from the rigid lines of the accepted political economy of the day, and his views were evidently wholly inconsistent with effective legislation for Ireland on the land question. If the principle of contract were to be simply affirmed and maintained in Ireland there would be no end to the grievances of a class at least of the people whose misfortune it was that they were not in a position to contract in perfect freedom with their landlords. But whatever objections might be urged to the juxtaposition of the trio Gladstone, Bright, and Lowe in the same Cabinet, their union, especially when the Government was strengthened by the adhesion to it of Lord Clarendon and Mr. Cardwell, at least indicated the coming together of all the elements of which the Liberal party was composed. Though the more advanced section of the party was not strong in the Cabinet, yet it had great faith—as events have demonstrated, unreasonably great—in Mr. Gladstone, and Mr. Bright was its idol. There was nothing at that time to trouble the party. All sections could unite in doing the work lying immediately before it, though under the influence it might be of different and even sometimes conflicting motives. The time for dissatisfaction was sure to come soon enough, but for the moment the leaders were both able to lead and the followers were ready to follow.

Mr. Gladstone and his colleagues entered office pledged to do justice to Ireland. Such a pledge implied the conviction on their part that the Irish suffered from injustice. The unity of the Empire was disturbed by periodical attempts at rebellion. There was possible a plea of justification for such attempts so long as Ireland was subjected to inequalities removable by the Legislature, and Mr. Gladstone undertook to remove them by legislating for Ireland in accordance with Irish ideas. It is to be regretted that his assumption of the task was accompanied by any such profession. It was right that injustice should be remedied, and that inequalities should be removed, but it was a misfortune that Ireland should be taught that her own will, or the arbitrary, as it well might be, resolution of the majority was the standard of right and wrong. Mr. Gladstone was or might have been aware that the Imperial Legislature would not be guided by Irish ideas in governing the sister island. He ought to have considered that the only consistent outcome of such a policy was Irish legislative independence, for of all Irish ideas that is the most ancient, the most persistent, and the one on behalf of which the country had been and was still likely to be most firmly and resolutely united. Of course it is true that Irish ideas constitute an element to be taken into account in legislating for Ireland, since without reference to it the most appropriate means of governing the Irish people so as to insure contentment and tranquillity could not be discovered. Mr. Gladstone's error consisted in laying too much emphasis on the wishes of the population, as if these themselves sufficed to constitute what was right. It is an error that has already wrought much evil, and may work still more, while it has given the enemies of the right hon. gentleman occasion to rejoice over him. Without its commission there could have been no foundation laid, or foothold obtained for the pretension that justice requires the endowment of a separate Catholic University, under the control of the Catholic hierarchy. The justification for the remedial legislation of the Government lay in the requirements of political rectitude and equality. No law of political justice of the rudest or most rudimentary kind could uphold the rightfulness of maintaining as for and on behalf of the nation a Church regarded with intense

hostility by four-fifths of the people. The clamant evil of
evictions, resented with such intense fury by the Irish, must
also, it was plain, be put a stop to, if there was to be social
repose in the country, and without social repose there could be
no political peace. There was need for no further special
reference to Irish ideas. The prominence that was given to them
as a warrant for legislative changes tempted the Irish people to
look for legislation in accordance with their preconceived notions,
as if the fact of being theirs was all that was required to justify
them. Just because they are sure to act upon this view in regard
to education, that problem has come to be one of exceeding
hardness to solve. If, as is far from unlikely, the Irish education
question should prove the rock whereon Mr. Gladstone's Administration splits and goes to pieces, it will be very much due to
the Premier's precipitancy that it will have become so.

Religious equality and justice to the tiller of the soil were
enough to justify all, and more than all that has been done with
reference to the Church and land in Ireland. Unfortunately,
however, in both cases it was sought to justify the measures as
exceptional, owing to the exceptional circumstances and position
of Ireland. The old British habit of compromise was at work,
and no doubt this way of putting matters conciliated the support
of some who might otherwise have remained aloof from if not
opposed to the Liberal party in its Irish legislation. But it was not
necessary, and events have proved that it was not accurate. The
Conservatives who saw in the assault upon the Irish Church an
attack upon Church establishments, and in the security given to
Irish tenants, the "confiscation" of the landlord's property were
true seers—truer than they would now like to believe. In dises-
tablishing the Irish Church a principle was asserted and applied
which has gained strength and influence since, and which will,
we may be sure, go on gaining still further. No doubt religious
equality was more flagrantly violated in Ireland than anywhere
else in the Empire, and it was right to begin with the overthrow
of Protestant ascendancy in the sister island. But it was neither
wise nor necessary to give the defenders of the Church and State
connexion the opportunity of alleging that the overthrow of
the State Church in Ireland was merely a measure of expediency,
or a simple bribe to keep the majority quiet. Accustomed to
view it in that light, as many more or less consciously were, it
became easy to convince them that the remedial legislation had
proved a failure, because peace was not at once insured in
Ireland. The opponents of the Government test the value of
the work done by its practical results. They assert that Mr. Gladstone has wholly failed to do for and in Ireland what he promised,
that Ireland still requires to be governed under an exceptional

system, that to secure the semblance of peace and order there the virtual suspension of the constitution is necessary. Such arguments have little force against the legislation of 1869 and 1870, but they are valid in the character of an *argumentum ad hominem* as against Mr. Gladstone. They have all the more force against the right honourable gentleman and his colleagues, because when symptoms of the old malady began to show themselves after the Upas tree had been in great part demolished, they seem to have lost their heads and rushed to the extreme of suspending the constitution in Ireland because of excesses in one or two of its provinces. The original fault, however, lay in so misreading the Irish character as to suppose that all the political ills to which the country had been heir for centuries could be removed and the nation made loyal and contented as by one magic stroke. Mr. Gladstone's historical imagination, cultivated as it has been by commerce with antiquity, ought to have enabled him better to judge of the probable results of legislative cures for evils deep-rooted in the soil through centuries.

Nevertheless the overthrow of the Irish Church, though it may not have been accomplished in the best or most fitting manner, was unquestionably a great work. We give Mr. Gladstone all credit for his courage and earnestness, as well as for the skill with which his Bill was drawn. Though it was introduced as an exceptional measure, the practical illustration thereby afforded of religious equality has done more to advance that great principle than the most brilliant and convincing theoretical expositions of its propriety continued even through years could ever have done. In fact, religious equality is now, we are entitled to say, recognised as part and parcel of the Liberal creed. It has become a real force in English politics. It has entered into the stream and swelled the volume of the waters, so that on all hands it is seen and acknowledged, even by those most antagonistic, that its full consistent application is only a work of time. The measure that embodied it in reference to the Irish Church was faithful to the principle. Only, as we have seen, there were mistakes committed in the way in which it was advocated and justified. There was an attempt at compromise, though happily the compromise did not affect the principle, but lay in the concomitant circumstances, in the accidents as it were of the situation.

Not less worthy of approval is the measure brought forward in 1870, to settle the long-standing abuses connected with the cultivation and possession of the Irish land by the tenantry. With but slight changes, our criticism of the Church extends also to the Land Act. There was the same needless prominence given to the claims of Irish ideas, the same search for grounds of compromise in order to justify action that was its own justification, and the same exaggerated expectations were fostered as to the results the change in the tenure of the land would induce. Yet in this case, as in the other, there was the application of a principle destined ere long to enter largely into the practical politics of the country. The agitations since originated and now existing for tenant right, the demand for compensation for improvements in both England and Scotland, prove that it was a mistake to suppose the question could be confined to Ireland. The evils of eviction were more intensely felt there than in other parts of the kingdom, where the hunger for the soil which is so strong in the Celtic race is less keen. But the application of the principle that the tenant is entitled to compensation for what of his own property he adds to, thereby permanently enriching the soil, as a cure for the special grievances of Ireland, was but the thin end of the wedge. Another principle became part and parcel of the Liberal creed, which was destined to work its way into prominence. There was in the mode of its application to Ireland much that was necessarily of a tentative character. But it was a case in which *Nulla vestigia retrorsum*. The step was taken, the principle was brought into view, and it has a future before it such as those who feebly dallied with it at the time had probably little idea of. We give all honour to the statesman who was the means of bringing to the front principles that must yet work mightily in the sphere of British politics, and help to transform the face of British society. In both instances the measures stood the test of not merely meeting the emergency for which they were designed, but also of resting upon sound and fruitful principles. There were certainly defects, some of them sufficiently notable in both ; but such as they were, they were the means of bringing into prominence principles that opened up new vistas to the Liberal party and the nation.

Two branches of "the Upas tree" which Mr. Gladstone entered office with a commission to destroy were hewn down by the blows dealt at Protestant and landlord ascendancy in the sessions of 1869 and 1870. And by assailing and overthrowing them as cumberers of the ground more was done than was at first intended, or perhaps even desired. For the principle of religious equality, as we have seen, was introduced into the sphere of practical politics, and the land question in all its breadth and extent was stirred if not definitely raised. The first is not likely to be got finally rid of till all State Churches disappear, and the second is assuming daily larger proportions. A great work was thus accomplished for which Liberals owe gratitude to the Gladstone Administration. As remedial measures, applying a healing policy to Irish discontent, their success has not indeed been brilliant. Ireland is neither satisfied, nor does she seem likely soon to be. Probably by slow degrees the conviction may grow steadily and surely in the mind of the Irish people that the British Legislature desires only their good, and is anxious to fulfil all the claims of right and justice. Once that conviction becomes general sedition will be deprived of its many feeders. But not only is that of necessity a work of time, of generations and it may be of centuries, its accomplishment must largely depend upon the education of the people. So long as the Irish continue under the pestilent influence of the Romish priesthood, and the cause of the Pope is, as more than ever of late it has come to be, identified with that of antagonism to all healthy progress, the old disease will abide. We have lately seen a revival of the demand for independence under the guise of Home Rule, and the feelings that make the cause of Home Rule popular, and may not improbably send a batch of Home Rulists to the House of Commons under the ballot, are not likely to die down very soon. Tested by immediate results, the healing policy has not therefore succeeded in effecting a cure. The short-sighted policy of the Government in ruling Ireland under a virtual suspension of the Constitution has even checked the natural healing and remedial process which the legislation on the Church and Land questions was fitted to encourage. The Conservative argument that Mr. Gladstone's mission has proved a failure thus possesses plausibility. Even those who look beyond immediate to remote consequences, while they anticipate permanent good to Ireland from the removal of crying wrongs, must admit with sorrow that the immediate results have not been what was hoped, and for that they feel that the Government is itself largely to blame. But in the meanwhile they are able to rejoice over the progress of religious equality and of more enlightened views regarding the land. As was to have been expected, the Irish are by no means satisfied with the Land Act as a final settlement of the question. Already a fresh agitation has been instituted for its alteration and amendment. They wish the Legislature to abolish the provisions that allow to a landlord and his tenant the power of contracting themselves out of the Act, so that its rules and regulations shall have no application to them. This liberty in the case of tenants, with rentals above a certain minimum, gives to the landlord the power of compelling his tenant to abandon the protection of the Act. Of course he need not do so unless he pleases, as it will be through his own arrangement if he be put in such a position. But why should it be allowed at all? Any contract of the kind should be illegal and *ipso facto* null and void. Though the Irish Land Act was in some respects a compromise, yet it professes to secure to the tenant his right of property in what he himself puts into the soil. He is therefore entitled to be protected in the possession of that right, if necessary against even his own weakness. The whole foundation of this legislation rested on the idea that the tenant was not in a position to contract with his landlord on free and equal terms. Obviously that idea is not fully applied, so long as it is left possible for the landlord to induce or compel his tenant to bargain himself out of the benefits of the Act. Of course, if we are prepared to be logical, the principle of a tenant's right of property in what he himself contributes to the fertility and wealth of the soil, carries us a good deal farther than the Irish Land Act has gone. It implies that the landlord has no right of property in the increasing value of the soil, when that is due to causes not supplied by him, and over which he has no control. The solution of the problem thus started can only be found when it is concluded that the State alone has a lawful, and the only lawful, claim to the added value due to the enterprise, action, and circumstances of the entire community. Only when the State shall resume possession of that whereof it is the proper owner, will the rights of all be fully protected and guaranteed. Meanwhile, though not prepared for any such thoroughgoing action by the Legislature, the tendency of public thought is towards that issue. The tenant farmers, as recent elections in Scotland teach us, are awakening to a consciousness of the stake they have in the question of tenant right. The demand for compensation for unexhausted improvements as the only guarantee for the effective development of the resources of the land, has been loudly urged in the north. The same demand is, though more slowly, forming in England, and the present Government itself appears inclined to take a step forward in this direction. The question has been fully raised, and whether or not there be legislation on it in the coming session, it will not lightly go to sleep again till some solution has been found. Though the Government may begin with the property of corporations, it is obvious they or their successors cannot stop there. The principle applied in the one case must find application generally. The abandonment of Mr. Goschen's Bill on county administration does not allow us to hope for much in the shape of earnest and consistent dealing with the land question from the present House of Commons; but the time must come when it will be no longer possible for Parliament to avoid dealing with it. This result, or the state of matters that makes this result necessary, we are entitled to attribute in great part to Mr. Gladstone's Irish legislation. The country has not been terrified by Mr. Disraeli's ingenious, if not very ingenuous denunciations of sacrilege, in the robbing of Churches, and confiscation in the limitation of the privileges of landlords. Such obviously insincere rhetorical devices call forth no shadow of dread. Mr. Gladstone has thus been the means, even to some degree unconsciously, of starting on the way to their solution great questions that involve great principles. He has made it the task of the Liberal party to apply these principles courageously and consistently. False Liberals will more and more shrink from their application; but we may rely upon the nation sending to St. Stephen's "true Liberals," not as defined by Mr. Disraeli, but men who have seen into the social and political maladies of the period, and who are far-sighted enough to suggest, and strong-minded enough to apply fitting remedies. When the Liberal party grapples earnestly with such tasks, its life will become more and more vigorous.

Had Mr. Gladstone's Administration terminated when it had given the country the Irish Church and Irish Land Acts it would have retired with honour, bearing with it the gratitude of the Liberal party and the country. There were no doubt faults and flaws in the workmanship in both cases. The tendency to compromise in order to win success was, as has been indicated, plainly visible in the management of these measures and in some of their details. But the great principles they embodied and illustrated were not to any considerable degree compromised with. The enthusiasm of the Liberal majority carried all before it. The Opposition was practically powerless, except for the influence it could exercise through the House of Lords. Whatever compromise was due to the Government was in the accidents, and not in the substance of their legislative measures. The hopes of Mr. Gladstone's enemies, who predicted that whenever the Irish Church was disestablished the various sections of the Liberal party would fall away from each other quarrelling over the spoil, had been disappointed. The majority remained almost intact, though naturally its enthusiasm was not quite so fresh and buoyant as at first. Mr. Gladstone had practically demonstrated that he could lead a party as well as inspire a nation with enthusiasm. At the time of the passing of the Land Bill the Gladstone Government was in the heyday of its power and popularity, and had it then resigned there would have been little but good to say of it so far as its legislation was concerned. But it was to have no such happy euthanasia. It was destined to live to commit many blunders, to disappoint the hopes of its best friends, and to give its enemies occasion to rejoice and triumph over it.

Whatever other minor causes may have contributed to bring discredit upon the Government, the first and the main source of the change in the estimation in which it was held by Liberals was its education policy. The English Education Bill was Mr.

Gladstone's first great compromise, and it was a compromise
with principles, and not in regard to any mere accidental
conditions. From the hour of the attempt to compromise
with his political opponents in regard to education dates
the beginning of the decline of the Gladstone Administration in public confidence and esteem. If the Prime Minister
were justified by the exigencies of his party, or by other considerations in postponing for a time dealing with the Irish
education problem—which he had indicated was the third
branch of the Upas tree that required to be hewn down—in
order that he might propose and carry the legislation urgently
required by the other portions of the United Kingdom, he ought,
as a prudent party leader, to have set himself to weld the elements
of his party, naturally shaken somewhat loose through the wear and
tear of the last two sessions. The way to do this obviously was to
continue in the paths he had already trodden. He had removed
two great Irish grievances by pursuing a policy of thoroughness.
His legislation had been based upon principles which, as genuinely
progressive, had a future before them. His Irish legislation
could only in fact be regarded as remedial, as truly healing, because
it proceeded upon principles sure to be universally accepted
ultimately, though for the moment the measures brought forward
were professedly applied as exceptional and represented as due
to exceptional circumstances. The same plan might have been
followed in regard to education. Had the Government gone
boldly forward to the construction of an education system founded
upon and faithfully applying the principle of State neutrality in
religion—that is to say, of religious equality, they could not
have failed to inspire fresh courage in their followers. Even had
they been defeated their defeat would have laid the foundation
of future triumph. They would have supplied a policy to their
party, and given it the opportunity of rallying the country to its
side. Unhappily the opposite course was the one actually
adopted. The principle on which Mr. Forster avowedly proceeded
was to take advantage of all existing provisions for supplying
education, and that the State should only supplement when
these were seen to be insufficient. Since the ground, when
occupied at all was almost wholly occupied by Church of
England schools, the effect, if not the intention, of such a policy
of compromise was to give to that Church an enormous increase
of strength and influence in the country. What was equivalent
to a fresh State endowment of religion, through the grants made
to the denominational schools, was systematically instituted.
The provisional system was made permanent, with all its inconsistencies and insufficiencies. Of course it is true it was not an
exclusive endowment of one sect picked out of a number to the

detriment and injury of all the rest. Denominational schools were to be assisted without regard to the character of the religious instruction offered in them. But though the endowment of all sects instead of only one may be more in harmony with religious equality than the endowment of one to the exclusion of all the others, this system of concurrent endowment made no account of those who could accept none of the shibboleths of the sects, who held that the State had nothing to do, in providing for the nation, with the distinctive specialities of any of the sects. Moreover, through the practical conditions existing and known to exist, denominationalism in this sense came to be equivalent to an endowment of the Church of England, the devotion of large sums of public money to the maintenance of schools in which that Church's creeds and catechisms were taught, which existed indeed mainly for the purpose of teaching these. We need not wonder then at the indignation of Dissenters. Mr. Gladstone and Mr. Forster found it pleasant to conciliate their political opponents, and did not hesitate to accept their aid in order to win victories over those who had proved their best friends. They were seduced by the delight of being well spoken of by those who used to revile and say all manner of evil against them falsely. The path of compromise was fully entered upon. A national system (falsely so called) was devised that was an amalgam of two inconsistent and opposing principles. The National and the Denominational, the compulsory and voluntary principles, were to meet together and embrace each other. Meanwhile a direct and powerful impulse was given to Denominationalism to increase still further. All over the country the Church of England turned to account the interval allowed her in order to build new schools, which coming into existence before a certain date were to be entitled to large aid from the State. The management was of course retained in denominational hands. The Church was willing, in consideration of the results, virtually to abandon her national claims; for in consenting to be dealt with as only one sect among a number, she practically confessed her own denominational and nonnational character. The State thus came to be the patron and supporter of schools over which it could exercise only an indirect control by means of the code that defined the conditions of the grants in aid. A system was continued and developed from being merely provisional and temporary into one of a permanent and established character which was calculated to perpetuate division in the educational sphere, and to create and promote constant dissensions. The rebellion of a section of the Liberal party was the natural result of such a policy of makeshifts.

The Dissenters were justified in accusing the Government of
betraying them. Their own aims were not indeed much nobler
than those of their opponents. They too thought more of winning
in the war of sects than of courageously applying national principles. Only by slow degrees do they seem to have awakened
to the bearings and import of the religious equality they professed
to champion. During the struggles in connexion with the
English Bill they were sadly lacking in clearness of aim and distinctness of purpose. The result might have been different if
from the first they had advocated national education organized
as for the nation and not for the sects. Had they from the first
insisted upon the compulsory creation of school boards in every
parish, so that the control of the education of the people should
have been altogether in the hands of the people, the State
sternly refusing to have anything to do with sectarian shibboleths of any kind, the Government would not, we believe, have
succeeded in imposing by help of the Tories the medley of Denominationalism and Nationalism devised by Mr. Gladstone
and Mr. Forster. The opposition to a genuine national scheme
would no doubt have been clamorous and noisy, but it would
only have been for a time. The country would ere long have
come to see the justice and wisdom of taking the control of the
education of the nation out of the hands of the Churches. Unfortunately the opportunity was lost, or rather thrown away. Mr.
Gladstone took his first great false step. The old influences that
cling to and exercise such mastery over him in spite of his
Liberalism, the influence of his Church training and sacerdotal
tendencies, were allowed to blind him to the teaching of true Liberalism. The right honourable gentleman has carried on his own
political education as Hegel said Schelling formed his philosophy,
in the view of the public. By slow degrees at one time, or
with convulsive leaps at another, and through we doubt not
many bitter conflicts with old prejudices and prepossessions, has
he advanced or been propelled forward on the Liberal path. On
the University Tests question, on Irish education, and on English
education, he has from his very sincerity been prone to become
a deviser of compromises, which, but for such influences, his clear
intellect must have led him to reject without a moment's hesitation. Since Mr. Bright's retirement from the Cabinet, this
uncertainty and indecision have been made more and more
prominent. The great evil resulting from such an idiosyncrasy
in the case of a party leader, is that he becomes the sport of circumstances and events. He does not lead, but is himself led.
His action is determined by the influences of the hour, and he
becomes a shuttlecock of political life and a waiter upon expediencies. With a leader of so subtle an intellect as Mr.

Gladstone, such a position is peculiarly perilous. His acute brain becomes the tool of his inclinations, for he can justify any course that seems convenient out of the abundant stores of his exhaustless casuistry. When the enthusiasm for a great cause or a great principle evaporates, the intellect that ought to point the way is apt to be converted into the slave of circumstances and external conditions. And thus the path of compromise comes to be the natural and inevitable roadway along which he travels, or rather in which he advances as it were at haphazard. There seems an irony of fate in the fact that the statesman who boldly applied the principle of religious equality in the disestablishment and disendowment of the Irish Church should have had to stand sponsor for the strange mixture of the compulsory and voluntary principles in education, whereby the Church of England was to obtain a fresh foothold in the country as a State-supported institution.

Since the English Bill became an Act the Government have had another opportunity of applying their education policy. The Scotch Education Bill which became law last session, and which was the issue of an educational struggle in Scotland carried on for a quarter of a century, was, we are glad to admit, an improvement on the English one. The Churches prevented Scotland getting an Education Bill all these years, and would have still prevented a settlement last session had they been able. Credit is therefore due to Mr. Young, the Scotch Lord Advocate, for the courage and persistence—his enemies call it obstinacy—he displayed in the conduct of this Bill. It is an advance upon the English Act, since it makes the election of School Boards universal, and thus provides a machinery for the creation of a genuine national system. But the evils of compromise were in it too. On the principle avowed by the Lord Advocate of "neither prescribing nor proscribing" religious instruction, it was left optional for the School Boards to introduce the teaching of the dominant sect in any and every locality. The result will probably be contests of exceeding bitterness in every parish where School Board elections take place. The partisans of Presbyterianism—the largely predominating sect—will support Presbyterian candidates; Episcopalians, Episcopalian ones; and Roman Catholics, Roman Catholic ones. Each of the several sects into which Presbyterianism again is divided, will probably put forward its own candidate. Thus a bone of contention, which will draw off attention from the main interests and objects that should occupy the electors and the members of the Boards, has been flung down among the Scotch, who, we may be sure, will snarl and wrangle over it with all the eagerness and bitterness which their polemical aptitude and theological zeal supply.

But not only have the Government thus sown the fruitful seeds of multitudinous conflicts and intense religious or theological and ecclesiastical discord, they have created a precedent which will make it difficult to deal with the Irish education problem in harmony with the principle of religious equality. If the Scotch people are allowed to decide as to the teaching of religion in the national schools, how refuse the like privilege to the Irish people? The fact that this must result, in the greater part of Ireland, in handing over the control of the schools to the management of the priests, is not a point which Parliament and the Government have left themselves at liberty to consider. The suspicion almost forces itself on the mind that the introduction of this way of solving the difficulty may have been designed for the very purpose of creating such a precedent for the behoof of Ireland. If this be not so, then Mr. Gladstone has exhibited deplorable feebleness in allowing the clamours of the Scotch, or of the bigoted portion of the population, to bring to nought the principles of Liberalism. There were other compromises besides this leading and most mischievous one in the Scotch Bill. The sacrifice of the money paid for centuries by the Scotch heritors or landowners in support of the parochial or old national schools by returning it into their pockets seemed very like a bribe to the land interest to get rid of its opposition, or at least to secure its neutrality. Unfortunately the bribe comes out of the pockets of the people, as the ratepayers must henceforth pay for the maintenance of the schools which the heritors were bound by every obligation, traditional and legal, to uphold.

Thus the educational policy of Mr. Gladstone has hitherto been one of shifts and compromises, the result of assumed party expediencies or supposed popular necessities, and in flagrant violation of the principles of progress. We have no doubt of the perfect personal sincerity of the Premier in applying such a policy. The disadvantage associated with Mr. Gladstone's leadership of the Liberal party consists in the fact that his impulsive and impressible nature, acted upon by his former Tory and Church training, readily makes him the sincere advocate of inconsistent compromises. He is too easily able to convince himself that he is perfectly right in any departure from Liberal principles which is found or deemed expedient. A policy of impulse may or may not be in accordance with progressive ideas. It is the misfortune of Mr. Gladstone to be always devising policies of impulse.

The natural effect of such a policy must be to weaken the confidence of the Liberal party in its leader. But there have been other things besides the want of thoroughness and the manifest inconsistency of his education policy in England and Scotland, that have tended to alienate Liberals from the present Prime Minister. His entire course in regard to Irish education has been tortuous in the extreme. After what took place when during the Ministry of Mr. Disraeli, Lord Mayo's "levelling-up" policy was suggested, which was so earnestly denounced by Mr. Gladstone, it might have been supposed there was no danger of the right hon. gentleman making a similar blunder. The voice of the nation pronounced emphatically against any attempt at redressing the evils of Protestant ascendancy by levelling-up the Catholics. "Concurrent endowments" in Ireland were indignantly discarded as soon as suggested. The correspondence between Lord Mayo and the Catholic bishops showed that nothing would satisfy the Irish Catholic hierarchy, except the endowment of a Catholic University over which the State should have no control, which should be entirely under the thumb of the bishops, who should have the right of appointing or a veto upon the appointment of the professors. Mr. Disraeli would never have brought forward such a scheme, and Lord Mayo, to his credit, steadily declined to give any countenance to the more extreme demands of the priests and bishops. Mr. Gladstone helped to increase the disfavour in which the Tory Government stood with the country, and to render his own triumph more certain and brilliant by his vigorous denunciations of the assumed "levelling-up" policy of the Conservatives. Yet the present Government has done very much to apply the justly abused policy of concurrent endowments since it took office. Of course, in a period of transition from the stage of Protestant ascendancy to religious equality, many things may be and may require to be done to soothe the sensitive susceptibilities of Irish Catholics, which may not be strictly consistent with a progressive policy. We pass over, therefore, such measures as the Glebe Loans Bill and the Maynooth College Bill in Ireland, and the Prison Ministers Bill in Great Britain, and say nothing of the extent to which the common school system of the former country is even now controlled by the priests. There is a more serious accusation than these supply, suspicious though some of them be, against the Gladstone Administration. The Prime Minister and his colleagues have perversely, and as they were well aware against the clearly declared will of the country, carried out the policy of concurrent endowments, of levelling-up, against which they formerly declaimed with so much seeming zeal and earnestness. "The phrase religious equality," remarked Mr. Gladstone, in reply to a question put to him in the course of last session, "admits of different interpretations. You may say that religious equality prevails conditionally or unconditionally." We presume the equality is unconditional when no religious sect has any favour shewn to it, and conditional when various denominations receive equal favours. Religious equality, that is to say, may be carried out either by levelling-down or by levelling-up. The former alternative was applied to Ireland in the Irish Church Act, though as the after-endowment of the disestablished Church, and of Maynooth College have proved, only partially. The latter is exemplified in some of our colonies, as for instance in Trinidad. In a despatch from Lord Kimberley, of the 6th January, 1871, to the Governor of Trinidad, his lordship writes: "The object which Her Majesty's Government desire to attain is, as you are aware, religious equality. Where, as in Jamaica, the most numerous Christian community on principle objects to State endowments for religion, equality cannot be attained except by entire withdrawal of such endowments. But where, as in Trinidad, no large proportion of the Christian population objects to religious endowments, but on the contrary there is a general desire to maintain them, Her Majesty's Government are ready to consent to the maintenance of State endowments, provided they be distributed equally amongst all denominations willing to accept them." His lordship proceeds to say that the Roman Catholics in Trinidad are twice as numerous as the Anglicans, and yet only receive about the same amount of money from the State. He therefore proposes to reduce the endowment of the latter, in order to increase that of the former, seeing the Government is not prepared to recommend any addition to the ecclesiastical expenditure. The same process ought, he suggests, to be applied in Barbadoes, Grenada, and St. Lucia.

The Government therefore adopt both theoretically and practically the alternative method of applying religious equality referred to by the Premier, apparently forgetting that " Christian communities" may not be the only classes of religionists who should be taken into account. Without pressing this consideration, it seems plain that levelling-up or levelling-down is a matter of the purest indifference to the Gladstone Administration. If we could suppose Ireland independent, and Mr. Gladstone the Irish Premier, he would doubtless establish and endow the Church of the majority, throwing sops the while to the Protestants in the shape of smaller endowments to keep them quiet. Since he is the Minister of Great Britain and Ireland, and the majority are strongly opposed to any such course, he finds it impossible to do this frankly and boldly. But he has applied to Ireland in various ways the levelling-up process, and there is reason to fear he may design to solve the Irish education problem on the principle of concurrent endowments. Unhappily, his education policy in England and Scotland affords a precedent for such a course in Ireland. Not the least objection which Liberals must have to the education policy of the Gladstone Government is that it has supplied such precedents. The country has been led into a position in which it will be impossible to act consistently upon Liberal principles without affording just and reasonable cause for complaint and discontent to the Irish. That is to say, the Minister who was to remedy Irish grievances has paved the way for the creation of others as formidable as any he has removed. No more serious accusation could be urged against the leader of the Liberal party than that he has rendered it impossible to carry out Liberal principles without giving Irish Catholics just ground for serious dissatisfaction. That is the position in which we now find ourselves. In England, the church which is numerically the most powerful, is helped by the Government to maintain its numerous schools, though instituted for denominational purposes; while in Scotland local majorities are left to determine whether religious instruction, and, if any, what, is to be given in the national schools. How is Great Britain to insist upon a purely secular system in Ireland in such circumstances, without giving occasion to the cry of unequal legislation? Yet the same principle applied to Ireland will make the Catholic priests the controllers of the greater portion of the national education.

Not content with landing the country and the legislature in this difficulty, in creating this well-nigh insoluble problem for legislation, the Premier has in other ways dealt in a most unsatisfactory manner with the subject of Irish education. It is impossible to contemplate without the gravest misgivings as to what may yet become the policy of the Premier in this matter. We refer mainly to his dealing with Mr. Fawcett in connexion with that gentleman's Trinity College (Dublin) Bill. A brief narrative will put this in a clear light.

Mr. Fawcett moved his first resolution on the subject, on 3rd August, 1869, proposing to free the scholarships and fellowships of the College from all religious disabilities. It was intimated at the same time, on the part of the authorities of the College, by Dr. Ball, that they had abandoned all notion of opposing the resolution. But Mr. Chichester Fortescue, then Chief Secretary for Ireland, instead of welcoming the opportunity for an amicable settlement thus presented, declared that Mr. Fawcett's scheme would not satisfy the Roman Catholics, whose objection was to mixed education, and whose grievance would not be removed if

Q 2

they were only enabled to obtain University degrees by that means. The following year, Mr. Fawcett introduced his Bill earlier in the session. Mr. Gladstone now took the matter into his own hands, and assumed high ground. He claimed that the Government had been intrusted by the country with the task of dealing with the state of Ireland, and that if so important a matter as education were to be handed over to the charge of a private member, it must be concluded the Government had lost the confidence of the House. But though treating the matter as one of confidence, Mr. Gladstone would not take the House of Commons into *his* confidence by explaining what he proposed to do. Mr. Fawcett reintroduced his Bill in 1871, but the Government managed to put off its consideration till too late in the session for any practical result, as it was the 2nd of August before the member for Brighton could secure a day for its discussion. The Prime Minister again opposed the proposed opening of Trinity College, on the ground that more was necessary to do justice to the Irish Catholics than would thereby be provided. But the House and the country were still kept in ignorance of the Ministerial intentions. This unsatisfactory mode of dealing with the matter had excited not a little apprehension, for although the Government disavowed any intention of creating a Roman Catholic University, they had never disavowed the purpose of constituting or endowing Roman Catholic colleges. The suspicions of the country have not been allayed by what passed last session. The undignified course then adopted, the evident eagerness of the Government to get rid of Mr. Fawcett's Bill at all hazards, the devices to gain that end that were adopted, and after intimating their intention of treating the question as one of confidence, their efforts to prevent a vote being fairly taken, must be fresh in the reader's memory. The second reading of Mr. Fawcett's Bill had been carried by a large majority, late in the month of March, Mr. Gladstone having so far yielded as to announce that the Government would not oppose the part of the Bill dealing with the abolition of tests, though resolutely opposed to the clauses providing for the reconstruction of the governing body of the University, on the ground that it would be a long time under them before the Catholic element would have any appreciable influence in the management of the University. Accordingly notice was given on the part of the Government, that when the Bill went into committee, or rather when the motion for going into committee came to be discussed, Lord Hartington would propose to divide the measure in two—the one dealing with the abolition of tests alone, and the other with the reconstruction of the governing body. . Intimation was made through a morning paper that this motion would be made a test of confidence, and that if beaten, the Government would resign. Passing over the objection to the source through which the anouncement was made, which at the time was demurred to as disrespectful to the House of Commons and inconsistent with the dignity of the Sovereign, the least to be expected was that having made the question one of confidence, the Government should have facilitated its discussion. Instead of that, every artifice was employed to stave off the subject when the 23rd of April arrived; and when success attended these tactics, the Prime Minister declined, though appealed to by Mr. Fawcett, to give that gentleman a Government day afterwards. Thus by tactics that are too familiar now to the House of Commons, Mr. Gladstone managed to prevent the matter from being brought to an issue. In the course of the early debates the Premier plainly declared that no reform would do justice to the Irish Catholics which did not enable them to obtain a University training for their sons in institutions where the religious influences they valued so highly were predominant. This was no new announcement on the part of the right hon. gentleman. So long ago as December, 1867, he had stated, at Southport, that the Irish Catholics were entitled to have separate Catholic institutions.

" If there be a Roman Catholic," he said, " and there are numbers of them, who hold in Ireland the very same opinion that the great bulk of us hold in England—viz., that we prefer having our children trained in establishments where their own religion is taught, these children are debarred from the privilege of a University degree, and that degree being a civil privilege, it comes to this, that there are still in Ireland civil disabilities on account of religious opinion. I own that if I were prohibited from sending my son to be trained in a school where his religion was taught, I should think it a great grievance. I ask you as good citizens, as just men, to place yourselves in the position of the Roman Catholics, or Presbyterians, who hold the opinion I have described, and I ask whether it can be said that we have yet given full and perfect equality in Ireland ?"

This implies that justice will only be done to the Irish Catholics by placing at their disposal, or giving them the means of instituting special Roman Catholic colleges for the training of their own youth. The same principles applied to elementary education would necessitate exclusively Catholic schools—schools that is, which under priestly control are pervaded by what is called a "Catholic atmosphere." The Irish Catholics, as explained in their manifesto of 1869, require " a distinct college (in Ireland) conducted upon purely Catholic principles." They have resolved to oppose by all the means in their power, " the extension and per

petuation of the mixed system of education, whether by the
creation of new institutions, the maintenance of old ones, or by
changing Trinity College, Dublin, into a mixed college." In
June, 1871, at a meeting at Maynooth, the priests and bishops
denounced the movement instituted for relieving the masters of the
National schools from absolute dependence on the managers, and
for freeing them from the liability to summary dismissal without
right of appeal or any means of redress. We have lately seen in
the case of the parish priest of Callan, that dependence on the
managers often means dependence on the will of the hierarchy,
and thereby the latter are able to get rid of any teacher who
essays to exercise the slightest measure of independence. They
threaten that the removal of this "indispensable safeguard of the
faith and morals of Catholic children," will lead to the "severance
of all connexion between the Catholic clergy and the Board of
Education."

We see then that what the Irish Catholics, as represented by
their bishops and priests, demand is the maintenance of a system
of education, both elementary and university, by the State for the
special behoof of the Roman Catholic Church. A system that
has been already overturned in Italy, France, Germany, and
even Austria, is sought to be instituted in Ireland. And we
see unhappily that the Gladstone Administration, instead of
scouting and denouncing so retrograde a policy, appear inclined
to promote it. Infidelity to Liberal principles could not be
more flagrant or more worthy of indignant reprobation. Of
course it is not to be supposed, after all his pledges, that Mr.
Gladstone will openly propose to create a Roman Catholic college
as a State institution. The fact that he has so long dallied with
the subject, and so frequently deferred it from session to session,
shows how thoroughly alive he is to the difficulties and dangers
of a compromise such as his own words indicate an intention of
submitting. But the time has come when the question can be no
longer delayed. The Government must deal with it during the
coming session. We cannot believe there is any truth in the
rumour circulated and possibly invented by political opponents—
that it is to be again got rid of for the session by the appointment
of a royal commission. There is no need for any commission, and
its appointment would be a flagrant evasion of an imperative duty.
Besides, the controversies on the subject are not to be set at rest
were there a score of commissions. The partisans of Ultramontanism, however often defeated, will never be silenced. The
controversy that has recently taken place on the subject of Ireland's need for a supply of university teaching, in the columns of
the *Times*, might and would be carried on interminably. Yet if

any one fact about Ireland be plain, it is that the Roman Catholic population are never likely to have so large a proportion of their sons fitted for, and anxious to obtain university education as the Protestant. This arises from the simple fact that the strength of the former lies in the poorer classes of the people, while that of the latter is mainly in the middle and the higher, except in Ulster, where Protestantism is more generally diffused among all classes. It is vain, therefore, to say that any very large element of the Catholic population is debarred from obtaining university training from the want of Roman Catholic colleges alone. If these existed, no doubt more Roman Catholics might seek the benefits of such an education for their children. But it is vain to hope that in any circumstances the mass of the Irish Catholic population will send their sons to the university, or that they will even do so in anything like the proportion in which it has been done by the poorer classes of the Scottish people. A commission to examine the question would only therefore be a device to put it off till a more convenient season, or to roll the duty of dealing with it upon another Government. That the Gladstone Administration should be deemed capable of so disingenuous a device only shows how much it has fallen in public esteem. There can be no doubt the delay that has already occurred in facing the problem is due to the conviction entertained by the Government of the exceeding difficulty of the task, owing to the absence of unanimity regarding it in the Liberal ranks. The Irish Liberals, as largely obedient to Cardinal Cullen, would not agree to any development of the system of mixed education. Nothing would please the Irish Catholics but a State-endowment of the Catholic religion under the guise of supporting education. Having destroyed Protestant ascendancy, Parliament and the Government are asked to lay the foundations of Roman Catholic ascendancy in Ireland. Of course, against all such schemes genuine Liberals must ever protest, and must use their utmost efforts to oppose and defeat them should they be brought forward. Here, then, was the occasion of a split in the Liberal party. Mr. Gladstone has been aware of this peril, and he has striven to avoid it by involving his plans regarding Irish education in mystery. This is the real cause of that policy of silence denounced by Dr. Ball and others as so injurious to the peace and tranquillity of Ireland. The Premier has shrunk from alienating either his Ultramontane or his Protestant supporters, and has by occasional dark hints encouraged the hopes alternately of both.

Conduct like this is unworthy, we need hardly say, not merely of a Liberal Government, but of honest and upright men. It has involved the Ministry in a tangled skein from which they will find it difficult to extricate themselves. As we write we hear a rumour that they will seek to escape the difficulty, which if not of their own creation, they have yet so greatly intensified, by a scheme worthy of Mr. Lowe's exceeding acuteness. Instead of adopting one of the alternative courses of either boldly supporting and extending mixed education, or of endowing sectarian institutions, another device may be tried. A suspensory Bill dealing with the property and endowments of Trinity College and of the Queen's Colleges, will, it is said, be introduced in the coming session, as was done in the case of the Irish Church. The Government will take into its own hands the control of the property, with a view to satisfy the wants of Ireland in regard to university education. Upon some plan not yet divulged, this property will afterwards be divided among Irish Protestants and Roman Catholics, in satisfaction of their supposed respective claims. With the amount thus bestowed on them, the Catholics may endow a sectarian college if they please, but whether they do or not, the Government will be able to say that it is in no way responsible for their action. Meanwhile, the State will probably provide a central university, modelled on the plan of the University of London, which shall be a mere examining Board. Applicants for degrees will require to pass the examinations of this Board, which will be the only lawful source for bestowing university degrees. Thereby the "civil right" of a degree will be conferred irrespective of creed, while the Catholics will be gratified by the institution—if they so decide—of a college of their own in which the preparatory training for their students would be supplied. If such should prove to be the Government plan, it must be admitted that it is preferable to the scheme of establishing State institutions for the purpose of training not good citizens, but good Catholics or Protestants, as the case may be. Such a scheme exhibits no slight ingenuity on the part of its authors. But in reality the State will all the same have bestowed the funds by which sectarian colleges might be endowed. If it evades the responsibility of an open patronage of such institutions, it will be morally responsible for them all the same. By an adroit device calculated and fitted to silence political opponents, it will have bestowed a sectarian religious system upon Ireland in accordance with the disavowed and denounced policy of concurrent endowment or levelling-up. Even if by such means the Gladstone Administration should succeed in evading the perils that threaten it in connexion with Irish education, we do not think the success of the plan will tend to make them any more the objects of trust to the Liberal party and the country.

In all this, however, we are dealing with a hypothetical future. Whatever be the upshot of the Irish education problem, we have seen that the general education policy of the Government has involved it in discredit and destroyed confidence in Mr. Gladstone and his colleagues. All through the dreary session of 1871 the effects were plainly evident. We do not go back upon that session in detail because the doings of the Government in its course have been already weighed in the balance and found grievously wanting in the pages of the *Westminster Review.* The tendency to compromise was developed in all directions. The Army Bill—the "great" measure of the session—has remained what it was then—a mere measure for the abolition of purchase. Our land forces are yet to be organized, and while the Powers of Europe are making strenuous efforts to add to their defensive capabilities, England, though spending forty millions sterling on her army and navy, continues very much as she was. Mr. Reed has lately proved in the *Times* that in regard to the navy we have been simply standing still, and the same seems to be true of the land forces as well. Last session the "great" measure of the period was the Ballot Bill, which became law after a series of changes that completely revolutionized its character and complexion. What was intended to be a measure of compulsory secrecy, was converted into a Bill for legalizing optional secrecy. The measure had been prepared with such negligence and listlessness that the necessity of enforcing secrecy by penalties does not seem to have occurred to its authors. The House of Commons refused to allow the omission to be supplied when it was discovered, and both Parliament and the country evidently shrank from the logical course of rendering the ballot a reality by making its secrecy inviolable. The fact that Mr. Gladstone himself had during the recess described the Ballot Bill as a measure to enable every man "to vote secretly if he liked," proved that the Prime Minister, only a few months before his Bill was introduced, did not contemplate any of those compulsory enactments without which he declared that the measure was a mere farce. The Ballot Bill which became law was a sham, and none of the Ministers seemed to know very much about it. The course of Mr. Gladstone himself, in relation to the ballot, is an illustration of his habitual facility of conviction and conversion. The ballot was espoused by him, as by several of his colleagues, from party motives and for party purposes. It was not anxiously desired by the country, which on the whole was apathetic. But it had for years been regarded as forming part of the orthodox Liberal programme, and as an orthodox Liberal Minister, Mr. Gladstone felt he must carry it. The process of reasoning by which he explained and justified his change of opinion on the Ballot is one of the recent curiosities of political life. He had always, he told the country on one occasion, held the doctrine that the franchise was a trust, and it was therefore right that the trustee should exercise it openly in view of those for whom as well as for himself he was acting. Such was the state of matters, but such it no longer is. The Reform Bill of 1867, by introducing Household Suffrage, converted the franchise from a trust into a property. It is no longer to be exercised by the individual voter on behalf of others, but only as for himself. There is no longer therefore any necessity for its public exercise. Without questioning Mr. Gladstone's personal belief in his own sincerity, we can hardly yet conceive that such an argument was seriously put forward. We cannot fancy that Mr. Gladstone believes the franchise is not a trust, using the word in any sensible and intelligible fashion. The voter is surely bound to exercise his vote as much now as ever for the good of the community and country. If we had Manhood instead of Household Suffrage, this would still be the case. But in reality, under the latter the proportion of voters to the non-voting population is, as Mr. Disraeli has repeatedly pointed out, still comparatively small. If the franchise was a trust before, it must be a trust still. The idea that it may be regarded as the property of the individual must logically lead to the justification of all manner of bribery and corruption. A man may do what he will with his own, and if he be not responsible to public opinion and his own conscience for the manner in which he discharges a public function, he may do with it what in his own view will bring him most benefit. If that were only a glass of beer or a sovereign, he must be entitled to barter his vote for either the one or the other as might best please him. Even, however, if Mr. Gladstone's premises were admitted, that the franchise has been transformed from a trust into a property, his conclusion does not follow. What does follow is, that the voter should be at liberty to do as he likes with his vote, and to give it either openly or secretly as he might choose. That is to say, there is no basis found in the new character of the vote for the compulsory secrecy alleged to be the principle of the Ballot.

We only adduce this remarkable process of reasoning as an apt illustration of Mr. Gladstone's facility of conviction. He is able on the slightest, or on what to most men would seem no grounds whatever, to satisfy himself that any course that seems expedient for the moment is right and proper. Such a disposition is the natural parent of policies of compromise, such as we have lately become so familiar with. Whatever the effects of the Ballot may be—and as yet no evidence is afforded that it will work for the good of the country—it will remain a scandal in English political history that it should have been adopted and promoted after the manner exemplified during the last two sessions of Parliament.

We have now traced the achievements of the Gladstone Administration in domestic politics during the four sessions in which it has guided the destinies of a great empire. We have seen that after the first flush of enthusiasm had passed away, the disposition to compromise came to the front. We have traced the influence of that disposition even in the great works of the first two sessions, which were based upon and exemplified genuine Liberal principles. We have seen it developed as time went on, and security in office made the Ministry negligent. We have at greater length traced out its mischievous effects on the Government's education policy, in which compromise was no longer in the accidents or circumstances of the measures brought forward, but in the principles of the measures themselves. And if we examine the course of the past two sessions and the conduct of the Gladstone Administration throughout them, we shall find that their legislative action has been of the same kind, exhibiting the same pernicious abandonment of distinct principles, and the same lack of clear conviction or intelligent comprehension of what the real mission of the leaders of the party of progress ought to be. The weakness of the Opposition and the *dolce far niente* policy of its leader—who, as one of his own party has lately accused him, has seemed to be rather in competition with than in opposition to the Prime Minister—have allowed the Government to do very much as it pleased. It has had nothing to fear from its political opponents, and the discontent of the Radicals, though active enough, has not been able to make itself formidable. The country has been submissive and generally apathetic. The faults and blunders of the Government have caused it annoyance on many occasions. It has felt discredited especially by the feebleness of the foreign policy of the Ministry, while it has more than once been stirred to irritation by the tortuous and inconsistent conduct of the Prime Minister. But on the whole the country has been largely indifferent to the politics and the political situations of the hour. Genuine earnestness in politics would almost appear to be dying out. As a people we are too much engrossed with money-making, and the haste to become rich too entirely occupies our thoughts and energies to allow us to pay great heed to national interests and international

relations unless at exceptional crises.   Only an apathetic country
manifoldly afflicted with *laissez-faire* could have tolerated so
patiently a Government that has been guilty of such manifold
and manifest failings as the Gladstone Administration.

That the Government has presumed upon this want of interest
in national affairs on the part of the country, has been evidenced
in many ways.   Mr. Gladstone is not a man to be indifferent to
public opinion—on several occasions both he and his colleagues
have manifested a painful servility which has tended to alienate
respect from them; and yet along with this servility there
has been at other times a disregard of the legitimate complaints and the justifiable indignation of public opinion.   The
same Administration which has swayed hither and thither at
the bidding of popular deputations in regard to the Contagious
Diseases Act, has shown itself defiant of the rights and convenience of the people in regard to the Epping Forest and
the Thames Embankment Bills.   No more discreditable spectacle
has been presented to the public view of late years than the
paltering with principle and conviction on the subject of the
first-named of these three measures.   We are no advocates of
that measure.   We have no faith in the virtue that requires
to be created and guarded by Act of Parliament.   But the
Government, it must be supposed, believed they were right when
they passed that Bill   They were entitled to make the
trial they attempted; but having done so, they ought surely to
have abided by their principles and convictions until the trial
had been fully made.   The Home Secretary, however, has
made it plain that if they had convictions on the matter,
they would suffer no inconvenience nor endure any risk to give
them practical effect.   Mr. Bruce's voice has been both for and
against the policy that had been avowed by the Ministry of which
he is a member, according as it suited the views of the rival
deputations by which he was beset.   The same disposition
to devise halting compromises as has been exemplified in so
much else has been also shown in measures like the Licensing
Bill and the Public Health Bills.   There has been in the
domestic legislation of the Government a meddlesomeness
in matters with which it had nothing to do that has been
often vexatious.   The pettiness begotten in men of narrow
natures, put into prominent positions of power and influence for
which they are ill fitted, has been exemplified in Messrs.
Ayrton and Bruce.   Yet though there is hardly a fault left for
these gentlemen to commit, though the insolence of the one
and the feebleness of the other have alike produced impatience
and resentment in the public mind, Mr. Gladstone clings with

womanish tenacity to his much-abused subordinates. His admirers are fond of telling us that in thus refusing to abandon his colleagues he exhibits the manly courage of a Palmerston; but there is a considerable distance between the shrewish obstinacy of the present Premier and the generous *camaraderie* of his predecessor in the Liberal leadership. The faults of an Ayrton would never have been tolerated by a Palmerston. Unfortunately the colleagues of the Prime Minister share his weaknesses and faults without his virtues. The same Ministry which has been so forward to legislate in the most inquisitorial manner upon trifles, has yet shrunk from grappling with duties that lay clearly before it. While we have had a Ballot Act and a Licensing Act, legal reform and local taxation have been left untouched.

If we turn from the contemplation of domestic policy to the management of our colonial and foreign affairs, a similar spectacle meets us. The Government of a great empire has been carried on less in the spirit of patriotic statesmen than in that of commercial clerks who only follow the routine of official precedent. In dealing with our colonies too much prominence has been given to an ill-judged economy. We do not advocate a policy of colonial dependence. Our colonies ought to be trained in habits of self-government and self-reliance; they ought to be taught to assume more and more the responsibilities of independent self-regulation and control. But that does not imply that they should be treated as needy poor relations, whose requirements are to be always met with a frigid but resolute refusal. It does not warrant such language as Lord Granville employed when, in answer to an application for an Imperial guarantee for a loan, he told the colony that England ought to ask money from them rather than they from England, and that as they governed themselves they must protect themselves. It does not justify the policy which wrung from Canada a consent to the surrender of her fishery rights and the abandonment of her claims on the United States for compensation for the Fenian raids concocted on American soil, by guaranteeing a railway loan. The entire spirit imported into our colonial relations by the present Government has been too much of this character, and has made the conclusion seem to many to be inevitable, that they desired nothing so much as to see the connexion between England and her colonies severed. Of late we are glad to admit there has been a change for the better. The present Under-Secretary for the Colonies has spoken of them and the connexion with the mother country in a different manner from that exemplified in the despatches of Earls Granville and Kimberley. We trust the change may grow still greater, and more and more in the right direction. Much, and it may be irremediable mischief has, however, been already done. In Canada, for example, there is an increasing conviction that England only desires to be rid of her troublesome dependencies. There is also a widespread idea that the mother country is afraid of the United States. The concessions made in the Alabama Treaty as well as the habitual tone of the Foreign Office towards the United States go far to justify the belief. The Government need to be reminded that national honour and national pride, though they may not seem marketable commodities, are yet precious possessions in even an economical light. The national self-respect has been lowered by recent events. Britain feels ill at ease with herself because she feels that she is no longer either feared or respected by others as she once was.

If this be made apparent by the colonial policy of Mr. Gladstone's Government its character has not been redeemed by its foreign policy. Though the action of the Government during the Franco-German war was generally prudent, there was a feebleness of tone as if proceeding from a dread of war, which in betraying itself made those who exhibited it powerless. We do not need to remind our readers of the surrender at discretion made by the Government when Russia demanded the sacrifice of what we had gained by the war in the Crimea. The country was bewildered and confused, and can scarcely yet believe the sacrifice has been made. Yet that we have yielded, and yielded under the influence of the fear of war, what would never have been asked of us had not the attitude and bearing of the Government satisfied Russia that it would yield, is too obvious to be denied. Since the Crimean war it has been too much the tendency of Great Britain to abdicate her functions as a European Power and to sink to a position of isolation and inaction. The Governments are not alone to blame, for they have been the too faithful reflex of the national indifference to all but our own material interests. The country, however, could not have found a fitter guide to console it in its lot than the statesman who sang "Happy England!" A leader of another stamp might have roused the nation to a more noble conception of its true functions instead of soothing its conscience into apathy in regard to the higher interests of mankind. Mr. Gladstone supplied what was necessary to apply a salve to the wounded pride of the country—suspicious that all was not as it should be—by his millennial doctrine of moral force.

But has not the Gladstone Administration atoned for the short-comings and blunders of its foreign policy by the sanction it has given to the solution of international difficulties by means of the introduction into international politics of the principle of arbi-tration ? Whatever consolation may be gathered from this has been unhappily marred by the manner of the sanction. The story of the Alabama arbitration is a record of blundering incapacity. From beginning to end we have only a series of vacillating com-promises. Arbitration, under certain circumstances, may prove a useful and beneficial method of settling differences between Governments and nations without necessity for the dread arbi-trament of war. But the manner in which the Alabama nego-tiations were conducted throughout involved the principle of arbitration itself in discredit. The country, far from feeling proud of this chapter in its recent history, views the whole matter with a sort of weary aversion. The very mention of the indirect claims and the supplementary treaty excites feelings of humilia-tion. It is not because we have to pay our millions for faults which we never committed, or because we have lost territory to which we felt we had every rightful claim, that we cannot join in the congratulations so profusely echoed by admirers of the Government. All that is bad enough, but worse remains behind. The tame submission to American arrogance, the aban-donment of our own just claims in case of offending American susceptibilities, the pressure put on Canada to make her do the same, together with the series of perverse blunders exhibited throughout the proceedings, have lowered the national self-respect.

We see the depths of discredit to which an Administration still left in possession of a large parliamentary majority may descend. Not only have the Premier and his colleagues lost the confidence of Liberals by their compromises in legislation, they have by the feebleness of their administration deprived them-selves to no small extent of the confidence of the nation also. And in the state of discredit into which the Government has fallen, it is not easy to see where the possibility of recovery lies. There is a promise of great things in the coming session. Ministers are to retrace their steps and retrieve their lost honour in the education question, by boldly asserting and applying the forgotten and despised—though once so highly honoured—principle of religious equality. They are to grapple firmly and thoroughly with the much-needed work of county administration and taxation. They are to take a step forward in the path towards a satisfactory handling of the land question. Much else they will do which will prove the thoroughness of their Liberalism. Such promises, however, were they ten times as great as they are, would scarcely excite enthusiasm in the country; we have had so much promise already that we have grown weary of looking for its fulfilment. And even though the Government were to undertake all that is now being suggested, it is felt that they will do it simply under the impulse of assumed party expediency. Confidence in the old genuine Liberalism of the Premier can with difficulty be re-vived. The part he has played in Irish education, his coquetting with Ultramontanism, and the avowed favour with which he regards the claims of the Irish Catholic hierarchy to control the national education, make it impossible for the hopes that have already been so cruelly disappointed again readily to spring to life. The country has abandoned the expectation of finding a national leader in Mr. Gladstone. But it was hoped that if he could not go before the people and raise their aspirations to a higher level, he might yet be trusted to fulfil honestly and impartially what was demanded by the people from their present stage of political culture. Even this minor rôle has not been fulfilled. Mismanagement and misrule have spread a spirit of mutiny throughout the departments, and the Government has been even accused of deceiving those whose interests it was bound to protect. Everywhere throughout the services of the State there is dissatisfaction and irritation. Uncertainty pervades every branch of the administration. The execution of the laws against even the most flagrant defiance of the State's authority is no longer sure. The very criminal classes are encouraged to presume on the feebleness of the administration. All the while ideas subversive of social organization, and that threaten the very existence of the State are fostered and diffused. Sometimes it might almost seem as if the time were coming when there shall be no ruler in England, but every man shall be left to do what seems right in his own eyes. It is this spirit of disorganization and disregard of law that requires to be checked. Active and ener-getic efforts need to be put forth to meet it. At no period of its history has the national prosperity been so great as now. We have been advancing, as Mr. Gladstone said not long ago, by leaps and bounds. And the prospect of further progress stretches forward in the vista of an indefinite future. At such a period national tran-quillity and contentment naturally prevail. For what they have done—and not less for what they have left undone—in fostering this prosperity, Ministers ought to receive all credit. Our relations with foreign States are disturbed by no shadow of threatening evil. Ministers have undoubtedly been anxiously solicitous to guard the country from mischievous and injurious complications abroad. And they have succeeded, though success has sometimes been bought with a great price. Still a powerful nation, if it is to continue powerful, must think of other aims than its material prosperity. Its Government ought to incite it to consider what it owes to the cause of human progress, while at the same time laying deep and broad the foundations of social order and political organization upon true and stable principles. The Gladstone Administration has not always borne this in mind. The immediate has been too constantly present with it. If it is to reattain the altitude from which it has declined, it must think more of the distant and remote, of the ultimate consequences as well as the immediate results, of its principles and policy.

CONTEMPORARY LITERATURE.

The Foreign Books noticed in the following sections are chiefly supplied by Messrs.
WILLIAMS & NORGATE, *Henrietta Street, Covent Garden, and* MR. NUTT, 270,
Strand.

THEOLOGY AND PHILOSOPHY.

MR. STATHAM has undertaken a difficult task, but he encounters it boldly, with no distrust in his power to sketch and
interpret it.[1] Beginning with the present position of Christianity, he
goes back to its earlier conditions, explains the meaning of the conflict
between religion and science, with the part to be taken in it; touches
upon theism, atheism and pantheism, expounds what he terms
humanism, and after illustrating the constancy of religious character,
points out the way to advance. The author is decidedly anti-christian
in belief and temper. In his opinion organised Christianity is an
insanity. There is no personal God, but an unknown force possibly,
which set all things we see and know in motion. Civilization is advancing, evolution is everywhere active; man, subject to inexorable
law, must work out his salvation, but he is utterly in the dark with
regard to the end of his best hopes and endeavours; for beneath a
universal and transcending power he merely lives and suffers, thinks
and triumphs, then vanishes away. The author asserts that the doctrines
of the efficacy of prayer and trust in divine Providence are the chief
foundations of *practical* Christianity, and professes that he can hardly
say we know whether Jesus ever had an individual existence or not. It
is easy to point out, as he does, the inconsistency of the professors of
popular Christianity with their alleged creed, and to take the common
ideas of it in order the more effectually to show their unsoundness.
All this is usual with public lecturers. But the true genius of Christianity is a different thing from that which is often professed or
preached. The manner in which Mr. Statham accounts for the success of Christianity at first, which he finds in the conditions of the
Roman empire, conditions which made it adaptable to our barbarous
Teutonic forefathers, is an able, if not completely successful sketch.
Excluding Christianity as an important element of civilization, he
attributes the latter to science or the positive philosophy. In like
manner he all but ignores the emotional side of man's nature, denies
those intuitional tendencies for which many think no experience can
account or compensate, and supposes knowledge to be nothing more
than the co-ordinations of impressions made upon us, or sensations
produced in us individually by external objects. And when the

---

[1] "From Old to New. A Sketch of the Present Religious Position." In Eight
Lectures. By F. Reginald Statham. London : Longmans.

author has taken a personal God out of the universe he tell us "to work out our salvation." The majority of mankind find it hard, however, to do that, without belief in a moral Governor of the world, or in a blessed immortality. Few will agree with him in thinking that the feeling of uncertainty as to the end of our hopes and endeavours makes us heroes. The Apostle Paul and Martin Luther would not have been heroes had they laboured on amid doubt and uncertainty as though these feelings gave zest to their lives. The most intelligent expounders of the Christian religion admit that it has been grievously corrupted, that it has been encrusted with superstition, that existing Churches are bad representatives and exponents of it, and that it must be brought back to its pristine purity with such adaptation as a true philosophy suggests. They maintain, however, that its essence will survive and be still the leaven of corrupt humanity, purifying society, guiding civilization, ennobling culture. It is impossible for historic criticism to deny the personal existence of Jesus in the reign of Tiberius, or to resolve all his teachings into the accumulated precepts of the Essenes. Mr. Statham may do so in the face of the most convincing proof to the contrary; but he cannot be taken for a fair interpreter of the great figure that arose out of Judaism and realised the long-cherished Messianic hopes in a more exalted sense than prophets dreamt of even in their highest imaginings. To take the *organised* Christianity of the day, or indeed of any post-apostolic period, as the legitimate outcome of the religion shadowed forth by Jesus, is a one-sided procedure.

Mr. Mocatta's volume[1] contains brief portraits of no less than sixty-five characters mentioned in the Old Testament, from which he deduces precepts and examples. Virtues and vices are pointed out in connexion with personages, in order to encourage and warn. The book is one of practical lessons founded upon the Old Testament, especially on the individuals there spoken of. Abraham, Moses and David, as might be expected, are painted at some length, to illustrate family affection, faith, benevolence, parental duty, individual merit, temper, meditation, &c. The reader is treated to a series of short sermons, with a practical tendency throughout. The author seems to be unacquainted with the results of modern historical criticism applied to the Hebrew records, or if he be not, they are ignored. He is a believer in the literal truth of the narratives, and therefore in Samson's miraculous strength as well as Jonah's miraculous safety in the whale's belly. Seeing no mythical elements in the Old Testament, Eve, Cain, Lot, and others appear as simple historical persons. In like manner, and with the same want of perspicacity or knowledge, Ecclesiastes is cited as Solomon's, the Proverbs indiscriminately as his also, and the Psalms as David's compositions. The letter on immortality at the end of the book, also shows how erroneous are the writer's views on the sacred literature of the Jews and its contents, for nothing is better

[1] "Moral Biblical Gleanings and Practical Teachings. Illustrated by Biographical Sketches drawn from the Sacred Volume." By J. L. Mocatta. London: Trübner and Co.

established than the fact that the doctrine of immortality does not
appear in the canonical books. The reflections and reasonings of the
author are weak and commonplace, pietistic in tone, often expressed in
ungrammatical English, and betraying no firm grasp of any subject.
They possess but small value, and are wearisome. It is difficult to
see how a careful reader of the Bible can go along with one who
tells him that Jacob's character demands the highest admiration and
is every way worthy of imitation; that prayer may be offered as an
atonement; and that the Sabbath was piously kept during the reign
of David "since some of his beautiful and devout psalms are especially adapted to that day." The volume is the product of a feeble
mind, in which pious feeling supplies the place of healthy knowledge
and sound judgment.

Mr. Braithwaite's book[1] discusses a great number of questions in
brief chapters whose titles are not always happily chosen, because
they do not suggest or imply the nature of the contents. Nor do they
follow in an orderly or connected sequence. The first chapters, treating
of protoplasm and the Darwinian doctrine of evolution, present many
acute and strong objections to the theories of Huxley and Darwin.
The beginning of life is left unexplained by the former; the gap between the human mind and the highest intelligence of any lower
animal, by the latter. The remaining part of the book is occupied
with most of the leading topics in the Bible; the Hebrew idea of God,
Moses, miracles, inspiration, incarnation, good and evil, sacrifice,
ascension and intercession, body or mind, the Trinity, the Virgin Mary,
prayer, praise and thanksgiving. The author, having vigorous common
sense and a power of reflection far from common, perceives that man
is under the dominion of unchangeable divine laws, conformity to
which is his paramount duty; that there is no suspension of these
laws; and that all representations of the Almighty must be tested by
reason. He points out the erroneous representations both of the
Deity and of man given in Scripture, rejects the account of the fall,
the existence of the devil, the occurrence of miracles, propitiation by
sacrifice; and holds the simple humanity of Christ, whom he paints as
the ideal of mankind. He refuses to accept the resurrection of Jesus'
body or its ascension to heaven, as well as the doctrine of the Trinity;
but does not discard praise, prayer, thanksgiving, public worship intellectually conducted. The Church in his opinion should be an educating body. Religion should be undogmatic, and our current theology
purified of its superstitions. It is impossible not to go along with the
writer in most of his views. Adopting, as he does, a healthy tone of
belief, and a rational faith such as science approves, his book com-
mends itself to all who wish to arrive at the truth. It is marked by
ability and force, exhibiting good conclusions supported by cogent
arguments. He should not, however, speak of Moses as the author of
the Pentateuch and of the institutions it records. We think, too, that

[1] "Esse and Posse. A Comparison of Divine Eternal Laws and Powers, as
severally Indicated in Fact, Faith, and Record." By Henry Thomas Braithwaite,
M.A. London: Longmans and Co.

his language about the religion of the Jews under the Old Testament and their conceptions of God is too strong, and needs qualification. Putting the whole Jewish race in one category, he does not notice the gradations in their ideas of the Supreme, till under the prophets a pure Jehovism was arrived at. He is also partial to the spiritual culture of the Egyptians and Greeks, at the expense of that of the Jews. With regard to the connexion between the old dispensation and the new, he denies it altogether according to the deistical belief, asserting that the two religions are distinct; but it is no less true that the one is the continuation and outcome of the other. Nor is it correct to say that Jesus first proclaimed the true idea of God, and emancipated himself from the trammels of Judaism. The true idea of God in His essential attributes is not unknown to the Old Testament; and Jesus did not break away from all the observances of Judaism. The Apostle Paul first separated the two religions; but even *he* retained some of his Judaism, such as his notions of sacrifice and propitiation. We are glad, however, to see that the author is not ignorant of the fact, that later conceptions entertained by the immediate followers of Christ, have in many cases overlaid the primitive record, distorting its simplicity, and adding to both the words and deeds of the Founder of Christianity. Doubtless the history and teaching of Jesus have been burthened with fictions which he would have repudiated. In like manner Mr. Braithwaite rightly conjectures that Jesus' known preference of the parabolic form, prompted his followers to apply it also to his biography. This is especially manifest in the fourth gospel. Where most of the chapters are so good, it is with reluctance that we refer to the account of the fall of man, which is inadequately explained. The myth was not of Persian origin, as the author thinks; for with considerable likeness there is too much dissimilarity to the latter; both the Persian and the Jewish myths came from an older one. The twentieth chapter, Trinity in unity, is an ingenious but confused and fanciful one. Those on the Hebrew ideal, body or mind, prayer and praise, are excellent. Had the author employed a less vehement style of writing, refraining from the use of new and uncommon words, from wholesale phrases and clinching sentences, his book would have been better. A more cautious and moderate tone, though it might have lessened the strikingness of his language, would have rendered his arguments all the more weighty. His ideas are usually so correct as not to need a slashing diction, in which minute accuracy is in danger of being sacrificed to the love of effect.

The so-called Speaker's Commentary, prepared by bishops and other clergy of the Established Church, originated in a desire to meet the arguments of Bishop Colenso against the Mosaic authorship of the Pentateuch, and at the same time to settle the orthodox faith on a surer foundation by a good commentary on the various books of the Bible, resolving all difficulties, and putting to rest all doubts adverse to the received or traditional belief. In the preparation of such a work, the learning and orthodoxy of the Church of England have been concentrated. Immediately after the appearance of the Penta-

teuch portion, the Bishop of Natal began a critical examination of
it. Since his first part on Genesis, the second and third on Exodus
and Leviticus have appeared.[4] The able and right reverend critic goes
patiently and carefully through the notes on every chapter, as well as
the general introductions to the books, exposing the shallowness and
subterfuges of the commentators, commending their timid concessions, but pointing out their intentional avoidance of difficulties, and
imperfect scholarship. It is easy to see that he is immensely superior
to his opponents in all the qualifications of a good commentator.
Having devoted to the Old Testament far more time and study than
they, and being addicted to nothing but a candid search after truth,
he writes in the interests of biblical literature as well as rational
religion, and demolishes the advocates of a tottering cause with a
convincing power, totally unlike their feeble reasonings. But it had
been proved long before, that the Pentateuch was compiled out of
various documents of different ages, and that Moses neither wrote
nor put it together. Historical criticism is on the side of Colenso;
an effete traditionalism on that of the orthodox commentators whom
he refutes. We have seldom read pieces of more effective criticism
than those contained in these pamphlets. The bishop preserves his
usual calmness, while dealing blows that reduce the reverend champions of the Church's ancient faith to a position of hopeless defeat.
We regret, however, that he has seen fit to go along with Graf, Kuenen,
and others, in throwing the Levitical legislation, that is, nearly all the
book of Leviticus, together with large portions of Exodus, into the
Captivity and later times. By this means, the nature, extent,
and age of the Elohist is essentially changed. He may even become
Ezra; as De Lagarde strangely conjectures. The completion of the
Pentateuch and of Joshua cannot be brought so low without compulsion. This hypothesis of the later Levitical legislation dictates or
tinges various answers which the bishop makes to the statements of
the commentators. For example, "this mention of the evil spirit
Azazel, whether identical with Satan or not, is another sign of the
later origin of the L.L.; since the Jews appear to have first
adopted the notion of evil spirits from the Persian religion during
the captivity." This argument is inconclusive, because Azazel the
evil demon may be a remnant of the pre-Mosaic religion. Besides, it
is utterly improbable that the Jews should have supposed at the final
period of their religious education, that all the sins of the congregation could be consigned to an evil demon in the wilderness and so
expiated. That they had some notions of an evil spirit before the
captivity, appears from the book of Job. Again, in answering Mr.
Cook, the general editor of the whole commentary, Colenso assigns
to his trusty L. L. (later legislation) Exodus vii. 19, 20a, and viii. 3,
which are Elohistic. With such drawbacks as these, there can be no
doubt of the complete demolition which the commentators have

---

[4] "The New Bible Commentary by Bishops and other Clergy of the Anglican
Church, Critically Examined," by the Right Rev. J. W. Colenso, D.D., Bishop of
Natal. Part ii. Exodus. Part iii. Leviticus. London: Longmans and Co.

received from one who shows himself abreast of the latest critical results regarding the Old Testament.

Mr. George Combe's "Science and Religion"[3] is issued in a fifth edition, after the author's death, with the amendments and additions contained in his own copy, and a few corrections by his nephew, as well as by the editor. It is superfluous to criticise a book which first appeared as a pamphlet in 1847, though it has grown since then into much larger proportions. After defining the words science and religion, the author explains the physical elements of man, his mental organs and faculties, and the particular faculties of the mind. He next treats of God, of divine government in the physical and moral worlds, &c. An appendix consists of a number of papers, more or less directly phrenological and personal. The book is written with all the natural simplicity and benevolent spirit that characterise Mr. Combe's other publications. It starts from a theistic basis, and remains there. In discoursing on physical laws and the attention they deserve, on conformity to the purposes of the Creator, as evidenced by the structure of the brain and all the bodily functions, the author speaks like a wise monitor or practical philosopher, whose lessons are eminently salutary. In regard to all moral duties, his observations are judicious. The tendency of the book is excellent. But its science resolves itself mainly into phrenology ; and the head will hardly bear the weight of the mental structure which has been built upon and out of it by such men as Mr. Combe. His definition, too, of religion as a complex thing, is not adequate; for it turns out to be little else than the due cultivation of certain phrenological organs. As regards theology, the author's remarks are good and pertinent. He sees what mischief its advocates have done by perverting religion, and persecuting those who differ from them. The volume does not possess any high scientific character or form. It consists of a number of observations on man, God, and nature; but is neither comprehensive nor philosophical in the best sense of the term. Yet its lessons may instruct and benefit the reader, introducing him to a better acquaintance with his mental and bodily functions, in the proper exercise of which his duty as a man and citizen consists. Of revelation, Mr. Combe has no other conception than the original implantation of faculties and emotions, whose media are cerebral organs. Man becomes actively religious, not by believing in a book or in the inspiration of remarkable persons whose teachings mirror the Divine image more or less nearly, but by the due regulation of all his functions according to the divine laws of nature to which he is subjected. This is true in a sense, but hardly so even in the lower sense intended by the author, who has not risen to the height of the themes about which he speaks.

The so-called Athanasian Creed is still pertinaciously held by many clergymen of the Established Church, though it is absolutely indefensible on the grounds of reason or Scripture. A document written

³ "The Relation between Science and Religion." By George Combe. Edinburgh: Maclachlan and Stewart.

by some unknown writer, but purporting to proceed from Athanasius or to represent his views, is maintained as one of the Church's creeds, to be publicly recited on certain days for the edification of the people. Even its damnatory clauses are justified, however repugnant they be to the genius of the gospel. The pamphlet of Mr. Flower[*] and the sermon of Mr. Perowne[†] are unfavourable to the creed, both writers feeling the injustice of consigning to eternal perdition all persons who do not believe in certain metaphysical propositions respecting the Trinity. The former effectually disposes of the Dean of Norwich's pamphlet. The latter dwells mainly on the severance from the whole Catholic Church which the public recitation of the creed in the Church services brings about. Nor do they leave untouched the Scripture passages alleged in favour of the damnatory clauses, such as Mark xvi. 16, John iii. 18, viii. 24, &c. &c.; but point out the want of analogy between the belief here required, and that demanded for the creed's propositions. The spirit of both writers is moderate; their remarks upon the symbol pertinent. They speak the language of common sense against a document carrying intolerance on its front, and consigning to everlasting damnation all who cannot or will not gulp it down. As long as it is retained by the Church, it is a blot and disgrace, repelling from her communion many of the most conscientious Christians. Neither the layman nor the clergyman, however, goes far enough in his condemnation of the creed; or avoids betraying his weakness. Thus, Mr. Flower, in alluding to the passages in Mark and John, affirms that the condemnation there applied is "for unbelievers in the divinity and mission of Christ and nothing else, and if the denunciations of the creed had been thus limited, little or no exception could have been taken to it." Such interpretation is erroneous. In like manner, Mr. Perowne, undertaking to show what men must believe if they are to be saved, finds Christ requiring belief in himself, belief in his words, belief in his works; for which purpose quotations from the fourth gospel are adduced. But it is presumptuous to define the faith necessary to everlasting salvation. Christ himself furnished no warrant for it; and the fourth gospel cannot be taken as a true record of his words or works. Mr. Flower rightly argues, that the procession of the Holy Spirit laid down in the creed means *extraction*, not the sending forth as an ambassador; so that the Dean of Norwich and Bishop Ellicott avail themselves of a subterfuge in order to lessen the difference between the Eastern and Western Churches. He also reasons rightly in maintaining, that what is derived from a being of supreme power, must be inferior to him from whom it originates; so that the Creed teaches by implication the inferiority of the Holy Spirit to the other persons of the Trinity, while asserting that the three are co-equal. But a similar argument holds good in respect to the Son, of whom it is said he is " of the Father begotten (*a patre genitus,*

[*] " A Layman's Reasons for Discontinuing the Use of the Athanasian Creed." By J. W. Flower. London: Williams and Norgate.
[†] "The Athanasian Creed." A Sermon by J. J. Stewart Perowne, B.D. London: Strahan and Co.

analogous to, *a patre et filio procedens*)." Does not " begotten of the
Father," though it be designated "eternal generation," imply derivation and therefore inferiority ? We deny that " all Christians agree
without much hesitation in the Nicene Creed" as Mr. Flower says;
for what meaning has "God of God" in it, but a derived or inferior
God. The three Creeds of the Church are all objectionable on various
grounds. They fetter thought and have little to do with practical
religion. It were better for the Church to lay them aside in her
public services. That the Athanasian one will soon be discarded, is
certain, though the threatened accession of a few intolerants may follow
its removal. She can spare them and be stronger.

The " Common-place Philosopher," whose productions are numerous,
has just published a volume he calls, " Sea-side Musings,"* which
are in fact sermons, preached in Scotland by a clergyman belonging to the Established Church. As such, they present no peculiar
excellence or characteristic quality sufficient to recommend them to
the reader's notice. Wordy to excess, feeble in conception, tautological,
common-place, with the doctrines of orthodoxy implied or expressed
in them, they sustain the general character of the pulpit for literary
inferiority and narrowness of view. The first sermon, entitled
" Christianity ultimate and absolute truth," fastens upon the Pauline
doctrine of the Atonement as the vital thing—the catholic belief of
sacrifice by which alone men are to be saved. The preacher has no
conception of the Pauline ideas on this topic being a result and remnant of his Judaism. True to his orthodox instincts, Mr. Boyd finds
the essence of the gospel not in the teachings of Jesus, but in those
of Paul. Yet he holds that Jesus was God himself; and has arrived
at the marvellous knowledge of One Person in the Trinity, having the
special vocation to help us to live towards the rule of the gospel. In
the seventh sermon headed, " perfect through sufferings," the author
flounders about, promulgating all but blasphemous notions about the
Deity, while he states, that " the Godhead was made perfect by the
Incarnation of its Second Person." Not perceiving the true meaning
of the verb rendered ' to make perfect,' that is, ' to exalt to honour or
glory,' he seeks for far-fetched explanations which obscure the sense.
Again, in the discourse " The truth as it is in Jesus," he specifies the
resurrection of the body among the truths which he calls distinctively
Christian, though it has been long since established, that such a
tenet is unscientific, irrational, and unphilosophical. And it is wholly
incorrect to assert, that Paul opens up more fully the short and simple
statements of Christ. His teaching, so far from filling in the first
sketch or adding nothing new to it, is both different and new.
Ebionite, cannot be identified with Pauline, Christianity ; the moral
teaching of Jesus, who did not hold forth himself as the foundation of
true faith, with the dogmatic doctrine of one who based all upon trust
in him who was crucified and rose again. But the errors of the writer
before us are too numerous to be noticed. Nor is it worth while to

* " Sea-side Musings on Sundays and Week Days." By the Author of the
"Recreations of a Country Parson." London : Longmans and Co.

point them out. Ignorance of the Bible appears throughout. One who can assert that the doctrine of Paul is vitally the same as that of James and Peter, understands little of the epistles attributed to those authors. He even speaks of " a reconciled God in Christ," which is anti-biblical ; and brings up again the horrible notions in which some of the old Calvinists occasionally revelled (witness Boston in his Fourfold State), that the redeemed shall find a theme for exulting praise in the utter destruction of the wicked. " Which of you could be happy with your little child tossing on a bed of sleepless agony ? but when *Depart from me ye cursed* is said to them, there will be only *Amen to reply.*" Happily the human mind revolts against such theology. After this, it is no wonder to find the gross ignorance which attributes the cxix. Psalm to David, though it is a post-exile production ; or Ecclesiastes to Solomon's authorship. Taking advantage of the Prayer-book version of the Psalms, a whole sermon is founded on the text, " The Lord gave the word : great was the company of the preachers " (Psalm lxviii. 11) ; though a company of *women* telling abroad the news of a glorious victory are meant by the psalmist. When such effusions proceed from the pulpits of the land, it is natural for thinking men who do not like to paint the Deity in their own image, to find solace in their private reflections.

Dr. Matthew Arnold, wishing to find some literary production of the highest order which can be studied as a connected whole in our schools for the people, gets it in the Old Testament, in the last twenty-seven chapters of Isaiah;* a piece of great poetical beauty, exhibiting Hebrew literature in a high stage of advancement, of manageable length and attractive style; which may, in his opinion, be introduced into schools with effect, raising the taste and standard of the pupils. To prepare the piece for such purpose, the editor has made several changes in the common version, not extensive or radical ones ; because he wishes to preserve the English to which we are accustomed, as far as possible. In an excellent preface of considerable length, Dr. Arnold explains his object and method, making some appropriate observations on the revision of the English Bible. He has also subjoined notes and explanations, illustrating what he calls the local and temporary side of the prophecies in question. Small as it is, the volume is excellent in design and execution. The editor is an accomplished critic of English style ; and his changes are often improvements, though it is easy to see where he fails for want of a good knowledge of Hebrew. Thus he is incorrect in changing " who hath believed our report" (Isaiah, liii. 1), into, " who believed what we heard." It is the prophet's *message* that is meant. So also in the alteration of " she hath received at the Lord's hand double for all her sins" (xl. 2), into, " she receiveth of the Lord's hand double for all her rue." The old word *rue* cannot well be revived ; and the true sense is, that Israel's punishments are twice as much as her sins. According to the parallelism, something com-

---

* " The Great Prophecy of Israel's Restoration (Isaiah, Chapters 40-66), Arranged and Edited for Young Learners." By Matthew Arnold, D.C.L. London : Macmillan and Co.

pleted and past is referred to. " Her warfare is accomplished ;" " her iniquity is pardoned," "she hath received double," &c. Among the pertinent objections to several renderings adopted by Lowth and Mr. Cheyne, the last clause of xlii. 3, is adduced, which the latter has badly turned into, "He shall bring forth religion truthfully." But Dr. Arnold's own translation is not the best. The original words are not, "He shall declare judgment with truth ;" but, "He shall announce judgment according to truth." The writer's remarks on the prophecies as having two sides or two applications, a side towards the nation at the time, and a side towards the future of all mankind ; a primary application, and a secondary—are inexact and misleading. They convey the old doctrine of a double sense, which sound criticism has exploded. There is but one sense in the prophecies—that intended by the writer himself. Other persons may apply or adapt them to times and circumstances which the prophet did not mean ; but such is not their true sense. It is mere adaptation, often arbitrary and deceptive. The New Testament writers, indeed, have sanctioned such accommodation, because they were Jews that did not rise in this respect above the method of interpretation common in their day ; but it is not the less capricious.

The little treatise of Julius Doederlein [10] on the existence of God, is formally divided, consisting of short paragraphs arranged in logical connexion. The argument is of the *à priori* kind, which used to be more employed in England that it is now. It is not so palpable or convincing as the *à posteriori* one. Even in the hands of Dr. Samuel Clarke, it was not invulnerable to rigid logic. After stating the use and necessity of the proof, the former based upon the certainty of eternal life, the latter on unbelieving science, the author lays down as the foundation of his proof "something is," and proceeds to build up his structure upon it. The whole rests upon what he terms *Gefühle, i.e. feeling,* the means by which we arive at a perception of God. In other words, the idea of a Being whom we call the Absolute or God, is intuitional. *Something* implies *an All.* The reasoning is ingenious and able. As far as the existence of the Deity is capable of proof, the author succeeds in showing it. But the theme is scarcely susceptible of mathematical demonstration. The writer shows a good mastery of the subject ; and besides his own opinion, states the views of many others, all amounting to the same thing, viz., that the Absolute can only be felt. Why he should oppose Kant so strongly it is not easy to see ; for though the Kœnigsberg philosopher states that we have no proof of the certainty of an invisible Being ; his own moral argument rests upon feeling, as Heidingsfeld affirms with truth. The tractate of Doederlein will repay perusal.

In the little treatise of the late Max Wolff, [11] an important and

[10] "Gottes Dasein bewiesen am Wissen und Sein." Von Julius Doederlein, Erlangen : Eduard Besold.
[11] "Das Evangelium Johannes in seiner Bedeutung für Wissenschaft und Glauben." Von Max Wolff. Hamburg : Meissner.

very interesting question is discussed, viz., the relation of the fourth Gospel to science and faith. The sacred document may be viewed in two very different aspects; as deteriorating the nature and form of primitive Christianity, or as giving an expansion and elevation to the primitive conceptions, bringing out the true lineaments into a picture fitted for humanity. Herr Wolff recognises the later and non-apostolic authorship of the Gospel. Admitting the results of modern criticism in this department, his object is to set forth the religious value of the work. His work is divided into six chapters, containing the Christ-portrait of John, its antagonism to the characteristics of the synoptists, the religious worth of John's Gospel, the existing historical materials and the evangelist's treatment of them, the Gospel's authorship, and the concluding argument on John as the expression of Christianity, and modern humanity's consciousness. The book is marked by a thoughtful spirit, and is, in parts, very suggestive. Its perusal quickens and deepens a sense of the need of a Christianity which is able to satisfy the spiritual nature of man. The tone is moderate, more conservative than otherwise. Hence the author is far from refusing belief to the historical elements in the Gospel, though he sees clearly that they are meant to be in part the vehicles of certain ideas. This is pre-eminently the case with respect to the miracles of Jesus. In making the Logos incarnate in the man Jesus, Herr Wolff thinks that the unknown author has seized upon the best way of rendering Christianity the universal religion; for the Logos-faith is the faith of humanity. The Logos is not an individual being like us, though humanly formed and endowed with human feeling. He is the all of goodness and greatness, of light and salvation; all of the divine life that lies in humanity, united into one person. In other words, he is ideal humanity. The writer finds the connexion of ideal and historical actuality, of the Son of God with a historical individual, to be the essential mark and decided assertion of Christianity itself. Accordingly, he attributes a high importance to the Gospel, because its mysticism and speculation are but the basis and medium of a life of practical morality. In some respects the author has exaggerated the value of the sacred book, though he is essentially right in his general estimate of its deep religious importance. But it has led to erroneous dogmas, by using the name *Son of God* as the expression of a peculiar metaphysical relation, instead of the Messiah. Its christology is too metaphysical; and though it may serve as the basis of a rational worship to the highly cultivated, because it holds forth the union of humanity and deity, it is apt to foster superstition. If we cannot adopt all the statements of Herr Wolff, we can sympathise in most of them; while we regard the form in which the author of the fourth Gospel propounds the essence of Christianity as more consonant with humanity's aspirations than any other that has been propounded, higher and nobler than the Pauline; mystical indeed and speculative, but speculative in the direction of elevating and perfecting man.

" The Reunion of the Churches "[*]—*i.e.*, of the Roman Catholic, the Eastern, and the Anglican—is a fond dream of many earnest ecclesiastics at the present time, not destined to be realised as far as we can see. Assuming that Christ was the founder of the Church, which he was not if the Catholic church of the third, fourth, and fifth centuries is meant; or if any of the three great branches taken to represent it at the present time, or all three united, be intended ; an appeal is made to the eucharistic prayer contained in the fourth gospel (John xvii.). But the Christianity of the great orthodox churches mentioned, was founded by Paul rather than by the Master himself. Besides, it is doubtful whether the latter contemplated an organised body, the Church, as the depository and promulgator of his teachings. His doctrines were meant to leaven mankind, to purify and regenerate the world ; and his kingdom was to be a purely spiritual one, consisting in divine precepts subjugating all affections and passions to supreme love to God and man. The ancient Church of the third and fourth centuries, still more that of the succeeding ages, were worldly machinery with creeds and formulas elaborated by human logic. They embodied the opinions and traditions of men ; while they were set forth as the apostolic faith or the truth of God once delivered to the saints. The numerous sects and divisions of professing Christians are doubtless a stumbling-block to weak minds, and hinder the propagation of Christianity among the heathen. But were the union of the three Churches effected, the advancement and triumph of the Christian religion would scarcely follow. Outward unions are worth little, especially when they are brought about by the retention of the three most ancient creeds, by the incorporation of orthodox doctrines, and by minor compromises. The Church of the future will not be a body such as those labouring for it are now aiming at ; it must be a very different thing, with a basis purely ethical, divested of dogmatic propositions, the notion of apostolic succession, of episcopal ordination unbroken ; in short of the ceremonies and rites which encumber or crush true life. The venerable Döllinger is enthusiastic in his hopes of the reunion of existing Churches. His lectures on the subject are characterised by his wonted ability. The views in them are liberal. He surveys Church history in a truthful and fair spirit, showing how the efforts towards union at different times have been frustrated. The persons who were active in dividing Christendom are also described. The lectures are seven in number, interesting, readable, instructive. The author is a large-hearted Catholic, who is opposed to papal infallibility and the principles of the Jesuits ; who recognises good in Protestantism, and the advantages both of the German and English Reformations. The most attractive lectures to Englishmen will be the last two, on the English Reformation, and on difficulties and grounds of hope. Though our stand-point is totally different from the author's, we admire his courage and

---

[*] " Lectures on the Reunion of the Churches." By John J. I. von Döllinger, D.D., D.C.L., &c. Translated, with Preface, by H. N. Oxenham, M.A. London : Rivingtons.

talents. The work appears for the first time in an English translation by Mr. Oxenham, whose long preface evinces his full sympathy with the author. The lectures are well rendered and well
edited.

The late Mr. Forster left in MS. a curious book on " Biblical
Psychology,"[13] which has been published by his son. The materials
are ill-digested, and the whole subject inadequately treated. The
work is a collection of opinions, of interpretations of Bible passages,
and of several peculiar notions, so that the reader will be more confused
than instructed by the discussions. The author has no conception of
the diversities existing between the various writers of the Old Testament and of the New, cites incompetent authorities, and heaps up a
considerable quantity of irrelevant matter. In general, no light is
thrown upon the various topics he handles. They are rather obscured
by erroneous explanations. Both his psychology and philology are
frequently at fault. One important doctrine he tries to eliminate from
the Bible as though it were Platonic, viz., the immortal soul as a
personality or entity distinct from the body. Instead of placing
personal identity in this immortal entity, he supposes that it is maintained solely by the union of the spirit with a body, and is lost on
their separation. But the opinion concerning the immortality of the
soul is not repugnant to the doctrines of Scripture, as he asserts. It
is superfluous to point out the grave mistakes of the book ; or the
curious mixture of orthodox and heterodox notions it promulgates. When
the author believes that Samuel was really raised by the witch of
Endor in his natural body ; and that the doctrine of the Resurrection
was clearly recognised by the more eminent of the patriarchs and
prophets, he cannot be expected to prove a good expositor of Scripture. Traversing as he does a wide field, the living soul, personality,
Biblical demonology, the sepulchral and a future state, the mode of
treatment is loose, inexact, unsystematic. The work contrasts most
unfavourably with Delitzsch's on the same subject; though the latter
is far from being excellent or satisfactory.

Dr. Falconer's observations on St. Paul's voyage and shipwreck
narrated in the Acts of the Apostles, first published in 1817, have
been recently issued by a relative, with additional notes and criticisms.[14]
The editor has enlarged the little work with new matter suggested
or supplied by recent works. This adds to its value and completeness. The excellent publication of Mr. Smith, on the voyage of Paul,
forms the chief exposition of the subject since the first appearance of
Dr. Falconer's. Both together furnish all necessary information on
the description given in the Acts. The present editor controverts the

---

13 " Biblical Psychology in Four Parts." By the late Jonathan L. Forster.
Edited by his Son, Henry L. Forster. London : Longmans and Co.

14 " Dissertation on St. Paul's Voyage from Cæsarea to Puteoli: and on the
Apostle's Shipwreck on the Island Melite." By W. Falconer, M.D.   Third
Edition, with Additional Notes by Thomas Falconer, Esq.   London : Williams
and Norgate.

opinions of Mr. Smith on various points, and seeks to strengthen the view of his relative as to Meleda, an obscure island in the Adriatic, being meant by Melite; not the island of Malta. His arguments, however, do not avail; any more than those of Dr. Falconer. Perhaps he has unnecessarily increased the size of the book in some instances, by additions of trifling importance. Thus, Acts xxvii., xxviii., 1—10 need not have been printed at the end in three versions; Mr. Bryant's opinions do not deserve the notice which they often receive; while Deans Alford and Howson might well have been omitted as authorities worth quoting. As he is unacquainted with points of New Testament criticism, he should have refrained from any discussion of the Vatican reading εὐρακύλων in Acts xxvii. 14, whose correctness he needlessly questions; and have avoided the error of calling B. the Vatican *version.* But he has improved Dr. Falconer's essay, and done what he could to prevent its being forgotten beside the abler and more elaborate work of the late Mr. Smith.

The late Dr. R. Williams was a man of devout spirit, of a retiring disposition, though not afraid to come forth in public at the call of duty; brave and manly, generous and sensitive. He united in himself the characteristics of a keen controversialist and a spiritual believer. In point of doctrine he was all but orthodox; as a churchman he was decided in his opinions, and somewhat high. He appears to have been fond of composing prayers from his youth, and was engaged in preparing such a book as is now issued by his widow,[26] which consists of three parts, the first comprising Litanies, Psalms, Prayers and Creeds, arranged from ancient sources and partly from Bishop Andrewes's compilation; the second, ancient Collects and other prayers revised; the third, miscellaneous meditations and prayers. It would be unseemly to criticise a volume which has not had the benefit of the author's final corrections; and parts of which he might not have published. It breathes throughout the spirit of devotion; of faith in God's love and mercy to all. The antique cast of the language, and Dr. Williams' own diction, are not the best vehicles for modern prayers or litanies. It will not be supposed that liberal theologians will agree with many sentiments expressed in the volume, or with the creeds it exhibits. Though the Church of England formularies are often improved and shortened, the essential changes made in them are not numerous. The author was too much addicted to the perusal of the Church's former divines, such as the Andrewses and Taylors, to move far in the direction of innovation or reform. His theology was that of the past, rather than that of the enlightened present. Hence we are not surprised to find in the volume prayers for rain and fair weather; for deliverance from eternal death; from beholding the Judge's face darken; from being placed on the left hand; and from hearing the dread word, depart. In like manner, it is not strange to find vague and mystic language used of the "Spiritual

[26] "Psalms and Litanies, Counsels and Collects, for Devout Persons." By Rowland Williams, D.D. Edited by his Widow. London : Williams and Norgate.

Word, the Lord" of whom it is curiously said that "he shall judge
with glory both the quick and the dead." In these and similar
phrases, the theologian of an orthodox Church appears, who was not
prepared for *organic* change either in her liturgy or creeds.

Mr. Prime's book[16] informs us that for the last fifteen years a public
meeting for prayer has been held in Fulton Street, in the city of New
York. Two volumes already published have furnished reports of these
meetings; and the present one collects the reports at the end of fifteen
years. The editor regards the facts described as historical evidences
that men ask God for certain things and the answer comes. The narratives are curious; the characters mentioned very different. Clergymen, laymen, women, boys are presented to view, asking to be prayed
for, praying for others, relating sudden conversions, instantaneous
answers to petitions, and singular coincidences. The reader is introduced into the region of feeling. Enthusiasm and imagination produce
remarkable results. Philosophy takes a very different view of the
subject from that which Mr. Prime holds. The power of prayer to
change the heart of another or to induce God to change it, must be
resolved into the unalterable moral laws under which man is placed,
and to which he must yield. Its efficacy is internal, not objective. It
may, and often does, act beneficially on the petitioner himself, deepen-
ing his sense of dependence on the Infinite; but it acts on another
simply in accordance with psychological laws, by sympathy, by the
influence of emotion to call forth emotion. As to instantaneous conversions, they are phases of thought and feeling that cannot well be
analysed. In this volume the usual Calvinistic theology plays its part.
The complete corruption of human nature, the active interference of the
devil in tempting man, his everlasting perdition if he does not believe,
his grasping the righteousness of another in order to justification, are
sufficiently prominent. These notions are now excluded from the
domain of rational theology.

Mr. Street's "Restoration of Paths to Dwell in"[17] insists on the
necessity of re-editing the text of the Old Testament as well as of
revising the English translation. According to the author, Ezra was
the last editor, who left the books much as they now are. He
supposes that the current Christian ideas about the Old Testament
have been unduly influenced by the Greek version—*i.e.*, by Jewish
interpretations; and that the Jews are not good expositors of the Bible,
because "they have not the Spirit." The Church alone, which has
the Spirit, can rightly interpret it. The Church is virtually identified with the Anglican Establishment; and how she is to edit,
translate, and interpret, we learn from the sentence "The Old Testament Scriptures are valuable only as applicable to Christ." In
other words, the ideas of the New Testament are to be transferred to

[16] "Fifteen Years of Prayer in the Fulton-Street Meeting." By S. Irenæus
Prime. London: Sampson Low, and Co.
[17] "The Restoration of Paths to Dwell in. Essays on the Re-editing and
Interpretation of the Old Testament Scriptures." By the Rev. B. Street, B.A.
London: Strahan and Co.

the Old, and to dictate the right view of it. The author takes all the
Hebrew records as historical and literal; having no conception of
there being legends and myths in them. He is so orthodox as to say
that when *the Lord spake unto the fish* (Jonah ii. 10), "it was the
directing impulse of the Divine nature on a lower nature, like the
impact of the sound of a word on the ear." He also takes the Pentateuch to be Moses' production throughout. Essays which display
a total disregard or ignorance of the critical results arrived at by
modern scholars respecting the Old Testament, and the Pentateuch in
particular, cannot be expected to possess much value. Neither do
they. Whatever may have been the efforts of the writer to interpret the
Hebrew Scriptures, he has signally failed. The volume shows an
amount of perverse explanations of the Bible which is truly surprising.
Though there is an apparent anxiety to display knowledge of Hebrew
and of Greek, the scholarship is often incorrect, and no reliance can be
placed in it. As the principle or principles of interpretation are
erroneous, their outcome must be false. Examples of proposed rearrangement are given from Exodus xx., xxi., xxii., xxiii., xxxiv. 20.
The three chapters, xxi., xxii., xxiii. he would transfer to xxxiv. 29;
desiring to keep the moral law distinct from the Levitical ordinances,
and to have the former given by God to Moses during his first abode
on the Mount; the latter during his second abode. Such transposi-
tion must be at once rejected. Though the author dismisses what he so
misunderstands as to speak of Elohistic and Jehovistic *sects*, each
compiling a book for its own use; yet it is only by the light of these
documents that Exodus xix.—xxiv. can be understood, which are a
Jehovistic insertion, though the Jehovist seems to have used various
older documents. The Elohist makes Moses ascend the mountain only
once, and receive there a representation or vision of the tabernacle
with its belongings; the Jehovist makes him go up six times; the
last time to the top of the Mount, where Moses received the Ten Commandments., The various accounts are mythical. In order to maintain consistently the character of the Lord as he is described in both
Testaments, Mr. Street is forced to indulge in assumptions alien to the
Jewish records and injurious to the Jews themselves. Erroneously iden-
tifying the Jehovah of the one Testament with the Christ of the
other, he tries to make the descriptions of the former uniform. Hence
he misinterprets a great number of places where Jehovah commands or sanctions war, extermination, slaughter, and bloodshed,
including the instructions given to the Israelites about rooting out the
Canaanites. The morality of the invasion of Canaan is sought to be
justified on a wrong basis. Mr. Street does not see that the subjective
views of the writers shaped and coloured their descriptions of Jehovah,
so that there is no need for unnatural expositions of the language to
extract a right character of God out of it. He forces the records to
vindicate a consistent and just description of the Supreme Being,
because his notions of what a revelation is are erroneous; and resorts to
distinctions such as that between *the Lord spake* (Daber) and *the Lord
said* (Amar), which are unfounded; the former phrase not expressing,

any more than the latter, a direct communication from the Lord.
Both convey subjective ideas of the writers. Inspiration is not
understood by our divine, who speaks in the usual way of *inspired
writings* as if they were infallibly recorded; an error which compels
him to fly to violent interpretations. How unfitted Mr. Street is for
the duty of a critic or expositor of the Scriptures is evident from his
asserting that Elohim means *trustees* under an obligation to perform a
trust—*i.e.*, the blessed Trinity; as also that *the cool of the day*
(Genesis iii. 8) should be, "*spirit or grace for the day.*" Nor is his
Greek lore better than his Hebrew, since he proposes to render καρποτην
τοῦ πάσχα "*the celebration of the passover* in the temples its
present preparedness." The book contains a few good parts, such as
the 14th essay, and all in the 10th about the sacrifice of Christ. But
it is a great failure, and indicates no small presumption on the author's
part. To ignore the works of scholars who have thrown new light on
the Bible, and set forth instead crude notions as to its authorship and
contents; to rest in the exploded belief of the past rather than accept
the enlightened views of the present, is unwise, though it be the common way of the clergy. The sons of the Church cannot assert her high
functions or her possession of the Spirit to guide into all truth, while
they close their eyes against light and knowledge.

Holland has of late contributed to the science of Religion an
unusual number of important works, and we have pleasure in
welcoming another.[18] The author, now a professor in the Remon-
strant Seminary at Leyden, was already favourably known as an editor
of the *Theologisch Tijdschrift*, and the Author of a work on the
religion of Zoroaster, one of the series on "Voormaaniste Godsdiensten" issued by Kruseman of Haarlem. The religions discussed in
the present work have a peculiar scientific interest. The Egyptian
and Mesopotamian (in the more limited sense) are the oldest of the
cultured religions known to us, while those of Phœnicia and Israel
have, the one through Greece, the other through Christianity, contributed largely to the religious development of the race. These religions
must therefore be attentively studied before any one of the many
questions relating to the origin and growth of religious ideas can be
intelligently discussed. Mr. Tiele's work has not the value that
would belong to a dissertation on any of the above religions by a
Specialist, but it has the worth proper to the work of an independent
and vigorous thinker who has mastered the discussions and discoveries
of many Specialists, and woven the results into combinations of his
own. Mr. Tiele proposes to write a comparative history of old
religions, not a religious history of antiquity. He divides the religions
of the world into two classes, the old and the new, or the ancient
and the modern. The former follow the pre-historical or palæontolo-
gical, and their distinctive characteristic is particularism—they are
religions of the family, the nation, or the state. The characteristic of

[18] "Vergelijkende Geschiedenis van de Egyptische en Mesopotamische Godsdiensten," door C. P. Tiele. Amsterdam: P. N. Van Kampen.

the latter is universalism,—they seek to become religions of man. The first class comprehends every religion, even though it still survive, which is in its nature national; the second comprehends only Buddhism, Christianity, and Islamism. Hence, our author's plan embraces a comparative history, of all religions, except the three first named; and in the part before us he discusses a cycle of religions, which are classed as theocratic. His method is at once scientific and historical. He recognises the influence of each country, culture, political change and international intercourse. He begins in each case with the question of race, then describes the earliest known form of religion, and traces its successive changes with their real or supposed causes. The question of race is determined by language, customs, traditions, and religion. The divisions in Genesis x. are regarded as neither ethnographical nor geographical, but as culture-historical (pp. 20-24, 271, 425). The condition and course of the several religions are ascertained and described by a free and critical use of inscriptions and documents. The work is well-written, the style clear and attractive, and the chapters in which the several religions are characterized acute and comprehensive. Especially is this the case with the chapter, which is in Mr. Tiele's best style, on "the character of the Egyptian religion and its moral fruits." Our limits forbid any approach to detailed analysis or criticism, but we may notice one or two salient points in "Godsdiensten von Fenice en Israel." As respects the latter, he occupies very much the standpoint of Kuenen, though with many specific differences. He regards the Hebrew Jahvism as only "the ripe fruit, the last word of a long preparative development, to which the whole Mesopotamian race, inclusive of Egypt, had contributed" (p. 410). The Hebrews and the Phœnicians are considered as of kindred race, though their actual identity is not affirmed (p. 430). The traditions of the Patriarchs are explained as nature-myths. Abraham is the old heaven-god, the night-heaven; his wife, the moon-goddess; and they are the parents of the laughing day-heaven or sun-god, who is married to the fruitfulness of the earth, Rebekka (pp. 433-4). Jacob-Israel, the putative Patriarch of Israel in the narrower sense, was possibly originally a deity, and then a god of the year (pp. 431-33). The religions of Phœnicia and Israel were similar in character—had customs, conceptions, gods in common (pp. 425, 436, 517-21). The difference between the two religions lies not in their character but in their development. The O. T. exhibits a religion which arose first in the ninth century B.C. The Hebrews in Egypt did not worship Jehovah; and their knowledge of him was derived neither from the Egyptians nor from the Canaanites, but from the Kenites during the sojourn in the wilderness (pp. 532-60). He was originally a nature-god, the god of thunder (pp. 545-9); hence the Cherubim represent griffins who watch the treasure of heaven, the thunder-clouds which carry the concealed fire; while the oldest Israelitish feast, the so-called feast of Tabernacles, still indicates the old belief that in harvest the thunder and rain-god is the mightiest (pp. 550-1). The worship of Jehovah was introduced by Moses, who was, however, no monotheist and

s 2

cannot be regarded as the author of the decalogue, which rests on conceptions possible in the eighth or seventh century before Christ, but not in the fourteenth (pp. 561-65). From what has been said, Mr. Tiele's method and standpoint will be sufficiently evident. His presentation of the religion of Israel in its later course and manifestations is less conjectural, and possesses more actual interest; but sketch or criticism of it is not now possible. On many points both of exegesis, criticism, and historical construction, we should be inclined to differ from him. His insight into the religion of Israel seems to us, on the whole, hardly as keen and appreciative as into that of Egypt. But he gives us the results of his own and others' studies in the field of religious history and criticism in a lucid and intelligible form; and we commend his work to every student whether of the Old Testament or the old religions, certain that they will, whether agreeing with or differing from the author, find him always attractive and suggestive.

Professor Calderwood has published a text-book of moral philosophy,[19] similar to Dugald Stewart's Outlines, in which he presents the chief problems of ethical science, giving a summary of discussion under each, and properly allowing fundamental questions the greatest prominence. The subject is divided into five parts: man's moral nature as cognitive, impulses and restraints belonging to human nature, the will, moral sentiments, disorder of our moral nature; all belonging to the psychology of ethics. These are followed by the metaphysic of ethics, and applied ethics. The literature of the science is given fully under each paragraph, so that the handbook is designed to guide the reader in his private study, though its main purpose is to supply the wants of university students. Threading his way through the difficulties of the science with cautious but decided steps, the author gives a valuable summary of judgments, proofs, and conclusions. He holds the intuitional theory of moral distinctions, supposing that the law which decides what is right is so connected with the nature of the person, that the recognition of it is involved in intelligent self-direction. The source being found in the mind itself, the knowledge is immediate. This theory is explained and advocated in six chapters. The development theory is also stated and rejected, with the leading arguments of its ablest representatives. One of the best parts of the book is that on the will, whose freedom is maintained. We are glad to see a separate chapter on the disorder of our moral nature, where more temperate views are expressed than such as are usually held by Calvinistic divines. The intuitional theory is by no means so well described or maintained as it might be; while in speaking of conscience, there are loose expressions or inexact statements that cannot be justified. He says, for example, that conscience is a faculty that cannot be educated. But surely the conscience may be enlightened and developed. What is this but its education? Professor Calderwood also terms it an intellectual *power*

---

[19] "Handbook of Moral Philosophy." By H. Calderwood, L.L.D. London: Macmillan and Co.

or *faculty*, excluding feeling from its nature; which may be reasonably disputed. In explaining Spinoza's theory of ethics, the author gives as his language, "the human mind is constituted by certain modes of the divine attributes," which is incorrect. In the demonstration of Propos. xi. part ii. of the Ethics, Spinoza says, "the essence of man is constituted by certain attributes of God," and in a Corollary, "hence it follows that the human mind is a part of the infinite intellect of God." With the metaphysic of ethics the author deals most successfully. The work possesses an intrinsic value which must recommend it to philosophers and students. It leaves little to be desired in the way of outline. As a formidable opponent of the development and utilitarian theories the Professor will be welcomed by many. We could wish, however, that his style and diction were better. In the able sketch of the history of philosophic thought as to the source of our knowledge of moral truth, we observe no mention of the works of De Wette and Harless, though less important authors, such as Wayland, are mentioned.

Professor Bain has published a new edition of his "Mental and Moral Science,"[10] divided into two parts or volumes, of which the first contains Psychology and the history of Philosophy; the second, the theory of Ethics and the Ethical systems. The author's views are too well known to require an explanation at the present day; for they have been before the public for several years. The volumes contain a very full account of the mind and its states, as also an excellent history of the opinions entertained by all the leading philosophers. Dr. Bain is an advocate of the development theory of morals, of the will's non-freedom, of utility as the criterion of morality, and many other opinions coinciding in the main with those of Mr. J. S. Mill. The volumes are exceedingly valuable and full of acute remarks. They contain many examples of patient analysis and intellectual sagacity. To the student of philosophy they are indispensable. The essence of the whole of the author's doctrine lies in the chapter headed, "The Origin of Knowledge," where he argues with considerable acuteness against innate principles and in favour of experience. None can read Professor Bain's work without instruction or profit, for he investigates all the questions of mental and moral science with much ability, and furnishes answers to the arguments of other philosophers, or criticisms upon them which are highly suggestive. His discussion of the will, whether it be free or always determined by a leading motive, exemplifies dialectic skill of a high order.

An old student has brought together in a volume several tracts on philosophical problems, written at various times.[11] The first two are on Sir W. Hamilton's doctrine of Perception; the second having reference besides, to Dean Mansel's views on the same subject. While Hamilton

---

[10] "Mental and Moral Science." By Alexander Bain, LL.D. In 2 Volumes. London: Longmans & Co.

[11] "Leaves from my Writing Desk: being Tracts on the Question, What do we Know?" By an Old Student. London: Williams and Norgate.

holds that in the act of perception we are conscious of two things; of self as the perceiving subject, and of an external reality, in relation with our sense, as the object perceived; the author before us endeavours to show that we are not conscious of an external reality, but that consciousness in every case terminates with Self; that is, with the subject of the sensation to which perception is correlative. According to him, perception is not the consciousness of the existence of the body as a material organism, nor of matter generally; for all the qualities of matter—primary, secondary and secundo-primary—are mere modes of our own consciousness. He also contends that resistance to the locomotive energy is not a mode of consciousness that tells us directly of the existence of an external world. In short, perception is the consciousness of nothing that has an existence of its own, independent of modes of thought. It attests the existence of nothing but subjective phenomena. The third essay, after showing that sensations, though apparently external and independent of us in part, do not overthrow the belief in the existence of bodies without us, falls back on Causality as a primary principle, to account for the origin of sensations. The fourth is on the relativity of human knowledge, a phrase the author dislikes, because with the two propositions which are its root, there is often understood or insinuated the idea that the known is *modified* by the knowing; that the thing as known and the thing as it is being regarded, are not identical or convertible. The fifth is occupied with the question, whether our knowledge is bounded by our consciousness, which he answers in the negative. The last three tracts are concerned with the doctrine of Causation. In them, it is argued that there is a necessary connexion between physical causes; and that causation is not identical with necessary connexion. Here Mr. Mill's modification of Brown's doctrine is minutely canvassed. The final tract on Necessary Truth, unfolds such truth as it exists in the axioms of geometry and the fundamental laws of logic as well as in the law of causality. The author's knowledge is ample, his reflective power uncommon. All that he has written deserves perusal. His contribution to mental philosophy, though apparently small, is of some importance. Generally speaking, he is opposed to the empirical or experiential philosophy, favouring the *à priori* or intuitional. He finds primary or innate principles in the human mind; believes that there is in our conception existence external and internal; that our intellectual faculties can be trusted; and that absolute truth is within our reach. Thus he is no idealist either of the Berkeleyan or of a later school. The volume possesses sterling worth.

THE number of works on military subjects being translated by
English officers from foreign, and generally German, originals,
affords an index of the direction in which the course of military science
in England may be expected to set. It is known that already the
lessons taught by the Prussians in their recent successful war are being
rapidly learned by those who are responsible for the training of the
English army. The nature of the changes which are being contemplated will be understood from the following comments on the organization of the North German army by Colonel Newdigate,[1] the translator
of a work on the subject by an anonymous Prussian General. " Without referring to the splendid organization of the North German army,
and the perfection of the arrangement by which every portion is held
ready for mobilization in case of a sudden declaration of war, perhaps
the lesson which most immediately concerns ourselves is the change
which modern firearms has rendered necessary in the tactics of infantry.
A skirmishing system of fighting must in future take the place of
close line formations. The *company column* of the Prussians (their
tactical unit) appears to offer the greatest advantages for this description of fighting, and the success of their infantry in the last campaign
has in great measure been attributed to the *relations* existing *between
the company-officers and their men*." Colonel Graham,[2] in his preface
to his translation of Captain A. v. Boguslawski's work on the " Tactical
Deductions from the War of 1870-71," insists on the importance of
the same lesson, and also other like ones. He says, " The Prussian
company column is an excellent institution, and should be introduced
into our service, though in a somewhat modified form." Major Blume's[3]
work, translated by Major Jones, Professor of Military History at Sand-
hurst, giving an account of the operations of the German armies in
France, from Sedan to the end of the war, probably affords the most
reliable and precise account of those operations, from a purely military
point of view, which has as yet appeared. The work is based on the
journals of the Prussian head-quarter's staff, which were placed at the
author's disposal for the purpose. The writer says, that though
Prussia had foreseen for some time that war with France must come

[1] "The Army of the North German Confederation." Translated from the
Corrected Edition, by permission of the Author, by Colonel Edward Newdigate.
London : Henry S. King. 1872.
[2] "Tactical Deductions from the War of 1870-71." By A. V. Boguslawski.
Translated from the German by Colonel Lumley Graham. London : Henry S.
King. 1872.
[3] "The Operations of the German Armies in France, from Sedan to the End of
the War." By William Blume. Translated by Major E. M. Jones. Second
Edition. London ; Henry S. King. 1872.

sooner or later, still the suddenness with which it broke out in 1870
took her completely by surprise. The declaration of war was delivered
in Berlin on the 19th of July, the whole of the reserves having been
called in on the 14th. The French had the advantage of the initiative,
but as early as the 2nd of August the Germans had 450,000 men
formed in three armies in the narrow space between Trèves and Landau,
to be followed at once by another 100,000, while, exclusive of the
garrisons at fortresses, 400,000 remained available at home. The
lessons of the late war are not exclusively to be learnt from German
sources and German experience, as is proved by the interesting work
of Colonel A. Brialmont, translated by Lieutenant Charles A. Empson.
The subject is the apparently very technical one of "hasty entrenchments." The contents, however, are of great general interest, and
the military importance of the question can hardly be placed too
high. The following extract from the report of the operations of
the 2nd French corps at Gravelotte, will explain the purpose of the
work :

"If the losses of the 2nd corps at the battle of Gravelotte were comparatively inconsiderable, we owed this, no doubt, to the precautions taken to
shelter our soldiers by mounds of earth and by epaulments at important points,
and we owed it also to the instructions that every hollow or excavation of the
ground should be profited by, not for the purpose of keeping the troops lying
on the ground there, but so as to protect them while making them keep up
their fire. We have not yet seen so marked an example of the advantages
gained by this arrangement of hasty entrenchments. We commend it to the
attention of those who will hold commands in years to come."

Major-General von Mirus' work on "Cavalry Field-Duty,"[5] translated by Captain Frank Russell, stands, in some respects, on even a
higher level of importance than the books already noticed. The work
of Major-General von Mirus is the text-book of instruction in the
German cavalry. It is complete within its own limits, and gives instruction to the soldiers in matters not purely belonging to military
science. Thus the soldier is reminded that "a good way of impressing on
the memory the principles of field-duty is to endeavour to picture in
one's mind those situations or circumstances of war of which one has
heard or read, or to which the attention has been directed." "It is
the duty of every good soldier to protect women, children, and old
men." There is an interesting chapter on "Definitions and General
Principles," in which words are explained which are not always accurately understood by the civilian—such as, *cantonments, outposts,
patrols, defiles, convoys, beacons,* and *ambuscades.*

"A Series of Sketches,"[6] entitled "Soldiering and Scribbling," are
lively pictures of the realities of the soldier's life, though the writer

[4] "Hasty Intrenchments." By A. Brialmont. Translated by Charles A.
Empson. London : Henry S. King. 1872.
[5] "Cavalry Field Duty." By Major-General von Mirus. Translated by Captain
Frank S. Russell. London : Henry S. King. 1872.
[6] "Soldiering and Scribbling." A Series of Sketches. By Archibald Forbes.
London : Henry S. King. 1872.

honestly tells us in the preface that they do not represent his own
personal experiences. However they are sufficiently plausible, and
obviously based upon actual facts, to be interesting and indeed
instructive. For instance, under the heading "Soldiers' Wives," a
quantity of information is given which is not generally accessible.
The situation of a soldier married without leave is described in a very
vivid way. It is said that for one soldier who marries "with leave,"
at least half-a-dozen marry without leave. Sometimes a man applies
for leave, which is either refused or postponed. "Of late years a more
lenient policy has come into operation. A suitable applicant is permitted to marry at once, with the promise that his wife will be taken
'on the strength' in rotation, and meanwhile a little work is assigned
her to ease the hardship of her lot." "To get married without leave,
even although it be accompanied by no other infraction of discipline,
is a military crime coming under the head of disobedience to orders;
and I have known a man severely punished for the offence. Thus, I
have known a man get seven days' cells, involving the loss of his hair,
for a couple of hours' absence in the morning for the purpose of getting
married."

There are many concrete and apparently minute topics of International Law which have become of the most serious moment to
Continental nations owing to the events of the recent war, and yet
which are as yet imperfectly apprehended or cared for in this country.
To the discussion of these topics the writers in the *Revue de droit
International*, and among them pre-eminently M. G. Rolin-Jacquemyns,[7] have made most important contributions both by way of
original suggestion and of criticism upon other writers. The main
problems evolved by the actual circumstances attending the conduct
of the late war concerned (1) the treatment of non-combatants,
(2) the latitude of destruction permissible to an invading army,
(3) the occasions and limitations of a blockade and a bombardment,
(4) the weapons and instruments of war allowable, and (5) the limits
to making forced conditions of peace. As to many of these matters
in all their details, special treaties have been made at different epochs
and between particular countries for their regulation; among which
the Treaty of Paris and the Conventions of Geneva and St. Peters-
burg are most conspicuous. But in the absence of such treaties, or
in cases to which they do not apply, or in the finer details of their
execution, there is still large room left for the controversies of
jurists and politicians. These controversies have recently circled
round two fixed points, to one or other of which each different jurist
is disposed to give superior consideration, according to his own special
proclivities. One of these points is that of "necessity;" the other is
that of "humanity." In the present treatise M. Rolin-Jacquemyns
arranges the topics for consideration in a very convenient form for the
purpose of bringing the controverted aspects of them into distinct

[7] "De la Manière d'apprécier au point de vue du droit International les Faits
de la dernière Guerre." Par G. Rolin-Jacquemyns. Gand. 1872.

relief. His arrangement may be compendiously described as follows: International war is essentially the exercise of a right of self-defence owing its origin to *necessity*. Two principles regulate the laws of war, the one that of *necessity*, which justifies the employment of violence or guile within the limits needed to attain the object of the war, but which is tempered, even within those limits, by considerations of humanity; the other, that of *humanity*, in accordance with which the consequences of war ought not to be extended to peaceable portions of a population except under the restrictions imposed by the law of *necessity*. There are of course a variety of detailed "corollaries" from these principles which refer to the practical problems presented by the conduct of modern land wars. The main difficulty arises, as the writer points out, when the law of *necessity* seems to be in direct conflict with that of *humanity*, as in the case of the necessity presenting itself of cutting off communications by railway and telegraph; of punishing the inhabitants of districts collectively for offences of individual persons in their midst; and of levying imposts and forced contributions of all sorts. The writer suggests as a general basis for a solution of these questions, that in strictly military matters *necessity*, and, in administrative matters *humanity*, should lead the way as the guiding clue.

Mr. Ruskin's "Fors Clavigera"[*] still pursues its motley, erratic, and nondescript course. It is certainly lively reading, though the reader quite as often laughs at the writer as with him. Between truisms, puerilities, exaggerated statements of real truths, paradoxes, artistic descriptions (though the writer reminds us "his *forte* is really not description, but political economy"), and courageous skirmishings with the most complex problems of political economy, it is difficult to divine the exact result on the brain of the "workmen and labourers of Great Britain," which a systematic study of this series of publications is likely to have. Among other grotesque ideas, Mr. Ruskin pictures the set of advertisements which (if he did, in a moment of mental collapse, condescend to advertising) he would publish of his own work.

"You prefer exercising your independent judgment, and you expect me to assent to it, by paying for the insertion in all the penny papers of a paragraph that may win your confidence, as, for instance, 'Just published. The —th number of "Fors Clavigera," containing the most important information on the existing state of trade in Europe, and on all subjects interesting the British operative. Thousandth thousand. Price 7d.; seven for 3s. 0d. Proportional abatement on large orders. No intelligent workman should pass a day without acquainting himself with the entirely original views contained in these pages."

Mr. Ruskin seems to approve the list of books "with brief accounts of them," of which the present section in this *Review* presents a type.

---

* "Fors Clavigera. Letters to the Workmen and Labourers of Great Britain." By John Ruskin, LL.D. For June, July, August, September, October, November. M. G. Allen, Keston, Kent.

A valuable pamphlet is published by Mr. Spearman E. Farries,[9] on the subject of "Electoral Equality." The contending cries for minority representation and for equal electoral districts often leave too much on one side a class of facts of the greatest importance in a readjustment of the electoral franchise. This class of fact is contained in the general circumstances that no fixed and inelastic reform measure can make allowance for the change in the relative numerical and social weight of the different parts of the population represented. Some schemes of minority representation indeed either exclude the idea of local representation entirely, or extend the unit of the constituency to such a magnitude as greatly to reduce the effect of a variable population, while other schemes provide for a variable scale of representation in proportion to population. But the actual facts implied in the measure of relative change of population have not had sufficient attention fixed upon them. Mr. Farries, in establishing his main position, gives one numerical instance of the rate of change in population which is of much value. It is well known that borough constituencies grow much more rapidly as a rule than those in counties, and hence we find the latter are generally more evenly represented than the former. According to the last Census returns the boroughs have added in twenty years to their population, which in 1951 was 7,498,079, no less than 3,217,251; while the counties outside the boroughs started with a population of 10,188,030, and only increased in the same period by 1,550,248.

A comprehensive glance at all the phenomena of the present day, political, social, and religious, with an attempt to trace their mutual relations, and to discover their causes and consequences, is never devoid of a certain interest. Mr. Statham[10] has endeavoured in a series of lectures delivered at Edinburgh to classify all the social growths of the nineteenth century under five somewhat original heads. These heads are Lutheranism, Commercialism, Evangelicalism, Byronism, Humanitarianism. In the course of discussing the last of these heads, Mr. Statham briefly adverts to the *Politique* of M. Comte (with whom, by the way, he seems only to be acquainted through the medium of Mr. Mill) and takes care to save his last "growth" from a discreditable association with the great Frenchman's most characteristic speculations. The essays are marred by the form in which they were originally delivered,—that of lectures, which are unavoidably diffuse and prolix. Otherwise there is much acuteness of view and justness of criticism contained in the work, and such philosophic surveys are, on every ground, to be encouraged.

---

9 "Electoral Equality considered in relation to the Recent Returns as affecting England and Wales." By R. Spearman E. Farries. London: Longmans. 1872.

10 "The Social Growths of the Nineteenth Century: an Essay in the Science of Sociology." Being the substance of Four Lectures delivered in the Freemasons' Hall, Edinburgh, May, 1872. By F. Reginald Statham. London: Longmans. 1872.

The fifth Report" of the Executive Committee for "Amending the Law with respect to the Property of Married Women," contains matter equally important and interesting, as well as illustrative of the mode in which legislation is carried on in this country by driblets and parsimonious instalments. It is well known that the "Married Women's Property Act of 1870," though remedying certain kinds of injustice flowing from the existing law, yet was so mutilated during its passage through the two Houses that it resulted in a mass of anomalies and inconsistencies. The Committee charged with the duty of securing the more complete and effective measure were naturally alarmed last Session at the prospect of fresh piecemeal legislation which might give a plausible show of finally adjusting the whole matter, while really exaggerating the anomalies, or, at the best, putting off indefinitely a complete amending measure. This alarm was well justified, and it was by the efforts of the Committee that, with the help of Mr. J. Hinde Palmer, a most unsatisfactory measure of proposed reform introduced by Mr. Staveley Hill was effectually opposed and prevented from becoming law. The Bill of Mr. Hill seemed likely to have the ridiculous effect of preventing business creditors of the wife prior to matrimony sueing either husband or wife for debts due to them in the event of the profits being settled under the Act of 1870 on the wife.

It is very refreshing to find a writer like Mr. Counsellor Cronin," Editor of the *Binghamton Times,* New York, placing together a number of large problems calling for immediate solution which in this country are too much wont to be separated, those who most warmly espouse one problem often looking with hostility or suspicion on those who advocate any other, and the man who advocates all of them being the general foe of all men. Mr. Cronin points out, in clear, vigorous, but very temperate language, that the existing evils which render society corrupt and miserable can be traced, first, to the want of education; secondly, to the debased and dependent condition of woman; thirdly, to the despotic and unnatural pressure of the existing marriage laws; and, fourthly, to the unequal diffusion of wealth. We have so often and consistently pleaded the urgency of immediate and contemporaneous reforms in all these particulars, that we can do little more than note with satisfaction an indication that in America, at least, the close connexion of these different topics is distinctly apprehended. Mr. Cronin well says:—"Nature is constantly remedying wrongs, through man, without his conscious agency, which shows that she is working out a plan entirely independent of his concurrence. Man may aid this plan, and he may retard it, but he cannot permanently obstruct or control it, any more than he can permanently stop the descent of a river by obstructing its regular channel."

[11] "Fifth Annual Report of the Executive Committee for Amending the Law with respect to the Property of Married Women." Manchester. 1872.

[18] "The Reforms which should Precede, and the Results which must Follow, the Equal Distribution of Wealth." By David E. Cronin, Office of *Binghampton Times,* New York. 1872.

A vigorous monograph by *"Capricornus"*[19] is well worth the attention of all interested in emigration questions. It deals with the history of Australian legislation about land during the last forty years, and with the bearing of the results of that legislation on the present aspects of the land-market in Australia. Eighty years ago, our first penal settlements contemplated a gradual colonization of the country by reformed convicts. Forty years later the futility of these hopes was demonstrated, and a fresh developement had followed on the introduction of herds and flocks, which increased so rapidly as to compel a dispersion of population into the waste lands, and the first "squatting interest" appeared. It became obvious that the well-ordered class of the community were turned into Bedouins. Sir Richard Bourke, "the best governor that has come to Australia," "discerned in these seemingly lawless undertakings the promise of wealth, commerce, and extended empire, and his wisdom sought rather to regulate than to curb." On his representations, squatting was legalized by the impost of a small fee, and land was to be had in almost any quantity at five shillings per acre, no right of possession, real or implied, being thus conveyed, but the tenure being simply a permissive use of grass. On Sir Richard Bourke's return to England in 1837, he was succeeded by Sir George Gipps, who was the instrument chosen for carrying out a scheme of "colonization in mass," proposed by Mr. Gibbon Wakefield, by which it was proposed to convey segments of English population to Australia, and to expect the previous distinctions and relations to survive the transplanting to a new soil and a wholly diverse set of conditions. Land was to be sold at what was called "a sufficient price," or a "hired labour price," of from one pound per acre upwards. Of course the scheme broke down. As ship after ship reached the wharves of Adelaide, a scene of busy traffic ensued, which looked to the unthinking new-comers like an established commerce. The town seemed to all likely to be the focus of wealth. Land was bought up, and sold, and redivided, and resold, and all the evils of land-jobbing established themselves for two years, when "the money was all spent and the land and the buildings belonged to the money-lenders and the grog-sellers." The legacy which all Australia has inherited is a high price for land prohibitive of profitable occupation, and a stinted and jealous spirit in its disposal. Sir George Gipps organized a Survey Department under whose auspices the land was cut up, as it was wanted, into small portions inconvenient for intending settlers, and only calculated to promote competition. It was sold by auction, and thus every land-jobber could manipulate the market at his will. He then announced that each squatter, in lieu of rent, should be compelled to buy part of his run periodically at the price of a pound an acre. This roused the opposition of the squatters, and they combined to ask, not only for redress, but for regular leases, rights of pre-emption, and fixity of tenure. The granting of these by Parliament in 1846 practically locked

19 "Bush Essays." By Capricornus. Edinburgh: Adam and Charles Black. 1872.

up all the land, until the rush of gold-diggers in 1851 broke down the restrictions which had made it impossible for so much as a hut or a garden or a cow to belong to a poor man, in the face of the large squatters, who were, however, themselves almost entirely in the hands of the banks and money-lenders. As time went on, and the fresh masses of population began either to find out the truth that the gold-diggings grew less rather than more profitable, or to wish to settle permanently on homesteads of their own, the theory of "selection" began to be spoken of. All forms of fraudulent dealing in land and stock had been favoured by the rise in prices consequent upon the sudden increase of population, and the resulting fortunes which new-comers supposed to be the products of years of honest labour. " Runs " were bought on credit and " there are many stations which have ruined three or four different purchasers during the last fifteen years, and at the same time have realized handsome profits for the ingenious finan-ciers who turned the handle of the machine." In 1860 the hitherto inert legislatures and silent press took up the matter. The squatters held to their claim to fixity of tenure, the public clamoured for free selection, and the battle became too fierce for compromise. At last free selection was established by law ; and as the leases of 1840 fell in, the lands were thrown open, as well as (in Sydney) the whole of the crown lands. But the new leases were by no means satisfactory. It was permitted that selections might be made in different places by members of the same family ; and as each patch "selected" gave a claim to three times the area of grazing-land, fresh openings for "jobbing" were made. The grazing-lands were little regarded when they were granted ; but bad seasons, scanty markets, the want of patient farming experiment, and the discovery that grazing can be made much more profitable by fencing and by the introduction of foreign grasses, have made them preponderate in value over the arable lands. The remedy for present difficulties would seem to lie in selling rights "in the gross—that is, without picking"—at an "improving" price—an alteration, simply, of the conditions of selection from an agricultural to a grazing basis. Queensland passed a law with this tendency in 1868, while Victoria and South Australia held to the agricultural basis. But above all, the remedy lies in emigrants being content to take small allotments, and working them either in co-operation or with their individual capital, and not on credit. This class of emigrants has not been popular with the Sydney money-lenders, who have preferred to take bills for the lands and stocks which they have acquired by foreclosure, and which are not worth the nominally low price at which they are offered. Of the four modes of livelihood now open to a working emigrant, gold-digging does not offer occupation to many thousands of new hands, nor at large wages. The modern system of fenced grazing needs fewer and fewer hands ; public works are finished up to the extreme point to which Government Funds or Credit will allow ; and until the land-laws and agricultural science are improved, farming is unprofitable.

Periodical literature is generally necessarily so slight in texture that the republication of articles from even our best magazines is of questionable policy, except under special circumstances. Mr. William Gifford Palgrave's literary position and exceptional knowledge of the whole range of Mahometan life, however, constitute such a speciality, and the republication[14] of his contributions to *Fraser's Magazine*, the *Cornhill*, the *Quarterly*, and *Macmillan*, is a valuable boon to all who care to acquire substantial grounds for their views on the East and on our own Eastern policy. True, that for some readers' taste, Mr. Palgrave shows too fond a leaning towards Mahometanism as contrasted with Christianity, and a perhaps more than impartial faith in its capability of permanence, if not its final supremacy, when he writes, "I find, or seem to find, that Mahometanism—the nearest approach made by any set creed to what is called 'natural religion'—has perhaps, on the whole, less tendency than any other system I am yet acquainted with, to cramp and thwart the innate excellence of human nature." And again, "Islam, taken apart from the Government, exhibits very few symptoms of sickness, and none at all of decrepitude. . . . . A time may indeed be in store when all dogmatic systems will disappear, ... but till then . . . . we may with tolerable confidence assert that the 'Allah' of Arabia will not want worshippers, nor the Koran of its Prophet those who read, revere, and follow." The three first papers are on Mahometanism in the Levant, and contain a series of most interesting and informing descriptions of the large classes of society *seriatim;* the Civil Service, containing both the class most open to ordinary European acquaintance, but which is a compound of all that is bad in Turkish character combined with all that is bad in composite Western influences, and also a large body of men of the old sturdy Osmanlie caste, not wholly unadorned by European acquirements, who bring a conscience to their work, and whose conscience is that of Islam; the Army, of the military power and good order of which the author has a high opinion; the agricultural classes who form the deep and wide base of the Mahometan Levant, the conservative landholders and peasants who alike look to a revival of Mahometanism as the cure for all that they now suffer under—a revival with which Mr. Palgrave deals in a later chapter as an actual fact; the comparatively small class of Mahometan traders—for, since both interest and conditional contracts were strictly forbidden by the Prophet, trade is crippled, and the true believer has to resort to calling interest an augmentation of capital, and to such "dodges" as selling a cat with a bunch of grapes on its back for large sums, and understanding her to represent the product of next year's vintage; and lastly, the class which comprises the learned in the Law and in Religion, divisions necessarily as indistinguishable as the Law and Religion themselves. In his chapter on the Mahometan Revival, Mr. Palgrave enumerates four great "signs of the times," dating from the last fifteen or twenty years. The first is that from the public schools. Through-

---

[14] "Essays on Eastern Questions." By William Gifford Palgrave. London: Macmillan and Co. 1872.

out Turkey the Christian children and European tongues, learning, and science, have been almost entirely eliminated. The next sign is the great diminution in the use of alcoholic and fermented liquors—a sign of revival which has again and again been seen at different periods of Islamatic history; and, cognate to this, is a stricter observance of the great Ramadan Fast. That these two changes have their strong effect on Imperial policy is attested by the fact that in all public employments the number of Europeans, and indeed of Christians generally, is markedly smaller and is every day diminishing, while concessions for engineering undertakings promised to Europeans are, so far as may be, persistently thwarted or nullified in their execution. Add to this that on every hand mosques, colleges, schools, and chapels innumerable are throughout Turkey being repaired or built, and their endowments better administered for the ends for which they were originally set apart. Mr. Palgrave urges these facts on the attention of the rulers of Mahometan India, where the deep clefts which divide the two great sects of Mahometanism are bridged in the presence of the "infidel," and where Mr. Palgrave believes that the only possibility of safe, just, and durable rule lies in the institution of Muslim courts and Muslim educational establishments, under the supreme control of of our own Government. Throughout, Mr. Palgrave praises the moral character of the Mahometan populations as contrasted with that of the Christians under the Sultan's rule, and plainly expresses his belief that sympathy with the Christians is both misplaced and mischievous. A survey of the different sections of Greeks, Maronites, Melchites, Armenians, Copts, is of great interest, the latter two sects being represented as most worthy of respect, although " what social merits they have, they share with the Mahometan population around them; their vices are their own;" and the last advice offered to Western Christians is that they should " love their brethren at least wisely, before they love them perhaps too well." The past folly of their love, Mr. Palgrave avers, has consisted in complaints to the Government of outrages which have never taken place until the remonstrance suggested the idea of inflicting the injury. "The Abkasian Insurrection" reminds or informs the reader of the facts of an insurrection of a tribe of the Caucasus against Russian tyranny, ending in the necessary triumph of the greater power, and finally in the wholesale emigration of the whole nation 'of Abkasians from the lands held by them for two thousand years into territory where, "under the more tolerant rule of the Ottoman Sultan," they found a freedom which Russia always denies within her own limits. The view presented by the foregoing pages of the Arab mind and character, as influenced by the Mahometan system, is completed by essays on Omar, the poet, and Ta'abbet Shurran, the brigand, as representatives, severally, of the civilization and refinement, and of the barbarous energy by which Islam was cradled,—elements necessary to form a correct estimate of the value of the religion which has remodelled or crystallized the earlier national characteristics. It is always superfluous to say that Mr. Palgrave's matter is given in worthy, that is in lucid and most attractive, form.

Mr. Ralston continues his efforts to make the British public acquainted with Russian literature, and, in the present volume," offers an instalment of the results of past and future years of research into the stories, legends, riddles, proverbs, and epic, as well as lyric, poems which oral tradition has preserved among the Russian peasantry, prefacing his various sections by short accounts of the religious ideas attributed to the ancient Slavonians, the superstitions current among their descendants, and some of the manners and customs of the Russian peasantry. The work is intended chiefly to render available, to such students of mythology and folklore as do not read Russian, some part of the evidence bearing upon such subjects which has been collected in Russia. The life of the Russian peasantry can best be realized by a knowledge of the songs which, coming down from generation to generation, and forming an indispensable accompaniment to every phase of life from the cradle to the grave, leave on the mind of the English reader a singularly mournful and pathetic impression, in harmony with the sad monotony of Russian scenery and the, until lately, hopeless restrictions of Russian serfdom. Even the village dances are accompanied by songs descriptive of the death of the soldier far from home, or of the neglect of the wife lured away by the wandering youth ; while among the songs of love and marriage, come prayers from the bride that her husband will only beat her for a good cause, because neither father nor mother will be there to pity her tears. It is, of course, true that some songs show more lightness of heart ; but even were that not so, readers who care to acquaint themselves with life as it is among the Russian population, would turn with no less eagerness to Mr. Ralston's painstaking volume.

It is only the travels of men who are setting foot on hitherto untrodden soil that can be given to the world with any hope of pacific treatment. In our days the battle of the geographers blots out of memory the fury of even theological conflict. Captain Burton is not among the least bellicose of our travellers, and in the present volumes" he wages war with reviewers in his first introductory line, and with the Palestine Exploration Society and nearly all former travellers in Palestine in almost every page which he contributes to the miscellanies here collected. Under the circumstances anybody must hesitate to call that valuable which is at all events interesting, but Captain Burton believes himself to have furnished, with Mr. Drake's help, important contributions to the map of Northern Syria, and to the knowledge of disputed sites, and Mr. Keith Johnston appears to have so far sanctioned this belief as to incorporate some alterations in the map appended to these volumes. The party visited patches of hitherto unexplored country lying within two days' ride of great cities until now represented as blanks in the maps, but really full of interest for students, and only unknown because of their inability to furnish water, forage, and provisions, and because they are the home of malarious fevers and of Bedouins. A collection of neo-Syrian proverbs,

---

[13] "The Songs of the Russian People." By W. R. S. Ralston, M.A. London : Ellis and Green. 1872.

[14] "Unexplored Syria." By Richard F. Burton and Charles F. Tyrwhitt Drake." 2 vols. London : Tinsley Brothers. 1872.

Mr. Drake's essay upon "writing a roll of the law," a transcript of the Greek inscriptions in the Hauran mountain, and the description of Palmyra, are the portions of the work most likely to interest the non-geographical public.

It would seem impossible to get a glimpse into the past of Russia without a feeling of deep sadness; but perhaps of all things the saddest is to note the effect produced on the mind of a much-enduring educated man by life-long subjection to Russian military despotism. In 1825, when the Emperor Alexander died, leaving his throne, by his will, to his younger son, Nicolas, the strange blunder was made of taking the oath of allegiance to the elder son, Constantine, from men who knew full well that Constantine had resigned all claim to the throne. Numberless societies throughout educated Russia, beginning as mere literary associations, had gradually become the homes of aspirations for a Republic; and the time of hesitation and national bewilderment between the death of Alexander and the true accession of Nicolas, seemed a promising time for an attempt to "make a beginning." As a matter of course a half-formed plot, concocted by men who thought it possible to begin a revolution and not carry it on, and who had not even a leader to look to, had a termination which would be ludicrous for its futility had its consequences not been so ghastly for five men who were executed, and so crushing for more than a hundred who were exiled of the best Russian nobility. Baron Rosen,[17] who writes the pathetic account of his own and his companions' sufferings, is a strange example of the result of Russian training. No very active participator in the affair, and hopeless of success from the beginning, he was imprisoned in a casemate for a year or more, sent to Siberia to forced labour for more years, allowed to settle in Siberia on a pittance, sent as a common soldier to the Caucasus, and finally allowed to return home, after fourteen years, to pass the rest of his days under police surveillance. Yet he hopes his readers will see that he feels "neither bitterness nor anger, in thinking over the trials" he has suffered, but that he has only "lasting gratitude for all the unfailing kindness which has been shown to him and to his comrades in grievous times;" and would entreat them always to bear in mind the circumstances under which they were condemned and punished: "they then will see there was reason enough for our having been treated thus." Apart from this over-great meekness, the account of the life in Siberia, and of the beauty and resources of the country is attractive.

Mr. Mounsey,[18] when ordered from Vienna on a mission to the Court of Persia, found it so impossible to gather the requisite information as to his route and his equipment from the experience of his friends, in the absence of a "Murray," that he resolved to supply the lack by publishing his adventures on the way, and the information gathered during his residence in Persia. The romantic ideas of Persian scenery imprinted on the juvenile mind by the "Arabian Nights" are rudely dispelled by the realistic writers of the day, and Mr. Mounsey

[17] "Russian Conspirators in Siberia." By Baron R——, London: Smith, Elder and Co., 1872.

[18] "A Journey through the Caucasus and the Interior of Persia." By A. H. Mounsey, F.R.G.S. London: Smith, Elder and Co. 1872.

only once found them justified—at Ispahan, where, ruined and devastated by Afghan invaders as the city has been, the palace of Chehel Sitoon still stands, decorated with all that Eastern fancy could invent and Eastern art execute. The gorgeous dress and jewelry are still to be seen at Court, though mixed somewhat strangely with the most unpoetic modern productions; as, for instance, Mr. Mounsey saw the Shah wearing common brown cotton gloves and a twin diamond to the Koh-i-noor, and standing by a throne of sandal-wood thickly studded with large emeralds and cushioned with Manchester chintz. The impression left by Mr. Mounsey's book as to the extreme corruption of the Government officials of all grades, the bigotry and intolerance of the population, the squalor of life, the desert wretchedness of the country, with occasional oases of great beauty, and the universal decay of the kingdom, is most painful; but in his preface he expresses his hope that he may in no degree have diverted sympathy from the populations suffering from the famine. He would have it borne in mind that the Persian's character has been formed, to a very great extent, by the system of government under which he has long lived. "His disposition is amiable, intelligent, imaginative, and docile." Owing to exceptionally dry winters in 1870 and 1871, the crops failed, and for the past two years there has been a famine frightfully destructive of life. Mr. Mounsey's descriptions of scenery; of the great ruins at Persepolis; of the "Bab" sect—a Persian eruption of Socialism peculiarly obnoxious to the despotic government of the country, and which may possibly have been crushed out, since nothing has been heard of it for twenty years—of the Guebres or Parsees, who are persecuted and diminished in Persia, and are only happy to be helped by their wealthy Indian co-religionists to emigrate; of Persian life, which he seems to have taken pains to see;—all these will repay the reader of this volume. It is impossible that an Englishman should not find amusement in the ignorance of the Eastern nations he comes in contact with, even if he acknowledges as often as Mr. Mounsey does, that in England, too, all the world does not know much about Eastern life. Perhaps the most amusing instance of such ignorance that Mr. Mounsey records is that of an official who could not attain to any understanding of the telegraph system, until it was compared to a dog whose tail should be trodden on in Teheran, and should itself bark in London.

" 'Two Idle Apprentices'"[19] have used their idle time well in catering for the information no less than for the amusement o their readers. A very temperate picture of average life in the Temple, together with hints of its historical associations, leads the way, and is followed by descriptions of the Courts at Westminster, the Chancery Courts, the Old Bailey, country Sessions, their appearance, the forms of the proceedings in them, and specimens of every-day scenes in them. The sketches contained in these papers are exceedingly vivid, and the

---

[19] "Briefs and Papers. Sketches of the Bar, and of the Press." By Two Idle Apprentices. London: H. S. King and Co. 1872.

"good stories" chosen out of that bulk of legal anecdote which must surely rival the 1300 volumes of Cases, are generally very good. Useful knowledge, in the shape of explanations of legal terms and forms, is adroitly administered to the lay public, and to many an anxious country cousin or aspirant youth the detailed and moderate account of days in chambers and in court, of the varied experiences of circuit, and of the labour necessary to become even a "rising junior," might prove very useful. A glance into the editor's room when the "leaders" for the daily paper are being discussed, apportioned, and revised; a description of the joys and miseries of newspaper reporters as they follow good and bad public speakers; an account of the rise and progress of war correspondence and correspondents, together with papers on telegraphing, company-jobbing, and the "paste and scissors" work of a newspaper editor, complete the volume. As a specimen of its real or affected humour the last few lines will serve: "I have before me a letter received by the sub-editor of a daily paper, asking whether Oliver Cromwell founded the Society for the Propagation of the Gospel in Foreign Parts."

Dr. Bastian's[*] historical and critical investigation into the "legal relationships" prevailing in different parts of the world is an excellent sample of a mode of inquiry which is becoming increasingly familiar both in this country and in Germany, and from which the most prolific results may be anticipated. Dr. Bastian discusses in a series of separate chapters each of the great group of social facts or institutions upon which legal relations are or may be based. Such facts or institutions are Property, Feudalism, Marriage, Slavery, Revenge, Witchcraft and Magic, Manufacturing and Artistic Skill. Dr. Bastian's conception of law is entirely conformable to the comprehensive and elevated view of it always presented by the best writers among his countrymen, and not unknown (though still very strange) in England. "Just," says he, "as the individual organism is maintained and regulated in its vitality by physiological prescripts, so is the organism of society, through which the personal representatives of humanity are welded into political unity, maintained and regulated by prescripts taking the form of law. The philosophic definitions of law, just as those earlier ones of the vital force, may (so soon as natural science has progressed far enough to take up psychology into itself and so to become known as the common medium of what belongs at once to the universe and the earth) be reconstructed on a method of exact investigation and be exposed to the test supplied by rigid comparative processes." Some way has already been made in thus expounding the conception of the most dominant legal ideas. It has become customary to treat individual ownership to land as an exceptional vagary, or at any rate rather as a very recent discovery than as a primitive and obvious institution. Monogamic marriage is also now recognised as peculiar and exceptional, however high it may stand as a moral development. So with slavery and trade-castes. They are seen to recur

---

[*] "Die Rechtsverhältnisse bei verschiedenen Völkern der Erde. Ein Beitrag zur Vergleichenden Ethnologie." Von Prof. Dr. Bastian. Berlin: 1872.

almost ubiquitously at certain stages of society in all nations, though
under the most eccentric varieties in each. Dr. Bastian levies his
illustrations from the most varied and out-of-the-way people, extending
to Northern Africa, Mongolia, China, Mexico, Peru, Australia, Sparta,
and Iceland. An interesting feature in this book is an extract from a
code of Siamese laws, originally published by Dr. Bradley, the missionary. The following are seven classes of persons whom it is proper
to employ as bond-servants:—First, persons for whom money or other
property has been paid for their relief; second, the children of persons
in bondage for debt; third, parents transferred to their children as
pawn-servants; fourth, persons given to others as pawn-servants;
fifth, persons redeemed from prison or from capital punishment; sixth,
persons under pressure of famine who have given themselves as bond-
servants in consideration of being fed and clothed; seventh, persons
taken captive in war.

The treatise of Dr. Gneist[11] on the "Rechstaat" (an expression, by
the way, characteristically untranslateable into English) is interesting
both from the antecedents of the eminent writer and from the existing
situation of Germany. Dr. Gneist is a member of the German Parliament. He is also a political philosopher, and has written the
most exhaustive and accurate work in existence on the details of
English government. The present work exhibits to the full all the
elements which the author and his subject might be expected to contribute. Germany is recovering slowly though surely from the
almost distracting spasm of effort whereby her formal political unity
was brought about, her commercial unity substantiated, and her
territorial integrity asserted against France. Dr. Gneist approaches
his subject from a point of view which can only be understood by those
who are in some measure conversant with the history of the political
and philosophical schools of Germany, the influence of which has in these
regions been so profound. The second section (by way of specimen)
opens with the following proposition: "The 'Rechstaat' (or the completely developed State), in the historical and philosophical sense of
the term, is a matter of long and laborious creation, growing up by
incessant struggle with the original impulses of society, and in the
modern world can only be supported and recovered (when lost) by
means of such a struggle." Thereupon follows an investigation of
the natural and various wants of mankind, and the argument is
broached that, just as the life and activity of the individual man
subsists in the constant play and mutual action and reaction upon
each other of his feelings or desires and his duties, so the life of the
whole community is maintained and developed by the mutual action
and reaction of liberty and government. "As no individual man can
renounce his moral duty, so can no people renounce their political consciousness; man is essentially a ζῷον πολιτικόν." A noticeable
section of the work is occupied with a criticism of the general political
elements now present in France, under the rather startling title of
the "Negation of the 'Rechstaat' in French Constitutions." Dr.

---

11 "Der Rechstaat." Von Dr. Rudolf Gneist. Berlin: 1872.

Gneist says that "the radical characteristic of the French Government
remains identically the same under all modifications of forms. Under
all changes of Government there is the same impotency in law to
protect the individual against the executive, and this is due to the
incapacity in which the whole of society partakes to conceive any
Government exempt from the triumph of party." The problem before
the German jurists is the reconciliation of the claims and duties of the
central Government with the interests and independent life of the
several States.

Mr. Walter Bagehot's[22] new edition of his work on the English
Constitution is rendered more interesting than the first edition by an
introductory chapter bringing up his comments on the existing political condition, both in this and in other countries, to the most recent
date. Mr. Bagehot's position in the political world is very peculiar.
He is what may be called a satirical admirer of the British Constitution.
Probably there could not be compared with each other two minds
more antipathetic at every point than those of Mr. Walter Bagehot
and the late Sir William Blackstone; and yet they both agree in discovering all kinds of lurking advantages and delicate adaptations in
the British Constitution which are hidden from the eyes, not only of
the Radical demagogue, but of the professional Conservative. In his
introductory chapter Mr. Bagehot shows how the views he has expressed throughout his book derive illustration both from the existing
position of M. Thiers in France and from the present and late economical struggles of the United States. Mr. Bagehot says that, when
the first edition of his book was published, he had great difficulty in
persuading many people that it was possible in a non-monarchical
State for the real chief of the practical executive to be nominated and
to be removable by the vote of the National Assembly. "But now
France has given an example: M. Thiers is (with one exception) just
the *chef du pouvoir exécutif* that I endeavoured more than once in
this book to describe. He is appointed by and is removable by the
Assembly. He comes down and speaks in it just as our Premier does;
he is responsible for managing it just as our Premier is. No one can
any longer doubt the possibility of a republic in which the executive
and the legislative authorities are united and fixed; no one can assert
such an axiom to be the incommunicate attribute of a constitutional
monarchy." Mr. Bagehot, however, points out that in three ways
the example of France is at present unsatisfactory: First, because the
nation has no peculiar aptitude, but "possibly a peculiar inaptitude,"
for parliamentary government; secondly, the present polity of
France is not a copy of the whole effective part of the British Constitution, M. Thiers having no power to dissolve the Assembly; thirdly,
M. Thiers does not govern, as a parliamentary premier governs, as the
head of a party. "On the contrary, being the one person essential to
all parties, he selects ministers from all parties, he constructs a
cabinet in which no one minister agrees with any other in anything,

22 "The English Constitution." By Walter Bagehot. New Edition, with an
Additional Chapter. London: Henry S. King. 1872.

and with all the members of which he himself frequently disagrees." The instances taken from the existing economical situation of the United States have for their purpose to prove that the separation of the President from Congress tends to prevent thorough public discussion from accompanying the solution of taxation problems, and so to favour a disastrous policy.

The present educational movement in this country is, fortunately, signalized by the appearance of a very superior class of school books, prepared (as such books ought to be) by some of the best minds in the country. A good specimen of the class is the first volume of an historical course for schools, the subject being a "General Sketch of European History,"[13] and the author of this preliminary volume being Mr. Freeman. There has long been wanting such a compendious and accurate treatise upon a topic in the highest degree complicated and composite. The object of the present volume is "to trace out the general relations of different periods and different countries to one another, without going minutely into the affairs of any particular country." There is no break recognised between what is usually called Ancient and Modern History, and the great events are grasped in a manner considerably facilitating apprehension and retention by the student. Thus the later chapters are devoted to such general facts and events as "The Swabian Empires," the "Decline of the Empire," the "Greatness of Spain," the "Greatness of France," the "Rise of Russia," the "French Revolution," the "Reunion of Germany and Italy." The extreme compression which is necessitated by the plan of the work renders it rather severe reading, but as a whet to the curiosity or a book of reference it is likely to prove very valuable.

A simple didactic work on the detailed mechanism of the British Government, reliable for accuracy and yet intelligible to young students, may be heartily welcomed. Mr. Frederick Wicks[14] has prepared such a work, and it is hoped the subject of it will soon be an integral part of the education given in the elementary schools. The proceedings of the House of Commons, which so few young people not in daily contact with the newspapers even know or understand, are given by Mr. Wicks with great particularity. The whole process of administering justice, both in the civil and the criminal courts, and both by judges of the superior courts and by justices of the peace, is described, and the meaning and history of trial by jury and the Habeas Corpus Act are given with much detail. Under the head of "Local Administration" the mode of governing the City of London is indicated, and that of the method of the administration of counties and of provincial districts is alluded to, though perhaps a little too briefly, considering the importance of the subject under the advancing influence of the Local Government Board. The work concludes with a brief and readable sketch of the "Growth of the Constitution."

[13] "Historical Course for Schools." General Sketch of European History. Vol. I. By Edward A. Freeman, D.C.L. London: Macmillan and Co. 1872.

[14] "The British Constitution and Government." A Reading and Lesson Book for Senior Classes. By Frederick Wicks. London: Collings and Appleton. 1872.

In the present social condition of England, and, indeed, of Europe
generally, it is not easy to rate too highly the value of such partly
scientific and partly popular handbooks as M. Edmond About's* on
"Social Economy," now translated by Mr. W. F. Rae, a writer who
belongs to the rare class of translators who stamp the works they
produce with a fresh and novel merit due to their own originality of
mind. Mr. Rae's introduction describes the circumstances which led
to the production of the original work, and there are similar circumstances all around us in this country which ought to lead to the
large circulation of it. Two sets of opinions alone had invariably
been presented for the acceptance of the Parisian workmen; the one
giving them no hope of rising from a condition of comparative servitude to a state of independence, and inculcating contentment with
their lot as an absolute duty; the other set being wholly revolutionary and subversive, upholding an appeal to force as the only sure
means for attaining to comfort and opulence. Not being satisfied
with remaining as they were, nor prepared to have recourse to violence,
they professed themselves desirous of being instructed as to the real
state of the case and ready to hear both sides. One of their number,
who wrote on behalf of the others, asked M. About: "Is there no
science of social economy? Why have we never been taught it?
Are you versed in it? Can you teach it us? We do not ask for a
formal treatise, but a few hours of familiar talk about wealth, capital,
income, labour, wages, production, consumption, co-operation, taxation,
money; in fact, about the words which are dinned into our ears, sometimes to dishearten, sometimes to dupe us, but are never defined and
freed from all uncertainty." M. About consented to undertake the
task. Mr. Rae points out how M. About's aptitude for writing such
a work is beyond all question. "He is largely endowed with the
peculiarly French gift of rendering the most abstruse topics clear to
the meanest understanding, and of making entertaining reading out
of the driest and most unpromising materials. He succeeds best where
he has no personal views to propagate. His greatest failures have
been his political opinions and previsions. So marked have been some
of his blunders that there is danger of underrating his real powers."
The arguments in favour of free trade used by M. About in his chapter
on "Liberty" are fine specimens of racy political writing, as well as
singularly apposite in the present anomalous reaction of the most
enlightened country of the world in favour of protection :—

"Why should consumers—that is, all men—be condemned to pay dearly for
a bad or mediocre product when, by crossing the frontier, they can have a
better one at a low price? Why should the produce of corn be obliged to
sell his harvest at a low rate on this side of the frontier, when the foreigner
offers him a higher price for it on the other side? Why should the Parisian
be free to open a grocer's shop, and should not have the right to become a
baker, butcher, cab-driver, broker, publisher, printer, manager of public enter-
tainments? Is there any logical reason why certain kinds of production

---

* "Handbook of Social Economy, or the Worker's A B C." By Edmond
About. Translated from the last French Edition.

should be open to everyone, and certain others restricted to those who are privileged? Why, in a country of equality, should masters possess the right to combine to prevent a rise of wages, while workmen run the risk of heavy punishment should they unite to obtain an advance in wages? These are some of the questions which spontaneously presented themselves to the good sense of our new statesmen. They have taken up several others of which the enumeration would be too long here, but which are all under consideration, and which we shall see settled sooner or later."

Mr. Rae curtly remarks that the delusion of the Protective system is not wholly due to the teaching or tyranny of monarchs. "M. About has lived to learn that, in this matter, a republic can be as short-sighted as a monarchy."

Among the various classes of treatises that are issued from time to time on different branches of ethical philosophy and on education in connexion with it, there is a great lack of simple elementary books explaining, in simple language capable of being made serviceable in the conduct of popular education, the grounds of the relative value of moral acts and the relative mischievousness of immoral acts. Even in the higher schools and universities of the country this part of the moral training of the young is entirely neglected or only imparted to a few of the most promising students—that is, those who least stand in need of it—under the form of Paley's "Moral Philosophy" or Whewell's "Elements of Morality." It is one indirect advantage of the abandonment of the teaching of religion in schools that the necessity of giving organic instruction in the elements of moral science is forced upon public attention. The need for a supply of good text-books on the subject is an obvious result of this impulse, and the work of Mr. Charles Bray,* which has just reached a fourth edition, is a good specimen of the kind of books that are wanted. Mr. Bray's work, indeed, is quite as instructive to parents and guardians as to the young; and, in fact, the whole subject of moral and physical education is in such a retrograde, or rather stagnant, condition, when compared with its pressing importance, that it is scarcely possible to lay down the simplest and most obvious principles without seeming to publish a new gospel. Thus Mr. Bray, in his chapter on "Anger and Passion, and Energy of Character," commenting on the vicious inculcation of principles of retaliation, says, "the expression of this feeling of anger in petty revenge is often foolishly encouraged by nurses: 'Did the naughty stick fall down and hurt baby? *beat* naughty stick:' and even if a brother or sister is the offender, the same amiable spirit of retaliation is impressed." And, again, in a passage which is singularly appropriate to the needs of the present day, Mr. Bray writes:—"We should never give unnecessary pain to any creature, and certainly never inflict pain for the sake of pleasure to ourselves." If children were properly brought up in love and sympathy with all around, what is called "sport" would be not sport to them: there would be no pleasure in killing even what we require for our daily food. Battues on poor half-tame pheasants, tiger-shoot-

* "The Education of the Feelings." A Moral System, revised and abridged for secular schools. Fourth Edition. By Charles Bray. London: Longmans. 1872.

ings, and other such "sports" are only evidence of the semi-barbarous
age in which we live.   The questions at the end of each section
point to the practical nature of the work, and will be found of great
service to the instructor.

SCIENCE.

THERE is a striking similarity between some of Don Quixote's
famous deeds and the series of criticisms which the late Professor
de Morgan[1] has published in the *Athenæum* under the heading " A
Budget of Paradoxes," and which have been reprinted now in a separate
volume.   We have all heard how the Spanish knight broke his lance
with such foes as windmills and herds of sheep. The late Mr. de Morgan
thought herds of ignorant blockheads worthy of his steel.   There is,
however, this difference between the professor and the knight, that the
latter is always ignorant of the real character of his enemies and fights
in good faith, while the professor is perfectly aware that the objects
of his onslaught are, in all cases, either dunces or lunatics.   Nor does
he fight for victory ; all he tries for is to make others laugh at the
ignorance of the poor miserable men who have at various times propounded silly doctrines in metaphysics, ethics, and other branches of
philosophical inquiry, or who have believed themselves to have discovered
the solution of the various so-called " problems" in mathematics and
physics.   The circle-squarers, cube-duplicators, and angle-trisectors are
especially welcome targets for the professor's wit.   We confess that we
have felt extremely perplexed as to an answer to the simple question,
which is clearly the first as regards every literary production—viz., *cui
bono ?*   What possible good can be derived by anybody from a book
like this ?   The late Professor de Morgan was not only a man of the
highest position as a mathematician, but also a profound thinker on
many branches of metaphysical science and on general matters of contemporary interest.   His views deserve in the highest degree to be collected
from his scattered writings and to be preserved, but we must really most
earnestly protest against erecting literary monuments for every ignorant and conceited man who has published some scientific rubbish of
one sort or another.   Such a book gives them precisely that notoriety
which such vain individuals are seeking.   " My intention in publishing
this Budget in the *Athenæum*," says the author, " is to enable those
who have been puzzled by one or two discoverers to see how they look
in the lump."   The truth is, that the lump looks exactly like the first
or second ; they are all made on the same pattern, made up by ignorance
of the very first principles of the subject of their discoveries, stuffed
with conceit, and dressed in a garment of the most intrusive and
audacious impudence. Science should condemn every individual of the
class to utter oblivion ; she can only detract from her dignity by

---

[1] " A Budget of Paradoxes." By Augustus de Morgan.   London : 1872.
Longmans, Green & Co.

making fun of them. And is it really so very funny to hear of a man who wrote a letter to the professor in which he says :—" There are no limits in mathematics, and those that assert there are, are infinite ruffians, ignorant, lying blackguards. There is no differential calculus, no Taylor's theorem, no calculus of variations, &c., in mathematics. There is no quackery whatever in mathematics ; no $\frac{0}{0}$ equal to anything. What sheer ignorant blackguardism that !" &c. The professor considered it necessary to inform the reader that " the poor fellow died in the Cork Union." Another specimen of this kind of humour is the story of an agricultural labourer. He squared the circle and brought the proceeds to Professor de Morgan, who returned the papers to the man with a note, stating he had not the knowledge requisite to see in what the problem consisted. For answer the professor received a letter in which he was told that a person who could not see that he had done the thing should change his business and appropriate his time and attention to a Sunday-school, to learn what he could and keep the *little* children from *durting* their *close*. Of this exhilarating correspondence the late professor seems to have made a great deal. He says " these letters were printed for the amusement of the readers of *Notes and Queries,* and they will appear again in the sequel." Of such anecdotes and of the professor's fun and wit there is no end in the book. The editress of the Budget, Sophia de Morgan, has added to the book and, here and there, has used the pruning knife. She mentions one large omission ; it is an account of the quarrel between Sir James South and Mr. Troughton on the mounting, &c. of the equatorial telescope at Campden Hill. " At a future time," says the editress, " when the affair has passed entirely out of the memory of living astronomers, the appreciative sketch which is omitted in this edition of the Budget will be an interesting piece of history and study of character." Here we meet with the same mistake which has given us such a book as the Budget : the future historian of science will care as little for the squabble between South and Troughton as scientific men of the present generation care about hearing the history of, and obtaining minute information about, every ignorant circle-squarer or mad metaphysician who pestered professors with his discoveries or published them.

Instead of launching witticisms, critical sarcasm, and professorial indignation against the long row of circle-squarers and similar self-vaunted benefactors to science, we should strongly advise every one of them to study carefully Mr. Barnard Smith's[1] " Lessons in Arithmetic, Writing, and Spelling." A more excellent little work for a first introduction to knowledge cannot well be written. Mr. Smith's larger text-books on arithmetic and algebra are already most favourably known, and he has proved now that the difficulty of writing a text-book which begins *ab ovo* is really surmountable ; but we shall be much mistaken if this little book has not cost its author more thought and

[1] " Easy Lessons in Arithmetic, combining Exercises in Reading, Writing, Spelling, and Dictation." By the Rev. Barnard Smith, M.A. London : Macmillan & Co, 1872.

mental labour than any of his more elaborate text-books. The plan to combine arithmetical lessons with those in reading and spelling is perfectly novel, and it is worked out in accordance with the aims of our national schools; and we are convinced that its general introduction in all elementary schools throughout the country will produce great educational advantages.

Mr. Hensley's[3] book on the same subject takes its readers somewhat farther than Mr. Smith's. It is an introduction to a larger work by the author, but we may say that it will be found independently a really capital introductory arithmetic, preparing for more advanced study generally. The definitions are very clear and simple, but it would, in our opinion, have been better if the book had ended at page 64: the lessons on fractions are far too short, and brevity becomes here obscurity. We do not for a moment believe that a beginner will understand that because it takes two halves to make one and two quarters to make one half, he will "see that you have to invert or turn over the fractional divisor and multiply by it." The mechanical rule is given far too early, and should have been preceded by many more distinct examples.

The first appearance of Father Secchi's[4] great work on the sun was enthusiastically welcomed by astronomers a year or two ago. The author had not only himself enriched the store of knowledge about our luminary by independent researches of the very greatest merit, but it was expected from an astronomer of his distinction that we should obtain from him a clear impartial history and review of all the recent discoveries in solar physics. Father Secchi's original work, " Le Soleil," was undoubtedly a source of much information, and it certainly presented to educated men for the first time a scientific exposition of a great many established facts bearing on the subject, while its illustrations were of the highest order; but, unfortunately, general disappointment was felt among readers beyond Italy and France because the discoveries of men belonging to other nationalities were not treated with proper fairness, and because not only undue prominence was given even to the less important observations made by Father Secchi himself, but that, in fact, the greater portion of the contents of the original consisted wholly of Father Secchi's own observations and his own conclusions therefrom. The general opinion of truly enthusiastic students, admirers, and protectors of science has recently more and more pointed to the sad truth that the want of modesty and self-denial in most scientific men of the present day and their mutual jealousies are a blight upon the growth of science. It is, therefore, especially gratifying to see that Father Secchi has entrusted M. Schellen, whose work on spectroscopic astronomy has made him already well known in this country, with the preparation of

---

[3] " Figures made Easy ; a First Arithmetic Book." By Lewis Hensley, M.A. Oxford : At the Clarendon Press. 1872.

[4] " Die Sonne." Von P. A. Secchi. Authorisirte Deutsche Ausgabe und original Work, herausgegeben durch Dr. H. Schellen. Braunschweig : Georg Westermann. 1872.

an entirely new edition of his work in German, bringing the subject up to the most recent date, and has left it to him to discuss with thorough impartiality the merits of other astronomers who have devoted some practical work or theoretical investigation to the sun. M. Schellen has done his work remarkably well. This magnificent book is not a mere literary drawing-room ornament, although its beautiful photographs and coloured illustrations are in themselves works of art and deserve general admiration; but it is a really scientific work, in the same sense popular in which we give this epithet to such works as Humboldt's "Cosmos" or Lyell's "Principles of Geology," implying that the highest results of scientific research are expounded without the dry data which line the road to philosophical results, and without approach to that superficiality which is so much the characteristic of the "popular" science of our day. The method in which the whole of the vast matter is arranged has the merit of being extremely logical. The simple observational aspect of solar phenomena is given first, and the various mechanical implements are then described which have in recent times so much contributed to extending our previous knowledge by multiplying and refining the methods of obtaining the facts. Next follows a comparison and critical elaboration of the really valuable portion of the results, as bearing both upon the astronomical elements of the sun—viz., the axial rotations and inclinations of the solar equator to the ecliptic—and also upon those intrinsic peculiarities of solar phenomena—viz., spots, faculæ, corona, chromosphere, &c.—the observation and study of which has been the aim of the most distinguished men in recent times. The discussion of the results may now be pronounced to be in every respect satisfactory, impartial, and complete, so as to make this work on the sun a truly noble monument of modern scientific research. In a work of this kind some inaccuracies and shortcomings are to be expected. Thus an explanation of the peculiarities in the motion of sun spots when near the limb is rightly sought for in the existence of a refracting medium around the sun. This question has been thoroughly investigated by Carrington in the *Monthly Notices* (a fact with which Father Secchi and M. Schellen seem to be quite unacquainted), and also more recently by Peters. Father Secchi takes all credit for this explanation to himself, giving to Mr. Carrington some little doubtful praise for having pointed out the possibility of such an explanation. In another place Sir William Herschel's idea of connecting solar and terrestrial meteorological phenomena is mentioned, and the fact of their connexion represented as being beyond any doubt. But the thread on which this supposed connexion hangs at present is as yet very slight indeed; it is merely a hypothetical construction, favourable to the existence of such a connexion, of a few isolated observations, some of which are not at all beyond doubt. It would be more correct to say that the question of such a connexion might certainly be solved if photographic records of solar events were more facilitated than they are at present by European governments.

From the sun it is only natural to be reminded of a French work,[1]

[1] "The Forces of Nature." By Amédée Guillemin. Translated from the French

which has made its appearance in English under the auspices of our
renowned physicist and solar observer, Mr. Norman Lockyer. Mrs.
Lockyer has translated M. Guillemin's work on "The Forces of Nature,"
and Mr. Lockyer has edited and annotated it, besides making valuable
additions. We have repeatedly in these pages attempted to discourage
the production of the so-called "popular" introductions to scientific
subjects, and have tried to persuade our readers to seek knowledge in
the legitimate and recognised rudimentary text-books. Such books
will not appear dry to a student who earnestly seeks for sound information, and no information is sound or worth having which is not
gained by mental exertion. We therefore entered upon the perusal of
this work with divided thoughts; the book being introduced by an
editor with a first-rate scientific reputation, but on the other hand,
being dressed in the gaudy external dress which usually hides superficiality, ornamented with highly-coloured and exaggerated plates, and
bound in a manner which makes a preparatory toilet and a dress suit
indispensable for its perusal. We were, however, soon satisfied that
there is really a noble work hidden beneath these gorgeous para-
phernalia, which seem to be incidents inseparable from modern book-
production. If the reader of Mrs. Lockyer's translation has perception for the beautiful fluency of the language, the clearness and succinct-
ness of the sentences in which difficult subjects are often explained, and
the thoroughly technical manner in which complicated experimental
arrangements are described, he will be captivated by this charming
production, which is by no means without genuine scientific worth.
There is a peculiarity of tone throughout the work, which we cannot
but believe to have been, perhaps, imperceptibly given to the language
by the lady who has given us this translation; it is a tone of profound humility, of innocent wonder and deep admiration for the effects
of the natural forces represented before our eyes; it is the same tone
which has lent such power of attraction to the writings of the late
Mrs. Somerville, and which is as different from the didactic and
authoritative tone of the text-books as it is from the condescending
style of the professional science popularizers. We wish every success
to Mrs. Lockyer's beautiful translation, and may point out that several
chapters—for example, those on polarization (book iii. chap. xvi. and
xvii.)—will even to the advanced student preach well-known facts in a
new and instructive light; indeed, the whole of acoustics and optics
is treated in the most admirable manner. The woodcuts are numerous
and excellent, but some of the coloured plates are not quite in accordance
with what is seen in nature.

Professor Tyndall[s] has collected in one volume his various "Contributions to Molecular Physics in the Domain of Radiant Heat"
which appeared at different times in the *Transactions of the Royal
Society* and in the *Philosophical Magazine.* These papers are the

by Mrs. Norman Lockyer, and edited by J. Norman Lockyer, F.R.S. London:
Macmillan. 1872.
    [s] "Contributions to Molecular Physics in the Domain of Radiant Heat." By
John Tyndall. London: Longmans, Green & Co.

author's experimental researches, principally on the absorption and radiation of heat by gases and vapours; on the physical connexion of radiation, absorption, and conduction; on the relation of radiant heat to aqueous vapour; on the passage of radiant heat through dry and humid air; on luminous and obscure radiation; on calorescence or the transmutation of heat rays; and on the influence of colour and mechanical conditions on radiant heat, besides several papers on cognate matters. These researches have established Professor Tyndall's fame as a physicist, and although a critical discussion of several points—which, however, is clearly out of place here—might lead to conclusions somewhat different from those of Professor Tyndall (especially those regarding the action of air and that of aqueous vapour on radiant heat), we cannot but express our greatest admiration for these papers, which in this collected form are more accessible than they were previously, and the publication of which is an undoubted boon to students of science. A second recent publication which bears Professor Tyndall's name[1] as author, will probably be a source of great disappointment to everybody who has looked forward to the "International Scientific Series," which has been for some time announced, and of which this volume, "On the Forms of Water in Clouds and Rivers, Ice and Glaciers," is the first part. This book is, in our opinion, as unworthy of Professor Tyndall as it is unworthy of serious criticism; indeed, we feel almost convinced that it will be the worst, as it is the first, of the whole series. It is not stated that the contents of the book are lectures, although it appears that such is the case. Here and there we are reminded of experiments which the reader and the professor have made together—of things which we have seen together, but of which, in fact, most readers will know nothing whatsoever. The book is clearly "made up" in a hurry for publication; it contains the well-known, and often-repeated facts about glaciers, filling all but twenty-five pages of the whole book, and we have failed to discover a single sentence which would throw light "on the form of water" in clouds, for example, on which point the professor might certainly have told us something worth hearing.

Mr. Proctor's[2] work "On the Orbs Around Us" is a collection of very clearly-written essays on various astronomical and physical subjects. They are intelligent expositions of our present knowledge of the physical constitution of several planets, of meteors and meteor systems, discussions of cometary phenomena and cometary theories, and contain sound teaching on various other questions. Two essays, which are very pleasant to read, are devoted to the discussion, in the light of modern science, of the old question as to the existence of living creatures on the celestial bodies. The author drives here on a still dark road,

[1] "The Forms of Water in Clouds and Rivers, Ice and Glaciers." By John Tyndall. The International Scientific Series. Vol. 1. London: Henry S. King & Co. 1872.
[2] "The Orbs Around Us." By Richard A. Proctor, B.A. (Camb.) London: Longmans, Green & Co. 1872.

but the sparks and scintillations produced by his wheel are striking and suggestive of more light; and the sound of the wheel is often charmingly poetical without clatter. We regret to see no allusion to Zœllner's cometary theory in the chapters devoted to the subject, and think that a more general and simultaneous discussion of the several cometary theories recently propounded, by an astronomer of Mr. Proctor's acumen, would have been more valuable than the criticism bestowed upon that one theory which has the least probability of all.

Two works to which already, on previous occasions, attention has been directed are now completed. One is Professor Wolf's[9] "Manual of Mathematics," the other is Professor Everett's[10] English edition of Deschanel's "Physics." Professor Wolf continues to the end to make his "Manual of Mathematics" a "dictionary of worthies," and Professor Everett is in this last part more zealous than ever to scatter mathematical formulæ and applications of the differential calculus over a book evidently designed for the very beginner in the study of physics. Both works possess, however, many points of real merit, and form undoubtedly valuable additions to scientific literature.

Dr. Plath's "Astronomy for Ladies"[11] is in every respect a characteristic specimen of the result of the popularizing process in science. Twaddle from beginning to end. The author is a physician who has published some "letters of a physician to a young mother." They seem to have been pretty successful in a pecuniary respect—hence letters on astronomy. He explains the systems of great circles and all heavenly motions principally with the help of a soap-basin.

Professor Kohlrausch's[12] little work of practical instruction in the physical laboratory is, since the first edition has made its appearance, in the hands of every physicist in this country. There are many considerable additions in the new edition to which we should like to direct attention: the number of distinct investigations is increased by twenty-eight, the number of tables by eleven, and an important appendix has been added on the system of absolute measures in the various branches of physics where it has been applied. More and more of this excellent matter is the only wish we have to express to the distinguished author with reference to future editions, of which many are certain to follow.

Dr. Mailly[13] has published two memoirs, one on the history of

---

[9] "Handbuch der Mathematik, &c." Von Dr. Rudolf Wolf. Zürich: Schulthess. 1872. (London : Nutt.)

[10] "Deschanel's Natural Philosophy." By Professor Everett. Part iv. Sound and Light. London: Blackie and Son. 1872.

[11] "Sternkunde für Frauen." Von Dr. Wilhelm Plath. Braunschweig: Meyer. 1872. (London : Trübner.)

[12] "Leitfaden der Praktischen Physik." Von F. Kohlrausch. Leipzig: Teubner. (London : Nutt.) 1872.

[13] "Tableau de l'Astronomie dans l'Hemisphere Austral et dans l'Inde." Par E. Mailly. Bruxelles : F. Hayer. 1872.

"De l'Astronomie dans l'Académie Royale de Belgique." Rapport Séculaire, (1772—1872). Par E. Mailly. Bruxelles : F. Hayer. 1872.

astronomy in the southern hemisphere and India, the other on the astronomical work done by the Royal Academy in Belgium during the century from 1772 to 1872. They are extremely valuable contributions to the history of astronomy, and the portions referring to astronomical labours by Englishmen in India, at the Cape of Good Hope, and in Australia, are written in an appreciative and even enthusiastic tone.

Mr. Darwin's work on "The Expression of the Emotions in Man and Animals,"[14] the third of the *pièces justificatives* published by him in support or illustration of his theory of the origin of species by natural selection, does not seem to carry matters much further than they were before. The expressions by which some of the mammalia manifest their emotions, with the exception of a sort of rudimentary laughter in which certain monkeys are said to indulge and the weeping of some other animals, seem to have no analogy with those displayed by mankind, and their citation here serves rather to show how the same principles govern the outward manifestations of emotion wherever such occur. These principles, as laid down by Mr. Darwin, are as follows :—

"1. *The principle of serviceable associated habits.*—Certain complex actions are of direct or indirect service under certain states of the mind, in order to relieve or gratify certain sensations, desires, &c.; and whenever the same state of mind is induced, however feebly, there is a tendency by the force of habit and association for the same movements to be performed, though they may not then be of the least use. Some actions ordinarily associated through habit with certain states of the mind may be partially repressed through the will, and in such cases the muscles which are least under the separate control of the will are the most liable still to act, causing movements which we recognise as expression. In certain other cases the checking of one habitual movement requires other slight movements; and these are likewise expressive."

"2. *The principle of antithesis.*—Certain states of the mind lead to certain habitual actions, which are of service, as under our first principle. Now when a directly opposite state of mind is produced, there is a strong and involuntary tendency to the performance of movements of a directly opposite nature, though these are of no use; and such movements are in some cases highly expressive."

"3. *The principle of actions due to the constitution of the nervous system independently from the first of the will, and independently to a certain extent of habit.*—When the sensorium is strongly excited nerve-force is generated in excess, and is transmitted in certain definite directions depending on the connection of the nerve-cells, and partly on habit; or the supply of nerve-force may, as it appears, be interrupted. Effects are thus produced which we recognise as expressive. This third principle may, for the sake of brevity, be called that of the direct action of the nervous system." (Pp. 28, 29.)

It is by means of these three principles that Mr. Darwin endeavours to investigate the origin of the various expressions of emotion, and although in some cases, at any rate, we may admit that his reasoning

---

[14] "The Expression of the Emotions in Man and Animals." By Charles Darwin, M.A., F.R.S., &c. London : Murray. 1872. 8vo.

seems to be a little far-fetched, it is yet impossible to deny that in general it furnishes an ingenious and often happy explanation of very difficult matters—difficult, at least, unless we are prepared to accept the old notion that these outward expressions, with language, were given to man by a sort of inspiration, and not as Mr. Darwin maintains, in the chief cases acquired by our early progenitors and transmitted by them by inheritance to their offspring until they have at length become fixed and innate. The following summary of the origin of the expression of grief in the human face will serve to illustrate Mr. Darwin's treatment of his subject. Starting from the principle that screaming or crying out under painful or troublesome circumstances is a natural, and indeed useful, action common to man and most of the lower animals that are endowed with a voice, our author says:—

"When infants scream loudly from hunger or pain the circulation is affected and the eyes tend to become gorged with blood; consequently the muscles surrounding the eyes are strongly contracted as a protection: this action, in the course of many generations, has become firmly fixed and inherited, but when, with advancing years and culture, the habit of screaming is partially repressed, the muscles round the eyes still tend to contract whenever even slight distress is felt: of these muscles the pyramidals of the nose are less under the control of the will than are the others, and their contraction can be checked only by that of the central fasciæ of the frontal muscle. These latter fasciæ draw up the inner ends of the eyebrows and wrinkle the forehead in a peculiar manner, which we instantly recognise as the expression of guilt or anxiety." (P. 351.)

As examples of the application of the principle of antithesis Mr. Darwin cites the behaviour of dogs under certain circumstances. A dog approaching another dog or a strange man with inimical feelings "walks upright and very stiffly; his head is slightly raised, or not much lowered; the tail is held erect and quite rigid; the hairs bristle, especially along the neck and back; the pricked ears are directed forwards and the eyes have a fixed stare"—peculiarities or actions which may nearly all be explained as beneficial in the dog's intended attack upon his enemy. But let the animal approach his master or some other person to whom he is attached, and his whole bearing is precisely the reverse to that above described; but now not one of his "movements, so clearly expressive of affection, are of the least direct service to the animal," and Mr. Darwin considers that they are explicable "solely from being in complete opposition or antithesis to the attitude and movements which, from intelligible causes, are assumed when a dog intends to fight, and which, consequently, are expressive of anger. The different attitudes of cats when angry and when demonstrating their affection for their friends furnish Mr. Darwin with another illustration of this principle, upon which he also explains the human habit of shrugging the shoulders and throwing out the open hands as an expression of helplessness or of acquiescence in what cannot be avoided, the actions in this case being in complete contrast with those expressive of indignation and defiant resolve. It would be impossible to follow Mr. Darwin through his discussion of the expressions by which the motions of joy, tenderness, devotion, reflectiveness, sulkiness, hatred and anger, contempt and disgust, surprise, fear and horror, shame, and many others are manifested, expressions in which, according to Mr. Darwin, we have to do for the most part with a direct action of the nervous system, modified, of course, by other conditions and especially dependent on habit. But it may be mentioned that he devotes considerable space to the examination of the phenomenon of blushing, to which, indeed, as being apparently a peculiarly human manifestation, it seems to be fairly entitled. He considers blushing to be the expression of such emotions as arise from the quality which he denominates "self-attention" being more or less painfully affected. In this exceedingly imperfect sketch we have, of course, been quite unable to do justice to Mr. Darwin's work, which, like all his other writings, is full of interesting facts and ingenious arguments. Except as indicating the mode in which those gestures and changes of countenance which express the internal emotions may have gradually arisen and become fixed and intensified in man, even supposing his origin to have been as lowly and brutish as the theory of evolution would make it, we cannot see that it can do much towards the support of Mr. Darwin's published views as to the origin of species; but, as the author points out, the facts which he has gathered from all sources and countries with regard to the expression of emotion in man are of much importance, as they prove "that all the chief expressions exhibited by man are the same throughout the world," thus affording "a new argument in favour of the several races being descended from a single parent stock, which must have been almost completely human in structure, and to a large extent in mind, before the period at which the races diverged from each other." This volume is illustrated with a few good wood engravings and with numerous photographic portraits of individuals displaying various emotional expressions. Many of the latter are exceedingly good and effective; others are rather poor.

Of the volume of essays on subjects connected with natural selection published in 1870 by Mr. Wallace we are glad to notice the appearance of a second edition.[u] The author is entitled to speak with authority upon a theory of which he may claim to have been the joint originator with Mr. Darwin, and several of these essays, especially those founded on the author's own personal observations, are of great interest and value. So also in the present state of the public mind are the papers on the application of the law of natural selection to man. The alterations made in the present edition are few and of no very great importance.

Dr. Nicholson is really an exceedingly prolific writer upon subjects connected with natural history. Having given us a "Manual," an "Advanced Text-book," and an "Introductory Text-book of Zoology," an "Introduction to Biology," and the first part of a "Monograph of the British Graptolitidæ," so rapidly one after the other as almost to take

[u] "Contributions to the Theory of Natural Selection." A Series of Essays. By Alfred Russell Wallace. London: Macmillan. 1871. 8vo.

away one's breath, he comes upon us now with a "Manual of Palæontology,"[16] forming a handsome volume of some six hundred pages. It is
true that in most of these works a great deal of the ground covered in
each is the same; but, nevertheless, the industry required to work up the
same materials into so many different shapes is something considerable,
and in the present case the subject, although to a great extent the same,
is surveyed from a perfectly new point of view. This "Manual of
Palæontology" is divided by its author into four parts, of which the
first consists of a general introduction indicating the general nature and
objects of the study of that science, with an explanation of such
geological facts as are necessary for the comprehension of the succeeding
parts. In the second and third parts the author describes the various
groups of fossil animals and plants in their systematic order, commencing in each case with the lowest forms. The fourth part is an
essay on what the author denominates "Historical Palæontology"—
that is to say, an exposition of the various formations of the earth's
crust in ascending order, with an account of the fossil forms of animals
and plants characteristic of each of them. The work, which is intended for educational purposes, is well executed, and will be found
very useful. The illustrations are numerous, but a great part of them
are borrowed from D'Orbigny's "Cours Élémentaire."

Of a somewhat different quality is a little book on the same subject
as the preceding, entitled "Life in the Primeval World," by Mr. W. H.
Davenport Adams.[17] We are not acquainted with M. Meunier's
"Animaux d'Autrefois," upon which the work is said to be founded;
but, judging from this adaptation of it, it must be characterized by
considerable superficiality and pretentiousness. We must confess,
however, that Mr. Davenport does not seem to have been sufficiently
at home in the subject treated of to render him even a fair exponent
of M. Meunier's statements; for we notice in many places evident
mistranslations of the original French, showing that the translator is
unfamiliar with the technical terms employed. He also seems to be
rather careless, of which we have an instance at page 64, where we
are informed by implication that the *Mesopithecus* is "the single
fossil of Greece"—"*single*" here, we presume, being the translation of
"*singe*"—and again at page 18, where we are told that the post-ter-
tiary mammals are divisible "into three categories according to their
several conditions of existence," and then only get two categories
explained to us, the explanation of the second being as follows:—
"2nd. Other formidable animals there were, contemporaries, like the
former, of the Diluvium, which, having survived it, became contemporaries also of the modern Alluvium, yet have not come down to us.
Such are the ox, the horse, the buffalo, the common stag, and the
aurochs"! in which it seems pretty evident that we have the first

[16] "A Manual of Palæontology for the Use of Students." With a General
Introduction on the Principles of Palæontology. By Henry Alleyne Nicholson.
Edinburgh and London: Blackwood. 1872. 8vo.
[17] "Life in the Primeval World." Founded on Meunier's "Les Animaux
d'Autrefois." By W. H. Davenport Adams. London: Nelson. 1872. Small 8vo.

part of one paragraph and the latter part of another combined to produce a very curious statement. Some people may be inclined to believe that the ox and the horse still exist, and a few misguided individuals no doubt fancied that the joint of which they partook heartily on Christmas came out of the loin of the former animal. The buffalo, the common Stag, and the Aurochs are also generally supposed to have survived to the present day. Of this little volume more than half is occupied by an account of fossil mammalia, especial prominence being naturally given to the discoveries of Gaudry at Pikermi, and this part, if it were not disfigured by many blunders, would be useful. The invertebrata are very slightly treated, and the book concludes with a sketch of what is known of pre-historic man, especially in the South of France. The illustrations are numerous, and some of them good.

It is unfortunate for the author of this laborious volume [u] that we cannot, do as we may, approach the subject of it in any other spirit than one of disappointment. No doubt we are wrong, and other critics who have more farsightedness and self-control will accord to Dr. Thudichum that cheerful praise and encouragement which he so richly deserves. This manual is full of the closest and most patient labour, and of labour which no doubt is accurate, though we cannot speak with the full technical knowledge which alone can settle the latter point. On the contrary, we opened the work as physicians and pathologists, and we must confess that we found it dreary. It is not that it lacks facts; the work bristles with them. Only a ready reckoner could rival it on *that* ground. Still they seem stones to us who want bread; or shall we speak a little less severely, and liken them at best to that pulverized earth in which some northern nations have to find their sustenance? It is really as surprising as it is disappointing to see, on the whole, how little the chemical analysis of the body and its secretions has done for biology and medicine; and, on the other hand, we have not heard of any great enthusiasm which its results have produced among the chemists themselves. To say that chemical physiology has benefited nobody would of course be an exaggeration, and the least exaggeration under the circumstance would be very unkind. But, putting aside in physiology the analysis of the main course of digestion and in pathology the accidental occurrences of sugar and albumen in the urine, what great practical good have we been able to extract from the labours of our biological chemists? The field was a most inviting one; it seemed as if we had but to enter in and be full; yet its latter promise seems to be but barren. Of course this may be, and probably is, a somewhat one-sided view of the matter; but it is not one-sided enough to obscure our eyes to the kind and measure of grateful thanks which we owe to Dr. Thudichum for labours undertaken in a spirit which is the more to be prized as it has guided him into paths leading to no immediate reward, and carried

---

[u] "Manual of Chemical Physiology." By L. L. W. Thudichum, M.D.

him on in a course of unostentatious usefulness. For, whatever its results, the work has, of course, to be done.

This is the first part of a hand atlas of anatomy for the dissecting room, by Dr. Henle, of Gottingen,[*] and contains the bones, ligaments, and muscles. We are very much pleased with it indeed, and wish our own students could have something like it; the amount of translation required to adapt it for English use would not be great. Its great merit is that excellent drawings, heightened by partial tinting, are presented in so very handy and convenient a form, with interleaved descriptive matter. In fact, the Atlas seems to consist of the plates from Henle's systematic work on anatomy, collected together in a compact light volume for use actually in the dissecting-room. The plates are all that could be desired, very clear, very accurate, judiciously tinted with one colour, and, above all, very distinctly pointed with marks of reference. The Atlas might be used very profitably by students ignorant of German.

It is a great pleasure to see Professor Humphrey's admirable essays[**] reprinted in a collected form. With one exception, they are reprinted from the *Journal of Anatomy and Physiology*, a journal which is both a credit to the schools of anatomy in Great Britain, and the chief organ of their growth and advancement. We therefore feel that, while we owe much to many other anatomists in our own country, who, both for numbers and excellence, keep us abreast in this respect with other nations, yet we have an especial tenderness for the editors of the *Journal of Anatomy*, whose heavy labours give us, as it were, an accredited position in biological journalism. It is with Professor Humphrey's work that we have especially to deal at present, and we have the comfort of ascertaining not only from our own reading, but from the opinion of the first anatomists of the day, that the praise we would so willingly accord to Professor Humphrey, is again justified by this volume, which presents the results of extended and faithful work. But, of course, it is not by this smaller volume alone that Professor Humphrey holds his high eminence as an investigator and as a teacher. This volume is but a small part of a scheme of labour which has not only, as we have said, advanced the position of Great Britain as a home of science, but has really made the reputation of Cambridge as a school of biology. Professor Humphrey is the chief of those to whom Cambridge men owe this achievement, that their University has held its own with their great neighbours at Oxford. Both Universities have made rapid progress of late in biological teaching and discovery, and, owing to accidental causes, Cambridge started in the race at some disadvantage. But Professor Humphrey and his colleagues have, by their patient energy, reduced these disadvantages, and have not only supported, but advanced the honour of their *alma mater* in the race. It is to the abiding credit of the author of this volume that he, who had a rare opportunity of spending his days in refined and dignified ease, should have spurned

---

[*] "Anatomischer Hand-Atlas." Von Dr. J. Henle. Braunschwvig. 1872.
[**] "Observations in Myology." By G. M. Humphrey, M.D., F.R.S.

such delights, and chosen the laborious days which have won distinction, not for himself only, but for us all.

Dr. Austin Flint in presenting us with the first instalment of his treatise, which deals with the nervous system, says that his work[91] is designed to represent the existing state of physiological science, and he claims therefore to be judged by the high standard of 1872. We have very kindly feelings for Dr. Flint, who is one of the most distinguished and laborious members of the American profession. We therefore opened the present volume with great anticipations, and with the hope of giving it very high praise. Judged, however, by that high standard by which Dr. Flint would wish to be judged, we are bound to confess that we are somewhat disappointed, and that the praise we find ourselves able to give is scarcely of the highest. We are disposed to think, though in this we may be wrong, that a systematic writer on modern physiology ought to be something more than an able compiler of knowledge, that he ought himself to have contributed more than a little to the science of which he treats; at any rate, we think, he ought to have so gone over the whole ground, as an original observer, as to have that command over the experiments of others and that general sense of control over most of the points under discussion which should distinguish a really masterly writer. This note of real excellence, we are bound to say, is absent. Nor can the volume be said really to come abreast with the most recent state of our knowledge. So far as the most modern information is concerned, Dr. Flint is almost entirely indebted to the last edition of Longet, a work of considerable merit, no doubt, but scarcely all-sufficient for the present time. Moreover, when we ourselves turn to those sections which may serve as tests of an author's research we find great omissions. There is scarcely any discussion, and no first-hand discussion of the most recent investigations by Schiff into the functions of the anterior columns and other districts of the cord; and if we look again, under the much-vexed questions of Electrotomus, we find little that is new since the teaching of Rutherford in 1868. We are not partisans of Dr. Radcliffe's hypothesis, but no modern work on physiology can afford to leave him, as Dr. Flint leaves him, entirely unnoticed. We regard Dr. Flint's work, therefore, as a book very creditable to his industry, and one likely to be useful to ordinary students; but as an exponent of the latest and best results of the chief modern physiologists for advanced readers, we are constrained to pronounce it more than a little defective.

In this pamphlet[92] Mr. Garrod, who is already known as an investigator of animal physics, discusses the probable causes and conditions of the frequency of the heart-beat. The pamphlet is rather an indication of the author's views than any elaborate proof of them, but as such it shows a good deal of ingenious argument and sound groundwork. Mr. Garrod's chief thesis shortly put is that the heart always

---

[91] "The Physiology of Man." By Austin Flint, Jun., M.D. New York. 1872.
[92] "The Law of the Frequency of the Pulse." By A. H. Garrod. London: Lewis. 1872.

recommences to beat when the blood pressure in the systemic arteries has fallen a certain invariable proportion. The following reflections occur to us after reading the pamphlet carefully. We think that Mr. Garrod is correct in insisting, as he does, upon the right of the inquirer to account for the heart's movements on grounds strictly mechanical. But we think Mr. Garrod will agree with us that this is correct only so long as the organism investigated is in a normal state. The influence of the nervous system must, no doubt, be regarded as an agency accumulated upon the heart, and not essentially belonging to the original idea of the heart. It is an agency to bring the heart into correspondence with other complex forces elsewhere, and is to be regarded rather as a regulator of the heart than as a substantial part of its mechanism. In morbid conditions, however, it is clear that the nervous system may unduly oppress or stimulate the heart, as a horse may be hindered or irritated by a bad driver, and so multiform considerations of another kind are introduced. It certainly seems to us that Mr. Garrod's law, primarily true, does not hold good under the perturbations of many diseases which we can watch at the bedside, and may not hold good in all cases of experiment upon living animals.

This is one of those works which hardly admit of a brief notice.[*] It does not do to dismiss them superciliously, as they are very grave books indeed, and cost their authors no little thought and trouble. Moreover, they must, we suppose, have a strong cohort of readers and admirers. Still we think that an able man may spin any quantity of this kind of thing, "if he abandons himself to it;" and we do not think it tends to any increase of knowledge. If it tends to the edification of some we shall be glad to hear it. Professor Leupoldt's aim is to express as much of human health and disease as he can in terms of a metaphysical psychology and of a pantheistic theology. We are sorry not to feel more grateful for the result.

Dr. Hagen, a well-known authority upon mental diseases, and one who has given much of the attention of an industrious and accomplished mind to the study of medical jurisprudence, here presents us with a series of seven studies in two thin volumes.[†] We presume that the series is to be continued. In Part I. we find the following six essays:—(1) On the value and importance of psychology in the study and treatment of mental diseases; (2) On fixed ideas; (3) On the Maid of Orleans; (4) On folly; (5) On the psychological treatment of the insane; (6) "The end sanctifies the means." The second part contains one essay only—namely, an elaborate study of the career of Chorinsky, a notorious criminal of unsound mind. The several essays in Part I. are very readable; they have decided literary merit, they betoken some measure of general culture, and they are good from their more special point of view. The essay on "Narrheit," which we have

[*] "Ueber Geist und Leben in der Medicin." Von D. I. M. Leupoldt. Erlangen. 1872.

[†] "Studien." Theil; I. und II. Von Dr. Fredrich W. Hagen. Erlangen. 1870.

translated after some hesitation as "folly," shows a good deal of thought and delicacy of appreciation. The difference between a fool and a lunatic is a theme which admits of a good deal of interesting and humorous discussion of a kind which does not lend itself to quotation or condensation. The essay on the Maid of Orleans is, of course, another of those curious inquiries into the relations between genius and insanity which do not seem to us to lead to much, especially when carried on upon imperfect historical data. The titles of the other "studies" speak for themselves and are pleasant to read, even when we feel constrained to differ from some of the author's premises. He quotes Maudsley more than once, and, to our thinking, he had done well to have substituted some of Maudsley's philosophical groundwork in place of his own. But it is impossible to be angry with so "genial" a writer; we must take him and all others as we find them, provided only that their work is thorough and good of its kind. As to his fundamental conceptions we will remember, in Dr. Hagen's own words, "Denn ist es ein grosser Irrthum, zu glauben, falsche Theorie zu machen, sei ein Privilegium der Gelehrten. Gott bewahre: sie wachsen überall wild, wie die Brombeeren" (p. 165). The long study of Chorinsky is too loathsome to read with pleasure or to remember with any interest. We presume that some one must study such subjects minutely, but there is something sickening and repulsive in the calm reckoning up of the life of a wilful, libidinous youth, who never seems to have had the sound whippings he richly deserved when a boy; who gradually abandoned himself to the nastiest indulgences, and ended, no doubt, as diseased in mind as in body—as a demented paralytic.

One of the most difficult problems of modern education in medicine is to discover, first, how far subdivision of labour may be carried in pursuit of special learning and skill without losing that more general view of things which alone can enable us to use such special attainments to good effect; and, secondly, how to arrange preliminary education so as to give the best foundation to those who aim at special knowledge. Without a sound and preliminary education all special direction of the mind is an excess; with such a beginning, however, special domains of industry must be granted, the question of their definition, of course, remaining to be solved. Is the domain of throat diseases too narrow, or, on the other hand, is the domain of surgery, properly so called, too large for the work of special cultivation? These questions are as yet almost untouched, and, judging from the bemused state of our medical guilds, no clear prophecies on the matter are likely to come from them. Meanwhile, the students of mental diseases are proving their own case by the work they do, and before us we have a very remarkable specimen of it." This, it appears, is the second volume of Reports which within two years have been published for the West Riding Lunatic Asylum, and an excellent volume it is. The reproach of being mere administrators cannot at any rate be levelled at the Wakefield staff. Dr. Crichton Browne himself is well known as one, at least, of the

* "West Riding Asylum Reports." Edited by J. Crichton Browne, M.D.

most rising men of the day in his own department, and he seems to
have that faculty of commanding, of bringing well-organized work
out of others, which is really rare. In a sense, no doubt, this volume
is mainly Dr. Browne's own, and must acknowledge his inspiration ;
for, excepting a paper on the electric treatment of the insane by Dr.
Clifford Allbutt, of Leeds, and a paper we read with peculiar interest
from the veteran commissioner, Dr. W. A. F. Browne, on "Impair-
ment of Language"—excepting these, all the papers come from old and
present officers of the Asylum. Among them Dr. Browne modestly
occupies but his own twelfth part—at least in name. It is impossible
to deal with these papers individually, and, indeed, the merits of many
of them must essentially depend upon the record of experience, but
they impress us favourably. Favourably for this reason, that instead
of long-winded psychological discussions we have brief pointed essays
on practical subjects, which, hit or miss, at any rate have no
ambiguity about them. We may refer to a few points on which we,
too, have something to say, such as on the use of ergot in mania,
recommended in the first volume, and which we have used accordingly
with marked success; on the use of opium in melancholia, our
knowledge of which entirely bears out the views expressed in the
second volume; and on the ultimate or postponed effects of cranial
injuries, concerning which we, like Dr. Browne, have been led to some
conclusions not generally thought of.

Dr. Cappie, in his little treatise on sleep,* subjects the current
theories of the process of sleep to a somewhat searching criticism. He
moreover proposes a theory of his own which seems to him better calculated to account for the facts. Dr. Cappie, in opposition to Dr.
Burrows and others, is disposed to believe not only that the contents of
the cranium are constant in quantity, but that the compensatory power
of shifting accumulations of cerebro-spinal fluid cannot be called upon
for any great assistance in the matter. On this latter point, indeed,
we are disposed to agree with the author. Dr. Cappie regards wakeful-
ness as being a time of arterial and capillary flushing of the brain with
great rapidity of circulation, while sleep he regards, on the other hand,
as a time of venous stagnation, during which the large veins of the pia
mater must increase pressure upon the superficies of the cerebrum.
Sleep, as he says, has points of much resemblance to symptoms
of which pressure is an acknowledged cause. The author adduces in
his favour the ophthalmoscopic observations of Jackson, Jamieson and
Allbutt, who find during sleep that the arteries of the retina become
fine and nearly empty, while the veins become dark and enlarged.

Three capital papers delivered as popular sanitary lectures at
Dresden by the celebrated author Von Pettenkofer" have reached us.
Like Tyndall, Huxley, Faraday, and other men who are really eminent
in their own branches of science, the author is very happy in his
mode of bringing the latest result of his work and observation before a

* "The Causation of Sleep." By James Cappie, M.D.
" "Beziehungen d. Luft zu Kleidung Wohnung und Boden." Von Dr. Max v.
Pettenkofer. Braunschweig. 1872.

general audience. In these lectures, which we think would well repay translation, the conditions of the air as it exists in clothing, dwellings, and soil are brought before us with much ingenuity, and with a precision of expression and experiment which is too often conspicuous by its absence in common sanitary writing. Von Pettenkofer brings these matters vividly before the public also by that judicious combination of general views with well-chosen and very interesting particulars, which is a marked feature in the lectures of the other distinguished men we have mentioned; and which has the effect of awakening our observation in the commonest matters—in matters so close to us that we men and generations of men habitually overlook them, as the magistrate in "Oliver Twist" overlooked the inkstand because it was under his nose. Many of our commonest practices as says the author, are never thoroughly investigated, because they necessarily come into use long before any explanation is possible. We could not remain naked until a German philosopher arose to explain to us the relative values of clothing and the best modes of its application, so meanwhile we clothe ourselves partly according to "instinct," partly according to rough experience and fashion, and partly according to inherited habits. So it is also with our dwellings, and thus habits, often more or less irrational, become so fixed that no one at length dreams of their being subjected to scientific inquiry at all. Yet we must admit that every new fact, method or device to which rigorous investigation may lead will undoubtedly bring with it sooner or later a practically useful result. Hence nothing, however habitual to us, however it may seem to be grounded on routine experience, should claim immunity from close inductive study, nor should seem too common to receive the attention of the mind. Fortunately Englishmen are not likely to be lulled into any false sense of security by tailors or by architects; more likely are we to regard them as public enemies.

The readers of "The Archives of Clinical Medicine" will remember the recent appearance in that serial of an exhaustive essay by Dr. Max Salomon on the history of diabetes. This essay we are glad to see republished in a convenient form;[*] seeing that it is not only an essay of much merit in itself, but that it is also of a kind very much needed. Dr. Max Salomon divides for us the history of Glycosuria into three periods, an old, a mediæval, and a modern period. The early period concludes in the second half of the 17th century, when Thomas Willis discovered the sweet taste of diabetic urine. Diabetes insipidus and glycosuria were thenceforward distinguished, and the latter disease was more closely studied in the second or middle period. During this time, which Dr. Salomon calls the diagnostic stage, the disease was closely observed and worked out in its clinical aspects by such men as Willis, Dobson, and their followers. With the masterly treatise of Rollo the third or "scientifically therapeutic" stage set in, which is yet unfolding itself. Dr. Salomon's essay deals with the first two periods only, including however the work of Rollo in his analysis. He gives us a very succinct and thorough view of the course followed

---

[*] "Geschichte d. Glykosurie." Von Dr. Max Salomon.

in the slow tracking out of one of the most remarkable of diseases, and he adds one example more to the many which prove the great value which such studies would have for students, and for their teachers likewise at the present time. In our own schools the historical side of medicine is sadly neglected. With so many subjects claiming our attention, it is hard perhaps to see how we are to find room for any additional chair, but we would suggest that a brief historical sketch of a few of the main diseases might fitly be introduced in their proper places in the formal courses of the professors of medicine, thus giving a more scholarly and wider bearing to such lectures as compared with clinical lectures. For the history of medicine is not mere idle lore, but is itself a very high kind of teaching for those toiling in the present. As the pedestrian who has reached an eminence can gain by throwing his eyes backward upon the country which he has traversed, so a good general knowledge of the main course which our art has pursued cannot but be full of real inspiration for those who have to help in working out the scheme of its future development. We may burrow on industriously, seeing little but our instant task, and thus indeed progress in a way, but in a way we should admit to be a rather blind way.

Our duty as regards this volume may be either easy or difficult according to the claims our readers may make upon us. If it be only asked of us to say what books to turn to and which to avoid, then our task is light; but if we are asked farther to give shortly our opinion of the value of the author's statements, then we shall be found wanting. Mr. Lyons' book " is one of considerable merit, both in its mode of dealing with its subject, and also in the evidence it gives of the author's careful observation and large experience. It is a book therefore distinctly to be read and perpended. Our own experience of relapsing fever, gained as it has been, in England only, is, however, of little use in discussing the relapsing fever of the tropics, which evidently puts on a very different type. The attacks, which in our own country are continued in type, in the tropics are either remittent or intermittent, and the relapse follows the same characters as the primary attack. In this relapsing fever does but follow the course of the typhus and enteric fevers, which in the same climates take on likewise intermittent and remittent forms. In common with many others we had been in the habit of assuming that this modification of type was due to malarious causes. In this we were prepared, however, to find ourselves corrected, but we were not prepared to find a writer of Mr. Lyons' ability denying the malarious origin of all and any fevers *in toto*. This bold defiance of his we leave to be dealt with by those whose experience has lain in the so-called malarious districts. Meanwhile we can only say that Mr. Lyons writes not as the scribes, and that whether the author turn out right or wrong, the whole subject can but gain by a thorough discussion. No theories are too old or too privileged to escape question.

---

* "On Relapsing Fever." By R. T. Lyons. London. 1872.

This pamphlet [a] is a reprint of the paper read by the author to " The Epidemiological Society," and from its nature deserves the notice which many pamphlets of its size could hardly claim. Dr. Grieve is well known as the medical superintendent of the Hampstead Small-pox Hospital, where he has great opportunities for observation. Hence any conclusions of his must meet with wide recognition. He says (p. 5), "I wish it were possible to bring home to the minds and belief of the general public, my conviction regarding revaccination, namely, *that it is a sure protection against Small-pox.*" (Italics his own.) It appears that the nurses and servants of the hospital, when thus protected, escape all infection—an observation which has now stood the test of five-and-thirty years at the older institution at Highgate. Indeed, Dr. Grieve does but re-enforce the old teaching of Dr. Marson, and thus the interference of the Legislature is still amply justified. Dr. Grieve shows, among other things, that a temperate life is a very important factor in the chances of recovery from small-pox. His tables are based upon the notes of no less than 6000 cases.

We have so recently had occasion to speak with praise of the second edition of this handbook,[b] that we have now little more to do than to congratulate the author on the well-merited reception his book has received. The present edition is enlarged and in many ways improved ; a number of the editorial blemishes also, which disfigured the former editions, have been removed, though too many still remain. We have not the former edition at hand for immediate comparison, but the newer and more disputable points seem well handled, and brought up to the mark of recent knowledge. In a full notice of Dr. Chapman's treatment by Spinal Ice and Water bags, we regret that the author says nothing of any experience of his own ; this we regret because this method, which in many ways seems so promising, now requires extensive testing by other observers. We have still also to regret that while this and other physical means of cure are included, there should be no mention of an especially valuable one, namely, electricity. A brief well-considered section on the use of the interrupted and continuous currents would have been a great boon to practitioners, and might perhaps have been obtained at the hands of the author's accomplished colleague, Dr. Reynolds, did he himself feel unwilling to undertake it.

HISTORY AND BIOGRAPHY.

THERE is perhaps no instance in literature of a writer springing at once from entire obscurity to a renown so wide and so illustrious as that which Mr. Buckle attained by a single work. His early and lamented death, which left his book an incomplete memorial, awakened, even in those who rejected his views, profound sorrow for

---

[a] "On Vaccination." By R. Grieve, M.D.
[b] "Handbook of Therapeutics." By Sidney Ringer, M.D.

the withdrawal of his great powers. Yet his first volume, a mere preface to the projected work, exercised an incalculable influence upon the whole science of history. No views of history can ever be held again without being affected in one way or another by that commanding work. And almost before the time had come for dispassionate criticism of his theories, the writer had passed away from the criticism and the glory. The work which is now given to the public[1] will, if it cannot diminish the general regret at the universal loss, serve at least to illustrate the patient unswerving industry of the historian himself. The biographer has little to tell. Henry Buckle was throughout his life an impassioned student; his life is without incident. He was born in 1821, the son of wealthy parents. His constitution was so delicate that he was never able to undergo the hardships of a public school life or the competitive struggles of a university, but from the earliest period he set before himself the design of a literary career, which he followed with singleness of purpose to his death. At the age of twenty his book was already projected. He says in his diary, Oct. 15, 1812 :—

"I am determined from this day to devote all the energies I may have solely to the study of the history and literature of the Middle Ages. . . . . And ambition whispers to me the flattering hope that a prolonged series of industrious efforts, aided by talents certainly above mediocrity, may at last meet with success."

Fifteen years later the first volume of the history appeared. No one can read the extracts from his diary kept during this period without being struck by the immense range of subjects which he studied in subordination to his plan. Almost all the languages of Europe, including such exceptional languages as Danish, Russian, and Dutch, were mastered—at least sufficiently for literary purposes. Even phrenology, which few historians would think it obligatory upon them to learn, did not escape his attention. In his diary for January 27, 1852, there is this entry : "I intend now to begin the study of phrenology, to determine its bearings upon the philosophy of history." It is unnecessary to recall the profound attention with which his first volume was received. It is curious to learn that at first no publisher could be found for it, and that it was brought out at his own cost. The second volume was prepared with infinite care and labour—a labour that severely tried his delicate health. In order to recover from this, he undertook, at the recommendation of his friends, a journey in the East. But the physical exertion of Eastern travel proved too much for him, and in the spring of 1862 he died at Damascus. As all his studies tended to one point, the illustration of the great subject which he had set before himself from the first, so in the present volumes we have very little except examples of his wide and careful reading. There is a lecture upon the influence of women on the progress of knowledge, which was delivered at the Royal Institution

---

[1] "Miscellaneous and Posthumous Works of Henry Thomas Buckle." Edited with a Biographical Notice, by Helen Taylor. London: Longmans, Green and Co. 3 vols.

in 1858, and which is chiefly employed in showing the encouragement that women give to deductive thought, and the value of deductive thought to science; a review of Mill's "Liberty," and a letter concerning the celebrated Pooley's case. The remainder of the volumes consists of fragments, extracts from his common-place book, studies on different subjects, and references. These are left in the original order. They are the unworked material upon which the great mind was exercised. And whatever view the historian or reader may hold of Mr. Buckle's theories, the perusal of these volumes can only afford intense pleasure and much instruction.

There is something of sadness as well as of pleasure in receiving a posthumous work by a well-known writer. Most readers will be surprised at finding so complete an edition of Persius by the late Professor Conington as that which Mr. Nettleship has just brought out.[1] Many of course knew that Persius had been a favourite author with the late Professor of Latin, and some will have heard his lectures upon that subject, but the full commentary and the exquisite translation contained in this posthumous work will be a surprise to most readers. The translation is indeed exquisite. The opening lines of the prologue will be enough to show every one that we have here one of those efforts which form the high-water mark of translation. And the commentary is equal to the translation. Take for instance the notes on Sat. i. line 95; lines 107-123; Sat. iii. 34; Sat. iv. 40; and as instances of scholarly acuteness, Sat. v. 19, and Sat. vi. 39. But perhaps the best part of the book is the essay, originally a lecture, upon the Life and Writings of Persius. The comparison between Persius and Mr. Carlyle is striking and instructive, and the influence of Horace upon Persius is well and definitely traced. The care which Mr. Nettleship, amidst the "pressure of other work," has bestowed upon his literary legacy is visible in every page, and his own additions are most valuable. Some oversights there are, which a subsequent edition will doubtless remove, but the students of classical literature cannot be too grateful to him for the little delay with which he has given them this book, unquestionably the best English edition of a somewhat neglected Roman writer.

Old English literature continues to reappear in the publications of the Early English Text Society;[2] the works now before us are full of interest for the philologist and the antiquarian. The miscellany which Mr. Morris edits is of a mixed and composite character. It contains a "Bestiary" of the thirteenth century, from which many interesting facts in natural history may be learned—as, for instance,

[1] "The Satires of A. Persius Flaccus." With a Translation and Commentary. By John Conington, M.A. To which is prefixed "A Lecture on the Life and Writings of Persius." Edited by H. O. Nettleship, M.A. Oxford: At the Clarendon Press.

[2] "An Old English Miscellany." Edited by the Rev. R. Morris. The "Liflade of St. Juliana." Edited by the Rev. O. Cockayne. The "Select Works of Robert Crowley." Edited by J. M. Cowper. A "Treatise on the Astrolabe." By Geoffrey Chaucer. Edited by the Rev. W. W. Skeat. London: N. Trübner and Co.

that the lion in flight erases his track with his tail, and thus escapes to his den ; that sailors frequently mistake a whale for an island, and disembarking, kindle a fire upon his back ; and that when old elephants fall, the young raise them up by means of their " snouts." From each of these facts lessons are drawn for the edification of the reader. Sermons and ecclesiastical documents complete this volume. The most valuable portion is the glossarial index. The works of Robert Crowley, as edited by Mr. Cowper, contain the " Epigrams," the " Voyce of the Last Trumpet,"' and other writings by this author, who was a demy of Magdalene College, Oxford, in 1510. He was the first to print and publish the " Vision of William concerning Piers the Plowman." From being a printer he became Archdeacon of Hereford, and during his ecclesiastical career appears to have taken part in most of the controversies of the time. Amongst other things he objected to the use of the surplice, and is reported to have said with a vehemence worthy of later times, that he " would not be persuaded to minister in those conjuring garments of popery." Like most controversialists he lived to a good old age. His epigrams are mostly fragments of good advice against " bearhaytynge," " brawling." " blasphemous swerers," and the like ; generally these " epigrams," are intelligible, and marked by good sense. With reference to " bearbaytynge," he asks :—

> " What follye is thys,
>   To keep with daunger,
> A greate mastyfe dogge
> And a foule ouglye bear ?
> And to thys onelye ende
>   To se them two fyght
> Wyth terrible tearyuge
> A full ouglye syght."

And swearing he abominates—not only profane oaths, but idle inventions of idle brains, when some swear

> " By cocke and by pye,
>   And by the goose wyng ;
> By the crosse of the mouse sole,
>   And by saynte Chyckyn."

For the brawler he has no hope :—

> " What other men will iudge,
>   I can not tell ;
> But if he scape Tiburne
>   I thynke he will hange in hell."

He is also very severe upon the " commen drunkardes " who " dryncke lustelye" through "muche of the nighte." St. Paul warns us not to eat or drink with drunkards :—

> " But alas ! manye curates,
>   That shoulde vs thys tell,
> Do all their parishioners
>   In drynckynge excell."

The " Listade of St. Juliana," edited by Mr Cockayne, is the history of the martyr Juliana of the city of Nicomedia, who was persecuted by the love of Eleusius, a "wicked reeve," and also by the "devil Belial." But she endured steadfast to the end, and "blessed angels with her soul, singing, ascended towards heaven."

The Astrolabe of Geoffrey Chaucer is more interesting. The present edition contains several curious plates and a valuable introduction and glossary by Mr. Skeat. Mr. Skeat illustrates passages in the Canterbury Tales from this treatise upon the Astrolabe.

Mr. Froude's book[4] on the English in Ireland will be read by all who are interested in that beautiful and unhappy island. Mr. Froude has not won, nor is he likely to win, the love of the Irish people. But as a historian he is laborious and earnest. His analysis of the Irish Celtic character will at least be admitted to be a forcible one :—

"In the annals of ten centuries there is not a character, male or female, to be found belonging to them with sufficient hardness of texture to be carved into dramatic outline. Their temperaments are singularly impressionable, yet the impression is incapable of taking shape. They have little architecture of their own, and the forms introduced from England have been robbed of their grace. Their houses, from cabin to castle, are the most hideous in the world. No lines of beauty soften anywhere the forbidding harshness of their provincial towns ; no climbing rose or creeper dresses the naked walls of farmhouse or cottage. The sun never shone on a lovelier country as nature made it. They have pared its forests to the stump, till it shivers in damp and desolation. The perceptions of taste, which belong to the higher order of understanding, are as completely absent as truthfulness of spirit is absent, or cleanliness of person and habit. The Irish are the spendthrift sister of the Arian race. Yet there is notwithstanding a fascination about them in their own land, and in the sad and strange associations of their singular destiny."

And so Mr. Froude, with this theory of nationality, whether true or false, always before him, works out the history of the relationship between Ireland and England. Yet if his picture of Irish character is unpleasing to the Irish themselves, his history is little flattering to English statesmanship. No reader of this history can look back without indignation at the monstrous injustice of the Irish land laws and the Irish Established Church. English statesmen have erred again and again in their rule of Ireland, and Mr. Froude does not spare their errors. But he has not proved that he is justified in treating the Irish character as the chief cause of Irish unhappiness, and he is certainly wrong when he asserts that the English government of Ireland has been marred by an attempt to rule according to *Irish ideas.* It is the enforcement of *English ideas,* of English land, laws, and English ecclesiastical systems upon Ireland, that has served to make the people unhappy. Mr. Froude thinks that Cromwell alone knew how to govern Ireland, because he alone understood coercion. Yet although Mr. Froude has written his work with a theory of nationality as its central point, the book will do good. It treats with earnestness a subject which has become the jest of our statesmen. So long as Mr. Disraeli is met with applause when he treats the Irish

---

4 "The English in Ireland in the Eighteenth Century." By James Anthony Froude. London : Longmans, Green and Co.

[Vol. XCIX. No. CXCV.]— New Series, Vol. XLIII. No. I.   X

sadness as the result of " contiguity to a melancholy ocean," and Mr.
Lowe, at Glasgow, can raise a laugh at the poverty of the Claddagh
fishermen, and " great laughter " at the failure of their fisheries, any attempt to treat Irish history with earnestness must be welcome. But the
Irish people will not like Mr. Froude's book, nor can we wonder at it.

Miss Cusack's Life of O'Connell [1] shows the strong and passionate
attachment which the Irish have for the character and memory of the
Liberator. It is a large volume of 600 pages, which has been got up
with more show than taste. The Life is, however, very readable,
though of course one-sided. It is full and complete, from the infancy
to the death of O'Connell. Miss Cusack is, however, inexcusably
ignorant that Mr. Lecky, the historian, is an Irishman. Each page
has an illuminated margin, but the cover and some of the plates are
indescribably tawdry.

Mr. MacCarthy has written an account of the early life of
Shelley. [2] It is concerned chiefly with that period which was spent in
Ireland. He professes also to have discovered the fact that Shelley
wrote a poem upon the eve of his departure from Oxford, which was
unknown to Mr. Hogg. We cannot attach so much importance
to this as Mr. MacCarthy does, for even if he had discovered
the poem itself—which he has not done—we are not sure that the
gain to literature would have been very great. Certainly Shelley's
earlier poems are not equal to the later. And probably the poem
would be interesting only as a promise, which we can the better dis-
pense with as we have the full flower of his genius. Another discovery which Mr. MacCarthy has made is the name of Mr. P. B. Shelley
amongst the subscribers to the fund in favour of Mr. Finnerty, an
Irish patriot. This discovery, which is introduced with some typo-
graphical display, does not strike us as very important. Shelley, in
his warm-hearted, hot-headed youth, subscribed to many charities;
always when there was any hint of oppression. We have ourselves
" discovered" the name of P. B. Shelley amongst the subscribers to the
fund in behalf of Mr. Hone, who was tried for profane parodies of
the liturgy. Our author has certainly lessened the authority of Mr.
Hogg, but the literary flourish with which he heralds each incident is
not in good taste. The chief portion of the book is concerned with
what he is pleased to call " Shelley's Irish Campaign." It seems that
at the age of nineteen Shelley visited Ireland, and spoke at Fishamble-
street Theatre, Dublin, at a meeting of the Irish Catholics. Mr.
MacCarthy has incorporated in his book every notice of the meeting
which appeared in the current papers. Some of them are not without
interest. The *Freeman's Journal* said: " Mr. Shelley, an English
gentleman (very young), the son of a member of Parliament, rose to
address the meeting. He was received with great kindness, and declared
that the greatest misery this country endured was the Union Law, the

[1] " The Liberator ; his Life and Times." By F. H. Cusack. London: Longmans, Green and Co.
[2] " Shelley's Early Life." From Original Sources. By Denis Florence Mac-
Carthy. London : John Camden Hotten.

Penal Code, and the state of the representation. He drew a lively picture of the misery of the country, which he attributed to the unfortunate Act of Legislative Union." This is probably a true though brief account of the speech, and it does not contradict Mr. Hogg ("Life of Shelley," vol. ii. p. 108), who says of the meeting: "Poor Byashe made a speech, and proposed his scheme, but did not succeed." Mr. MacCarthy has not much more to tell us, nor has he much of importance to tell us at all. We were aware before that even as a boy Shelley was passionate and unguarded in his denunciations of tyranny in every aspect ; and although it may be interesting to know that the great Liberator was present in Fishamble-street when Shelley spoke, we do not forget that it was as a poet and not as an Irish patriot that Shelley won the love of all who are delighted with poetry and freedom.

The "Memoirs of Baron Stockmar" are in some respects disappointing, and intelligibly so. He has been so highly spoken of by great persons and great personages, he has been so widely looked upon as the confidant and the adviser of those who are supposed to move the strings of State, his life was spent amongst the most notorious and the most influential of so many countries that we come to his memoirs with the expectation of becoming acquainted with a rare and remarkable character. And although we do this, there is still left in our minds a feeling of disappointment. We wonder how Baron Stockmar managed to convince so many people of his foresight, his shrewdness, and his ability. He is received in every Court as a friend and an adviser. At the Belgian and English Courts he was considered a family friend. It is certain, too, that he never abused this position. Professor Max Müller says: "He was content to remain through life the unknown friend and benefactor of the Sovereigns whom he served." He attributes his success partly to his entire truthfulness, and partly to the "rare art of telling the truth, even to kings, without offence." Queen Victoria pays her tribute to the Baron. "The Queen," she says, "can never forget the assistance given by the Baron to the young couple in regulating their movements and general mode of life, and in directing the education of their children." ("Early Years of H.R.H. the Prince Consort," p. 186.) And the King of the Belgians wrote of him: "Il a été mon fidèle soutien et ami. Je ne nie point qu'il est plutôt mon ami que mon serviteur." But a better testimony is that of Baron Bunsen, who called him "one of the finest politicians of Germany and Europe." Of such a man we might naturally wish to learn much, but in these volumes we learn but little. His son says: "My father was content to remain always half-hidden before the eyes of posterity. Faithful to his spirit, this book also lifts the veil but a little." Yet the memoirs are not without considerable interest. Stockmar had two political ideals—noble ones both—the union of Germany under Prussia, and a unity of purpose between Germany and England. These are seen throughout his memoirs. Indeed almost everywhere where we can see his

† "Memoirs of Baron Stockmar." By his Son, Baron E. von Stockmar. Edited by F. Max Müller. 2 vols. London : Longmans, Green and Co.

views they are sound and just. Those upon English representative government are exceptional. But people who like to read about Courts—and there are still some—will find these volumes more instructive than the majority of books that come from such quarters. They are, for instance, more instructive than Lady Clementina Davies's "Recollections," though not so amusing. Lady Clementina belonged to a family allied to the Stuarts and the Bourbons. Her father, Lord Maurice Drummond, spent many years at the Court of Louis XVI. and Marie Antoinette. Lady Clementina has an amusing story of the "last Queen of France," who shocked the Court by falling off a donkey, and by sending for the mistress of the ceremonies to inquire as to which was to rise first, the Queen or the ass. The book, indeed, is full of the most agreeable and polite anecdotes, and is concerned chiefly with the highest circles. It contains little of interest, and nothing which is not readable.

Sir Bernard Burke has written another work [8] upon the subject which so delights him—the history of the aristocracy. The title of the book is taken from the first article, which forms about a sixth of the volume, and which consists of a gossiping analysis of the peerage. The other chapters are stories of different families and aristocratic feuds of all times, from the rival pretensions of Scrope and Grosvenor to the Aberdeen romance. Sir Bernard quotes from Dibdin the description of the great book battle in 1812, when the Marquis of Blandford and Earl Spencer valiantly contended for the possession of the unique copy of Boccaccio's Decameron, which the Marquis obtained for 2260*l*. Sir Bernard gives the further history of this costly volume. Seven years later the Marquis was obliged to sell his collection, and the Decameron was purchased by Earl Spencer, through Messrs. Longman and Co., for 918*l*., and is now one of the curiosities of the library at Althorp. There is also an interesting chapter upon the extinction of the families of illustrious men. The list of great men unrepresented amongst us is very large. There is no living descendant, in the male line, of Chaucer, Shakspeare, Milton, Cowley, Dryden, Pope, Goldsmith, Scott, Byron, Sir Philip Sydney, Sir W. Raleigh, Drake, Cromwell, Bacon, Locke, Newton, Hume, Gibbon, Macaulay. Sir Bernard traces the extinction of these families and of many more. Most of those mentioned were married and had children, but their descendants in the male line are all gone.

Mr. Sandford published at intervals during the last two years estimates of the personal character of each of the English monarchs. These appeared in the *Spectator* newspaper, and have now been collected and published in a continuous series.[10] They form a history pleasant to read and not devoid of instruction. Mr. Sandford has not

---

[8] " Recollections of Society." By Lady Clementina Davies. 2 vols. London : Hurst and Blackett.
[9] " The Rise of Great Families." By Sir Bernard Burke, Ulster King of Arms. London : Longmans, Green and Co.
[10] " Estimates of the English Kings. From William the Conqueror to George III." By J. Langton Sandford. London : Longmans, Green and Co.

gone to original sources for information, nor is there any profound research visible in his work; but he has read the best authorities upon each subject, and formed his own conclusions. Hence he is enabled to say, "I do not think that my view of any king's character will be found quite identical with that taken by any preceding writer." The "Estimates" are well written, and leave a distinct portrait of each monarch upon the reader's mind, the later portraits being naturally more vivid. Where we have had an opportunity of comparing Mr. Sandford's work with that of other writers, we find his judgment correct and independent. Most readers are familiar with the work entitled the "Greatest of the Plantagenets," by an anonymous writer. Strangely enough, Mr. Sandford had not met with it when he wrote his estimate of Edward I. In its general conclusions he concurs, but he does not assign to Edward unreservedly the first place amongst our mediæval kings. Nevertheless, Mr. Sandford describes very excellently the true earnestness of Edward's mind, his strong personal identification with the law, and his supreme power of organization. In the estimate of Henry VIII. the author does not by any means follow servilely in Mr. Froude's footsteps. Indeed, he thinks Mr. Froude errs by a theory "which is too artificial to meet the misgivings of broad common sense and of instinctive morality." He himself considers the basis of Henry's character to have been his physical constitution, his powerful and healthy *physique*. To this he traces most of his vigorous and impetuous acts; and thus it was, he thinks, that personal will took the place of any rule of life in the policy of the king. The best "Estimate" is that of Oliver Cromwell, with whom Mr. Sandford cannot conceal his sympathy. He traces the power of this uncrowned monarch to his breadth of mind and width of view. We cannot follow Mr. Sandford in his delineation of Cromwell's patience, consideration for others, and religious toleration, but we commend this article as the best in an otherwise interesting, well-written book.

Our next work, "Cabinet Portraits,"[11] has been compiled in the same way as Mr. Sandford's "Estimates," though the characters depicted are those with which we are more familiar. Mr. Reid says that he has striven to the utmost to divest himself of all political partisanship in these pages, and we think he has very fairly succeeded. He is candid and outspoken; he is almost merciless in his dissection of character—perhaps more so than usual in his dissection of Liberal characters. His portrait of the Duke of Argyle, with his unbounded pride of race, his provincialism of feeling, and his ambition of oratorical fame, is undoubtedly good. So, too, is the portrait of Mr. Bright; and as Mr. Reid speaks from personal knowledge, we will quote his description of John Bright in Parliament:—

"We have watched the faces of the men to whom is committed the government of the British Empire, and of the 'strangers' permitted to join with them—strangers including Princes of the Blood, peers of long descent, the

---

[11] "Cabinet Portraits: Sketches of Statesmen." By T. W. Reid. London: Henry S. King and Co.

ministers of foreign countries, and the leaders of the Church; we have watched them, as slowly, word by word, he was rolling forth the magnificent peroration of one of his great speeches, and we have seen upon their countenances such a rapt and almost awe-stricken expression as one might have expected to see on the faces of a Hebrew congregation before whom an Isaiah was delivering himself of his heaven-born visions."

Mr. Reid is also successful in his portraits of Mr. Disraeli and Mr. Gladstone; perhaps he does not do full justice to the latter, but he does more than justice to Mr. Gathorne Hardy, who is certainly not the eminent statesman that Mr. Reid believes him to be. But, taken as a whole, this book of Cabinet Portraits is creditable to the fairness of its author. The portraits are drawn from a close personal observation of the public life of the men criticized, and may be read with interest even by political partisans.

The remarkable memoirs of Leonora Christina [12] have already passed through several Danish and German editions, and are now offered to an English public. Their history is curious. They were discovered only a few years ago amongst the papers of Count Waldstein, her lineal descendant, and their authenticity was established by a comparison of the manuscript with known specimens of the handwriting of the authoress. The first edition appeared, therefore, in Danish, in 1869, and a second in 1871. Herr Ziegler translated the work into German, and it now appears for the first time in English. A brief sketch of the chequered life of Leonora forms an introduction to her memoirs. She was the daughter of Christian IV. and Kirstine Munk, with whom he was morganatically united. At eight years of age she was promised to Corfits Ulfeldt, the seventh child of an old and distinguished family, which had no less than seventeen children. His youth had been spent abroad, and he became a great favourite with King Christian, who gave him his daughter Leonora. After several successful diplomatic missions abroad, he rose to the influential position of Lord High Steward of Denmark, a position which he abused for his own aggrandizement, whereby he lost the confidence of the King, and was finally refused admission to court. Denmark was still an elective monarchy, and, upon the death of King Christian, Ulfeldt was the President of the Regency. By his efforts the monarchy was conferred upon Frederic III. But a quarrel soon ensued between the King and the High Steward, and the difficulties having become further complicated, Ulfeldt and Leonora fled to Holland. Here he treacherously took measures with the Swedes against his own country. The result of this in the end was that he was obliged to fly. He had lent large sums of money to Charles II. of England, and he desired Leonora, who was a cousin of Charles once removed, to go to England and claim it. She did so, but was sent back by Charles to Denmark without the money. The next twenty-two years she spent in prison at Copenhagen. One year after her arrest

her husband died. During her captivity she wrote the history of all
the prison incidents which amused or terrified her, and the result is
the memoir, which has only recently been made public. Her chief
trouble seems to have been the difficulty of passing her time, and the
dread of what might be in store for her. A broken wooden spoon
found her some occupation, for, by means of a piece of glass, she converted the spoon handle into a pin with two prongs, whereon she
made ribbon, taking the silk from the border of her night dress.
A piece of pewter she converted into an inkstand. Indeed, all the
miserable devices which beguile the intolerable vacuity of prison life
are mentioned here. They are varied only by the gross brutality of
the prison governor and the petty tyranny of the prison attendants.
After her liberation in 1685 Leonora had a royal manor at Maribo
granted to her as a residence.

The history of Maximilian, late Emperor of Mexico," shows that
even in modern times royalty runs the same risk in an unsettled
country as it did two hundred years ago. Mr. Chynoweth has drawn
up in a short compass and with great clearness a history of the events
which led to the execution of Maximilian. He deals briefly but lucidly
with the Empire under Iturbide, and with the Republican era up to
the signing of the "Convention of London" in 1861. The machinations
of France and the designs of Napoleon are made manifest, and the
preliminaries themselves of the Empire are a prediction of its fall. At
first there was a possibility that the unfortunate Emperor might have
ruled the country for its advantage and his own security. He showed
signs of possessing liberal principles, which would have conciliated to
him the great body of the people. Nay, they began to regard him as
the saviour of their country, and to look for a time when war should
cease and political contentions die out. Unfortunately their hopes
were not to meet with a realization. The clerical party trembled at
their own prospective failure under the Empire; they were impatient
to repain the enormous landed property of the Church, and by a
system of insidious flattery they gained the Emperor's ear, and
gradually alienated him from the liberal body of the people. Then
general confidence fell away ; a system of guerilla warfare was organized
against his troops, and the path was opened to the impending catastrophe. This catastrophe was hastened by the fatal and cruel decree
which he issued in the autumn of 1865. This decree, carried out to
the very letter, condemned to capital punishment any one convicted
" only of the act of belonging to an armed band." The consequences
were indeed terrible. Many of the most respectable and pacific
of the community were shot, and it is said that 11,000 men in the
Republican army, after falling prisoners of war, were slain in cold
blood, without the slightest inquiry of any kind. One commander
of a French division, after a great slaughter of a surprised camp, stated
in his despatch to Marshal Bazaine that his men had made a free use

10 "The Fall of Maximilian, Late Emperor of Mexico." By W. Harris
Chynoweth, Twenty-five Years Resident in Mexico. London: Published by the
Author.

of the bayonet, and *that they had taken no prisoners.* The end of
these horrors was not far distant, and the morning of June the 19th,
1867, witnessed the execution of the amiable but weak Maximilian.
It is described as a morning of more than usual splendour, and as the
mournful cortège left the garden of the Capuchinas, Maximilian,
enthusiastic to the last, could not refrain from expressing his admiration. Turning to the advocate Ortega, he exclaimed : " What a
beautiful sky ! It is just like this that I should have wished the day
of my death to be." A few minutes later, and Mexico was without
an Emperor. To the clear narrative of events Mr. Chynoweth has
appended a report of the defence made by the advocates for Maximilian, and of their persevering efforts in his behalf at the seat of the
republican government.

Mr. Rush was the American minister at the Court of London from
1817 to 1825. In 1833 he published his memoirs of residence, both
in America and England, where it went through two editions. The
book has, however, been long out of print, and it is now republished,[14]
with occasional notes, by his son. Mr. Rush was a popular resident
in England, and although always loyal to his own country, and animated at all times by "an American spirit," he was deservedly respected
by the English. Mr. Rush's notes are extremely interesting. He
was much impressed with his first view of London, though disappointed in the general exterior of the dwelling-houses. The noise and
tumult of the streets surprised him, the strange yet familiar faces and
accent perplexed and tantalized him. Shortly he dined at Lord
Castlereagh's. He was surprised to find French the language of conversation, and, we may add, that so are we; for it is well known that
Lord Castlereagh spoke it execrably—even worse than English. Most
people will be surprised to learn that the first subject which the American minister had to bring before the notice of the English Government was a claim for compensation for slaves. But it behoves us to
remember that the accursed system of slavery did not begin with the
Americans, but with ourselves, whilst America was but a colony of
Englishmen. Mr. Rush was not long in presenting his letters of cre-
dence to the Prince Regent, and was much pleased with his reception.
He was not so pleased with the deputations which waited upon him,
the "palace drums and fifes," the "royal waits and music," the
"king's marrow-bones and cleavers," all of whom presented an address
and *had a book to show.* But it is impossible for us to record the
various impressions which Court life made upon Mr. Rush. He describes everything with grace and *naïveté.* His diary at the Court of
Louis Philippe is equally good. He was there during the revolution
of 1848, and saw much of Lamartine and De Tocqueville. We can
cordially recommend the book to our readers, and wish to add that
not the least pleasing part of it is the manly and kindly accompaniment of notes which Mr. Benjamin Rush has included in the
volume.

---

[14] " Recollections of the English and French Courts, 1817-1849." By Richard
Rush. Edited by his Son, Benjamin Rush. London : Hamilton, Adams and Co.

Our next work[14] takes us from the atmosphere of Courts to that of country parsonages. The Hares were two brothers, who have found fervent admirers, and who have had some influence upon religious minds. The best known of the two was Julius Hare. His range of influence lay in the same direction as that of Coleridge. Like Coleridge and F. D. Maurice, he was among the first to feel one wave of thought that came from Germany, and to communicate it to others in England. He was himself an accomplished German scholar, and possessed something of the German philosophy, combined with Italian elegance. In 1827 he published, in conjunction with his brother Augustus, "Guesses at Truth," a work which gained considerable and deserved success. The lives of these two brothers form the chief subject of the present book. The biographical portion is compiled from letters and journals of different members of the family, and was commenced many years ago by the widow of Augustus. The work has been continued by her son, who has made his mother the central figure. It is well done, from a literary point of view; but the thought, which would have been deemed daring thirty years ago, seems now to lack vigour and originality. Yet it is certain that both the brothers were men of lofty and tender character and of considerable intellectual refinement; but even refinement does not atone for the absence of power. Indeed, the school of Coleridge is apt to mistake culture for nerve—an error which Coleridge himself would never have committed. We may connect with these memorials the letters[15] of Mr. Tayler, a Presbyterian minister, but we confess that we think them far more instructive reading than the somewhat effeminate and sentimental writings of the Hares. In 1834 his congregation allowed him to spend some months at a German university. Here he attended the lectures of the Professors, and became acquainted with Otfried Müller and Ewald. Of the latter he says:—

"I am exceedingly pleased with Ewald and his lectures. He is not a mere philologist. There is a spirit of philosophy in his lectures. He converges the various lights of his attainments to illustrate the origin and connexion of the manners and institutions of the infancy of mankind. He is remarkably amiable and unaffected in his manners; in countenance a little resembling James Martineau, but with a softer expression."

He says again:—

"The Church of England is in no high repute among the learned theologians of Germany. It is literally true that the mention of "our Episcopal Church," as they call it, almost universally raises a smile on the countenance of the speaker. Its excessive and ill-distributed wealth, its sinecures and pluralities, its rigid and immovable orthodoxy, its obstinate resistance to the light which should break in upon it from the progress which knowledge and liberality are making in the world, its political character and its close involution with the aristocracy, are subjects of universal censure and astonishment."

---

[14] "Memorials of a Quiet Life." By Augustus J. C. Hare. 2 vols. London: Strahan and Co.

[15] "Letters of John James Tayler, B.A." Edited by John Hamilton Thom. 2 vols. London: Williams and Norgate.

Of Schlegel he says :—

"He loses a little on a nearer approach, being vain and coxcombical almost to the ludicrous, though he is now considerably advanced in years."

In the same letter he says :—

"We are also acquainted in Bonn with a very agreeable person, the grandson of the celebrated Mendelssohn, the contemporary and friend of Lessing and Lavater, who, you know, was called the Jewish Socrates. He lectures upon ancient and modern geography."

In 1840 Mr. Tayler was elected Professor of Ecclesiastical History in New College, Manchester. Of this College he subsequently became Principal—an office which he held until his death, in 1869. He was upon intimate terms with Baron Bunsen, and the second volume contains some of his correspondence with that distinguished scholar. It contains also letters to Crabb Robinson, Mr. Martineau, and Mr. Hutton. They are all characterized by a wise and liberal spirit, and by a profound and scholarly knowledge of philosophical subjects.

The work which shall next occupy us is one which has already gone through two editions in Germany. It is a History of German Literature in the Nineteenth Century." Herr Gottschall very properly recognises three divisions in the general tendency of this literature— the Classical, the Romantic, and the Modern. The Classical school created an artistic form upon the ancient models, the Romantic derived its inspiration from mediæval traditions, the Modern school strives to unite the artistic perfection of the ancients with the poetry of the present. The representatives of the Classical school are Göthe, Schiller, and Jean Paul Richter. We think that Herr Gottschall is quite right in assigning Jean Paul a place in the Classical school, though some classical writers would have repudiated the relationship. He belonged to it by the intensity of his convictions and the loftiness of his moral energy, which separated him entirely from the Romanticists. The license of his style and the wildness of his humour render his proper position at first sight obscure. But he is the necessary complement of Göthe and Schiller. He united Schiller's moral force and Göthe's subjective contemplation in the bright focus of his own humour. The object of his culture, however, was neither the ethical aim which Schiller set before himself, nor the æsthetical goal which attracted Göthe. It was an inward poise and harmony of the spiritual elements. Feeling took the place with him of Schiller's volition and Göthe's contemplation.

At the head of the Romantic school stood Fichte, Schelling, and the two Schlegels. Herr Gottschall brings well before us the principles of this school, especially as they manifested themselves in its two prophets Novalis and Tieck. The mysticism, the melancholy, and the "*schwärmerei*" of these amiable writers become attractive under the pen of the historian. This school ends, according to Herr Gottschall,

---

[17] Die deutsche Nationalliteratur des neunzehnten Jahrhunderts. Literarhistorisch und kritisch dargestellt. Von Rudolf Gottschall. Vier Bände: Breslau. London : D. Nutt.

with Eichendorff and Von Platen. By form, Von Platen is classical; in spirit, he is still under the influence of Schlegel. We differ very considerably from Herr Gottschall in his estimate of Von Platen. Perhaps no German poet has had so little justice done him by his countrymen. Savagely attacked by Heine in the second volume of his *Reisebilder*, unappreciated by his contemporaries, he is placed now in a position which he would certainly have deprecated, the rear of the Romantic school. How little he deserves this position his "Songs of the Poles" show. At any rate, with his poems, and those of Karl and Immerman, the Romantic school of German poetry passed away, and with Heine we enter upon the new era. Of Heine, Herr Gottschall says :—

"Heine marks the resolution and dissolution of German Romance, the extreme point of its spiritual chaos, the vigorous transmutation of its fancy into the life of the present. But whilst his irony builds up the unreal dream-world, and again annihilates it, it is not the fascination of decay which gives the last impression, but over the ruin there comes the enchanting breeze and odour of new times—the breath of the future is felt, a joyous Hellenic life rises from the Gothic dust. It is true this Hellenism is frivolous and wanton ; the Phrynes play a great part in it ; Homer and Sophocles are not there ; form and morality are absent ; the death-despising heroism of Marathon and Salamis does not belong to it ; but it has the cynical wit of Diogenes, the brightness of the Aristophanic parabasis, and all the divine mischief of an unrestrained darling of the Muses. Wit—sovereign, unerring wit—is the intellectual solvent which effects the dissolution of old epochs and obsolete circumstance. Of this resolving wit Heinrich Heine is the incarnation."

The history of the modern epoch occupies three out of the four volumes, and is fully told. The influence of the Hegelian school upon modern philosophy and literature, upon science and society, is brought out under the names of those who have led it along its various channels. The lyrical poetry of Uhland, Müller, Grün, Freiligrath, and Geibel is referred in each case to its own school, a general conspectus is given of the modern drama and the modern novel, and the book closes with a well-grounded hope that there lies before the spirit of German literature a future of yet better and more joyous development. The whole history is written in a lucid and charming style, and affords, we believe, the best general view of the latest German literature in all its branches.

The sad story of the Thirty Years' War in Germany has been often told, at least in part. It has now been told again[14] in a series of live lectures by Dr. Trench. He gives some vivid pictures from that unhappy time, and a clear outline of events. One interesting feature of the book is owing to the well-known etymological studies of the author, who shows with great skill the large deposit of military words which that deluge of war left in the language of the people. But through all the horrors which he has to relate, Dr. Trench keeps the mind of his hearer directed towards the good time which was so

[14] "Gustavus Adolphus in Germany, and Other Lectures on the Thirty Years' War." By Richard Chenevix Trench, Archbishop of Dublin. London : Macmillan and Co.

long afterwards to come. He takes the reader a sad and dreary way, but he himself never forgets "that he is travelling by a road which will lead him at last to the War of Liberation, to Sadowa and Sedou."

Dr. Grotefend's "Manual of Historic Chronology,"[19] should be named rather, a "Manual of Ecclesiastical Chronology." It is, in fact, a complete and scientific history of the Ecclesiastical Calendar, the Easter cycle, the cycle of the Sunday Letters, the Golden Number, and the Epact. This history is followed by a series of eighteen tables and two glossaries of Latin and German terms belonging to the Calendar. The book appears to be compiled with great care and accuracy, and will doubtless be useful as an authority for establishing dates.

Dr. Jacob Herz, a short memoir of whose life[20] is now before us, was a medical man of Erlangen, distinguished alike for his professional success and his humane philanthropy. He belonged to a Hebrew family, once wealthy, but during his boyhood reduced to poverty, so that he himself with great difficulty was enabled to pursue his university career. He did so, however, with such earnestness that he attracted the attention of the authorities, and was finally elected to an official position in the University of Erlangen—the first Jew who was ever so honoured in Bavaria. His exertions on behalf of the wounded in the late war were the proximate cause of his death.

Herr Lehmann, in a very interesting essay,[21] has given an analysis of the character of the great historian Gervinus. He has combined this with a short biographical sketch of the man himself. Neither enthusiasm for his subject nor admiration for his friend are wanting, and the whole is a tribute which is not unworthy of the great writer it celebrates. Herr Lehmann says:—

"He held fast and immovably to his belief with an iron consistency, which was, perhaps, at times exaggerated; he never made a concession to the judgment of the vulgar, he never strove for their favour, which, with his dazzling ability, he might easily have won. He was a man, 'if we take him for all in all,' a man without a parallel, a man who will live in the memory of a just posterity as a bright example of fidelity to conviction, and as one of the chief ornaments of German science."

We have now but little space to deal with the remaining books of this quarter.

The Irish State Papers for the three years 1603-1606[22] form a bulky volume, published under the direction of the Master of the Rolls. They are introduced by a long descriptive preface, and conclude with a full general index. The papers themselves refer chiefly to the administration of Sir Arthur Chichester and the noblemen who were engaged with him in the conduct of public affairs. They synchronize

[19] "Handbuch der historischen Chronologie des deutschen Mittalalters und der Neuzeit." Von Dr. H. Grotefend, Hannover. London: D. Nutt.
[20] "Doctor Jacob Herz. Zur Erinnerung für Seine Freunde." Erlangen.
[21] "Georg Gottfried Gervinus, Versuch einer Charakteristik." Von Emil Lehmann, Hamburg. London: D. Nutt.
[22] "Calendar of State Papers, Relating to Ireland, of the Reign of James I., 1603-1606." Edited by the Rev. C. W. Russell, D.D., and John Prendergast, Esq., Barrister-at-law. London: Longman and Co.

with the Carew papers, and may be regarded as forming a part of the same historical picture.

The Domestic Series of State Papers of the reigns of Elizabeth and James[73] are now completed in a final volume of Addenda. These calendars include all the historic material of the period hitherto discovered in the Public Record Office. This volume has a general index.

The second part of the fourth volume of the State Papers of the reign of Henry VIII.[74] has also appeared. This huge volume has neither preface nor index. An index will probably be given in the closing part.

The Clarendon Papers preserved in the Bodleian Library, Oxford, have now been fully catalogued and analysed. The first volume[75] refers to documents which reach up to the year 1649. They begin with the year 1523. They are partly original State Papers, and partly the private correspondence of Lord Clarendon.

The second volume of the Clarendon Catalogue[76] refers to the period 1649-1654. The plan of the work is the same as that of the Calendars of State Papers published under the direction of the Master of the Rolls.

Mr. Lumly has reached in his edition the fourth volume of the "Polychronicon."[77] This strange medley of history and fiction is accompanied by two English translations—one that of John Trevisa, and the other the work of an unknown writer of the fifteenth century. There is at present no index.

The index to the supplementary series of the Wellington Despatches[78] forms the fifteenth volume of that series, and is excellently arranged.

Mr. S. Owen, Reader in Indian Law and History at Oxford, has published in a connected form the substance of a course of lectures delivered by him at Oxford on the history of the Mogul Empire, and Maratha rule in India.[79] The work forms a concise and intelligible history of India to the year 1761.

Mr. Sherring's book[80] is an attempt to give a detailed account of

[73] "Calendar of State Papers, Domestic Series, of the Reigns of Elizabeth and James I." Addenda, 1580-1625. Edited by M. A. E. Green. London: Longman and Co.

[74] "Letters and Papers, Foreign and Domestic, of the Reign of Henry VIII." Edited by J. S. Brewer, M.A. London: Longman and Co.

[75] "Calendar of the Clarendon State Papers Preserved in the Bodleian Library." Vol. I., Edited by Rev. O. Ogle, M.A., and W. H. Bliss, B.C.L., under the direction of Rev. H. Coxe, M.A., Bodley's Librarian.

[76] "Calendar of the Clarendon State Papers Preserved in the Bodleian Library." Vol. II. Edited by the Rev. W. D. Macray, under the direction of Rev. H. Coxe, Bodley's Librarian. Oxford: At the Clarendon Press.

[77] "Polychronicon Ranulphi Higden, Monachi Cestrensis." Edited by R. J. B. Lumly. M.A. London: Longman and Co. Vol. I.

[78] "Supplementary Despatches, &c., of F.M. the Duke of Wellington, K.G." Edited by his Son. Vol. XV. Index. London: John Murray.

[79] "India on the Eve of the British Conquest." By Sidney Owen, M.A. London: W. H. Allen and Co.

[80] "Hindu Tribes and Castes as represented in Benares." By Rev. M. A. Sherring, M.A., Calcutta. London: Trübner and Co.

the castes in India; and he has chosen Benares as his representative town, because, being a sacred town, it draws to itself members of every caste. As far as a single town can avail Mr. Sherring has thoroughly accomplished his self-imposed task.

BELLES LETTRES.

WE think it right to say that we know nothing personally of Mr. Samuel Tinsley. We have, however, much pleasure in complying with his request, and accordingly draw attention to his new method of publishing novels. Any reform in this direction is welcome. He has further favoured us with three pamphlets. One of these consists of a letter to the editor of the *Times* on three-volume novels, whilst " The Publisher's Circular," as he calls his preface to the " Mistress of Langdale Hall,"[1] explains his own system. As these pamphlets form quite a literature of their own, apart from the actual novel, we shall deal with them separately. Hitherto in these columns we have only dealt with the literary aspect of the novel, for once we shall treat of the commercial. And here let us say, that as far as we have from actual experience been able to test Mr. Tinsley's statements, we have found him invariably correct. We should have thought, however, that his estimate of the profits on an edition of a three volume novel was calculated rather too high ("The Publisher's Circular," p. xi.). Mr. Tinsley certainly discloses a state of things very different to what we are accustomed to read in the works of novelists themselves. There the hero pays off his Oxford and Cambridge debts with the proceeds of his first novel. But what does Mr. Tinsley say about the sale of the average three-volume novel? We quote his own prosaic, but, we believe, very truthful words :—" In the case of the average run of novels, the sale of five hundred copies is considered a success; very often it does not reach two hundred and fifty." (p. xi.) But Mr. Tinsley's revelations on the subject of payment are still more instructive. He tells us (p. iii.) that instead of being paid the author often pays. Never was the modern Gospel of " buy in the cheapest, and sell in the dearest market," so thoroughly carried out as in Paternoster Row. The publisher in fact mulcts both author and public. Mr. Samuel Tinsley steps forward to remedy this state of things. Instead of charging the public thirty-one shillings and sixpence, he gives them precisely the same amount of matter in a more convenient form for four shillings. So far so good. Mr. Tinsley is evidently a benefactor to the public, and we hope the public will be grateful. But what about

---

[1] I. " The Mistress of Langdale Hall." A Romance of the West Riding. By Rosa Mackenzie Kettle. London: Samuel Tinsley. 1872. II. " The Publisher's Circular." (Prefixed to the Mistress of Langdale Hall). Same Publisher. III. " Three Volume Novels." A Letter to the Editor of the *Times*. By Samuel Tinsley. Same Publisher. IV. " The Publishing System." By Samuel Tinsley. Same Publisher. London. 1872.

the author ? Mr. Tinsley is silent, for he probably knows that no one
will care about such a person. But all this time we are keeping Mr.
Tinsley's new four-shilling volume waiting. We are bound to say that
he has made good his word. "The Mistress of Langdale Hall," both as
regards quantity and quality, is not merely equal to the general three-
volume novel, but is decidedly very greatly superior to the majority of such works. Further, the book is printed in a clear legible
type, and on good paper. The binding is substantial and tasteful. The
illustrations would have been better omitted, and we could have done
without the repetition of the figure 4 on the side and back, which has the
appearance of a shop ticket. So far for the exterior. With regard to the
"reading," as children say, if this is Miss Kettle's first production, it
is full of promise. She knows more of the world and its ways than the
generality of young novelists. Her characters are by no means of a
conventional type. She has evidently drawn from her own observation,
and not copied from books. Her conversations are good, but her descriptions of Yorkshire scenery are still better. She is filled, too, with
that proper enthusiasm about Yorkshire and everything Yorkshire,
which ought to make the book especially acceptable throughout all the
three Ridings. Her mistakes are those, however, of the three volume
novelist, without his excuse. Now the great objection to the three-
volume novel is from a literary and not a commercial point of view.
The author is obliged to spin out his story to comply with the demands
of his publisher. Everything is sacrificed for the sake of completing
the tale of volumes. Padding, irrelevant incidents, commonplace
conversations, are all introduced, especially in the third volume, to
make "copy." Now Miss Kettle's story would be twice as interesting
if it were reduced by three quarters. Her conversations, as we have said,
are good, but we may have too much of a good thing, especially when it
is mere talk for talk's sake. Her descriptions of scenery are also excellent, but they would be far more effective if they did not occur quite
so frequently, and were not so much alike. Repetition fatigues.
Further, Miss Kettle is often very careless and slipshod in style.
Still, in spite of these shortcomings, her novel is decidedly interesting.
If Mr. Samuel Tinsley can continue to give the public works of such
genuine merit as "The Mistress of Langdale Hall," we wish him every
success in his new undertaking.

We wish that we could give the same praise to Mr. Tinsley's next
four-shilling novel. Vulgarity is the keynote of "Puttyput's Protégée."[1] Mr. Tinsley no doubt wishes to consult the tastes of a
great number of readers. There are people who admire vulgarity,
and mistake slang for humour. It was but the other day we happened
to be at one of the largest fairs in the Midland counties. The great
attraction was a booth with a stage, on which two seedy clowns, a
wretched-looking harlequin, and a creature supposed to be a columbine,
performed. The whole affair was as painful as it was disgusting. But
the crowd was in ecstasies. It yelled with delight when the two

---

[1] "Puttyput's Protégée." A Story in Three Books. By Henry George
Churchill. With Illustrations by Wallis Mackay. London : Samuel Tinsley. 1872.

clowns knocked each other over. So with the present volume. There
will be readers who will enjoy its vulgarity. By long experience we
have found that reproof is of no avail. Some of its readers, however,
will, in time, perhaps, learn to appreciate something better and nobler,
and even the author himself may come to look back with sorrow upon
his present performance.

"'The town of Shallerton ends as abruptly as some books do," are
the opening words in "Miriam's Marriage."[3] If the author had said
"as some novels begin," we think it would have been far more
appropriate. The abruptness, however, of "Miriam's Marriage" is
only felt at the beginning. The story is particularly well told. The
opposite characters of the two sisters, Miriam and Nancy, are admirably
discriminated. The best character, however, as far as literary workmanship is concerned, is that of Mr. Purton. He is a sketch which
Miss Austen might not be ashamed to own. The picture of his
dining-room is perfect. It reveals the man. We at once recognise
the kind of person, who loves to live in a low, dark room, with the
ceiling crossed by heavy beams, and the walls adorned with "gloomy
oil pictures of unknown but classical subjects," filled in with olive
green trees in the foreground, and clouds more like a slate quarry than
anything else in the sky. It was upon those old oil pictures that not
only Mr. Purton's reputation for his wealth, but his very dignity,
rested. As Mrs. Macquoid remarks, old oil pictures with cracked
surfaces are, in some people's eyes, a decided sign of wealth. Still
better is the account of his marriage trip in the third volume. Mrs.
Macquoid never descends into mere burlesque. Her humour is
genuine. The scene in which Mr. Purton finds out that his bride is
not a lady, but a lady's maid, and is confronted by her former mistress,
is touched in with very light and delicate strokes. In the hands of a
less able writer the scene must have inevitably degenerated into mere
farce. Then for the first time is Mr. Purton's selfish nature thoroughly
revealed. A reconciliation is, however, patched up. "There's hardly
a man in ten thousand who would forgive such a deception," observes
Mr. Purton. "Then I am sorry for the men," retorts his bride.
The other minor sketches are all equally well done. Thus Joe the
groom is at once brought before us, "with his hair like a bird's nest,"
and Miss Topper, whose false curls, dangling over her eyes, "made
her look like an antiquated Blenheim spaniel," is hit off by a single
stroke. But the interest of the story centres in Miriam's so-called
marriage with Godfrey Brendon, and its consequences. Here Mrs.
Macquoid is seen at her best.

When we read the title, "Yarndale, an Unsensational Story,"[4] we
hoped that we might discover a new writer who would lift us
into a higher atmosphere, who would interest us, not so much
by the plot, as by the graces of style, by the charm of high
ideas, by vivid pictures of natural scenery, and, above all, by

[3] "Miriam's Marriage." By Katharine S. Macquoid. Author of "Patty."
London : Smith, Elder & Co. 1872.
[4] "Yarndale." An Unsensational Story. London : Longmans, Green & Co. 1572.

carefully drawn characters. For it must be confessed that the ordinary novel has no claim to any place in literature. How many of the novels, which come out every week, will be known in fifty years? We had hoped, we repeat, to have found something different in "Yarndale," but are doomed to disappointment. It is simply an average novel, written probably by a clergyman, who is evidently well acquainted with Lancashire and its cotton-lords, and its "hands." Its humour is of the boisterous slap-on-the-back style, which belongs to the imitators of Dickens. Here and there we meet with chapters such as "The Man who does the Butchering," "The Oratorio," "The Election," "The Sportsman's Breakfast," which would have done admirably by themselves in a Magazine. The writer knows the Lancashire dialect, and uses it with effect. The best and most natural characters are, the great cotton-spinner Sir Timothy Brierly, knight and ex-mayor of Yarndale, who says "that the flame of my affection for my wife is still burning brightly on the altar of my heart, on an average" (vol. i. p. 278); Mr. Shorland, another Yarndale cotton lord, and the rich heiress, Miss Trumpington. As a story the chapters are far too disconnected, and are held together by far too slight a thread. Yet if any one wishes to know something of Lancashire and its cotton-lords, and the miserable state of the factory "hands," a few hours will not be misspent on "Yarndale."

There has lately been a run upon precious stones amongst our novelists. Mr. Trollope has recently given us "The Eustace Diamonds," and now Mr. Francillon comes forward with his " Pearl and Emerald.'" " Frightfully improbable!" every reader will, we suppose, say at the end of every chapter. "I know it," replies Mr. Francillon, " but mine is a tale of Gotham, and my characters are Gothamites." But the Gothamites are not quite such fools as Mr. Francillon thinks. If he will only turn to such a common work as Murray's " Handbook of Nottinghamshire," he will, under Gotham, find the true meaning of the tale which he quotes, and discover that the Gothamites were a great deal sharper than their neighbours. As for his *credo quia impossibile* argument, we imagined that this was only applied to things divine and supernatural, and we suppose he does not wish us to believe that there is anything very divine about Mr. Grode, or supernatural about old Nathan Levi. The truth is, Mr. Francillon should not have given us his reasons. He has written a very clever amusing story, and should not have condescended to bandy words with his readers about its probabilities and improbabilities. Certainly it strikes us as improbable that a shrewd business man, like old Grode, should have attracted the attention of a whole room full of Jews, brokers, and second-hand dealers by bidding for a picture of a magpie by an unknown artist. He would naturally have sent a commission through some agent. There is not the most unpractical bookworm in the world who does not know that if he was to walk into Messrs. Sotheby and Wilkinson's auction-rooms, and begin

---

* " Pearl and Emerald." A Tale of Gotham. By R. E. Francillon. With Four Illustrations. London : Smith, Elder & Co. 1872.

bidding, he would at once attract the attention of all the second-hand booksellers. And if an unpractical bookworm knows this, how much more does a practical man of business? But putting aside all questions of the sort, the story is excellently told. Mr. Francillon has a bright, lively style. He contrives to hold the threads of the story well together. He has, too, a quick eye not only for sketching mere externals, but for character. Some of the scenes during the artistic career of the hero are admirably done.

We have conscientiously read every page of "The True History of Joshua Davidson,"[6] and read it, too, we may add, with much interest, but we fear with little profit. We have not the slightest idea what the author means. Nor do we think the author himself knows what he means. In the last page but one he confesses that his mind is "unpiloted and unanchored," and his concluding words are a petition for some one to enlighten him on his doubts. This we cannot pretend to do. We can here merely deal with his work from a literary point of view. It is no more a novel than one of Mr. Jenkins's stories, to which there is a family resemblance. No attempt is made to interest us either by plot, or character, or dialogue. The whole interest centres upon class strife. We have no doubt that there are plenty of clergymen like Mr. Grand, plenty of artisans like Joshua Davidson, and plenty of girls like Mary Prinsep. We fear that the pictures which the author has drawn of the squalid scenes in the back courts in London are too true. The author, as far as we can judge, appears to be perfectly orthodox, but whether the orthodox party will thank him for his book, and especially for his portrait of Mr. Grand, is very doubtful.

We must give both the authoress and the publishers of "Una"[7] a word of praise. The authoress first. She has written a really readable novel, without too much of the "goody" element, which may be safely placed in the hands of all young girls. She does not possess any very great dramatic power, nor has she any particular talent for character drawing, but she has a clear, vivid style of her own which carries us along, and never allows our attention to flag. And now for the publishers. We have to thank them for giving us a novel, as the best American publishing houses do, with the pages cut. A book ought no more to be sent out without the pages being cut than without its binding. We can only say that we shall always first turn to those novels which are ready cut for us by the binder, before those through which we have to hack our way with a paper-knife.

The words, "Reprinted from the *Sunday Magazine*," may, perhaps, account for the peculiar tone of certain passages in Miss Fraser-Tytler's new novel, "Margaret."[8] Sterne used to call Romanism his bread and cheese. Whenever he was at a loss for a subject for a

[6] "The True History of Joshua Davidson." London : Strahan & Co. 1872.
[7] "Una, or the Early Marriage." A Domestic Tale. By Harriette Bowra. Authoress of "Redlands." London : Hodder and Stoughton, 1872.
[8] "Margaret." By C. C. Fraser-Tytler. Author of "Jasmine Leigh." Reprinted from the *Sunday Magazine*. London : Strahan & Co. 1872.

sermon he used to attack the Pope. Here he had an unlimited field
for his imagination, here he was sure of delighting his audience.
Darwin is now the Pope for our *Sunday Magazine* novelist. Baiting
an atheist is the new Sunday sport. Here is Miss Fraser-Tytler's
description of the beast :—

> "Any one who has any knowledge of the human countenance, or its diverse
> expressions, must know the peculiar cast of an atheist's face ; the brow,
> devoid of all grandeur, the fixed and soulless expression of the eye, the look
> of stern calculation, the intense materialism of his creed, or no creed, per-
> vading all." (vol. i. p. 252.)

Every one will, we are sure, recognise the truth of this photograph.
The atheist is, of course, worried in the orthodox way for the amusement of a fashionable dinner-party. His "peculiar cast of face" is of
no use to him. His "look of stern calculation" avails him nothing.
He is allowed no peace from the soup to the dessert. He's badgered
between each course. He is driven from pillar to post, that is to say,
from Huxley to Darwin. He in vain takes refuge in molecules and
carbonic acid. Lastly, he and all the materialists are overthrown with
a crushing argument about the First Cause. This great victory, we
may remark, is achieved by a young girl, who informs us that she is
totally ignorant of all scientific matters.

Mrs. Craven's "Fleurange,"* like Miss Fraser-Tytler's "Margaret,"
is a didactic story. But in the one case cultured Catholicism, and in
the other raw Protestantism, leaven and inform the stories. In
"Fleurange," there is not a word of controversy, whilst "Margaret"
bristles with religious arguments. In short, "Fleurange" is spiritual,
"Margaret" goody. And in reading the two tales—in spite of our
natural leaning to Protestantism, in spite of all the noble services
which it has rendered to humanity—we find ourselves almost echoing
the famous saying, that Romanism is the only religion fit for the
artist and the poet. If we could persuade ourselves to use the term
"dangerous" in the sense in which theologians use it, we should say
that "Fleurange" is a most dangerous book. Miss Fraser-Tytler's
novel, although the heroine so easily and so triumphantly overthrows
Materialism, is by no means dangerous. It will make no converts to
Protestantism worth having. No one with the slightest sense will be
convinced by the defeats of such a scarecrow as Miss Fraser-Tytler
tries to frighten us with. On the other hand, "Fleurange" is sure
to make many proselytes. The unobtrusive piety, the real devotion,
the wide charity, the culture, which shine out on every page, gradually
win us to the writer's faith. If these are the results of Catholicism,
then it is a religion which is worth something, the reader will say.
And many a one dissatisfied with the coldness of Protestantism, the
apathy of its "professors" for anything but its emoluments, the
bitter and barren squabbles about the merest trifles, will read "Fleurange" with a delight and a rapture which they in vain seek for in
our professedly orthodox novels.

---

* "Fleurange." By Mrs. Augustus Craven. Translated from the French by
Emily Bowles. London : Smith, Elder & Co. 1872.

We must deal with the remaining novels before us more briefly than we could wish. Mar Travers, we suppose, stands for some lady's name, and "The Spinsters of Blatchington,"[10] we also suppose, is a first attempt at novel-writing. If this is the case, there are indications and promises of far better things. The story improves as it goes on, and the dialogue is a great deal better in the second volume than in the first. The character-drawing is good. The personages behave, with one exception, with thorough consistency. They are the every-day sort of people whom we are in the habit of meeting. They read the *Pall Mall Gazette* and the *Saturday Review*, and discuss the subjects of the hour with good sense. The love-making, too, is good. And we follow the fortunes of Molly Blomfield with real interest until, in the last chapter, she becomes Mrs. Thorold.

"Martin's Vineyard"[11] is thoroughly artistic in its workmanship. The author lingers lovingly over each description. It is easy to see that she has added stroke after stroke until each picture was finished. Shore, and orchard, and pasture-land are all painted in with minute touches. The effect is certainly striking. The children also are painted in with the same careful hand. The authoress evidently loves children and childhood, and is thoroughly at home amongst the scenes which she describes.

Mr. Horace Field is already well-known by his philanthropic works. There is a certain eloquence about all which he writes. The charm of tenderness pervades his books. "Glitter and Gold"[12] will, we think, be quite as popular as its predecessors. The author's aim is to show the power of Christ as seen in its influence on the social man, in short in the social order of the day. The book may be recommended for Sunday reading.

"The Insidious Thief,"[13] we hardly need say, means drink. The book might have been brought out by the Temperance Society. It probably may do some good, though we think it hardly requires two hundred and fifty pages to show the ill effects of drunkenness. Had the tale been compressed into half a dozen short chapters and circulated as a tract, it might have found its way into many households. It possesses not the slightest literary merit, but probably this is an advantage, considering the class of readers to whom it appeals.

"Honor Blake,"[14] takes its title from its heroine, one of the most genuine characters, whom we have for a long time met with in fiction. The scenes abroad are sketched with great spirit. The chapter "Bayonne," in the first volume, is alone worth scores of ordinary

---

[10] "The Spinsters of Blatchington." By Mar Travers. London: Henry S. King & Co. 1872.

[11] "Martin's Vineyard." By Agnes Harrison. London: Sampson Low, Marston, Low and Searle. 1872.

[12] "Glitter and Gold." By Horace Field, B.A. Author of "A Home for the Homeless," &c. &c. London: Longmans, Green & Co. 1872.

[13] "The Insidious Thief. A Tale for Humble Folk." By One of Themselves. London: Samuel Tinsley. 1872.

[14] "Honor Blake. The Story of a Plain Woman." By Mrs. R. H. Keatinge. London: Henry S. King & Co. 1872.

circulating novels. Mrs. Keatinge can describe the wild coast scenery and the fir woods with the same skill with which she can paint Honor's first ball. The episode about the Simmonds family, and the story of the forged cheque are also told, the first with some humour, and the second with some dramatic power. Altogether we can honestly recommend "Honor Blake" as a fairly amusing story, free alike from sensation on one hand, or any morbid tone on the other.

The author of the "Memoirs of Mrs. Lætitia Boothby,"[15] has done his work by no means badly, but it is easy to see that he has had a very uphill fight to maintain. Even Thackeray's great genius cannot prevent "Esmond" from sometimes becoming wearisome. We discover that these imitations of a past time and a past style are imitations. Yet Mr. Clark Russell is not a bad imitator. He has in many places caught the spirit of the times and the persons whom he represents. It is not his fault if he cannot make electroplate look like silver. It is only justice to add that the book, like all Messrs. King and Co.'s works, is most artistically got up.

Of the various tales in "Times and Places,"[16] we like "The Two Brothers" the best. But the sentiments in all of them are unimpeachable, and the moral good. It is a pity that the author should spoil the general effect by attempting to be witty.

"The Seagull Rock"[17] is a book for boys with a Robinson Crusoe turn of mind. There are plenty of adventures to satisfy the most adventurous. There are, too, the most wonderful woodcuts of shipwrecks and savages, two things which always delight a boy's heart.

The one novel which alone will make its mark on the age, the one book which will outlive all its fellows, the book from which future generations will learn not only our outward lives, our daily doings, but our inmost thoughts and aspirations—we mean of course "Middlemarch"[18]—has reached us too late for anything but a cursory and insufficient notice. As to its supreme literary merits, there can be but one opinion. Upon this point critics are unanimous. Style has never reached such perfection of art. Humour of so rare a quality has not been given to the world since the days of Shakspeare. In fact, the standard of English literature has been distinctly raised. No novelist can for the future write a novel of any pretensions without knowing that it will be weighed in the balance against such a work of art as "Middlemarch." There will probably always be a difference of opinion as to which should be put upon the highest pedestal, "Middlemarch" or "Romola." "Middlemarch" is more likely to appeal to the general public, "Romola" to the cultivated few. "Romola," in

[15] "Memoirs of Mrs. Letitia Boothby." Written by Herself. Edited by Clark Russell. London: Henry S. King & Co. 1872.

[16] "Times and Places; or, our History." By A. Stone. London: Trübner & Co. 1872.

[17] "The Seagull Rock." Translated from the French of M. Jules Sandeau. By Robert Black, M.A. London: Sampson Low, Marston, Low, & Searle. 1872.

[18] "Middlemarch. A Study of English Provincial Life." By George Eliot. London: William Blackwood & Sons. 1872.

its scenery, its passions, its times, its religious conflicts, is too far away from us, but "Middlemarch" comes home direct to our hearts with its English scenery, its English clouds and English meadows, with its groups of homely faces such as we know and love, and, above all, with the questions of the hour, which so perplex us. And here comes the point, how far is "Middlemarch" to be received as a contribution to social ethics.

"If we had not seen Mr. Tennyson's name and those of his publishers on the title-page, we should have imagined that 'Gareth and Lynette' had been written by some one who had caught the poet-laureate's mannerism, without possessing any of his power." This would have been an impertinent, but by no means an unfair criticism on the last Arthurian Idyl" which Mr. Tennyson has given the world. Perhaps it is difficult in judging it to be quite fair. It is impossible for us to say how the new idyl will look when it falls into its proper place and relation with the others. We should not think of judging an arch without reference to the aisle in which it forms a part. Mr. Tennyson may very fairly say that we are not his proper critics: and we fully admit his plea. We cannot possibly judge the present poem in the way which the next generation will do, when they see the Idyls as one noble whole, and not as we have done, piecemeal. Having said this much by way of caution, we make no hesitation in avowing that we think "Gareth and Lynette" is utterly unworthy of Tennyson. We care for neither Gareth nor Lynette. Gareth is a prig, and Lynette is a scold. Gareth is introduced to us as one of those insufferable prodigies who are going to put the world to rights, without having any conception of what is right or wrong. His first step is, if not to tell a lie, at least to act one. His next is, of course, single-handed, to overcome six men. His love-affairs are so strangely managed that we do not know whom he marries, and are almost afraid that he commits bigamy. The poem itself is as faulty in details as in conception.

> "Who walks thro' fire, will hardly heed the smoke,"

is a mere Tupperism.

> "Knights who sliced a red life-bubbling way
> Through twenty folds of twisted dragon,"

might have been written by the late Alexander Smith or King Cambyses.

> "The birds made
> Melody on branch, and melody in mid-air."

They certainly do not make melody in this particular line.

> "Lightly was her slender nose
> Tip-tilted, like the petal of a flower."

As everybody had something to do with tilting at Arthur's court, Lynette's nose may just as well tilt as anything else. But we have

---

[19] "Gareth and Lynette," &c. By Alfred Tennyson, D.C.L., Poet Laureate. London: Strahan and Co. 1872.

not the heart to proceed. It is painful to have to make such comments. We shall say nothing further, though nearly every other page calls for criticism, either from some absurdity, some false metaphor, or some new-coined word, which grates upon the ear. And what have we to set against all these flaws and shortcomings? One or two exquisite and subtle passages, which no other living poet could have written but Tennyson. First comes the description of Camelot:

> "Far off they saw the silver-misty morn,
> Rolling her smoke about the royal mount,
> That rose between the forest and the field.
> At times the summit of the high city flashed;
> At times the spires and turrets halfway down
> Prick'd thro' the mist; at times the great gate shone
> Only, that opened on the field below;
> Anon, the whole fair city had disappeared."

Of course we need not explain the allegory to the reader, for, as the old Seer says,

> "The city is built
> To music, therefore never built at all,
> And, therefore, built for ever."

Once more. In the encounter between Gareth and the knight calling himself "The Star of Evening," we have the following fine image:

> "Gareth panted hard, and his great heart,
> Foredooming all his trouble was in vain,
> Labour'd within him, for he seem'd as one
> That all in later, sadder age begins
> To war against ill uses of a life;
> But those from all his life arise, and cry,
> 'Thou hast made us lords, and canst not put us down.'"

This is very fine, but it is spoilt by the setting. We are so sickened with the constant brain-hewing, blood-shedding, bone-breaking, and shambles talk, that we are hardly in the humour to appreciate its beauty. "The Last Tournament," which completes the present volume, has long since been public property. We have no wish to disturb the general verdict which criticism has passed upon the poem. We will rather recall a very beautiful passage, which is far more beautiful detached than when taken with the context.

> "Fell, as the crest of some slow-arching wave,
> Heard in dead night along the table shore,
> Drops flats, and after the great waters break,
> Whitening for half a league, and thin themselves
> Far over sands marbled with moon and cloud."

This is a perfect picture, and shows the most consummate delicacy and mastery of touch. Mr. Tennyson has here proved that words are more powerful than colours. Once more, to show how skilfully Mr. Tennyson can use words which are not in common use, let us call attention to his delicious phrase, "the garnet-headed yaffingale." The "yaffingale," we may remark, is the provincial term in the New Forest for the common green woodpecker, which in the Forest of Arden—Shakspeare's Warwickshire Arden — is called the "ickle," and in Sherwood Forest—Robin Hood's forest—is known as the "knicker-pecker." All three words are onomatopoetic, and refer to the woodpecker's peculiar shrill laughing cry; but Mr. Tennyson has, with a poet's instinct, chosen the most beautiful, which he may have heard in the Isle of Wight from some rustic, close to his own home at Faring-ford.

Mr. Wade Robinson[20] is already well known as a writer of graceful poetry. The present volume will certainly increase his reputation. There is both freshness and feeling in all his pieces. Here, for instance, is a pretty idea:

> "Past me the spring's first butterfly ranged on his yellow wings—
> A primrose gone alive with joy, to dance with living things."—(p. 73).

There was not the slightest occasion for Mr. Robinson to add a note, and say that he wrote the lines long before he had seen Mrs. Browning's famous

> "large white butterflies,
> Which look as if the May-flower had caught life,
> And palpitated forth upon the wind."

No critic with a particle of insight would accuse him of plagiarism. Mrs. Browning's lines, although they have been so much admired, have always appeared to us far from perfect. In the first place, the mind does not readily catch the resemblance between "large white butterflies"—to the size of which our attention has been specially called—and the excessively small and delicate flowers of the may, of which it would take half-a-dozen to make even a moderate butterfly. One flower might, perhaps, make a small moth. In the next place, "palpitating" is far from felicitous. To talk about a palpitating butterfly appears to us about as unnatural as to say, as we lately heard a woman say, that the hippopotamus had pupped. Of the two similes, we decidedly think that Mr. Robinson's is the happiest.

We shall not condemn the author of "Nuova Italia,"[21] but allow him to perform that task for himself. Here are his reflections upon foreign cookery and cooks:

> "Their cooks—the villains! *chefs*, indeed, yclept,—
> Ought to be forced to drink their own *potage*,
> Ought with a cat's-tail to be soundly whipt,
> And sent to bed to sup on their own *rage*."—(p. 217).

If our First Commissioner of Works wrote poetry, it could not be much more vulgar.

"Aspects of Authorship"[77] bears on its title-page two names, Mr.

[20] "Songs in God's World." By Wade Robinson, Author of "Loveland," &c. London: Longmans, Green, and Co. 1872.

[21] "Nuova Italia, or Tours and Retours through France, Switzerland, Italy, and Sicily." A Poem in Ten Cantos. By Nomentino, F.R.G.S. London: Longmans, Green and Co. 1872.

[77] "Aspects of Authorship; or, Book Marks and Book Makers." By Francis Jacox. London: Hodder and Stoughton. 1872.

Francis Jacox and Mr. Nicias Foxear. One appears to have written the prose and the other the poetry. It is, however, easy to see that they both are the same words. If authors trifle with their own names, they must not be surprised if the public trifles with them. The book, however, is a much better book than might be expected from such a display of affectation on the title-page. The first three chapters are the weakest; and, as far as we are concerned, the least interesting. For our own part, we do not care to know that Maturin used to write his plays with a red wafer stuck on his forehead, and that Dibdin composed " Jolly Dick, the Lamplighter," when having his hair brushed. This is literary twaddle with a vengeance. Very much better is the fourth chapter, entitled " Bookish." The fatal mistake which is made in our days is the idea that we can obtain that knowledge from books which can only be gained from experience in the world and intercourse with our fellows. The words of Rivarol will bear remembering, " Un homme qui pense en sait toujours plus long qu'un homme qui apprend ; un homme qui agit vaut mille fois mieux qu'un homme qui pense." Lessing separated Gelehrsamkeit—mere book-learning—from Weisheit, and Charron made a wide distinction between the *sage* and the *savant*. The man who is merely literary, and nothing else, is a detestable creature. When one meets him, we are inclined to sympathize with Gray's sarcasm, " learning never should be encouraged, as it only draws fools out of their obscurity." Equally good, too, are the author's chapters on composition. It is, perhaps, just worth remembering in these days, when novelists produce three or four volumes a year, that the world's great authors have written slowly and painfully. Who now reads Lope de Vega, who dictated faster than the copyist could write ? Who now knows the name of Faria, who could in a single day compose a hundred different addresses of congratulation and condolence ? On the other hand, the *Maximes* of La Rochefoucauld were corrected thirty times. Petrarch polished his smallest pieces again and again. The Cambridge MS. of Milton's " Lycidas " is full of alterations. The Ferrara MS. of " Ariosto " has been altered over and over again. Nothing for nothing is this world's inexorable law in literature as in everything else. " Nothing has been sent to me in my sleep," said Goethe. Equally interesting, and equally full of information, is the writer's chapter on authors' marriages. Poets and philosophers have not, as a rule, it must be confessed, lived very happily in the marriage state. From Socrates and Xantippe down to Shelley and Harriet Westbrook, they and their wives have been strangely assorted couples. Is the author to marry a clever woman, and then find out with M. de Bonald, " A un homme l'esprit il ne faut qu'une femme de sens : c'est trop de deux esprits dans une maison ?" Shall he, on the other hand, marry a she-fool, like the one mentioned by De Tocqueville, who ran away whenever she saw Bonaparte coming, " because he was always talking his tiresome politics ?" These are mysteries with which we will not meddle. Those who care to investigate the subject should consult Mr. Jacox's pages, where they will find the matrimonial follies of poets, artists, and philosophers duly catalogued. But the most interesting chapter is decidedly that which Mr. Jacox calls by the slangy title of "A Hard Crust." Why did he not at once say "Hard Cheese," as it deals with the literary man's means of livelihood, and would not have been much more vulgar? All those who are thinking of adopting literature as a profession should certainly read this chapter. We can only say with Milverton, in "Friends in Council," that a crossing-sweeper's occupation is better. There are several other chapters, especially the one upon style, on which we should have liked to make some remarks, but space fails us. "Aspects of Authorship" is a book cram full of matter, which may be taken up at any spare five minutes, and from which something is sure to be learnt. We regret to find from the preface that the work has been written upon a bed of sickness; and, taking this circumstance into consideration, the book is in every way most creditable to its industrious and painstaking author.

"A Plea for Culture" is the first of Mr. Higginson's Essays.[a] We did not know that culture required any plea, but from Mr. Higginson's opening words we learn that the spread of culture is causing considerable alarm in the States. Culture and the Almighty dollar are at war. Culture does not make money, does not strike oil. Mr. Higginson tries to allay the panic. At present, as he observes, American scholars are not such monsters of learning. They have not yet an "indecent acquaintance" with the classics. Most of them, as he observes, might hope by reasonable non-industry to forget all they know in a year. Mr. Higginson proceeds to show that if culture does not make money, it does what is infinitely of far more importance, makes men. For culture, of course, means not mere knowledge but intellectual grasp, judgment, character. His remarks upon university education, and the true aim of a university, are excellent, and go to the heart of the matter. If Mr. Higginson has not already seen it, we should most strongly advise him to read the Rector of Lincoln's (Mr. Pattison's) speech at the meeting of the University Reformers lately held at the Freemasons' Tavern, an epitome of which he may find in *The Academy* for December 1st, 1872, page 460. In that speech Mr. Higginson will see his own views still further carried out to their legitimate consequences. Mr. Higginson does not give us a very bright picture of intellectual life in the States. When Emerson lectures in the western towns, the enterprising manager of the hall gets up a dance at the same time—"Tickets to lecture and ball one dollar." The great need in the States is not, Mr. Higginson thinks, the want of an international copyright law, nor of libraries nor museums, but the want of an atmosphere of sympathy in intellectual aims. An artist, and by an artist Mr. Higginson means an author, "can afford to be poor, but not companionless. No one can live entirely on his own ideal. The man who is compelled by his constitution to view literature as an art is more lonely in America than even the painter or sculptor, and he has no Italy for a refuge."—p. 10. And yet all great artists

[a] "Atlantic Essays." By Thomas Wentworth Higginson. London: Sampson Low, Marston, Low, and Searle. 1872.

have lived upon their ideal. Still, it is highly probable that sensitive artistic natures will feel their isolation greater in America than in any other country which the world has yet known. Hawthorne, by his own confession, was driven out of America. The typical American loves what is death to the artist. "I can't abide Naples; there's no noise nor racket as there is in New York," exclaimed the American lady. Mr. Higginson proceeds to show that it is political knowledge which is valued in the States. There politics are imbibed through the pores of the skin, and learnt in one's sleep; but the artist has no more in common with the average Yankee politician than with a New York dry goods dealer. Yet Mr. Higginson plucks up heart of grace. He sees, as we do, better things in store. He points out that Agassiz endeared himself to the best of his adopted fellow countrymen when he declined a lucrative offer, on the ground that he had no time to make money. He adds, too, that though in America there may be a want of cultivated sympathy with the higher intellectual pursuits, yet respect is felt for them. Mr. Higginson has firm faith in the future. He can discern a place for America in art. As he truly says, "Everything is here, between these Atlantic and Pacific shores, save only the perfected utterance that comes with years. Between Shakspeare in his cradle and Shakspeare in Hamlet there was needed but an interval of time, and the same sublime condition is all that lies between the America of toil and the America of art."—(p. 22). He warns his countrymen, however, that nothing can be done by affectation or spasm. They must loyally accept the essential laws of art, which have from eternity been the same. Mr. Higginson again takes up the subject in another admirable essay, "Americanism in Literature," and again warns his countrymen against the same faults, as well as that of mere imitation. Of course, there has necessarily been a stage in American literature when it was imitative. This stage, has, however, been outgrown. American authors have discovered what Emerson has always so strongly insisted upon, that at home there is virgin gold. And in this essay, too, we find what, perhaps, had better have been stated in the "Plea for Culture,"—that for moral courage the people have always been in advance of the Universities. He reminds us how slavery found its advocates within college walls. He reminds us how culture shunned Parker and Phillips. The real answer to this accusation is, that the Universities do not then fulfil their proper purpose, and that something is mistaken for culture which is precisely the reverse of culture. It would require an essay as long as Mr. Higginson's whole volume to examine the causes why the Universities so thoroughly fail to instil that faith, that courage, that toleration, which should be the results of culture. We would, however, refer Mr. Higginson to a most able paper on "Oxford Studies," by the Rector of Lincoln (Mr. Pattison), in the first volume of "The Oxford Essays." He will there find many of those points which he has merely touched upon more fully worked out. Mr. Higginson's own essays are so suggestive that we hardly know to which especially to turn, for it is impossible to examine them all. In "Literature as an Art" he well points out that the average literary productions of the day have no more to do with literature than a writ has. As he says—

" Words afford a more delicious music than the chords of any instrument. They are susceptible of richer colours than any painter's palette; and that they should be used merely for the transportation of intelligence, as a wheel-barrow carries bricks, is not enough. The highest aspect of literature assimilates it to painting and music. Beyond and above all the domain of use is beauty, and to aim at this makes literature an art." (p. 28).

Mr. Higginson is never tired of repeating this lesson. In another place he says, " Words in a master's hand seem more than words. He can double or quadruple their power by skill in using" (p. 30). As the old verse ran, " Herbis ac stellis vis est, sed maxima verbis." Yet Mr. Higginson is no admirer of art for art's sake. On this point he is most emphatic. He tells his countrymen that the same Puritan spirit which has triumphed in war and triumphed in politics must also triumph in literature. This time, however, it must be the Puritanism not of Cromwell but of Milton. As he says, " The foundation of all true greatness is in the conscience. . . . . . . The invigorating air of great moral principles must breathe through all our literature. All culture, all art without moral nature, must be but rootless flowers, such as flaunt round a nation's decay" (p. 46). We most deeply regret that we have not space to do more than call attention to the rest of Mr. Higginson's essays. " Ought Women to learn the Alphabet " should be read by everybody who takes an interest in the most important movement of the day. It is full of that wit which is truth. " A Charge with Prince Rupert " abounds with picturesque painting. We do not feel certain that the whole events of the time, in spite of modern researches, are sufficiently well known to quite justify the writer's high estimate of the Prince and his cavaliers. The true history of our civil war has yet to be written. " Fayal and the Portuguese" is a most lively and vivid account of that island. It is a model sketch. The two next essays are, perhaps, the best in the volume—" The Greek Goddesses," and " Sappho,"—both of which should be read in conjunction with " Ought Women to learn the Alphabet." They each supplement the other. The last essay, " On an Old Latin Text-Book," is a most able and eloquent defence of classical studies. Mr. Higginson does not require our aid. And here we must unwillingly conclude our most inadequate notice of a book which will most assuredly help to raise the standard of American literature. Mr. Higginson's own style is, after Hawthorne's, the best which America has yet produced. He possesses simplicity, directness, and grace. We most strongly recommend this volume of essays, not to be merely read, but to be studied. It is as sound in substance as it is graceful in expression.

The greatest improvement which has lately taken place in English literature has certainly been amongst school books, if the works which Dr. Morris, Mr. Abbott, and Mr. Hales give us come under such a title. Thirty years ago English grammar was not taught. No boy was expected to parse an English sentence, or to derive an English word. English authors were banished. Now everything is altered.

Rugby masters are now publishing plays of Shakespeare, which illustrate the poet not only with quotations from Æschylus and Sophocles, but from Browning, Tennyson, and George Eliot. Dr. Morris gives us an English grammar," as readable and as interesting as a novel. It would be a total mistake to suppose that the book is merely a school-book. No educated person can possibly read it without learning much. There is not an uninteresting page in the book. Dr. Morris not only teaches us much which is new, but he has the great merit of presenting old things in a new light. Thus in his chapter on the History of the English Language he takes two groups of words, referring for instance either to animals, the elements, or the arts, and places those of English origin opposite to those of Romance origin. In this way any one of average intelligence can form conclusions for himself. Thus Dr. Morris gives us a group of words of English origin referring to agriculture, containing "plough, share, furrow, rake, harrow, sickle, scythe, sheaf, barn, flail, waggon, wain, cart, wheel, spoke, nave, yoke." Opposite to this group stands the solitary word of Romance origin "coulter" (p. 37). If the reader will, however, cast his eye lower down the same page, he will find two groups of words referring to food, in which those of Romance origin preponderate. We need not draw the conclusions, which every reader of "Ivanhoe" can anticipate. We wish that Dr. Morris in his list of farm implements had noticed some of the words which Sir Anthony Fitzherbert uses in "The Boke of Husbandry" [1523], in his two chapters.—"To knowe the Names of all the Partes of the Plowe," and "The necessary Thynges that belong to a Ploughe, Carte, and Wagone." It would be interesting to notice which words we had lost, and which we had retained. A greater change, however, is going on amongst agricultural words since the introduction of machinery, and especially of steam, than amongst, perhaps, any other class. Out of the words which Dr. Morris has given probably "sickle" and "flail," will in a few years become obsolete, being supplanted by "reaping machines," or "reapers," as they are called, and "steam thrashing-machines," or "steamers." Every group of words which Dr. Morris has given is equally instructive and interesting. The whole volume deserves the highest praise.

Equally good, too, are "Specimens of Early English,"" which Dr. Morris has edited in conjunction with Mr. Skeat. How exhaustive the notes are may be judged by the following :—

Stikes, paths, ways, A. S. *stig*, a way, path ; *stigan* (pret *stáh*, pp. *gestigen*), to go, climb, ascend ; whence *stile* (A.S. *stigel*), *stirrup* (A.S. *stig-ráp*, i.e. mounting-rope,) *stair* (A.S. *stæger*). Cf. O .E. *stegh* = Prov. E. *stie, steye, stee,* a ladder." (p. 239).

Now when language is taught in this way, it is as interesting as a

" "Historical Outlines of English Accidence." Comprising Chapters on the History and Development of the Language, and on Word-Formation. By the Rev. Richard Morris, LL.D. London : Macmillan and Co. 1872.

" "Specimens of Early English." A New and Revised Edition, with Introduction, Notes and Glossarial Index. By the Rev. Richard Morris, LL.D., and the Rev. Walter Skeat, M.A. Part II. From Robert of Gloucester to Gower, A.D. 1298—A.D. 1393. Oxford : The Clarendon Press. 1872.

problem in chess. "Staggers" is, we may add, provincially used in some parts of Lincolnshire for stairs. To take one more example—

"*Irchons* = *urchins*, hedgehogs (we still have *sea-urchin*) from F. *hérisson*, O. F. *eriçon*, from Lat. *ericius*, a hedgehog. We find also in Latin the forms *eris* and *erinaceus*. The A. S. term for hedgehog is *igil* (connected by Curtius with the Gk. *έχῖνος*). (p. 292).

To learn by word-building like this, can be nothing else but an amusement to an intelligent boy. The spelling "irchin," we may remark, is retained in the "English Expositor," by H. C. [1617], whilst "urchin" and "orchin" are still very common provincialisms throughout the Midland and Northern counties for hedgehog. Wherever we have turned to in the volume we have found the same care bestowed upon the smallest points. No difficulty is passed over. The specimens which are given of early English poetry are well worth reading for their own sake. There is a charming little lyric called "Spring Time" (p. 48), which Mr. Skeat has modernized with much skill and taste.

"Streams from Hidden Sources"[26] has evidently been not only a labour of love, but a labour of a lifetime to Mr. Ranking. We are, unfortunately, living too far away from either the British Museum or the Bodleian Libraries to verify his references. But where we have been able to test his accuracy we have found him correct. And Mr. Ranking adds to scholarship the graces of a cultivated style. His criticisms are particularly sound. His own narrative is marked by feeling, originality, and, above all, by a delicate appreciation of the beauty of archaic words. No one, except the author of "The Earthly Paradise," has rescued so many of these long-forgotten but most beautiful words and phrases, which are to be found in the pages of our Elizabethan writers. And Mr. Ranking uses them without the slightest affectation or straining. One of the most beautiful of the stories which Mr. Ranking has reset for us, is that of "Sir Urre of Hungary." Short as it is, it is too long for our pages. But we cannot refrain from paying our tribute of praise to Mr. Ranking's graceful introduction, and to his keen appreciation of the nobleness of the character of Launcelot. We can only regret with Mr. Ranking that neither Tennyson nor Morris should have dealt with this most pathetic episode in Launcelot's history. The other stories in the volume are equally well told, and all show the same spirit of industrious research, the same keen criticism, the same poetic insight, and the same depth of religious feeling.

In noticing, last quarter, the very excellent version of "Juvenal" in the "Ancient Classics for English Readers" Series, we expressed a doubt how far the great Roman satirist could ever be realized to the mere English reader. We also called attention to the fact how far happier the great Greek comic poet had been in his translators. This quarter Mr. Collins has given us an "Aristophanes,"[27] which will, we

---

[26] "Streams from Hidden Sources." By H. Montgomerie Ranking. London : Henry S. King and Co. 1872.

[27] "Aristophanes." (Ancient Classics for English Readers Series). By the Rev. W. Lucas Collins, M.A. London : William Blackwood and Sons. 1872.

think, not inadequately present the author of the most brilliant comedies which the world has yet seen to the English public. The task, however, is much easier than that of presenting Juvenal. It is impossible to give by a translation the full force and weight of such moral poems as Juvenal's Satires are, but it is by no means impossible to give the plot of a play, to set before us the most striking and amusing situations, to pick out the most brilliant dialogues, and, may we say such a thing, the "larks," the high jinks, and the horse-play. This Mr. Collins, by the help of Frere's admirable translation, has done. But it would be a great piece of injustice to give all the credit to Frere. Mr. Collins has evidently also caught the true Aristophanic tone. There is an excellent version by him from the chorus of women in the "Thesmophoriazusæ," beginning—

"They're always abusing the women,
As a terrible plague to men;
They say we're the root of all evil,
And repeat it again and again."

for which we regret we cannot find room, as the last part is a great deal more humorous than the first. We generally find ourselves agreeing with Mr. Collins's criticism. But we can hardly go with him in his depreciation of "The Birds." "The Birds" and "The Clouds" have always proved to us what a genuine poet Aristophanes really was. How comes it, by the way, that Mr. Collins omits all reference to Mr. Courthope's really brilliant parody, when he mentions Planché's very tame travesty? In conclusion, let us recommend the present volume to the English reader as certainly one of the most spirited and one of the most amusing volumes in "The Ancient Classics for English Readers" Series.

Some time since we called attention to the Rev. James Stormonth's excellent "Etymological Dictionary." We have now from him "A School Etymological Dictionary,"[a] on a smaller scale. The derivations are particularly good. But either Mr. Stormonth has omitted many words, or we have looked in the wrong place for them. He should remember that, in our large manufacturing towns, like Manchester, Birmingham, and Sheffield, there are a great number of well-to-do persons, especially ladies, who cannot write a common letter without a dictionary. We should advise him to add to the utility of his work by giving more of those words, which, though in common use, are still a puzzle to a great number of worthy people.

From Henley-on-Thames Grammar School comes a volume of "Latin Prose Exercises."[b] We cannot pretend, by a mere cursory inspection, to judge of its merits. Time and experience will alone

[a] "The School Etymological Dictionary and Word Book." Combining the Advantages of an Ordinary Pronouncing School Dictionary, and an Etymological Spelling-Book, for Use in Schools. By the Rev. James Stormonth. London: William Blackwood and Sons. 1872.

[b] "Latin Prose Exercises." For Beginners and Junior Forms of Schools. By R. Prowde Smith, B.A., Assistant Master at the Grammar School, Henley-on-Thames. London: Rivingtons. 1872.

decide. It comes out, however, under good auspices. And if Mr. Prowde Smith can write as good books for boys as the Head Master can for scholars, Henley-on-Thames Grammar School will soon become as illustrious as other schools on the same stream.

Dr. Andrew Wood's translation of Horace's Epistles and Art of Poetry[30] requires no special remarks. It is neither very good nor very bad. If his version calls for no praise, it deserves no blame. It has formed the recreation of the leisure hours of a busy professional man, who evidently has a sincere liking for Horace and a taste for English poetry.

From Messrs. Smith, Elder, and Co. we have to acknowledge two new editions of the "Plébiscite,"[31] and "Jane Eyre,"[32] in a convenient form and handsomely bound.

ART.

DR. MAX SCHASLER'S "Critical History of Æsthetic"[1] is one of the most important of recent contributions to the literature of art. The author begins with the beginning, *i.e.*, with Plato, and carries us down to the latest moment of publication, so that the volumes now before us form a complete work independent of that philosophy of the beautiful and of art which is announced to follow in connexion, and which has, we believe, already appeared. It will be seen from the use of the word "critical" that Dr. Schasler maintains (in opposition to Vischer) the possibility of tracing an organic development in this science. In his opening chapter he suggests that the "History of Æsthetic" may be divided into three great epochs. First, the period of intuitive (unsystematic) perception; secondly, the period of reasonable system; finally, the period of philosophical speculation. Consequently ancient æsthetic is comprised in the first period, in the second is placed the philosophy of the seventeenth and eighteenth centuries, whilst the third division embraces the æsthetic of the nineteenth century up to the present time. In each period we have again corresponding subdivisions of unsystematic, systematic, and speculative treatment. These subdivisions are not only somewhat unnecessary and confusing to the reader, but frequently oblige the writer to force his facts to suit their situation. For example, the term "intuitive or systematic"

[30] "The Epistles and Art of Poetry of Horace." Translated into English Metre. By Andrew Wood, M.D., F.R.S.E. Edinburgh: William P. Nimmo. 1872.

[31] "The Story of the Plébiscite; Told by one of the Seven Million Five Hundred Thousand who Voted 'Yes.'" From the French of MM. Erckmann-Chatrian. London: Smith, Elder and Co. 1872.

[32] "Life and Works of Charlotte Brontë and Her Sisters." An Illustrated Edition in Seven Volumes. Volume I. Jane Eyre. By Currer Bell. London: Smith, Elder and Co. 1872.

[1] "Aesthetik als Philosophie des Schönen und der Kunst." Erster Band: kritische Geschichte der Aesthetik von Plato bis auf die neueste Zeit. Von Dr. Max Schasler. Nicolaische Verlagsbuchhandlung. 1872.

applied to the æsthetic of the Greeks may perhaps be suitable as regards
Plotinus, but can only be adapted to Plato with difficulty, whilst as to
Aristotle it is in nowise fitting. Here, too, it may be noticed in
passing that Katharsis is taken by Dr. Schasler according to the old
interpretation of purifying the emotions, and he does not seem to be
aware that this interpretation has been challenged and made at least
doubtful by Professor Bernays, who assigns to the expression a totally
different meaning. After the decay of the æsthetic of the ancients we
have a blank of something like a thousand years, the consequence of a
total change in sentiment respecting art. The unity of the ancient
point of view was set aside to make way for the middle-age spirit,
which, sharply dividing soul from body, bound art to the service of
spiritual content. The æsthetic interest was absorbed by the theological. With the Renaissance movement the yoke was cast off, and
art was once again set free, but not until it had, so to say, run through
the whole domain of nature did the necessity make itself felt for the
construction of a theory of the then complete content. At this point
Dr. Schasler enters on the second period in the history of æsthetic, which
receives at his hands, as might be expected, even more exhaustive treatment than the first. And here again we find that his scheme has become a Procrustean bed. Giants are compressed to fit it, dwarfs are
stretched to fill it. Undue weight is attached to the importance of the
speculations of Herbert and Schopenhauer, simply because the scheme
demanded representatives of realism to act over against the idealism of
Hegel, and the position assigned to Schopenhauer is in itself awkward.
He is ranked in the second group (that of the reasonable systematizers)
of the second division, and yet, as every one knows, his æsthetic is
nearly related to that of Plato. To Hegel Dr. Schasler (who is the
sub-president of the Berlin Philosophical Society, the stronghold of
Hegelianism) does no more than justice. He even seems to lay an unnecessary stress on his want of acquaintance with the practical details
of art, but he acknowledges that the æsthetic of Hegel is a vast
treasure store, full of pregnant thoughts and deep insight into the very
essence of art. The task which our author reserves for himself is that
of placing on a sound basis the æsthetic of the future, by attempting
a fusion of the two opposing forces, idealism and realism, in so far as
they affect the theory of the arts. At this point he closes the present
work. We have pointed out that the desire to methodize and co-
ordinate according to a preconceived scheme has uncomfortably
fettered Dr Schasler; but we must not forget to emphasize the value
of his historical analysis. He has come to the rescue of the student
who has hitherto been obliged to collect and arrange for himself the
great variety of æsthetic theories which exist scattered about in the
writings of different authors. In the labour of digesting and analysing
he has been well served by the same instinct for completeness and
unity which has forced him to submit himself so unquestioningly to
his preconceived scheme, and he has produced a work which is likely
to be extremely valuable as a book of reference in a department of
literature in which such a work was greatly needed.

The fifth edition of Kugler's well-known Handbook of the History of Art' has been carefully re-edited by the author's most distinguished pupil and friend, Dr. Wilhelm Lübke. The fact that this work, in spite of formidable competition, still maintains its high position as the best text-book on the subject speaks for itself. Like Dr. Schasler's History of Æsthetic, this handbook is another example of the extraordinary talent for organization of which the Germans now give evidence in every department of literature and life. The period of production has ceased, but the national activity is only diverted into other channels; it has turned to the labour of consolidating the results already obtained. No pains have been spared by Dr. Lübke to bring this work up to the level of present knowledge; but complete success in the achievement of an undertaking of so gigantic a nature cannot be looked for at the hands of any one or any two men. The framework is perfect, the general design could not be bettered; it is admirably convenient and handy as to form, but the filling in of the details frequently leaves something to be desired. For example, the chapter on France, under the heading of *Die bildende Kunst in der zweiten Hälfte des 10 Jahrh.,* is very imperfect. Why select as the most important works of Jean Cousin as a sculptor, *einige portrait-figuren im Museum von Paris,* and leave unmentioned the tomb of Admiral Chabot, the noblest piece of French sculpture produced at that time, which long tradition, recently confirmed, gives to Cousin as his *chef d'œuvre?* And again, why, as regards the same artist, quote his painting of the Last Judgment in the Louvre, and omit the Entombment, a far finer work by his hand, in the Museum of Mainz? Such flaws as these can only be detected by careful testing of special points by special knowledge, and this serves to show that wide-spread co-operation on the plan adopted by Julius Meyer in his excellent Kunstler Lexikon, can alone ensure the attainment of perfection in the execution of works of so vast and comprehensive a nature.

The translator of a History of Sculpture[2] should be a person conversant not only with the language in which it is written, but with the subject of which it treats. A translation of such a book should be (if it is intended for the use of students) a new edition. When we find in the present volumes that the section on Ancient Art contains no mention of the sculptures from Priene; of the Diadumenos found at Vaison, and now in the British Museum; or of the sculptures recently unearthed at Ephesus, we cannot but regard the information it contains as very imperfect. But it is not only from this point of view that we are forced to look with dissatisfaction on the work before us. The pages not only abound with misprints, and with words which do not give the exact meaning of the original, and to which no milder term can be applied than that of mistranslations, but there exist whole sentences calculated to convey the most erroneous impressions. Here are a few instances quoted from a long list now lying before us. On

[1] "Handbuch der Kunstgeschichte." Von Franz Kugler. Fünfte Auflage. Stuttgart: Ebner und Seubert. 1872.

[2] "History of Sculpture," by Dr. Wilhelm Lübke. Translated by F. E. Bunnett. London: Smith, Elder & Co. 1872.

p. 141, l. 10, occurs the assertion that the citizens of Apollonia, in commemoration of a victory, dedicated a bronze group *to* Olympia; on p. 79, l. 1, we learn that works by Bupalus and Athenis *are* to be seen at Delos (we only wish they were!); on p. 81, l. 1, that a statue of Juno *is* at Delos; on p. 125, l. 7, that the atelier erected for Phidias by the Elians has been carefully preserved, and is shown to travellers, which is as if one were to say that Noah's ark can still be inspected on the top of Mount Ararat. This is really worse even than mistranslation, for it betrays want of education, coupled with an amount of headlong haste in translating which it is vexatious to see displaying itself in a work upon which the publisher has apparently spared no pains or expense.

This Catalogue of the Ivories in the South Kensington Museum[6] is admirably got up in every respect. The photographs are perfection, and the descriptions are just what they should be, which is rare merit, for there are very few who know exactly how to describe, who know exactly what points require special emphasis in order to aid the labours of identification and comparison. It may, however, be urged that a little more method in the preface, and a chronological arrangement of the catalogue, would have facilitated the use of the work for the purposes of study. We must also point out an erroneous statement which occurs in a foot-note on page lvii. of the preface. The writer, Mr. William Maskell, says, speaking of the Roman de la Rose, " It was written somewhere about the year 1300, by Guillaume de Lorris and Jean de Meung." Now this implies that the joint authors were cotemporaries, whereas de Lorris, who wrote the first 4500 lines, died in 1262, nearly ten years before De Meung (who continued the poem forty years after) was born. Then Mr. Maskell goes on to say, " It (the Roman de la Rose) was frequently moralized: in France by Clement Marot." The truth is, it was not " moralized " by Marot at all. In 1526 he revised the poem, substituting French of his day for words and expressions then already obsolete; but it was " moralized " in 1500 by Jean Moliuet, who has helped us to recollect the fact by the four doggerel lines with which he commences his performance :—

> "C'est le Roman de la Rose
> Moralisé, cler et net,
> Translaté de rime en prose
> Par vostre humble Molinet."

Sir Charles Bell's Anatomy of Expression[7] is one of those rare books which, though written upon a special subject, may be perused with pleasure by the general reader. The present issue is a reprint of the third edition, which was published after the death of the author. He had entirely recomposed the original work, and enriched the text with various notes and extracts from the journal which he had kept

[6] " A Description of the Ancient and Mediæval Ivories in the South Kensington Museum." Chapman and Hall. London: 1872.

[7] " The Anatomy and Philosophy of Expression." By Sir Charles Bell, K.H. (Sixth edition.) Bohn. London: 1872.

during his visit to Italy in 1840, whither he had gone expressly to
verify the assertions concerning the principles of criticism on art
which were contained in his essays. The interest of the later editions
is derived from these alterations, corrections, and additions, for in
point of beauty, both of letter-press and illustrations, none of them
can stand a comparison with the original published in 1800. The
copy now lying before us has been somewhat carelessly put together,
for at page 224 a blank of eight pages occurs, which is filled by the
repetition of pages 217 to 224.

The author of "Etruscan Inscriptions' Analysed and Translated,"
informs us in the brief preface which he has prefixed to his work, that
his object has been to show that the language employed in these inscriptions is an ancient form of German, in corroboration of an argument derived from independent sources, to prove that the Etruscans
were a branch of the Teutonic race. Lord Crawford adds that in a
work which he is about to issue on a much more important subject,
he has employed "the ancient German" as an instrument of etymological and mythological comparison and analysis in a manner which
can only be justified by adduction of proof that the language stands
upon a par in point of antiquity and importance with Greek and Latin,
Zendic and Sanskrit, and that its written or rather engraved monuments are centuries older than the Gospels of Ulphilas. It is greatly
to be regretted that so much labour and erudition should have been
bestowed by Lord Crawford on so untenable a theory, and it is addi-
tionally unfortunate that he should have selected the present moment
for publication, when at last the long puzzling riddle has been successfully solved. One of the most interesting of recent announcements in
the world of letters is, that the labours of Corssen have at last met
with their due reward, in the establishment of the fact that Etruscan
is to be read as a dialect of Latin.

The pilgrimage made round London by Mr. Blanchard Jerrold and
M. Gustave Doré has given us the most splendid gift-book of the
season.' A book in which the triumphantly popular characteristics
of M. Doré's facile pencil are conspicuously exhibited with every perfection of skilled engraving and printing, and in the full advantage of
luxurious broad-sheets of cream-tinted paper. Mr. Jerrold's accompanying text is sufficiently pleasant light reading, and is attractive
from the total absence of the moral or literary affectations which
usually beset writers on a theme like this. He describes the scenes
shifting before him, and almost invariably leaves them to point their
own moral. They stand clearly out before us in that objective reality
which is full of the deepest suggestiveness to those who choose to look
for it. The public are too familiar with the brilliant qualities of
M. Doré's work for them to need any note of distinction here. They
do not desert him in this new task. We find him always ready,

    ' "Etruscan Inscriptions, analysed, translated and commented on." By Alex-
ander, Earl of Crawford and Balcarres, Lord Lindsay, &c. Murray. London : 1872.
    ' "London." By Gustave Doré and Blanchard Jerrold. London : Grant and
Co. 1872.

always clear and intelligible, always seizing the most salient points of his subject with unerring swiftness, always arranging it with an eye trained and accustomed to watch for picturesque effect. In the docks, in the Parks, at the opera, at a penny gaff, all the intermediate shades between abject poverty and the pride of wealth find in M. Doré the same quick-witted, sharp, unsympathetic observer. He is one of the most successful of modern artists, and of the most successful he is perhaps one of the emptiest. He gives us sketches in which the commonest, the vulgarest external features are set down with an unsparing and vigorous hand. In this, if we are content with this, he is supreme, but if we look beyond these sharply-defined outlines we find a blank. It is rarely indeed that he handles any subject in such a way that we are tempted to ask him to give us more in it, so that we may dwell upon it longer; we are generally satisfied with a glance, with a minute's amusement and wonder. But in the present work M. Doré now and again (as, for instance, in the sleeping group which heads chap. xxi.) touches matter so full of pathos, that we are drawn instinctively to ponder it, and dwell long and inquisitively upon the lines which present it to us with such a semblance of fitting solemnity and grandeur. It is with a deep sense of dissatisfaction and disappointment that we turn away; our long scrutiny has yielded us nothing beyond the sharp-cut, unvarying, inexorable first impression.

The publishers of "The Picture Gallery" and "The Picture Gallery of Sacred Art"[1] are carrying out a very laudable enterprise. Both works are issued in monthly parts, each of which contains three photographs from the works of masters of reputation. The moderate price (one shilling a number) places the publication within the reach of persons of very moderate means. The selection appears to be made with care and judgment, and in the case of Sacred Art embraces the works of French, Italian, Spanish, English, and German artists, while the Picture Gallery illustrates English art during the past and present centuries. The photographs are, of course, not all equally good, some having been taken from engravings of average merit, whilst others are direct from the pictures or from excellent reproductions. We are glad to see that the Saint Cecilia and Saint Catharine of Domenichino have found a place in the Sacred Series.

The translation of M. Jules Verne's "Twenty Thousand Leagues under the Sea"[2] is written with much liveliness, and the illustrations are excellent in their way. Taking it as a whole it is perhaps one of the cleverest boys' books which have appeared of late years. The plot of the story will remind older readers of the means by which such strange fascination was imparted to About's "L'Homme à l'Oreille Cassé." In both works the whole force of real experience and carefully constructed scientific detail is brought to bear on the elaboration of an impossibility which is indeed only just impossible. By these

---

[1] "The Picture Gallery of Sacred Art." "The Picture Gallery." Sampson Low and Marston. London : 1872.

[2] "Twenty Thousand Leagues under the Sea." By Jules Verne. Sampson Low, Marston and Co. London : 1873.

means the author maintains an unrelaxing hold upon his reader's imagination, so that whilst he knows that the story is fiction he can hardly persuade himself that it is not fact. If he makes his escape from the charm, it is but for a moment; the author soon re-asserts his power, and holds us entranced with excitement and expectation as to the course which the ship Nautilus will take, and the adventures with which she will meet in her submarine voyage.

"The Pleasant History of Reynard the Fox"[10] is always welcome in any language. This English edition, from the translation of the late Mr. Thomas Roscoe, will be found a very useful book for children. It is of a convenient size and overflows with illustrations.

In "The Chatterbox" and "The Children's Prize"[11] we find ourselves at once on a lower level, but both these volumes seem to be modest, unassuming attempts to meet the demand for cheap popular children's books of an unobjectionable character.

Mr. Young's architectural studies and designs[12] contain many bits which are likely to be suggestive to intending builders with Gothic propensities. Here and there detached portions occur which are not only good from a constructive point of view, but promise to please the eye when they appear in all the uncompromising reality of stone and mortar. For the most part the details are heavy, and it cannot be too often impressed on the English architect that what is ponderous is not necessarily solid.

---

[10] "The Pleasant History of Reynard the Fox." Translated by the late Thomas Roscoe. Sampson Low, Marston and Co. London: 1873.

[11] "The Chatterbox." W. W. Gardner. London: 1872. "The Children's Prize." W. W. Gardner. London: 1872.

[12] "Picturesque Architectural Studies." By William Young, Architect. E. and F. N. Spon. London: 1872.

THE

WESTMINSTER

AND

FOREIGN QUARTERLY

REVIEW.

APRIL 1, 1873.

ART. I.—THE NATIONAL IMPORTANCE OF SCIENTIFIC RESEARCH.

NEARLY all great modern scientific discoveries have been made by teachers of science and others, who spent a large portion of their lives in experimental investigation, searching for new truths, and not by persons who have hit upon them by accident. The greatest discoveries in physics and chemistry in modern times were made chiefly by such men as Newton, Cavendish, Scheele, Priestley, Oersted, Volta, Davy, and Faraday; all great workers in science.

It is by observing matter and its forces under new conditions that many discoveries are made; thus Priestley placed some oxide of mercury in an inverted glass vessel, and heated it by means of a lens and the sun's rays, and discovered Oxygen. Oxygen was nearly discovered by Eck de Sulsbach three hundred years before; he heated six pounds of an amalgam of silver and mercury, and converted the latter metal into a red oxide like cinnabar, and he remarked, "a spirit is united with the metal, and what proves it is this, that this artificial cinnabar submitted to distillation, disengages that spirit." The "spirit" was evidently oxygen.

Some kinds of discoveries are made by observing the phenomena of bodies placed under special conditions by those operations of nature over which we have little or no control. All our knowledge of astronomy, and much of that of geology and physiology, was acquired in this way.

In nearly all modern discoveries of importance, in physics or chemistry, long and difficult investigations had to be made in order to completely establish their truth. When Crookes discovered Thallium, he saw the first sign of its existence as a momentary flash of green light in a spectroscope, but he had to expend upon the subject several years of most difficult labour, and a considerable sum of money, in order to prove the correctness of his suspicion that he had discovered a new metal.

Discoveries differ from inventions; a scientific discovery is a newly found truth in science, which in the great majority of cases is not in the form of a saleable commodity, but may be used for the purposes of ordinary scientific instruction. An invention is usually a combination and application to some useful or desired purpose of scientific truths which have been previously discovered.

Immediately a discovery is made it becomes published and incorporated in all the ordinary text-books of science; and in this way such books have become filled with valuable knowledge acquired by researches in past times, and this accumulated learning is ready for dissemination by teachers of science, and for inventors to apply to useful purposes. All this knowledge (which is of enormous value, and has cost a vast amount of intellect and labour) has been given freely to the nation without money and without price.

The most abstract and apparently trivial experiments in original research have in some cases led to inventions and results of national importance. The contractions of a frog's leg in the experiments of Galvani, and the movements of a magnetic needle in those of Oersted, have already led to the expenditure of many millions of pounds in laying telegraph wires over many parts of the earth, and to an immense extension of international intercourse. But the original experiment of Oersted was not discovered without labour; it was only arrived at after many years of research.

The discovery in olden times of the attractive properties of a fragment of iron-ore, was the basis of the invention of the mariner's-compass, which greatly improved navigation, and led to nearly all the chief maritime discoveries which have since been made. It enabled sailing vessels to venture freely out of sight of land, and to traverse the open ocean with even greater safety than to sail near the shore. By its means Columbus crossed the Atlantic Ocean and discovered America. By its means also, Vasco de Gama sailed round the Cape of Good Hope and discovered a new route to India; and in the year 1500, another Portuguese Captain, Cabral, was driven across the Atlantic, discovered Brazil, and was enabled by the aid of the magnet, to send back a ship to Lisbon with news of the discovery. By its assistance also, Magellan discovered Patagonia and the South Pacific Ocean ; and by the completion of that voyage the earth was first circumnavigated and proved to be a globe. With the aid of the same means, others discovered Australia and New Zealand, and ultimately completed the maritime geography of the whole world. By the same means, at the present time, every mariner directs with certainty the course of his ship, and innumerable cargoes of enormous aggregate value, are safely conveyed to all parts of the globe.

The geographical discoveries of the Portuguese, made by means of the magnet, produced great national results ; they profoundly changed the balance of power and wealth amongst the European nations, by changing the direction of navigation and of the great streams of commerce between Europe and the East. They gave a mortal blow to Italy and the cities of the Mediterranean, by transferring Eastern commerce to Spain and Portugal ; and Egypt ceased to be the greatest route of commerce from Europe to India.

The discovery of the properties of a mixture of nitre, sulphur, and charcoal, which occurred at about the same time as the invention of the mariner's-compass, led to the use of gunpowder, which changed the whole method of warfare, and made mere animal strength a less advantage in fighting.

Never were nations so rapidly enriched as those of Spain and Portugal by means of the magnet and gunpowder. Spain brought home immense quantities of gold and silver from Mexico ; Portugal imported diamonds from Brazil, and riches of all kinds from India and the East.

Scientific discovery has in all ages been a most powerful agent of civilization and human progress. The discovery of the black liquid which a solution of nut-galls produces when mixed with green-vitriol, led to the invention of writing-ink ; and a knowledge of the properties of ink and paper prepared the way for the invention of printing, by means of which learning has been spread all over the earth.

The apparently insignificant property possessed by amber, of attracting feathers immediately after it has been rubbed, was known twenty-four hundred years ago, and led in modern times to the discovery of electricity. In still later times, Dr. Franklin, by means of a kite, charged a bottle with lightning, examined it, and proved lightning and electricity to be identical. This knowledge, joined to the further discovery, that electricity would pass freely through metals, led to the invention of the lightning conductor, by means of which all our great buildings, ships, lighthouses, arsenals, and powder magazines are effectually protected from lightning.

"Coming events cast their shadows before:" the discovery of the instant transmission of electricity along wires foreshadowed the invention of the electric telegraph. About the year 1815, Oersted, a Danish philosopher, after fifteen years of study and experiment, to ascertain the relation of electricity to magnetism, discovered that if a freely suspended magnetic needle was supported parallel to a wire, and an electric current then passed through the wire, the needle moved and placed itself at right-angles to the current. This discovery, coupled with the previous one of the electric conductivity of metals, formed the indispensable foundation of all our present electric telegraphs.

Original research is more productive of new industries and inventions than any other kind of labour. The researches of Volta, Faraday, and many other investigators, have led to the process of electro-plating, the use of electric lights for lighthouses, and the great system of telegraphs. Those of Davy, Wedgwood, and others, respecting the action of light upon salts of silver, have led to the modern processes of photography, which are now in use almost everywhere. The discovery of zinc by Paracelsus, has been followed by the use of that metal in galvanic batteries, and the great use of "galvanized" iron for telegraph wires, for roofing, and many other purposes. The discovery of nickel by Cronstedt has led to the great modern use of German-silver in the construction of electro-plated and other articles. The discovery of chlorine by Scheele formed the basis of nearly all our modern processes of bleaching cotton and other fabrics. The discovery of gun-cotton and nitro-glycerine has led to the use of those substances in blasting rocks and in warfare. The discovery of oxygen by Priestley, has enabled us to understand and improve in a great number of ways, the numerous manufacturing, agricultural, and other processes in which that substance operates. The discoveries of gutta-percha and India-rubber were the origin of the great use of those substances in telegraph cables, and in a multitude of useful articles. The discovery of chloroform and anæsthetics, has led to their use for the purpose of alleviating human suffering. The discovery of phosphorus led to the erection of the large manufactories of that substance and of lucifer-matches, and to the use of those matches all over the earth. The discovery by Sir Isaac Newton of the decomposition of light by means of a prism, has led in recent times to the invention of the spectroscope; to the use of that instrument in the Bessemer-steel process; to the discovery of four new metals, thallium, rubidium, cæsium, and indium, and to the most wonderful discovery of the composition of the sun and distant heavenly bodies.

Even the invention of the steam-engine was partly a consequence of previous researches of scientific men. Watt himself stated in his pamphlet entitled "A Plain Story," that he could not have perfected his engine, had not Dr. Black and others previously discovered what amount of heat was rendered latent by the conversion of water into steam. Had not the steam-engine been developed, it is clear that railways, steam-ships, and all the numerous uses to which that noble instrument is now applied, would have been comparatively unknown. The discoveries of nitric-acid, hydrochloric-acid, oil of vitriol, and washing-soda, by the alchemists and early chemists in their researches, led to the erection of the numerous great manufactories of those substances which now exist in England and in other civilized countries. There is probably not an art, process, or manufacture, which is not largely due to scientific discovery, and if we trace them back to their source, we nearly always find them originate in scientific research.

Discovery is usually the basis of invention; a man cannot generally invent an improvement unless he possesses scientific knowledge, and for that knowledge he must in nearly all cases resort to a scientific book or teacher. Nearly all the pure scientific knowledge contained in books was obtained by original research, and the great bulk of valuable patented inventions was made with the aid of that information. The discovery of a single substance, such as oil of vitriol, or washing-soda, has led to the formation of many valuable inventions, patented or otherwise, and to the establishment of more than one hundred manufactories.

Judging by means of the experience already acquired, we cannot reasonably expect that discoveries fraught with such momentous consequences as those of magnetism, or of galvanism and electro-magnetism, will be made very often. The progress of scientific discovery is gradual; we have at present but glimpses of the new world of truth which is being revealed to us by means of research; we are only at the very commencement of a knowledge of the inherent properties of matter and its forces, and consequently the methods we employ to utilize them are extremely imperfect. Discoveries probably remain to be made which will enable us to convert the various forces into each other without division or loss; at present we can scarcely do so in any instance. By the steam-engine, that marvellous result of modern intellect, we only obtain available for our uses about one-eighth of the mechanical power producible by coal. Matter has a general property of subdividing forces; if we put one force into a substance or machine, it produces many effects, not only those we want, but those also we do not want: when we heat a piece of iron, the heat produces a number of changes, mechanical, electric, magnetic, and chemical, and it is by means of what is termed the "internal resistance" of bodies that these effects are produced, and we know but little of that property. The explosive action in a gas-engine produces not only the mechanical force we desire, but also a quantity of heat we do not want, and at a cost of a portion of the gas. In a similar manner, in the steam-engine much of the heat of the coal is converted into forces which are lost; a large amount of it is uselessly expended in warming the machine itself and the surrounding atmosphere; much also is lost by friction. Discoveries probably also remain to be made which will enable us to completely utilize solar heat and tidal energy. The total amount of solar heat which falls upon this earth in twenty-four hours, would, if converted into mechanical power, be equal to that of an immense number of horses; the average of that which falls annually upon a square foot of terrestrial surface would lift fifty-two tons weight one mile high. The total mechanical value of the tidal energy of all the water on this globe is also an amazing amount.

That "knowledge is power" is an old maxim, but that *new knowledge is new power* is a new maxim which scientific discovery has impressed upon us. By means of discoveries we have acquired new powers; by those of Electricity we have acquired the power of conversing with each other at unlimited distances, and by means of those in Optics we are enabled to analyze the composition, and perceive some of the physical changes of the most distant heavenly bodies.

Experience in science has shown that it is by means of inventions based upon *new* discoveries that the greatest utilities are obtained, rather than by the exercise of invention upon knowledge acquired long ago. The knowledge obtained by research in ancient times has been largely exhausted for the purposes of invention by modern inventors, and what we very greatly require now is *new* knowledge. Experience in science also leads us to believe that the extent of possible discovery is as boundless as Nature, and that an immense amount of new knowledge may yet be discovered. Every discoverer of repute could supply a copious list of investigations yet to be made.

A very great amount of the wealth of this nation has been obtained by the application of scientific knowledge to the substances and forces by which we are surrounded. Who can estimate the money-value of the application of such knowledge to coal, by enabling it to produce mechanical power in the steam-engine and gas-engine; to evolve light by means of coal-gas; to yield the beautiful aniline dyes; and to be used as a source of ammonia ?

Nearly every manufacturer in this country is deriving from scientific discoveries advantages for which there has been made little or no payment to the discoverers. The makers of coal-tar-dyes and the dyers of wool and silk are using Mitscherlich's discovery of nitro-benzine. Manufacturers of picric acid and "French purple" have enjoyed the fruits of the labours of Dr. Stenhouse. Makers of chlorate of potash are profiting largely by the discoveries of Scheele, Gay-Lussac, and others. The various telegraph companies, copper-smelters, and makers of copper telegraph wire, are using Dr. Matthiessen's discovery of the influence of impurities on the electric conducting power of copper. Phosphorus-makers are reaping the reward of the labours of Gahn and Scheele. The makers of electro-plate and of German-silver are deriving great profits from the labours of Faraday and Gay-Lussac. Makers of Bessemer-steel enjoy advantages derived from the spectrum discoveries of Kirchhoff. Iron and copper-smelters, metallurgists, dyers, calico-printers, bleachers, brewers, makers of vinegar, white-lead, red-lead, varnishes, colours, soaps, green-vitriol, phosphorus, oil of vitriol, and many others, are deriving benefit from the discoveries of Priestley and Scheele. Physicians also are receiving the reward of the labours of Soubeiran, Liebig, and Dumas, in the discovery of chloroform; of the researches of Fourcroy, Vauquelin, Pelletier, and others, in the discovery of quinine; and of many other chemists, in the discovery of numerous remedial substances.

The great pecuniary benefits arising from the applications of science are generally reaped in the first instance by the great manufacturers, agriculturists, merchants, and capitalists. Countless fortunes have been made by means of processes and manufactures based upon scientific discovery. The pecuniary profits of the great manufacturers of cotton, copper, iron, pottery, beer, sugar, glass, spirits, vinegar, gutta-percha, india-rubber, gun-cotton, the various metals, machinery, electro-plate, washing soda, German silver, brass, phosphorus, manures, the common acids, the various chemicals, and a multitude of other substances and articles, have been extremely great. The pecuniary advantages of the use of the electric telegraph and railways to merchants;—the gains of capitalists by money invested in railways, telegraphs, steam-ships, gasworks, iron shipbuilding, engineering, and other great applications of science, have been enormous. The money expended upon the construction of railways alone in this country has already amounted to more than five hundred and fifty millions of pounds, and the total receipts upon British railways has reached forty-three millions per annum.

In a general way, the greatest pecuniary benefits arising from science, sooner or later go to enrich the possessors of land. The demand created for coal, iron, lime, building-stone, and all the metals, by the industrial applications of science, has greatly increased the value of land under which those substances lie. The value of cultivated land has been everywhere increased by the discoveries of agricultural chemistry. Land has also been required for railways in nearly all parts of the kingdom, and has thereby been considerably raised in value. Discoveries produce inventions, inventions give rise to processes and manufactures, the employment of workmen and others, and the erection of workshops and dwellings, and these have rapidly increased the value of building ground. In Lancashire the value of such ground has been greatly increased by the invention of the steam-engine, the discovery of chlorine, and their application to the cotton manufacture. In all the great manufacturing districts, and in all the chief centres of industry, a similar result has occurred. Wherever a railway has been constructed in Great Britain, the value of land has increased in consequence of the increased facilities of communication. All these great additions to the value of land are largely due to the unpaid labours of scientific discoverers, and it may be said that this nation has largely gained its wealth, and is still living in a great degree on the products of those labours. Those great additions to the value of land are also permanent, are continually increasing, and are largely independent of any exertion on the part of the owners.

There is not a man in this kingdom who has not derived some advantage, in one way or another, from scientific research. The advantages of gas light, rapid postal service and transmission of goods, railway travelling, cotton apparel, photography, cheap pottery, improved medicine and surgery, Australian preserved meats, &c. &c., have been reaped more or less by everyone, even the very paupers. Science has also, by developing new processes, given employment to whole armies of workmen in numerous arts, manufactures, and occupations. About a quarter of a million persons are employed on the railways alone in Great Britain, besides those who were engaged in their construction; and in the postal-department alone of the telegraph service of this country more than fifteen thousand operatives are employed. Chemical works also find employment for twenty-six thousand, and gasworks for ten thousand work people.

It would be altogether a false argument to say that the practical benefits derived from the labours of discoverers by the different classes of the community are small or imaginary, because the discoveries and the benefits are not immediately connected. We know that the consumers of tea in this country derive benefit from the grower of that herb in China through the hands of a series of intervening agents, as certainly as if they received the tea direct from his hands.

Much of the wealth of this country, resulting from science, has been very easily obtained by its possessors. That acquired by means of our coal has especially been obtained without commensurate effort. To draw upon a mine of coal is much like drawing upon a bank of money, because coal is a great store of power; it differs from nearly all other abundant substances by containing an immense amount of latent chemical energy, which may at any moment, and with scarcely any expenditure of labour on our part, be converted into heat and mechanical power in the steam-engine. Every piece of coal contains sufficient latent power to lift itself a height of more than two thousand miles, but it costs only a small proportion of that power to extract and raise it from the mine. We do not mean by these remarks to imply that the wealth accruing from this great store of power in coal, is derived chiefly by the owners of coal mines.

An excess of money or power, obtained without commensurate effort, fails to properly develop the intelligence of its possessor, and nations have been hastened to ruin in this way. The wealth of the upper classes of this nation has, by decoying from study undisciplined young men at our old Universities, kept down the general standard of scientific instruction throughout the country, and by leading to neglect of scientific research, is now retarding our progress in arts, manufactures, commerce, and civilization. The great poverty of the working classes is also producing similar effects by retarding education, and increasing the great want of skilled labour of which our inventors, manufacturers, and others so strongly complain in the working of their scientific processes. Had a just share of the great amount of money gained by the applications of science to useful purposes, been applied to the payment and maintenance of scientific discoverers, as it should have been, the wealthy would have been more intelligent, the poor would have had more employment and money, and the happiness and civilization of all would have been greater.

Of the great multitude of rich manufacturers, merchants, capitalists, and landowners in this country, who have derived such great pecuniary benefits from original scientific research, we believe there is scarcely a man existing who has ever given to a scientific society, institution, or investigator, a single thousand pounds for the aid of pure research in experimental physics or chemistry; the nearest approach to exceptions are a very few wealthy persons who have devoted themselves personally to scientific discovery. Many of those manufacturers and others would however willingly give money towards such an object, if they understood the value and necessity of scientific research.

Whilst many millions of pounds are annually expended in

this country upon religious, philanthropic, and other good objects, there is scarcely a scientific society or institution (with the exception of the British Association), which expends even the small sum of five hundred pounds a year on pure experimental research in physics or chemistry. In the Royal Institution of Great Britain, the average annual expenses relating to experimental research, including salaries to assistants in the laboratory, from the year 1867 to 1871, did not amount to two hundred and fifty pounds.

Considering the multiplicity and variety of philanthropic institutions and bequests in this country, and the great effect original scientific research has in ameliorating the condition of mankind, and reducing the amount of human misery, it is surprising that no wealthy philanthropic individual has bequeathed funds for the endowment of an institution for pure research in physics or chemistry. In America, the "Smithsonian Institution" was founded at Washington by a benevolent and patriotic person, " for the increase and diffusion of knowledge among men," and one of the objects of that institution is " to enlarge the existing stock of knowledge by the addition of new truths;" and a portion of its plan is "to stimulate men of talent to make original researches, by offering suitable rewards for memoirs containing new truths," and " to appropriate annually a portion of the income for particular researches."

Many persons in this country look upon scientific research, either as a hobby, or as a refined intellectual pursuit, and do not view it as an important or essential element of National greatness and progress. Persons in general in this country also consider such research as unpractical, but this is simply in consequence of their ignorance of the subject; if discoveries were commercial commodities, the practical character of research would then be within their comprehension. Scientific discoverers may be considered the most practical men in existence, because their labours give rise to greater and more numerous practical results than those of any other persons. A man who cultivates plants for the purpose of obtaining the seed, is quite as practical a person as he who converts that seed into vegetables fit for human consumption.

In addition to the great benefits accruing from original research to all classes of society, our Governments have also derived immense advantages from the same source. The revenues have been greatly increased by the universal advantages conferred upon all kinds of industry and commerce by scientific knowledge. The additional taxes upon increased incomes arising from agriculture, arts, manufactures, mines; increased value of land and rents; investments in railway, telegraph, steam-ship, and other companies, have been extremely great. From the sale of Patents alone, a surplus sum of nearly six hundred thousand pounds has already accumulated. Our Governments are also indebted to original research for the use of percussion-powder, gun-cotton, improvements in cannon, projectiles, rifles, armour-plated ships, the ocean telegraph, field telegraph, rapid postal communication, the speedy transport of troops and war material, and a multitude of other advantages. The value of science to Governments in the prevention of war by means of more ready correspondence through telegraphs is incalculable.

As the knowledge resulting from scientific inquiry has been of such immense value to this nation, one would suppose that such inquiry would be greatly encouraged and highly rewarded. The reverse is, however, the case ; research in physics and chemistry has for years been declining in this country, chiefly in conse-quence of the neglect with which it has been treated. Most of our ablest investigators in those subjects have ceased to make researches. Several also, Faraday, Graham, Matthiessen, and Miller, have died, and others have not arisen to supply their places. Able discoverers are rare, and the loss of even a few such men in a country is a national calamity. At the present time the proportion of such men amongst us wholly engaged in research is less than one in a million of the population.

Whilst the number of original researches in physical and chemical science has been increasing on the Continent, especially in Germany, it has been decreasing in England. The Journal of the Chemical Society, which was formerly filled with original researches made by British chemists, is now almost entirely occupied with the abstracts only of researches made elsewhere, and we are rapidly becoming dependent upon foreign nations for a supply of new scientific knowledge. According to a statement of Dr. E. Frankland, the number of published scientific researches in the year 1866 was in Germany 777, France 245, and Great Britain 127.

It is more difficult to carry on original research in England now than it was twenty years ago, because scientific employments of a much more lucrative kind have greatly multiplied, and attract men of science from pursuing discovery ; the means also for prosecuting research have not increased, whilst the expenses of living have become much greater ; nearly all other useful oc-cupations have advanced and left scientific inquiry behind.

Whilst vast sums of money are spent upon the applications of science in military and naval affairs, research itself is neglected : the superstructure is attended to, but the foundations are left to decay. Our Governments have as yet made no payment for the labour of pure research in experimental physics or chemistry ;

they have given a thousand pounds a year to be distributed by
the Royal Society amongst scientific investigators, but a grant
from this sum is an unprofitable gift to accept, because it is only
sufficient to partly pay expenses out of pocket for chemicals and
apparatus, and allows nothing for skill or labour. Investigators
frequently, for this reason, do not avail themselves of the fund.

So defective are the arrangements of our Governments
with regard to science, that gentlemen comparatively ignorant
of it are appointed to decide the various scientific questions of
national importance that arise, and to direct scientific men in
their own special departments. Quite recently (May 1872), a
memorial, signed by the eminent investigator, Sir William
Thomson, was sent by the British Association to the Lords of
the Treasury, applying for 150l. to continue researches on the
tides ; but notwithstanding that we spend immense sums of money
on ships, and a knowledge of the tides is essential to the safety of
those costly vessels, the small sum asked for so important a purpose
was refused. Not one of the gentlemen appointed to consider
this application is known as an authority in scientific research.
Another recent instance, that of the First Commissioner of
Works, and the eminent botanist, Dr. Hooker, is so well known
that we abstain from describing it. The teachers of science also
in nearly all our Grammar-schools, are subject to the direction of
unscientific head-masters, who are appointed in accordance with
the recommendations of Government Commissioners, with power
to choose the scientific books and control the method of teaching science in those schools.

Want of recognition of the value of science has been so general
in this country, that it is quite pleasing to quote a somewhat
different case from *The Illustrated London News*, January 4,
1873—viz., that of Archibald Smith, LL.D., F.R.S., who recently
died. That gentleman was an investigator in pure mathematical
science, and devoted the latter part of his life to the application
of his mathematics in the computation, reduction, and discussion
of the deviation of the mariner's-compass in wooden and iron
ships, and made practical deductions therefrom in the construction of those vessels.

He published those practical applications of his scientific knowledge in the form of an Admiralty Manual, which was afterwards
republished in various languages. Her Majesty's Government,
not long ago, "requested his acceptance of a gift of two thousand
pounds, not as a reward, but as a mark of appreciation of the
value of his researches, and of the influence they were exercising
on the maritime interests of England and of the world at
large."

The case of Dr. J. Stenhouse, F.R.S., is one of rather an

opposite kind. That gentleman devoted his life throughout to pure investigations in organic chemistry, and published several of his researches in the Philosophical Transactions of the Royal Society. His discoveries are very numerous, and although not much applied to practical uses by himself, the results of his researches on Lichens, and on the yellow gum of Botany Bay, have been applied extensively by others in the manufacture of "French-purple" and picric acid, and will doubtless continue to be applied to valuable uses by other persons. He held the Government appointment of Assayer to the Royal Mint, London, an office for several years unprofitable to him, but of rapidly increasing remunerative value, and which would now have been worth 1200*l*. a year; but after the decease of his colleague Dr. Miller in 1870, that office, which was then worth to him about 600*l*. a year, was abolished by the Chancellor of the Exchequer, and he lost the appointment, receiving, however, 500*l.* as compensation. An application was therefore made to the Government, and a partial recompense to him was obtained, by her Majesty granting him one hundred pounds a year " for eminence in chemical attainments, and on account of loss by suppression of office in the Mint."

The only difference in these two instances was, that in the second there was a very much greater amount of pure research and discovery, and a much smaller degree of applied knowledge.*

These instances also illustrate the statement, that however great an amount of valuable knowledge in pure science a man may discover and publish, or however freely he may provide others with the materials of invention and wealth, if he never invents anything, nor applies his knowledge to useful purposes, he is usually less rewarded even than an inventor.

In harmony with these instances, we find that it is not the pure sciences, but the concrete and the applied ones, such as meteorology, geology, natural history, &c., in the Meteorological Department, the Geological Survey, the British and South Kensington Museums, the Geological Museum, &c., which have received the greatest degree of support from our Governments.

It is believed to be a duty of the state to provide and pay for pure scientific research for the following reasons :— because the results of such labour are indispensable to national welfare and progress ; because the results are of immense value to the nation, and especially to the Government ; because nearly the whole pecuniary benefit of it goes to the nation, and scarcely any to the discoverer ; because research cannot be efficiently

* See "Royal Society Catalogue of Scientific Papers," vol. v. pp. 717 and 819.

provided for by means of voluntary effort; and because there appears to be scarcely any other way (except by application of University revenues) in which discoverers can be satisfactorily paid for their labour.

There are also many experiments, investigations, and explorations bearing upon scientific discovery, which neither private individuals, nor even corporate bodies, such as the Royal Society, the British Association, or Geographical Society, can effectually make, and which only a Government can carry out, such as Arctic expeditions, trigonometrical surveys, deep-sea dredging operations, magnetic observations, determinations of longitude, meteorological and astronomical observations, researches on tides, observations of earthquakes, determinations of the height of mountains and of the density of the crust of the earth, experiments on the best form of ships, geographical explorations, and many others.

It is clear from the enormous advantages which this nation has already derived from scientific discovery in physics and chemistry, pursued with only the aid of the very limited means of private persons, that had research in those subjects been sufficiently supported, the manufactures, arts, commerce, wealth, and civilization of this country would have been much greater than they are; emigration also of the industrious classes, pauperism and crime, would have been much less. The amount of knowledge and riches obtainable by means of research and invention, is practically unlimited, and it is astonishing that this immense source of industry and wealth in a nation should have been so neglected by our Governments, and permitted to decline; but the most probable explanation is, that our rulers have been ignorant of its great value, and of their duty to utilize it. The practical value of new scientific knowledge is infinitely greater than that of our coal supply, because it would not only enable us to obtain from coal several times the amount of available heat and mechanical power we now secure, but also to apply to our wants the numerous other materials composing the crust of this globe and the contents of our oceans; also all terrestrial forces, the internal heat, the tidal energy and atmospheric currents, and the immense amount of power this earth is continually receiving from the sun.

It is reasonable to suppose that Universities should be fountains of new theoretical scientific knowledge, as well as be the disseminators of it, and that they (especially the old ones with their rich endowments) would be certain to promote scientific research, as being especially a part of their functions; but such is not the case. Our Universities have not established any professorships of original research; they make no payment for such labour, nor reimburse any expenditure incurred in such occupation, and afford but little facility for the prosecution of pure scientific inquiry. Further, they discourage scientific discovery by giving the greatest emoluments, and the highest honours in science they have to bestow, to young men who have never made a single original research, or discovered a single new fact in science. The money paid in the form of comparatively sinecure fellowships, or retiring pensions to young men in Oxford alone, "now amounts to about eighty or ninety thousand pounds a-year." It may be objected, that young men are not capable of doing original research, but as they do it in German Universities, they can also do it in England if they are properly disciplined, and are not decoyed from industry by the possession or expectation of wealth. A man who has never made a scientific research is not the most worthy recipient of the highest scientific honour, and in Germany it would not be given to him ; he is not properly disciplined in the detection of error or the discernment of truth in matters of science ; he is deficient in accuracy of scientific judgment, and in the true spirit of scientific inquiry.

As the subject of this paper is scientific *research*, it is unnecessary to speak of what has been done during the last few years at our old Universities and great public schools, in the erection of laboratories, and in other ways for the promotion of science, as it has been for the purposes of instruction, and not of original research. No amount of ordinary instruction in science will remedy the evils caused by want of original inquiry, because such instruction does not produce new knowledge, but only disseminates that already possessed.

That discoverers are not treated by us as we treat other valuable members of the community is quite clear; either a physician, a judge, divine, lawyer, or railway superintendent of high ability, obtains from one to many thousand pounds a-year, but a discoverer in pure physics or chemistry is, in scarcely any case, paid anything for his labour. The discoverer, Faraday, received for his scientific lectures only 200*l*. a-year and apartments, during many years, and absolutely nothing for his great discoveries; and during the remainder of his life he only received a few hundred pounds per annum, including a pension of 300*l*. a-year from Government. A general of our army receives 2000*l*. and a Field Marshal, 4400*l*. a-year (see "Whitaker's Almanack," 1873, pp. 121 and 138). A head master of either of the great public schools obtains from 3000*l*. a-year upwards. An Archbishop of Canterbury receives 15,000*l*. a-year, besides a great amount of influence and power in the form of patronage to 189 livings, a palatial residence, and a seat in the House of Peers. A Bishop of London has

10,000*l.*, the patronage of 98 livings, a palace, and a seat in the House of Lords. (See the "Clergy List," also "Whitaker's Almanack," 1873, p. 155, and "Walford's County Families," 1872, pp. 173 and 610.) We leave our readers to judge to what extent these instances illustrate the statement that discoverers are not treated by us as we treat other valuable members of the community.

It is well known that had Faraday chosen, he might certainly have made a large income as a consulting chemist and scientific advocate, but the love of truth for truth's sake alone was strong in him, and he spontaneously abandoned that course in order to pursue the more important national employment of pure research. It was a statement of his, "I cannot afford to become rich." Discoverers are generally poor, because they are not paid for their labour ; and a man cannot usually pursue with success, pure scientific research and money, because such research occupies a very great amount of time.

It is scarcely credible that in a wealthy and civilized country, whilst the non-productive classes are most properly protected in the enjoyment of titles and material wealth which they have not earned, the greatest scientific discoverers and benefactors of the nation are constrained to live in a state of comparative poverty whilst working for the pecuniary and other advantages of those classes, and of manufacturers, capitalists, landowners, and the nation in general. By these remarks it is not intended to imply that discoverers are intentionally neglected ; but that the circumstances are a disgrace to the nation, and do not reflect any credit upon the governing classes, or especially upon those who reap the greatest advantage.

The men who are rewarded the most highly in this country are not always those who yield the greatest services to the nation, but frequently those who render the most immediate or most apparent benefit ; such short-sighted policy as this cannot produce the greatest degree of success. The national services of a great discoverer are immense, and probably not equalled by those of any man. Who can estimate the value of the commercial, social, moral, political, and other great advantages to the world, of the discovery of the principle of electro-magnetism, which enabled the invention of the electric telegraph to be made ? The men we pay the highest are not those who discover knowledge, but those who use or apply it ; physicians, judges, bishops, lawyers, railway-managers, military and naval officers, and head masters of schools, are all gentlemen who render great services to the nation, by using, diffusing, and applying knowledge already possessed.

Why do scientific investigators in general pursue difficult

researches if there is no payment for such labour?—First, from a spirit of inquiry; and second, to obtain high repute in their profession as teachers, &c. No scientific man who entertains a strong sense of the dignity of science, and who in his occupation as a teacher or otherwise, continually perceives the incompleteness of our knowledge of the properties of matter, would willingly spare any amount of labour in order to make that knowledge more complete, especially as he knows that scientific discoveries are of great value to mankind. If such men had not made discoveries, we should have been without even the conveniences of life, and in a state of comparative barbarism. It need hardly be said that it requires great self-sacrifice on the part of comparatively poor persons, to make difficult, expensive, and often dangerous investigations, without receiving any payment.

It might be supposed that investigators would patent and sell their discoveries; but discoveries in pure science cannot usually be patented or sold, because they have not been converted by invention into commercial commodities. It would also be less to public advantage if investigators were to neglect the more important occupation of discovering new knowledge in order to apply that knowledge to practical uses. It requires a higher quality of mental power to discover new truths, than to utilize them by means of invention; and men who can invent are far more numerous than those who are able to discover. A discoverer creates new knowledge, but an inventor only applies it. Discoveries are also generally much more valuable than inventions, because a single discovery (that of gutta-percha for example), not unfrequently forms the basis of many inventions.

Some persons have suggested that scientific men should keep their discoveries secret, but this would generally be a greater disadvantage to the investigator even than publishing them, and the nation would not then derive the benefit:—discoveries also being often capable of numerous applications, and not being in a saleable shape, cannot usually be monopolized by any one. Discovery is eminently national work, and discoveries are national property. New scientific knowledge is like a powerful light; it cannot be hidden.

Other persons suppose that investigators should be satisfied with the fame of their discoveries, and not require any payment; but this is a most unfair supposition, because no man can live without means, and every useful person deserves to be paid for his labour. Ought the late Duke of Wellington to have been satisfied with the fame alone of his exploits, without being paid any salary? Ought a Bishop to be content with the renown of his eloquence, without receiving any payment for his services?

It has been suggested that an investigator, if he is a man of practical ability, is very often put into an office, the duties of which he can efficiently discharge, and yet have leisure for original research—as in the case of the late Dr. Graham, the eminent Master of the Mint,* our Astronomers Royal, &c.—and thus obtain his reward. But this is a very imperfect plan, because research is very difficult, and to be carried out fully requires the whole of a man's time and attention; the investigator would also be taken from more important work to do that which is of less value to the nation, and which might be performed by a more suitable person; appointments also of the kind referred to are much too few in number. Such a plan as this, of relegating important national work to odd hours spared from official duties, is a makeshift, and quite unworthy of this nation.

Probably the most satisfactory way of rewarding scientific discoverers and serving national interests at the same time, would be to create salaried professorships of original research, and appoint discoverers of repute to fill them.

The great difficulty of determining from what source discoverers should be paid for their labours, arises from the fact that all classes of the community share in the benefit. It is evident they should be paid from a source towards which all classes either directly or indirectly contribute, and therefore from some national fund. The persons who first use new scientific knowledge are the compilers of scientific books, and teachers of science; but these only disseminate the knowledge, and do not derive from it any great pecuniary advantage—they are only the agents for supplying the knowledge to others. The persons who first convert such knowledge into valuable commercial commodities are inventors, and manufacturers who have received scientific education or advice; but those who derive the greatest pecuniary benefit from it, and who should therefore either directly or indirectly pay in the largest degree for it, are the great manufacturers, capitalists, and landowners. Whilst the question as to what class of persons shall primarily bear the expense of research is being settled, discoverers themselves are suffering great injustice, research is declining, and our manufactures and commerce are passing into the hands of foreign nations.

What the amount of loss and disadvantage suffered by this nation, through want of encouragement of scientific inquiry is, cannot be estimated, but it is certainly enormous. Had even a very moderate amount of payment been made for such labours, and the expenses out of pocket paid in full, the amount of research performed would have been greatly increased. Under

* The Mastership of the Mint is no longer given to scientific men.

present circumstances, many promising young men, fitted to become good investigators, have been driven out of science altogether. Even amongst our most able discoverers, scarcely one who has not possessed private means has continued research beyond the middle age of life, because such labour enables no provision to be made for old age; and all those who have left have devoted themselves to less important but more lucrative occupations—some to lecturing or teaching, others to compiling scientific books, some to practise as scientific advocates or consulting chemists; some to work out inventions, some to become scientific Commissioners or inspectors of chemical works, others to become manufacturers, patent-agents, managers of works, &c. Most of these gentlemen have been obliged to abandon research at a period of life when their faculties were in the most perfect state for continuing it.

Meanwhile our manufacturers and others in all directions are asking for improvements in their machines and processes; employers of steam-engines want to obtain more power from the coals; makers of washing-soda wish to recover their lost sulphur; copper-smelters want to utilize the "copper-smoke;" glass makers wish to prevent bad colour in their glass; iron-puddlers want to economize heat; gas companies are desirous of diminishing the leakage of gas; iron-smelters wish to avoid the evil effects of impurities in the iron; manufacturers in general want to utilize their waste products, and prevent their polluting the streams and atmosphere; and so on without end. And inventors are continually trying to supply these demands, by exercising their skill in every possible way, with the aid of the scientific information contained in books; but after putting manufacturers and themselves to great expense, they very frequently fail, not through want of skill, but through want of new knowledge, attainable only by means of pure research. Judging from the vast amount of inventive skill already expended upon the steam-engine, and the small proportion of available mechanical power yet obtained from the coals consumed in it, it is highly probable that a machine for completely converting heat into mechanical force cannot be invented until more scientific knowledge is discovered.

The progress of invention depends upon that of discovery, and these various inventions wanted by manufacturers and others, cannot be perfected until suitable knowledge is found. Every invention has its own appropriate discoveries, by means of which alone can it be perfected; it was not possible to perfect the idea of an electric telegraph before the discoveries of Volta and Oersted were made. An unlimited number of inventions cannot be made by means of a limited amount of scientific knowledge;.

and our present stock of such information applicable to invention, is very insufficient.

In consequence of this want of new knowledge, manufacturers continue to suffer losses which might be avoided; the high prices of useful articles are maintained; defects in their quality are not improved; preventable accidents continue to happen; the health of workmen continues to suffer; many means of curing diseases remain unknown; medical practice remains full of empiricism, &c. &c. The great sewage question is apparently in this predicament; we are probably trying to solve it without first discovering the requisite knowledge; inventors, engineers, and consulting chemists, have racked their brains and have not been able to devise a satisfactory remedy, and the health of the entire population of this country is suffering. If we so neglect the means of ameliorating our condition we deserve to suffer. One would suppose that cholera, contagious diseases, colliery accidents, pollution of air and water, enormous waste of heat from fires, and a multitude of other evils which depend upon physical and chemical conditions, are of but little importance, that we should so neglect one of the most effectual means of preventing them; and it is perfectly clear that by neglecting to aid research, those who gain so much money and advantage 'from science, are sacrificing national interests (and their own) on an immense scale to personal aggrandizement.

It must not be supposed from these remarks, that discoveries which will enable a man to make any particular invention, can be produced to order; that is only true to a very limited extent. Men are beggars of nature, and must not expect to be permitted to choose her gifts, or dictate what secrets shall be disclosed. We may however be certain that if we acquire a very much greater supply of new scientific knowledge, we shall then be able to perfect many good inventions, though not exactly of the kind we wish, or in the way we expect. The great sewage question may perhaps be solved in quite an unexpected way, possibly by the discovery of some substance capable of precipitating ammonia and organic matter from their solutions.

What is the reason that scientific research is not encouraged in England? It is chiefly ignorance. There is not a good and important subject, understood by the public, which is not in this country greatly assisted, nor a valuable public servant, whose labours are understood, who does not receive liberal payment and reward; and scientific research and discoverers therefore are neglected, not wilfully, nor because persons are unwilling to encourage good objects, but because scientific discovery and its great value to the nation are so little known. Scarcely a member of our legislature, or of our Universities, is fully acquainted with the national importance of scientific discovery, and it would probably be impossible to find a subject of such great magnitude so little understood. Comparatively few persons have clear ideas of the essential differences between scientific instruction, research, and invention.

Scientific research can only be successfully pursued by employing the highest motive—viz., a love of truth in preference to all things; and this is a condition which very few persons really understand, and a principle which a still smaller number practise. Men in this country are so accustomed to be actuated by the less noble motive of immediate self-interest or of some apparent practical result, that they cannot perceive that in scientific research the most valuable results can only be obtained by employing the highest motive. However necessary and effective the motive of self-interest or of apparent practical result may be in the ordinary affairs of life, it will not enable a man to make many discoveries, because it leads him away from those which are possible, to search for others which may nor may not be possible. The beginnings of discoveries are often so very small, that it requires acute senses and observation in order to perceive them; and if the mind is preoccupied with a desire to discover some particular practical object, new phenomena are overlooked. When Faraday discovered magneto-electricity, the first effect he obtained was so very feeble that he could scarcely perceive it. In discovery, man must follow where Nature leads. Some of the greatest practical realities of this age had their origin, not in a search after utilities, but in a search after pure truth, entirely irrespective of any utilities to which it might lead.

Another cause of the want of encouragement of research, is the natural selfishness which exists, though in very different degrees, in all men. Many wealthy persons wish things to remain as they are. Many manufacturers would not aid research unless they could monopolize its advantages. Students also generally prefer those subjects which are best rewarded, and do not sufficiently consider their intrinsic value. The love of truth for truth's sake alone is very weak in most men, and but few men make the greatest public good their chief object of life. Englishmen in general care less for new scientific knowledge than for the new inventions which result from it.

The extreme ignorance in this country of the value of scientific research, is largely due to the narrowness of the "practical" character of the English mind; men cannot perceive the deep-seated and universal sources of their wealth, and they prefer those occupations which yield the most obvious remunerative results. It is also partly due to scientific investigators themselves not having pleaded their own cause; such men have been so absorbed in the more important occupation of discovery, that they have, probably more than any other class of persons, neglected to enforce the just claims of their own subject. It is however chiefly caused by the influence of misapplied wealth, operating through the old Universities and large public schools. The sons of the wealthy are most of them educated at those institutions, and according to evidence supplied by University authorities to Royal Commissioners, many persons send their sons to those places for other purposes than to acquire learning, and allow them too much money. The considerable wealth of these young men supplies them with attractions which decoy them from industrious study, and the wishes of the parents and students have been largely acquiesced in by the tutors and college authorities. At our old Universities also, physical and chemical knowledge is very much less rewarded than some other subjects, though latterly a considerable improvement has been made in this respect, but even now there is not a University in the kingdom in which a knowledge of scientific research is necessary in order to obtain the highest scientific honour. In these various ways physical and chemical science has been kept very low in our chief seats of learning; and scientific research is wholly neglected by the governing authorities.

The Universities practically determine the kind and amount of scientific instruction in the schools generally of this country, because the boys in the schools are prepared for those institutions in the subjects only which the Universities require, and thus the old Universities have largely been the cause of the low standard of scientific knowledge throughout the country. The members of our Government, also the head masters of nearly all the Grammar schools, and the upper classes generally in this country, having been mostly educated at our great public schools and old Universities, have remained comparatively ignorant of science, and still less acquainted with scientific research.

Unless a powerful remedy is promptly applied, the present decline of research is likely to continue, because the pursuit of it is continually becoming more difficult, and our scientific investigators are becoming more painfully conscious of the injustice of their position. And should research go on decreasing, and that of other nations increase, we shall probably continue to fall behind foreign countries in improvements in arts, manufactures, commerce, and all the advantages that flow from science.

The industry of the Germans in scientific research is quite remarkable, as may easily be seen by an inspection of a recent volume of the Journal of the Chemical Society, or of the *Chemical News*; they are availing themselves of the great fountain of knowledge to a much greater extent than ourselves, and are already beginning to reap the reward. Within the last three or four years they have succeeded, by means of researches, in making alizarine, the colouring principle of madder. "England produces immense quantities of benzene, the greatest part of which goes to Germany, there to be converted into aniline dyes, a considerable quantity of which goes back to England. No other country is so far advanced in the manufacture of the coal-tar colours as Germany. The quantity of alizarine manufactured by the German makers far surpasses the English production." (See "Alizarine, Natural and Artificial," by F. Versmann. New York, 1873.) Statements of this kind are frequently published, and made by our manufacturers and others, of the departure of branch after branch of our manufactures to Germany, and of the continually increasing importation of German-made articles.

To remedy this state of things we require a general encouragement of pure scientific inquiry by the State and the Universities. It is thought by some persons who have given special attention to the subject that the State ought to encourage such research and science in general, by appointing a Minister of Science possessing scientific knowledge and good administrative ability; a scientific council to advise our Governments in all important matters relating to science; and by establishing State laboratories for pure scientific inquiry, with discoverers of repute in them wholly engaged in research in their respective subjects. It may be difficult to determine the expediency of giving effect to this proposal, but we do not hesitate to urge that some of the funds of each of our Universities should be applied to pure scientific discovery, by the foundation of professorships of original research, and that the highest honours in science should only be given to students who have made a good original research in pure science. The Royal Commission for the Advancement of Science is, however, collecting evidence on the subject from all the leading scientific investigators in the kingdom, and will soon issue a Report containing their recommendations.

In addition to these means, local efforts might be made to encourage research in each great centre of industry; those efforts being excited by issuing a prospectus of the following kind:—

Proposal to Found a Laboratory of pure Scientific Research in ——.

As the manufacturers, merchants, capitalists, land-owners, and the public generally, of this town and district have derived, and are still deriving, great pecuniary and other benefits from the discovery of new knowledge by means of pure research in the sciences of Physics and Chemistry ; and as in consequence of the great neglect of such research in this country, and the increased cultivation of it in other lands, especially in Germany, our commerce is suffering, and a great many evils in manufacturing and other operations, in sanitary and many other matters dependent upon physical and chemical conditions, remain unremedied ; it is proposed to found a Local Laboratory of original research in those sciences, and to employ one or more discoverers of repute, with assistants and every suitable appliance in them, who shall be wholly engaged in such labour in their respective sciences.

It may be objected that no corporate body can enter into the question of the relative merits of different discoverers proposed to be appointed as professors of original research in such laboratories, but this question is largely decided by the public opinion of scientific men. Any man who had published many original papers in the first-class scientific periodicals or journals of scientific societies, would of course be a discoverer of repute ; and any investigator who had published a number of papers in the Philosophical Transactions of the Royal Society might be considered one of the highest ability.

The great difficulty to be surmounted in carrying out any of these schemes, is the very general ignorance in this country of the value and necessity of research, and this can only be overcome by scientific men themselves performing their duty of enlightening the public on the subject. On the other hand, it must not be forgotten that whilst scientific discoverers are waiting for justice, they hold to a great extent the key of the future prosperity of this nation in their hands.

ART. II.—MR. GLADSTONE'S "DEFENCE OF THE FAITH."

*Address Delivered at the Distribution of Prizes in the Liver-
pool Collegiate Institution*, Dec. 21st, 1872, by the Right
Hon. W. E. GLADSTONE, First Lord of the Treasury. With
an Introduction and Illustrative Passages. London: John
Murray. 1873.

IT is not our general custom to review speeches—or "Addresses"
as they are now-a-days called—by public men, however
eminent. They form a legitimate subject of criticism to the
newspaper press, to which indeed they supply a large portion of
its materials; criticism which, however vigorous and able, is yet
almost always necessarily delivered in much the same off-hand
style as the language commented on. To examine such utterances
minutely in the pages of a Review would be evidently unfair.
To speak plain truth, we are most of us in the habit of delivering ourselves in the course of this mortal life of many superficial views, hasty generalizations, indifferent logic, and other
matter which if not absolute nonsense, yet, as the old phrase is,
"runs very much up into it." With ordinary men this kind of
talk finds its natural vent in the domestic circle or the commerce
of society. With what are called public men, it is discharged at
Mechanics' Institutes, Collegiate Institutions, Liberal and Conservative Demonstrations or Agricultural dinners. And there is
this to be said by way of excuse in the latter case, that on these
public platforms and occasions it is not always discharged
voluntarily.

If then Mr. Gladstone had chosen *proprio motu*, or yielding
to a mild compulsion had felt himself called upon, to address some
observations upon any subject under the sun to a room full of
good young Liverpool men or Sunday-school children, and had
allowed these observations to find their way to the public through
the medium of the daily papers, we should hardly have felt that
it was within our province to offer a remark. Not that we
would be supposed to insinuate that under these circumstances
he might, as far as we were concerned, have talked nonsense with
impunity. On the contrary, we venture to think—having some
experience of his speeches—that an off-hand effort of this kind
would have been better than the present performance; and we
willingly concede that, even when talking on topics which he
appears to us not to have maturely considered, he never talks
nonsense. All we mean is, that a speech of this kind, whatever

it might have contained, would not have been a fair subject for more than passing observation. We are informed, however, through the reports in the papers, that this address was, contrary to the well-known practice of the Premier, either read or delivered from very copious notes. He himself speaks of its delivery as "no matter of mere compliment or ceremony, but as one of very serious duty." What is of more moment, it has since been deliberately published, either by its author or with its author's sanction, with the addition of illustrative passages, an introduction, and some fresh matter. An address issued in this form, with its author's imprimatur, becomes to all intents and purposes a book, and it does not matter for the purposes of criticism whether it is a large or a small one. Or rather, as we shall directly endeavour to show, the publication of a small book or pamphlet, if that name be preferred, by such a man on such topics renders his utterances in some respects even more noteworthy than if they had been embodied in a large one.

We must at once say that we think it a subject of regret that Mr. Gladstone should have introduced into an address of this kind topics which he himself admits that he was quite unable to deal · satisfactorily with in his limits ; and still more a subject of regret that he should have given these crude remarks of his to the world in an authorized form. It is true that he shows symptoms of great alarm, and to individuals as well as to crowds afflicted by a sense of panic much may be pardoned. Nor can it be said that he is alarmed without a cause, that this panic is an unreasonable one. Since his theological views were definitely formed some forty years ago—and we are sure that no man's views have ever been more honestly formed—since the time when as we suppose he would say they were "determined," a great movement has been going on in the minds of men as honest, as thoughtful, and in many cases as able as himself, distinctly hostile to several of the main conclusions which he then arrived at, and which early training and subsequent habit have imprinted in his mind in the form of axioms. A keen observer, he has noticed this movement, and is greatly puzzled at it. And more than this, in his peculiar position—we think we are doing him no injustice in venturing the suggestion—what he sees can scarcely fail to be specially irritating to him. His feelings must be those with which we may imagine a virtuous Roman statesman of the time of the Antonines contemplating the rapid spread of a new and to him incomprehensible delusion like Christianity. Here is a man who has taken a great part, not seldom the leading part, in all the vast social and political movements of a whole generation, and who is suddenly brought face to face with a movement incalculably more important than

any of those with which he has had to deal, in which he
can take no part, which is indeed running in a direction
entirely opposite to his most cherished convictions, and threatening what he holds to be the most firmly established truths.
In 1834, and for years afterwards, he tells us plaintively,
" there seemed to be a public proclamation of the established
harmony between Science and Religion " (that is, orthodox
Christianity). And why, he asks in effect, cannot this be so
in 1873? Ah, why indeed? The evil, we fancy, dates from
a period anterior even to 1834. Why was this dangerous path
of divergence from Scripture ever entered upon by science?
There was a time, less than a hundred years ago, when science
and Revelation were in perfect accord on the subject of the
Cosmogony of Genesis. Why are they not so now? We think
we could find some examples of still earlier disagreement between the two. We wonder it had not occurred to the author,
though it will be no news to our readers, that a possible explanation of the phenomenon may be found in the fact that science is
progressive, that the science of 1873 is not in all respects the
same thing as the science of 1834. We were, however, pointing
to what may be, nay, what must be, the feelings of one in Mr.
Gladstone's almost unique position among us, when contemplating this to him portentous inroad of free-thought. He is puzzled,
for reasons of his own, and for very much better reasons he is
probably annoyed, and certainly alarmed.

Yet a moment's reflection should have shown him that before
taking part in the conflict he ought to have made sure that he
had something worth hearing to say. For he might very well
have said nothing ; which we think would have been under the
circumstances the wisest course to pursue. Or he might have
prepared a short argument directed against the weak places of
Mr. Herbert Spencer and Dr. Strauss, which would at any rate
have been received with that respectful attention which is sure
to greet everything from Mr. Gladstone's pen. The one thing
he ought not to have done is to make just such a speech, or
rather to publish just such a pamphlet as that now before
us. Because what it amounts to, in point of fact, is simply this,
that he himself is entirely opposed to what Mr. Buckle termed
" the sceptical spirit " in religion, and that he looks upon certain
extreme manifestations of it with a disfavour which we will
admit that we ourselves in some degree sympathize with. At
the same time he has given this opinion under circumstances
which prevent him from backing it with his reasons, he himself,
indeed, carefully informing us not only that he has not got the
time, but that he has not got the requisite capacity. Now we
think that this way of treatment is—to use the words of Mr.

Affable Hawk in the *Game of Speculation*—" too much to be enough." We do not think that it is likely to be serviceable to the author, or to the cause supported by him, while we think that he has not taken into account the danger from his point of view of making use of it.

No human being, as far as we know, has ever accused or even suspected Mr. Gladstone of being what is commonly called an Infidel. Some ridiculous persons have, from time to time, written to ask him whether he is a Roman Catholic, and by a strange perversity, he has written answers which though perfectly satisfactory to all reasonable minds—which indeed needed no satisfaction on the point—were always of a nature to leave it open to those who raised the question to assert that they were mere evasions. No doubt he might urge, in the words of Dr. Johnson, that he had furnished people with a reason, and was not bound to furnish them with an understanding. But then unfortunately there are a great number of people without understandings, and in condescension to their weakness it might have been just as well to say in plain language, " I am not a Roman Catholic." With regard to scepticism, he has taken a much more decided course. He has, as it were, issued a proclamation, or we may say launched a Bull against it : for that is what this lecture amounts to. But why do this (since he had not to free himself from any suspicion of complicity with the views animadverted on), except from a mere burning desire and impulse, prompted by panic, to proclaim his opinions, "quodcumque animo flagrante liberet," from the housetops ?—a course scarcely worthy of a Prime Minister who is at the same time a thinker. For though Mr. Gladstone seems to sneer at the term, we have no hesitation in applying it to him. There is indeed a third solution, involving a motive which may have influenced him, almost without his having acknowledged it to himself. We would not be supposed to hint that as Henry VIII. and James I. of England issued royal manifestoes in support of established but disputed views of their day—both of them, by the way, being directed against the damnable opinions of certain Germans—so Mr. Gladstone, to whose office has accrued so much of the kingly power of former days, may have thought of reviving in his own favour the quasi-royal function of denouncing religious error. But it is possible that the motive which has induced him to announce in this way his personal views may not be altogether dissimilar to that which influenced Henry VIII. and James I. He may think that from one in his exceptional position a mere warning against certain opinions may have great effect, especially on the young, and that he is bound to give this warning. We should respect such a notion as this, like any other honest and conscientious one, but we should think it a complete mistake. It is a mistake not unlikely to be made by persons who are conscious of exercising an immense influence in the sphere of politics. Yet it is not too much to say that in the present day, and in civilized countries, a mere announcement of opinion on the part of any man whatever, on a subject lying outside his own sphere, will have no appreciable weight, as it certainly deserves to have none. We have used the term "in civilized countries," because we can quite believe that if the Sovereign of Japan, or even the Emperor of Russia, were to announce to-morrow his conversion to a new religion, a great number of his subjects might be led to imitate him. But while it is quite certain that Mr. Gladstone's change of opinion on the subject of the Irish Church, for instance, induced a great number of other people to change their opinions, we hold it as equally certain that neither he nor Prince Bismarck, neither the Emperor William nor General Grant, will by a mere announcement of his views on theology or science or art, be able in the long run to influence the mind of any human being outside the small circle of his friends, acquaintance, and dependents. We should have thought that Mr. Gladstone would have known this, and that he would have been able to distinguish between the large circulation sure to be commanded by any utterances of his on such subjects, and the permanent effects likely to be produced. If he does not see this, if he thinks that the numerous editions of his pamphlet which have been called for are a satisfactory symptom of the good which it is working, he resembles the ingenious gentlemen who draw up the reports of certain Bible and Tract Societies, and who inform us how chestsfull of these publications are "eagerly sought for" by the heathen of such and such a locality into whose hands they are emptied, without being able to tell us that a single genuine case of conversion has resulted. On the other hand, while not a single man or woman will be converted from or prevented from falling into infidelity by learning that the Prime Minister has a special horror of it, we are reminded of what Hume tells us of Henry VIII., " As the controversy became more illustrious by Henry's entering the lists, he drew still more the attention of mankind ; and the Lutheran doctrine daily acquired new converts in every part of Europe." The effect of James's work was in the long run precisely similar. What result can be expected to follow from his mere denunciation (admittedly without an attempt at refutation) of the opinions of Strauss and others? Evidently that an English translation of Strauss's latest work will be among the first announcements of what is called the " publishing season;" that Mr. Winwood Reade's book, which was, we believe, for some time after its appearance a drug in the market, will have received an impetus like that communicated some years ago by the same hand to " Ecce Homo ;" that many educated persons who had heard vaguely of Mr. Herbert Spencer will purchase his " First Principles," and what is more read it, and what is still more may not be "shocked" at it, or may even be "beguiled and attracted" by it. Most people know the story of the Irish priest who on confessing the ostler, asked him whether he had ever greased the horses' teeth to prevent their eating the beans. "Never !" was the indignant reply. On the occasion of the next confession, the question being repeated, elicited the answer that Pat had of late frequently indulged in the practice. "Why, who could have put such a wicked idea into your head ?" "Faith, to be sure it was your reverence !"

We now proceed to offer a few remarks upon that portion of the address to which we have been alluding. And lest it be thought that we are dealing too hardly with the expressions used, and cross-questioning too closely the ideas which may be supposed to lie behind them, we must repeat that we are commenting upon a published and corrected work, issued from the press for a particular and a very definite purpose. True it is a short one ; but its shortness forms no plea in bar of such criticism. There is no excuse for falling into confusion in the course of a few pages. Whether Mr. Gladstone's ideas are clear on the subjects of which he treats, we shall see directly. At page 11 of the pamphlet is to be found the first symptom of alarm, and, we think we may add, of confusion. The author objects to professors of the natural sciences claiming for them in a pre-eminent or exclusive sense the name of " science."

"So that a man who observes and reasons upon plants or animals, the constituent parts of the globe, or of the celestial system, is a man of science ; but to observe and reason upon history, upon philosophy in its older sense, or upon theology, establishes no such title, though the very same process of collecting and digesting facts and of drawing inferences from them is pursued in one case and in the other ; and though it seems sufficiently absurd to hold that there is a science of the human body, but that there can be no science of the mind or soul."

We find it difficult to deal with this sentence, coming from the pen of a Prime Minister. If it reached us as a fragment of a prose exercise sent up for correction by a pupil of the Liverpool Collegiate Institution we should be at our ease, because we should feel entitled to administer to him some such elementary observations as the following :—

"You will find it, as a general rule, much better not to quarrel

with the accepted use of words. You are either wanting to restore to Science the meaning which it used to bear, that of
Scientia, knowledge of all kinds, a change which it is hopeless to
attempt to make ; or else (and this really seems what you do intend) you are for including under it branches of human inquiry
which have no more to do with it than playing on a violin has to
do with driving a steam-engine. Of course, as you know, definitions often shade into one another, and with regard to History,
which you have mentioned, though it is not yet a science, there
is no doubt that some historians often pursue their investigations
in what may be called a scientific method. Such men might perhaps, without violence, be styled scientific men. But with regard
to what you call ' philosophy in its older sense ' (which means
Metaphysics) and Theology, there is no doubt whatever. They
are not sciences in the modern acceptation of the term : indeed
the term excludes them as certainly as the definition ' Animals '
excludes ' Plants,' as the word England necessarily excludes all portions of the territory known as France. For the term science is now
employed in reference to a collection of phenomena which can be
verified, and which can be exhibited as possessing some mutual
connexion, so that from the occurrence of such and such antecedents we can invariably infer such and such results. Now from
their very nature Metaphysics and Theology fall outside this
definition. Nor are any of the experimental methods essential
to the verification of facts capable of being employed in regard
to the statements which their professors set before us—these
alleged facts being in truth legitimate subjects of dispute. They
are attempts in the direction of Ontology, a strange word to you
perhaps ; they deal, that is to say, with things as they are supposed to *be*, not merely to *seem* to us, and what are called transcendental truths, beyond the reach of verification, and consequently of science. And no amount of ingenious reasoning based
upon assumptions more or less reasonable can be compared with
' the process of collecting and digesting facts and drawing inferences from them.' We may then soothe your wounded feelings
by calling the Theologian a man of great reasoning powers, a
man of genius, &c.—as indeed many such a one has been—but
we cannot admit him as a scientific man without altering the
accepted meaning of the word ; and after all, this would not serve
your purpose, for we should immediately have to invent some
new word to mark the difference of method which separates him
from ' the professor of the natural sciences.'

" Just one word more about that passage in which you talk of
the ' absurdity of holding that there can be no science of the
mind or soul.' Who says that there *can* be no science of the
mind or soul ? All that is asserted is that there *is* not one.

You must be aware that there are some subjects of study which have not as yet been admitted to the full rank of Sciences, either because a sufficient number of verified facts falling within their domain have not been collected, or because, though we are in possession of a great number of facts, we have not as yet been able to systematize them in any way. Of this latter class were until very lately political economy, geology, and even chemistry; to this class still belongs sociology. Psychology is still an imperfect science, and must remain in that condition as long as the nature of the most elementary operations of the mind is a subject of dispute between contending schools. It has not at present got out of the hands of what you call 'philosophy in its older sense;' and this, though scientific methods are being applied to it by such men as Professor Bain, Mr. Herbert Spencer, and others. Nobody, I repeat, says that there *can* be no such science. You had better cut out this part of your very promising theme, and devote this evening to reading the introduction to Lewes's Biographical History of Philosophy."

At page 22, after telling us that it is not his intention to treat of the differences which separate Christian Churches and sects from each other, the author thus proceeds to break ground on the subject of modern Scepticism :—

" It is not now only the Christian Church, or only the Holy Scripture, or only Christianity which is attacked. The disposition is boldly proclaimed to deal alike with root and branch, and to snap utterly the ties, which under the still venerable name of religion, unite man with the unseen world, and lighten the struggles and the woes of life by the hope of a better land."

This must mean that there are now-a-days persons who deny the existence of a personal God—or rather who deny that there are any sufficient reasons for supposing the existence of such a Being—and who hold similar views as to a future state ; who, like Strauss, consider every form of worship and every species of prayer to be not merely so much idle breath spent upon the air but misspent in the sense of being wholly unworthy of the dignity of man. No doubt there are many who hold this sort of creed, driven to it by an honest exercise of their faculties, whether for adequate reasons, or not, is another matter. The point to be considered in connexion with this reference to them is not whether they are or not mistaken, but whether Mr. Gladstone has correctly described the results which would have to be accepted by those who embrace their teaching. He tells us that it snaps the ties with the unseen world, *which lighten the struggles and the woes of life by the hope of a better world.* Now this is the truth, but not the whole truth. It is precisely one of those statements which by carefully leaving out of sight one of the most important elements in the question, give an entirely false and distorted view of it. We consider this matter of so much importance that although we have recently adverted to it in the pages of this Review, we shall make no apology for again devoting a few words to it.

To speak quite plainly : which would be to the ultimate advantage of mankind generally, that Dr. Strauss should turn out to be right, or that the Church of England should turn out to be right? Dr. Strauss tells us that at the close of this life we shall cease to be. Whether there are or are not grounds for this opinion, is, we must repeat, altogether beside the question. What we want to ask is — Does this view of Dr. Strauss's offer such a very appalling look-out to a reasonable man? Many millions of human beings hold it, by the bye. No doubt the *prospect* of future non-existence may not be an altogether pleasant element to mingle with our ideas for a few short years to come; but by no ingenuity can non-existence itself be represented as unpleasant. It was our condition, if we may so express it, when Cyrus and Cambyses "made all that pother," when Romans and Carthaginians contended for the mastery of the world; as Lucretius long ago pointed out—

> " Et velut anteacto nil tempore sensimus ægri
>   Ad confligendum venientibus undique Pœnis.
>
>   . . . .
>
>   Sic ubi non erimus, cum corporis atque animai
>   Discidium fuerit, quibus e sumus uniter apti
>   Scilicet haud nobis quicquam qui non erimus tum
>   Accidere omnino poterit sensumque movere
>   Non si terra mari miscebitur et mare cœlo."—III. 844, sqq.

On the other hand, the Christian Churches teach us that there is such a place as hell, a scene of endless and excruciating torment; and not only this, but that it is the ultimate destination of by far the greater part of the human race. Founding themselves as they do upon the literal interpretation of the New Testament, we think they are unquestionably right in teaching this; for, indeed, we can extract no other meaning from several distinct utterances of Jesus, and other passages of Scripture; and if these be toned down into a sense different from the plain obvious one, a similar mode of interpretation may be applied to other parts of Scripture, with the effect of loosening the foundations of all dogmas. Now we are by no means asserting either that there is no hell or that the bulk of mankind are not bound thither. But what we do assert, if not without fear of contradiction, at any rate without fear of refutation, is that it

is much to be hoped that there is no future at all for us rather
than such a future as this. A Universe without a sentient
Deity, and without a future existence,* is a much more cheerful
prospect for man than a Universe governed by such a Deity as
Orthodoxy paints ; one who chooses, or is compelled, to torture
the bulk of us for ever and ever. And more than this, even
those who deem themselves to have a well-founded assurance of
eternal happiness must, except upon the supposition of their
being utterly selfish and degraded, welcome a discovery, if such
a one could be made, which should deprive them of this prospect,
on the condition of relieving countless millions of others from a
fate at which imagination stands aghast. In other words, it is
not quite honest—for the " orthodox Christian " that is to say—
to talk of those who preach the doctrine of universal extinction
as robbing certain people of the hope of a better world, while
carefully suppressing the effect of such a doctrine, if it could be
shown to be true, in delivering a very much greater number of
others from a worse one. Not of course that we accuse
Mr. Gladstone of anything like conscious misstatement. He is
merely giving utterance to the commonplaces of his creed, which
he has imbibed, and now gives forth again, without having set
himself seriously to consider whether they altogether correctly
represent his creed viewed as a whole. Yet if the subject were
one to which he could devote his intellect cleared from the
disfiguring mists of prepossession, that ἀχλὺς τῆς ψυχῆς of which
Plato speaks, who so ready as he to scatter such sophisms (and
half-truths are often sophisms) in half a dozen sentences? Let
him transfer himself in imagination to the planet Mercury—we
are not afraid of repeating an illustration which we gave last
January—and there let him be called upon to decide which of
two disputed beliefs offers the most *desirable* prospect (that is
the point) for the Mercurians ; one which consigns them all to
the sleep of death, or another, holding out (if you please) to all
the hope of heaven, but, as a matter of fact and of revelation,
teaching that the greater part will go to hell. He could give
only one answer. A demonstration of Strauss's Universum
would be to the Mercurians generally not the best conceivable
tidings, but at any rate infinitely better tidings than proof of the
truth of the system set forth, say in the Longer and Shorter
Catechisms. How then can this be different at Liverpool ?
How could Mr. Gladstone go over there, and in the presence of

---

* It has been urged, *e.g.*, by Bishop Butler, that it would not *necessarily*
follow because there was no God there could therefore be no hell. It is to
meet this that we have inserted in the above sentence the words " and without a future existence." The point itself we have not space to notice further.
It does not affect our argument.

a number of young men *imply* that Atheism and annihilation
are a black look-out for the race compared with what he as an
orthodox man must believe to be the average prospect for the
individual? How, believing Straussism to be untrue—and our
argument does not touch the truth or falsehood of the respective
creeds—could he from his stand-point represent it as anything
else than "a pleasing dream," "tidings for humanity too good
to be true," "an enticing self-delusion," from which, because
untrue, it was desirable for the young men to guard themselves?

In the above extract, as we have just said, we understand the
author to refer to certain extreme forms of unbelief amounting
to Atheism. We should not have thought it at first sight good
policy, from his point of view, to direct special attention to these.
We should have thought that there were other, and, if we may
be permitted to say so, more reasonable issues raised by the
spirit of free inquiry in the present day equally hostile to some
of the main dogmas of Mr. Gladstone's creed, and much more
likely to exercise the minds of young men; doubts, for instance,
as to the inspiration, in the orthodox sense, of the Old and New
Testaments, which he passes by with an incidental allusion.
Would it not have been well, if this system of warning and
caution is held to be of any use, to have warned and cautioned
his audience (containing, it would seem from page 10, some Jews)
against these? However, we shall directly see what his object
was in dwelling with particular emphasis upon sceptical views of
an extreme kind. What we would here observe, is that he is
not happy in his illustrations of what constitute these extreme
views, and that he includes among speculations which deal root
and branch with religion some which appear to us by no means
necessarily to have that effect.

The paragraph to which we allude follows immediately upon
the sentence last quoted from the address, and deals exclusively
with Mr. Herbert Spencer. Mr. Spencer will be able to inform
us, if he should condescend to do so, whether Mr. Gladstone has
upon the whole correctly apprehended the spirit of his teaching.
We have our opinion on the subject, but (especially with this
pamphlet before us) we entertain a strong aversion to mere expressions of opinion on these topics: and to justify ours by our
reasons would require more space than we have at our disposal.
We will, however, notice one statement, which is indeed the key-
note to the tune of the whole paragraph "Upon the ground of
what is termed evolution, God is relieved of the labour of creation."
Now is it true that the doctrine of evolution is fatal to religion?
That it would be fatal to orthodox Christianity we admit (though
some orthodox people have denied even this); but teaching

which is hostile to something more than Christianity has been distinctly referred to. We have forborne, by the way, from criticising such expressions as "attacking," "proclaiming a disposition to deal alike with root and branch," though they are open to some comment. The philosophy of Mr. Spencer, for instance—its truth or falseness being quite beside the question—is an attack upon orthodox religion only in the same sense that Galileo's theory was an attack on the Book of Joshua, and geology an attack on the Book of Genesis. However, in what sense is the doctrine of evolution, as advocated by its chief apostle, hostile to religion ? And what is meant by such expressions as God being " relieved of the labour of creation," " being discharged, in the name of unchangeable laws, from governing the world " ? Merely, if the matter be looked into, that, as science advances, conceptions of God and of his mode of working are being continually suggested to us, more and more removed from the notions entertained by savages. The same cry has for centuries greeted every fresh scientific discovery, and every speculation following in the wake of scientific discovery. " Why, this would be banishing God from the universe !" All this is so well set forth by Mr. Spencer himself in the very book referred to, " First Principles," and is besides so familiar to readers of this Review, that we may be excused from dwelling at length upon it. Not indeed but that the doctrine of evolution may be held by many Atheists, but that is not the point ; the point is whether the man who holds it must necessarily be an Atheist. We say no. If all Mr. Spencer's speculations, and, we may add, all those of Mr. Darwin, and the "spontaneous generation," to use a common term, vouched for by Dr. Bastian, should be proved to be true, a God, that is, a particular conception of God, would be indeed put an end to. That is to say, the modus operandi of the great First Cause would be shown to be different from that imagined by theologians ; his *immanence* in the affairs of the universe would remain undisturbed in the mind of him who was otherwise convinced of it ; it would not be disproved by the evolution theory ; in other words, it might be held with the evolution theory. The fact is that early education and subsequent very conscientious investigation have impressed Mr. Gladstone with a strong belief in a Deity acting in a particular way. Any argument directed to show that the operations of the First Cause are carried out in a different (and, as we think, far grander and more awe-inspiring way) become to his mind immediate and necessary attacks upon the idea of a God. If a party of European sailors were to make an attack upon the painted idol of a tribe of savages, the latter would probably think that if they did not succeed in defending it no God would be left in the universe.

Nay, we have plenty of people in the same state of mind among ourselves. For instance, there is a caste among us, receiving several millions of national money annually in return for the discharge, among other duties, of that of calling forth rain and sunshine by their invocations; many of whom, with a number of others, would hold that to suppose that rain and fine weather are governed by fixed laws is a decided confession of Atheism. It is to them inexpressibly awful and blasphemous to think of their Deity "being relieved of the labour" of watching their prayers, "being discharged in the name of unchangeable laws," from the function of withholding and distributing his showers as the surplus weight of human importunity may incline the balance in one direction or the other.

We will conclude this part of our notice by commending to Mr. Gladstone's attention the words of an eminent man of science, who is at the same time a sincere and devout believer in God, Dr. Carpenter :—

> "There is surely nothing more atheistical in the idea that the Creator, instead of originating each race by a distinct and separate act (the notion commonly entertained), gave to the first created monad those properties by the continued action of which, through countless ages, a man would be evolved, than there is in the idea to which we are irresistibly led by physiological study, that the first cell-germ of the human ovum is endowed with such properties as enable it to become developed into a human baby in the course of a few months."

And again :—

> "As the tendency of each of these great doctrines—the Newtonian law of Gravitation and the Nebular Hypothesis of Laplace—was pronounced in the first instance to be atheistic, whilst in the end each has been accepted as an expression of our best and highest knowledge of the Creator's action in the physical universe, so it will ultimately be with the doctrine of organic evolution; which will come to be viewed as presenting a far grander notion of creative design than the idea of special interposition required to remedy the irregular working of a machine imperfectly constructed in the first instance.*

We must decline to follow the author through the summary which he gives of certain opinions of Dr. Strauss. We are not concerned in defending Dr. Strauss, and we do not consider this the occasion, even if we had the space, to offer any criticism on his last work. Mr. Gladstone must suppose that he is fulfilling

---

* *Contemporary Review*, Oct. 1872. It is true that in these passages Dr. Carpenter is not specially referring to Mr. Spencer's particular theory. We have quoted his remarks as generally confirming our own, and as bearing on Mr. Gladstone's whole tone of theological thought.

some good purpose by telling a number of people, who might
otherwise learn nothing about it, what it is that a certain learned
German believes. " What can the purpose be ?" we can suppose
some one asking, who had heard of the intention, but had not
seen the lecture. The design is perfectly plain, and is indeed
unmistakeably set forth by the author. It is to frighten his
audience and readers, to communicate to others some of the
horror with which he himself views these theories, an object
which he thinks can be effected by the mere announcement of
them ; just as a person would deem it sufficient to give us notice
of a precipice lying a few yards before us, in order to prevent
our moving in that direction in the middle of a fog, without
feeling himself called on to explain that it was a disagreeable
thing to be dashed to pieces. And further to tell them that
this is the result to which Free-thought, if once indulged in,
must lead.

" Neither can I profess to feel an unmixed regret at their (these
astonishing assertions) being forced thus eagerly and thus early into
notice ; because it is to be hoped that they will cause a shock and
a reaction, and will compel many who may have too lightly valued
the inheritance so dearly bought for them and may have entered
upon dangerous paths, to consider, while there is yet time, whither
those paths will lead them."—p. 25.

Now we are not quite sure that this is either sound policy or
sound reasoning. In the first place, everybody (the young men
at Liverpool of course included) knows us a matter of fact that
views not in the main dissimilar to those of Dr. Strauss are held
by a considerable number of educated, and we are bound to
suppose conscientious persons ; and it does not therefore by any
means follow that a mere announcement of their existence will
cause a shock of horror. Nor do we think, by the way, that they
ought to be looked upon with horror, or in any other light than
as being mistaken opinions In the next place, even supposing
them to excite the feeling which Mr. Gladstone desires to
produce, it does not follow that the exhibition of them will, much
less that it ought to, divert young people from the path of Free
Inquiry. Free Inquiry, if once entered on, knows nothing of
consequences ; and the question here resolves itself into one, as
to whether people ought to inquire at all ; the old dispute between
Free-thought and Authority. But, putting aside this, there is an
assumption here which we have often met with, to the effect
that no form of Theism, no belief in a future, no religion of any
kind, is tenable apart from Revelation ; that there is no possible
" Via Media," as Mr. Henry Rogers puts it, between Orthodoxy
and Atheism. We believe this opinion to be false in theory and
false in fact. We do not think it true that persons who have

conceived doubts about the plenary Inspiration of Scripture, or
the divinity of Jesus, either will or logically ought to find their
way to a Universum, any more than we believe that persons who
begin to doubt about the infallibility of the Pope are on their
way to the most extreme forms of Calvinism, or that those who
have discarded the divine right of kings will end by shooting the
Bishop of London and setting fire to the Mansion House.

In view of the spirit of denial which is abroad, and which
challenges all religion, the author now proceeds "to offer a few
suggestions, in the hope that they may not be wholly without
their use." These suggestions are the most curious feature in
this publication. That a clever man should utter them on the
spur of the moment, at a distribution of prizes, would not be
wonderful. But that any one with a capacity above that of
a writer in the *Record* newspaper should have deliberately
printed and given them to the world, with the idea that they
might be "of use" in deterring young men from scepticism,
exceeds our comprehension.

" You will hear in your after-life much of the duty and delight of
following free thought ; and in truth the man who does not value the
freedom of his thoughts deserves to be described as Homer describes
the slave; he is but half a man. St. Paul, I suppose, was a teacher
of free thought when he bade his converts to prove all things; but it
seems he went terribly astray when he proceeded to bid them ' hold
fast that which is good;' for he evidently assumed that there was
something by which they could hold fast. And so he bade Timothy
keep that which was committed to his charge, and another apostle
has instructed us to ' earnestly contend for the faith which was once
delivered to the saints.' But the free thought of which we now hear
so much seems too often to mean thought roving and vagrant rather
than free; like Delos, in the ancient legend, drifting on the seas of
Greece, without a root, a direction, or a home."—p. 20.

We answer that certainly Paul was a teacher of free thought, if,
when he bade his converts to prove all things, he meant to
tell them honestly to exercise their faculties upon whatever
was submitted to them. If he meant something else, he was
not teaching free thought. In any case he was quite justified in
bidding them "hold fast that which is good." He had arrived
at certain conclusions, and he naturally thought them "good;"
and thinking them so he did not "go terribly astray," but, on
the contrary, we cheerfully admit, was quite right in urging upon
his converts and upon Timothy, who all agreed with him, the
necessity of holding them fast, and conforming their lives to
them. We should not think ourselves going terribly astray if
we urged upon Mr. Gladstone to hold fast to our common
Liberal principles, and not to sacrifice them on ecclesiastical

and educational questions to the Tories. So, as staunch Liberals, we might tell young men entering on public life, as far as possible "to prove all things" in politics; but if by this we meant that it is sinful to be a Tory, we should be talking what is now admitted to be absurd in the case of Politics, but is not yet seen to be absurd in the case of Theology. We are sorry to say that we cannot quite make out what this introduction of Paul and Jude has really got to do with the question of free thought. Unless it be implied that a man who proceeds to "prove all things" is bound to arrive at a conclusion to which he can "hold fast;" which is as nearly nonsense as anything which we should venture in imagination to charge upon Mr. Gladstone. An inquirer is not always bound to arrive at a conclusion; or, we may say, that a man who is irresistibly led to this, that we are necessarily in a state of ignorance and uncertainty about many things believed in by Mr. Gladstone, arrives at *a* conclusion, to which he holds fast; and to argue that it is not a good one is to beg the whole question. If it be implied that the particular conclusions which Paul arrived at, we also are bound on inquiry to hold as good— i.e., as good conclusions, this is only a roundabout way of stating the Dogma of Authority.

The author now proceeds to tell us, very truly, that we ought not to form an exaggerated estimate of the age in which we live. If the object of this be to warn us that we ought not to be sure that the beliefs, theological, &c., at which we have arrived may not be upset by a future age, the warning is sound enough, though, to be sure, it is capable of more than one application. If the meaning be that we ought not to think the present age a vast deal wiser than any preceding age, we think this is altogether unsound. The illustration which he has himself given, and which has been much commented on, is not to the point. He says that as much mental strength and application have perhaps been required to perfect the violin as to perfect the steam-engine. Very likely. And this may be a good answer to those who affirm that the individual men of the present age are intellectually superior to those of the past ages. But we have not met with any persons who affirm this: at any rate, this is not a view generally held by those who talk of the "advancement" of the nineteenth century. The man who invented the first plough, or the first rudder, may have been a greater mechanical genius than either Stephenson or Brunel. Euclid of Megara and Archimedes were almost certainly greater geniuses than the senior wrangler of last January, or the head pupil of the Ecole Polytechnique. Yet if Archimedes came to life again, the merest tyro in engineering would be capable of giving him lessons, and Euclid would have a great deal to learn from a senior optime. Nobody says that we are taller men than our ancestors ; but what is said, and with truth, is that we see further, owing to our standing on their shoulders. As a contemporary very well put it, the partners in a firm which has traded successfully for a long time will be richer men than their predecessors, though the men now carrying it on may be inferior to those who started it. It is probable then that the views entertained on vexed questions in the present age will be upon the whole more worthy of notice than those acquiesced in fifteen hundred years ago ; just as it is probable that, if the world continues to advance, many of our speculations on theological, political, social, and other questions will, fifteen hundred years hence, be looked upon as ridiculous— ridiculous, that is to say, in respect to any one *then* putting them forward. And this is all that we understand reasonable men to mean when they talk of the intellectual advancement of their own time.

The next paragraph is still more singular.

" Again, my friends, you will hear much to the effect that the divisions among Christians render it impossible to say what Christianity is, and so destroy all certainty as to what is the true religion. But if the divisions among Christians are remarkable, not less so is their unity in the greatest doctrines that they hold. Well nigh fifteen hundred years—years of a more sustained activity than the world had ever before seen—have passed away since the great controversies concerning the Deity and the Person of the Redeemer were, after a long agony, determined. As before that time in a manner less defined, but adequate for their day, so ever since that time, amid all chance and change, more, ay, many more, than ninety-nine in every hundred Christians have with one voice confessed the Deity and Incarnation of our Lord as the cardinal and central truths of our religion. . Surely there is some comfort here, some sense of brotherhood ; some glory due to the past, some hope for the times that are to come."—pp. 27, 28.

Surely it cannot be intended by this to imply that because the Council of Nice arrived at certain conclusions as to the divinity of a Being who lived three centuries before its epoch, therefore we are bound to accept those conclusions. After his warning addressed to an age of steam-engines, Mr. Gladstone is not going to claim infallibility for an age of almost universal ignorance, darkness, and superstition. We cannot suppose that, as a Protestant writer, he meant this ; yet it is rather difficult to say what he did mean. Mr. Gladstone knows perfectly well that the prelates who "determined" the divinity of Christ would have been equally ready to "determine" the existence of witches and the reality of demoniacal possession, that the whole universe was, in fact, full of demons, some of which might be swallowed

in eating a lettuce, that there were such things as Phœnixes and
weir-wolves, that the whole of the Heathen Mythology was true,
and that the heathen gods were devils, that a body could not
act where it was not, that the earth was flat, and had been
created in six days, that the sun sank hissing in the ocean on
the further side of the pillars of Hercules. We are not therefore
compelled to attach any more weight to the conclusions which
they arrived at on theological matters than to those which they
would certainly have arrived at on other matters, unless upon
certain assumptions which Mr. Gladstone is not entitled to make.
We cannot suppose then that he meant this. Further on we
are told that it must be a great comfort to Christians to feel that
a vast majority of them are agreed upon certain propositions.
No doubt in a sense this is true, just as it is a comfort to find
oneself alongside of a number of other people in a battle, or a
popular rising, or on the benches of the House of Commons. That
numbers impart courage is a truism; but if it be implied that
the society of others should confirm us in our beliefs, it is not
too much to say that this idea has served to keep alive all the
religious error, and nerved the hands of men to all the acts of
religious persecution known in history. We have not space
to pursue the subject, if it need to be pursued. Suffice it that
the young men might have been very properly warned, even by
Mr. Gladstone, that it did not at all follow that *because* ninety-
nine out of every hundred Christians believe in the divinity of
Jesus (if the fact be so), therefore they ought to accept the
doctrine, for that history exhibited examples of beliefs held by
a much greater number of people for a much greater number of
years, which yet turned out to be mere delusions.

We take the general meaning of the paragraph to be that
there are some points of extreme importance on which all
Christians agree, and that those who say that they do not know
what Christianity is, in consequence of the numerous divisions
among its professors, may be referred to these points as constituting
its essentials. A Christian, it is implied, is a man who holds such
and such dogmas common to the Catholic and Protestant Churches:
a statement which involves this further one, that differences and
divisions on all other points are comparatively unimportant. We
wish we could think that the majority of Christians were as
liberal in the definition of their own name as Mr. Gladstone is;
but as a matter of fact they are not. Five out of every ten
of them would immediately repudiate his definition of the term
except as used in its rough popular sense. A Roman Catholic
would by no means admit that a man who holds the propositions
common to Catholicism and Protestantism is a true Christian.
He requires assent to a number of other propositions, some of

them of scarcely less importance; and he requires that assent should be given to all of these on entirely other and different grounds. On the other hand, a vast number of Protestants not only deny the name of Christian, in its proper sense, to the head of the rival Church, but actually style him Antichrist. As long as large sections of the so-called Christian world talk of each other in this fashion, and differences so wide separate them, it is idle to say that certainty as to what is the true religion is not, we will not say destroyed, but greatly obscured.

The author next touches on "one more of the favourite fallacies of the day—the opinion and boast of some that man is not responsible for his belief." We admit that we are victims to this fallacy, if such it be. We are quite sure that a man is not answerable (that is to say, ought not according to human conceptions of justice to be made to answer) for his belief. The question is, what is meant by belief? It has always been held by those who uphold this view that the belief in question must be an honest one: the result arrived at by the mind after a candid and impartial, though it may be necessarily somewhat rough and ready investigation: and this definition implies that "self-love and passion," "pride and perverseness," and every other disturbing cause, influence, and prejudice has been silenced as far as it lies in human infirmity to do so. For this sort of belief alone do we claim immunity from responsibility. Any views otherwise formed we look on as mere "Idola," for the formation of which and the consequences of which man is distinctly responsible. The author appears to entertain at bottom very much our opinion; only that he uses the word "belief" in the same sense as that in which we have employed the term "Idolon," and thus renders the advocates of the non-responsibility view further responsible for a view which they do not entertain. We must add that we do not think him happy in his illustration. "Should we, in common life, ask a body of swindlers for an opinion upon swindling? or of gamblers for an opinion upon gambling? or of misers upon bounty?" We *should* ask one of these persons—*e.g.*, a swindler, what he thought about swindling, in the sense in which the suggestion is offered here; that is to say, if we believed we could ascertain from him what was his inmost conviction about swindling, and how he had arrived at it. And in the event, which we think would be a unique one in a civilized community, of his having *honestly* (if we may use the term) come by a belief that swindling was right, we should hold him not responsible to a Higher Power, while we should at the same time clap him into prison. In fact, we take a view as nearly as possible the exact opposite of that which we understand Mr. Gladstone to hold on this point. We believe

that man is responsible to *man* for his outward acts in cases
where he is not responsible to *God.* And we believe that the
same rule would apply to inward acts (as Mr. Gladstone defines
opinions), but that of course we can infer these only from some
external expression of them. Was General Washington an
honest man or a criminal? Every one will reply an honest man.
Suppose he had failed—and success or failure have no bearing
on his honesty—would the English Government have been justified in imprisoning him? Certainly. Would he have been a
criminal in the eyes of the Supreme? We cannot think so.
Now suppose it had been possible for the English Government
by some machinery to have got at his opinions before, as the
French say, "they had received a commencement of execution"—
opinions, we will say, virtuous and patriotic in the highest
degree, and justified, as things have gone, by the event, to the
effect that it would be much better that the British should be
driven out and that the American colonies should be self-
governed—it might have been in the highest degree necessary
and proper to seize and imprison, or even shoot, a man likely to
exercise so strong an influence. As far as we can judge, no soul
purer in intention than that of Charlotte Corday ever went up
to God, yet man was perfectly right in putting her to death for
stabbing Marat. But however this be, we must not be diverted
from pointing out what is inferred in this paragraph, not indeed
in exact words, but it is impossible to avoid seeing what is meant,
especially when the whole spirit of the address is considered.
"And if in matters of religion we allow pride and perverseness
to raise a cloud between us and the truth so that we see it not,
the false opinion that we form is but the index of that perverseness and that pride, and both for them, and for it as their
offspring, we shall be justly held responsible" (pp. 28, 29). This
is quite true, but it is impossible, as we have just said, not to see
distinctly what is pointed at. That a man will be justly
responsible for any errors into which he may fall if without
consideration he indulges in doubts about or arrives at a
conclusion hostile to orthodox Christianity, for instance, we have
admitted, and no one disputes. Indeed, we will go further than
this, and allow that even if he should turn out to be right in the
main as to his doubts or his hostility, he will be blameable for
having taken up opinions which, so to speak, only accidentally
turn out to be right. But the insinuation here is that in
religious matters only pride and perverseness can raise a cloud
between us and "the Truth." (What, we may ask with Pilate,
is the truth?) which is only another way of saying that it is
inconceivable to Mr. Gladstone how any man after investigating

these matters can honestly arrive at any other conclusion than that of Mr. Gladstone.

The lecture concludes with a few maxims which we can take no exception to, which were perhaps suitable to the occasion, but which we should have thought it hardly worth while to print. Indeed they are of the kind most usually found in manuscript, on the ruled pages of copy-books. We must except one sentence which, after turning it about in every way, we give up. "Do not too readily assume that to us have been opened royal roads to truth, which were heretofore hidden from the whole family of man; for the opening of such roads would not be so much in favour as caprice." There is perhaps a misprint here. We must also call attention to the concluding sentence, in which the author manages to vanish, characteristically, in a cloud. "Eschewing a servile adherence to the past, regard it with reverence and gratitude; and accept its accumulations alike in the inward and the outward spheres, as the patrimony which it is your part in life both to preserve and to improve." Here we have a notable example of that "language, grave and majestic, but of vague and uncertain import," which Lord Macaulay long ago pointed out as one of the characteristics of the eminent man who was once the "hope of the Tories" and is now sometimes the despair of the Liberals. What is meant by its being our part in life to preserve the accumulations of the past? A great part of our duty in life consists in sweeping away these accumulations. The founder of Mr. Gladstone's own creed commenced by virtually making a clean sweep of a great part of the Mosaic law. The teaching of the Apostles to the heathen was directed to the entire subversion of all the accumulations of preceding ages known under the name of mythology. "Brûlez ce que tu a adoré, et adore ce que tu a brûlé," was the advice given to Clovis; and precisely similar is the advice given in the present day by the missionary to the Buddhist and the Confucian. When we gave up burning and drowning witches, we made a clean sweep of all the accumulations, learning, lore, observations, experiences, experiments, rules, which had become collected, in and out of books, on the subject, during a great number of centuries. The word "accumulations" here means such as have value, such as deserve to be retained. But then how is this value to be ascertained except by inquiry of the freest kind? So amended, the sentence may mean "Do not be for pulling down beliefs, &c., because they are old." And this may be good advice to give in certain quarters; but if it have any reference to the sceptical spirit of the age, then there is a misapprehension of the real tendency of that spirit, which is not to pull down what is old, but what rests upon insufficient foundations.

Having thus indicated and commented on the salient points of this pamphlet (which reached us too late for notice in our January number) we should have liked to add a few words by way of conclusion. We should have wished to point out to Mr. Gladstone what really are the points at which his faith is seriously assailed; what really are, in our humble opinion, the issues which science, or if he pleases Scepticism, is fairly entitled to submit to Theology in the present day. But our limits have been reached, and we fear exceeded. We hope that, in his own words, we have "united plain speaking with personal respect," though we will not add, with him, that "this though an obvious is not an easy duty; for it is impossible to view certain states of mind as other than the results of strong though honest self-delusion ;" because we do not see why it should be other than an easy duty to speak with respect of those who in our opinion are mistaken, that is to say, who differ from us, which we presume is all that is here intended. We must, however, add iu conclusion that if it has been the author's purpose " to place on record his conviction that belief cannot now be defended by reticence any more than by railing," he has succeeded at the same time in accomplishing another purpose—namely, in giving us an additional proof, if any were needed, that it can derive no help from mere expressions of individual opinion, however eminent the individual, and however temperate his expressions may be. And if, as he further tells us, the time has come when the faith can no longer " be defended exclusively. by its standing army, by priests and ministers of religion ;" if, that is, volunteers are called for, it is surely desirable that they should come prepared to do something more than proclaim their allegiance to the cause, else they may perhaps be rather in the way than otherwise, and had better after all leave the matter in the hands of the regular forces. We will take the liberty of concluding with a metaphor of our own, which Mr. Gladstone's classical reading will at once render intelligible to him. The ancients, as he knows, used to utter loud cries and make other noises with the view of preventing an Eclipse of the moon. It is not by similar proceedings that, in the present day, any man or any body of men will succeed in warding off an Eclipse of the faith.

Art. III.—Venetian Painting.

IT was a fact of the greatest importance for the complete development of the arts in Italy that painting in Venice reached maturity later than in Rome, Florence, and Milan. Owing to this circumstance one chief aspect of the Renaissance —its material magnificence and freedom—received consummate treatment at the hands of Titian, Tintoretto, Veronese. To idealize the sensualities of the universe; to achieve for colour what the Florentines had done for form; to invest the external splendours of human life at one of its most gorgeous epochs with the dignity of the highest art; to vindicate the long forgotten title of the body to respect; to prove the sanity and the majesty of the flesh, was what these giant spirits lived to do.

Venice was precisely fitted for the accomplishment of this task. Free, isolated, wealthy, powerful; famous throughout Europe for the pomp of her state equipage, and for the magnificent immorality of her private manners; ruled by a prudent aristocracy, who spent vast resources on public shows and on the maintenance of a more than imperial civil splendour: Venice, with her street pavement of liquid chrysoprase, with her palaces of porphyry and marble, her frescoed façades, her quays and squares aglow with the brilliant costumes of the Levant, her lagoons afloat with the galleys of all nations, her churches floored with mosaics, her silvery domes, and ceilings glittering with sculptures bathed in molten gold: Venice luxurious in the light and colour of a transparent atmosphere, arched over by the broad expanse of a sky which nothing bounded but the horizon of sea and plain, and which was reflected, in all its gorgeousness of sunrise and sunset, upon the glassy surface of smooth waters: Venice asleep like a coral-reef of opal or of pearl upon the bosom of a waveless lake, an apocalyptic sea of glass—here and here only on the face of the whole globe was the unique city in which the pomp and pride of worldly life might combine with the lustre of the physical universe to create and stimulate in the artist a sense of the permanent value of colour, of the surpassing attractiveness of pageantry. There is colour in flowers. Gardens of tulips are radiant, and Alpine valleys touch the soul with the pathos of their pure and gemlike hues. Therefore the painters of Flanders and of Valdarno, John Van Eyck and Fra Angelico, penetrated some of the secrets of the world of colour.

But what are the purples and scarlets and blues of the iris,
the anemone, or the columbine, dispersed among deep meadow
grasses, or trained in quiet cloister garden beds when compared
with that melodrama of flame and gold and rose and orange and
azure which the sunset or the sunrise of Venice yields almost
daily to the eye? The Venetians had no green fields and trees,
no garden borders, no flowers to teach them the tender suggestiveness, the quaint poetry of isolated or contrasted tints. No.
Their meadows were the fruitless furrows of the changeful sea,
hued like a peacock's neck; they called the pearl shells of the
Lido flowers, "fior di mare;" nothing distracted their attention
from the symphonies of light and colour which their sea and sky,
one sphere of ever-shifting rainbow hues, one prism as wide as
the world, presented to them. It was in consequence of this
that the Venetians conceived colour heroically on a vast scale,
not as a matter of missal-margins or of subordinate decoration,
but as a theme worthy in itself of a sublime development.
In the same way, hedged in by no narrowing hills, contracted by no city walls, stifled by no dusty streets, but open
to the liberal airs of heaven and of the sea, the Venetians
understood space, and imagined almost illimitable pictures.
Light, colour, air, immensity—that is the theatre on which
the figures of the Venetian painters in their proud humanity
are made to move. Shelley's description of a Venetian sunset
in "Julian and Maddalo," is so true to the scenery which
inspired the art of the great masters, that it may be quoted as a
preface to what we have to say about their specific qualities.

> " As those who pause on some delightful way,
>   Though bent on pleasant pilgrimage, we stood
>   Looking upon the evening and the flood
>   Which lay between the city and the shore,
>   Paved with the image of the sky; the hoar
>   And airy Alps, towards the north, appeared,
>   Through mist, a heaven-sustaining bulwark reared
>   Between the east and west: and half the sky
>   Was roofed with clouds of rich emblazoury,
>   Dark purple at the zenith, which still grew
>   Down the steep west into a wondrous hue
>   Brighter than burning gold, even to the rent
>   Where the swift sun yet paused in his descent
>   Among the many-folded hills—they were
>   Those famous Euganean hills, which bear,
>   As seen from Lido through the harbour piles,
>   The likeness of a clump of peaked isles—
>   And then, as if the earth and sea had been
>   Dissolved into one lake of fire, were seen

Those mountains towering, as from waves of flame,
Around the vaporous sun, from which there came
The inmost purple spirit of light, and made
Their very peaks transparent."

That passage strikes the key-note to Venetian painting. With the poem of Shelley we may compare the following extract from a letter addressed from Venice in May, 1544, to Titian, by one of the most utterly worthless and unprincipled of literary banditti who have ever disgraced humanity, and who nevertheless was solemnized to the spirit of true poetry by the grandiose aspect of Nature as it appeared to him in Venice. That Pietro Arctino should have so deeply felt the splendour of natural beauty in an age when even the greatest artists and poets sought for inspiration in human life more than in the material universe is a significant fact, and seems to prove the natural fatality which made Venice the cradle of the Art of Nature.

"Having, my dear gossip, to the injury of my custom, supped alone ; or, to speak better, in the company of this quartan fever, which will not let me taste the flavour of any food, I rose from table sated with the same ennui with which I had sat down. In this mood I went and leaned my arms upon the sill outside my window, and throwing my chest and nearly all my body on the marble, gave myself up to the contemplation of the marvellous spectacle presented by the innumerable boats, filled with foreigners as well as people of the place, which gave delight not merely to the gazers, but also to the grand canal itself, which delights everybody that ploughs its waters. From this animated scene, all of a sudden, like a man who from mere ennui does not know how to occupy his mind, I turned my eyes to heaven, which, from the moment that God made it has never been adorned with such painted loveliness of lights and shadows. The whole region of the air was what those who envy you, because they are unable to be you, would fain express. To begin with, the buildings of Venice, though of solid stone, seemed made of some ethereal substance. Then the sky was full of variety, here clear and ardent, there dulled and overclouded. What marvellous clouds there were ! Masses of them in the centre of the picture hung above the houseroofs, while the immediate part was formed of a grey tint inclining to dark. I marvelled at the varied colours they displayed. The nearer masses burned with flames of sunlight ; the more remote blushed with a blaze of crimson lees afire. O how splendidly did nature's pencil treat and dispose that airy landscape, keeping the sky apart from the palaces, just as Titian does! On one side the sky showed a greenish blue, on another a bluish green, invented verily by the caprice of nature, who is mistress of the greatest masters. With her lights and her darks, there she was harmonizing, toning, and bringing out into relief, just as she wished. Seeing which, I who knew that your pencil is the spirit of your inmost soul, cried aloud thrice or four times, ' O Titian, where are you now ?' "

In order more fully to understand the destiny of Venice in Art, we may consider how different as a city she was, tranquil in her tyranny, serene in undisturbed prosperity, inhabited by merchants who were kings, and by a freeborn nation who had never seen war at their gates, from Florence, every inch of whose domain could tell of civil struggles, whose passionate aspirations after liberty ended in the despotism of the vulgar Medicean dynasty, whose repeated revolutions had slavery for their invariable catastrophe, whose grim grey palaces and austere churches bore on their fronts the stamp of the middle ages; whose spirit incarnated itself in Dante the exile; whose enslavement forced from Michael Angelo those groans of a tortured Titan which he expressed in marble and in fresco.

It is not an insignificant, though a slight detail, that the predominant colour of Florence is a sombre and cold brown, while the predominant colour of Venice is that of mother-of-pearl which conceals within its general whiteness every tint that can be placed upon the palette of a painter. To represent in art the spiritual strivings of the Renaissance was the task of Florence and her sons; to leave a pompous monument of Renaissance splendour was the achievement of Venice. Without Venice the modern world could not have produced that flower of healthful and unconscious beauty in painting which is worthy to stand beside the serene product of the sinless Greek genius in sculpture. Athene from her Parthenon stretches the hand to Venezia enthroned in the ducal palace. The broad brows and earnest eyes of the Hellenic goddess are of one divine birth and lineage with the golden hair and proud pose of the Sea-queen.

It is in the heart of Venice, in the House of the Republic, in the so-called Ducal Palace, that the Venetian painters, considered as the interpreters of proud magnificence, fulfilled their function with the most surprising success. Centuries contributed to make the ducal palace what it is. The massive colonnades and gothic loggias on which it rests, date from the 13th century; their sculptures belong to the age when Nicolo Pisano's genius was still in the ascendant. The square fabric of the palace, so beautiful in the irregularity of its pointed windows, so singular in its mosaic diaper of pink and white, was designed at the same early period. But the inner court and the façade which parts the lateral canal, display the handiwork of Sansovino, a Florentine of the Renaissance, who adopted Venice as his home, and whose talent, excited by the magnificence of the Republic, created a style of architecture almost arrogant in its fusion of a broad and vast design with superfluity of costly decoration. The halls of the palace—spacious chambers where the Senate assembled, where

Ambassadors approached the Doge, where the Council of Ten deliberated, and the Council of Three conducted their inquisition, are walled and roofed with pictures of inestimable value, encased in framework of sculptured oak, overlaid with solid gold. Supreme art, art in which fiery imagination vies with delicate and tender skill, is made in these proud halls the minister of mundane pomp. That the gold brocade of the ducal uniform, that the scarlet and crimson of the Venetian noble, may be duly harmonized by the richness of their surroundings, it was necessary that canvases measured by the score of square yards, and made priceless by the authentic handiwork of Titian, Tintoretto, Veronese, should blaze upon the gilded walls and roofs. A more insolent display of public wealth, a more lavish outpouring of human genius in the service of mere pageantry, cannot possibly be imagined. Supreme over all allegories and histories depicted in those multitudes of paintings, sits Venezia herself enthroned and crowned, the personification of haughtiness and power. Figured as a regal lady, with golden hair tightly knotted beneath a diadem around a small head proudly poised upon her upright throat and ample shoulders, Venice there takes her chair of state under resplendent canopies, as mistress of the ocean, to whom Tritons and sea nymphs and Neptune offer pearls ; as empress of the globe, at whose footstool wait Justice with the sword, and Peace with the olive-branch; as queen of heaven, exalted to the clouds. They have made her a goddess, those great painters,—have produced a mythus, and personified in native beauty that bride of the sea, their love, their lady. On every side, above, around, wherever you turn in these vast saloons, are seen the deeds of Venice, whether painted histories of her triumphs over the Emperors, the Popes, the Turks, or allegories of her grandeur—stupendous scenes in which the Doges Grimani and Loredani and Gritti and Contarini and Friuli and Dandoli, perform acts of faith, with St. Mark for their protector and with Venezia for their patroness. Surging multitudes of Saints in Paradise, massed together by Tintoretto and by Palma for the display of imposing effects of light, grand attitudes, gorgeous nudities, and mundane pomp of many-hued apparel, mingle with elaborate mythologies of Greek and Roman origin, fantastic arabesques, and charming episodes of pure idyllic painting. Religion in these pictures was a matter of parade, an adjunct to the costly public life of the Republic. We need not conclude that it was unreal. Such as it was, the religion painted by the Venetian masters is indeed as real as that of Fra Angelico or Albert Dürer. But it was the faith, not of humble men or of mystics, not of profound thinkers or ecstatic visionaries, so much as of courtiers and soldiers, and merchants and statesmen, to whom religion was an element of life, a function among other functions, not a thing apart, a consecration of the universe, a source of separate and supreme vitality. That Tintoretto could have painted the saints in glory, a countless multitude of surging forms, a sea whereof the waves are souls, as a mere background to state ceremony, shows the prosaic point of view, the positive and realistic attitude of mind, from which the Venetian masters started when they approached a religious subject. Paradise is a fact, reasoned Tintoretto ; and it is easier to fill a quarter of an acre of canvas with a picture of Paradise than of any other subject, because the figures can be so conveniently arranged in concentric tiers round Christ and Madonna in glory; therefore I will fill that end of the Council Chamber with my Paradise. Without more ado he did it. There is a picture by Guardi, which represents a kind of masked ball taking place in this chamber. The gentlemen are in periwigs and long waistcoats ; the ladies wear hoops, patches, fans, high heels, and powder. Bowing, promenading, flirting, diplomatizing, they parade about ; while from the billowy surge of saints, Moses with the Tables of the Law, St. Bartholomew holding up his poor flayed skin, the Magdalen with her dishevelled hair and adoration of ecstatic penitence, look down upon them. Tintoretto must have foreseen that the world of living pettiness and passion would perpetually jostle with his world of painted sublimities and sanctities in that vast hall. Yet he did not on that account shrink from the task. Paradise existed ; therefore it could be painted : if it filled the space better than another subject, put it in the place appointed : if the fine ladies and gentlemen below feel out of harmony with the celestial host, so much the worse for them.

In the Ducal Palace the Venetian Art of the Renaissance culminates. That art has been described as decorative; and truly here at all events it lends itself to the purpose of gorgeous ornamentation. Yet long before it culminated in this final splendour, the painting of Venice had been forming a tradition of pompous art in which the spirit of the Renaissance as the spirit of free enjoyment and magnificent expansion found its expression. To trace the history of Venetian painting is to follow through its several stages the growth of that mastery over colour and physical magnificence which blossomed finally in the works of Titian and his contemporaries. Under the Vivarini family of Murano the Venetian School of painting began with the imitation of pure nature, and with the selection from the natural world of all that it possessed of brilliant, luminous, salient with qualities of strength and splendour. No other painters of the fourteenth century in

Italy employed such glowing colours, or showed such predilection for the careful representation of fruits, rich stuffs, architectural canopies, jewels, landscape backgrounds. Their piety,
unlike the mystical asceticism of the Sienese and Florentine
masters, is marked by sanity, solidity, vivacity, joyousness. Our
Lady and her court of saints live, move, and breathe as if on earth.
They do not swim before ecstatic eyes as in the visions of
Angelico or Duccio. There is no atmosphere of tranced solemnity
surrounding them like that which gives peculiar charm to the
pietistic pictures of Van Eyck and Memling—artists who, by the
way, are more nearly allied than any others to the spirit of the
first age of Venetian painting.* What the Vivarini began, the
two Bellini, with Crivelli, Carpaccio, Mansueti, Basaiti, Catena,
Cima da Conegliano, Bissolo, continued. Bright colours in dresses,
distinct and sunny landscapes, broad backgrounds of architecture,
polished armour, gilded cornices, young faces of fisher boys and
country girls, grave faces of old men brown with sea-wind and
sunlight, withered faces of women hearty in a hale old age, the
superb manhood of Venetian senators, the dignity of patrician
ladies, the gracefulness of children, the rosy whiteness and
amber-coloured tresses and black eyes of the daughters of the
Adriatic and lagoons—these are the source of inspiration to the
Venetians of the second period. Mantegna, a few miles distant,
at Padua, was working out his ideal of severely classical design.
But he scarcely touched the manner of the Venetians with his
influence, though Gian Bellini was his son-in-law, and though
his genius, in grasp of matter and in management of thought,
soared far above his neighbours. Leonardo at Milan was working out his problems of psychology in painting and offering to
the world solutions of the gravest difficulties in the delineation
of the spirit by expression. Yet not a trace of Leonardo's subtle
play of light and shadow upon thoughtful features can be discerned in the work of the Bellini. Their function was a different
one. All the externals of a full and sumptuous existence
fascinated their imagination. The problems that they undertook
to solve were wholly in the region of colouring—how to depict
the world as it is seen, a mirage of varying lustre and of melting
hues, a pageant substantial to the touch and concrete to the eyes,
a combination of forms defined by colours more than outlines.

---

* The conditions of art in Flanders—wealthy, bourgeois, proud, free—were
not dissimilar to those of art in Venice. The misty flats of Belgium have
some of the atmospheric qualities of Venice. It is the different ἤθος of the
Flemish and Venetian nature which distinguishes their painting. As Van Eyck
is to the Vivarini, so is Rubens to Paolo Veronese.

Very instructive are the wall-pictures of this period, painted not in fresco but on canvas by Carpaccio, Gentile Bellini, and their scholars, for the decoration of the Scuole or Guildhalls of the Companies of St. Ursula and Sta. Croce. They bring before us the life of Venice in all its complexity. They indicate the tendency of the Venetian masters to express the shows and splendours of the actual world, rather than to realize an ideal of the fancy or to search the secrets of the soul of man.

Gian Bellini brought the art of this second period of Venetian painting to perfection. In his altar-pictures the reverential spirit of early Italian art is combined with a feeling for colour and a dexterity in its treatment peculiar to Venice. Bellini cannot properly be called a master of the Renaissance. He falls into the same category as Francia, Fra Bartolommeo, Fra Angelico, Perugino, who adhered to mediæval modes of thought and sentiment, while attaining at isolated points to the freedom of the Renaissance. Bellini's ground of superiority was colour. In him the colorists of Venice found a perfect master, and no one has surpassed him in the difficult art of giving tone to pure and luminous tints in complex combination. There is one picture of Bellini's at Venice in the Church of San Zaccaria, Madonna enthroned beneath a gilded canopy with Saints, in which the art of the colorist may be said to culminate in unsurpassable perfection. The whole painting is bathed in a soft but luminous haze of gold; yet each figure has its own individuality of treatment—the glowing fire of St. Peter contrasting with the pearly coolness of the drapery and flesh-tints of the Magdalen. No brushwork is perceptible. The whole surface and substance has been elaborated into one harmonious homogeneous richness of tone that defies analysis. Between this picture, so strong in its smoothness, and any masterpiece of Velasquez, so rugged in its strength, what a wide abyss of inadequate half-achievements, of smooth feebleness and feeble ruggedness, exists! Giorgione, did we but possess enough of his authentic work to judge by, would be found the first true painter of the Renaissance among the Venetians—the inaugurator of the third and great period. But he died young, at the age of thirty-six, the inheritor of unfulfilled renown. The part he played in the development of Venetian art was similar to that of Marlowe in the history of our drama. He first cut painting wholly adrift from mediæval moorings and launched it on the waves of the Renaissance liberty. While equal as a colorist to Bellini, though in a different and more sensuous region, Giorgione by the boldness and inventiveness of his conception, proved himself a painter of the calibre of Titian. His drawings, like those of his great successors, are miracles of form evolved without outline by massive distributions of light and

shade, suggestive of colouring. Time has destroyed his frescoes.
Criticism has reduced the number of his genuine easel pictures
to half-a-dozen. He exists as a great name. Of the undisputed
pictures by Giorgione the grandest is his Monk at the Clavichord,
in the Pitti Palace at Florence. The young man has his fingers
on the keys; he is modulating in a mood of grave and sustained
emotion; his head is turned away towards an old man who
stands by him. On his other side is a boy. These two figures
are but foils and adjuncts to the musician in the middle; and
the whole interest of his face lies in its intense emotion—the
very soul of music, as expressed in Browning's Abt Vogler, passing through his eyes. This power of painting the portrait of a
soul in one of its deepest moments, possessed by Giorgione, is
displayed again in the so-called *Begrüssung* of the Dresden
Gallery. The picture is a large landscape. Jacob and Rachel
meet and salute each other with a kiss. But the shepherd lying
beneath the shade of a chestnut tree near a well at a little distance has a whole Arcadia of intense yearning in the eyes of
sympathy with which he gazes on the lovers. Fate has dealt less
unkindly with Titian, Tintoretto, Veronese, than with Giorgione.
The works of these supreme artists, in whom the Venetian Renaissance culminated, have been preserved to us in vast numbers
and in excellent condition. Chronologically speaking, Titian
precedes Tintoretto, and Tintoretto is somewhat anterior to
Veronese. But for the purpose of criticism the three painters
may be considered together as the representatives of three marked
aspects in the Venetian Renaissance.

Let us first briefly characterize their qualities, and then proceed to more detailed remarks upon their several styles.

Tintoretto, called by the Italians the Thunderbolt of Painting,
because of his vehement impulsiveness and rapidity of execution,
soars above his brethren in the faculty of pure imagination. It
was he too who brought to its perfection the poetry of chiaroscuro, expressing moods of passion and emotion by brusque lights
and luminous half shadows and opaque darkness, as unmistakeably as Beethoven by contrasted chords. Veronese elevated
pageantry to the height of art. His domain is noonday sunlight ablaze on gorgeous dresses and Palladian architecture.
Titian, in a wise harmony, without the Æschylean fury of Tintoretto or the sumptuous arrogance of Veronese, realized the ideal
of pure beauty. Continuing the traditions of Bellini and Giorgione, with a breadth of treatment, a wisdom of moderation, a
vigour and intensity of well balanced genius peculiar to himself,
Titian gave to colour in landscape and the human form a sublime yet sensuous poetry which no other painter in the world
has reached. In his Assumption of the Virgin, his Bacchus and

Ariadne, his Venus of the Tribune, his allegory of the Three
Ages, Titian achieved the most consummate triumphs of
Venetian art. Tintoretto and Veronese are both of them excessive: the imagination of Tintoretto is too passionate, too
scathing ; the sense of splendour in Veronese is overpoweringly
pompous; Titian's exquisite humanity, his large and sane nature,
gives their proper value to the imaginative and the pompous
elements of Venetian art without exaggerating either. In his
masterpieces composition, thought, colour, sentiment are carried
to their ultimate perfection, as the many-sided expression of one
imaginative intuition, by which the supreme artist gives one harmonious tone to all the parts of his production. Titian, the
Venetian Sophocles, has infused into his painting the spirit
of music, the Dorian mood of flutes and soft recorders, making
his power incarnate in a form of grace.

Round these great men—Titian, the Sophocles of painting,
perfect in his harmonizing faculty, unrivalled in his empire over
colour ; Tintoretto, the archangel of Chiaroscuro, the Titan
of audacious composition, the priest of a passionate imagination ;
Veronese, the poet of insolent and worldly pomp—are grouped
a host of secondary but distinguished painters : the two Palmas,
idyllic Bonifazio, Paris Bordone, the Robusti, the Caliari, the
Bassani, and others whom it would be tedious to mention. One
breath, one afflatus inspired them all. Superior or inferior as
they may relatively be among themselves, each bears the indubi-
table stamp of the Venetian Renaissance, and produces work of
a quality that raises him to a high rank among the artists of the
world. In the same way the spirit of the Renaissance passing
ver the dramatists of our Elizabethan era, enabled intellects of
average force to take rank in the company of the noblest.
Ford, Massinger, Heywood, Decker, Webster, Tourneur, Marston,
are seated on the steps of the throne at the feet of Shakspeare, Marlowe, Jonson, Fletcher.

In order to penetrate the characteristics of Venetian art more
thoroughly, it will be needful to enter into detailed criticism of
the three chief masters who command the school. To begin
with Veronese : What is the world of objects to which he introduces us ?

His canvases are nearly always large, filled with figures of the
size of life, massed together in brilliant groups, or extended
beneath white marble colonnades, enclosing spaces of blue sky
and silvery cloud. Armour, shot colours in satins and silks,
brocaded canopies, banners, plate, fruit, sceptres, crowns, everything in fact that the sun can shine upon, form the habitual furniture of his pictures. Rearing horses, dogs, dwarfs, cats, when
occasion serves, are brought in to add reality, vivacity, grotesque-

ness to his scenes. His men and women are large, well-propor-
tioned, vigorous, eminent for pose and gesture rather than for
grace and loveliness, distinguished by adult rather than adoles-
cent charms. Veronese has no choice type of beauty. We find
in him on the contrary a somewhat coarse display of animal
force in men, and of superb voluptuousness in women. He
prefers to paint women draped in gorgeous raiment, as if he
had not felt the majestic beauty of statuesque nudity. His
noblest creatures are men of about twenty-five, manly, brawny,
full of nerve and vigour. In all this Veronese is not unlike
Rubens. But he never, like Rubens, appears to us gross,
sensual, fleshly; he remains proud, pompous, powerful. He
raises neither repulsion nor desire, but displays with the cold
strength of art the empire of the mundane spirit. All that
is refulgent in pageantry, all the equipage of arrogant wealth, the
lust of the eye and the pride of life, such vision as the fiend
offered to Christ on the mountain of temptation, this is
Veronese's realm.

Again, he has no flashes of imagination like Tintoretto; but
his grip on the realities of the world, his faculty for poetizing
prosaic magnificence, is greater. Veronese is precisely the painter
suited to a nation of bankers, in whom the associations of the
counting-house and the exchange mingled with the responsibilities of the Senate and the passions of princes. Veronese
never painted vehement emotions. There are no brusque
movements, no extended arms, like those of Tintoretto's
Magdalen in the Pietà at Milan. His Christs and Maries and
martyrs of all sorts are composed, serious, courtly, well-fed,
sleek personages, who, like people of the world accidentally
overtaken by some tragic misfortune, do not stoop to distortions
or express more than a grave surprise, a decorous sense of pain.
The Venetian Rothschilds undoubtedly preferred the sumptuous
to the imaginative treatment of sacred subjects. To do him
justice, Veronese does not make what would in his case have
been the mistake of choosing the tragedies of the Bible for representation in his pictures. It is the story of Esther, with its
royal audiences, coronations, processions; the marriage feast of
Cana; the banquet in the house of Levi, that he selects by
preference. Even these he removes into a region far from biblical associations. His *mise en scène* is invariably an idealization
of Italian luxury—vast open palace courts and loggias, crowded
with guests in splendid attire and with magnificent lacqueys.
The same love of display led him to delight in allegory—not
allegory of the deep and mystic order, but of the pompous and
processional, in which Venice appears enthroned among the
deities, or Jupiter fulminates against the vices, or the Genii of

the arts are personified as handsome women and blooming boys.
Tintoretto is not at home in this somewhat crass atmosphere of
mundane splendour. He requires more thought and fancy as
a stimulus to creation. He cannot be contented to reproduce
even in the most lustrous combination what he sees around him
of gorgeous and magnificent and vigorous. There must be some
scope for poetry in the conception, for audacity in the composition, something in the subject which can rouse the prophetic
faculty and evoke the seer in the artist; or Tintoretto does not rise
to his own altitude. Accordingly we find that Tintoretto, in
abrupt contrast with Veronese, selects by preference the most
tragic and dramatic subjects that can be found in sacred or profane history.* The Crucifixion with its agonizing Deity and
prostrate groups of women sunk below the grief of tears; the
temptation of Christ in the wilderness, with its passionate contrast of the grey-robed Man of Sorrows and the ruby-winged
voluptuous fiend; the temptation of Adam in Eden, a luxurious
idyll of the fascination of the spirit by the flesh; paradise, a tempest
of souls, a drift of saints and angels, "ruining" like Lucretian
atoms or golddust in sunbeams "along the illimitable inane," and
driven by the celestial whirlwind that performs the movement of
the spheres; the destruction of the world, in which all the fountains and rivers and lakes and oceans of earth have formed one
foaming cataract, that thunders with cities and nations in its rapids
down a bottomless gulf, while all the winds and hurricanes of
the air have grown into one furious blast that carries souls like
dead leaves up to judgment; the plague of the fiery serpents—
multitudes encoiled and writhing on a burning waste of sand;
the Massacre of the Innocents, with its spilth of blood on slippery
pavements of porphyry and serpentine; the Delivery of the
Tables of the Law to Moses amid cloud on Mount Sinai—a
white, ecstatic, lightning-smitten man emerging in the splendour
of apparent Godhead; the anguish of the Magdalen above her
martyred God; the solemn silence of Christ before Pilate;
the rushing of the wings of Seraphim; the clangour of the

---

* Perhaps the most profound characteristic of Tintoretto is that he attempts
to depict situations that are eminently poetic. The poet imagines a situation
in which spiritual or emotional life is paramount, and a sense of the body subordinate. The painter selects a situation in which the body is of first importance, and a spiritual or emotional activity is suggested. But Tintoretto
grapples immediately with poetic ideas, and often fails in his attempt to realize
them completely. Michael Angelo did the same. His sculpture in San Lorenzo,
compared with Greek sculpture, is an invasion of the proper domain of poetry
or music. Moses, in the picture of the Golden Calf in Santa Maria dell' Orto,
is a poem and not a true picture. The lean pale ecstatic stretching out his
emaciated arms, presents no beauty of attitude or outline. Energy of thought
is conspicuous in the figure.

Trump that wakes the Dead : these are the awful and soul-
stirring themes that Tintoretto handles with the ease of mastery.
He is the poet of infinity and passion; the Prospero of arch-
angelic Ariels; the Faust of spiritual Helens; the majestic
scene-painter of a theatre as high and broad and deep as heaven
and earth and hell. But it is not only in the region of the vast
and tempestuous and tragic that Tintoretto finds himself at
home. He is equal to every task that can be imposed upon the
imagination. Provided only that the spiritual fount be stirred,
the jet of living water gushes forth pure, inexhaustible, and
limpid. In his Marriage of Bacchus and Ariadne, that most
perfect idyll of the sensuous fancy from which sensuality is
absent; in his Temptation of Adam, that symphony of greys
and browns and ivory more lustrous than the crimson and the
gold of sunset skies; in his miracle of St. Agnes, that lamb-like
maiden with her snow-white lamb among the soldiers and the
courtiers and the priests of Rome, Tintoretto has added one
more proof that the fiery genius of Titanic artists can pierce
and irradiate the placid and the tender secrets of the soul
with more consummate mastery than falls to the lot of those
who make tranquillity their special province. Paolo Veronese
never penetrated to this inner shrine of beauty, this Holiest of
Holies where the Sister Graces dwell. He could not paint
waxen limbs, with silver lights and golden, and transparent
mysteries of shadow, like those of Bacchus, Eve, and Ariadne.
Titian himself was powerless to imagine movement like that of
Aphrodite floating in the air above the lovers, or of Madonna
adjuring Christ in the Paradiso, or of Christ himself judging by
the silent simplicity of his divine attitude the worldly judge at
whose tribunal he stands, or of the tempter raising his jewelled
arms aloft to dazzle with meretricious lustre the impassive God
above him, or of Eve leaning in irresistible seductiveness against
the fatal tree, or of St. Mark down-rushing through the air to
save the slave that cried to him, or of the Mary who has fallen
asleep with folded hands from utter exhaustion of agony at the
foot of the Cross. It is in these attitudes, movements, gestures,
that Tintoretto makes the human body an index and symbol of
the profoundest, most tragic, most poetic, most delicious thought
and feeling of the inmost soul. In daylight radiancy of
colour, he is surpassed, perhaps, by Veronese. In perfect
mastery of every portion of his art, in solidity of execution, in
firm unwavering grip upon his subject, he falls below the level of
Titian. Hundreds of his pictures are unworthy of his genius—
hurriedly designed, rapidly dashed in, studied by candlelight,
with brusque effects of abnormal light and shadow, hastily
daubed with colours that have not stood the test of time. He is

a gigantic improvisatore—a Gustavo Doré or a John Martin on the scale of Michael Angelo : that is the worst thing we can say of him. But in the swift intuitions of the spirit, in the purities and sublimities of the prophet-poet's soul, neither Veronese nor Titian can approach him.

How, lastly, are we to speak of Titian? Who shall seize on the salient characteristics of an artist whose glory it is to offer nothing over-prominent, who keeps the middle path of sanity and perfection? Just as complete health may be defined as the absence of any obtrusive sensation, just as virtue has been defined as the just proportion between two extravagances, so is the art of Titian a golden mediocrity of joy unbroken by brusque movements of the passions, a well-tempered harmony in which no thrilling note suggests the possibility of discord. When we think of Titian we are irresistibly led to think of music. His Assumption of the Madonna, the greatest single picture in the world, if we exclude Raphael's Madonna di San Sisto, may best be described as a symphony—a symphony of colour, in which every hue is brought into melodious play ; a symphony of movement in which every line communicates celestial sense of rhythm ; a symphony of light in which there is no cloud ; a symphony of joy in which saints, angels, and God himself sing Hallelujah. Tintoretto, in the Scuola di San Rocco, has painted an Assumption of the Virgin with characteristic energy and impulsiveness. A group of agitated men around an open tomb ; a rush of air and clash of seraph wings above; a blaze of light; a woman borne with sideways swaying figure from darkness into splendour; that is his picture: all brio, bustle, speed. Quickly conceived, carelessly executed, this painting bears the emphatic impress of its author's impetuous soul. But Titian has worked on a different method. On the earth among the apostles there is energy and action enough ; ardent faces straining upward, impatient men raising impotent arms, and vainly divesting themselves of their raiment as if they too might follow her they love. In heaven is splendour that eclipses half of the archangel who holds the crown, and reveals the Father of Spirits in a halo of golden glory. Between earth and heaven, amid a choir of angelic children, stands that mighty mother of the faith of Christ, that personified Humanity, who was Mary and is now a goddess, ecstatic yet tranquil, not yet accustomed to the skies, but far above the grossness and the incapacities of earth. The grand style can go no further than in this picture, serene, composed, meditated, enduring, yet full of dramatic energy and of profound feeling.

To talk about Titian is a kind of profanity. He does not stir the imagination like Tintoretto, or sting the senses, or awake

unquenchable ardours in the souL   But he gives to the mind joy
of which it can never weary, pure, well-balanced pleasures that
cannot satiate, a satisfaction not to be repented of, a sweetness
that will not pall.   It is easy to tire of Veronese; it is possible
to be fatigued by Tintoretto; Titian waits not for moods or
humours in the spectator.   Like Nature, like Pheidias, he is
imperishable.

In the course of this attempt to analyse the specific qualities
of Tintoretto, Veronese, and Titian, we have wandered from
the main subject we proposed to treat,—the character of
the Renaissance as exemplified by the Venetian masters.
It was necessary to do so, because the points of difference
between them are personal, while their point of accord is
complete participation in the spirit of Renaissance liberty.
Nowhere in Italy was art more absolutely emancipated from
servile obedience to ecclesiastical traditions than at Venice.
Nowhere was the Christian history treated with a more vivid
realism, harmonized more naturally with pagan mythology, or
more completely disinfected of mediæval mysticism.   The frank
liberty, the scientific positivism, the absolute sincerity, the candid
and joyous acceptance of all facts in human and physical nature,
which were the greatest qualities of the Renaissance, found no
obstacle whatever to their free development in Venice.

The Umbrian pietism which influenced Raphael in his boyhood
and from which he broke off too abruptly in his manhood, the
gloomy prophecy of Savonarola which steeped the soul of
Michael Angelo in melancholy, the psychological preoccupation
of Leonardo, were alike unknown at Venice.   Titian, Veronese,
Tintoretto, were courtiers, men of the world, children of the
people, men of pleasure ; wealthy, urbane, independent ; were all
these by turns ; but were never monks, or mystics, or philosophers.
In the Renaissance-spirit which possessed them religion found
a place ; sensuality was not rejected, but the religion was sane and
manly; the sensuality was vigorous and virile.   In a word
Humanity, that marvellous complex of what we call flesh and
spirit, lived in them and was mirrored in their hearts with absolute
limpidity.   There is no prudery, no effeminacy, no licence, no
hypocrisy, no morbidity either of superabundant sensualism or of
exaggerated asceticism in their strong, concrete, splendid pageant
of the newly discovered world.

Art. IV.—Henry Murger, the Bohemian.

1. *Œuvres Complètes de Henry Murger.* Paris: 1855, &c.
2. *Histoire de Henri Murger.* Par "Trois Buveurs d'Eau." Paris: 1862.
3. *Henri Murger.* Par M. Pelloquet. Paris: 1861.
4. *Murger et la Bohème.* Par A. Delvau. Paris: 1866.
5. *Contemporains.* Par E. Mirecourt. Paris: 1857.

THIS is a story of "Bohemian life" in its strangest and extremest form. In every age and in all countries the men who have followed art as a calling—whether with the pencil, the chisel, or the pen—have been wont to rebel against the chafing trammels of the conventionalities that society in its own general interest has imposed upon its members, and have sought, in isolated cliques, to shut out the turmoil and the rush of this busy work-a-day world; and, as in some secluded haven where the lusts of gold and pride and power are not, have given themselves wholly and solely to the worship of pure art, finding strength to bear defeats in the companionship of fellow-workers, courage to endure privations and to compel success in their very dreams and illusions. There is always something fascinating about the history of those who, worshipping strange gods and having peculiar standards of their own as to the purposes and utility of being, lead lives apart from the routine of ordinary mortals. And if this rule applies to the swarthy gipsy as he lies in the free night air by the fitful gleam of his camp fireside, it applies with a threefold greater force to those other Bohemians who, amid the pent-up closeness of a civilized city, have founded inaccessible communities of their own. "Bohemian life," wrote Murger, "is possible nowhere but in Paris." This was scarcely true; but old Paris, above all in the Quartier Latin, with its quaint huge houses, each standing as a fortress against the Philistines of the outer world—its thoughtless students, its grisette-loves, its *halles*, its cafés, its cheap pleasures, its sunshine and its joyousness, was the very home of a picturesque Bohemia. At the time, too, of which we are writing, from a variety of causes, political and other, a strong reaction had arisen against the materialism of the day; numbers of young men had, in different cliques, banded themselves together to follow "Art for Art's sake," and their joys, their miseries, their day-dreams, and their rare successes present us with a marvellous picture, in which the lights and shadows stand out in bold relief. We are told that since literature has been elevated into a profession the wretchedness of Grub Street has disappeared. There are certainly more prizes now for the competitors, but there are as certainly more blanks; and we shall find that the struggles of an Otway, a Savage, a Chatterton, or a Goldsmith are fairly rivalled in interest by the history of those young Frenchmen who, in our own times, and in "the most civilized city of the world," adopted, careless of the cost, the melancholy motto—" The Academy, the hospital, or the Morgue !"

Henry Murger was born at Paris upon the 24th of March, 1822, in a house in the Rue St. George, of which his father was the *concierge*, or porter. Though the family name was of German origin, Murger *père* came from Savoy ; he had fought in the French army in the disastrous campaign of 1815, and wishing to remain in France, had settled in Paris, where he married a young French work-girl, so that on both sides Henry was of the humblest extraction. Shortly after the birth of their only son the proprietor of the house turned the family suddenly adrift into the streets, though Murger had served him long and faithfully ; but after a few weeks' misery, he obtained another situation as porter in one of the fine houses in the Rue de Trois Frères, and here he was allowed, for he was an energetic man, fonder of crossing his legs than his arms, to commence business on his own account as a tailor, a trade almost proverbially associated with the German porters of Paris.

Henry was a fine child, chubby and beautiful, with an odd knack of making friends among his elders and social betters, and as soon as he could toddle about his beauty became the boast of the *quartier*, and as "the little boy in blue" he was everywhere known, for his mother took a pride in dressing him becomingly. Nor did the good woman's ambition stop here ; with a quick motherly instinct, not unmingled with personal pride, she declared that her darling was no common child, and determined that he was destined to become a *monsieur*, not a mere tradesman, and this project, spite of the querulous objections of the father, who looked upon her prophecies as absurd motherly vanity, she kept steadily in view.

Two artistic families of distinction, the Garcias and the Lablaches, resided in the house of which his father was the porter, and the ladies spoiled the little fellow, who was so much brighter and fresher than Parisian children wont. Pauline Garcia, afterwards as Malibran to be so famous, was just about his own age, and the two children were inseparable. Thus his first years were divided between the pleasant poverty of home and the graceful elegance of artistic and witty society, to which, doubtless, much of his own peculiar humour was afterwards due. Then there was the childish love with his cousin Angèle, which he himself sung when, growing older, she became ashamed of her graceless sweetheart. Smile at it as we will in after years when we see it in other children, this child-love is part and parcel of all our lives, and very potent to their future colouring.

TO COUSIN ANGELINE.

"We both have left behind us the early
    years that seem
The sweetest and the fairest in their
    innocence divine.
I often count them over, but oh I do
    you ever dream
Of the happy days of childhood, O
    my cousin Angeline !

"Those days are very distant, and
    already many times
The passing years have touched us
    with their soft wings as a sign,
And all our ringing gladness, with its
    laughter-pealing chimes,
Has fled, alas ! for ever, O my cousin
    Angeline !

"A class of noisy scholars, from books
    and ferules fled,
We sang the ancient carol, but with
    sinister design,
'We'll go no more a-Maying, for the
    hawthorn trees are dead ;'
We'll go no more a-Maying, O my
    cousin Angeline !

"But happier far than I am, you have
    never had to part
From sweet maternal tending care,
    from the hearth-side's holy shrine ;
Oh keep a minted purity deep buried
    in your heart,
Tho' never more in my heart, O my
    cousin Angeline !

"With work to keep you company
    throughout the livelong day,
At eve the white-winged angels in
    guardian hosts combine
To watch your girlish slumbers, while
    celestial visions stray
From the heavens to your pillow,
    O my cousin Angeline !

"Your voice is low and pleasant, and
    your eyes are softly coy,
While love and human kindness
    through all your glances shine,

A MA COUSINE ANGÈLE.

" Nous avons tous les deux laissé derrière
    nous
Une époque où la vie est bien bon et
    bien belle,
Je m'en souviens encor, nous en sou-
    venons-nous
De notre enfance heureuse ! ô ma
    cousine Angèle !

" Ils sont bien loin ces jours, et déjà bien
    des fois
Les ans nous ont touchés en passant
    de leur aile ;
Et notre gaîté blonde aux grands éclats
    de voix,
Hélas ! s'est envolée, ô ma cousine
    Angèle !

" Ecoliers turbulents de la classe
    échappés,
Pour danser en chantant l'antique
    ritournelle.
'Nous n'irons plus aux bois, les
    lauriers sont coupés,'
Nous n'irons plus aux bois, ô ma
    cousine Angèle !

" Plus heureuse que moi, vous n'avez
    pas quitté
Le foyer de famille, et la voix mater-
    nelle ;
Conserve à votre cœur la sainte piété,
Qui n'est plus dans le mien, ô ma
    cousine Angèle !

" Vous avez le travail pour compagnon
    le jour,
La nuit un ange blanc vous couvre
    de son aile,
Et des songes bénis descendent, tour à
    tour,
Du ciel à votre lit, ô ma cousine
    Angèle !

" Votre parole est douce, ainsi que votre
    nom ;
L'esprit de la bonté dans vos yeux
    se révèle,

O sweet sixteen ! your maiden years
  have fill'd the house with joy,
And with youth as with a perfume,
  O my cousin Angeline |

" O long ago when New Year came, the
  day was very pleasant,
For I had hoarded up my store to
  purchase something fine,
And breathlessly and joyously I ran to
  give my present,
Though never of the dearest, O my
  cousin Angeline |

" But since that distant period the devil,
  as they say,
Has taken up his sojourn in this
  empty purse of mine,
I hail blind Plutus lustily, but he's
  deaf, too, when I pray.
For he never seems to hear me,
  O my cousin Angeline !

" You will have nothing from me, alas !
  my dear, to-day ;
No picture-teeming keepsake, in
  scarlet robes ashine,
No rich and costly trifles, no gems of
  purest ray,
Not even sugar'd bon-bons, O my
  cousin Angeline !

" You will have nothing from me but a
  kiss a brother might
Press on your snowy forehead, from
  these luckless lips of mine.
And then these sorry verses, that to-
  morrow or to-night
You'll doubtless have forgotten, O
  my cousin Angeline !"

Et vous seize ans fleuris embaument la
  maison,
D'un parfum de jeunesse—ô ma
  cousine Angèle !

" Autrefois quand venait le jour de l'an
  nouveau.
Selon le contenu de ma pauvre
  escarcelle,
J'arrivais tout joyeux vous offrir mes
  cadeau,
Qui ne coûtait pas cher—ô ma
  cousine Angèle !

" Mais depuis ce temps-là le diable,
  comme on dit,
S'est logé dans ma bourse, et vaine-
  ment j'appelle
Plutus, l'aveugle dieu, que je crois
  sourd aussi,
Car il ne m'entend pas, ô ma
  cousine Angèle !

" Donc, vous n'aurez de moi nul présent
  aujourd'hui,
Ni keepsake éclatant, ni riche baga-
  telle,
Ni bijou ciselé par quelque Cellini,
  Et ni bon-bons sucrés—ô ma cousine
  Angèle !

" Vous n'aurez rien de moi qu'un serre-
  ment de main,
On qu'un baiser au front, étrenne
  fraternelle,
Et puis ces pauvres vers, que ce soir ou
  demain,
Vous oublirez sans doute, ô ma
  cousine Angèle !"

The boy's day-dreams took after his life. He invested the
gaiety of Parisian poverty with a marvellous joyousness; the
marionette shows and penny theatres became halls of dazzling
splendour; the grisettes and students were endowed with all the
fancies of an only child who lived much with the fairies ; the
world was very happy, beautiful and bright, full of loving friends
with outstretched helping hands, to be trusted evermore ; of
glorious prizes to be longed for, and forthwith obtained ; and so
down the gamut of every childish dream. But the Paris world
was more than this for Murger—it was a world to be painted, to
be sung, to be immortalized in some way, and by him. For
beyond his mother's petting flatteries he heard a voice that
whispered, "Son of a tailor, thou shalt be a poet ! The Pari-
sians shall sing thy verses, as the fishers of Sorento those of Tasso.
Thou shalt be one of the chosen whom women crown with roses
and men with laurels. Thou shalt be loved and applauded. Go

onward, child, to glory; onward towards love!" but the fairies whispered nothing of misery and starvation and neglect and sickness.

All the education that was paid for in money—nay, in sous—was received at a little primary school, where he learned to write a pretty hand, an advantage more than counterbalanced by a detestable style, and an orthography beyond even the common sins of the French *bourgeois*, to be unlearned afterwards by years of painful labour. At school, however, one of the "Professors," a boy not much older than himself, who had at twelve exhausted all the capabilities of the establishment, and had been retained in a condition of proud slavery as a lofty ensample to the others, took much interest in young Murger, directed his out-of-school studies, and strengthened his artistic cravings.

There were fierce battles fought at this time between his father and mother, the former declaring that the lad should follow his own calling, and the latter by every womanly ruse endeavouring to compass her ends, and cunningly seeking allies among those who were not to be daunted by fear of domestic brawls. The owners of the houses on either side, Isabey, the painter, and M. de Jouy, of the Academy, had taken a fancy to the sprightly boy, and lent all their influence to the mother's petition. M. de Jouy, a literary man of the old school, who had in his back yard built a temple to Voltaire, and who quaintly filled his library with glass flagons in the shape of books, containing exquisite wines and fine liquors, lettered "Spirit of Montesquieu," "Spirit of Rousseau," &c., obtained him the offer of a situation, and finally, when Henry was only fourteen years old, his father consented that he should become an office boy to an attorney, at the moderate salary of twenty francs a month, and Madame Murger, overjoyed beyond measure at seeing her darling on the highroad to becoming a *monsieur*, was probably more gratified at the prospect than the boy himself.

In the office he met two other lads of his own age, and a pretty life they must have led the worthy attorney. The brothers Bisson like Henry hated desk-work, and were determined to become artists of some grade, but they were already further on the road to their aspirations. Living next door to a houseful of painters they had forthwith determined to paint. This enthusiasm was infectious, Murger became as eager as any. Directly office hours were over the three lads, with their portfolios under their arms, rushed off to the nearest gratuitous art-school, and later on Murger managed to crib an hour or two in the daytime for the same purpose. Whenever their master's back was turned, or when there was a pause in the engrossing of deeds and the spoiling of stamped paper, there were new pictures and poems to be discussed, stormy disputes as to the comparative merits of Lamartine and Hugo. For some time Henry thought he had found in painting the fitting medium to express the thoughts that since childhood had thronged his brain ; and he laboured very zealously, though with little result, except as to the detriment of the attorney's purchased service. The brothers Bisson had, however, found their true vocation, and throwing title-deeds and briefs to the four winds of heaven, they determined to starve upon art, rather than upon the scanty wage the law afforded. Murger still joined them every evening, sketching with all the zeal of fancy, scribbling his first verses as random genius prompted. He had no inducements now to stop at home, his loving mother was dead, and his father was daily becoming more sullen and morose. The poems and sketches were hoarded safely out of his sight, but one unlucky day he was surprised in the composition of a sonnet, and his father angrily demanded the reason of those foolish lines,—probably they were difficult of comprehension—and, but little satisfied with the explanation rendered, vowed that unless Henry's pen were for the future used exclusively for law notes and minutes, it would be withdrawn altogether from his hand, and a needle substituted. This feeling was, after all, only a grotesque exaggeration, brutal maybe in this instance, of the dread with which every parent regards art as a career, and the biography of every artist—poet, painter, sculptor or musician, shows a similar family reluctance. Perhaps, as M. Th. Gautier urges in one of his most charming *causeries,* the parents are in the right after all. To what a sad, precarious, miserable existence, leaving aside altogether the mere question of money-earning, does a lad pledge himself when he selects art as a profession. From that day he is, in a degree, separated from his fellows. He is a spectator rather than an actor upon the human stage. He is subject to the same hopes, the same passions, the same emotions as other men, and in a finer degree ; but he must pause even in his torment to analyse them all. He must dream of an ideal he can never reach, he must yearn for her through toilsome hours, through long drawn out years of defeat and suffering, and when at length he clasps her, it will probably be in time only to perish upon her bosom, worn out with battling and with sheer exhaustion. And what after all if he were but pretender, a mere dreamer, if his calling should prove abortive, and his efforts die stillborn ? To Murger's father, however, it was probably a calculation of the comparative earnings of a tailor's apprentice, and an unpublished, unpublishable poet's. The world he knew must have clothes, and did not much care about poetry till it had the stamp of fashion and popularity to recommend it.

E E 2

Besides these quarrels with his father there were repeated scoldings for the youngster when he entered the office. It was scarcely possible that he could sit up all night with his books and his sketches—for his daily business occupation forced him into habits of nocturnal study that clave to him through life—and turn up fresh and punctual in the morning; that when he looked upon the weakest of his sonnets as of infinitely greater importance than the weightiest office deeds, his duties could be satisfactorily performed. Storms were brewing in all directions till old M. Jouy came again to the rescue with the promise of a secretaryship to Count Tolstoy, which was to leave him some considerable time for the bent of his natural inclinations. At this period Henry is introduced to us for the first time in veritable history by Lelioux, one of the "Trois Buveurs d'Eau," who afterwards in the "Histoire de Murger," related what each personally knew :—

"I saw Murger for the first time towards the end of 1839 ; he was then about sixteen. I have only to shut my eyes to see again clearly and distinctly all the details of that first visit. The key was in the lock ; Murger had knocked softly, and then entered, tranquil and smiling. He was a stout young lad, beardless, chubby-cheeked, and rosy, whose whole appearance, puffy rather than brawny, betrayed a lymphatic temperament. His brown eyes were very open, and looked around with a placid *naïveté*. His friendliness, juvenile as it was, was as exempt from embarrassment as from overboldness. 'M. Pottier is not in ?' he asked. 'No, monsieur,' replied I ; 'Pottier only comes back at night.' 'Oh, I am one of his friends,' he continued, taking possession of a chair, and pulling all the essentials for a cigarette out of his pocket ; 'he was my master at the school of M. ——. He met me the other morning, and engaged me to come and see him ; besides, he told me that you lived together, and that you wrote for the papers and the theatres, and advised me to come and have a chat with you.' 'Ah ! you write verses too ?' 'I try,' he answered, endeavouring to laugh at himself. . . . I was only nineteen, and at that time there was no other literature for us but 'verses'—we allowed the great poets only to write prose."

After chatting for two hours, Henry began to read his verses, "ten, eleven, thirteen, fourteen syllables to each line, rarely twelve !" and these were continued until Pottier entered. Pottier had left his unprofitable "professorship" to follow the precarious calling of literature. Slightly older than the others, he was almost worshipped by the small clique ; "good at everything, enthusiastic about everything, able to learn anything in two hours, to comprehend anything in a day, to do anything in a week. This prodigious facility of assimilating his genius to all forms and subjects falsified our predictions. Would he be a

Désaugiers, a Béranger, a Casimir Delavigne, or a Lamartine? Alas and alas! to this day his verses have never been published."

An acquaintance so pleasantly begun soon ripened into a warm friendship, and Murger came to their rooms almost every day, for now that his mother was dead he only slept at home. Lelioux's room was his asylum on the *rive droite*, while the Bissons' studio was his refuge on the *rive gauche*; in the first he kept a desk, in the second an easel; and when the attorney sent him out during office hours to make business calls to either the east or the west, he used to drop in upon one set of friends or the other, and steal an hour or so to cultivate one of the two arts. These double studies lasted for some time, until one of the Bissons told him frankly that he was altogether wasting his time in endeavouring to become a painter. Murger took the advice in good part, and henceforth gave all his thoughts to poetry. He had still much to learn, and not a little to forget, for neither his style nor his grammar was at present pure. But night and day he laboured, proud of his productions till a fortnight afterwards he tore them up in disgust. "I can finish nothing," he used to say, and even his friends' approbation vexed him, for he felt that his genius was infinitely superior to his performance. First one sheet of verses and then another would be tossed into the fire, till at the year's end his desk would be completely emptied. These poetical studies led him into a curious mania, which he himself has described in an autobiographical sketch:—

"This was one of the many fancies of this singular lad: he used to purchase all the thin little volumes in green and blue that in the spring and autumn appeared upon the quay bookstalls. Not a single hemistiche was published but he soon got scent of it. He argued that it was necessary to keep oneself *au courant* with the progress of poetry, the fact really being that he wished to judge if he were himself as strong as the authors of the 'Midnight Moanings' and 'Matutinal Memories.' Every time he purchased one of these wretched little volumes he assembled all the poetasters of his acquaintance, and proceeded to read the new poems aloud, and when his own opinion and that of his admirers turned in favour of his own verse he was contented, and accepted the superiority they voted him without a contest."

This mania, melancholy enough in the long run, must however have introduced him to the works of Alfred de Musset, Hégésippe Moreau, Emile Deschamps, and Sainte-Beuve; but the most memorable purchase he made was that of Banville's "Cariatides." When this poem was read aloud, it caused a kind of stupor among the audience; they knew that Banville was only nineteen, and they felt terribly defeated and out-distanced. After a painful silence, Murger shouted, " I swear I'll see this Banville ; Nadar knows him, and he shall introduce me I"

Murger's relations with his father and his master were daily becoming more unpleasant, and there was doubtless a general feeling of relief when, in 1839, M. de Jouy obtained him the promised appointment as secretary to Count Tolstoy. It was fully understood that time should be allowed the lad for study, and the salary of forty francs a month, small as it was, did not imply any great amount of labour. From this monthly allowance his father deducted thirty francs as payment for board and lodging.

Murger made favourable way with his new patron, the official correspondent of the Russian Ministry of Public Instruction, but nothing he did pleased his father, and to make matters worse he fell violently in love at this time—a fatal passion that was to embitter his life—to be fully treated of hereafter ; and what with his love, and his studies in his friends' rooms, his habits became irregular. One night he was late, his father grumbled ; the next night he was later, his father thundered ; on the third night he did not turn up at all, and when he appeared in the morning his father refused him admittance altogether, and bade him shift for himself in the future—and he was an outcast with the whole of his worldly possessions on his back, principally in the shape of a greatcoat of hairy yellow stuff, made by the parental hands, for too many years alas, to be a well known feature of the Quartier Latin. Still he was nothing daunted. Full of love and poetry, and singing a pæan to liberty, he rushed to Lelioux's room and took up his abode there permanently. Hitherto he had never known actual want or misery, but he had burnt his ships, there was now no return. For better or worse he was one of the Bohemian brotherhood.

It is worth while pausing for a moment to examine the world into which he was entering—the battle in which his life was staked to play out to the end. At no other time and in no other place had there ever existed such a literary Bohemia as that which from various causes sprang up in Paris after the events of the year 1830. The profession of Art in its every branch had, from want perhaps of other religion, been elevated into a passionately eager worship, and its followers struggled against the material necessities of existence—all but absolute—against the wearisomeness of years of laborious apprenticeship, against the gibes of friends and the utter indifference of the public, with only their genius and their hopes to aid them in the battle. Many died of misery ere their fame had been achieved, before their books had been printed or their pictures seen —and they were heard of no more. But some few rose to supreme eminence, and these represent the others; for does not every general's tomb bear an epitaph beneath which a thousand brave soldiers lie sleeping? Abridging the eloquent words of Charles de Molly, there are, apart from all idea of loss or gain, of dirge or pæan, few battles as glorious as this; to renounce constantly, and without a shade of regret, often even joyously, the advantages of wealth and influence with which so many callings abound ; to live above petty interests and puerile vanities in the lofty world of Art ; to give every thought to austere contemplation, to passionate enthusiasm, to painful study ; to accept all privations so that one day, we know not when, the ideal we bear within ourselves may be realized ;—" this is to act nobly, and lives such as these are worthy of being told, nay, worthy of being sung, for there is a poem in this courage, in this faith !"

Side by side with these young artists who fashioned their thoughts laboriously so as to give them the very form of their dreams, who battled for the holiest things in this world, the Good, the True, the Beautiful, there were then, as there are now, a crowd of audacious mediocrities, self-styled painters, poets, and sculptors, who profess the same aims, but who have never comprehended, never even tried to comprehend, the fact that a masterpiece costs much time and the most indefatigable labour. These are they who never having produced an idea under any possible form, complain of their obscurity and their misery with a bitter hatred to all whom either genius or talent has led to fortune—and who conceal their moral incapacity and their insurmountable idleness in the smoky depths of some low tavern. Ask them what they have ever done, by what profound study they have acquired the right of discussing men and ideas, and they reply by foul-mouthed declamations upon the miseries of the times, and the injustice of their contemporaries, upon the lucky chance or the cunning intrigue through which the others have surpassed them.

The room in which Murger took refuge was a little attic in the Rue d'Auvergne ; it was so low that an ordinary man could not enter in his hat, and was occupied chiefly by Lelioux's bed— he was luxurious—by an old bureau, full of precious papers, and by books and broken pipes. The inmates were only able to "seat themselves morally," but then they made lyric poetry and had a thousand dreams and illusions to keep them steadfast in their purpose. The cold winter of 1839-40, pleasant enough in snugly curtained drawing-rooms, was a trying season for the poets ;—and there were, he tells us, alas, more poets in Paris than gas-lamps, with every chance of an increase if the police failed to interfere. Little by little their scanty furniture disappeared to

thaw out the frost, and one especially bitter night the cold was
so intense that a drawerful of precious manuscripts was sacrificed.
They were luckier in the possession of this garret than another
of their clique, poor Karol, whose residence was in the "Avenue
de St. Cloud, in the third tree to the left after leaving the
Bois de Boulogne, and on the fifth branch." Heaven alone
knows how they all lived! Literary work does not drop readily
into the hands of young poetasters of seventeen who have voted
prose a degradation. Murger was at all events more fortunate
than some of the others, and his regular income of forty francs a
month obtained him the sobriquet of the "Capitalist." He laboured
incessantly at his art, and learned something of prosody and grammar, but the only poem with which he was at this time at all
satisfied, a dismal prose precursor of the *Vie de Bohème*, em-
blematically christened the "Via Dolorosa," went the round
of the Paris publishers in vain—and in maturer years he never
cared to print it. There were other struggling artists living in
the house, notably the actor Lureau, who played the rôle of
heavy father at the minor theatres, and performed the character
still more thoroughly at home, where he had a wife and seven
children depending on his seventy francs a month. This scanty
income he eked out by addressing envelopes at twenty-five cents
the hundred ; and every morning Murger and Lelioux used to
write two or three hundred of these for the wage of a cup of
café-au-lait. There were, however, two occasions of splendid
extravagance. Once when the friendly editor of the *Gazette
de la Jeunesse* inserted, and actually paid for, Murger's first
contribution. And again, when Lelioux drew, also for the first
time, his half share in the author's profits of *La Justice de paix,*
a vaudeville played at a suburban theatre. The friends arrived
at the cashier's desk in a state of nervous anxiety, for at the
first representation they had been the only occupants of the
boxes, the other author occupying the dress-circle, a comrade
holding the stalls, while the gallery resounded with the applause
of six friendly *claqueurs.* With a success like this the piece had
run for eighteen nights ; and the four per cent. on the receipts,
legally allotted to the authors, amounted to twenty-seven francs—
thirteen francs and a half each, the exact price of the paper and
the *pour boire* to the prompter..
   Still Murger was advancing gradually in his art, and his style
daily became more assured ; and though nothing of this early
period was intrinsically worth preservation, he felt that he had
mastered the rudiments and technicalities of poetry. As before
and after, he worked through. the night and slept during the
day—an arrangement, by the way, that doubtless led to some
comfort in the economy of beds ; he had discovered that coffee

appeased hunger and excited the imagination, and with coffee and these midnight vigils he undermined his constitution. Candles were at this time about his only extravagance. At night he used to light his whole stock of them, laying a sheet of paper by each before he began to compose : walking to and fro he would write a line in one form upon one sheet, in a different form upon a second, and so on through the five or six, merging them eventually into one completed whole—not a pleasant habit this for his luckless companions who slept, or tried to sleep, as nature bade, from eve to morn.

This was the true garret life of which Béranger sang "the attic where one is so happy at twenty,"—"the snug little kingdom up three pair of stairs,"—though "snugness" is an idea belonging to the English version. But dearer than even friendship or the Muse was the enthusiastic passion of love. For the last eighteen months his comrades had heard this love-story daily—"to be continued to-morrow." Even before this the poet's necessity of loving some one, of finding sympathy somewhere, had induced him to renew his childish companionship with his cousin Angèle, and at this period the verses we have before quoted were written, but now as he says, "she could not bear him." The other love with Marie was the one that coloured his whole afterlife, that was to be reproduced in all his works with the same certainty as that she was to be the heroine and himself the hero. The beautiful story of *Les Amours d'Olivier* contains, according to the unanimous testimony of his earliest friends the true history of this unfortunate passion, for Olivier as usual, may in a stronger degree than usual, is Henry Murger.

After he had been placed in the attorney's office, his father thought it desirable that he should obtain a knowledge of book-keeping, and he was sent to a professor in the neighbourhood, one M. Duchampy, for instruction. A dissolute man this professor, a *roué*, a gambler, and a drunkard, who at the age of forty-six married a young girl to whom he had before behaved atrociously. His wife, Marie, now about four-and-twenty, had those languorous graces so often betokening a loving temperament disappointed of its ideal and feeding upon dreams. Her soft eyes, of an indecisive blue, were sometimes, though rarely, illumed with a sudden flash of compressed passion which lent also an animated colour to her ordinarily pale cheeks. Her smile seemed to beseech a confidence for a life of poignant suffering. When Murger took his lessons, she was always in the room busied with a thousand coquettish household cares, and it not unnaturally happened that he learned little of the science of double-entry, but fell, as a romantic schoolboy could scarcely fail to do, most violently in love with his professor's wife. It was the old story—a loving lad, an idle wily woman—ennui-dispelling amusement on the one part, a mad devotion that tinged the whole of a life's career on the other. One evening when they chanced to be alone, she poured forth a pitiful tale of the sufferings that burthened a wasted and uncomprehended existence. The boy's heart was full of compassion for her wrongs, of yearnings to share her troubles; very eager to show that some one at least could sympathize, he flung himself upon his knees, and with sobs that broke his utterance, and did but lend a stronger fervour to it, he burst out with a confession of his mad love, with all the eloquence of a first passion. She listened with averted face, but from that evening they were Marie and Henry to each other.

Six months' constant attendance had in spite of himself taught Murger as much book-keeping as the professor was capable of imparting, and he was told that his further attendance as a pupil would be useless, though his master added, the oftener he came as a friend the more welcome would he be made; and, as before, his visits were of almost nightly occurrence. M. Duchampy divined the motives clearly enough, for on surprising a platonic letter to his wife, commencing "Ma sœur," he took it to her with a brutal jest, and complacently let events go their own way, more especially as Henry's presence at home left him leisure to pursue a villanous fraud he was then concocting. After a twelvemonth this scheme was discovered by the police, and he fled for very life to England, leaving his wife alone in Paris without a sou, and without a friend but her boy-lover, who flew at once to her rescue. For eighteen months his love had been of the purest, he had seen her daily from the morning till the evening—this time he remained with her from the evening till the morning, as a protector more than as a lover, for justice was already upon her track as an accomplice in her husband's machinations. Seeing the liberty of his darling threatened, and having neither money nor asylum of his own, Murger ran to one of his friends, the elder Bisson, who offered him the use of a little room that adjoined his studio. Here for some months the two lovers hid themselves from the world, their poverty being in the eyes of one, at all events, far more than counterbalanced by the fulfilment of his dearest dreams. The little attic became a fairy palace, the single rickety old arm-chair was large enough for two, and the scanty "bread of gaiety" was very sweet indeed when there was some one with whom to share it. Then there were long Sunday excursions into the pleasant country around Paris, when the trees and the flowers and the streams had new meanings of their own, the singing birds sweeter melodies. It was the dreamland that comes to most men once, to brighten a few weeks, to bless or curse an afterlife. Limitless protestations of love, wonderful hopes of a rosy future when fame and glory would justify its choice, were poured hour by hour into her ears by a lover all unconscious of the yawn upon his mistress's face. In the evening Bisson would sometimes leave his neighbouring easel and look in to rally them both merrily upon their happiness, becoming so friendly that he found it pleasanter to pay his visits in the morning when Murger was out altogether, till finally one afternoon when the young poet came back from work, he found, instead of Marie, a laconic note, saying that she was wearied of the poverty and misery of the life they had been leading, and that, as she thought the police had discovered her abode, she was going to take refuge with a relation, whose address it was perhaps safer to conceal, and of whose existence Murger had never before heard mention. Full of forebodings for her safety, though with no manner of distrust as to her loyalty, he rushed to Bisson's studio. The painter received him with an embarrassed air, and offered but feeble consolation. Not a new story this—a first friend, a first mistress—love them both and lose them both.

Still he had no suspicions. For a week he sought her far and near. Was she ill, he wondered, or imprisoned? At last he met her walking with Bisson. This sudden revelation of treason struck a chill through all his veins, and, clutching for support at a passing carriage, he fell senseless to the ground. Bisson stopped the cab and sent him home, where he arrived still in a dull, heavy lethargy, and the *concierge* put him to bed. He awoke in a fever. There were faces gibing at him everywhere through the darkness—two faces, his mistress's and his friend's. There were voices, two voices, in peals of mocking laughter ringing through the room. The coverlet pressed on him like a sheet of heated lead, and springing from his couch, he opened the window. It was snowing hard outside, but the clear winter moonlight streamed in, and the faces and the voices were gone, but the desolation of solitude was almost more painful, for the moonbeams played with the ribbons and the toilet trifles that she had left strewn about, with their old chair, their little bed, crueller memories these than all the phantasms. He tried again to close his eyes, if he could not sleep, at least to shut out vision; but the pillow on which he laid his head was still odorous with the perfume of her hair. " I cannot rest here !" and flinging on some garments, he rushed out into the pitiless winter night. It was snowing faster now, and he hurried on, stopping awhile at the Fontaine de Jean Goujon, snow-covered, with fantastic garments deep-fringed and white, to think in his heavy stupor how unlike it was to the warm summer time, when this was a pleasant trysting spot. On, on through the vilest slums of midnight Paris, with a kind of stolid wonder at the tawdry women, the hideous men, whom not even the cold could drive out of the streets. At length, in sheer exhaustion, burning with fever and benumbed with cold, for his scanty garments were sodden with the snow, he halted in a low market-place. Two women standing by a soup stall saw him. "Look, Marie!" cried one, "what a pretty lad he is; why, the child is frozen to death; he should not be here alone." "Marie! where is Marie?" he shouted, snatching at the word, and half recovering his senses. The good wives bade him stay by their warm stove, and tried to persuade him to swallow some hot soup. At this moment a young artist who had come abroad in search of a miserable face for a study, passed by. He recognised Murger, and led him by the arm into a café. There was a bottle half full of brandy on the table. Murger seized a tumbler and drained the bottle dry, and then began an incoherent account of his miseries: in a few months he had lost his mother's love, the shelter of his father's roof, his mistress, and his friend. And then he babbled his verses to Marie. "Poor fellow," said the painter, "I, too, had a Marie once," as he carried him to Lelioux's room.

The Bohemians were but rough nurses, still they watched by his bedside till he was better. The fever, for a time, was gone, but his whole nature was changed. He had entered bitterly into manhood, and had, alas! lost faith in the purity of woman. His smile now had something of grief about it, his genius was saddened, his kindliness tempered with irony. They bore with him tenderly, and humoured all his fancies, scraped sous together to buy him little dainties, tried to wile him out of his melancholy, and brought him news of Marie. She had gone to England disguised as a man, and having cut her curls off, sent them to him as a parting gift; they had seen Bisson with another girl. "Ah!" cried Murger, in half relief, "I knew he never loved her." But, in spite of all their efforts, he again relapsed, and they had to bear him to the hospital. How many times was he to enter those gloomy doors in after years?

His illness was long and tedious, but the Sisters of Mercy were very kind and gentle. "O, good little Sister!" he cries, "how good you were, and how beautiful, when you came to sprinkle holy water on us. We used to watch you from afar, walking softly and noiselessly under those gloomy roofs, draped in your white veils, which made such lovely folds around you, and which my friend Jacques admired so much. A good Sister you were, the Beatrice of that hell. Your soothing consolations were so sweet that we all complained, whenever we had the chance, so as only to be consoled by you."

But the sights and sounds entered into his soul, and one of his saddest, most painful poems, describes this hospital life ; one stanza will suffice :—

"We may doze, we may sleep, we may wake
And the same sights come to our eyes,
For even our visions must take
Their themes from the groans and the sighs.
Let them vary the beds as they will,
Can the voices of sickness be still ?
Can they stifle the pitiful pain
Of a brother who moans for relief—
A living link of the awful chain
That is forged by the laws of grief."

"Ici qu'on dorme ou qu'on veille,
Toujours même spectacle à voir,
Devenant écho pour l'oreille,
Le rêve est pour l'œil un miroir.
Rien ne se tait, rien ne s'efface,
Et l'on est toujours face à face
La plaie aux flancs et l'œil en pleurs,
Quelque frère en misère humaine,
Anneau vivant de cette chaîne
Qui forge la loi des douleurs."

Early in the spring of 1841 he was allowed to leave the hospital, but the doctors warned him :—"Do not think yourself cured—the cure will take a long time, and will depend entirely upon the care you have of your health. Live regularly, abstain from coffee and go to bed early." Advice easy of fulfilment to most men, but impossible to Murger. He came back gaily from the sick ward to his old life of joyous misery. Count Tolstoy had kept the secretaryship open, with its certain, if meagre emolument. The Bohemians, who had spent all the time allowed to visitors by Murger's bedside, welcomed him back heartily. Shortly after his return the young poet Noël, was introduced to the circle, and Lelioux, Noël, and Murger began a new brotherly intercourse, sharing alike the difficulties of bed and board. The two tried, but in vain, to break Murger of his old love for midnight study, and for the intellectual excitement that the extravagant abuse of coffee produced. They went even so far as to draw down the blinds, fasten the shutters, and light the candles in the daytime ; but the Muse was not to be deceived by this ingenious stratagem. These nocturnal vigils conduced more and more to ill health, but inspiration came to him only in the evening, and disappeared with the flush of daylight, and nature and sleep were compelled to yield to the pleasure, the necessity of creation.

In personal appearance he was no longer the same rosy, merry lad who had burst into Lelioux's room. Privations and miseries, real sorrows and fictitious griefs, had blanched his cheeks and wrinkled his skin prematurely ; and that ' 'many-coloured beard" with which he afterwards endowed his favourite hero Rodolpho, was making itself visible, and already characterized his physiognomy.

With the same sworn disdain for prose as unworthy of a serious effort, he returned more eagerly than ever to his poetical

studies. Nadar speaks with a touching pathos of that "small
band of poets *à outrance* but still absolutely unpublished,
meeting in a garret without vests or boot-soles, despairing of
nothing, of neither their morrow, nor their genius, nor their
neighbour's genius, nor the publisher who was some day to make
such gracious overtures, nor success, nor fair ladies, nor fortune—
of nothing, if it were not of that evening's dinner—too readily
convinced, moreover, as to the question of next day's breakfast.
All of them poets save one, for I alone wrote in prose; all in-
toxicated with hope and gaiety and courage; all radiant with
the joys of youth and spirits; all brave and loyal."

Under the disguise of Melchior, in the story entitled *Un poëte
de Gouttière*, Murger has given us a vivid, if rather fanciful
sketch of his own hopes and dreams at this time :—

"This deplorable mania for poetry, originating in a stormy first-love,
was encouraged by his friends, who compared him to Lamartine. In
many secret communings with his modesty, which, like that of others,
was only the hypocrisy of pride, he avowed that he would one day
justify the comparison. If by chance a doubt arose in his mind as to
the truth of his vocation, it was speedily dispelled by the perusal of
one of his own poems, and in this darling offspring of his heart-thoughts
he would exhibit an infinite delight. He wept, he sighed, he clapped
his hands, he ran to the glass to see if he had not already an aureole
upon his brow, and he saw it. These follies were not inherent to his
nature, but had been inculcated by the friends among whom he lived,
who assured him daily that he was summoned to the loftiest poetical
destinies. When other acquaintances, in the name of 'common sense'
and reason, tried to demonstrate the folly of these proceedings, he
readily snatched up the glove. He had, he cried, a mission to fulfil,
for poets are the high priests of humanity, and were he to die upon
the road he vowed he would never deny the worship he professed. He
had, moreover, a fixed idea: he wished to raise a superb poetical monument to the memory of his first love, on the front of which he would
place his mistress's name, and so bequeath her to posterity with the
memories of Laura and Beatrice. . . . . He used to read the fragments
of this love psalm upon a table covered with the *débris* of their
grand passion."

For the old gloves and ribbons and feminine garnerings had been
carefully preserved as holy relics, and years afterwards his friends
used to see them fastened up above his little bed. With the
account of these love relics the truth of the sketch perhaps ends,
but the sequel, if romantic, is too pathetic to be omitted. After
two years had elapsed a relative left him sufficient money to
publish the volume that was to immortalize his first love and
himself. His friends were summoned to a banquet to salute the
first proof-sheets—dear to every young poet's heart—with be-

fitting honours, and one of these friends, by a strange chance, actually brought with him the fugitive Marie, who had just returned from England. She heard the lines complacently, and told her former lover that she would have preferred a new dress and a pair of boots to all the poetry in the world.—" What, my dear, you have really written all that for me ! Ah well, they certainly are very amusing." " Very," replied Melchior ; " I have loved you in verse for two years, now I will love you in prose,"—and in the morning he withdrew the manuscript from the printer's hands. He loved her in prose for six weeks, and then spent what little of the legacy there was left in learning book-keeping, so as to qualify himself for a clerkship in a money-changer's office.

To return, however, to the every-day lives of the Bohemian brotherhood. Scarcely more than boys, they were solely dependent upon their own efforts for bread, these efforts almost invariably failing them : they dined uncertainly ; they lived or starved upon credit ; but still there were merry gatherings in each other's attics, where their tipple was oftenest "unfiltered water," and where mentally they fed upon what they thought nectar meet for gods, for here their poems were rehearsed, compared, corrected, criticised, and praised. And then on Sundays, " hiding their aureoles and for the moment disguising themselves as young *bourgeois,*" they deigned to mix with the common world, and ran, as wild shop-lads might, to the woods of Villa d'Avray—" our woods of Villa d'Avray." One avenue there was that was supremely theirs, where, lying each under his own tree, each improvised an opera—(words and music too, O Shade of Verdi !)—a hymn to Nature and Springtime. " La Jeunesse n'a qu'un temps" was the motto of the day :—

" The sun of all our dreams should set
  Upon the dawn of reason,
So love and sing a moment yet,
  For youth is but a season !

" Breastplated as with patience round,
  Oh what is fate at twenty ?
When scant-earned food's more grateful found
  Than all the bread of plenty ;
When ringing jests and chorus'd songs
  Laugh troubles down as treason—
To merry tunes we'll set our wrongs,
  For youth is but a season !

" And if a loving sweetheart we
  Have won, through Cupid's chances,
To light the flames of poesy
  Before our burning glances,

" Notre avenir doit éclore
  Un soleil de nos vingt ans !
Aimons et chantons encore ;
  La Jeunesse n'a qu'un temps.

" Cuirassés de patience
  Contre le mauvais destin,
De courage et l'espérance
  Nous pétrissons notre pain ;
Notre humeur insoucieuse
  Aux fanfares de nos chants
Rend la misère joyeuse,
  La Jeunesse n'a qu'un temps !

" Si la maîtresse choisie
  Qui nous aime par hasard,
Fait fleurir la poésie
  Aux flammes de son regard,

We'll vow that she is passing fair,
Be sceptical of treason,
And love her, faithless though she were,
For youth is but a reason!

"And since all charming joys below
Of mortal love and beauty,
Must go where summer roses go
When they have done their duty;
Since Springtime rains a golden flood
Of flowers, oh more the reason
To pluck the blossom in the bud,
For youth is but a season!"

Lol mchant gré d'être belle,
Sans nous faire de tourments,
Almons-la, même infidèle ...
La Jeunesse n'a qu'un temps.

"Puisque les plus belles choses,
Les amours et la beauté,
Comme les lis et les roses
N'ont qu'une saison d'été.
Quand mai tont en fleurs abore
Le drapeau vert du printemps,
Aimons et chantons encore :
La Jeunesse n'a qu'un temps."

This brotherly life—a fraternity if ever there was one—when all suffered together, together were happy, when purse and roof and bed were held in common—led in December, 1841, to a further extension of the principle in the foundation of the famous little society—the "Buveurs d'Eau."

"There existed," Murger tells us, "under the title of Buveurs d'Eau, a small society of young men, who, associating their hopes and their labours, endeavoured to establish in this artistic life the traditions of independent thought and serious action, so easily forgotten when artists have to struggle against the allurements of passing fashion and the seductions of trade. The founders of this little solitary sect had been drawn towards each other by the random haphazards of a great town. All children of poor parents, they had entered upon their apprenticeship to poverty at a very early age. Already toiling for bread, though scarcely more than children, the hours allotted to recreation were given over to serious thought. Entering a career proverbially difficult, and under circumstances the least conducive to success, the Buveurs d'Eau boldly faced together misery and suffering. But the principal fault of this association was the complete isolation of its members from the influences of the outer world, which ended for them at the walls of their studios or their studies. The atmosphere became asphyxiated, and those who entered in from outside cried, 'Open the windows. There is a stifling need of fresh air.'"

The main idea of this society was its community—for the material wants of life the members depended the one on the other, as they had long done, but the law of a common purse, though existing, was never absolutely enforced. They were, however, all devotees of art, worshipping "art for art's sake," with every hope and ambition subordinate to art, bound to produce themselves, and to aid others to produce, with what influence of money, interest, or encouragement they had at hand; and this was carried so far, that if a member considered that the possession of a certain book, the viewing of a certain performance or a certain picture, in any way essential, the rest helped him to the fulfilment of his desire. The outside world was shunned as much as possible, and all new acquaintances rigorously avoided. Though art was the one aim of each man's life, it was enjoined on each to earn, if possible by labour that should not defile his art, enough for bare subsistence. They derived their name of " Buveurs d'Eau" from the glass of water that each member drank when he took the pledges of the society; and at their formal monthly gatherings nothing but water was permitted to be supplied. The regulation did not go further than this, and was adopted on this occasion so as to put all on a level in regard to the cost of entertainment. From these meetings politics were absolutely tabooed. At the end of every year each member was obliged to submit to the society at least one work of conscientious study as proof of an earnest and serious attempt.

The "Buveurs d'Eau" were at the same time quite ready to exchange this state of existence for a better, so long as the change could be effected without prejudicing their ideas upon art. They were men, and very young men too, and the severance from the pleasures and delights of their age was often painful, but they resisted outer temptation thoroughly, and placed all their delights and pleasures in art itself.

Of this society Noël was the president, Murger the secretary, and Christ the assistant-secretary and *treasurer.* The members were few in number, but terribly in earnest. There was Karol, the "mother of the Bohemians," who watched over them as tenderly as if they had been his children, and whose door was ever on the latch, so as to afford a speedier entrance to the distressed:—whose ambition it was, he used to say, "to make three periods of my life; the first for literature; after having won the name of a great poet, I shall seize the sword and deliver my noble country (he always wished to believe himself a Pole); I shall then occupy my mind with philosophy and legislation." There were the two Desbrosses, one of whom, Christ, the treasurer, a sculptor, was now designing ornaments for a marble-mason's establishment; the other, Gothique, a painter, whose only present earnings arose from the manufacture of tradesmen's signboards. There was Chabot, also a sculptor, serving much the same apprenticeship as Christ. Among the literary aspirants there was Lelioux, who used to don the sacred cap of liberty whenever he recited his verses—Noël, Murger himself, and Nadar, who alone of the starving brotherhood deigned from the first to write in prose.

The early period of the society's existence appeared joyous enough to Murger, when he looked back upon it in after days of comparative comfort; but to others of the set it was a wretchedness so unimaginable, so unnatural, that, even when long years had passed away, its memory seemed like the impossible phantom of some half-forgotten nightmare. The health of all the members was more or less affected by the severity of the struggle ; the lives of three were lost ; the hospital came to be looked upon as a sheltering haven where health and courage might be recruited and renewed, and to it the Bohemians went, in rotation, every few months.

Taking the joyous side of this life first, we find that occasional successes were exaggerated into fame and fortune ; that weeks of cruel starvation were forgotten on those happy occasions, few and far between, when they dined the whole day long, and went merrily to the *halle* in the evening. Love, too, was not forbidden by their monastic rules ; nay, was considered rather essential than otherwise to the progress of true art. With never-failing gaiety they treated their defeaters—the pitiless picture dealers, editors, and publishers—as Philistines dead to all hope of future art salvation. As before, there were still the pleasant Sunday rambles, and, as soon as the Bohemians discovered the Café Momus, they originated a kind of club, open and frequented from dawn to midnight. Quickly, however, after its adoption by the clique the café was rendered unbearable to the staider and wealthier guests, and even the *garçon*, Murger tells us, was driven into idiocy in the flower of his age. It was in vain that the proprietor complained ; till, frantic with despair, he one night formally enunciated his griefs as follows : that one of the band was in the habit of coming early in the morning, and seizing all the papers in the establishment, carrying this usurped prerogative to such a point that he became unbearably angry if a single wrapper was removed by another hand than his, and depriving all the other *habitués* till dinner time of the organs of public opinion, till, in fact, they scarcely knew the names of the members of the present cabinet. That this same member had forced the café to subscribe to a paper of which he was the editor by calling out steadily, every quarter of an hour, ' Waiter, bring me the *Castor*,' till a general curiosity was excited, and there was such an outcry for the *Castor* that they had been absolutely obliged to subscribe, but, as it turned out to be a fashion journal, no one ever cared to read it. That the Bohemians monopolized the one tric-trac board, and that, when it was asked for, they replied, " The tric-trac is *en lecture ;* call to-morrow." That not only were their orders meagre in the extreme, but that upon the absurd pretext that they could not countenance an immoral connexion between coffee and chicory, they had brought thither their private machine and materials, and made their own coffee, to the discredit and loss of the establishment. That one of the painters had introduced his easel, and had even summoned models of divers sexes ; that one of the musicians talked of bringing his piano bodily, and that he had, by slipping a card into the illuminated lantern outside, upon which was written—

Gratuitous instruction given to ladies and gentlemen in vocal and instrumental music : apply at the counter—

caused the café to be thronged all night long by persons of neglected costume, asking where they had to go. And that, finally, not content with destroying the *garçon's* reason, they had so corrupted that unhappy boy's morals that he had addressed some impassioned verses to the lady at the counter, beseeching her to forget her duties as a wife and as a mother, the disorder of the style being only too evidently due to the pernicious influence of another member.

This is a sketch from the "Bohemians," true enough in substance, if grotesque in manner, but the time had not yet come to write of these things pleasantly, as Murger explains in the introductory verses to his great work :—

<table>
<tr><td>

" Like a child of true Bohemia,
  Playing bravely out my part,
Friends, I march for ever forward
  On the great high-road of Art !

" And for staff to aid my journey,
  As a true Bohemian ought,
I have faith in long endurance ;
  Without that I should have nought.

" Ah ! the road was gay and smiling
  To the early steps of youth ;
Now, alas ! I see it clearly
  In the frost-cold light of truth :

" For I see it strait and gloomy,
  With no havens of retreat,
And I hear my comrades calling.
  As they march with bleeding feet ;

" And I hear the shouts of anguish,
  And the shrieks of utter woe,
Of the stragglers in the distance,
  Yet I onward, onward go !

" Till at last I cross the borders,
  And with worn feet in the brook,—
Friends, the hurricane is over ;
  Now I dare to write my book :"

</td><td>

" Comme un enfant de Bohème,
  Marchant toujours au hasard,
Ami, je marche de même,
  Sur le grand chemin de l'art.

" Et pour bâton de voyage,
  Comme le bohémien,
J'ai l'espoir et le courage,
  Sans cela je n'aurai rien.

" Car cette route si belle
  Quand je fis mes premiers pas,
Maintenant je la vois telle,
  Telle qu'elle existe hélas :

" Je la vois étroite et sombre,
  Et déjà j'entends les cris
De mes compagnons dans l'ombre
  Qui marchent les pieds meurtris ;

" J'entends leurs chants de misère,
  J'entends la plainte de mort,
De ceux qui restent derrière,
  Et pourtant j'avance encor !

" Et debout sur le rivage,
  Les pieds mouillés par le flot,—
Ami, c'est après l'orage
  Que j'ai tracé mon tableau."

</td></tr>
</table>

The story Murger tells in his letters, written at this period from day to day—the series forming a vivid autobiography—is vastly different in its painful realism. We abridge the most characteristic of these letters into a kind of sequential diary :—

" *14th December,* 1841.—Lelioux has joined the staff of the *Audience* (as a law reporter). He is in a good way if you like ;—drinks nothing but pure Bordeaux, eats *pâté de foie gras,* lives in a splendid apart-

ment, wears a cashmere dressing gown, and writes two-thirds of a
verse per diem—I am told he is very happy. Poor fellow, I pity him!
We often speak of thee, of thy ex-beard O Vandal, of thy poems O Great
Man! In talking thus the time passes but the appetite remains, and
then we go to bed to dream we are dining with Véfour. Karol, ex-
Don Juan of the Quartier Latin, ci-devant poet, philosopher, generalis-
simo, &c., is but a pleasant memory left in an atmosphere of disagreeable things—he seems to have grown grave—and his gravity is
justified. The Desbrosses spend half the day starving with hunger,
the other half starving with cold. As to your humble servant he has,
alas! consumed his monthly forty francs in a fortnight, but he has
happily forty sous left to carry him on till next pay day. His existence during this first fortnight has been a round of beefsteaks, and
wax-sunlights, Havanna cigars and embroidered shirts, bon-bons and
biscuits :—to-day he has only his landlord to pay and his shoemaker!

"*6th March*, 1842—For three days I have eaten nothing but dry
bread. Will you forgive me ?—I took twenty francs out of the sixty
received. Then I set to work to eat copiously, and I paid my most
pressing debts. I have never before been so wretched. As to T., he
repays the thirty francs he owes me by fourteen sous and fourteen sous—
droll, isn't it ? Without Christ, who has four days this week given
me dinner and breakfast, I know not what would have become of me!

" *21st March*, 1842.—Carissimo!!! Eve was perfectly right to eat
the forbidden fruit, and Voltaire was not in the wrong when he said
that the world went on very well as it all happened ! I vow I wont
abate one iota of this. Were you only present now, but judge ! . . . .
I swim in a golden sea, in an ocean of fifty-cent pieces, in a veritable
exhibition of kings and queens of all countries and all profiles. I wash
my hands in the Pactolus—and with almond soap. I wear gloves of
many colours, frockcoats and pantaloons ditto ditto. Mark you,
friend, the poets are but vain babblers when they pretend that life is
dark and gloomy. What should they, forsooth, who all day long yell
miserere nobis know of life at all. They do not even dream of the
existence of a crowd of delights which I am at present tasting. They
have never fully understood the joy of hearing a cabman ask for a
pour boire. They know not there is a perfume in Havanna cigars,
light in costly wax-tapers, music in the gracious crackling of too tight
a boot and varnished. Ha! ha! all that I feel, I see, I hear! You,
O meagre great one, would no longer recognise your fat Fleming. He
has vanished into dust and space with his old coat and his battered
boots :—

> *An owl he died, but as a phœnix rose.*

What a pretty Latin verse that would make—I know it would.

" It is in this wise, O my friend ! at this present hour His Lofty and
Most Puissant Highness the Viscount de la Tour d'Auvergne (a title
from his dwelling) is dazzling. The beggars hang upon his steps, they
cry aloud to him for alms, and he tosses them a franc. The women
ask for nothing, and yet he addresses them a smile, and what a smile!
Behold! O mighty man, my position ! Life I swear is beautiful ! This
cloud of five-franc pieces which has burst upon me came like a
hurricane from the north—a magnificent aurora borealis !!! My

patron put 350 francs into my hand for the poem I had written to the Czar, and promised me 150 more. I ran to Rothschild to cash my cheque, from there to the library, from there to the tailor, from there to the restaurant, from there to the theatre, from there to the café, from there home, where I plunged me into new sheets and dreamed that I was Emperor of Morocco and married to the Bank of France.

"*25th March*, 1842.—Luck has again departed; you will see a number of the *Age d'or* (a children's journal conducted by Lelioux) which I am filling at *two francs the page*. O profanation!

"*Hospital St. Louis*, 23rd *May*, 1842.—Again at the hospital! I awoke one night as if on fire. I lit a candle and saw that I was red from head to foot—as red as a boiled lobster, neither more nor less. In the morning I ran to the hospital, where I now am. The doctors are totally amazed at my case. They say it is a *purpura*. I should think it was; the purple of the Roman emperors was never so purple as my skin.*

"*30th May*, 1842.—My malady is in a state of reaction, and science does not seem to know much about it. There are a thousand trumpets blaring in my ears. They bleed me, re-bleed me, poultice me—and all in vain. I consume as much arsenic as three boulevard melodramas. . . . . I have written to Douché to tell him that, being in want of money, I will let him have my story of *Rouet* for ten francs—and I have had no reply. Ah, they are sad things, these cold friendships! If you are in funds send me a post-office order for five francs, for I foresee the moment when the Desbrosses will bring me no more tobacco. I am vexed, my poor friend, at always bleeding you, whether near or distant."

(In July we find him out of the hospital, momentarily better.)

"*8th July*, 1842.—I read and re-read Chénier, and—I confide in you, never betray me—to try and seize an intuition of harmony I read aloud—yes very much aloud—Horace, Virgil, and other ancients; not that I can in the slightest degree comprehend their meaning, but to me their very metrical cadence is full of charms.

"*22nd September*, 1842.—(This letter contains melancholy forebodings that he will lose his situation on account of a misunderstanding that was afterwards rectified. He had been offered a *superb* situation in a canvas warehouse.) 800 francs per annum and lodgings. The duties are to begin at seven in the morning and often never finish. I am not yet quite wretched enough to accept it. My father, with whom I had again been on speaking terms, has again broken all relations with me. He has seen me wanting bread, and he has never offered me any, though he held money of mine. He has seen my boots in tatters, and he has made me comprehend that he was not flattered by my visits. Again I am literally an orphan, face to face with misery; and yet, my friend, I swear to you that when I am ever so little

* The *purpura*—an uncommon disease, rarer however in France than England—is generally brought on by a miserably insufficient diet, and that of salted and unwholesome provisions; by the want of proper rest, and by an overstrain of mental power. As in Murger's case, it is apt to ruin the constitution and to sow the seeds of a permanent malady.

satisfied with my work I am ready to clap my hands to existence. O
poor creatures that we are! You say that *you* are discouraged.
Discouragement! I know it, too, and the dolorous anguish of doubt I
For three months now and more I have been able to do nothing. I
am incapable of writing twenty lines for a miserable children's paper.
My brain is a void—as empty as a tomb. I have tried to awake the
demon of intelligence by material means. There are nights when I
have taken six ounces of coffee to convince more than ever of my
powerlessness—and this has lasted for six months! I feel the purpura
coming on again. Come weal, come woe, I am too far advanced to
recoil. Everything is against me, none the less I will remain in the
arena; the wild beasts will devour me—let them.   .

"*10th Nov.*, 1842.—I have spent another month in the hospital; you
know that, and you know why. My red skin, my *purpura*, has resisted
all possible attacks. I am soaked in sulphur, I eat it, I drink it, and
the said purpura insists upon appearing regularly every Thursday,
which is monstrous to Science, who opens her large round eyes without
seeing a whit the clearer. In short, at the end of a month I left the
hospital, and both Chintrœuil and Le Gothique took my place there.
Gay this, is it not? Alas! yes, always the same song. Our existence
is like a ballad. Now all goes well, now all goes ill; then better, then
worse, but the refrain is ever the same—'misery, misery, misery.' . . .
. . . Five days since I was walking in a street, dreaming of Marie;
suddenly a woman came out of a turning. It was she! My heart
almost broke from my breast; I clutched hold of something, or I
should have fallen. She paled slightly, and went her way. Alas!
now I dream of her ten times more than ever, and love her as much as
I loved her two years ago. God knows how long a time it will take
me to chase this miserable folly from my head and from my brain.

"*17th Nov.*, 1842.—I am better at present, and working like a
madman at a dramatic poem (subject of course Marie). If you have
at your disposal a number of pretty harmonious names enclose them
in your next, for at present I have found none suitable, and my heroes
and heroines are called 1, 2, 3, 4, 5, &c. &c. Scarcely picturesque."

December finds him in the hospital again.

"*15th April*, 1843.—I have not written for so long because I have
been in such trouble. First of all, I have, by my own fault, it is true,
lost my situation. I had determined to finish my prologue to 'Marie'
by a Saturday, and on Saturday morning I had still a hundred verses
to write. I thought my *patron* could do without me for a day, and I
remained at home, and completed my work. When I went again next
day, he thanked me for my services, and there and then dismissed me.
I have been much bullied by my landlord, to whom I owe two quarters
rent, and it would take more ingenuity than I am master of to pay
one. The bailiffs, too, are after me for 'T.'s business. Altogether, for
the last three weeks I have lived in hell. . . . . . We are cramped
with hunger. We have spent the last sous. I must find a ditch
somewhere and blow my brains out.

"*7th May*, 1843.—My purpura worse than ever. Before entering the hospital this time I was obliged to hand over my furniture to my landlord for 75 francs due, and I shall have neither bed nor board when I go out. But I have grand projects in my head, glorious projects, which, if they succeed, will make me a man of consequence."

Directly Murger came out of the hospital he met Jules Fleury, afterwards as Champfleury to be a distinguished novelist, and having already some footing in the press. With the true Bohemian spirit, Fleury at once offered to share his allowance from home and his rooms with the needy poet, and for six months they were as Orestes and Pylades. Fleury, though idle, had an intensely realistic genius, and was in every way the direct opposite to Murger. "Write prose!" he cried, "write prose, man, or you will die of starvation!" Eighteen months before, after an evening's brilliant conversation, where Murger had excelled himself in paradox and humour and kindly cynicism, even his clique of young poetasters had cried out this same advice. But it took a year and a half's misery to effect the reformation. To return, however, to their meeting; Champfleury afterwards in his *Contes d'Automne* draws a charming picture of this joint life. It is too humorous to be in any way abbreviated :—

"It is now nine years since we were living together in the proud possession of a joint income of 70 francs a month. Full of confidence in the future, we had hired, in the Rue de Vaugirard, a little room at 300 francs. Youth is no arithmetician. You had spoken to the concierge so loftily of our sumptuous furniture that he let you have the room at once without requiring references. You brought with you six plates (three of them china), a Shakespeare, Victor Hugo's works, a superannuated chest of drawers, and a cap of Liberty. By the oddest chance I had *two* mattresses, 150 volumes, a sofa, two chairs, a table, and, to crown all, a skull. The first week passed delightfully ; we never went out ; we worked hard and smoked hard. I find amongst my old papers a scrap, upon which these words are written—

"BEATRICE,
"A Drama in Five Acts,
"By
"HENRY MURGER.
"As Performed at the ——— Theatre,
"The — of ———, 18—.

This was a leaf torn out from an old blank book, for you had a bad habit of wasting all our paper in scribbling the titles of plays, putting the important word 'performed,' so as to judge of the effect."

Then came days of great scarcity.

"After a long discussion, each hurling reproaches at the other for his inane prodigality, we agreed that as soon as our income of 70 francs came to hand, the strictest account of our outgoings should be kept.

Now, among my old papers I also discovered the ACCOUNT BOOK. It is simple, touching, laconic, and full of memories. We were wonderfully exact upon the first day of every month. I read on the 1st Nov., 1843 : ' Paid to Madame Bastion for tobacco, 2 francs.' We also paid the grocer, the restaurant (it was a restaurant !), the coal merchant, &c. The 1st was quite a feast day. I wasted 85 centimes at the café, a mad extravagance that brought a series of remonstrances upon me all the evening, but that very day you, to my horror, invested 65 centimes in pipes !

"On the 2nd we paid our laundress the large sum of 5 francs. I walked across the Pont des Arts as if I were an Academician, and proudly entered the Café Momus. We had but just discovered that benevolent establishment which gave us a *demi-tasse* for 25 cents.

"On the 3rd you decided that as long as the 75 francs lasted, we should cook for ourselves. Consequently you bought a saucepan, some thyme, and some bay-leaves, and, as might have been expected from a poet, you used far too much bay—the soup tasted of nothing else. We also laid in a stock of potatoes, with tea, coffee, sugar as usual.

"It was with much strong language and gnashing of teeth that we entered the expenses of the 4th.

"Why on earth did you ever allow me to go out with my pocket so full of money ? You had gone to Dagneaux to spend 25 cents. What the deuce could Dagneaux give you for 25 cents ? Ah, how dear the cheapest pleasures are ? Under the pretext of going to Belleville to see a drama—with an order of course—by one of our set, I took two omnibuses—one to go, one to return. Two omnibuses ! I was well punished for my prodigality, for 3 francs 75 cents dropped through a hole in my pocket. How did I dare to go home to face your wrath ? The two omnibuses alone deserved the severest reproach, but the 3·75 ! I had been lost if I had not disarmed your anger by beginning with the plot of the play.

"And yet the very next morning, without thinking of these terrible losses, we lent our friend G—, who really seemed to look upon us as his bankers (the house of Murger & Co.), the enormous sum of 35 sous. I have often puzzled my brain to discover by what insidious means G— had succeeded in winning our confidence, and I can find none but the inexperience of foolish youth ; for ten days afterwards he coolly came again, and again demanded exactly the same sum.

"Until the 8th November, we added up the sum total correctly at the bottom of each page. It then amounted to 40·01, but then the addition stops, for we did not dare to face the total any longer. Upon the 10th November you bought a thimble ; now without being a very acute observer, it is impossible to doubt the momentary appearance of a lady in the establishment, though certainly you might urge that many men do occupy their leisure moments in mending their own clothes.

"On the morning of the 14th M. Credit returns. He pays a visit to the grocer, the tobacconist, and the coal-chandler. He is by no

means badly received by the grocer's daughter—nay, warmly—for were
not you with him? Did he die, though, about the 17th, for I find
'frock-coat, 3 francs' entered to our credit? These 3 francs came
from the Mont-de-Piété—a heartless monster this, worthy rather
of the title Mont-sans-Piété! Heaven knows we suffered enough from
the machinations of his minions! Alas! it was my only frock-coat
that we pawned, apparently for the purpose of lending that insatiable
U— half the pittance we received.

"On the 19th we sold some books. Fortune must have smiled upon
the sale, for the pot was again set a-boiling with a fowl and plenty of
bay-leaves.

"M. Credit seems to have continued his foraging excursions in
search of provisions with a dignified composure. He makes daily
requisitions in all directions till the 1st December, when he actually
pays his debts in full.

"Ah me! what a pity that our little register is interrupted
brusquely at the end of one month—only that November! Why
not more? If we had continued to keep our book there would have
been so many signposts to guide us back again to youthful ways.

"O happy times! when from our little balcony we could catch a
glimpse of one tree of all the garden of the Luxemburg, and that by
craning over at the risk of life and limb!"

This meeting with Champfleury was the first real stroke of
fortune in Murger's career, though some time elapsed before
the result became apparent. In the succeeding letters to his
country friend, he apologizes for writing tales for insignificant
journals, and pieces for the minor theatres, "as literary crimes
to be carefully concealed under a *nom de plume*—a sorry resort,
may be ; but then what can I do? I have no situation, and I
must live. After all, it may perhaps open up the way for the
serious labours I will never, never abandon." But even anent
these "literary crimes" there is the usual story of rejection from
editor and manager. "Sad replies, my friend, 'a charming piece,
delicious couplets, and many regrets that they are not quite
suitable.'"

On the 19th January, 1844, he is again in despair. A temporary coolness had arisen between him and Champfleury, and
they had parted company. Nadar, however, offered the use of a
room, and Murger had obtained a berth upon the *Journal de
Commerce*, with a salary of fifty francs a month for eight hours'
work a day, Sundays and holidays included.

"17th *March*, 1844.—From Scylla to Charybdis; misery is more
terrible than ever with me, and around me. My situation at the
Commerce led to nothing. I am again thrown on the streets. It is
horrible! I am overwhelmed with discouragements. A few days
more of this wretchedness, and I will either blow my brains out,

or ship as a common sailor. Forgive my despair. It is the cry of *finis*."

The Bohemians saw that there was something radically wrong with Murger's health, and, poor as they were, they subscribed enough to send him into the country, to stay awhile with the friend with whom he corresponded. Three months' complete rest—he only wrote one couplet the whole time—pure air and good food restored him to health and spirits; but immediately after his return, the melancholy death in the hospital of Christ, the young sculptor, whose work already exhibited splendid promise, struck a terrible blow of grief and foreboding into the heart of every Bohemian, and by none was the loss more painfully felt than by Murger.

"*26th July*, 1844.—Still unfortunate, but more than ever determined to the struggle. Count Tolstoy has done nothing, wishes to do nothing for me. My father says I ought to feel ashamed of my position, and take a situation as a domestic servant. I can hope for no employment. I have no clothes in which to call upon any one; and to make matters worse, my old complaint has returned. I don't want to go to the hospital at present; we have had enough of that. Give me your sincere advice upon the old plan of going to sea.

"*15th August*, 1844.—At last a letter which is not a narrative of miseries. Bad luck is wearied out. These are the facts, our friendship is too old for any dissimulation. I wrote to Madame Rothschild to ask for a berth in her husband's bank. I did not obtain the place, but she sent me fifty francs in a very kind and delicate manner—and I took them. I then bought some clothes and was able to go abroad again. My father, too, gave me a nearly complete second suit. I called on Count Tolstoy on Saturday, who presented me with twenty francs, and on the Sunday wrote to ask if I would like to occupy my old place. Didn't I just accept his offer!! The Count also, not liking the paletot I wore, gave me another forty francs to buy a coat. Lelioux has had a story bespoken by a novelist, and we are writing it conjointly. A third is nearly ready; that will give us 125 francs each."

These letters cover a period of four years, and trace Murger's history for that period most succinctly. Jules Janin has remarked, that while his prose is gay, his verse is of the saddest—nor can we wonder at it, when we consider that the poems were mostly written during these four years—the prose after he had crossed the rubicon of misery. "Write prose or die!" Champfleury had exclaimed, for the poet now like other men has to earn his daily bread; if he cannot earn it—and what poet can without an apprenticeship as long as Joseph's, with the reward more than twice deferred?—he will starve; if he starve too long he will die. There is not much poetry about the sufferings of modern misery. Hitherto scarcely any of Murger's writings had got abroad, and though he was two-and-twenty years of age, his name was still unknown beyond the small Bohemian circle. But these four years had been most potent to the framing of his life. He is still to undergo the same sufferings, the same delights, the same labours, but upon a larger stage ; and gradually he is to leave Bohemia behind him till it becomes a pleasant youthful memory, by no means unprofitable or irksome in the telling.

Beyond what we have given in the foregoing pages, these letters show that the society of Buveurs d'Eau had been formally dissolved. While the respect of each member for individual aspiration had been religiously observed, it was difficult to establish a well-defined demarcation between the form of a work and its tendency—difficult to admire without reserve, to praise without restriction the poem, the picture, the statue, which were each but a symbol of one idea that all could not partake. The annual exhibition "of serious attempts at pure art" led to stormy discussions, and finally it was determined to, in form, dissolve the society, though for every practical purpose as to material support and mutual encouragement, the members were for many years to come still bound together. There are, too, in these letters a few laughing allusions to two passing love-adventures with Louise and Christine, mere effervescences of youthful gallantry, but to be noted for the beautiful poem in which their names are associated with Marie :—

MEMORIES.

"Have you forgotten, O Louise,
Our little garden's leafy shrine,
And that long evening 'neath the trees
When your small hand stole into mine?
When both our lips did half beseech
The words that were not spoken yet,
For you and I were all to each :
O tell me, dear, do you forget?

"Have you forgotten, O Marie,
The fountain with its voice sonorous?
The golden light on land and sea,
That flung its mystic mantle o'er us?
The rings we changed when last we swore
We would be faithful till we met?
O, these and many memories more,
O tell me, dear, do you forget?

"Have you forgotten, O Christine,
The rosy boudoir's sweet delights?
The little room that lay between
The earth and sky, the long May nights,—

RENOVARE.

"Avez-vous oublié, Louise,
Le coin fleuri du vieux jardin,
Où certain soir ma main s'est mise
Pleine d'émoi dans votre main?
Nos lèvres cherchaient nos paroles,
Nos genoux touchaient nos genoux ;
Nous étions unis nous les mules—
Dites, vous en souvenez-vous?

"Avez-vous oublié, Marie,
L'échange de nos deux anneaux,
Les soleils d'or dans la prairie,
Les bois plein d'ombre, et plein d'oiseaux,
La fontaine au bassin sonore?
Où nous avions nos rendezvous?
Des ces lieux, et d'autres encore,
Dites, vous en souvenez-vous?

"Avez-vous oublié, Christine,
Le boudoir rose et parfumé,
L'humble chambre de ciel voisine,
Les jours d'avril, les nuits de mai?

Clear nights when every glittering star
Said, ' Sweet, unveil like us, and let
Your beauty daze us from afar.'
O tell me, dear, do you forget ?

" Louise is dead, and, lack-a-day,
To vice Marie has stretch'd her hand,
And pale Christine has gone away
To bloom in some sweet southern land !
Louise, Marie, Christine, you seem
As dead and gone, to me, all three ;
Our love is but a ruin'd dream,
And only to be dreamt by me.

Ces claires nuits où les étoiles
Semblaient vous dire : ainsi que nous,
Belle, laissez tomber vos voiles—
Dites, vous en souvenez-vous !

" Louise est morte, hélas, Marie
A la débauche tend la main ;
La pâle Christine est partie
Refleurir au soleil romain.
Louise, Marie, et Christine,
Pour moi sont mortes toutes trois ;
Notre amour n'est qu'une ruine,
Et seul j'y pense quelquefois.

Early in the new year, 1845, he was introduced by Champfleury to an obscure paper entitled the *Moniteur de la Mode*, where he got some kind of footing, inasmuch as his novelettes and those of his friends were accepted, mostly for a wage of gratified vanity and theatrical orders. The *Mode* had but a flickering existence and was succeeded by the *Castor*, which was so crammed by the Bohemians with romantic "copy," that the few subscribers, seeing bonnets and fichus altogether neglected, withdrew their support. Champfleury in *Madlle. Mariette* gives us an account of another journal also open to the fraternity. The editor, St. Charnay, was an old man of sixty, who had spent his life in similar undertakings, but who nevertheless continued to surround himself with young men, and thus gave his paper a tone of originality. The luckless débutants were cautiously held in hand by various ingenious means. They were paid at the lowest possible rate, so as to leave them no time for idleness. They were told of the marvellous successes of the great men who had before this passed through his hands on the way to fame, and yet were taught that out of his magic circle there was at present no possible hope of existence. No personal friendships were allowed to interfere with the conduct of his journal ; he admitted the most violent attacks, but disapproved of enthusiasm. A contributor was obliged to send in at least ten slashing articles before he was allowed to pay a friend a compliment, and when at last the kindly notice appeared it was always more than counterbalanced by some insulting remarks elsewhere. " More than once all the staff came to blows, and, as an ex-guardsman, M. St. Charnay encouraged this high tone, and contributed considerably to the literary hurricane."

In February, 1845, Murger ventured to call at the office of the *Artiste*, and in less than five minutes he had won the friendship of Arsène Houssaye, always ready, when possible, to aid a struggler. Looking over some verses that Murger brought with him, he declared that the author was cousin-german to Alfred de Musset, and he commenced reading them aloud to attract tho attention of Gérard de Nerval, who was busy at his desk writing perilous travels into some distant country. Nerval stopped short before his period was rounded off, tossed his pen into the air, and swore that Murger was one of themselves. Two poems were immediately accepted, and a tale bespoken; but the kindly editor objected to the uncouthness of the poet's signature; how-ever, by transposing an *i* into a *y*, and by placing a trema over the u (*ü*), *Henry Mürger* was pronounced to be sufficiently picturesque, even for the columns of the *Artiste*. He had been baptized Henri Murger, but as, in future, adopting only half the change of his literary godfather, he invariably signed himself HENRY MURGER, we have, for the sake of uniformity, so styled him from the first.

Encouraged by this success Murger threw a dozen canards into the box of the *Corsaire*, and had the pleasure of seeing them defile, one after another, in the columns of that paper.

The *Corsaire*, a lively little journal originally named *Satan*, had a double staff of contributors—the politicians and the novelists, and after a few trial contributions Murger was regularly num-bered iu the latter department, with Banville, Baudélaire, Fiorentino and others, with all of whom he subsequently be-came intimate,—his friendship with Nerval eventually leading them to start a joint establishment in the Rue Notre Dame de Lorette.

The first story of any length he contributed to the *Corsaire* was *Orbasson le Confident*, about which a curious anecdote is related. At the time of the Revolution of February Count Tolstoy was so overburthened with work that he requested his secretary to aid him in writing his despatches. Setting to work zealously he finished the official letters and then betook himself to the eighth chapter of *Orbasson*, for which the printers were waiting. This done he directed his correspondence, and in error sent the secret despatch destined to the Czar to the editor of the *Corsaire*. "Sire,—The Revolution is triumphant; Louis Philippe and his family have fled. M. Lamartine, Ledru-Rollin have— &c. &c." If Niennaitre was astounded at this official intelligence the Czar was not less perplexed at the news he had so anxiously expected taking the undecipherable form of an odd chapter of a sensational story, with the promise "to be continued in the following number."

These several and signal successes seem at first almost to have alarmed Murger. He still writes plaintively of the "necessity of sacrificing to vile prose," and holds out many hopes of shortly completing his volume of poems. With the proceeds, however small, of his contributions to these journals, and the more re-

munerative if less ambitious work in magazines for milliners
and children, his life became more comfortable, his existence
more assured. The old days of a forced choice between the
streets and the hospital had departed, and the *Corsaire*, in which
he was forming a style, a manner, a *genre* altogether his own, was
proving itself a little door that should open upon a great public.
He had now but scanty time for poetry, but then the daily hack-
work, so fatally dulling to most imaginative geniuses, was rapidly
executed, without leaving a suspicion of its influence upon his
mind, and the best of his prose writings were still autobiographical.

In 1848 the *Corsaire* published the famous *Scènes de la Vie
Bohème*, written by Murger from night to night, painting the
life he had led, the life he was daily leading. For this masterpiece he received fifteen francs a *feuilleton*, and there were in
all twenty-three *feuilletons*—not quite fourteen pounds. This
Vie Bohème came out very quietly, making a sensation certainly
among the men of his calling, but being scarcely noticed by the
general public. As soon as the series was completed in the
Corsaire a bookseller gave 500 francs for the copyright and
struck off 70,000 copies!—altogether something under thirty-four
pounds for one of the most popular books of modern times, and
that after the author had been in the profession for ten years!

The *Vie Bohème* stands apart from all preceding works. In
it the author explored unknown solitudes, discovered a fresh
world, full of gaiety and tears, of ringing laughter and the
starkest poverty, of hopes unutterably eager, and of miseries that
are indicated rather than described. Soon after it was presented
to the public in a collected form it took France by storm.
as "Pickwick" just before had captured the English mind.

Each chapter in the strange volume is a work complete in
itself, yet the chapters lead one into the other, till the whole,
with its quips, its jests, its delicate shades of humour and its fine
strokes of wit, forms one of the gayest naïvest books of even this
century of fantasies.

A dry analysis would be useless and tedious. Our present
sketch is biographical, not critical, and we have only space for a
few autobiographical excerpts. The *Vie Bohème* has moreover
been treated at full length in a former number. (*Westminster
Review*, January, 1861.)

Round Rodolphe, the "man of letters," and his comrade,
Marcel, our most immediate interest clings. With scarcely a
coat to his back—at the bravest his costume is "plaid trousers,
a grey hat, a red tie, a white glove and a black one," Rodolphe
(a Murger under the thinnest possible disguise), is yet the
editor of *L'Echarpe d'Iris*, the famous fashion journal, which

gives the *ton* to Paris and the world. It is almost impossible to compress the story of his hunt after "that ferocious animal the 5-franc piece," essential to the treating at the Grands-eaux de Versailles, of a brilliant conquest just achieved, without losing all the natural and rollicking fun of the story. He has just five hours to find this necessary 5-franc piece—"20 sous an hour, like the horses in the Bois de Boulogne." He must at once see his friends. He first visits an influential critic, who, up to his eyes in work, is in sad want of assistance. " Did you see the new piece at the Odéon last night ?" "See, it ! why, I'm the Odéon's public." " Can you write me the plot of the play ?" " Of course I can, I have a creditor's own memory." And in a few minutes the plot was ready. "Oh ! this is too short !" " Well ! put in some dashes and your own criticism." " Alas ! I have no time for criticism, and then my real opinion would not occupy much space—stick in an adjective every three words." "Yes—shall I add my private opinions on tragedy generally. I have printed them twice in two different papers." " Bah ! that don't matter. How many lines do your opinions occupy ?" " Forty"—(" Good, thought Rodolphe, I have given him 20 francs worth of copy, he can't refuse me the 5 francs.") " I must warn you though, that my opinions are not altogether novel. I have yelled them out in every café in Paris; there is not a *garçon* who doesn't know them by heart !" " What matter ! is there anything new in the world except virtue ? Thunder and lightning, I still want two columns ! Have you any paradoxes ?" " Well, I have, but they're scarcely my own—at least I bought them from a poor friend in the last stage of misery for 50 cents each—they have never appeared yet." (" Hah ! hah ! thought Rodolphe, I can ask 10 francs apiece; why, paradoxes at present are as dear as partridges")—and he scribbled some thirty lines. "Oh ! they're first-rate," said the critic; "kindly add ' it is only at the hulks that we find absolute honesty !'—that will just complete the quantity." The influential critic listened gratefully to the requested loan, but hadn't a farthing in the house. At last he gave Rodolphe a Bossuet, a bust of M. Odilon Barrot—"the widow's own gift, I swear !"—and some odd volumes of poetry; and on these, after much persuasion as to their utility and beauty, a poor washerwoman was induced to lend 2 francs. The other money was obtained with still greater ingenuity, and jingling the 5 francs in his pockets, Rodolphe meets his brilliant conquest punctually at five o'clock, and astounds her by his liberality.

One night they give a grand party; this is their invitation card :—

" MM. Rodolphe and Marcel request the honour of your company upon Saturday evening next, being Christmas-eve. There will be laughter.

"P.S. Youth is but a season."

We abstract a few items from the enclosed programme; too long, unfortunately, to be quoted in its entirety:—

"At 7 the salon will be thrown open for lively and animated conversation. At 8 a general promenade in the neighbouring salons of the gifted author of *Montagnes en Bouches*, a charming comedy, recently rejected by the Odéon. At 8·30 M. Alexander Schaunard, the distinguished virtuoso, will perform upon the piano his inimitable symphony, 'The influence of the colour BLUE on the Fine Arts.' At 10 M. Tristran, man of letters, will record the story of his early loves, M. Schaunard accompanying him on the piano. At 2, opening of the sports and organization of the dances, which will be carried on till morning. At 6, sunrise and final chorus.

"Throughout the evening the ventilators will be open.

"N.B. Any person attempting to read or recite verses will be promptly turned out of the room, and handed over to the custody of the police. Visitors are earnestly requested *not* to carry away the candle-ends."

This party had been so often promised and discussed that the two hosts were fairly ashamed to postpone it any more. They would spend a hundred francs upon this glorious entertainment—they had a week to find the money. Paris had many resources—surely it could be done. Day by day their hopes dwindle, till on the morning of the entertainment they pledge their wardrobes with a tailor for 15 francs. This opens up new difficulties, but Rodolphe comes over to his neighbour Collie, and explains that as the *host*, a black coat was to him absolutely essential. "Will you lend me yours?" "But," pleaded Collie, "a black coat is equally essential to a guest." "Oh, nonsense, don't stand upon ceremony with us, I willingly permit you to come in a paletot." "You know I never had a paletot!" "Well, if you are so particular, perhaps you wouldn't mind staying at home for the evening, and lending me your coat. You see I must be there. Or if you will come, come as you like in your shirt-sleeves, you'll pass muster as a tried and faithful domestic," and half by persuasion, half by force he effected his purpose. They prepared the room by chalking it into four compartments, so as to avoid all chance of quarrels between the different branches of "men of letters;" thus:—

| CÔTÉ DES POÈTES. | ROMANTIQUES. |
| CÔTÉ DES PROSATEURS. | CLASSIQUES. |

The only chair was set aside for the "influential critic;" and all the books written by any of the guests coming in the evening were placed conspicuously upon the table.

Never had such a charming evening been spent, and never
was festivity so talked of in the future.

Marcel, the joint host of this successful entertainment was the
famous painter of that huge picture, the " Passage of the Red
Sea," which had for so many years been obstinately rejected by
the Hanging Committee of the *Exposition*. It was sent in the
second time as " Crossing the Rubicon," but Pharaoh was recognised under the disguise of Cæsar, and dismissed with all the
honours due to him. Again, the Egyptians were metamorphosed
into Grenadier Guards, the Red Sea into winter snow, and the
" Passage de la Bérézina" stood complete, but the Hanging Committee were too well acquainted with a singular many-coloured
horse, upon which Marcel used to test his experiments in colours,
to be deceived. It had now undergone a fresh modification as the
" Passage des Panoramas." " If they reject you again," cried
Marcel, " may all the vermilion of the Red Sea mount to their
faces and cover them with shame ;" when it was purchased by a
dealer—" for less than the price of the original cobalt"—as a
signboard for a provision merchant's shop, and here Marcel saw
it suspended in mid-air, a steamboat had been painted in, and it
was described as the " Port of Marseilles." There was an
astounded crowd round it as he passed, and, returning home
delighted with his triumph and oblivious of official defeats, he
murmured " *Vox populi vox dei est.*"

There is another story of which he is the hero. One of the
brotherhood had been asked to dine with a deputy, and all felt
personally concerned. A black coat was absolutely essential, and
the *black* coat (it was really blue) which Rodolphe had so adroitly
borrowed, and which had at once been adopted by the Bohemians
generally, had gone, as well it might, to the tailor's. They were
discussing the question perplexedly, when a respectable tradesman arrived, anxious to have his portrait painted. He sat down.
They all looked at the coat he had on, then at each other. The
" Roman costume," he was told, was more fashionable, and he
was invested with an old dressing-gown, while the Deputy's
guest, already over-due, offered to hang the coat up in the cloak-
room, and putting it on outside, quietly went to his dinner-party.
Many were the stratagems by which the worthy sugar manufacturer was detained till midnight, and by which he was induced
to order in a splendid and costly repast.

There are many privations and miseries in the volume, but
they are rendered entertaining by the extraordinary shifts and
contrivances to which they give rise, and are altogether forgotten
in the glorious memories of wealth and sudden splendour, when
the Bohemians seem to have dined the whole day long, when
they cried out like poor Jacques Desbrosse, " Oh ! I shall never

have had enough." There was one special Christmas-eve when, with their sweethearts, they met at the Café Momus, and not finding a sou in any of their pockets, determined to test the utmost confidence of the lady at the counter, and to celebrate the festive season duly, to have a banquet that should cost as near 100,000 francs as her endurance would allow. By degrees her suspicions became aroused; but by the time the bill had exceeded all human forbearance, and had been presented, the guests were far superior to the cares of totals and additions.

But the charm of the *Vie Bohème*, after its never-failing gaiety, lies in the tenderness and the beauty of its love scenes. In connexion with the student we naturally have the grisette— now, alas! no more—devoted in her love, facile in her conquests, industrious and happy in her labours and privations. To Mimi and Musette we owe all the pathos of the volume. We may, after a colourless fashion, compress the gayer episodes—Rodolphe writing Mimi a gown, and, at her solicitation, adding, with so many more columns of matter, so many more flounces and furbelows; but it is impossible to deal in this meagre manner with the pathetic chapters. Mimi was Rodolphe's mistress, and her love, affected only by too long a bout of starvation, for she was fond of dress and pleasure, is merely a reproduction from real life. "The scene at the hospital," says Banville, "so poignant with misery, is completely true. Poor Mimi had lived too long among the poets, till she naturally came to die at the hospital as a poet might." But it is in Musette that Murger is happiest. Her character is that of Marie, and his years-long dreams of Marie, with the loves of early days, came back to him in the "Chanson de Musette." "I would," cries M. Alexandre Dumas *fils*, "willingly give all my novels to have written this one song to Musette."

"Yesterday summer's earliest swallow
  Brought thoughts of climes and
    springs sublime,
Till dreamful thoughts of her did follow
  Who loved me when she had the
    time;
And all day long I stay'd me here
  And watched with a half sacred glow
The almanack of that old year
  When each one loved the other so !

"O youth ! you are not wholly dead,
  Nor, sweet one, is remembrance o'er,
And if I only heard your tread
  My heart would leap towards the
    door.
E'en now it trembles with a thrill
  Of joy to dream you might relent,
That we might break together still
  The happy bread of fond content.

"Hier, en voyant une hirondelle
  Qui nous ramenait le printemps,
Je me suis rappellé la belle
  Qui m'aima quand elle eût le temps ;
Et pendant toute la journée
  Pensif, je suis resté devant
Le vieil almanach de l'année
  Où nous nous sommes aimés tant !

"Non, ma jeunesse n'est pas morte,
  Il n'est pas morte ton souvenir ;
Et si te frappais à ma porte,
  Mon cœur, Musette, irait t'ouvrir ;
Puisqu'à ton nom toujours il tremble,
  Muse de l'infidélité,
Reviens encore manger ensemble
  Le pain béni de la gaîté.

" The furniture of our old room,
As if all trusty friends and true,
Have cast aside their air of gloom
At merest hopes of meeting you.
Oh I come and are them all; alas!
They've mourn'd enough in lone
  despair—
The little bed, the mighty glass,
Where you so often drank my share!

" Again you'd wear the simple gown
Which then was grand enough to
  please,
And, as on Sundays, from the town,
We'd start in search of streams and
  trees.
At night to some love bower we'd bring
A flagon, cheap, but oh I how rare,
Where, sweet, your song would wet its
  wing
Before it vanish'd in the air.

" And Nature, who bears ne'er a spite,
For all the pranks that you have
  play'd,
Will not refuse a moon to light
And gild our kisses in the shade;
But prodigal of all her store,
Around, beneath us, and above,
You'll find her ready, as of yore,
To smile again upon our love.

" Musette, when richer friends grew
  strange,
Bethought of him who loved her best,
And did return awhile for change,
A stray bird to the ancient nest.
Alas ! with e'en the greeting kiss
Our fond love vanish'd in a sigh,
Each felt that something was amiss—
You were not you, and I not I.

" Farewell for aye I my lost, my dear,
For you are dead, and dead your
  lover,
And both our youths lie buried here
In this old almanack's torn cover.
'Tis only when we stir the dust
Of some dear day that in it lies,
That memory gives us back in trust
The keys of our lost paradise."

" Les meubles de notre chambrette,
Ces vieux amis de notre amour,
Déjà prennent un air de fête
Au seul espoir de ton retour—
Viens, tu reconnaîtras ma chère,
Tous ceux qu'en deuil mit ton départ,
Le petit lit, et le grand verre
Où ta buvais souvent ma part.

" Tu remettras la robe blanche
Dont tu te parais autrefois,
Et comme autrefois les dimanche
Nous irons courir dans les bois.
Amis le soir sous la tonnelle,
Nous boirons encor ce vin clair,
Où ta chanson mouillait son aile
Avant de s'envoler dans l'air.

" Dieu, qui ne garde pas rancune
Aux méchants tours que tu m'as faits,
Ne refusera pas la lune
A ses baisers sous les bosquets.
Tu retrouveras la nature
Toujours aussi belle et toujours,
O ma charmante créature,
Prête à sourire à nos amours.

" Musette qui s'est souvenue,
La carnaval est fini,
Un beau matin est revenu,
Oiseau volage à l'ancien nid :
Mais en embrassant l'infidèle,
Mon cœur n'a plus senti d'émoi,
Et Musette, qui n'est plus elle,
Dixit que je n'étais plus moi.

" Adieu, va-t'en chère adorée,
Bien morts avec l'amour dernier,
Notre jeunesse est enterrée
Au fond du vieux calendrier.
Ce n'est plus qu'en fouillant la cendre
Des beaux jours qu'il a contenus,
Qu'un souvenir pourra nous rendre
Le clef des paradis perdus !"

The penultimate verse was not yet realized, but ten years after her flight Marie did return, and with her came the disenchantment.

" La Jeunesse n'a qu'un temps " is the title of the last chapter. The Bohemians are all making their way in the world—their pictures are selling, and editors are fighting for their contributions; the old life, with its miseries, its joys, and its ringing laughter has drifted to the rear. " It is over," said the painter,

'"La jeunesse n'a qu'un temps'—where are you dining to-night?" 'If you like," replied Rodolphe, " we will dine for twelve sous at our old restaurant in the Rue de From off the coarsest earthen-ware, where long ago we used to leave off so hungry when we had finished all they gave us." "Not I, faith !" cried Marcel, " I'll willingly look back upon the past, but it must be over a bottle of good wine, and seated in a cozy arm-chair. What would you, my dear fellow ? I am corrupted. I love good things no longer !"

This is the end of the *Vie Bohème*, and the book was the end of Murger's career as a true Bohemian. Looking back for a moment at the old members of the little society, the *Buveurs d'Eau*, how many had fought their way upwards, how many had perished in the struggle ? Christ had died in the hospital ; Chabot had died in the hospital ; a third had gone to his native town to beg the bread he could not find in Paris. Karol, the kindliest of all, had expired in Constantinople, without a friend or franc to aid him in his extremity, after months of starvation in his futile endeavours to get pupils for French ; Jules de la Madeleon was dead ; Gérard de Nerval had, like Chatterton, grown weary of the struggle, and, seeking a like escape, had perished in his pride. Of the others, Murger and Noël were alone beginning to be known, the rest were still in the glooming. *Vive la Bohème !*

Of the actual persons typified in the book the end was at least as melancholy. Marcel became a picture dealer ; Schaunard has made a large fortune as a fishmonger ; Musette, the Musette of the story not of the song, vends toilet articles ; and Mimi is dead.

Not yet famous, for the *Vie Bohème* at first made its way slowly, Murger was now a writer well considered by editors. He continued his connexion with the *Corsaire*, and with Champfleury and Charles Hugo took part in the editorial management of the *Événement*, and shortly afterwards of the *Dix Décembre*, in which two journals respectively appeared the *Amours d'Olivier*, and the *Souper des Funérailles ;* but he was scarcely adapted for editorial duties. The *Figaro* relates an anecdote, that when he came to the office he would yawn uneasily for half an hour, and finally pulling out a five-franc piece, toss it into the air : " heads you must write the article ;—tails I will do it on Monday—or some other day !"—and so the question would be settled.

His circumstances had now much improved. He could afford to forego Tolstoy's allowance altogether, and he took comfortable chambers in the Rue Mazarin, where Banville, Baudélaire, Champfleury, Arsène Houssaye, Pierre Dupont, Alfred Vernet,

and many other men of note attended as in a club on Wednesday
evenings; and where the gentler sex was chiefly represented by the
grandest queen who ever reigned over Bohemia, that famous
model whom Adolphe Yvon has immortalized, and for whose
amusement the *Résurrection de Lazare* was afterwards written
by three of the clique.

As soon as the success of the *Vie Bohème* became indisputable
M. Th. Barrière, then a rising young dramatist, offered to assist
the author in adapting the story to the stage.   The collabora-
tion was accepted, and the five acts were in 1849 carried to the
Variétés; but the actors, frightened at the novelty of the situations and at the production of such a piece at a vaudeville
theatre, prophesied a fiasco.   At the first night's performance all
the surviving *Buveurs d'Eau* were present, each feeling as
though a work of his own were at stake.   Madlle. Thuillier, who
took the part of the heroine, was the very counterpart of the
actual Mimi, and it seemed to the brotherhood as though she
had come to life again.   "All at once," writes Banville, "my
blood rushed to my face, and I felt my knees tremble under
me. . . . . Oh! how pale, how white, with her dying hands—
fair as a lily amid the deep gloom of the scenery.   It was Mimi
herself, snatched by I know not what sacrifice of love from the
rigid grasp of death!"   "When she was dead," says Nadar,
"and we heard the cry of her lover, thinking with a brutal selfishness of nothing but the loss he personally had sustained, 'O my
youth, it is you they are burying!' the egotism of the shriek
seemed to freeze the blood in my veins.   I ran to Murger—'You
have won a glorious, a legitimate success, but in the name of all
the love you bear us cut out that last atrocious sentence!'
'Certainly not,' he replied, 'it is Nature.'   At the end of
every act the applause had gradually increased till the curtain
fell amid a perfect roar of enthusiasm."   The production of this
play was followed by an absolute rage for books and dramas
upon Bohemian life—every minor theatre and every petty journal
reproduced Murger's work in one pirated form or another.   Yet
at the same time the author's future was assured.   M. Buloz,
the autocratic editor of the *Revue des Deux Mondes*, opened to
him the pages of the most influential periodical in Europe, then
in the zenith of its glory; and shortly afterwards his services
were bespoken for the *Moniteur*.   Henceforth he had but to
write what he would, and gather in a golden harvest.   But his
wants were small, he had an extreme distaste for the mechanical
drudgery of work in which his whole sympathy was not enlisted,
and he contented himself in the future with an income of from
three to four thousand francs a year.

In the August of 1851, Murger met Madame Anaïs, a lady

whose loving companionship was to sweeten the remainder of
his days. Some few of his letters to her have been published;
but charming as they are in their gracious abandon and pleasant
familiarity, we can only quote from them most scantily: " Your
pen seems to share the timidity of your life; where I had hoped
to see *mon ami,* I find *mon voisin.* Ah, sweet! you have a
lively and charming mind. One harmonious law seems to
govern all the movements of your gracious being, and each of your
gestures is a cadence. Your glances at once provoke me and
rebuke me. Your hand is soft to my lips, and your lips are soft
to my kisses. But why is your heart like a letter enfolded in
thirty-six envelopes, of which you will only unseal thirty-five?"
In July, 1853, the correspondence shows that he was on a visit
to Algiers—the first time he had ever left France—"in the land
of the Arabian Nights, where I have picked up all manner of
Arab words, to tell you how I love you in the language of the
East." Then follows a list of presents far beyond the prudent
limits of his scanty purse, including even all manner of fantasies
for her in her turn to give her friends.

Immediately after his return from Algiers, Murger commenced
the *Buveurs d'Eau* a very painful *pendant* to the gay and
sparkling merriment of the *Vie Bohème.* This volume was due
rather to a general and profound study of human nature than to
the characteristics of actual personages and the idiosyncrasies of
individuals. As a work of art, it is undeniably superior to the
first, but as a readable, mirth-compelling fiction, far below it.
The "Buveurs d'Eau" contains three tales round which the characters are grouped, and these tales prove Murger to have been
as true a master of pathos as of kindly, laughter-splitting caricature. The "Buveurs d'Eau" of his fiction were of course
founded upon the members of their old society, and like them
were bound by the same stern rules, fired by the same lofty
ideal. By this time, however, regarding it retrospectively, he
perceived clearly that their isolation, their many self-imposed
abnegations, their terrible miseries, did not altogether afford the
speediest method of arriving at their ends:—

" We have among us poets whose muses are stuttering still, but they
stutter boldly. There are others whose works, already accentuated,
prove themselves children of a grand race. As to our poverty we accept
it submissively, as we accept the cold in winter, only our cold is of
the severest. Hope to us is no poetic figure, as allegory depicts her;
she is but a sorry companion, consoling us with her sighs rather than
with her songs. We are like children who are not accustomed to see
playthings. We economize our joys, and make them last as long as
possible, and when the sound of them is dead we listen for the echo.

Do we believe that some day some one or something will result from our association ? The future will show. Has there ever been a great artist among us ? I doubt it; when our muses breathe their songs we see that they are scant of breath ; our productions savour of the earth, and so far they are weakly. Thus we do not think that we can produce great things, but our productions will be at least sincere. . . . . . The definitive formula of modern art will one day be discovered ; in the meantime there are patient students laboriously struggling, as thorough as men can be in an age of unbelief, living apart from the din of theory-mongers, very careless of puerile triumph, and humbly resigned to their modest lot. Of these are we; it is our one merit, and it is a merit."

Shortly after the publication of the " Buveurs d'Eau," Murger retired from the *Revue des Deux Mondes;* writing in future chiefly for the *Moniteur.* It has been a disputed point among critics as to how far his connexion with this staid and grave *Revue* acted upon his genius, as to whether it did not in some degree weaken the sprightliness of his sparkling humour. The short tales that had appeared here and elsewhere were now collected by M. Lévy, and published in volumes as *Scènes de la Vie Compagne, Scènes de la Jeunesse, La Romance de toutes les Femmes,* and that other Bohemian story, *Le Pays Latin.*

In the year 1855 he gave up his residence in Paris altogether, and went to live at Marlotta, near the forest of Fontainebleau, where for the last five years he had found a country sojourn whenever he had had leisure and opportunity ; of this spot Michelet somewhere says, "many men have remained here captured and engulfed. They came for a month and rested till death took them." So it was with Murger. He adopted all the habits of a country life, and became a mighty huntsman ; he did not attempt to conceal his aspirations ; on the contrary his ordinary costume would have made a Nimrod wild with envy— " boots up to his hips, a melon-shaped helmet, a dress of spangled green, a gun, a game-bag, and a dog," accoutrements that excited not a little admiration when, as was his wont when duty called him to Paris, he appeared in them on the boulevards. At Marlotta he had a pretty little villa, half-buried in jessamine and roses, with two doors, one opening on the road for general use, the other strictly private, leading straight into the country, very convenient when he started for the chase, more so still when he returned, for alas, this ardent passion for sport was, like so many other of his loves, of a purely platonic nature ; he was never known to have slain with his own hands a single bird or beast fit for human food. The countryside was and is full

of pleasant stories anent his sporting career. For example,
a hare had made her form in a neighbouring potato field.
Murger took possession of the hare ; henceforth it was his hare :
every day at sunrise he rose to hunt the animal, and he hunted
it unremittingly until the evening. This lasted all the summer,
as the other sportsmen had agreed to hold the animal sacred.
One day, however, some strangers were down shooting with the
keeper. A hare sprang out of a hedge, one of the strangers
quickly raised his gun, and the keeper had but just time to strike
it into the air. " Good heavens, Monsieur ! would you kill
Murger's hare ?" " Murger's hare ! ah ! well, I will merely leave
my card upon him," and with his second barrel he took off the
hare's left ear.

Still the sport, such as it was, entertained Murger immensely,
and he hated the dull season, more than once harmlessly encroach-
ing upon the forbidden time. It was only to Madame Anais
that he ever confessed his impotence as a sportsman, and that
in the gentlest manner. Writing to her from the country, he
says, " Bring me my Saturday's article in the *Figaro*, and bring,
above all else, your gentleness of happy days ; and, by the way,
if you really want to taste any game, I think it would be prudent
to buy some in Paris and bring it with you too."

There was other game which he was still obliged to pursue—
cet animal féroce qu'on appelle la pièce de cent sous. He worked
now only when he felt inclined, and took life very pleasantly,
but the last days of each month were always times of poverty.
His correspondence is full of laughing descriptions of duns and
debts and shifts. Even the dog Mirza was supposed to feel the
advent of these evil days, and with a paw, guided by Murger's
hand, wrote thus plaintively, " My dear Mistress,—It seems that
unhappy times are approaching. My master talks of suppressing
my morning *pâté*, and actually wishes to hire me out to a shepherd, so that I may earn enough money for my own support, but
as I have an evil reputation of loving cutlets, they wont trust
me to watch the sheep. If you should happen to come across a
pretty dog-collar, set round with diamonds, costing not more than
25 sous, bring it me.—CHIENNE MIRZA."

Murger now at last found time to return to the completion of
that volume of poems which had been his life-dream, and which
was, he thought, to make his reputation anew, and he prepared
it for the press with more hopes of attracting an audience than
he ever before possessed.

From the first page to the last the volume is laden with melancholy, for in his poems he could only speak what his heart
prompted. There is a sadness of hope long deferred even in
the jesting and cynical dedication to the reader :—

"O friendly reader ! who hast boldly dared,
  In daylight, too, and by the price
  assured,
In this small tome to openly invest,—
In thy posterity may'st thou be blest !
And in each rapidly succeeding child
Oh ! may that pleasant face, so blandly
  mild,
Without an after-touch be clearly
  traced !
And may thy spouse be frugal, friend,
  and chaste ;
And like the Spartan dames of high
  degree
May she mark linen well, and well
  make tea !
In trade and private life may every
  friend
Be slow to borrow, very quick to lend !
May'st thou ne'er gamble ; gambling,
  may'st thou win,
And touch the token of thy neighbours'
  sin !
Then proudly on a tomb of marble
  white,
In golden letters, loving hands shall
  write :—
'Here lies the man who, when he
  lived, paid down
For one small book of modern verse a
  crown !' "

" Ami lecteur, qui viens d'entre dans la
  boutique
Où l'on vend ce volume, et qui l'as
  acheté,
Sans marchander d'un sou, malgré son
  prix modique,
Sois béni, bon lecteur, dans ta postérité !
Que ton épouse reste économe et
  pudique,
Que le fruit de son sein soit ton por-
  trait flaté,
Sans retouche ; et, pareille à la matron
  antique,
Qu'elle marque le linge, et fasse bien le
  thé !
Que ton cellier soit plein du vin de la
  comète !
Qu'on n'emprunte pas d'argent—et
  qu'on t'en prête !
Que le hrelan te suivre autour des
  tapis verts ;
Et qu'un jour sur ta tumbe, en marbre
  Carrare
Un burin d'or inscrive *hic jacet* l'homme
  rare
Qui payait d'un écu trois cent pages
  de vers ! "

But through all its pages *Les Nuits d'hiver*, with its despairs, its melancholies, its disenchantments, and even its occasional weaknesses, is a picture of the strange life that Murger had led ; giving us something of his purest heart's blood, of his soul's deepest tenderness ; caressing, and yet in a manner spurning, the passion to which his boyhood, his life, had been a victim ; till in the last song of all, the *Testament*, he bursts forth with an out-wrung cry of indignation, with a cynicism that is half real, half hysteric, against the love that he had cast into the dust to be trampled by a worthless woman's silken slippers. Bequeathing all his goods to his mistress,—this time not Anais, or Louise, or Christine, but Marie herself—he bids the executor bear her the news of his death, and ask her to his funeral, "but if in her clear eyes a single tear should tremble you must tear the will in two—the legacy was not for her !" and the priests when they came to assist at the ceremony were to be warned that their presence was useless—" Tell them I've read Voltaire !"

Full still of the old Bohemian motto—"the Academy, the Morgue, or the Hospital !"—he trusted that this volume would proclaim aloud so blatantly that neither officialdom nor favour could stifle it, his indisputable right to be numbered among the " Forty Immortals"; yet it was, perhaps, in the fitness of things that the historian of Bohemia should reach the last rather than the first of these three goals.

Honours, however, did at last begin to fall upon him; in Michaelmas, 1860, the government granted him a small pension; and in the January of 1861, as a further recognition of his services he received the cross of the Legion of Honour. But these gifts came too late.

On the 14th January, 1861, he was seized by an attack of what he thought was gout in his left leg, but the doctors pronounced it to be an *artérite*, which would rapidly, they prophesied, cause the mortification of the member. He was moved from Marlotta to the little room in Paris he had just taken. The symptoms rapidly became worse; he had no loving friends at hand; his purse was empty; and on the 26th he was carried to the hospital. On the road thither he cried, "Take me first into the chapel; that will do me more good, for I think God is stronger than the physicians!" In the little chapel's quiet gloom the impious cry of "having read Voltaire" was forgotten, and again "a little boy in blue" it seemed as though he was kneeling once more beside his mother's feet. At the Maison Dubois he occupied bed No. 14. "Ah, No. 14," he said when they laid him in it, "it was in a No. 14 that poor Jacques died!" The doctors forbade him to talk. He tried to scribble a line to a friend—"Ravel and the others advised me to go to the Maison Dubois—I would have liked St. Louis better. I am more at home there. Excuse . . . ."

By this time the news had reached his friends and the public— all Paris was in consternation when they heard that one of their most promising writers was dying in a common hospital. Was it not enough that Hégésippe Moreau and Gustave Planché should have died within those dreary walls so recently?

All day long his friends called to see him or to gather tidings of him. One of the youngest insisted upon watching over the patient's sick couch day and night, though warned that the malady might be fatally contagious. M. Walewski on the part of the government sent 500 francs to procure any delicacies the doctors might allow, and the Société des Gens de Lettres were anxious to do the same. M. Ravel, the kindly actor, as much a favourite in London as in Paris, slipped a hundred-franc note into the dressing-table drawer. When it was found there Murger was very pleased, and said, with a smile through all his pain, "Ask Ravel who was the author of that act; he wont betray him!"

Murger's death was miserably painful, for mortification set in rapidly. On Sunday, the 28th, he received extreme unction, and on the evening of Monday, the 29th January, he passed away,

murmuring "*Pas de musique, pas de bruit, pas de Bohème.*"
The news ran rapidly through Paris, for all were in a state of
anxious expectancy. There was a grand ball at the Hôtel de
Ville. "Murger can't live till the morning," said a doctor to the
crowd who thronged round him for the latest bulletin. "No,
thank you," replied a young lady to her partner; "Murger is
dying; I can dance no more to-night."

On Wednesday, the 31st, the funeral took place. M. Walewski
was charged with all the preparations. Three thousand persons,
bareheaded, and one hundred carriages, followed the corpse to
the grave. The Ministers of State and Public Instruction were
all represented, as well as the Academy and the other learned
bodies; and close behind the hearse, arm in arm, walked the
three surviving *Buveurs d'Eau.* "He was escorted even to
the cemetery by the music of the regiment that killed him."
"Is it the funeral of a millionaire, Monsieur?" asked a curious
gossip. "No, Madame; it is the funeral of a pauper poet!"—
of a poet whose poems were published for the first time upon
the day of his death, and who died, just as his talents were
becoming duly recognised, at the age of thirty-nine, from the
effects of the want and misery of the unaided struggles of his
youth.

Next day they opened a subscription to erect a handsome
monument to Murger's memory. Long ago he had asked for
bread; now they gave him a stone of the costliest!

Art. V.—Charity Schools.

1. *An Essay on Charity Schools.* By Bertrand de Mandeville. 1716.

2. *Report of the Endowed Schools Commission*, presented to
   the Education Department of the Privy Council, 1872.

3. *Educational Hospital Reform. The Scheme of the Edin
   burgh Merchant Company.* A paper read before the
   British Association, by Thomas J. Boyd, F.R.S.E., Master
   of the Merchants Company.

OUR recent experiments in public education, the zeal and
fulness with which they have been discussed, and the
universal interest which they have excited, will probably render
this a very memorable age to future generations. Yet they ought
not to blind us to the fact that there have been earlier periods
of educational enthusiasm and revival. Long before the sixty
years' struggle—begun by Lancaster and Bell, and completed in
Mr. Forster's great measure of 1870—had ended in placing the
provision for general elementary instruction on a basis commensurate with the needs of the poor of England, there were in
our history at least two notable epochs of educational activity,
each of which in its own way has left enduring traces on the
intellectual growth, and on the social institutions of our own
time.

The first of these was the Tudor period, in which originated
the larger number of our Grammar Schools. Before the
accession of Henry VIII., there were but thirty-five such institutions in England, including Eton, Carlisle, and Winchester,
and a few others which had been founded as chantries, or were
otherwise connected with Ecclesiastical Establishments. But it
was the dissolution of the monasteries which at once gave the
impetus to the establishment of such schools, and furnished the
means of sustaining them. And it is a fortunate circumstance
for England that the same event which set free large resources
for these special uses, happened to coincide with the revival
of learning, with the Protestant Reformation, and with the
quickening of intellectual energy and of the spirit of inquiry
throughout the land. During Henry's reign, sixty-three foundation schools, including St. Paul's, Ipswich, Bruton, Manchester,
and most of those specially attached to cathedrals, were set up.
In Edward VI.'s reign, besides Christ's Hospital, the great schools
of Birmingham, Sherborne, Sedbergh, Leeds, Skipton, Ilminster,
Tunbridge, and others, to the number of fifty, were established.

Even in Mary's time nineteen new foundations were added to the list, of which the only existing institutions of any fame are those at York and at Brentwood ; while the long life of Elizabeth is distinguished by the addition of 138 to the number—Westminster, Merchant Taylor's, Wakefield, Aldenham, Croydon, being amongst the best known. Eighty-three other Grammar Schools were founded in the time of James I., of which a few, such as the Charterhouse, Doncaster, and Dulwich, are still important ; but, since that time, though many foundations bearing the name of Grammar Schools have sprung into existence, they are, with few exceptions poorly endowed and historically insignificant. One uniform purpose, however, is manifest in the testaments, the deeds of gift, and the early statutes by which the career of these schools was intended to be shaped. It is to encourage the pursuit of a liberal education, founded on the ancient languages—then the only studies which had been so far formulated and systematized as to possess a disciplinal character. It is almost invariably stipulated in the instruments of foundation, that the master is to be a learned man ; that he shall be apt and godly, qualified to instruct in good letters, and good manners ; and that he shall receive as his pupils children of all ranks.

But it is notable that by the end of the seventeenth century, a great change seems to have come over the minds of testators and benevolent people in regard to this matter of education. The endowed schools, which owe their origin to this period, aim no longer at the general diffusion of a liberal education, or at the encouragement of all classes in the common pursuit of knowledge and culture. They are for a limited number of the poor, but for the poor alone. They are designed rather to repress than to stimulate intellectual ambition, and consciously or unconsciously, they were adapted less to bring rich and poor together than to set up new barriers between them. There has been no period of our history, in which the social separation of classes has been more marked and more jealous than at the beginning of the eighteenth century. The disappearance of the last vestiges of feudalism under the legislation of Charles II. and of William, synchronized with the steady growth among the upper and middle classes of a kind of social conservatism, which was none the less strong because the legal securities for its maintenance were passing away. A fear lest the poor should forget the duties of their station, and encroach upon the privileges of the rich, is very evident in much of the literature and some of the legislation of the age. And there is no more significant token of the changed feeling with which the rich had come to regard the poor than the simple fact that whereas in the sixteenth century Englishmen founded Grammar Schools, in the eighteenth they founded Charity Schools.

What truly noble product even of philanthropy was to be expected in an age so barren of faith and earnestness, as that in which Pope, Warburton, and Bolingbroke were the philosophers, and Tillotson, Hoadley, and Atterbury the divines? One reads the classical discourses, the moral essays, the cold evidential theology, the half-hearted apologetic literature, wherewith the clergy of that day feebly strove to check the prevailing Deism; and one is thus well prepared to find as the natural correlative of such a condition of religious life, an ignoble conception of the conditions of intellectual life in a nation, as well as of the mental claims of the poor. To men who were content with the stately and pompous orthodoxy of the time for themselves, it seemed natural that the religion of a poor man should be neither intellectual or emotional, but severely practical. A code of precepts about virtue and morality, learned by heart and enforced at school would, it was hoped, restrain the vices of the poor, keep them in due subordination to their superiors, and make them industrious, respectful, and contented. There was unquestionable kindliness, and a desire for the welfare of the poor; but the benevolence was restrained and modified by a fear lest too much education should in any way imperil the stability of the social fabric, which, whatever its defects, was on the whole a safe and comfortable residence for the classes most interested in the establishment of the schools. This conflict of motive will be seen in the case of Bishop Butler, who, preaching in St. Paul's on behalf of the Charity Schools of London, commended them to the benevolence of the citizens on these grounds—

"Their design was not in any sort to remove poor children out of the rank in which they were born, but keeping them in it, to give them the assistance which their circumstances plainly called for; by educating them in the principles of religion as well as of civil life, and likewise making some sort of provision for their maintenance, under which last I include clothing them, giving them such learning—if it is to be called by that name—as may qualify them for some common employment, and placing them out to it as they grow up."

And he goes on to anticipate the objection of those who fear that a little book learning will set these children above their station, by showing how well calculated the system of clothing the children in a distinctive dress, and making them public objects of charity is to neutralize this objection; for "it will, so far from encouraging vanity or ambition, have quite the contrary effect, when they grow up, and ever after, remind them of their rank."

One after another of the prelates and dignitaries who preached the annual Whitsun sermon before the charity children and their patrons in London, insisted on the same view of the character and work of the schools. Kennett, Bishop of Peterborough, himself while a curate at St. Botolph, Aldgate, the founder of the first charity school in London, in his sermon (1706), speaks with pardonable enthusiasm, as to the novel spectacle which had thus been provided for the gratification of rich people with kindly instincts—

"I cannot but commend the prudence of the Governors and Trustees of this charity, that they keep up an anniversary meeting of these poor children, to come from every quarter of our two cities and their larger suburbs, to walk in decent couples through the streets, led by the ministers, the pastors over the lambs of the flock, and then at last folded, as it were, in the courts of God's House; to see them clothed with neatness and set off with good manners, and by humility and piety made all glorious within; to hear them reading the psalms distinctly, making the responses audibly; turning readily to the chapters, reciting more perfectly their catechism and some useful exposition of it, and singing forth the psalms and hymns in a melodious manner. O what a Christian entertainment is this! a spectacle far beyond the vanities of the stage or music-house, or any worldly pomp whatever!"

Dean Stanhope, in his sermon of the previous year, had been careful to define the educational aims of these schools:

"It is not a knowledge of empty speculation or wanton curiosity that I stand here an advocate for, such as may render the youth brought up in it pragmatical and busy, dangerous and troublesome to others and disposed to think of themselves more highly than they ought to think; but it is a knowledge tending to make them just and peaceable, useful and industrious, necessary to qualify them for getting their daily bread."

And Dr. Robinson, Bishop of London, in 1714, gave a strong, and as it has proved, wholly superfluous warning to the patrons of these schools, against carrying the instruction a step beyond the rudiments:

"It is doubtless your intention that these objects of your charity be so educated as that they may hereafter become useful in inferior stations, and therefore whatever exceeds now what may reasonably be expected to be their lot afterwards, may be too much, and ought to be avoided; lest instead of the principles of piety they should, by your too great indulgence, imbibe those of pride."

It would be easy to multiply evidence of this kind, as to the spirit in which Charity Schools originated, from the sermons of the clergy, as well as from the writings and correspondence of clerically-minded laymen, like Robert Nelson, the author of the "Fasts and Festivals," who took great interest in the movement, and who at the request of the local trustees in Bath and elsewhere, drew up the rules for the religious instruction and discipline of the schools. There is in all alike evinced more of patronage than of sympathy, more of stern churchmanship than of religious earnestness, and a general desire to make the charity schools instruments rather in the maintenance of the social order, than in promoting the mental or spiritual wellbeing of the scholars.

So Edward Colston, the tutelary saint of Bristol, in whose honour pious orgies are still annually celebrated in that city, founded and endowed in 1708, a hospital school. In his settlement he not only gave the usual orders respecting the learning of the Catechism, and the diligent attendance of the children at Church twice on every Sunday and Saint's day; but further ordained that the apprentice premium to be given to a boy on leaving school was to be paid only, if the master to whom he was bound was in all respects conformable to the Established Church. Moreover he ordered that "in case the parents of any boy in the Hospital shall prevail on him to go or be present at any conventicle or meeting on *pretence of religious worship*, or by word or action prevail with or deter any child from attending the public worship according to the religion established in the Church of England, then it shall be lawful for the Trustees to expel such child and to take away his clothing." He proceeds to add several minatory clauses addressed to any possible future Trustees who should consent to the education of boys in any other than an orthodox way—"it being entirely contrary to my inclinations that any of the boys should be educated in fanaticism, or in principles any way repugnant to those of your present Established Church."

This jealous and exclusive temper is characteristic of many of the so-called "pious foundations" of that age. The Toleration Act had recently forced English Churchmen to recognise dissent as a fact, and to many it was a most unpleasant fact. All efforts to incorporate Puritanism into the organic life of the English Church had finally failed after the Act of Uniformity. Henceforth the Conformist and the Nonconformist must go different ways; and the desire on the part of the ruling classes to attach the poor to that English Church which so many people of the Puritan middle classes had sullenly forsaken, found expression in the erection of schools of a type wholly new to Englishmen. In the charity schools, at least, all remonstrance would be silenced. Within the walls of a schoolroom raised by the benevolence of Churchmen, and filled with children whose very dress betokened their dependence, the clergyman and his allies were supreme.

"God bless the Squire and his relations,
And make us keep our proper stations,"

was the general sentiment pervading the schools. A little
reading, writing, and mechanical summing were taught; but there
was a careful avoidance of geography, of history, of literature of
poetry, of everything calculated to exalt the imagination, or
kindle thought, as being unsuited to the objects of the institution. In place of these there was much church-going on Sundays
and holidays; a ceaseless repetition of the words of the Prayer
Book, notably of those of the Catechism, which, though antiquated in form and unintelligible to a child without much explanation, were never explained, and yet are still supposed by many
of the clergy to exercise a sort of talismanic power or virtue in forming the mind of a devout Churchman. That wonderful formulary
is surrounded by so mystic a halo of tradition, affection, and
religious controversy, that it is difficult to look at it with fresh
eyes, and ask ourselves what thoughts it actually conveys into
a child's mind, and how far it is instrumental in producing, we
will not say the effects designed by an intelligent Christian
teacher, but any intellectual or moral impression whatever. There
are many clergy who though disposed to abandon it as a text-
book of theology, nevertheless cleave to a touching faith in its
moral teaching. They are accustomed, for example, to refer to
the answers to the two questions, "What is thy duty towards
God?" and "What is thy duty to thy neighbour?" as admirable
compendiums of Christian duty; and as embodying in a
practical and useful form the whole meaning of the Ten Commandments. How the Catechism fulfils this purpose may be
judged from a single clause in the "Duty to my neighbour."
"To submit myself to all my governors, teachers, spiritual
pastors and masters; to order myself lowly and reverently before
my betters," words which, whatever be their worth *per se*, can
hardly be regarded as a fair paraphrase of any one of the in-
junctions in the second table of the law.

It is not a little curious, in the light of modern experience, to
turn back to contemporary comments on this new experiment.
Bertrand de Mandeville appended in 1716 to his famous book
the "Fable of the Bees," an essay on what to him was the fashionable folly of the day, the establishment of charity schools. "After
his sour fashion" he denounced generally the system of endowments by which rich and vain men sought to purchase immortality, defrauded their natural heirs, crowded treasure into what
he called the dead stock of the kingdom, and encumbered the
world with useless and inelastic institutions, designed rather to
glorify themselves than to benefit society. With special emphasis
he pointed to the endowment, two years before, of the Radclyffe

Library at Oxford, which he attributed to pride and vulgar ostentation, and to an ignoble wish to purchase in the cheapest market the homage and veneration of posterity :—

"Had this British Æsculapius followed arms, behaved himself in five-and-twenty sieges and as many battles with the bravery of an Alexander . . . . or devoting himself to the Muses sacrificed his pleasure, his rest, and his health to literature and the toils of learning, or else abandoning all worldly interest, excelled in probity, temperance, and austerity, and ever trod in the strictest path of virtue, he could not so effectually have provided for the eternity of his name, as after a voluptuous life and the luxurious gratification of his passions he has now done without any trouble or self-denial, only by the choice in the disposal of his money when he was forced to leave it. In the Universities men are profoundly skilled in human nature; they know what it is their benefactors want, and there extraordinary bounties shall always meet with an extraordinary recompense, and the measure of the gift is always the standard of their praises."

And in like manner the cynic goes on to examine the causes which brought charity schools so much into vogue. One of them is a sort of æsthetic gratification which good people derive from the sight of a row of charity children in the street or in the gallery of a church.

"It is diverting to the eye to see children well-matched march two and two in good order, and to have them all whole and tight in the same clothes and trimming must add to the comeliness of the sight; and what makes it still more generally entertaining is the imaginary share which even servants and the meanest in the parish have in it, to whom it costs nothing. In all this there is a shadow of property that tickles everybody, but more especially those who actually contribute and had a great hand in advancing the pious work."

He complains also that the actual government gets into the hands of mean, fussy, and self-important people. To such persons he says :—

"There is great satisfaction in ordering and directing. There is a melodious sound in the word Governor that is charming to mean people. Everybody admires sway and superiority, even *imperium in belluas* has its delights; there is a pleasure in ruling over anything, and it is this chiefly that supports human nature in the tedious slavery of schoolmasters. But if there be the least satisfaction in governing the children it must be ravishing to govern the schoolmaster himself. What fine things are said and perhaps wrote to a Governor, when a schoolmaster is to be chosen. How the praises tickle, and how pleasant it is not to find out the fulsomeness of the flattery, the stiffness of the expressions, or the pedantry of the style."

And he roundly asserts that as far as the upper classes are concerned, the chief motive in the establishment of the schools has been the desire to strengthen a party :—

" Why must our concern for religion be eternally made a cloke to hide our real drifts and worldly intentions ? Would both parties agree to pull off the mask, we should soon discover that whatever they pretend to, they aim at nothing so much in charity-schools as to strengthen their party ; and that the great sticklers for the Church, by educating children in the principles of religion mean inspiring them with a superlative veneration for the clergy of the Church of England, and a strong aversion and immortal animosity against all that dissent from it. To be assured of this, we are but to mind on the one hand what divines are most admired for their charity sermons and most fond to preach them, and, on the other, whether of late years we have had any riots or party scuffles among the mob, in which the youth of a famous hospital in this city were not always the most forward ringleaders."

These passionate utterances do not, however, represent the prevailing feeling either of Mandeville's age or of any which has succeeded it. Charity schools of this kind rapidly multiplied during the last century and the beginning of this, and they are still flourishing. They are founded on a conception of education, partly religious and partly feudal, but almost wholly ignoble and humiliating. And they exist to our own day in striking contrast to the grammar school foundations of earlier generations. The charity school children were to be sedulously discouraged from learning more than is supposed to be necessary to the discharge of the humblest duties of life. But the scholars in the grammar school were either to be the sons of gentlemen or are to be treated as such. They were to be brought within the reach of the highest cultivation that the nation can afford, they were to be encouraged to proceed from school to the Universities ; and special provision was always made to tempt into this higher region of learning and gentlemen the child of the yeoman and the peasant, in order that, if quickwitted and diligent, he too may be trained up to serve God in Church and State.

One fact deserves special notice in reviewing the history and condition of these two classes of institutions. Those of the one class are confined exclusively to boys, those of the other are designed for both sexes, almost equally. And the public authorities who have lately been called on to investigate the condition of endowed educational foundations, with a view to their re-organization under the Act of 1869, find themselves in the presence of this curious and anomalous fact :—all the endowed schools which aim at a high or generous ideal of education are appropriated to boys only, all the endowed foundations in the kingdom which are open to girls are charity schools only. In most of them the avowed aim is to make good domestic servants, and to this end much sewing and household work are required ; but in none of them is the educational aim higher or more liberal than that of

II H 2

a good national school, and in very few is it so high. Grotesque and striking as has been the failure of institutions of this kind to produce skilled domestic servants, it must yet be owned that kindly and religious people have been quite as ready to recognise the claims of poor girls as of boys to the sort of training which was presumed best fitted for a humble station, and to make them useful menials to the rich. But there is scarcely a record in all the elaborate reports of the Schools Inquiry Commission or Charity Commission of a single old endowment in England which deliberately contemplates an advanced education for a girl; which recognises her claim to intellectual culture, or shows any solicitude about her grammar, "good literature," or "godly learning." A girl is not expected to serve God in Church or State, and is therefore not invited to the University or the grammar school; but she may, if poor, be wanted to contribute to the comfort of her "betters," as an apprentice or servant, and the charity schools are therefore open to her.

Roughly it may be computed that there are in England nearly eight hundred institutions, which at one time or other in their history have professed to give higher than elementary instruction; and that the total revenues, even if the value of the sites and buildings be included, fall a little short of 400,000*l.* per annum. The later charity schools, on the other hand, which have never contemplated higher instruction in any form are much more numerous, amounting to about two thousand; but they are much poorer, and their gross annual income scarcely exceeds 100,000*l.*

The Schools Inquiry Commission reported fully on all the schools of the former group; but except for statistical purposes, those of the latter did not fall within the scope of the report. The provisions of the Endowed Schools Act of 1869, however, extend to both, and include all educational endowments whatever. Clause 29 expressly states that:—"For the purposes of this Act endowments attached to any school for the payment of apprenticeship fees, or for the advancement in life, or for the maintenance or clothing or otherwise for the benefit of children educated at such school, shall be deemed to be educational endowments." Thus the law evidently contemplates the reform and adaptation to the purposes of organized secondary instruction, not only the grammar schools which were designed to give such instruction, but also all other educational foundations.

The Endowed Schools Act declares in its preamble that its object is "to carry into effect the main designs of the founders, *by placing a liberal education within the reach of all classes.*" It thus puts its own interpretation upon those designs, credits the Nelsons and the Kennetts of last century with large and generous educational objects which those worthies certainly did not entertain, and which their successors, the clergy, and parochial and municipal authorities who still manage charity schools and administer patronage, are most reluctant to recognise.

We gather from the report of the Endowed Schools Commission that though this general intention of the Act was plain in 1869, and although a large and bold adaptation of ancient foundations to modern uses was then expected and deemed necessary by statesmen of all parties, and by all who had studied the evidence on the subject, in practice it has been found that the country is hardly prepared for the reception of this reform. Formidable local opposition seems everywhere to compass those who attempt to set the Act in motion, and this opposition is directed not so much to the particular mode in which, in given cases, it is proposed to apply the power of the Commission, as to the Act itself, and to the principles on which it is based. The Committee of the House of Commons recently appointed to investigate the operation of the Act seems to be bringing this fact into greater prominence. All the Commissioners and their assistants testify that though considerable local sympathy is to be found in regard to moderate reforms, the full application of the principles laid down by the Schools Inquiry Report, and endorsed by so many experienced witnesses, seems to the average Englishman little short of impiety and sacrilege.

In these circumstances it becomes advisable to recall attention to those principles which underlie the whole question, and to look with fresh eyes on a problem which can, in fact, never lose its interest for thoughtful men—how to combine reverence for the past with faith in the future, a sincere respect for the spirit of ancient bequests, with a statesmanlike diagnosis of the defects and intellectual wants of our own time. There is no civilized community in the world which leave so large a liberty to the discretion and caprice of testators as our own. Our statute law and our judicial procedure have alike assumed that the State was interested in encouraging the accumulation of wealth, and that to this end it was wise to legalize bequests of almost all kinds, and to interpret wills in the way most favourable to the presumed wishes of testators. The community, in fact, expresses its willingness to receive bequests for public objects on any conditions, without reserving to itself the privilege which is possessed by every other legatee to refuse the gift if the conditions are unacceptable. While each generation claims the right to overhaul ruthlessly the legislation of the past, however solemnly it has been enacted by wise and ancient Parliaments, there is one legislator, who though self-appointed, and possibly not gifted either with wisdom or forethought, is allowed to escape the common fate of oblivion.

Your "pious founder" lays down ordinances for the government of an institution which he professes to bequeath as part of a national provision for a public purpose, and these ordinances are commonly presumed to possess a sacredness which does not attach to any other laws. It is irreligious to touch them. It is confiscation to apply his wealth to new, even if to cognate objects. How far does a man by the mere accident of his possessing wealth, and not caring much about his natural heirs, acquire the right to impose upon all posterity crude theories about education or demoralizing and injurious institutions under the name of charities? Philosophy may have its misgivings as to this question. But sentiment sweeps it abruptly away as irreverent and shocking. Natural piety comes to the aid of instinctive Conservatism. "Let us at least fence off one region from the encroachments of revolution. And so far as endowments are concerned, let the living be contentedly governed by the dead."

That traditional sentiments like this will not bear close or rational scrutiny, and that like other of the *idola tribûs* of which Bacon warns us, they will disappear with the spread of a sounder political education in England, can scarcely be doubted. It is manifest that the only condition on which a State can wisely accept bequests for charitable or educational uses, is that she shall reserve to herself the power to criticise and amend the terms of such bequests, and when necessary to modify the means by which these ends can be best attained. If this were done resolutely in the case of all endowments half a century old, it is probable that a good many of the pettier and more selfish forms of bequest, those, *e.g.*, for sermons on a founder's birthday, or for dresses with a founder's badge, would be discouraged, and this would be a clear moral gain. But all the wiser and nobler forms of bequest would probably be greatly multiplied if it once became known that pains would be taken to preserve their vitality and to prevent them from degenerating into abuses. We do no real honour to the founder of a charity when we perpetuate in detail arrangements which, however well adapted to his age, are harmful or ridiculous when carried out under the altered conditions of ours. On the contrary, the truest compliment we can pay to his memory is to assume that if he were living now, he would be as anxious to render the highest service to this generation as he was to benefit his own, and would rejoice to see measures taken for the attainment of this end.*

---

* An interesting illustration of this is furnished by the recent splendid gift of 400,000*l.* devoted by Sir Josiah Mason to the foundation of a Science College in Birmingham. The *Spectator* of December 14, 1872, after describing in detail the object of this foundation, gives the following facts and com-

" The letter killeth, but the spirit giveth life," is as true in regard to the careful provisions in the wills of our ancestors as

ments in relation to the manner in which the trust is to be managed:—" A large and generous design like this, in favour of an object of indisputable public utility, is no novelty in the history of foundations. And yet it alone has not been found in practice to be an adequate safeguard against subsequent mismanagement and stagnation. As one looks back, not without sadness, at the record of endowments started in a similar spirit, it is impossible to forget that many of them have failed in their objects and become public nuisances, and that this result has been mainly attributable to two causes, which the most generous benefactor, when destitute of political foresight, is apt to overlook. One of them is, that a body of trustees named in the founder's deed, and allowed to renew itself by perpetual coöptation, becomes in the course of years a narrow clique, practically irresponsible, out of harmony with the outside world, and disposed to administer the property rather as a private trust than with a view to the public interests. Another and graver evil is that the precise statutes and arrangements decreed by the founder are assumed to be of perpetual obligation, and that no provision is ever made for revising them from time to time, and abrogating those which are virtually obsolete. But for the operation of these two causes, endowed foundations might preserve the same vitality as other English institutions, and there would be little or no need for periodical Royal Commissions to report on gross abuses and to recommend revolutionary measures. It is interesting to inquire what provisions are contained in Sir J. Mason's deed of foundation in regard to each of these particulars.

" The total number in the future governing body is to be eleven, of whom the founder nominates six during his lifetime, and the Town Council of Birmingham is to elect five after his death. As vacancies occur in the number of official or representative trustees, they are to be filled up by further election by the Town Council; and when the number of original trustees is reduced to four, their places are to be supplied by coöptation among the whole body, in which it is evident that the representatives of the Council will each time be in the majority. Thus the trust will be invigorated by the constant infusion of new representative elements, and the administration of the funds will always be in the hands of a body directly responsible to the community for whose benefit the institution is designed.

" And with a view to render his regulations and provisions better adapted to the requirements of future times, there occurs in this deed an important and unique stipulation.

" ' Provided always that it shall be lawful for the said Josiah Mason at any time or times during his life, and after his decease for the Trustees *within two years after each successive period of fifteen years, from time to time to alter or vary the trusts and provisions* herein contained, in any or all of the particulars following, that is to say, the number of the trustees, the number and functions of the Council, the age at and the conditions on which regular students shall be admitted, and shall leave the institution, the proportion of income to be applied to scholarships, exhibitions, prizes, premiums, and gratuities, and the preference of regular students born in the boroughs of Birmingham and Kidderminster.' And it further appears that the only parts of his present intentions (other than the general design to promote scientific instruction), which he declares to be fundamental and unalterable, are that the Governors shall be Protestant laymen, that no theological teaching shall be given in the college, and that no religious test shall be applied either to teachers or students."

in regard to the words of our highest teachers. And we of this generation find ourselves set free, alike by the teachings of experience and by the enactments of modern legislation, to ask ourselves, how educational endowments may yet continue to fulfil great public objects without losing any of their distinctive excellences, and may prove a link to unite what is freshest and most vigorous in the future, with what is noblest in the present and in the past.

> " The old order changeth, yielding place to new,
> And God fulfils Himself in many ways,
> Lest one good custom should corrupt the world."

The prominent object in the minds of the founders of endowed schools, was the diffusion of knowledge, and in the case of the charity schools, the special relief and benefit of the poor. These two purposes are perennially wise and beneficent. Yet the mode of accomplishing them must be very different in two ages, of which one, like our own, has a national public provision for elementary instruction, and another possessed no such provision. The hospitium of a monastery ceased to be a valuable institution at the enactment of a Poor Law, and the *raison d'être* of a charity school disappeared no less completely with the Education Act. The State has now accepted the duty of seeing that primary instruction shall be placed within the reach of all the children of the poor ; and has also made legal arrangements which furnish a safer guarantee for the efficiency of such instruction than could possibly be provided by an endowment. It may be reasonably presumed, therefore, that a benevolent testator in these days would not think it expedient to bequeath money for primary education in any form. Seeing, however, that the endowments exist, they must be used. And before determining how they should be used, it may be well to look at some of the evidence which has been collected respecting the existing condition of these foundations, and as to the way in which they now serve either to promote education or to help the poor.

It would seem from this evidence that while most of the Hospital and Charity Schools are relatively of less value now than ever, they have also contrived to develop some positive evils peculiarly their own. The Schools Inquiry Commission report that :—

" There are schools largely endowed which board and lodge as well as clothe the scholars. Such are Colston's Hospital (net income 3400*l.*) ; Queen Elizabeth's Hospital (5000*l.*) at Bristol ; Christ's Hospital, Lincoln (2200*l.*) ; Cheetham's Hospital, Manchester (2600*l.*) ; Henshaw's Blue School at Oldham (2200*l.*) ; Old Swinford Hospital (2000*l.*) ; those in Westminster—viz., Grey Coat Hospital (2000*l.*) ;

Green Coat (700*l.*); Emanuel Hospital (700*l.*); Aske's Hospital, Hoxton (5000*l.*); Bancroft's Hospital, Stepney (2000*l.*); the Great Hospital Schools at Norwich (1700*l.*); and many others of smaller amount. Mr. Fearon visited and inspected six which lay in his district. In some, as in the Emanuel and Grey Coat Hospitals, an English education only is given; in others, as in Bancroft's and Aske's, Latin, Euclid, algebra, and French are added. 'The discipline and order in these schools are almost always excellent, but the boys show much less quickness and intelligence under examination—they are much more apathetic and drowsy than day scholars.' 'There is not,' Mr. Fearon believes, 'in any one of these Hospital Schools' (in his district) 'any admission examination.' The result is, the majority of these boys come in at the age of eight or nine years totally ignorant. 'Their parents,' said one of the masters to Mr. Fearon, 'look forward to getting them before they are ten years old into one of the hospitals, and make no attempt to educate them previously. There is a certain class of persons who can always make pretty sure of getting their children in. Such are messengers in the House of Commons or House of Lords, or persons in the employ of the Governors. Similarly, Mr. Stanton was informed the boys at the two Bristol hospitals are mostly sons of the workmen or servants of the electors.'

"Many of these endowments are, as has been shown, very large. They were given to promote education and to assist in the maintenance and advancement in life of children while and after receiving such education. They now act largely, though indirectly, in discouragement of education, and they are applied very frequently to the relief of classes of persons who could hardly have been regarded by the founders as within the immediate purview of their intentions. Whether it be desirable to spend such large sums in relieving parents, &c., at the pleasure of irresponsible trustees, not of the most destitute class or even of a destitute class at all, of all cost for the boarding and clothing of some of their children, is to say the least a very doubtful question; but this much appears certain—that if the admissions were made a reward of merit and a means of progress to the scholars in primary schools; if the education were put, by the enforcement of good entrance examination, on a level superior to that of a national school; if day scholars were admitted, some on payment and some freely, winning their freedom by competition, the 'Blue Schools' and others of the same class throughout the country would be quite as certainly as now fulfilling every intention of their founders, and would be exercising a far wider and safer beneficence."*

In these guarded sentences the Commissioners have stated the case against the hospital schools with almost needless moderation. They have not pointed out that pieces of patronage so valuable as nominations to these foundations, worth —including clothing, food, and apprenticeship—100*l.* to 150*l.*

---

* Report of Schools Inquiry Commission, vol. i. p. 914.

to the parent of each child, are very highly prized by trustees, and are objects of some importance to many parents, who though not necessarily the poorest or most deserving, have nevertheless access to those gentlemen, and influence enough to urge their claims. Hence it is notorious that in Bristol and other places this local patronage has been used as a reward for political services, and that canvassing and other forms of solicitation have done much to pauperize the artizan and lower middle class, and to diminish their self-respect. Nor does the Report dwell on the fact that though a nomination to a hospital school is very acceptable to a selfish parent, it is no boon, but oftener a source of degradation and trouble to the child. The educational aim in schools of this class is never high. The life lived in them is for the most part joyless and uninteresting. The children are dressed in a hideous costume : they are subject to many restraints of a humiliating kind, which are presumed to be appropriate in a charity school, but which would not be tolerated in a free and open boarding school by parents who paid for their children's maintenance. The fact that all the scholars come from one class, and that a low one, causes the tone of thinking and of social life to become narrow and enervating, and the absence of stimulus, aid, or supervision from without renders the teachers satisfied with educational results of the most meagre kind.*

On this point the testimony of the Master of the Merchant Company in Edinburgh, in regard to the great hospital schools. which have long been conspicuous ornaments of that city, is very striking. By the energy of the Merchant Company these rich foundations, with an annual revenue of nearly 22,000*l.*, have lately been entirely remodelled, the hospital system abandoned, and a completely reorganized system of secondary schools for the whole city established in its stead. But of the state of things which existed before this reform was effected, Mr. Boyd, in a pamphlet whose title is placed at the head of this article, says :—

"For upwards of a quarter of a century there has been a growing feeling in Scotland against what is known as the Hospital System, and happily people generally are now coming to believe in the truth of the saying that children should be brought up in families not in flocks.

* In these respects it must be owned that the most conspicuous hospital school in England, Christ's Hospital, is a remarkable exception to the rule. The dress of a Bluecoat boy is the one charity dress in the whole country which has no dishonouring associations, and of which the wearers are always proud. But this is mainly because Christ's Hospital has long given a liberal education. In this respect it differs from all other foundations of the purely eleemosynary or hospital type in the country.

The education of large numbers of children apart from their parents, relatives, or friends, and without their having almost any intercourse with other persons, except the officials of the hospital establishments, was a system unnatural in itself, and not calculated to make them in after life useful members of society. With whatever zeal those who were so brought up might be trained morally and intellectually, many were found on the completion of their education to be devoid of that general intelligence which is acquired from intercourse with friends in the home circle; and when they left the hospitals to begin the business of life they were as a rule unable to take their places with others whose scholastic training had not been superior, but carried on under happier circumstances. Altogether, it was felt that in the return for the large sum of money expended upon them comparatively small benefits were derived."

Nor are the day schools of the "charity" class which exist for gratuitous education and for clothing only in any more satisfactory a condition than the hospitals. They are more numerous, and they are as a rule far less richly endowed. They are to be found in many parishes existing side by side with national schools, in others with national schools more or less clumsily grafted on them; and in many more, especially in rural districts, they serve as substitutes for such schools. But in almost all cases they seem to be rather hindrances than helps to the education of the district in which they are placed. For if the endowment is employed to relieve the children of fees, it does harm to the parents, and produces, according to the universal testimony of inspectors, irregular attendance and general negligence. If, as often happens, it just suffices to prevent the school from claiming the Government grant, it serves to keep the school out of the reach of the stimulus of inspection; it satisfies itself with an untrained and worthless teacher, whose income is not dependent, like that of an ordinary schoolmaster, on the results he produces, and who has little or no motive for exertion; moreover, in this case the local endowment is in effect given over as a present to that impersonal entity the British Treasury; and is utterly wasted as far as the fulfilment of any local educational purpose is concerned. And to the extent to which the possession of a school endowment diminishes the necessity for a rate or for local subscriptions, it not only serves as a relief to the richer inhabitants, who have no right to be beneficiaries of a charity; but it deprives the school of that watchful local supervision which is always the correlative of local contributions.

Other usages are to be found lingering in charity schools, which have been abandoned in all healthy modern institutions, and which experience has shown to be unfitted for continuance. The system of paying a premium to apprentice a good boy at the end of his school-life was kindly and wisely devised, and has in past years done good service. It was, in fact, the only way in which a poor boy could be introduced into a reputable trade. But the conditions of industrial life have greatly altered. Juvenile labour has since risen in price; and masters in all except the highest trades are glad to receive respectable boys and to teach them their art and mystery in return for such services as they can render, without demanding any payment whatever. In fact, under our present industrial conditions masters are more at a premium than apprentices. Yet in many places the system of paying premiums is kept up, merely because there are endowments to support it. In these cases the apprenticing is a colorable transaction altogether ; the money is granted and the indenture made out to some tradesman specially favoured by the trustees, and not unfrequently to one of themselves. In other cases it is nominally received by the tradesman, but returned, according to a private understanding, into the hands of the parents. Sometimes the sum paid as premium is given back in the form of wages. In Wakefield the Commissioners reported that a handsome sum was given out, of a charity to each governor's apprentice, on the completion of his term ; that it was usually spent in a great feast at a public-house, and that this practice had become a source of vice and a public scandal. But in scarcely any case is it shown that the practice of granting premiums to schoolboys at fourteen is really helpful to them in obtaining introduction to a higher trade than they would otherwise be likely to enter.

It is the universal testimony of official inspectors that the endowed elementary schools are many degrees worse than others, and that in the presence of a national provision for primary education they have become superfluous if not mischievous. It is highly inexpedient to withdraw children who need elementary instruction only from the national and other schools in which that instruction is given under public supervision, and on conditions which guarantee its excellence. It is clearly wasteful to keep up small establishments which give a less efficient education at a much greater cost per head merely because the endowment, dating from a time when there were no State-aided schools, was originally and very properly designed for that purpose. And while the Conscience Clause, the right to be relieved from dogmatic religious instruction, or from enforced Church attendance, has been publicly recognised as the legitimate privilege of the poor man, it is very undesirable that a class of elementary schools should continue to exist in which this right is systematically refused. For it need hardly be said that in the charity schools as a rule there is no Conscience Clause. To accept the clothing, and to be relieved of the school fee, is to forfeit all claim for consideration; and it often happens that in a school where a few paying scholars are admitted as well as the "blue boys" on the foundation, the former enjoy the freedom, while it is denied to the latter. Thus the payment of a fee purchases the privilege of exemption from religious teaching, and the poorer boys come to regard the enforcement of such teaching as one of the incidents of their poverty, or as a part of the price they pay as the recipients of charity—an arrangement as dishonouring to religion itself as it is unjust and harsh to conscientious parents. In fact, it is becoming daily more evident that the strenuous efforts made by the clergy to use the schools as instruments for attracting children to the Church, and retaining them in it, have conspicuously failed in their object. More than three-fourths of the children in the elementary schools of England have been under the direct control of the clergy, and have been more or less subjected to that "distinctive Church teaching" to which on platforms in Episcopal charges and in religious periodicals so much importance is attached. Yet the class to which these children belong is more completely alienated than any other in the community from the English Church. The scholars whose attendance at church has been enforced as part of the school discipline, almost invariably quit the Church for ever when they leave school. And no student of human nature can wonder at this. The hard aggressive teaching of Church dogma by creeds and formularies, and by compulsory church attendance, defeats its own purpose. No children are attracted, or are ever likely to be attracted to a religious body by such means. They may come in time to like and to study the creeds of a Church, because they have in childhood learned to love it as an institution, and because they have owed to its services some enjoyment or spiritual awakening. But nobody ever comes in later life to love the Church as an institution because he has first been taught her doctrines and formularies as school lessons.

On the whole, it may be safely said that the charity school of the eighteenth century type is, relatively to the requirements of our day, a superfluous and costly anachronism. In so far as it gives clothing and maintenance, it gives them on a wrong principle and on humiliating conditions; it encourages jobbing and mean patronage on the side of the trustee, and subserviency, falsehood, and loss of personal independence on the part of the parent. And in so far as it is a place of education, it is nearly always vulgar and illiberal, carefully withholding from the scholar, on some sectarian or social grounds, intellectual advantages to which by modern legislation he has become entitled as one of a nation of free men.

In the light of these facts it is not difficult to see what are the wisest and fittest purposes to which these endowments may be applied. We have learned by this time that while education is a good thing, almsgiving, however disguised, is an almost unmingled evil. It is the first duty of the Legislature, therefore, to reduce to a minimum the eleemosynary and so-called "charitable" elements in these foundations, and to develop to the utmost their educational character. And in doing this it is plain that the endowments, whether originally designed for primary or for advanced instruction, should be made to serve some purpose which the ordinary system of public elementary schools cannot fulfil. They should either be converted into secondary schools, or, if the endowment be too small, should be used as a special fund for the encouragement in the ordinary national school of higher instruction than such a school generally contemplates.

Our national provision for the elementary instruction of the children of the poor is now nearly complete, so far as the supply of schoolrooms and teachers can make it so. It only requires development, increased watchfulness on the part of the School Boards, and the constant maintenance of a high and improving ideal of education on the part of the central and examining body at the Privy Council office, to render it one of the most efficient in Europe. Our highest or University education is also daily improving, and exercising a greater and more widely spread influence over the intellectual life of the country. Neither has become what it is, or would ever have become so, by the voluntary system—by depending on the operation of the great law of supply and demand. The student at the University is helped and encouraged by large and magnificent endowments, the poor man's child is aided by local rates and a Government grant, which for his own purpose are far better than an endowment; but our secondary or intermediate education is scandalously inefficient. It is aided by no public subsidies, it is subject to no public supervision. It is carried on without system or authority; often by pretentious and utterly unqualified persons, who take up the business of teaching as a trade, who seek only to flatter the vanity of ignorant parents, and who have an utterly false and ignoble conception of what good education means.

The establishment of an organized system of public secondary schools both for boys and girls, by which we may bridge over the gulf which now separates the primary school from the University has been elaborately recommended and enforced by the Schools Inquiry Commission, with a view to meet this grave defect. That report pointed out that schools of the several grades, if once provided by endowment or otherwise with appropriate buildings and teaching apparatus, and subjected to the superintendence of a responsible local body, would be self-supporting, at lower fees than are now paid in the unsatisfactory private schools. And if the endowment is large enough to provide more than the building, it cannot (in the opinion of the Commissioners) be better spent than in scholarships or exhibitions, designed partly to attract into the schools as free scholars children of promise from humbler places of instruction; and partly to encourage the further advancement of the scholars, by helping them to higher schools or to the Universities, and paying their fees. In the published schemes of the Commissioners we observe the constant provision that a certain proportion, varying from 10 to 20 per cent. of the whole number of scholars, shall be free ; and that of places on the foundation, a goodly number shall always be reserved for "children of the public elementary schools" of the district.

Such a use of the endowments is calculated not only to supply a great national want, but it is especially called for in the interests of the poor. The present system, it is true, gives to a small number of the more importunate of the poor free instruction and occasional maintenance. But it wholly fails to give to the poor that which as a class they most need—access on equal and honourable terms to the same educational advantages which others, in a higher class, are receiving and paying for at good schools. The poor man who has five children, of whom one evinces exceptional ability and fondness for reading, has no need of a charity school for any one of them. For four he may receive, on payment of two or three pence a week, a useful and appropriate education in a public elementary school ; and for the fifth, he wants—not a hospital or a special institution for poor boys—but admission into a good school, such as is largely frequented by those who are likely to choose intellectual pursuits, and is adapted to their requirements. Into such a school, if he comes as a foundationer chosen by merit, he enters with honour, since his success in the examination outweighs any social disadvantage he would otherwise have experienced. The presence of others who do not originally belong to his own class is a necessary condition of his own advancement. He at least has no reason to feel jealous of the extension to others of some of the advantages of the endowment : for he has as much to gain from free

association in study with those who have had greater home
advantages, as they can possibly gain in intellectual stimulus
from him.

It is to the work of reorganizing the endowed foundations of
England on this basis that the Commission now engaged in
administering the Endowed Schools Act have set their hands.
If we may judge from the report which they presented to
Parliament last year, they have sought to accomplish four or
five distinct objects. (1) The grading of schools, with a view to
economy of means and teaching power; (2) the abolition of the
system of nomination or patronage, and the substitution for it
of a system of free places attainable by merit; (3) the extension
of the benefits of endowed schools to girls; (4) the quickening
and invigorating of the life of the schools by annual examination and report; and (5) the introduction of new and popular
elements into the governing bodies. But the same report is also
a disheartening confession of failure, a record of difficulty, of
opposition, and of controversy.

The Commissioners pathetically say, "Our experience in attempting to work the Act has shown that the country was hardly
prepared for its reception;" and they proceed to recount the
hindrances which they have met in their work, notably from the
Corporation of the City of London, always more distinguished
for an acute sensibility to its own dignity and privileges than
for any perception of national or intellectual interests. From
this body, and from the trustees of various rich foundations in
Bristol and elsewhere, it would seem that the Commissioners
have received determined opposition in the attempt to change
and modernize the constitution of certain hospital schools.
That opposition is not always candid; for the true *grievamen* of
the Corporation in the case of Emanuel Hospital and of other
trustees against the Commission is, that their own patronage
and exclusive right to the management are likely to be interfered with by the schemes. It is not, however, considered politic
to give prominence to this objection. So it is found more convenient to put forth an impassioned plea against the "robbery
of the poor," the "violation of the sacred wishes of the dead,"
and other wrongs which are more likely to be present to the
imagination than to the reason of the British public. And in
the absence of further investigation and more generally diffused
knowledge of the subject, declamation of this kind, when urged
by powerful bodies, naturally falls on many sympathetic ears.
That some of the objects contemplated by the "pious founder"
could not possibly be now fulfilled, even if we desired it; that
others, if fulfilled, would in our day be productive of nothing
but mischief; that if he was as wise and benevolent as he is

expected to have been, and could be consulted now, he would probably wish to adapt his gifts as carefully to the experience and wants of this age, as he did to the experience and wants of his own : but that in his unavoidable absence, it is the duty of the State as supreme trustee to undertake this duty for him, and to do it boldly and effectively, are truths which at present are very imperfectly recognised, because they conflict with the vague sentiment of reverence for the dead which naturally colours the notions of all of us, and which so easily passes for a respectable principle of action until it is examined. But they will become more and more clearly recognised as the study of the subject extends ; and they are not disputed by any one who has taken the trouble to read the abundant evidence so laboriously collected by the Schools Inquiry Commission. " I remember," says Bishop Temple, in a remarkable letter which he has lately addressed to the citizens of Exeter on the subject, " the extreme divergence of views in the Schools Inquiry Commission when it first met. And yet in the end we never had one difference of opinion on what we should recommend."

It is perhaps inevitable that in vindicating their policy the Endowed Schools Commissioners and their friends have given excessive prominence to those provisions of their schemes which are designed for the special benefit of the clever and aspiring scholars, especially from the poorer ranks. They have been earnestly denounced for taking away the heritage of the poor, and they have naturally felt challenged to show that the poor, defined for practical purposes " as scholars in public elementary schools," would derive special benefits from the intended changes. But the true vindication of a great and systematic reform in charitable foundations rests on far deeper grounds. It is a poor conception of the worth of knowledge to a State, which regards it chiefly as a means whereby men may be lifted out of one social rank into another. The highest aim of the philosopher and teacher, is so to diffuse learning and culture in the State that it shall become the heritage of each man, that it shall be felt as appropriate for the lower as for the higher employments of life ; that it shall seek, not to tempt men out of the position which they happen to fill, but to make them happy and useful in it. That was an ignoble and degrading theory of charity which, in the last century, set up schools in order that the poor might be kept in their places, made conscious of their dependence, and sternly forbidden to aspire higher. But it would hardly be less ignoble, if we were now to fabricate a system whose chief aim was to foster the vulgar instinct for social superiority, and so to aggravate the restlessness of an unquiet and struggling age. Incidentally every good and well devised system of public in-

struction should provide facilities for the advancement of all
who possess special gifts, and leisure, and inclination to turn
them to account. But the highest purpose of such a system
should ever be to provide appropriate discipline and wise teaching for all classes, mainly for those who wish rather to adorn
their own rank than to make their acquirements a means of
rising to a higher. Mr. Forster and Professor Huxley have said
enough about the ladder from the gutter to the University.
Such a ladder may fitly form a part, though only a small part
of the machinery of national education. But as one looks wist-
fully forward to the end of all the present experiments and controversies, it is difficult to repress the hope that some yet wider
and higher view of our national responsibilities may ultimately
prevail; and that we may come to regard our whole machinery
for the instruction of the people in the light in which Bacon
desired to view it :—" Not as a couch whereon to rest a searching
and restless spirit, nor as a terrace for a wandering and variable
mind to walk up and down with a fair prospect, nor as a tower of
State for a proud mind to rest itself upon, nor a fort or commanding ground for strife and contention, nor a shop for profit or sale ;
but rather as a rich storehouse for the glory of the Creator of
all things, and for the relief of man's estate."

ART. VI.—IRRESPONSIBLE MINISTERS—BARON
STOCKMAR.

Memoirs of Baron Stockmar. By his Son, Baron E. VON
STOCKMAR. Translated from the German by G. A. M.
Edited by F. MAX MÜLLER. Two vols. London : Long-
mans, Green, and Co. 1872.

WE may say of this book, as Dr. Newman said of "Ecce
Homo," that it is remarkable because it has excited remark.
That indeed it was certain to do. The memoirs of inmates of
palaces are always sure to find readers ; and as this memoir is of
one who lived amongst ourselves and is still recollected, and
the Royal Household of which he was a member is that of our
own reigning Sovereign, the announcement of its intended publication bespoke for it a wide circle of readers. The book,
therefore, was eagerly expected, and the disappointment felt on
its perusal was proportionately great. It contains little of those
matters which generally form the interest of books of this class.
There are no *chroniques scandaleuses*—no Court gossip—not

many or important details of the lives, opinions, habits, or feelings of the illustrious family in which Stockmar lived. "My father," says Baron E. von Stockmar, in his sketch of the elder Stockmar's life, "was content always to remain half-hidden before the eyes of posterity. Faithful to his spirit, this book also lifts the veil but a little." Professor Müller in his preface confesses that he experienced "a certain disappointment at not finding more of the inner life of the man, who but rarely lets us see all that he thought and felt." "It is clear also," he continues, "that his son has not published all that he might have published." It is equally true, as we shall presently show, that Baron E. von Stockmar has published much which he ought not to have published. The book on its first appearance in Germany formed the subject of a paper both in the *Edinburgh* and in the *Quarterly Review*. That in the *Edinburgh Review** is evidently written by one as intimately acquainted with the private life of the Palace as was Stockmar himself. Both this paper and that in the *Quarterly Review†* are distinguished by a tone of official reticence and cautious reserve, as if their writers were aware of the presence in the book of matters to which public attention had best not be directed, and which, if dealt with at all, must only be alluded to with the utmost delicacy and caution. In truth the value of the book lies in this, that it contains some noteworthy revelations as to the practical working of the monarchical element in our constitution, during the present reign, and more especially in the lifetime of the Prince Consort. It is to these parts of the book, and to Stockmar's opinions on English politics and statesmen, and not those portions to which other reviews of it have been mainly confined, that we propose to call our readers' attention.

Stockmar's position in England was this—the secret and irresponsible minister of a constitutional sovereign. Such a position is utterly inconsistent with the theory of our constitution, and with parliamentary government. It is to be hoped that, now the existence of such an anomalous evil in our own time is revealed by publication of this book, Parliamentary and public opinion will prevent the existence of any such person in the future. Professor Müller in his preface admits that "Statesmen were fully justified in regarding Stockmar's situation with suspicion,"‡ but he says that Stockmar's "exceptional character" enabled him to fill his "exceptional position" without the mischievous results which would surely have followed had that position been filled by an ordinary man. It is due to Stockmar's memory to

---

* *Edinburgh Review*, No. 272, 1872.
† *Quarterly Review*, No. 266, 1872.   ‡ "Editor's Preface," p. xii.

acknowledge that his illustrious Mistress has recorded her conviction, that " Rarely has it fallen to the lot of queen or prince to be blest with so real a friend, in the best sense of that word, with so wise, so judicious, so honest a counsellor."[*]

King Leopold also, the sovereign to whom Stockmar first stood in this peculiar relation, wrote of him, " *Il a été mon fidèle soutien et ami.*"[†]   Again, three of our Premiers with whom Stockmar was intimately associated during his connexion with England, and to whom it is plain he was often playing the part of a secret and irresponsible leader of opposition, have left a similar testimony as to him.   Lord Melbourne told the Queen, "Stockmar is not only an excellent man, but also one of the most sensible men I have ever met with."[‡]

Lord Palmerston, it is said, disliked Stockmar.   He certainly, as we shall see further on, had very good reason for so doing; but, as Mr. Cobden in his dying moments said, " Palmerston was always a very generous enemy;" and Baron Bunsen relates that "the remark had been made how seldom it was that a wholly disinterested action was met with in political men, to which Palmerston observed, 'I have never but once met a perfectly disinterested man of this kind, and that is Stockmar.' "[§]

Lord Aberdeen also said of Stockmar, "I have known men as clever, as discreet, as good, and with as much judgment, but I never knew any one who united all these qualities as he did."[||]

We have, in justice to Stockmar's memory, given him the benefit of these testimonies.   In justice to ourselves, we must remark that similar testimony from the three other Premiers of his time is conspicuous by its absence.   These three men, each intellectually superior to the three we have quoted, and each distinguished by his knowledge of the English Constitution and of historic precedent, and as practical statesmen by their adherence to the guidance of these lights, were—the late Earl of Derby, Earl Russell, and the late Sir Robert Peel.   No doubt these statesmen justly disliked the position held by Stockmar, and probably they did not conceal the fact.   Lord Derby Stockmar condemns "as a frivolous aristocrat."[¶]   An aristocrat Lord Derby was; the arrogance which lay deep in his character—"he could not, it was said, deal with common men as his equals"—no doubt displayed itself unmistakably towards one whom he considered—and from his point of view rightly—as a low-born adventurer holding an unconstitutional position.   Frivolity, however, can never be imputed to Lord Derby by any

* " Editor's Preface," p. lv.   † Ibid. p. xiii.   ‡ Ibid. p. xlv.
§ " Memoirs of Baron Bunsen." vol. ii. p. 189.
|| "Preface," p. xv.   ¶ " Memoirs," vol. ii. p. 446.

Englishman of whatever party, or by any foreigner who really understands the position which for more than thirty years Lord Derby filled. Stockmar's accusation reminds us of Sir R. Peel's sarcastic remark in reference to a similar complaint made by certain Radical members—"Often have I heard the noble lord taunted with his aristocratic demeanour. I rather think I should hear fewer complaints on that score if he were a less powerful opponent." Lord Russell is referred to by Stockmar in depreciatory terms.* For Peel alone, of all English statesmen, Stockmar felt respect and even admiration ; but even Peel he called "sharp but short-sighted—a Myops."† Peel, whom the biographer describes as "formal, suspicious, and reserved," on his part thought Stockmar's manner "too free," and the following story certainly proves he was right :—

"One day," relates Stockmar, "I had brought Peel to talk of an important political event, in which he himself had been concerned. He was just about to make some interesting disclosures, only the last word of the secret was wanting when he paused. To help him, I exclaimed, 'Well, don't gulp it down.' This disconcerted him ; he made an odd face, and broke off."‡

Premising that Stockmar's objects were the Crown, not the country—Belgium and Germany, not England—we are willing to admit that he acted wisely and conscientiously in the anomalous character he filled. Our objection is to the position, not to the man. It would have been bad enough if such a situation had been filled by an Englishman. That Stockmar was by birth, and in aims and spirit continued to be, a foreigner, aggravated tenfold the mischiefs of his anomalous and unconstitutional position. It was said by Lord Russell, when Premier, of Lord Palmerston as Foreign Secretary, "My noble friend will not be the minister of Austria—he will not be the minister of Russia—and he will not be the minister of France—but he will be the minister of England."§ Whatever we may think of Lord Palmerston's foreign policy, or of his occasional errors, his colleague no doubt accurately described it ; but while this was the aim and spirit of England's Minister for foreign affairs, the private cabinet of the Queen contained a minister the purpose of whose life was to be the minister of Belgium—the minister of Germany.

"Stockmar," says Professor Müller, "had two political ideals—first, to see Germany united under Prussia ; secondly, to help to establish a unity of purpose between Germany and England."|| This was not the policy of any English cabinet or minister ; but

---

* "Memoirs," pp. 446, 448, 547.   † Ibid. pp. 428, 429.   ‡ Ibid. p. 419.
§ "House of Commons Debates on Foreign Policy, 1850."
|| "Translator's Preface," p. xv.

Stockmar had not only a foreign policy of his own for England, which he might have promoted concurrently with that of the English cabinet—he was directly opposed to the policy of the known and responsible Foreign Minister of England.

"The one-sided alliance," continues Professor Müller, "of England with France, as conceived by Lord Palmerston, was in Stockmar's eyes the beginning of endless complications. It would have broken his heart had he lived to see all its consequences."[*]

Joined to this opposition to Lord Palmerston's policy was a personal dislike to that essentially English statesman, which attained such a pitch as to cause Stockmar to impute insanity to our Foreign Secretary.[†] Although these memoirs profess "to lift the veil but a little," they reveal enough to show that these feelings were shared in and acted on by Prince Albert.[‡] In addition to his separate foreign policy, German and not English in its aim and object, Stockmar had this other great disqualification for an adviser of any constitutional sovereign—especially of an English sovereign, and pre-eminently for one reigning under the Constitution as modified since 1832—viz, a profound dislike, arising in great part from a foreigner's ignorance of Parliamentary Government and the free life and debate of English party politics.[§] He desired that the Sovereign should possess a large share of personal power in the government—certainly at least to the same extent as before 1832. To the fact that Stockmar held these views, natural to a German brought up in a petty despotic state and attached to its court, and to his influence over the Prince Consort, is no doubt to be attributed the anti-popular tone which was scarcely concealed in some of the Prince's speeches, especially the notorious one made at the Trinity House, 9th June, 1855, comparing constitutional with despotic governments, and composed on Single Speech Hamilton's recommendation—"When you produce an instance to illustrate, let the instance be in itself invidious as well as illustratory." These views, joined to a scarcely concealed contempt for the English people, their character and institutions, in a great degree deprive of value Stockmar's opinions on English statesmen and politics. We may remark in passing that they are equally held by his son and biographer.||

Having stated Stockmar's position in England and our objections to it, we proceed to make good our assertions by examining, so far as they relate to England and Englishmen, these singularly confused and ill-arranged Memoirs.

---

* "Translator's Preface," p. xvii.   † "Memoir," vol. ii. p. 438.
‡ Ibid. pp. 458, 476.   § Ibid. vol. ii. ch. 25, 26, 27; especially p. 645 et seq.
|| Vide the "Memoir," *passim,* and especially vol. ii. p. 450 et seq.

Stockmar, to his credit be it remembered, was a self-made man. His father appears to have held some minor judicial office in the Duchy of Saxe-Coburg-Gotha. Christian Frederick, the subject of these Memoirs, was born at Coburg, 22nd August, 1787. He commenced a university career in 1805, and studied medicine until 1810. To this study Stockmar and his friends seem to have attributed much of his after-success. "It was a clever stroke," he writes in 1853, "to have originally studied medicine. Without the knowledge thus acquired, without the psychological· and physiological experiences which I thus obtained, my *savoir faire* would often have gone begging."[*]

For a few years he practised as a physician and acted as director of a military hospital. While thus engaged he formed an acquaintance with Prince Leopold of Saxe-Coburg—afterwards King of the Belgians—and when the marriage of the Prince with the Princess Charlotte of England was settled, Stockmar received the appointment of his physician in ordinary. The Prince and his physician arrived in England in 1816, and shortly afterwards Stockmar thus describes his position to one of his sisters :—"I seem to be here to care for others more than myself, and am well content with this destiny." Our antipathy to Stockmar's position and opinions does not prevent our frankly admitting that throughout a long life this continued to be his destiny, and that he was always well content with it.

From physician Stockmar became the secretary of Prince Leopold, and continued in his service until he passed into that of our present Sovereign. After Leopold became king, Stockmar held in Belgium a similar objectionable and anomalous position to that he afterwards held in England. Much of his time was spent in this country, and at our Court he seems to have been a real, though unacknowledged minister for the promotion of Belgian and German interests; and there are, as we shall see, traces of his having been mixed up with the political intrigues of the Court of William IV. and Adelaide. While holding this position, Stockmar became acquainted with the Duke of Wellington, and amongst his papers was found the following estimate of the Duke as a minister, to the general truth of which we assent :—

"Blinded by the language of his admirers, and too much elated to estimate correctly his own powers, he impatiently, and of his own accord, abandoned the proud position of victorious general to exchange it for the most painful position which a human being can occupy—viz. the management of the affairs of a great nation, with insufficient mental gifts and inadequate knowledge. He had hardly forced him-

* "Biographical Sketch," p xli.

self upon the nation as Prime Minister, intending to add the glory of a statesman to that of a warrior, when he succeeded by his manner of conducting business in shaking the confidence of the people. With laughable infatuation he sedulously improved every opportunity of proving to the world the hopeless incapacity which made it impossible for him to seize the natural connexion between cause and effect. With a rare *naïveté*, he confessed publicly and without hesitation the mistaken conclusions he had come to in the weightiest affairs of State; mistakes which the commonest understanding could have discovered, which filled the impartial with pitying astonishment, and caused terror and consternation even amongst the host of his flatterers and partizans. Yet so strong and so great was the preconceived opinion of the people in his favour, that only the irresistible proofs furnished by the man's own actions could gradually shake this opinion. It required the full force and obstinacy of this strange self-deception in Wellington, it required the full measure of his activity and iron persistency, in order at last by a perpetual reiteration of errors and mistakes, to create in the people the firm conviction that the Duke of Wellington was one of the least adroit and most mischievous ministers that England ever had."*

We must dissent from the statement that the duke forced himself upon the country as Prime Minister. On the breakdown of Lord Goderich, it was Lord Lyndhurst who suggested to George IV. that he should send for the Duke,† who, after his refusal to serve under Canning, does not appear to have been in communication with the King. The country, still dazzled by the glare of the Duke's victories, was—as Stockmar himself admits—only too glad to welcome him as minister. Stockmar accurately describes the mixture of incapacity and naïveté in the duke's manner of conducting business. It was especially evident when acting as leader of the House of Lords. For an illustration of this we are indebted to "The Handbook of Parliamentary Anecdote," a work we have before had occasion to notice. On the memorable evening in November, 1830, when the Duke pronounced his extravagant eulogy on the unreformed parliament, even the usually unruffled quiet of the House of Lords was disturbed. The fact forced itself on the Duke's notice, and he inquired of the colleague next to him—"Have I said anything I ought not to have said?" "You have simply announced the downfall of your ministry," was the reply. A characteristic trait of the Duke's want of foresight and of his blunt naïveté is given in a letter from the Princess Lieven to, apparently, King Leopold. She is describing a dinner-party at the Pavilion,

---

* "Memoirs," vol. i. pp. 129, 130.
† Vide "Memoir of Lord Lyndhurst," *The Times*, Oct. 13, 1863, reprinted in the "Mornings of the Recess," vol. ii. p. 1; see also Lord Campbell's "Life of Lord Lyndhurst," and the review of it in *The Times*.

Brighton, during which the news came of the success of the Belgian Revolution :—"The Duke of Wellington came, very calm, very certain that Belgian affairs would be settled, and that Brussels would surrender. After dinner a messenger arrived from London with the news that the king's army had retired. He was overcome—prostrate. '*Devilish bad job,*' said he."*

Some revelations are made by Stockmar as to Wellington's interference with the home affairs of France, in a short paper on "Wellington and Polignac." This paper strengthens Lord Palmerston's statement, published in his Life by Lord Dalling,† that Wellington wrote urgently to Charles X. to allow Polignac to lay before him a report on the dangers of his, the king's, position—in other words, had recommended Polignac as Minister. Stockmar relates that in July, 1829, an old lady of the Ultra-Royalist party, and a friend of George IV., came to London and saw the King. Immediately afterwards a rumour spread that a change of Ministry in France was intended, and Polignac was named as head of the new Cabinet. This rumour was disbelieved by competent judges, but certain it is that on 8th August following the too celebrated Polignac Cabinet was formed. Stockmar acquits Wellington of having formally given advice to the French Ministry recommending the Ordinances of July, which led to the fall of the restored monarchy. He expresses, however, his firm conviction that both George IV. and Wellington foresaw those measures and approved of them, and that Charles X. and his ministers were thereby confirmed and encouraged in their intentions. In proof of this he quotes a statement made at the end of March, 1830, by George IV., "with tears in his eyes," to "a distinguished person"—probably Prince Leopold :—"If," said the King, "Charles X. does not adhere to the path upon which he has entered he is lost and I fear he will be, because there are signs that many of his own courtiers are already advising him to abandon that path."‡

Stockmar further states, as a fact apparently within his own knowledge, that Charles X. feared nothing so much as the overthrow of the Wellington Cabinet and the loss of the moral support in the carrying out of his views which he would thereby sustain. Wellington by the aid he gave to the creation of the Polignac Ministry, whose reactionary policy caused the Revolution of July and so changed the whole position of European politics, brought about "the exact reverse of what he intended." This proved him, in Stockmar's opinion, to be "the most shortsighted

* "Memoirs," vol. i. p. 145.   † "Life," vol. i. p. 330.
‡ "Memoirs," vol. i. p. 133.

statesman that has existed for a long time." In the latter years of Wellington's life Stockmar modified this unfavourable opinion.

"When Wellington died, Stockmar," says his biographer, "lamented the loss of an universally recognised authority, which had latterly proved itself a firm support of the monarchy."*

In connexion with Stockmar's estimate of Wellington it will be convenient to refer to his estimate of Sir Robert Peel. It was published at the time of Peel's death in the *Deutsche Zeitung*, with Stockmar's name subscribed, "a thing most unusual for him." We regret that we can give only a short extract.

"Peel's mind and character rested on moral foundations, which I have not seen once shaken, either in his public or private life. From these foundations rose that never-failing spring of fairness, honesty, kindness, moderation and regard for others which Peel showed to all men and under all circumstances. On these foundations grew that love of country which pervaded his whole being. . . . . I have been told, or I have read it somewhere, that Peel was the most successful type of political mediocrity. In accepting this estimate of my departed friend as perfectly true, I ask Heaven to relieve all ministers within and without Europe of their superiority, and to endow them with Peel's mediocrity; and I ask this for the welfare of all nations, and in the firm conviction that ninety-nine hundredths of the higher political affairs can be properly and successfully conducted by such ministers only as possess Peel's mediocrity."†

This sketch is followed by an extract from a letter of Peel's to Stockmar—written in 1848—in reference to the socialist movements on the continent. The following extract is not without interest and application at the present time.

"Anti-social dreams have never lasted long; in our time they must become still shorter, for, numerically, too many have a binding interest to uphold principles which alone render human society possible. A victory of communistic theories over the institutions of property I consider as altogether impossible: if, however, against my expectations, it should appear that one or the other nation wishes to be governed according to communistic principles, the only thing we can do is not to envy it."‡

We cannot resist the temptation of making the following extract from a letter of Lord Palmerston's. It is eminently characteristic of the man, and of the thorough contempt which he, an aristocrat and Tory "dyed in the wool," felt for the Radical supporters of the Whig Government of which he was a member. Notice of a motion relating to the pension paid by

---

* "Memoirs," vol. i, p. 135.   † Ibid. vol. ii. p. 418 et seq.
‡ Ibid. p. 427, 428.

this country to the King of the Belgians had been given by one whose name these memoirs may preserve from " that deep gloom into which everything useless passes," Sir Samuel Whalley, a retired mad-doctor, who in one Parliament sat for Marylebone. Lord Palmerston, writing of this motion to Stockmar, says :—

" I must and shall assert that the House of Commons has no more right to inquire into the details of the debts and engagements which the King of the Belgians considers himself bound to satisfy, than they have to ask Sir Samuel Whalley how he disposed of the fees which his mad patients used to pay him before he began to practice upon the foolish constituents who have sent him to Parliament."*

In Lord Palmerston's later days a coincidence in names may have suggested to him that the constituency of a cathedral city may be even more foolish than that of a metropolitan borough, in that they have sent, not once, but many times, to represent them in the House of Commons, not a mad doctor, but one who ought to be his patient.

From May, 1834, to the same month in 1837, Stockmar was absent from England, but there are indications of his having been mixed up during this absence with the intrigues of the Court to get rid of the Whig Ministry. That Stockmar was at least well aware of this design of the Court is proved by one of his letters written, apparently to King Leopold, immediately after the events of 1832.

" John Bull has once more put Grey into the saddle. How long he will remain there is another question. The circumstances under which Grey's resignation took place must have contributed not a little to make the King exceedingly unpopular. After the exertions which the King made personally in favour of Wellington, it is impossible that he can longer have any real inclination for Grey ; the present ministry, therefore, must be regarded by him as one forced upon him by public opinion, and he will seek the first opportunity to get rid of it. To this must be added, that the Queen, the Fitzclarences, the ladies-in-waiting, Salisbury and Howe—all of them keep up the connexion with Wellington. The latter will not find it difficult, as soon as the Reform Bill has been settled, to beat the ministers on some other question in the House of Lords, and thereupon make a second attempt to upset Grey."†

The opportunity of getting rid of the hated Whigs did not arrive until November, 1834, when the death of Earl Spencer, and the consequent removal of Lord Althorp to the House of Lords, afforded the King a pretext for dismissing them. Stockmar was, as we have said, then absent from England, but

---

* " Memoirs," vol. i. p. 305.   † Ibid. pp. 272, 273.

amongst his papers were found two papers relating to this event,
which the author of these Memoirs has thought it right to publish—viz, a memorandum by the King, and another by Lord
Palmerston. The possession of these papers by Stockmar, a
foreigner, indicates that after his usual mole-like fashion he was
secretly engaged in promoting or advising the dismissal of the
Ministry. Probably his then master, the King of the Belgians,
with the mistaken view of promoting the interests of his niece,
the heiress presumptive, would have preferred seeing England
made once more to bow her neck under the yoke of Wellington
and the Tories, who were more likely than the Whigs to strive
to preserve and uphold the prerogatives of the Crown, and to
keep down the growing power of the Reformed House of
Commons. To do this was Stockmar's ideal in English politics,
and probably, therefore, that also of Leopold. Lord Palmerston's
memorandum is dated "Foreign Office, Nov. 15th, 1834," and
seems to be a circular to the diplomatic agents of England
abroad. Stockmar seems sometimes to have irregularly acted in
this capacity, and his possession of this memorandum alone
would not prove his complicity in these unworthy intrigues.
Far different is the case with regard to the King's memorandum.
The author of these Memoirs says of it :—

"In January, 1835, King William felt himself moved to hand over
to his minister, Sir R. Peel, a complete statement in writing, not only
of his proceedings in the last crisis [the dismissal of the Whigs] but
of his whole home and foreign policy since his accession ! (of his
'general proceedings,' as he comprehensively termed it). This document Sir R. Peel showed at the time, as it seems, only to the Duke of
Wellington; it is hardly known in England, and has never been published."*

Now, how and why did Stockmar become possessed of this
paper? Sir R. Peel, with his usual caution, showed it at the
time only to the Duke of Wellington. He did not think proper to publish or refer to it in that portion of his autobiographical
papers which relates to the affairs of 1834-5. Since his death
his literary executors have continued to observe the same reserve.
There appears to be no reason why the King should have given a
copy of this highly confidential paper to Stockmar merely as
a former secretary of Leopold, and then one of his unrecognised
advisers. Moreover, unless the author of these Memoirs wishes
to intimate that this was one of those things which Stockmar
"sometimes succeeded in accomplishing," but which he himself
says, he had " to conceal as if they had been crimes," why are these

<hr/>

* "Memoirs," vol. i. p. 313.

papers published in these volumes, which profess to be memoirs
of Stockmar, and not a political history of his times? We
shall therefore freely quote from, and comment on them. If
in so doing we seem to depart from the design of this paper,
we must lay the blame on the author who has introduced into
his work a digression so interesting, but to the memoirs of Stockmar so irrelevant, except on our theory of his being concerned
in the matter. We will deal first with Lord Palmerston's
memorandum, as being the earlier in date. He says :—

"The Government have not resigned but are dismissed, not in consequence of having proposed any measure of which the King disapproved, and which they nevertheless would not give up—but because
it is thought they are not strong enough in the Commons to carry on
the business of the country, and their places are to be filled by men
who are notoriously weak and unpopular in the Lower House, however
strong they may be in the Upper one.

"It is impossible not to conclude that this is a preconcerted measure, and therefore it may be taken for granted that the Duke of
Wellington is prepared at once to undertake the task of forming a
Government. Peel is abroad, but it is not likely that he should
have gone without a previous understanding, one way or the other, with
the Duke as to what he would do if such a crisis were to arise."[*]

Lord Brougham, in his celebrated speech on this change of
Ministry, more than intimates that the dismissal of the Whigs
and the restoration of Wellington had long been a common
topic of conversation in the Royal circle, and Lord Palmerston is
no doubt right in saying that this change of Ministry was a preconcerted measure ; but all the evidence shows that he is unjust
to Peel in accusing him of complicity in the plot.

We make another extract from Lord Palmerston's paper for
the sake of the illustration it gives of his deep-rooted and
genuine hatred of really Liberal men and measures :—

"I lament this event, because I can see nothing but mischief arising
out of it, and all merely to gratify the ambition of the Duke of
Wellington and the prejudices or sordid feelings of his followers.
Either Parliament will be dissolved, or it will not. If not, the Opposition will be most virulent and powerful, and the Government will
soon be beaten ; and in the meantime Whigs and Radicals will be jum-
bled together, and the former will be led on by party passion to identify
themselves too much with the latter. Besides, a dissolution will
always be considered as hanging over our heads, and men will be
making violent speeches, and giving extravagant pledges to curry favour
with their constituents with a view to the next election. If, on the other
hand, an immediate dissolution takes place, there will be no limit to

* "Memoirs," vol. i. p. 309.

the fury of opposite factions. The Tories may win fifty or sixty votes, and the majority will consist of men who have pledged themselves on the hustings chin deep for triennial Parliaments, ballot, and universal suffrage; and a fine state we shall then be in, with a House of Commons that will follow no ministers who will not propose measures of this extravagant kind."*

We have said that our author has published much which he ought not to have published, and here is a proof of it. This paper was certainly intended for confidential circulation only, and it is not said that permission to publish it has been given by the Foreign Office or by Lord Palmerston's representatives, and they must regret its publication. Interesting it undoubtedly is, but it will not enhance Lord Palmerston's reputation for sincerity. It is an additional proof, if any be needed, that he, a Tory in heart, for years continued to be a member of Liberal Ministries, and that such a Ministry, under his presidency, was what Mr. Disraeli termed the so-called Conservative Ministry of Sir Robert Peel—" an organized hypocrisy."

Let us now turn to the royal memorandum. M. E. von Stockmar, with his usual scorn and contempt for everything English, says of it:—

"If King William's views were not in themselves remarkable, still his memoir is of value from the facts it contains and the insight it gives into the machinery of a constitutional government. King William's style abounds to overflowing in what is called in England Parliamentary circumlocution, in which, instead of direct simple expressions, bombastic paraphrases are always chosen, which become in the end intolerably prolix and dull, and are enough to drive a foreigner to despair. The whole document is disfigured by such mere verbiage and wearisome repetitions."†

We are not concerned to defend the literary style and execution of this paper, but we think our author is not justified in attributing its style to the King himself, simply for this reason, that we do not believe his Majesty could have produced anything so good. Comparing this paper with the letters of Sir Herbert Taylor, written both in his own name and in that of the King, which are published in "The Correspondence of William IV. and Earl Grey," we have no hesitation in attributing its authorship to Sir Herbert. It is entitled "A Statement of his Majesty's general proceedings, and of the principles by which he was guided from the period of his Accession, 1830, to that of the recent change in the Administration, Jan. 14, 1835." It occupies thirty-six printed pages,‡ and at a length which partially

* "Memoirs," vol. i. pp. 309, 310.   † Ibid. p. 314.   ‡ Ibid. pp. 314–350.

justifies M. E. von Stockmar's uncomplimentary description discusses the events of the reign. We do not propose to weary our readers with the whole of it, but only to quote and comment on its more noteworthy passages. We learn from this paper that the King's ideal of statesmanship was that the country should be governed by political principles and measures "such as had been approved by his father." It establishes the truth of the rumours current at the time as to the efforts made by the King's private and irresponsible advisers to persuade him to *emancipate* himself—the word is his own—from Earl Grey and the Whigs.[*] It reveals also that the King, as was natural and consistent in one who thought it possible, after the passing of the first Reform Act, to govern England on the principles of George III., felt obliged—

"to give his most earnest and vigilant attention to the progress of measures emanating from a Government deemed *popular;* and he cannot, he continues, charge himself with having neglected so essential a part of his duty, nor with having hesitated to remonstrate and to object as far as the circumstances in which he was placed would admit."

The Royal clemency thus rejoices over signs of repentance in some of the leading Whigs. Whether it be true, or merely what his Majesty wished to be true, what follows is amusing.

"His Majesty is bound to do Earl Grey and Viscount Melbourne and *some* of their colleagues the justice to say that . . . . although they have erred in introducing too extensive a measure of Reform, he verily believes them to have become in the progress of their ministerial duties sensible of this error, and earnestly desirous of checking those who persisted in a course of which they had not equally discovered the destructive tendency."

Then follows a long and very laboured defence of the dismissal of the Whig Ministry. It completely justifies Lord Palmerston's description of it as "a preconcerted measure." On the receipt from Lord Melbourne of an account of the critical state of Earl Spencer—

"the King's first conclusion was that Lord Melbourne (who had, as well as Lord Grey, attached, after the secession of Mr. Stanley, a paramount importance to Lord Althorp's services in the House of Commons) would resign whenever the contemplated event should take place; but in the next letter, as far as his Majesty recollects (for he has not reserved any copies) Lord Melbourne stated a hope that Lord Althorp might be prevailed upon to continue in the Administration, although a member of the House of Lords ; and his Majesty's answer

---

* "Memoirs," pp. 317, 325.

did not give any opinion that this would facilitate the arrangement to be made. *In fact, his Majesty did not contemplate the possibility of Lord Melbourne's submitting any that would prove satisfactory; and, when he intimated his intention of coming to Brighton, his Majesty had persuaded himself that he was coming to tender his resignation, and had made up his mind to accept it.*"

This statement suggests the following questions : Why should the King, without any intimation from Lord Melbourne that such was his purpose, assume that he would resign ?   Why could not his Majesty contemplate the possibility of Lord Melbourne submitting any arrangement which would prove satisfactory— except because it was a foregone conclusion in the Royal mind that no arrangement he would or could propose should be satisfactory ?   In candour his Majesty should have added to his statement that he had made up his mind to accept Lord Melbourne's resignation another—viz., that he had determined unless Lord Melbourne resigned to dismiss him.

We resume our extracts from the memorandum. Those of our readers who remember "The Correspondence of George III. with Lord North " will see in the son, as in the father, a fussy desire to interfere with the management of the House of Commons, joined with perfect ignorance of its tone and temper and the qualifications necessary for a successful parliamentary leader or speaker.

"Lord Melbourne came to the King on November 13th. The only arrangement which his lordship brought forward, as he stated, *with the concurrent opinion and advice of all his colleagues and those most competent to suggest any opinion with respect to the feelings of the House of Commons was that* Lord John Russell should succeed Lord Althorp as leader. His Majesty objected strongly to Lord John Russell; he stated, without reserve, his opinion that he had not the abilities which qualified him for the task, and observed that he would make a wretched figure when opposed by Sir Robert Peel and Mr. Stanley."

We have so lately and so fully considered Lord John Russell in his character as leader of the House of Commons, that we feel it unnecessary to say more on this remarkable display of kingly ignorance and presumption than to refer to what we have already written.*

" Lord Melbourne—continues the memorandum—thought the King laid more stress than was justifiable upon the necessity of being a good speaker or ready debater; these being advantages which Lord Althorp did not possess, while he exercised an extraordinary influence in the House of Commons. He did not mean to say that Lord John Russell or any other member of the Government could, in this respect, effectually replace Lord Althorp; but he did not allow that there was any reason to apprehend that the business of the Government might not be carried on satisfactorily."

What follows is decisive as to the King's foregone conclusion to dismiss his ministers:—

"The King objected equally, if not more, to Mr. Abercomby, whose name appeared also to have been suggested to Lord Melbourne, as well as Sir John Hobhouse, and Lord Melbourne did not seem to think either eligible, any more than Mr. Spring Rice, whose name his Majesty stated he expected to have been proposed to him; Lord Melbourne therefore persisted in urging preforably the nomination of Lord John Russell, but his Majesty had further objections."

The pretext under which the King endeavoured to veil his predetermination to get rid of the Whigs was Lord John's then recent declaration as to the Irish Church, which, in Lord Derby's phrase, "upset the coach." We will not weary our readers with the royal views on that subject, nor with further extracts from this "Statement," which, out of regard to the King's reputation, we wish had not been given to the public. Coupled with his letters to Earl Grey, it completely destroys the illusions about "William the Reformer," as he was called in the early part of his reign, and on his own confession convicts "the Sailor King," not only of being in heart opposed to the great measure of his ministers, but of want of fairness and straightforwardness in his dealings with them. We cannot, however, dismiss this unfortunate document without making the following excerpt as to Lord Brougham, concerning whom, after all that has been said on the subject, it is interesting to learn his Majesty's opinion in his own words:—

"Nor did his Majesty conceal from Lord Melbourne that the injudicious and extravagant conduct of Lord Brougham had tended to shake his confidence in the course which might be pursued by the administration of which he formed so prominent and so active a feature, and in its consistency."

The Whig Ministry being thus dismissed, the Duke of Wellington was sent for to form another. He, however, had learned something by experience, and refused to be the premier. The Peel-Wellington Ministry was then with the greatest difficulty constructed, to drag on a miserable existence till the following April, when it met its Nemesis. This is the latest, and it probably will be the last, exercise of the Royal Prerogative in dismissing a Ministry, independent of the will of Parliament. The results of the experiment do not raise our opinion of the judgment, not only of William IV., who wished to govern England on the principle of George III., but also of Stockmar

and others like minded with him, who think that the Crown
should personally take a part in the government, independent
of, if not in opposition to, Parliament. That Stockmar was in
some degree one of the King's secret ill-advisers in this matter
we think probable, for the reasons we have given. The probability is strengthened by the fact that, as we shall see later on,
he was afterwards concerned in advising the dismissal by prerogative of Lord Palmerston.

Baron E. von Stockmar refers to this dismissal as a proof
that the English Sovereign "is not a mere nodding mandarin,"
and has "an important sphere of political duty," and with the
usual ignorance and rashness of foreigners in dealing with
English politics, he attempts to show from this case that our
constitutional doctrine of ministerial responsibility "is both
morally and practically nonsense." We will give his own
words :—

"When King William dismissed the Whig ministry, the Duke of
Wellington wrote to Sir Robert Peel that, in his opinion, the new
ministers were not in any way responsible for the conflict of the King
with their predecessors, as this was a matter which had been concluded
before his Majesty sent for him (the Duke). [*Peel's Memoirs*, vol. ii.
p. 23.] Peel stated in reply, that he was well aware that by his acceptance of office he became technically, if not morally, responsible for the
dissolution of the preceding Government, although he had not the
remotest concern in it. Todd (" Parliamentary Government," p. 124)
praises the more perfect correctness of view, inasmuch as a Constitutional King cannot undertake any act of government without some
one being responsible for it. In those words of Peel's, however, there
is the distinct admission that the responsibility of the new ministry
for the dismissal of the old one *was both morally and practically nonsense*. They proved, moreover, how important in fact is the function
of the Crown in a crisis of this kind. It appears from the above that
the English sovereign has an important sphere of duty."*

The doctrine of ministerial responsibility was admirably stated
and enforced by Lord Brougham, in his speech on the dismissal
of Lord Melbourne, to which we have before referred, and by
Lord Russell and the other Ministers in the debates relating to
Prince Albert's position (31st January, 1854), and may be thus
summed up :—Ministers are responsible for every State transaction of the Sovereign ; if they do not wish to undertake the responsibility they must resign. The House of Commons can give
practical effect to this responsibility by a vote of want of confidence
in, or an address for the removal of, Ministers—*e g.*, in 1835—the
House, before proceeding to any other business, could have
shown its disapproval of the dismissal of the Whig Ministry by

---

* " Memoirs," vol. i. pp. 379, 380, 381.

one or other of these votes, and so removed the Peel Cabinet. Ministerial responsibility, therefore, notwithstanding the dogmatic assertions of M. E. von Stockmar, is neither morally nor practically nonsense.

Stockmar's more intimate and influential connexion with the English Court commenced in May, 1837. Some time previously it had been arranged by King Leopold that from the 24th of that month, the eighteenth birthday of the Princess Victoria, when as heiress presumptive she attained her majority, Stockmar "should reside in England as the trusty helper and adviser of the Princess." He accordingly arrived in England on the 25th May. William IV. had been taken seriously ill a few days before, and on the 20th June he died. Stockmar remained in England for more than a year after the Queen's accession.

"His external position," says his biographer, "was an undefined one; circumstances would hardly have admitted of any other, nor would another have suited or satisfied him. . . . . Upon us devolves the task of describing the manner of his activity on the delicate English *terrain*, and in the difficult period of the first years of Queen Victoria's reign."[*]

What, then, was the manner of Stockmar's activity? We are told that—

"Stockmar's clear insight made him carefully avoid every interference with English affairs of State. Had he so interfered, he would have acted in direct opposition to the opinion of *King Leopold, who employed him,* and would at once have rendered his position in England impossible. . . . . He had nevertheless many opportunities of obtaining an insight into State affairs."

What follows is significant:—

"It is true that a confidential person of this kind may now and then indirectly exercise an influence over affairs with which it is neither his duty nor his desire to interfere; and where the confidence reposed is not limited to certain special objects, such a person may at times be called upon to express directly an opinion upon affairs of this kind."[†]

Considering that this book avowedly "lifts the veil but a little," we think that this passage, if it stood alone, justifies our designating Stockmar as the "*secret and irresponsible Minister of a constitutional Sovereign.*" He was so even before the arrival of Prince Albert, in a far greater degree after that event, and more and more so as the Prince was gradually allowed to exercise an influence in English politics. In the following passage the veil is lifted a little more:—

"Stockmar was the familiar and confidential friend of the Royal

* "Memoirs," vol. i. p. 379.   † Ibid. pp. 356, 357.

couple, who discussed everything with him, the little as well as the great, and claimed his advice and assistance for the one as well as the other."[*]

And still higher in what follows :—

"He felt called upon to exchange the part of a quiet observer for that of a quiet co-operator only when the personal interests of the royal families, or of the Crown in England and Belgium, or the vital interests of Belgium were called in question."

In fact the situation filled by Stockmar in the English Court was that well known in German Courts, and described in this book (vol. i. p. 379) as Cabinet Councillor of the Crown, but which before the present reign was wholly unknown in England. With this office Stockmar united that of unrecognised Minister for Belgium and Germany.

It was not long after the accession of the new Sovereign before her unconstitutional Minister assumed the part of leader of Opposition to her constitutional Premier, Lord Melbourne. As chief of the party in power, Lord Melbourne, like every English statesman so situated, paid due regard to party interests. The Queen placed in him, and—as all parties agree—justly, almost filial confidence, and was in all things guided by him. Stockmar, on the other hand, endeavoured to impress upon the Queen " that she was Queen of the entire people, and that it was her duty to hold herself free from the bonds of any party." " On this point," says the biographer, " Stockmar was not agreed with Melbourne, and had many a dispute with him thereon."[†]

This advice may have been well intended and sound in itself, our objection to it is that it was given by a foreigner, the avowed employé of a foreign Sovereign, in opposition to the advice of the Queen's constitutional and natural adviser ; and by one who could so forget himself and his position as to designate her Minister to the youthful Sovereign by the nickname of the *Poco-curante.* The annoyance caused to Lord Melbourne by Stockmar and his position may be judged by his remark :—" King Leopold and Stockmar are very good and intelligent people, but I dislike very much to hear it said by my friends that I am influenced by them—we know it is not true, but still I dislike to hear it said."[‡] Nor was the uneasiness caused by Stockmar's anomalous position felt by Lord Melbourne alone.

"One day the Speaker of the House of Commons, Mr. Abercomby, declared to the Premier that he felt it would be his duty to call attention in Parliament to the unconstitutional position of that foreigner Stockmar. Melbourne replied, that Stockmar was a person who filled a gap caused by circumstances in certain relations, with his (Melbourne's) knowledge and approval. Lord Melbourne related the circumstance to Stockmar, who exclaimed, "Tell Abercomby to bring forward his motion against me in Parliament; I shall know how to defend myself."[*]

Notwithstanding the probability given to this story by Lord Brougham's description of Mr. Speaker Abercomby as a man who got on in the world by ever making himself disagreeable, we cannot receive it as historical. It is not likely that the Speaker would have announced his intention to do that which his position and all its traditions would prevent his doing, or that the House, then led by Lord John Russell, and with Sir Robert Peel as leader of the Opposition, would have permitted their Speaker to take a course so wholly unprecedented. The truth we take to be this—that both in the House and in the country there was a general uneasiness as to Stockmar's position; that the Speaker knowing this, and himself sharing the general feeling, told Lord Melbourne that it was likely the attention of Parliament would be called to the subject; and that Lord Melbourne, whose invariable remark on hearing that anybody intended doing anything was "Can't you leave it alone?" dissuaded from his intention whoever thought of raising the question. The invincible ignorance of foreigners as to English officials and customs accounts for the mythical shape which the story assumes in this book. Anyhow the story, be the truth contained in it much or little, shows with what jealousy Stockmar's position was regarded by English politicians.

From the summer of 1838 until January, 1840, Stockmar was engaged in attendance on Prince Albert, for the purpose of preparing him for the position it was hoped he would fill. It is to be regretted that King Leopold, who selected Stockmar for this delicate position, should have chosen a foreigner, and one not only inclined to high views of kingly authority, but devoted to other interests than those of the country of which the Prince was to become the first citizen. It was natural that King Leopold, by birth a foreigner and by position a foreign sovereign, should make such a choice; but had the interests of England been his first object he would have chosen an Englishman.

In January, 1840, Stockmar returned to England in the capacity of Prince Albert's plenipotentiary to negociate the treaty of marriage with Lord Palmerston on behalf of the Queen. From the blame heartily bestowed by Stockmar on all parties for the reduction by Parliament of the proposed annuity to the

---

[*] "Memoirs," vol. i. pp. 397, 398.

Prince, it is clear that it was a grievous disappointment both to
the Prince and his adviser. Stockmar accuses even his favourite
Peel of having in this case allowed "party feeling and passion to
get the better of higher political considerations."* We thought
at the time, and on reading this book our previous judgment is
confirmed, that in the then state of the country—*i.e.*, a financial
crisis, a stagnation of commercial industry, and among the
working classes almost universally a strong feeling for the
Charter, with a disposition to enforce its adoption by physical
force, Sir Robert Peel, by giving his influence in favour of the
smaller sum, and so diminishing the burdens imposed by the
Royal establishment on the taxes raised from an overburdened
and exhausted people, showed himself a truer friend than the
Whigs to the Queen and the Prince, as well as to the country.
As foreigners, of course neither the Prince or Stockmar would
know or understand the state of things which led Peel to take
the course he did. The defeat of the Government measure as to
the Prince's annuity led Stockmar, in his office of Cabinet Councillor to the Crown, to the irregular act of attempting through a lady
to open negociations with the Opposition to facilitate the passing
of the bill settling the Prince's rank and precedence.† These
negociations failed, but Stockmar's advice in the matter was
taken by the Ministers. The part of the bill settling the
Prince's rank was abandoned, and as in the case of the
marriage of the Princess Charlotte with Prince Leopold, Prince
Albert's precedence was defined by an Order in Council.‡
This advice being strictly according to precedent, the Ministers
were justified in taking it, notwithstanding the quarter whence
it came. Stockmar took the same highly objectionable course
of negociating between the Queen and Prince and the Opposition
with regard to the Regency Bill of 1840, the appointment of the
Royal household at the change of Ministers in 1841,§ and in
short, in all matters relating to the interests of the Crown or the
Royal family.∥ Intense desire was felt by the German clique in
the palace, and by their connexions abroad, that the Regency
should be vested in Prince Albert alone, and not in the Prince
and a council of regency. The latter plan seems to have been
that first contemplated by the Ministers, as it certainly was desired, and properly desired, by the surviving sons of George III.¶
In the event of the Queen's death immediately after the birth of
an heir, the minority would have lasted eighteen years. The
Regency Act, as passed through the intrigues of Stockmar, made
Prince Albert sole regent. The Prince, therefore, would for those

---

* "Memoirs," vol. ii. p. 28.   † Ibid. p. 34.   ‡ Ibid. p. 35.
§ Ibid. pp. 38–45.   ∥ Ibid. pp. 60–65.   ¶ Ibid. p. 45.

eighteen years have been in all but name king of England. The character of the man—his talent, his strong will, his leaning towards prerogative, if not absolutism—the supremo regard he always felt for Germany in preference to England—the influence over the Prince of Stockmar, who thought "a king of this country with the necessary capacity had it in his power to be his own prime minister"[*]—Stockmar's dislike, felt no doubt equally by his royal pupil, to Parliamentary government—his contemptuous estimate of English statesmen and the English people—all these forces working together, would in all probability have made the history of this country from 1840 to 1858 and onwards, very different to what it has been. Looking at the dangers we have escaped, we cannot be too thankful that we were saved from such a destiny. The Prince in a letter to his father (24th July, 1840), writes—"There has been much trouble to carry the matter [the Regency Bill] through, for all sorts of intrigues were at work; and had not Stockmar gained the Opposition for the Ministers, it might have ended as did the 50,000*l.*"[†] To enable him to gain this much desired object, Stockmar seems to have intrigued to secure the influence of *The Times.*[‡]

In September, 1841, the Whigs, evidently to Stockmar's great satisfaction, were driven from office, and Sir Robert Peel came in. It is interesting to note the light in which Stockmar viewed the new Minister:—

"I place (he writes) great reliance on Peel's capacity as a statesman. Want of confidence in himself and in others appears to me to be his weak point. I should consider him, therefore, better fitted for quiet than for stormy times; anyhow, he will in a far higher degree than his predecessor, be Prime Minister in the true sense of the word, and placing the confidence that I do in his honesty, I hope that the Royal Prerogative will be far better maintained by him than by Melbourne. I know for certain, however, that Peel does not yet believe that he possesses the confidence of the Queen to the extent which he wishes and requires. The Prince, on the other hand, he considers as his friend. [What follows shows how the events of 1840 rankled in the German mind.] It is remarkable that the Prince should have had this opportunity of heaping coals of fire on the head of Peel, who reduced the Prince's income by 20,000*l.*, and did his best to deprive him of his rank."[§]

All likelihood of a regency now disappeared; and encouraged by what he believed to be Peel's views of prerogative, Stockmar set to work to secure for the Prince the same position in another form.

---

* "Memoirs," vol. i. p. 380.   † Ibid. vol. ii. p. 45.
‡ Ibid. p. 44.   § Ibid. pp. 54, 55.

When Stockmar returned to England in September, 1841 (says his biographer), he had, as we see from his notes, long negociations with Peel on *the re-establishment* of the constitutional authority of the Queen and on the position of the Prince.

" It was my maxim (he writes) that the Prince is the necessary private secretary of the Queen. This view had been accepted by the late Lord Grey, Abercomby, and Lord John Russell. Peel allowed that position to the Prince, at least *de facto*, but from that time I constantly preached to the Queen that the first favourable opportunity ought to be seized, in order to obtain a legal sanction for that position of the Prince, and in order to define by a Bill, the place, the rights, the duties of a Prince Consort, thus filling up a gap which existed in the Constitution. There was another motive for this—viz., to render unnecessary the wish of the Queen, expressed in December 1841, to bestow on the Prince the title of King. I was of opinion that by the bestowal of an idle kingly title, the Prince would be brought into a false position with regard to the nation and his own children."

" Peel, as Stockmar relates, considered not only the kingly title, but also the legal definition of the position of the Prince, unadvisable on account of the difficulties to be experienced in Parliament. The wish of the Queen with regard to the title had not remained a *secret and the enemies were already mischievously rejoicing over the expected result*. [We wish the biographer had enlightened us as to whom he designates by the word 'enemies.' We presume he means English statesmen.] The following words of Lady Palmerston were reported to Peel : ' If Peel listens to the wish of the Queen, he is lost—he will be beaten in Parliament. If he resists the Queen, there will be a breach between her Majesty and him.' But Peel was too prudent and the Queen too temperate to allow either the one or the other to come to pass. The result was that nothing was done in order to regulate the position of the Prince by law."*

This passage, we think, justifies us in attributing to Stockmar's influence the fact that the Prince defined his own position "as private secretary of the Sovereign, and her permanent minister."† The idea of a permanent minister is as entirely in accordance with Stockmar's opinions and aims as it is unknown to the English Constitution, and repugnant to it in its later developments.

Considering that in three hundred years there had been only two Prince Consorts—that the prospect of there being another seemed remote—that in the case of William III. the elevation

---

* "Memoirs," vol. ii. pp. 494, 495. Our readers will please to bear in mind this mention of Lady Palmerston in connexion with the enemies alluded to, when they read what we hereafter say as to the relations between Lord Palmerston and Prince Albert.

† In his letter to the Duke of Wellington respecting the office of Commander-in-Chief, published in the Introduction to " Speeches and Addresses of the Prince Consort," p. 73, and quoted in these "Memoirs," vol. ii. pp. 487, 488.

of a foreigner, the husband of a Queen Regnant to Regal equality with his wife, and the consequent embroilment of England in foreign politics, was one of the drawbacks to the enormous advantages of the Revolution of 1688 — the Queen's constitutional advisers of 1841 acted most wisely, and strictly in accordance with all English tradition and precedent, in resisting the proposal of her unconstitutional adviser to define by positive enactment the position of a Prince Consort, and in leaving it to be developed and modified by the free action of time and circumstances. A later passage in these memoirs shows that nothing short of the Prince's complete regal equality with the Queen would have satisfied Stockmar—if indeed he did not desire that there should exist between them, as in ordinary marriages, subserviency of the wife to the husband. The passage referred to relates to the Parliamentary debates of January, 1854, on the Prince Consort's interference in affairs relating to the Russian War. Lord Campbell, then Lord Chief Justice, said in the House of Lords that " It was not as a Privy Councillor that his Royal Highness had to give counsel, but it was as the *alter ego*, as the Consort of the Queen of Great Britain." Of course it could not be expected that Lord Campbell would miss an opportunity of uttering as uncontrovertible law a dictum so pleasing to princely ears, but which the merest tyro in the law knows to be not only unsupported by a single rag of authority in any decided case or text-book, but to be repugnant to the whole tenor and spirit of all those authorities. The courtly doctrines of Lord Campbell were not, however, strong enough to please Stockmar.

" Ministers (he writes) have not shown themselves as firm, as determined as I could have wished, and as without danger they might have been. The only one who was not afraid to utter the bare maxim that the husband is necessarily the *alter ego* of the wife, was the Lord Chief Justice, Lord Campbell, but he did not uphold or carry perfectly through this doctrine."*

Like the French courtiers who were *plus Royalistes que le Roi*, Lord Campbell and Stockmar in their zeal for the Prince's dignity and power went far beyond, indeed contrary to, his own estimate of the duties inseparable from his position. In his letter to the Duke of Wellington, to which we have before referred, the Prince writing of himself says :—

" The husband should entirely sink his own individual existence in that of his wife ; that he should aim at no power by himself or for himself ; should shun ostentation ; assume no separate responsibility before the public, but make his position entirely a part of hers."

---

* " Memoirs," vol. ii. pp. 501, 504.

This was written in. 1850, but as the appetite for power grows by what it feeds on, it may be that in 1854 Stockmar's opinion was that then held by the Prince.

Had Stockmar succeeded in gaining a legally defined position and powers for the Prince, we are left in no doubt as to the use the Prince, guided by Stockmar, would have made of it. We have said that aversion to parliamentary government was one of Stockmar's great characteristics. Of this these volumes contain abundant proof. Thus he writes in 1851 :—

"The evil from which we suffer since the Reform Bill is always becoming greater. I mean the growing omnipotence of the House of Commons and its interference with things belonging to the executive. In order to check this evil we want a series of able Premiers ; the line which separates a Republic from a Constitutional Monarchy is not sufficiently appreciated, and therefore it is not sufficiently defended. To defend it, however, is the first duty of the Ministry. This defence must take place at any moment when the representatives of the people avail themselves knowingly or unknowingly of the forms of the Constitution in order to imperil it or its essence, and to carry the country unobserved by the multitude into another form of government. At every such attempt, the Minister must offer the most serious opposition to the House of Commons. He must openly profess this principle : ' You have a Constitution which the majority of the people wishes to see preserved, and I shall not allow a minority to use the omnipotence which the House of Commons has long aspired to in order to cheat the majority of the nation, and deprive it of its good right.' "•

This was the tone which our German philosopher—the Cabinet Councillor of the Crown—would have had "an able Premier" assume towards the House of Commons. When this superficial critic of English Parliaments and statesmen thus spoke of the evils of the growing power of the House of Commons since the Reform Bill, and in the next sentence of the representatives of the people trying to cheat the majority of the nation of its good right, did it not occur to him that this growing power of the House of Commons was the result of its having been made by the Reform Bill more of a representative body, and that it was the influence of the majority of the electors sending the majority of the House of Commons which causes it to attain more and more of control over the executive ? This same letter concludes with the following supercilious outburst—"This English mania of making all political wisdom to consist in the art of satisfying Parliament, and of tricking it by clever speeches, makes me sick."†

• "Memoirs," vol. ii. pp. 448, 440, 450.   † Ibid. p. 450.

Supposing our German critic would have condescended to listen to any benighted Englishman on the working of our institutions, we should have commended to his notice Lord Macaulay's vindication of Parliamentary Government which we quoted in our last number,* but we presume that the High Prerogative German would have considered the English statesman tainted with, to use a phrase common in France during the Second Empire, "the virus of Parliamentarism."

This was not a mere thoughtless effusion in a hasty letter. It was Stockmar's deliberate judgment, thus repeated towards the close of his life:—

"Since the Reform Bill [he writes July 26, 1858] suddenly admitted a greater mass of democratic matter into the House of Commons than had been compatible with the former practice of government, a democratic party has arisen who aim at the omnipotence of the House of Commons. They have in view, and try to effect the annulling of the theory and practice of the English Constitution before 1830. Whenever, since the Reform, the Whigs have held the reins, they have allied themselves with this party, have governed with their aid, and existed through their favour. In the short intervals in which the so-called Tories were in power they followed their predecessors in practice, whatever their own theoretical creed might be. With the single exception of Peel, I may say that all the ministers whom I have known since 1830 have intentionally and unintentionally laboured to destroy the Constitution before 1830. . . . . I do not despair, but it is enough to make one low-spirited and afraid when one considers to *what Ministers and to what an absurd usurping House of Commons* the fate of England is at present entrusted."†

We therefore can perfectly well judge what would have been the result of Prince Albert's attaining the position which Stockmar sought for him. All English ministers since 1830, Peel excepted, are condemned because they have wisely given way to the growing demands of public opinion as soon as they have been satisfied that that opinion has been unmistakeably expressed. No premier would have been sufficiently "able" in Stockmar's view, but the "Permanent Minister," the Prince himself, and, as he certainly possessed the "necessary capacity," no doubt he would have been instigated by Stockmar to make himself his own Prime Minister. To what a dead lock should we have been brought! On the one side an irremoveable minister devoted to foreign interests, with absolutist sympathies and even tendencies, striving to restore the constitution as it existed before 1830. On the other hand the Parliament and the people set on attaining year by year more and more of free and self-determined govern-

---

* Vide the *Westminster Review*, Jan. 1873, pp. 52, 53.
† "Memoirs," vol. ii. pp. 545, 546, 547.

ment, and yearly more and more inclined to the principle of
non-intervention in foreign politics. Stockmar's ideal, and perhaps that of the Prince also, of the relation between the Executive and Parliament is best represented by that which existed a
few years ago between the Parliament of Prussia and Bismarck,
to which England and her Parliament would never have submitted. The House of Commons is condemned by Stockmar as
"absurb and usurping," but the tree is known by its fruits, and
future generations, judging by that test the House of Commons
as it was constituted from 1832 to 1868, will not be inclined to
think that England would have been better governed by two
clever and ambitious Germans. Let us hear the testimony of
one of our ablest statesmen as to the labours of the House of
Commons during that period. It is that of one by no means
favourable to the democratic spirit or party, or disposed servilely
to flatter either Parliament or people.

"I can remember the time myself [*i.e.*, Stockmar's golden age, the
ante-Reform period before 1830], when the House of Commons was
regarded, not as representing the wishes and forwarding the views of
the bulk of the English people, but as the greatest obstacle in the way
of carrying out improvements which were desired by them, and that
was not merely the opinion of the working classes; it was an opinion
shared to a great extent by the education and property of the country,
and but for which conviction the Reform Bill would never have passed
into law. Let me ask, Have not the results fulfilled and exceeded the
expectations of the most sanguine prophet of that time? Look at the
noble work—the heroic work—which the House of Commons has performed within these thirty-five years. It has gone through and revised every institution of this country; it has scanned our trade, our
colonies, our laws, and our municipal institutions; everything that was
complained of, everything that had grown distasteful, has been touched
with success and moderation by the amending hand."[*]

The truth of this no one well informed on the subject can
dispute, and the re-Reformed Parliament has not shown itself
less fruitful in noble and heroic work than its predecessor.
Would one of Stockmar's "able premiers," acting on the principles of Lords Castlereagh and Liverpool, with a Parliament
submissive to his dictation, have done as well for England as
"this absurd and usurping House of Commons?"

The great object of Stockmar, however, in seeking to gain this
defined position and power for Prince Albert was not only to
oppose the progress of popular power in England, but to enable
the Prince, hardly if at all checked or controlled by Parliament
or Ministers, to employ in Continental politics and intrigues the

* "Speeches and Letters on Reform," by the Rt. Hon. R. Lowe, M.P.,
p. 51.

power and influence of England in favour of the interests of
Belgium and Germany. These were the great interests of
Stockmar's life. The greater part of the second volume is filled
with details relating to the politics of Belgium and Germany, to
"Stockmar's German policy," to "Prince Albert's German policy,"
all interesting to the German readers for whom this book was
originally published, but which have little or no interest for the
great majority of Englishmen. To them the value of this portion
of the Memoirs is the light it throws on the relations between
Lord Palmerston and Prince Albert, and to these we now propose
to call attention.

Narrating the circumstances which in December, 1851, led to
the memorable event of Lord Palmerston's dismissal by the
Queen, or rather by the Prince, for his recognition of the government of Louis Napoleon after the *coup d'état*, our biographer
thus, to use his own phrase, "lifts the veil a little :"—

"A certain antagonism had long existed between Palmerston and
the Prince Consort. The Prince could not approve of the restless,
interfering, and demonstrative line of policy which the Minister since
1848 had adopted more and more, *which offended the Continental
governments*, injured England, and benefited nobody. *The Prince
stood up for the right of supervision belonging to the Crown* in foreign
politics. This was again displeasing to the self-willed lord, and the
means and artifices he employed to escape from that control did not
improve matters."[*]

The following extracts from Stockmar's correspondence show
the estimation in which the English statesman was held in the
Palace. In November, 1851, Stockmar writes—"I think the
man has been some time insane." And again, on December
22nd :—

"Ever since I returned here, therefore, for the last two months, he
[Palmerston] has been guilty of follies which confirm me more and
more in my firm opinion that he is not quite right in his mind. The
Prince might have been strongly tempted to rush in and throw him
over, but he quite agreed with my advice, which was that he ought to
remain a mere spectator, as I feel certain that if Palmerston requires
another thrust his colleagues themselves will give it."[†]

The Prince did not long remain a mere spectator :—

"Immediately after the *coup d'état* the Queen and the Prince,"
writes M. E. von Stockmar, "discussed the line of policy to be observed by England with regard to this event. *It was settled* that it
must be a policy of abstinence and of neutrality. The Queen wrote in
this sense to Lord John Russell, who declared his entire agreement."[‡]

This, if true—and no doubt it is—is instructive. The policy
of England on a grave question of foreign policy is settled in a

---

* "Memoirs," vol. ii. p. 452.   † Ibid. p. 453.   ‡ Ibid. p. 460.

matrimonial *tête-à-tête*, without reference to the advice or opinions of any of her Majesty's constitutional advisers, although *they* are responsible to Parliament and the country for the foreign policy of England. The Prime Minister is told what the policy of his Cabinet must be, and he agrees, perhaps because he cannot help himself. Though the constitutional advisers were not, the un-constitutional adviser no doubt was, consulted. The result, as we all remember, was Lord Palmerston's dismissal. What follows is an instructive comment on the value of royal interference with Ministers, of irresponsible advisers, and of the amateur states-manship of foreigners in English politics.

"It has been Palmerston's maxim for a long time (writes Stockmar in October, 1854), that an alliance between France and England could hold the rest of Europe in check. From this his maxim I explain to myself his wild experiment of publicly approving the *coup d'état* of Louis Napoleon immediately after its success, which was contrary to his duty as Minister, and his attempt at establishing a political under-standing with the Napoleons, in spite of the general condemnation of the events of December. In order to be just, I must admit that he, at that time, saw more keenly into the future than all of *us*, as *we* saw through glasses darkened by indignation at the *coup d'état*. The Russian madness certainly made the Franco-English alliance a politi-cal necessity, and Palmerston may justly say that he recognised that necessity sooner than *we*. He certainly had the better of *us*."*

By the *us* is doubtless meant the Prince and Stockmar. Notwithstanding that Lord Palmerston's sanity was thus established against the doubts cast on it by Stockmar, neither he nor the Prince seem to have learned wisdom by the ex-perience of their errors in 1851. The formation of the Aberdeen-Russell Ministry seems to have been watched by Stockmar with jealousy and distrust,† and his biographer "lifts the veil" enough for us to see that Prince Albert and Stockmar were opposed to the foreign policy of the authorised and re-sponsible Ministers. Writing of the Russian War, he says:—

"The efforts of the Prince Consort against the course of events were in vain. His policy was simply this—he wished to see the war averted through a common action of the Four Powers; the danger of an ex-clusive alliance with France, and the precarious nature of such an alliance, was perfectly clear to him. On the one side he had to fight against the excessive confidence of Aberdeen, who always supposed the best intentions in Russia, and was inclined to believe every word of the Emperor Nicholas, and therefore did not act with sufficient decision against Russia for the maintenance of peace. Aberdeen used to say, that even if Russia were not honest, one ought to treat one's enemies as if they were honest. The Prince admitted the truth of this in a certain sense, but he added that one need not believe in their honesty. On the other hand, it was his duty to watch Palmerston, who was always spinning new threads in the interest of the French alliance. . . . . It gave him particular pleasure to support such French wishes as might be most unpalatable to the Court. He could thus take his revenge for what he had suffered for Louis Napoleon in 1851. All these circumstances naturally increased the tension in his relations to the Prince Consort. Curiously enough, circumstances happened in December, 1858, as in that of 1851, which still more embittered that relation."*

It is only necessary to call to mind Mr. Cobden's dying testimony to Lord Palmerston to see what a mistaken estimate of him was formed by the courtier who wrote this, in supposing that his policy with regard to France was dictated by a petty desire to revenge himself and annoy the Prince. Those who come after us will no doubt think that the Anglo-French alliance during the Second Empire was the best element in the foreign policy alike of Napoleon III. and of Lord Palmerston, and the opinion of it attributed in this extract to Prince Albert will not enhance his reputation as a far-seeing statesman. The circumstances referred to as embittering the relations between him and Lord Palmerston were the Prince's interference with the conduct of the Russian War. As to the extent of this meddling the biographer does not in the least lift the veil, though we have a shadowy and not very correct sketch of the state of public feeling on the matter, and of the parliamentary debates on it. This sketch embraces a long dissertation on the causes of the Prince's general unpopularity in England, written in the sneering and contemptuous tone usual in the author when referring to Englishmen.† On one transaction of this period it was doubtless in the biographer's power to have lifted the veil, but he has not thought proper to do so. It was at the time in political circles matter of common report and belief, that after the death of Lord Raglan, Lord Palmerston was desirous of appointing as his successor to the command-in-chief of the forces in the East Lord Clyde, then Sir Colin Campbell; that the appointment was opposed by Prince Albert on the pretext that Sir Colin was not of sufficiently good family to command the British army ; that, to please the Prince, the command was given to an aristocratic nonentity and Court favourite, who held a command in the Household Brigade. The result was the minor part played by England in the decisive events of the war, and the consequent loss of national prestige. This, however, was shortly afterwards recovered by the brilliant success of Sir Colin Campbell in crushing the Indian mutiny. The appointment to the Indian command not being coveted or

---

desired by Court favourites nor dictated by Royal prejudices.
If this report were true, the transaction casts equal discredit on
the Prince and Lord Palmerston. It was the Minister's duty to
the country to have resigned; had he done so, and stated to
Parliament that his reason for resigning was that his advice as
to the conduct of the war was overruled by an irresponsible influence behind the Throne, that influence would have received
a decisive check, and the Minister would have been carried back
to power by the irresistible will of the nation. If the story is
untrue, it would have been better for the sake of the memories
of the Prince, of Lord Palmerston, and of Stockmar, to have
referred to and refuted it.

With the close of the Crimean war Stockmar's active influence
in English politics seems to have ceased, and being then seventy
years of age, he finally returned to Germany, where he died in
1863, not long outliving his royal friend and pupil.

As we said at the opening of this paper, these Memoirs contain
some noteworthy revelations as to the practical working of the
monarchical element in our Constitution. We do not undervalue
the value of that element. Nothing we see of the working of
the Republican system established in America, or of the nominal
Republic in France, would induce us to change for a Government
Republican in name the one which we now possess, and which
to appropriate, in a relation different to that in which its author
used it, a phrase of Mr. Bright's, we should call a Monarchical
Republic. We differ from most of what the writer of these
Memoirs says of our system and mode of Government, but we
assent to his assertion, and the facts he relates prove it, that the
Sovereign "is not a mere nodding mandarin." Equally clear is
it from those facts that the Sovereign commits a great mistake
whenever he of his own will and judgment interferes with his
responsible ministers, and dissents from the judgment they have
formed on their wider experience and more intimate acquaintance
with Parliament and the country. The royal dismissals of the
Melbourne Ministry, and of Lord Palmerston, are sufficient proofs
of this. In England a parliamentary vote remedies the errors of
the Sovereign. America could not get rid of Andrew Johnson;
France in M. Thiers, experiences the working of the institution
Stockmar would have imposed upon us—viz., a head of the State
his own Prime Minister, who cannot be got rid of without a political convulsion. Part of the price we pay, as these volumes show,
for the inestimable blessing of an hereditary chief of the State,
is the occasional accession of a female Sovereign and, through her
marriage, the falling of the royal authority into the hands of a
clever and ambitious foreigner, whose sympathies are with other
countries, and whose ideas of government are alien to those of
Englishmen. It is clear also that our system of parliamentary

government does not so completely, as has hitherto been generally thought, prevent the existence and influence of Court favourites and secret and irresponsible Ministers. These are no doubt evils. The remedy for them is not to be sought in abolishing the monarchical element in our Constitution, but in the further development of that "omnipotence of the House of Commons" so repugnant to Stockmar, and others like him, and the increasing influence of an enlightened constituency enlarged from time to time as circumstances require upon their representatives in Parliament.

We have spoken freely of Stockmar's position, of the evils inseparable from it, and of his many errors, but we repeat we believe that in that position he acted on a pure and conscientious, though narrow and mistaken judgment. To us his career is one of the most melancholy of which we have ever read. Towards its close he thus describes it :—

"The peculiarity of my position compelled me always anxiously to efface the best things I attempted, and sometimes succeeded in accomplishing, and to conceal them as if they had been crimes. Like a thief in the night I have often laid the seed-corn in the earth, and when the plants grew up and could be seen, I knew how to ascribe the merit to others, and I was forced to do so."*

This is a sad retrospect for one who struck those associated with him as being "one of the best political heads in Europe," but it was the inevitable result of the course Stockmar consented to pursue. The servants of a free State, Russell or Derby, Peel or Gladstone, O'Connell or Cobden, Thiers or Guizot, Cavour or Ricasoli, Washington or Lincoln, who serve their country in the light of day, and subject to the control and inspection of public opinion, may occasionally for the time be misunderstood, be unfavourably judged, and have their wise and well intended measures at one time thwarted; at others appropriated by rivals, but in the end they enjoy the fruit of their labours, oft late reaped, yet long enduring, in the respect and consideration paid to their acknowledged benefactors by successive generations of the people. They, on the other hand, who, like Stockmar, devote themselves to the secret service of families and dynasties, to the intrigues of Courts, or to unacknowledged diplomacy, must be content, like Stockmar, to lead what one of his friends called *une existence souterraine anonyme,*† and as they draw near to the grave to feel like him, that what they have really been will soon be unknown to any one.

* "Biographical Sketch," vol. i. p. cx. † Ibid., p. cix.

Art. VII.—"Our Seamen."

1. *Our Seamen.* An *Appeal.* By Samuel Plimsoll, M.P. Virtue and Co. 1873.
2. *Parliamentary Papers.* Board of Trade Abstracts of Wrecks, Casualties, and Collisions, 1862 to 1872. Hansard.
3. *Parliamentary Debates.* The *Times* Newspaper, 5th March, 1873.

THE conditions under which in some respects the trading ships of this country have for several years past found employment, have for a length of time been present to the minds of many persons more favourably placed for observing them than for commanding the public ear. We purpose devoting a chapter to them.

It will we fear be seen that the condition of our merchant shipping has become one of practical anarchy, excusable to us as a nation only in so far as the facts of the case are insufficiently notorious to influence the public sentiment. We shall probably find that this impugned condition is largely influenced by the facilities arising from extreme competition in the business of marine assurance. And we shall deem it within our province to discuss the question of an adequate remedy.

If we can suppose a state of things in which the sea risk of any maritime adventure should be borne by the persons severally interested in it, the shipowner taking that of his ship and freight, the merchant that of his cargo, we should have in existence a guarantee of the best kind for the presence of the many elements, moral and material, which enter into the constitution of seaworthy fleets, and reducing casualties to a minimum. And to the extent to which the practice of assurance usurps these conditions, the motives which lead up to them are intruded upon and counteracted. Theoretical perfection would then consist in rendering the contract of assurance legally void, and forbidding the business of underwriting under pains and penalties. But for practical ends it is necessary to admit that sea assurance, sanctioned as it is by a venerable age, has been and must continue to be an indispensable handmaid of commerce, and that it supplies one of the requisite conditions on which that important constituent of civilization can in any wide sense of the term exist. No statesman, no essayist, no economist would be capable of the folly of proposing that a business so

nicely adapted to the world's needs should be either morally
or legally discountenanced. And we think that no one
fully cognizant of the numberless ramifications which enter
into the consideration of the subject, would seriously maintain
the possibility of controlling or regulating it from without.
There is a point *up to* which the interests of the marine
adventurer and those of the underwriter are in harmonious
co-operation towards a given result, *beyond* which the latter is a
mere victim of circumstances which he is powerless to influence
or control. We shall find strong reason to believe that the
high pressure conditions of modern commerce, and the presence
of excessive competition among underwriters, have disturbed this
necessary co-operation with results which challenge investigation
in the interests of society.

We do not quite go the length of Mr. Bright in his recognition of the sacredness of free competition. There are, however, degrees in these things, and so long as our vital organs are
left uninvaded, we are willing, in a general way, to accept his now
historic dictum, that adulteration is only one of its many forms.
If our clothier gives us shoddy when we have paid for cloth,
or our shilling razor when tried adopts a harsher view of its
obligations than we bargained for, we deem it a sufficient retaliation upon our tormentors if we pass them by when we are next
in the market. But our temper becomes slightly vindictive
when we find ourselves the victim of Hamburg sherry, and
it would rise to a point not readily controlled, if we found
ourselves by unusual luck on dry land again after a voyage
in some ship, the conditions of which we might have seen
reason to believe were so nicely calculated as to prevent the
expectation of our being ever again heard of; and we should
begin to think that if the conditions of business were such as to
leave possibilities of this kind subject to no greater check than
the difficulty of finding persons capable of practising them, the
time had clearly arrived for discussing the question involved in
them as one of public concern.

Our readers are well aware that our proclivities lead us in
quite an opposite direction from that of being the advocates of
paternal government. But if there is one thing more absurd
than to invoke it helplessly on the occasion of every petty dislo-
cation of the social machine, it is to elevate the absence of it
into the dignity of an inelastic principle to which the plainest
considerations of expediency and even the dictates of humanity
are to give place. If in the course of our observations we
find ourselves under the necessity of viewing the conditions of
our subject as something which legislation alone can correct, we
shall in its proper place not lose sight of the obligation on us to

justify our opinion. We hesitate indeed to make the admission too absolutely even with respect to mere property, that its continuous and wholesale destruction should, if plainly avoidable, constitute something outside the legitimate province of authority to take cognizance of; but if we find reason to think that sailors', and often passengers' lives are the counters with which the game of some shipowners and others is being played, a case will have been established which, unless capable of being successfully contradicted and openly discredited, will appeal to Parliament for a remedy with the endorsement of a whole community.

Our propositions then are these—

That life is recklessly sacrificed and property squandered in maritime enterprise as now conducted, and that there are strong reasons to connect this result with the multiplied facilities for effecting marine assurance.

That any effort to counteract these evils indirectly by regulating or controlling the contract of insurance or otherwise would be inexpedient as well as impracticable.

That there remains the necessity of legislation framed directly to cope with them, and which should include provision for a compulsory classification of shipping under the direct responsibility and control of the Government.

The greater portion of what we have now written had taken shape and consistency for the purpose of publication in this Review before the appearance of the remarkable volume the name of which stands first of those set down at the head of this paper. We willingly surrender our place in the main attack to the earnest and worthy gentleman whose name it bears, and shall chiefly seek our vindication for what we advance in its pages. We are aware that certain of the allegations set out by him are assumed by some shipowners to be directed against themselves, and are about to become the occasion of proceedings at law. We shall not knowingly make any of these the subject of reference, but we hold it a mere affectation of delicacy carrying this reticence to the point of tying up the whole question, pregnant as it is with issues of life and death to a considerable class of our fellow-citizens, until certain selected passages forming an inconsiderable proportion of the bulk of the volume are dealt with by the occasionally protracted processes of our Courts.

Our first proposition aptly finds its illustration in Mr. Plimsoll's pages. It is indeed difficult to quote from them without diluting the effect of a demonstration built up layer by layer, and pointing irresistibly towards the one conclusion. But it will be convenient at this stage to extract for ourselves from the Board of Trade returns the annexed particulars, which are not there exhibited in

any one table, but which we have condensed for easy reference :—

Year.	Wrecks and Casualties on the coasts of these Islands.	Of which involving Loss of Life.	Lives Lost.	Wreck and Casualties abroad.	Of which involving Loss of Life.	Lives Lost.
1567	2090	245	1100	935	105	1671
1869	1747	177	720	935	158	1426
1609	2114	183	800	961	195	1682
1870	1502	101	676	1208	174	2255
1871	1575	110	530	1754	212	1659
Total Lives lost on Home Coast			3832	Total Lives lost abroad		8093

Or say a grand total in 5 years of 12,525 lives.

NOTE.—In all but the second of these columns the figures have
reference to British ships only. It is also right to notice that the
second and fifth columns include every variety of incident from a
trivial casualty to a disaster. The lives lost abroad for 1870 include
those on board H.M.S *Captain.*

Now these statistics, considerable as they may appear—and a
loss of 12,525 lives in five years *is* somewhat considerable—do
not necessarily prove the insufficiency of the wrecked or lost
vessels, either in respect of management, material, or equipment.
In exhibiting therefore this sad muster-roll, we still require the
link of independent observation and inquiry to connect the two
things. This then is a quotation given by Mr. Plimsoll from the
pages of the *Lifeboat* for Nov. 1, 1870 :—

" We have repeatedly through the medium of this journal strongly
called attention to the terribly rotten state of many of the [wrecked]
ships above twenty years old ; in too many instances on such vessels
getting ashore their crews perish before there is any possibility of getting out the lifeboat from the shore to their help."*

And again here is an extract from the Board of Trade report
applicable to the coast losses of 1871 (original, p. 7) :—

" It will be seen from table 10 distinguishing the wrecks, &c., on or
near the coasts of the United Kingdom according to the force of the
wind at the time at which they happened, that in 1871, 856 happened
when the wind was at force 6 or under—that is to say, when the force
of the wind did not exceed a strong breeze, in which the ship could carry

---

* We restrict ourselves to the portion of this quotation which embodies the
results of direct observation on the part of the officers of the Royal National
Lifeboat Institution, omitting some statistics which, doubtless the result of
inadvertence, appear to have been inaccurately transcribed from the abstracts
of the Board of Trade.

single reefs and topgallant sails; that 149 happened with the wind at
forces 7 and 8, or a moderate fresh gale, when a ship if properly found,
manned, and navigated, can keep the sea with safety."

And again from the same authority we extract these figures
(Returns for 1871, p. 5), covering a period of ten years, and which
exhibit the causes of wreck resulting in *total* loss on our own
coasts :—

In	Stress of weather.	Inattention, carelessness, and neglect.	Defects in ships and equipments.	Various and unknown causes.
1862				
1863				
1864				
1865 There were ves-				
1866 sels totally lost				
1867 from the annexed				
1868 causes.				
1869				
1870				
1871				

In	Stress of weather.	Inattention, carelessness, and neglect.	Defects in ships and equipments.	Various and unknown causes.
1862	249	72	26	116
1863	332	61	31	79
1864	163	69	39	95
1865	245	99	38	88
1866	276	125	74	87
1867	385	106	65	100
1868	265	87	71	104
1869	325	60	74	127
1870	160	77	63	111
1871	137	09	44	118
	2530	1419	1025	

Exhibiting a total of 1419 losses within this period from causes
so closely allied as "inattention, carelessness, and neglect," and
"defects in ships and equipments." We say closely allied for the
reason that we do not believe in the possibility of creating any
sentiment of pride in his calling, or any feeling of conscientious
regard for the property under his charge, in the mind of any captain to whose hands you consign the command of a rotten and
worthless tub. And probably we should be entitled to claim no
small contribution from the column exhibiting loss from unknown
causes towards the two which precede it, if nicer discrimination
were possible in the circumstances.

We conclude with this quotation from the same authoritative
source :—

"Of the 308 total losses from causes other than collisions on and
near the coasts of the United Kingdom in 1871, 137 happened when
the wind was, as appeared from the wreck reports, at force 9 or upwards (a strong gale); 44 arose from defects in the ship or in her equipments (and of these 44 no less than 25 appear to have foundered from
unseaworthiness);* 99 appear from the reports made by the officers
on the coasts to have been caused by inattention, carelessness, or neglect; and the remainder appear to have arisen from various other
causes."

It is of course impossible outside the borders of a novel to ac-

---

* The italics are ours.

quire such a knowledge of people's private affairs as would enable any one to show that the more considerable proportion of
these losses had their moving cause in over-insurance. Mr.
Plimsoll gives (pp. 35, 36) some remarkable instances of the
kind which he has taken pains to ascertain ; and although no one
in daily familiarity with underwriting doubts the fact that they
are in respect of a certain class of insurers representative ones,
proof of any such allegation strictly so called is rarely if ever to
be met with in any form in which it could be safely used to illustrate our argument. The facilities for compassing over-insurance
without detection are at all events so great, they are so
beyond the scope of remedy capable of being devised by any ingenuity of legislation, and the moral reprobation attached to the
act has got to be looked on as so inconsiderable, that it would be
wonderful indeed if any one could be made to believe that those
whose rotten fleets come within the confines of these various extracts would shrink from the comparatively venial irregularity of
practising tricks upon underwriters.

To many it may possess the interest of novelty if we follow the
process of effecting assurance on a ship or her contents. Mr.
Plimsoll does so very effectively, and his letter-press description is
so illustrated and connected by original documents in facsimile from which the name of the assured is alone expunged,
that even those of his readers who know not the city find themselves on a level with the most experienced. In the absence of
similar aid we must do our best by way of ordinary description.

The shipowner or freighter who requires his property afloat
covered by assurance usually employs an insurance broker, who
proceeds to compress the particulars of the required transaction
on the upper half of an oblong piece of paper about 7 by 2½
inches, and which contains his name, the date, the ship's name,
the amount to be covered, the voyage, the interest or subject of
assurance—*i.e.*, whether the body of the ship, the freight, or the
cargo, and usually the rate at which he expects it to
be taken. This paper, technically known as the "slip," he takes
round either to Lloyd's, a large room in the east wing of the
Royal Exchange, and exclusively the home of individual underwriters operating on their own account ; or to one or more of the
numerous marine assurance companies,—or it may be to both—
and each underwriter to whom it is "shown," if satisfied with
the risk and the rate, sets down on the lower half of it, the amount
he is content to *underwrite* in figures with his initials attached.
As a means of estimating the quality of the ship by which the
risk is sought to attach, the underwriter before initialling generally refers to one or more Register books periodically issued by
various societies, in which such vessels as are voluntarily sub-

mitted by their owners for the purpose, are, after due survey and approval, classed in grades which vary in relation to their age, construction, material, and the like. If the vessel holds a good class in " Lloyd's Register," or the " Underwriters' Registry of Liverpool," or the " Bureau Veritas of Paris," as the chief of these books are respectively termed, the underwriter in practice accepts the record thereof as obviating any need of further or more special inquiry on his own account, and the risk is taken at ordinary rates. But if the vessel either occupies a low class or is altogether unclassed, it is nevertheless almost always possible to get the business done at an extra rate more or less considerable.

Excusing ourselves for a momentary digression, we must here observe that it has always occurred to us as rather remarkable that in neither of these classification societies have the immense sea assurance interests of this city outside Lloyd's—in other words, the great Marine Assurance Corporations of London—either part or lot, or the smallest voice, vote, or control. And what is perhaps even more so is the unquestioning complacency with which the situation is accepted. The prospect of waning dividends may possibly disturb it, and suggest to those who have these vast interests in their keeping a view of their obligations in this respect scarcely compatible with a mere mechanical acceptance of other people's work.

To resume our description. The risk is universally recognised as passing to the underwriter immediately he initials the slip, but it is yet necessary to complete the transaction in regular and legal form. The broker therefore proceeds now more leisurely, and having obtained a form of marine policy with the proper revenue stamp attached, and the printed portion of which expresses in old-fashioned phraseology the terms common to all contracts of sea assurance, he fills up its blank spaces from the *slip* with the details peculiar to the operation in hand ; but whereas these mostly occupy their place on the slip in abbreviations understood only by the initiated, they are now expanded at full length. The policy so prepared is then presented with the slip to the same underwriters as before, or rather to those of them who sit at Lloyd's, and each of whom in his turn draws a pen through his initials on the *slip*, and signs the *policy* which cancels and supersedes it. Public companies, on the other hand, all of whose operations take place outside the "room," as Lloyd's is familiarly called, and each one of which has its own paid underwriter with an office to himself, invariably issue separate policies, prepared by their own clerks, for the whole or any portion of risks underwritten on their behalf. For example, if in a total operation of 20,000*l.* there is say 15,000 done at Lloyd's, spread among fifty names taking 300*l.* each, and 5000*l.* in full done with a single company, the transaction, although comprised in *one* ship, would be represented by *two* policies—one for the 15,000*l.*, which would be signed by the fifty names in their turn, each writer setting down 300*l.*, the limit of his individual obligation, in a line with his name—the other for the 5000*l.*, which would simply bear the signature of one or two directors or responsible officers of the issuing company, as representing the whole amount taken by it. The delivery of the two completely signed policies by the broker to his principal, and the payment by the latter of the premium or price of saddling the underwriter with the sea risk of his adventure, would, leaving aside needless detail, complete the operation.

Now the incidents which affect the question of price in underwriting are so various and intangible, that notwithstanding the efforts of able men to formulate and drill them into figures, we are of those who think that no ingenuity can successfully compass the effort to class marine risks among the exacter sciences in the sense in which those of fire and life have found a place in them. It, however, calls for no special education in matters of assurance to perceive that a fundamental element of success in any department of it, is the acquisition of a number of transactions sufficing to spread the risk over a tolerably wide surface.

But if the multiplication of assurance offices, and the addition of new underwriting members to Lloyd's have, as we suspect they have, of late years had the effect of supplying the thing in which they deal in excess of the market demand for it, two conflicting impulses at once confront each other in the underwriter's mind, as thus: "Here is a risk offered me at a rate or price which I believe to be inadequate. Therefore I should refuse it. But if I keep on rejecting business on such grounds, I shall not have enough left to maintain that spread or extent of risk which is an essential of a wholesome underwriting account. Moreover the ship may arrive. I shall therefore chance it." Here that demoralization sets in which results in business of all sorts being too readily clutched—in the antecedents and incidents of a risk ceasing to be scanned—in the unscrupulous having their path cleared for them so long as their contribution to the daily tale of premiums helps to sustain the sum total of an otherwise perhaps waning business, and—by an easy transition—in rotten and overladen fleets and manslaughtered ships' companies; which *has* resulted in Mr. Plimsoll's appeal; which *will* we hope result, and that without needless delay, in a competent answer to it.

A conception of the underwriter's business of which the tradition still happily prevails, is one which regards it as at all events partly founded on the presumed honour and integrity of his client. The more these things can be made to hold their place in it side by side with other necessary conditions, the better it will be for all who have to do with it. Our present concern with it—as a subject-in-chief, we may take it in hand on some subsequent occasion—extends no further than the point at which it affords too convenient an opportunity to the unprincipled to disregard obligations in which the whole community have an interest. But we cannot help expressing our belief that the gentlemen who in some respects so ably fill their posts in the chief marine offices of this city, have it in their power to do a great deal which they omit to do, towards restoring the vitality of the honourable tradition of which we have spoken, and in which they have a common concern with the outside world. Let them search the pages of the law reports, thickly interspersed as they are with insurance trials for the last few years, and when they disintegrate them sufficiently to recognise the significant majority of instances in which the vexation, the sense of unfairness, and the expense resulting from these proceedings, have their first cause in the scarcely disavowed misrepresentation or concealment of some "sharp" but perhaps nominally respectable broker, we would ask them what is the usual practice when the same performer next comes to do business. In any healthy state of things what turn would his reception take by the profession generally? In most other walks of life we venture to think the answer would be easy. At the bar, or in the army, he could only do things of a like kind at the cost of professional ruin as well as social extinction. Is our information correct that in this one, which there is the strongest motive even of mere expediency to fortify with the sanctions which appeal to men of honour, and which, if they existed, few would have the courage, even if they had the disposition, to disregard, his reputation is in many instances recognised not as a treasure which he is bound to hold sacred, but as a fund on which he is at liberty to draw from time to time until it is exhausted, and that the severity of multiplied competition* forbids the rejection of at all events more *good* business from such a source?

As one of other measures advocated in the ultimate interests of seamen, Mr. Plimsoll urges the view (p. 36) that "in no case should a shipowner (legally we presume) be allowed to insure his ship for more than two-thirds of its value properly ascertained." He suggests that a certain sum per ton measurement should only be allowed, and that it should vary with class, age, and certain

---

* Some half dozen of the companies formed within the last few years took their rise in the "development of business caused by the opening of the Suez Canal" (see any number of prospectuses), the true fact of the case being that the concentration of risk in comparatively few vessels resulting from the Canal Trade militated directly against the interests of underwriting.

other defined considerations. And he is of opinion that there would be no difficulty in the Board of Trade tabulating a scale for the purpose. We are glad, however, to notice in a subsequent page of the work that these suggestions are in the meantime put forward merely tentatively. For our own part we are convinced, as we have already indicated, that any such restriction would be impossible in practice, and not in all instances desirable even if it were possible. The assumption that the trade of shipowner can under any circumstances be so removed above ordinary vicissitude as to be on all occasions exempt from the presence in it of struggling, withal it may be honest and conscientious men, is one with which we decline to credit Mr. Plimsoll even in view of the paragraph by which he has almost obviously forced himself to sustain it. Troublous years follow prosperous ones. The equivalents of a shipowner's property pass temporarily into third hands. With free scope, honest purpose, and a little time he can shake himself clear; but surround his policies, which in the case supposed are of the essence of his security, with vitiatory complications which the banker or money lender would refuse to understand, and you may at once bring him face to face with his creditors. Again, he might wish to carry into effect some repairs or improvements in his ships, which although not technically imperative by any rules which any system of classification might impose, he might at the same time deem necessary to their perfect seaworthiness. It would plainly be impossible to construct any tabulated scale adapted to every contingency of this kind, and he might be obliged to fall back on the reflection :—" I cannot afford the uncovered risk of this new outlay, the limit prescribed in the tabulated scale does not permit me to transfer it to·underwriters, I must therefore with considerable regret and recognition of the danger of so doing postpone it to a more convenient season." And even if the restriction were desirable in itself, the dozen modes of evading it without possibility of check would prove a fatal objection to it in practice, and these are of the essence of our argument as to the futility of approaching a subject calling for plain right down handling by a devious and misleading route. A vessel's hull may even be under-insured, while at the same time a gross sum may be done on the aggregate of any particular adventure of which she forms a part, which would still leave a clear pecuniary benefit derivable from her loss. Chartered freight contracted for even before the arrival of the vessel at the port of loading, is a recognised insurable interest, so are ships' stores, outfit, profit, passage money, cash advances, and many such matters scarcely possible to be dealt with by any scale or on any principle of tabulation. These are in nearly every instance effected on valued policies, and therefore practically indisputable, whatever extravagances, to use a mild term, may come to light when loss occurs. Moreover marine assurance is one of the few descriptions of business which is independent of locality. The same operation may be repeated, or operations having the same object in view may be multiplied, at home and abroad, in Holland or Paris, in China or Bombay, in London or Liverpool, as in twenty other places, and on the hypothesis of dishonest intent the double loss collected without a chance of detection. The number of transactions already sent to be covered abroad by brokers operating in the interests of underwriters in Holland and elsewhere are already very considerable, and might find ample scope for increase in the event of the business being made the subject of artificial restrictions in this country. And again the instances are so frequent in which policies pass into the hands of innocent holders for value that any obligation to search into the incidents of their inception in every instance of casualty, would be found a serious interruption to commerce in any case, but it is one which would be found intolerable if accompanied by the conviction that it was after all fruitlessly suffered.

We have for reasons already indicated avoided strengthening our argument by many illustrations which we might have derived from the results of Mr. Plimsoll's personal inquiry and investigation; but if we have been so far successful in our intention it will have been seen that rotten and unseaworthy ships form too conspicuous a proportion of the merchant fleet of this country; and we have advanced reasons for believing that the suggestion of reaching and correcting it through exercising control over the contract of insurance, would be as ineffective in practice as in our belief it would be erroneous in principle.

What then is the true direction in which a remedy is to be sought for a state of things which quite plainly cannot be left alone?

The appointment of a Royal Commission will doubtless be conceded by Government with results which will appear in good time; but unless we are to suppose the existence of a general conspiracy in the interests of untruth, there is surely already before us a sufficiency of admitted material to sustain a discussion which it may be hoped will be fruitful for good, both in eliciting and educating opinion as to the best way in which the questions involved in it should be approached, without the necessity of waiting for what may be found in some yet distant Parliamentary report.

Mr. Plimsoll, supported by the more influential sections of the newspaper press, says we are to seek this remedy in a system of compulsory official classification. So far we agree with him. But when in advocating the adoption by Government of the necessary measures to give effect to this view, he proceeds (pp. 62, 63) to propose that it should only take up the ground not already occupied by "Lloyd's Register," and other private and irresponsible systems, we deem it of importance before public opinion acquires an immovable bias on the question, to be permitted to show cause against a conclusion we should strongly deplore ; one which we fear would serve merely as a convenient absorbent of the public sentiment now thoroughly aroused, while relegating the real difficulty to some distant day when circumstances might be less favourable for grappling with it.

At present "Lloyd's Register" of classification, taking it as the chief of its kind, is an institution existing by voluntary support, whose customers so to speak come to its door, and so long as they are satisfied it is under no obligation to adapt either its constitution or its proceedings to any supposed demands of external criticism. But when it is proposed to afford it official recognition in the capacity suggested by Mr. Plimsoll and others, it becomes proper to scrutinize its title to so important a place in the public economy, and to recollect that half its board of management are the nominees of shipowners (a point overlooked by Mr. Plimsoll in his description of its constitution, p. 60), and are mostly shipowners and builders themselves.

In saying this many will think with us that we sufficiently imply the condemnation of any such proposition as that under notice. Others will probably meet it with the argument, if we may so call it, of the intensely respectable character of these institutions—for we presume their constituents are tolerably alike, although we have not the means at hand of informing ourselves as to that of the "Liverpool Registry." We admit it ; although the term in its corporate application is not so proverbially an equivalent for fidelity in the discharge of occasionally invidious duties as to tempt us into accepting it at any extravagant valuation. But there is something so insidious in the influences which operate on this question—it is so difficult even for good men in such positions to define the point at which regard for the interests of themselves or their class should merge in their larger obligation to society; it is in practice so impossible to impeach them if they should occasionally elect the less praiseworthy alternative—that it is surely better to provide at the outset that any Government system which may be created by new legislation should obtain what professional help it requires by the simple expedient of paying for it; and leaving private institutions to follow their own devices, become in its application uniform, comprehensive, and compulsory.

Mr. Plimsoll does not afford us any indication of his views in detail on this part of his subject, but we cannot help suspecting that they would bear reconsideration. One of two things must happen—the three systems he speaks of must either work independently of each other, each one following its own devices, or they must conform to a common standard for the preservation of which official guarantees would have to be taken. Our contention is that in the first alternative they would all alike be a source of mischief and confusion; in the second, two out of the three would be superfluous.

The two chief English Registers have doubtless able men on their staff, but whose abilities would perhaps possess more favourable conditions for their exercise were there neither fear nor favour to expect from the owners of any of the ships which come under their view; they have their machinery in working use, and they contain within themselves the potentialities of good and efficient public service. And while we may not presume to dictate to them what course they should follow in any given eventuality, it would seem at least probable that if the establishment of a uniform system were inflexibly persisted in by the Legislature they would recognise the logic of facts and would hesitate to maintain a purposeless rivalry. What therefore one would hope to see in any new scheme of Government classification would be a frank endeavour to arrive at a friendly arrangement with the Register Committee or Committees whereby the Government should take over their working staff, leases and obligations, and that from the date of such transfer they should in their existing constitutions stand dissolved.

The disposition at the moment, one which Mr. Plimsoll doubtless in good faith helps to sustain, is to accept the work of these Committees as something almost above and beyond criticism. Such is far from being the impression of many who are favourably placed for forming an opinion, and looking to the gravity of its bearing on present circumstances we should regard it as deplorable if it were accepted off hand by the eye of faith and suffered to pervade and emasculate any result of Parliamentary action.

The writer of a letter to the *Times* in November, 1871, asserted without contradiction that in the " Official Wreck Register for 1870 " he had (excluding craft under 90 tons) counted fifty-eight British owned ships as having sailed within the year without being again heard of, and that of the number not fewer than *twenty-four* bore the class of A 1 at Lloyd's. Some of these may have been overloaded or undermanned, but from any point of view the proportion is remarkable, and may possibly lead to some little reflection before the acceptance of ready-made conclusions on the phase of our subject under immediate notice. Mr. Plimsoll himself is of opinion (p. 59), with respect at all events to steamers, that well built and found and properly manned and

loaded, they *cannot* founder at sea. In our opinion the remark
should apply almost in an equal degree to sailing vessels.

Respect for judicial proprieties forbids us the possibility of
strengthening our position by reference to the incidents of a remarkable lawsuit, the arguments of which have been concluded
in the Court of Queen's Bench sitting at Guildhall, the day on
which we write, but which must be presumed as still pending
because tried with inconclusive result. In short, we feel present
to our minds the same danger, the same difficulty, the same feeling of injustice to our case by what we are compelled to withhold,
and a necessity for the same caution in dwelling on these things
by any selection of particular instances, as Mr. Plimsoll has found
in another department of his work.

Our author we think fails to dispose satisfactorily of the
objector who said (p. 63), "that as Government would probably
sanction the surveys of Lloyd's, &c., and the other Committee, it
would amount to a recognition of private institutions." For our
own part such recognition in many conceivable forms of it would
fill us with no alarm. But in the present instance we consider
the objection a sound one, and one which is not removed by the
rather inadequate analogies which immediately follow it. There
may truly enough be no great distinction in point of principle
between authorizing a private institution to test a chain-cable
and to class a ship—for to save needless quotation, this is the
comparison instituted by Mr. Plimsoll—but there is in practice
all the difference between a simple mechanical act capable almost
of being performed by an intelligent labourer, and the conduct of
a system requiring for its proper discharge the educated skill of
an engineer and the ability of an administrator.

There is no reason any longer to assume the indifference of
Parliament to the subject of "Our Seamen," but Mr. Plimsoll
has in his work plied them so irresistibly with cognate instances
which exhibit their jealous care for other classes of the community, that in the absence of any early intention to legislate for
our seafaring population, the most ordinary regard for consistency
would almost compel a repeal of the numerous Acts which
surround the toiler ashore with competent safeguards in nearly
every walk of life. And the like consideration supplies our
justification if we required it, for the attitude we have assumed
on this question. If we were arguing for the first time in
support of some new theory of legislative interference in apparent
disregard of principles for which this Review has always had consistent regard, it might be necessary to enter with some elaboration
into the reasons which seemed to vindicate the exception.
But for present purposes there is no further obligation on us than
to observe that we are not claiming to be the patentees of a new

invention, and that we are content to rely on the faultless
analogies with which Mr. Plimsoll has in this respect
supplied us.

We perceive that Mr. Plimsoll promises to bring in a short Bill
during the present session of Parliament in order to deal with
the more flagrant and easily remediable of the practices which he
has taken in hand to rectify. This is professedly intended as a
temporary measure, and if it matured into an Act it would
doubtless be with the intention of becoming absorbed in and
superseded by the larger enactment which we are bound to expect
from the Legislature as a result of the labours of the Commission
now we hope about to be called into existence. We are therefore conscious that much of what we now say may seem to have
less concern with the subject in any aspect of it likely to be of
imminent interest, than with the more exhaustive controversies
which we may be sure will anticipate and accompany the remoter
efforts of Parliament upon it. But we shall nevertheless proceed
with our present intention, in the hope that our work may not be
altogether superfluous in slicing off some of the rougher edges of
the block for the more finished artists who have afterwards to
come in and perfect the design.

In view then of contemplated legislation on the subject, be it
impending or remote, we propose to devote our attention to and
so far as necessary recapitulate the considerations which in our
view should regulate its action, the evils with which it can
adequately cope, and the nature of the shortcomings which should
be more especially the subject of recognition in any Bill framed
to give competent relief to the public conscience now keenly
alive to its responsibilities towards seamen.

We maintain then that the importance of the proposed object
calls for the creation of a special Government department in
which the best administrative ability and practical skill for the
purpose in view should find a place. And there will be the less
occasion for the Chancellor of the Exchequer to feel unhappy
at the prospect, inasmuch as there cannot be the shade of a doubt
—and in this we are in accord with Mr. Plimsoll—that any such
department will after a possibly trifling deficit at first starting,
become not merely self-supporting, but a positive source of
revenue to the country.

We think a fundamental regulation of the department should
be that every vessel registered in this country and employed
for carrying passengers or cargo should, after the preparation of
a proper set of rules and grades of classification and the creation
of administrative machinery necessary to their operation, be
under compulsion to find a place in one or the other of them.
Each successive grade from and under the highest should corre-

spond to proportionate disqualifications in respect of passenger traffic as well as of the voyages they might undertake, and the descriptions of cargo for which they might compete, and failing the competency of any vessel to enter the *lowest* she should be required to be broken up, or if permitted to be used as a hulk, or for any similar purpose in harbour, should be dismantled, and proper safeguards under penalty taken against her re-equipment.

We have already expressed our views as to the attitude which we should desire to see the Government assume towards private Committees of Registration, but if it were found that these were resolved to retain their separate existence for the convenience of such owners as should continue to desire the voluntary in addition to the compulsory classification, it might still be hoped that a sentiment of friendly co-operation might prevail in view of the common object of improving the general character of our merchant fleet. But whether helped or hindered by others, we trust that no considerations of supposed expediency will influence the Government against pursuing with inflexible purpose the determination that their own system, if they are to have one, administered by their own officers, will alone have accorded it the privilege of granting such certificates as shall constitute a compliance with the law. There is the more need to insist and dwell on this point, as a responsible Minister of the Crown is Chairman of Lloyd's as well as a member of the committee of management of one of the private Register Committees; and although the positions are probably little more than honorary, and we have the sincerest belief in the rectitude of the right hon. gentleman's motives, it is well known how these things operate on the minds and opinions of weaker brethren, and it is clearly one point entered against the dispassionate consideration of this subject in official circles, that there should be in existence any circumstances calculated to suggest the merest shade of bias one way or the other.

Any supposed difficulty in acquiring and educating a proper staff of surveyors for the work, will seem preposterous to any one cognizant of the number of able and often accomplished seafaring men, not mere mariners, on the look-out for shore appointments of the better sort. Indeed all the trouble the Government would be under any real necessity of taking upon itself, supposing Parliament to have done its work, would consist in looking out some gentleman of the stamp and calibre of Mr. Scudamore, giving him the Act of Parliament to read when passed, *carte blanche,* a proper salary, and an intimation to set about his business.

We shall shortly express our views as to the attitude legislation should assume towards some of the causes of unseaworthi-

ness classed by our author under certain specified headings, the
order of which we shall mostly preserve.

UNDERMANNING.—We are in accord with the view which
regards the difficulty of dealing with this subject by any
inflexible regulation, but join in the advocacy of requiring
compulsory returns from owners, as well for the guidance of
charterers and underwriters as for the purpose of constituting a
possible basis of future legislation.

BAD STOWAGE, alike of outward bound ships and arrivals,
should be watched by officers of our supposed department, and
when reported and proved as involving or to have involved
danger, but not otherwise, should be a subject of penalty. All
arrivals with grain in bulk and the like should be strictly dealt
with in this respect, and the absence of proper longitudinal
divisions and other needful precautions made severely punishable.

DECKLOADING, similarly to the question of manning, is difficult
to provide for by rule and compass, but it would very much lose
its importance in the presence of efficient rules against overloading, to which we shall presently come.

DEFICIENT ENGINE POWER IN STEAMERS is a question which
will have to be considered relatively to the manner in which the
vessels are sparred and rigged. For example, any steam vessel
equipped in this respect similarly to the s.s. Great Britain
would simply be a first-class sailing-ship, with engines for use or
surplusage as convenience might dictate. The gradation of
class granted to these vessels must then begin at the point where
the essentials of an efficient sailing-vessel are partially sacrificed
to the presumed sufficiency of the steam power; it must consequently have regard to the relation of power to tonnage in
all vessels of which the equipment aloft has been calculated on
this principle.

OVER INSURANCE.—The difficulty, or, as we think, the impossibility of operating on our main question by setting legislative
bounds to transactions in marine assurance, is a question which
has already sufficiently occupied our attention.

DEFECTIVE CONSTRUCTION—IMPROPER LENGTHENING—WANT
OF REPAIR—constitute subjects to which the experience and rules
of the older registries would prove the most convenient guide, at
all events to commence work upon, and therefore do not call
for special remark. Some of the few things which would call
for a trifling share of attention under this head are best sketched
off thus. " Our Seamen " (p. 37):—

" After I had concluded my speech in moving the second reading
[a Bill to prevent overloading] a member accosted me in the lobby and
said, 'Mr. Plimsoll, you were mistaken in that statement of yours?'
'What statement?' I answered. 'Oh! that where you said a ship-

owner had lost ten ships in less than three years from overloading.'
'I mentioned no names,' I said. 'No; but I know who you meant;
it was Mr. ——, of ——. He is one of my constituents, and a very
respectable man indeed. It is not his fault, it is the fault of the man
who built his ships; for one of them was surveyed in London, and was
found to be put together with devils; Mr. —— knew nothing about
it, I assure you.' 'Devils?' I said. 'Yes.' 'I don't know what
you mean.' 'Oh, devils are sham bolts, you know; that is, when they
ought to be copper, the head and about an inch of the shaft are of
copper, and the rest is iron.' "

The term would also seem to apply to a dummy bolt about
an inch and a half in length with a head like a real one inserted
into the timbers, not to hold them together, but merely for make-
believe. An instructive sketch of this latter kind is given
opposite page 37, and we can truly say that the contrivance
vindicates its peculiar baptism.

OVERLOADING is a subject to which Mr. Plimsoll has devoted
a great deal of space, and not more than is warranted by its
importance, for it seems to have been of all others the most
fertile source of disaster. We extract but two from a storehouse
of instances, some of them not easily read without emotion, with
which his case is supported (p. 52):—

"On occasion of one of my visits to a port in the north I was met
by a gentleman who knew what my errand there was likely to be, and
he said, 'Oh, Mr. Plimsoll, you should have been here yesterday, a
vessel went down the river so deeply loaded that everybody who saw
her expects to hear of her being lost. She was loaded under the personal directions of her owner, and the captain himself said to me, "Isn't
it shameful, sir, to send men with families to sea in a vessel loaded like
that?" Poor fellow, it is much if ever he reaches port.'
"Mr. C. B——k said, as he saw her, 'That ship will never reach her
destination.'
"Mr. J. D. said, 'She did not look to be more than twelve or
fourteen inches out of the water.'
"Mr. J. H., a policeman, said to his colleague, 'Dear me! how
deep she is!'
"Mr. W. B. said to a friend, standing by his side, 'Dear me, this
vessel appears very deep in the water.'
"Mr. J. S. said, 'It strikes me she is dangerously deep.'
"The captain called on his friend Mr. J. H., who said he (the
captain) was greatly depressed in spirits. He told him (Mr. H.)
'that he' (the captain) 'had measured her side loaded, and she was only
twenty inches out of the water.' He also asked his friend to look
after his (the captain's) wife. Mr. H. gave him some rockets in case
of the worst, and then they shook hands and parted.
"Mr. J. N. and —— C., two workmen, said to each other, 'that
they would not go in that ship if the owner would give them the ship.'
And J. L., another workman, said, 'He'd rather go to prison than go

in that ship ;' and lastly, two of the wives of two of the sailors at least, begged the owner ' not to send the vessel to sea so deep.'

"She was sent. The men were some of them threatened, and one at least had a promise of ten shillings extra per month wages to induce him to go. As she steamed away the police-boat left her ; the police had been on board to overawe the men into going. As the police-boat left her side two of the men, deciding at the last moment that they would rather be taken to prison, hailed the police and begged to be taken by them. The police said ' they could not interfere,' and the ship sailed. My friend was in great anxiety, and told me that if it came on to blow the ship could not live.

"It did blow a good half-gale all the day after (Sunday); the ship sailed on Saturday. I was looking seaward from the promontory on which the ruins of T—— Castle stands, with a heavy heart. The wind was not above force 7—nothing to hurt a well found and properly loaded vessel. I had often been out in much worse weather ; but then this vessel was not properly loaded (and her owner stood to gain over 2000l. clear if she went down, by over-insurance), and I knew that there were many others almost as unfit as she was to encounter rough weather—ships so rotten, that if they struck they would go to pieces at once ; ships so overloaded, that every sea would make a clean sweep over them, sending tons and tons of water into her hold every time, until the end came.

"On Monday we heard of a ship in distress having been seen ; rockets had been sent up by her ; it was feared she was lost. On Tuesday a nameboard of a boat was picked up, and this was all that was ever heard of her.

"Mr. D——d was quite correct. On the Saturday he saw his wife reading the newspaper, and said to her, ' Look out for the —— in a day or two. I saw her go out of the river. She is sure to be lost.' She was lost, and nearly twenty men returned home never more."

Then again (p. 53) :—

" The L——, a large ship, was sailing on a long voyage from a port in Wales with a cargo of coal. Mr. B. called a friend's attention to her state. She was a good ship, but terribly deep in the water. Mr. B. said, ' Now is it possible that that vessel can reach her destination unless the sea is smooth as a millpond the whole way ?'

" The sea does not appear to have been as smooth as a millpond, for that ship was never heard of again, and twenty-eight of our poor hardworking, brave fellow-subjects never more returned to gladden their poor wives and play with their children."

If this practice has been the sailor's worst enemy, it at all events befriends him to the extent of being the one most easily counteracted. Nor should the needful steps having this end in view be delayed for the more elaborate consideration which the question of seaworthiness will undergo, at we fear the rather distant day when it will be ripe as a whole for Parliamentary treatment. We are unable to think of any valid objection to an authoritatively fixed load-line, which should be required to be conspicuously painted of a fixed length and depth, and of a colour in sufficient contrast with that of the ship's hull. Its exact measurement from the covering-board of the waterways should also be entered in a certificate to be granted to the captain as a check upon any alteration in repainting his ship; and the production of which on demand to any officer or surveyor of the department of classification should be made compulsory.

In our belief suggestions which have been offered in some of the newspapers and which favour an attempt to adapt the load-line to differences of season, or alternatively advocate its being left to the caprice of the shipowner on condition of his depth of free-board being declared at the Customs before commencing to load, would fail to meet the demands of the situation. There would possibly enough be an occasional hardship in laying down an arbitrary rule on the subject, but it must be balanced against the unquestionable evil of leaving things as they are, and if the latter weighs down the scale, its correction by the only means effectively possible becomes a necessity. Moreover all experience shows us that after a little preliminary fuss in such matters, commerce has never been slow in devising modes of reconciling itself to the inevitable.

If we err in the advocacy of an inflexible maximum load-line, we at all events do so in good company. There is, for example, the Chamber of Commerce of Newcastle on Tyne and Gateshead, an institution in which we are probably safe in assuming that shipowners themselves are not unrepresented. This is the unqualified language in which on 15th March, 1870, they petitioned Parliament on the subject.*

"Your petitioners regret that no provision is made in the [Navigation] Bill to determine the maximum load-line of ships and steamers. Recent experience has shown how much property is lost, and how many valuable lives are sacrificed by overloading. The extent of the evil arising from such cause, in the absence of all inquiry into vessels lost at sea (except in some isolated cases), cannot be estimated, and your petitioners feel that legislative measures alone can lessen this evil, and that the proposed provision of sec. 313 recording the draught of water of a sea-going ship is insufficient, and that none of the proposals herein made can be held to relieve the shipowner of his existing responsibility. Your petitioners would observe, that however perfect the measure may otherwise be, if it be without distinct provisions to meet the evils resulting from overloading, it fails to deal with one of the most distinct and recognised deficiencies in the Merchant Shipping Service."

And again this is the assertion of Mr. W. W. Rundell,

* " *Our Seamen,*" pp. 65, 66.

of Liverpool, in addressing the *Shipping and Mercantile Gazette* of that town, June 7th, 1870.*

"Mr. Plimsoll's proposal has met with a large amount of support from the owners of sailing vessels in this town. The Committee of the Liverpool Shipowners' Association have, I understand, unanimously supported this part of the Bill, as they consider that while the restrictions upon loading will not affect those who already load their ships reasonably, it will act as a decided check on the unscrupulous owner or charterer, and will tend by the greater safety which will follow, to reduce the general rate of marine assurance."

ADEQUACY OF GROUND TACKLE constitutes a division which we add of our own motion, as it does not come clearly within any of those which we have made the subject of remark. It is as important as any of them, and should have a defined and necessary place as a condition of the issue of a class of any grade.

In offering these various suggestions we cannot omit placing ourselves in front of an apparent difficulty which we are unable to allege we have thought out sufficiently to pretend that our opinions are altogether formed upon it ; and it is this. Suppose laws having these various objects in view are passed, and regulations framed in the spirit of them, what attitude must they take towards vessels registered (in the Custom House sense of the term) outside our jurisdiction, but which come to these shores for the purpose of competing in our trade? Would it be fair to English owners that a quasi-protection should be conceded to the foreigner by permitting him to come into our ports for the purpose of discharging overloaded cargoes out of rotten ships? Or would it be a law which could be practically enforced that no ships except those bearing the supposed class of our Government should be permitted access to any portion of our carrying trade?

We shall be glad to see the question discussed, but we think the solution of it would rest between these extremes. We think it would be impossible to insist on the possession of a class as a necessary qualification for arriving here with an inward cargo. The vessel and the cargo would come, and what could be done with them? We think it would be fairly competent to our authorities to put the matter in this shape. "We cannot very well send you back again with a cargo you have brought into our harbour, and you must therefore be allowed to discharge it. So far as concerns that purpose we shall not therefore trouble ourselves about the quality of your ship, but we shall estimate the excess freight you earn by loading beyond the line which our law per-

---

* "Our Seamen," p. 70.

mils, and *that* we shall require you to forfeit to our revenue. Moreover the immediate object of your arrival being accomplished, we shall not suffer you to perpetuate a trade *from* our ports otherwise than on the terms to which ships of our own subjects are compelled to submit. You must then either go through the necessary surveys and obtain our class, the conditions attached to which you must accept, or when you set sail again you must do so in ballast." By adherence to this principle we should place before foreign owners a powerful incentive to obtain admission to our official class register. To the extent to which they might avail themselves of this permission the equilibrium of impartial competition would be restored; to the extent to which they might prefer to neglect it their capabilities of privileged competition would be neutralized.

A word or two more before we leave this branch of the subject. If some compulsion could be included in the direction of providing seamen afloat with such trifling amount of extra cubic space as would afford them a better promise of comfort and a possibility of acquiring self-respect, it would represent a moral and even material gain out of all proportion to the apparently inconsiderable importance of the suggestion. Who shall say what latent possibilities it may not contain of inducing many good and sober fellows into the service whose habits forbid the possibility of adaptation to the dens by courtesy known as "the forecastle" now to be found in too many ships. And looking to the statistics of the Board of Trade which indicate the immense number of losses from "inattention, carelessness, and neglect," qualities rather obviously suggestive of demoralized ships' companies, we cannot deem it superfluous to suggest that in any new regulations it should be made somebody's business to follow up to prosecution and punishment the blundering incapacity which is so disastrous and fatal in its results. At all events, either do this or let us never again hear of railway pointsmen being placed on their trial for manslaughter.

Any Government system of classification should be represented by competent gentlemen in every important seaport in the world where facilities exist for dry inspection of shipping, and who should be empowered to grant certificates of classification or to conduct the necessary time surveys for vessels already classed in the United Kingdom. The Bureau Veritas of Paris and Brussels, an institution constituted for similar purposes to those carried out by the private Register Committees of this country, and whose operations from a European point of view are of at least equal importance with those of any of them, has no difficulty in finding gentlemen of talent and ability to carry out similar objects.

We are as ready to admit that some of these things will be
difficult to provide for in every necessary detail, as we are
impelled to deny that they are impracticable or that the difficulties will prove insuperable. The reason the great offices of State
in this country are bestowed on presumably able men is, we suppose, with a view to difficulties when they occur being triumphed
over.

We have at this stage the advantage of perusing the Parliamentary debate of March 4th, on Mr. Plimsoll's motion
"That an humble address be presented to her Majesty, praying
that she will be pleased to issue a Royal Commission to inquire
into the condition of and certain practices connected with
the commercial marine of the United Kingdom." The motion
has been withdrawn on the promise of the Government to
take the necessary steps without delay for the formation of a
Commission, but we regret our inability to find in the contributions to the debate of the official representatives of the Government anything to permit us to suppose that they are alive either
to the gravity of the allegations with which it will be the
province of the Commission to deal, or to the stringency of
the remedy which will be called for on the hypothesis of
their truth. Mr. Plimsoll may have quoted a few extracts
from official abstracts and elsewhere, which would have been
improved by some qualifying explanations, but these do not form
especially conspicuous portions of his volume ; and if he informs
us as the result of painstaking and obviously protracted personal
investigation that the evidence which can be produced on the
part of "gentlemen of high character in Cardiff, Newcastle,
Greenock, Port Glasgow, London, Sunderland, Hull, Liverpool,
and other places, who are longing for the opportunity of telling a
Royal Commission what they know, but whose lips are now
sealed by the terrible law of libel, and that when that Commission (if granted by the Government) reports, they will disclose a
state of things wholly disgraceful, shameful, and afflicting;" we
prefer at all events to suspend our judgment, in preference
to yielding to the ready cry, that a man of transparent honesty
and truth has, with a full sense of the responsibility resting upon
him, even gravely exaggerated his case. It may not be necessary
to take any severe view of the feeble machinery with which it is
proposed to open the inquiry in presence of the pledge that statutory powers of compulsory summons and of examining witnesses on oath will be added, if subsequently called for ; but
it appears to us to betray an ignorance of the world which people
have come to look upon as the peculiar attribute of a Liberal
administration, to suppose that the evidence which alone could
sustain the grave charges now under view, is of the kind which

persons are accustomed to volunteer at their own risk. The
gentlemen who can give this evidence have no right to be
invited to place themselves in the invidious attitude of amateur
informers. Nor is moral courage of so exuberant a growth as to
warrant any safe calculation of its ready presence on all such
occasions. If the Commission were issued under statutory
powers its summons would issue to the willing and unwilling
alike, so that there would be no external means of distinguishing
between the one and the other—a measure of protection to
which the former are fully entitled—and we trust that superfine
distinctions about making the inquiry "inquisitorial," will
not be permitted to have the effect of needlessly delaying
the step necessary to convert it into what we should prefer
to call an investigation.

One or two observations in the speech of the Right Hon. the
President of the Board of Trade calls for notice. He says—

"The dark colours in which the hon. gentleman had painted the
system might be relieved by his mentioning that insurance, as he was
informed, was falling more and more into the hands of powerful companies, very different from the feeble underwriters with trifling interests
who no doubt existed, companies with capital, able to hold their own
against fraud and criminality. Lloyd's Salvage Association, moreover,
conferred great benefit on the underwriting and shipping community
by its searching investigation into suspicious cases."

Now companies, whether powerful or otherwise, can only hold
their own against fraud and criminality through the instrumentality of a court of justice. In the few instances in which there is
evidence to sustain a criminal prosecution in connexion with any
barratrous or fraudulent act at sea, juries are we think fairly entitled to the admission that as a rule they fulfil their duty. But
then it must be recollected that these instances are rare—that the
crime is usually one the incidents of which can be readily
grasped—that a thing which is openly and avowedly crime is, we
are glad to say, outside the sympathies of the respectable men of
whom the panels are commonly composed—and that this kind of
charge is usually so expensive in respect of the materials necessary to its substantiation, that it is never entered upon unless in the
presence of evidence of a nature conclusive and overwhelming.
But when we come to the kind of fraud which keeps itself on
the safe side of actual crime, and which, whether avowed or
merely implied, is a considerable ingredient of no small proportion of the civil actions with which underwriters are concerned, it
is scarcely an exaggeration to say that the number of instances in
which the verdict is rooted in justice is so inconsiderable, that an
assurance office so far as it is unsheltered by some point within
the province of the judges to deal with, is practically beyond the
pale and protection of the law. "Then why did he take the

man's money if he didn't like the risk?" is the less elaborate
summing up which usually follows that of the Bench, and in which
the merits of a carefully argued case are condensed with the
supreme judicial instinct of perhaps some eminent cheesemonger.
And the extent to which we are asked to rely on the active
energies of Lloyd's Salvage Association is something not justified
by the conditions under which that body operates in the pursuit
of its "searching investigation into suspicious cases." As a matter of fact it only so operates when moved by individual members,
underwriters, or companies, who are required to guarantee all expenses of their doing so. Say for instance, that a vessel is bound
to this country carrying a cargo the property of a firm of London
merchants. The captain, for fraudulent ends of his own, scuttles
her in mid-ocean under circumstances of suspicion which renders
it probable that by a considerable expenditure of money on the
task the crime may be brought home to him. The merchant,
who is innocent of all participation in it, suffers either by
himself or his underwriters the entire loss of his goods. But this
being sustained he has no greater motive beyond that of mere
vindictiveness in seeing the crime punished, than any other person in or out of London. Yet we are given to understand that
the Salvage Association with its competent officers and ample
funds will not spend a five pound note in such a cause except at '
the request and expense of the last person of all others who
should be called on to add to a loss which has already weighed
heavily upon him. Several years ago there was an instance in
which this principle of action was departed from, and a difficult
and rather notorious case followed up at the proper expense of
the Association, but we believe this was avowedly made an exception to a general rule, one which has not been repeated in
any subsequent instance, and which although there may be an
absence of any formal resolution to that effect, there is, we believe,
no intention to repeat. The Association is primarily and professedly one for dealing with material salvage, and it owes no
obligation in respect of that which it may do or leave undone
to any one beyond the circle of its own subscribers. The facts
correspond to the theory, and the result is a dangerous immunity
to frauds of the particular class under notice.

If we have described these things correctly—and our words are
open to challenge—where, we ask, is there anything in them to
excuse the official complacency which finds it superfluous to care
for such matters because it seems they are supposed to be cared
for already?

We have then felt it our duty to recognise the gravity of the
circumstances which have called both for the "appeal" and the
motion of the junior member for Derby. Where we have differed

from him has been rather in the extent than the nature of their
proper remedy, and we have done so in the confidence that so far
as there may be found in our remarks anything worthy of attention, they will be considered without foregone purpose, and with
a single eye to the completeness of the result.

Those of our readers who have not obtained Mr. Plimsoll's
volume for themselves had better lose no time in doing so.
They will feel when they have read it that they have not only
fulfilled a righteous obligation in acquainting themselves with
facts in connexion with which every man in this country in
possession of a Parliamentary vote has a plain responsibility
before him, but that having regard to its merely literary aspect
they have at the same time whiled away a few pleasant hours
in the process. There is almost a Biblical simplicity and force
in the language of the book, in keeping with the wholesomeness
of sentiment which pervades it. Its author's name is now a
household word, and his disinterested courage has met with a
warmth of public recognition which a good man may justly
value. But the internal evidence to be found in his pages
makes it abundantly obvious that no such motive was present
to his mind, and that no such prospect cheered him, when with
the fidelity of a knight-errant added to the sober determination
of a man of business, he turned to his self-appointed task.

A word before we conclude is due in commendation of the
beautifully clear diagrams, &c. in facsimile with which "Our
Seamen" is illustrated, and which appear to have been taken by
the heliotype process.

Art. VIII.—Irish University Education and the Ministerial Crisis.

PARLIAMENTARY history is fertile in surprises. The Session
which began so quietly and seemed to offer to the Government the prospect—if they would only be decorously dull—
of continued power and prosperity, suddenly became transformed.
Within a month from the opening of Parliament there was eager
and agitated excitement of political parties. Ministerial crisis,
probable dissolution, change of Government, became topics of
universal interest and concern. After a discussion of four nights,
which assumed the character and dimensions of a great party
debate, the Ministry were defeated on their Irish University
Bill. Resignation speedily followed, the alternative course of a
dissolution scarcely commending itself as prudent in all the

circumstances. The leader of the Opposition when appealed
to in the usual constitutional course, declined the honour
to which he was called. It only remained then for the Government to resume office in order to conduct the national
business. But though they are thus able to protract their
reign for some time longer, they can only do so with the
view of preparing for the dissolution and appeal to the country
that have become almost inevitable.* Their Bill is lost, and as,
by circumstances partly of their own devising and partly independent of them, the Ministry staked their existence upon its
fate, they will be compelled to invite the judgment of the nation
upon their policy and career. It was scarcely conceivable that
even Mr. Disraeli's eagerness for office, or the necessity for
"blooding the hounds," by a taste of the spoils of office, should
have led the Opposition to assume again the responsibilities
without the power of government in a House of Commons
which still counts a Liberal majority of at least ninety. The
speech of Mr. Gathorne Hardy on the second night of the late
debate showed that the Conservatives look forward with sanguine
confidence to the results of a general election. Both parties
are thus on different grounds interested in an early dissolution.
The defeat of the Government compels Mr. Gladstone, if he
remains in office, to appeal from the decision of the House of
Commons to the country on his Irish Education policy. The
leaders of the Opposition, on their part, glad of the opportunity
of raising an issue that will excite sectarian bigotry and religious
prejudice, count upon these influences and the dissatisfaction
with the Gladstone Administration aroused during its tenure of
office to produce a reversal of the verdict of the autumn of 1868.
They are wise in their generation, for the circumstances and
issues are more favourable to them than only a few weeks ago
seemed possible of origin. The defeat of the Government on the
second reading of their Irish University Bill, though not much
of a surprise at the last, was certainly what no one ventured to
anticipate when the measure was introduced. There is a mystery
in the sudden and complete change of sentiment and opinion
that occurred in the interval which is not easily explained.
After Mr. Gladstone's masterly speech in introducing it—one of
the right hon. gentleman's greatest oratorical efforts—the
Bill—to use the Premier's own simile—was "on the crest of the
wave." Even Mr. Horsman, who so furiously assailed it in the
debate on the second reading, was for at least two days after the

---

* It is not of course necessary that the Ministry should contemplate an
early dissolution. But whether they do so or not, the circumstances and their
changed position after defeat on the measure of the Session make a dissolution
almost inevitable as we say.

speech its ardent admirer. He wrote to the *The Times* in language of glowing eulogy of the measure, which seemed to him fitted to "crown the work" of the present Parliament in doing justice to Ireland by a masterpiece of "wise" and "generous" legislation. *The Times,* and the Liberal press as a whole, after a little hesitation, followed in the same course. So general was the approval that nobody thought of doubting its success. In a few days all was changed. The voices of hostility and denunciation were no longer confined to the ranks of the political opponents of the Government. Gradually the sounds of opposition swelled into a chorus of abuse. Nobody, even among those who had before approved, had a word to say for the Bill. The Irish Catholic prelates pronounced against it, and when it was known that the measure must therefore fail to satisfy those for whom it was mainly designed, the general volume of antagonism "grew mightily and prevailed." It is intelligible that many who were by no menus enthusiastic for the Bill, but were willing to tolerate or even vote for it, if by so doing the alleged grievances of the Irish Catholics were removed, should have changed their attitude when they found that such an idea was fallacious. But though this accounts for the revolution of view in question to some extent, it is far from doing so altogether. Among the opponents of the measure, who were before its eulogists, were many who cared little for the Catholic attitude. It would be unjust to charge the responsibility for their inconsistency upon the Prime Minister, as if due to omissions in his explanatory statement, which were only observed when the Bill itself was perused. No candid hearer of Mr. Gladstone's speech can deny that it contained a faithful and a remarkably full account of the provisions and character of the Bill. All the objectionable features afterwards enlarged upon in the debate were explained by the right hon. gentleman. Other circumstances must supply the reason why the measure in so short a time passed from "the crest" to the "trough of the wave." And some of these, we fear, will not be found altogether creditable to those to whom they apply.

If the defeat of the Government on the second reading meant and involved the loss of the measure, and an immediate change of Ministry, it might not perhaps be necessary that we should venture at any detail into the question. But an appeal to the country on a scheme of Academical Education Reform is a curious and unwonted phenomenon, and such an appeal whatever may be urged to the contrary must be made sooner or later. The constituencies might not be able to return a very trustworthy answer if the matter were limited to the rearrangement of the means for supplying Ireland with University instruction. But not only has the question been widened out by the circumstances from an academical and educational to a

political one, but there are general principles involved in its
settlement which it is fitting that the country should decide
upon. It would be unfortunate if there should be any uncertain
sound returned in regard to these. Hence it is desirable to make
plain so far as possible what these principles are, and how they were
affected by the Bill brought into Parliament by Mr. Gladstone.
We confess we view the loss of the Bill with some little regret.
It contained much that was obnoxious, not a little that was fitted
to arouse the indignation of the friends of education, some things
that would have proved damaging and mischievous, and at least
one provision which would have applied a policy directly at
variance with the policy now pursued towards Ultramontanism
by nearly every Continental Government. We believe there
should never have been, as there need never have been, any
occasion for a Bill of the kind. University reform in Ireland
was doubtless essential, and might have been effected at least
three years ago. Had Mr. Fawcett's Bill for the regulation of
Trinity College and Dublin University been then accepted by
the Government, and passed by Parliament with some additions
and modifications, all that was necessary might have been accomplished without agitation, and without inflaming religious animo-
sities or exciting sectarian prejudicies. But the course pursued
by Mr. Gladstone rendered a larger scheme of reform indispensable. After the Premier's speeches and Parliamentary tactics
in relation to Irish University education, which were traced out
in the last number of the "Westminster Review,"[*] it was no longer
possible for the Government to avoid dealing with the question.
The arguments of Mr. Horsman and others, to show that
legislation was unnecessary, were disposed of by Mr. Gladstone's observations in closing the debate. An Irish University
Bill was a necessity to the Government, but it was a self-imposed
necessity which need never have arisen. After the Premier's
speech, in which the old statement that the Irish Catholics had
an educational grievance was reiterated, and it was added that
the state of education in Ireland was "scandalously bad," the
necessity was made more imperative. Irish University Reform
has become both a Government and a Parliamentary question, and it is deeply to be regretted that it is so. Still the facts
being what they are, "something must be done." Successive
Governments have, by both word and action, admitted that the
British Legislature owes in this matter a heavy debt to Ireland,
more particularly to the Irish Catholics. The Queen's Speech
acknowledged that the rights of conscience are not under existing
arrangements duly respected. Parliament has virtually, if not
expressly, made a like acknowledgment. The question is there-

---

[*] No. LXXXV. Article on "The Gladstone Administration."

fore one that must impede legislation, and trammel the action of
our legislators, until by some plan or device which must assume
the character of a compromise, it can be taken out of the
way. The longer the "grievance" is permitted to remain, the
greater will the discontent of the Irish Catholics grow. They
have been offered a settlement, and have refused it. The offer
is the maximum of concession which any English Ministry could
venture to propose, and it included much more than Parliament
would have granted. The fact that so much was proposed to be
given them, emboldened them to ask for more. Nothing, the
Irish prelates plainly say, will satisfy them but an endowment,
an endowment not only of their College or University, but also
of their intermediate schools preparatory for the University. It is
needless to say that the Irish Catholics, in making such demands,
are crying for the moon. No Government, whether Tory or
Liberal, dare venture to revive the exploded policy of concurrent
endowment. Two members of the present Ministry—the President of the Board of Trade and the Chief Secretary for Ireland
—intimated their approval of the principle in the late debates.
Mr. Disraeli, as leader of the Opposition, in his buoyant and
vitriolic speech, did the same. But that is a subject on which
the country has fully made up its mind, and it did not need the
solemn appeal of the Prime Minister against any such policy, to
make sure that the nation will have none of it. But while this
is so, and the Irish Catholics, on the principle of the Scotch
proverb, which advises a demand for a gown in order to be sure
of getting a sleeve, must know they are asking what cannot be
granted ; the Bill of the Government has given them a pretext
for making very large requests. It is, in this view, a premium
on agitation. It encourages further demands. There will be no
rest or peace in Ireland till the question is got out of the way.
The Irish policy of the Gladstone Administration has borne its
bitter fruits. It is too late to repudiate the mischievous idea
of governing Ireland "according to Irish ideas." The mischief
has been already done. The Irish have been taught to measure
the legislation that will be granted by the magnitude of the
outcry they raise. Mr. Gladstone's large promises, his denunciations of the Upas tree, his profession that his policy would be
moulded upon "Irish ideas," have at last come home to
roost. Had Ireland been taught by the legislation on the Church
and the land, that what she would alone receive, and alone need
ask for, are measures based upon the principles of political justice,
we should not have been in the present muddle. It is the fatal
habit of compromise illustrated in the accidents and concomitants
of the Government's Irish policy that has brought our present
difficulties. The same habit was illustrated in the foiled
University Bill. But it would have been possible so to alter and

mould that measure in Committee that it might have proved
innocent, if not highly beneficial or useful. To have passed a
Bill that would have closed agitation, stopped the mouths of the
Irish prelates, made plain the final attitude of the Legislature
towards Irish University Education, and taken the question out
of the hands of party politicians, would have been worth some
sacrifice even of consistency. The blundering tactics of the
Government spoiled the prospect, once so hopeful, and insured
their defeat. When Mr. Gladstone found the Irish Catholics
were against him and the prelates irreconcilable, he set up Mr.
Cardwell to abandon those features of the Bill which attracted
Catholic support. This decided the Irish Catholic members to vote against the second reading of the Bill, and it
was the support of the Irish Catholic members, with a small
sprinkling of English and Scotch Liberals, that gave the Opposition their small majority. The leader of the Opposition had
not ventured to test the question as one of confidence or censure. The amendment of the member for King's Lynn was not
a practical proposal, and it was found convenient by Mr. Disraeli
virtually to disown it. Obviously if the Bill was to be accepted at
all, it was unreasonable to expect that Government should name
the members of the governing body of the new University before
it was known whether there was to be any such council. Mr.
Bourke's resolution was in fact dead before it was born, and
there was no other semblance of a party motion. The issue
thus came to be simply whether the Bill should be read
a second time or not. And if by an error of tactics, curious
in so experienced a Parliamentarian as the Prime Minister, the
right hon. gentleman had not repelled the confidence of the Irish
Catholic members who would otherwise have voted for the
second reading — for the prelates had declared the Bill might
be made acceptable by amendments — the second reading
would have been carried by a sufficient majority. Ministers
might then have withdrawn the Bill if they despaired of passing
such a measure as they deemed essential, or they might have
gone into Committee to discuss its various proposals on their
merits, as Mr. Gladstone professed his desire to do. Large
amendments would assuredly have been requisite, but none
greater than those that transformed the Conservative Reform
Bill of 1867 into a measure of household suffrage. The opportunity
was lost or thrown away, and the question of Irish University Education must sooner or later be appealed to the country.

The Bill which for a time brought us face to face with a dissolution and a general election, was described by Mr. Fawcett as a
compromise which tried to please everybody and ended by
pleasing no one. It bore on every feature and in every clause
the marks of Mr. Gladstone's too subtle intellect. No one

could agree upon a description of its fundamental principles. The interpretations of it were indeed of an inconsistent and self-contradictory character. It was a Bill for "the advancement of learning," but that vague definition of its purport throw no light on the manner in which the object was to be fulfilled. To "advance learning" by fettering the freedom of professors, imposing new tests more odious than the religious tests that were to be swept away, and by putting under a ban some of the most important branches of a liberal education, was a decided novelty. But none of these provisions were essential. None of them therefore contained the principle of the measure. It might be said that the centralization of University instruction, by founding and equipping a central University with which a number of colleges that might be either denominational or secular, was the main characteristic of the Bill. The fact that the Government, as Mr. Fortescue averred, looked forward to the Irish Catholics winning in time a large if not a preponderant influence over the governing body of the new University, and therefore over the whole system of University Education in Ireland, seemed to involve that the principle of the measure was the reconciliation of mixed with denominational education, with unhappily a strong bias towards the latter. There can be little question the Ministry themselves at the outset held this characteristic to be essential to their scheme. But when they found the proffered bait was not swallowed, that the prospect of crippling and ultimately destroying the Queen's colleges, overthrowing the Queen's University, and reducing the dignity and proportions of Trinity College, Dublin, was not enough to satisfy the arrogant requirements of a haughty priesthood, they sought out a new device. Mr. Harcourt, rejoicing in the prospect of the Attorney-Generalship, was permitted to announce the startling discovery that the principle of the Bill, "the only principle," he said, "on which he could or would support the second reading, was to affirm, consolidate, and extend the system of mixed and united education in Ireland." The ingenuity which this discovery betokened, deserves the reward which rumour says awaits the honourable member. We do not doubt that it might have been possible to make the Bill what he said. Only because we believe that might have been done, could we approve the acceptance of the compromise it embodied for one moment. But to say that through much alteration, and after many amendments, it might have been made to work in favour of mixed and united education, is very different from admitting that the extension of that system was the main principle of the Bill.

The Bill as introduced may be divided into two parts, the part which removed existing disabilities and the part which was con-

structive or reconstructive. So far as it merely did the former
it was objected to by no one. In abolishing tests, opening the
fellowships and scholarships of Trinity College, Dublin, to all
competitors irrespective of their religious opinions, and separating
the Theological Faculty from Trinity, it would have secured the
support of all Liberals and even of most Conservatives. Mr.
Fawcett's Bill did very much under this head what the Government proposed to do, and Trinity College, Dublin, fully accepted
the principles of that measure. Unhappily, the Government
were not satisfied with removing existing disabilities; they
sought to impose new ones. By what have been called the
"gagging clauses," power was to be granted to the Council
or Governing Body of the University "to question, reprimand,
or punish by suspension, deprivation, or otherwise, any professor,
teacher, examiner, or other person having authority in the University, who, when in discharge of his functions as a University
officer, may by word of mouth, writing, *or otherwise* be held by
them to have wilfully given offence to the religious convictions
of any member of the University." Professors would lecture
and teach with the threat held over them *in terrorem* of loss
of office for perfectly innocent observations and illustrations.
The capability of Catholics to discern insult and offence to their
religious convictions in the most legitimate arguments in ethics
or the most pertinent illustrations from history is boundless;
and a Council which might be determined to exercise punitive
discipline for such offences—on the motion, say, of Cardinal
Cullen—would obviously render freedom in teaching philosophy
and history impossible. It was a logical corollary therefore
from the bestowal of such a power on the Council to prohibit,
or at least to discourage the cultivation of these branches of
learning. Accordingly it was declared that the University
should have no power to examine or to appoint any person as
professor or teacher in modern history or moral and mental
philosophy. The highest honours and the most lucrative emoluments in the University were to be opened to competitors who
might be innocent of a knowledge of ethics and metaphysics and
of modern history. Of course the result must have been the practical discouragement of these branches of culture; the degrees
of the new University must consequently have been deteriorated,
if not rendered worthless. A Faculty of Arts, which it was
Mr. Gladstone's main object to establish, without philosophy and
history, must have been a maimed and distorted image of what
such a faculty ought to be. What has Ireland done, it might
be well asked, to be punished after this fashion? The country
which produced a Hutcheson and a Berkeley, and which now
ranks distinguished metaphysicians among the fellows and tutors

of its chief college, deserves better of a Government calling itself
Liberal, than to see its University instruction condemned to intellectual barrenness and its University degrees made a laughing-
stock among the universities of Europe, under the plea that it
was done for "the advancement of learning." No wonder the
House of Commons burst into incredulous laughter when Mr.
Gladstone made the announcement in his most solemn and
serious manner. To fetter professors by making criminal their
unintentional offences against the "religious convictions" of any
member of the University, to create a faculty of arts from which
moral and mental philosophy and modern history were excluded,
to make University degrees independent of all knowledge of
these branches, and above all—as is laid down in a further clause—
to prohibit the disqualification of candidates for holding "*any
particular theory in modern history, moral or mental philosophy,
law, medicine, or any other branch of learning,*" are strange
ways of "advancing learning." Such proposals unhappily do
not cease to be mischievous by the fact of their rejection, when
they have emanated from a responsible Government, particularly from a Liberal Government. Irish Catholics are now
able to adduce the 'authority of the most Liberal Government
Britain has ever had, for the assertion that it is impossible for non-
Catholic teachers and professors to give instruction in philosophy
and history without affording them reasonable ground for offence.
Philosophy and history must be taught only by professors fresh
stamped from Cardinal Cullen's orthodox mint; for though a
Liberal Government has declared these branches of culture non-
essential, Catholics are too acute to believe anything of the kind.
Only, the philosophy and history fit for the ears of the faithful
must emanate from their own fellow-religionists. We fear the cause
of learning and culture in Ireland has received a heavy blow from
the well-intentioned blundering of the Gladstone Government.

The second or constructive portion of the Bill was not
liable to such serious objections as the first, though on some
points it would have been necessary to amend it. The general
object of this part of the measure was to create a new central
University, to be both a teaching and an examining institution,
to which existing colleges and others, it might be afterwards
created, should be affiliated. In his comprehensive introductory
statement Mr. Gladstone sought by an elaborate historical argument to prove that the founders of University instruction in
Ireland aimed from the outset at the establishment of a complete system, the head of which should be a University in
Dublin with a body of subordinate colleges attached scattered
over the country. From the unsettled character of the times,
and the vicissitudes to which Ireland was exposed at the hands of

foreign invaders or her own home factions, it was impossible to
realize the great conception. Trinity College, Dublin, under such a
system, would only have been one of the subordinate institutions,
the University of Dublin which had come to be merged in as
united to the College being the head. In order in these more
peaceful and settled times to realize the historical idea, Mr.
Gladstone therefore separated Trinity from the University. The
former would remain a college as before, while the latter was to
become a body corporate bearing the name of " The University of
Dublin," and having all the rights and privileges of a corporation. This body it was proposed to endow largely out of the
funds of Trinity, the property of the Disestablished Church and
the Consolidated Fund. It would have become the great degree-bestowing body of Ireland, and would have had a complete
equipment of professors, scholarships, fellowships, and the other
requisites of a well equipped University. For the regulation
of its affairs, a " University Council " was to be instituted, to
which would pass all powers and privileges exercised by the
provost and senior fellows of Trinity in regard to the control and
regulation of the University. Now as this great teaching and
examining body, the head and model for all Ireland, would
naturally determine the character and value of Irish University
degrees and of Irish University culture, it was obviously of
the last moment how the governing body that was to regulate its affairs was constituted. If the Irish Catholics, if
Cardinal Cullen and the Ultramontanists, could manage by any
device to gain a majority on the Council, it is plain the control
of Irish University instruction might easily and naturally pass
into their hands. Parliament was therefore entitled and bound
to be jealous on this point. The Queen's University, Dublin,
was within two years to be dissolved and incorporated with the
University of Dublin ; and though two of the three Queen's
Colleges were to be allowed to remain, Galway College was to
be dissolved before 1876, while of course Belfast and Cork
Colleges would be affiliated to Dublin University, as also, it was
expected, would be the Roman Catholic University of Dublin.
The University Council would thus have been the supreme
source of academical culture, the fountain of academical honour,
and the origin of all University distinctions in Ireland. The
proposal of the Government was to govern the University
by a Council of twenty-eight ordinary members appointed in the
first instance by her Majesty ; that is to say, by the Ministry of
the day, supplemented by an indefinite number of collegiate
members. Thus in the first instance, and for a period of ten
years, there must have been a government of the University by
a body which, if not itself political, owed its appointment to a

political source, and as the Lord Lieutenant was to be the Chancellor of the University it is difficult to see how the management could have been other than of a political character. As the institution of a new University by the Crown acting on the advice of the Minister of the day must in any case necessitate the appointment of a governing body more or less political in its origin, we do not so strongly object to this portion of the Ministerial proposal. But a new element came into consideration in connexion with the collegiate members. Every college of the University having fifty of its members matriculated as scholars of the University was to be entitled to return one person as a collegiate member of the Council, and if it had one hundred and fifty members so matriculated it might return two. An opening was thus made by which, as by an avenue, the Irish Catholics might have gained large and even determining powers over the University Council. From the analogy of the Irish National Board of Education, it may be concluded that in selecting ordinary members the Government would have had regard to the religious opinions of the candidates. An attempt would probably be made to balance the Protestant by the Roman Catholic element so as to please both. Both Roman Catholics and Protestants would have sought to win influence if they could through their representatives in the deliberations of the Council. The means of adding to the number of their representatives would be found through the collegiate members. Colleges might be affiliated to the University with this as the principal object in view. In Ireland, as in other countries, there are a number of educational institutions which assume the lofty title of college, though they are in reality nothing better than private boarding-schools. We do not suppose that immediately on the passing of the Bill a multitude of these would have sought affiliation to the new University in the manner anticipated by some members of the House of Commons. Before the debate on the second reading began, Mr. Gladstone intimated with a view to allay such fears, that he was prepared to make the affiliation of the colleges to the central University conditional on approval by the Crown. This might have been to some degree a safeguard. But the transfer of the power of affiliation from the Council to the Castle, as was the substance of the proposal, would not really have made much difference. The atmosphere of the Castle is not so free from suspicion of intrigue that we could welcome the change as any enormous improvement. There can be little doubt the collegiate members would have represented religious prejudices and sectarian prepossessions more than anything else. And there is no reason why in the course of a few years the dexterous management of Cardinal Cullen might

not have secured complete control, through a majority subject
to Ultramontane influences, in the University Council, and
therefore over Irish University Education.

As the Bill has been lost it is not necessary that we should go
further into its details. Enough has been said to show its
general character and probable effects, and to enable us to illustrate from it the struggle of conflicting principles which Irish
University education involves. It was pre-eminently Mr. Gladstone's workmanship, and after all that had gone before, its failure
made the right hon. gentleman's resignation inevitable. He
could not with self-respect or without grave detriment to his
political character have done otherwise. It was natural for his
admirers in the press and the House of Commons to counsel a
different course. It was true that the vote against the Bill did
not necessarily involve a vote of censure on the Government's
general policy, or imply that they had lost the confidence of
Parliament. It would probably have been practicable to obtain—
as Mr. Gilpin benevolently designed — a vote of the House
affirming that the Liberal majority retained its confidence in the
general policy of the Ministry, notwithstanding the vote of the
12th ult. But the acceptance of such a loophole of escape from
a situation of his own making, after failing disastrously with a
measure designed to complete a broad scheme of general policy
applied to Ireland, would have been alike undignified and unworthy of a great statesman. The Prime Minister's mind was
evidently full of forebodings of the issue before him from the
moment of the change that swept over public opinion in regard
to his measure. His speech at the banquet to Mr. Locke King
at Croydon on the 5th ult. proved that. He vindicated the character and career of his Ministry as if expectant of an early
termination of its existence. His demeanour and bearing also
in his impressive speech at the close of the debate conveyed
anticipations of the coming event which had been casting its
shadow before for some days previously. The right hon.
gentleman spoke with a weight and solemnity that betokened
his full appreciation of the crisis, and his conviction that the
fact of his Irish Bill being weighed in the balance and found
wanting could only have the one result. That result will be
the reference of the question who shall govern England to the
constituencies through a general election. The country will be
called upon to sit in judgment on the Gladstone Administration.
Through the delay between the resignation necessitated by the
defeat of the University Bill and the general election—during
which the Ministry must to some extent be a Government on
sufferance—the issue to be decided may seem to be apart from and
to have little or no reference to that Bill. The spokesmen of the

late Government in the press endeavour to represent the matter thus. They tell us that the nation is called upon to decide between two sets of statesmen and two political parties in view of their general principles and past services. Therefore they logically ask the constituencies to take into account only the career of the Gladstone Administration, its great legislative achievements, and the virtues and abilities of its members. If we might trust the gushing language of its eulogists these are such as to render the result sure. It may seem expedient in a merely party light to stake the matter on this issue. But to ask us to blot out of remembrance the Irish educational policy of the Ministry, which is really what is done, is to demand what it is impossible to grant. That is inwrought with the character and career of the Government, and the University Bill was only its final outcome. Yet even in a party light we do not think Mr. Gladstone need object to have his Ministry tested by that measure. For with all its evils and defects it proved one thing which it is gratifying to learn: it helped to remove the prevalent impression that Mr. Gladstone was prepared to gratify the Ultramontane party in Ireland at all hazards. There was much in Mr. Gladstone's language that seemed to warrant, if not even to compel to such a conclusion. The refusal to accept Mr. Fawcett's Bill, the repeated admission of a great educational grievance affecting the Irish Catholics, the almost tropical vehemence of the right hon. gentleman's language about the Upas tree, and the eagerness with which he insisted upon the necessity of bestowing powers and privileges upon the Irish Catholics beyond what they now possess were naturally believed to indicate if not subservience to Ultramontane designs, yet a readiness to play into the hands of the Ultramontane party. The excited imaginations of fervent Protestants represented the Premier as in close alliance with Cardinal Cullen. He was seriously believed by many to take his instructions direct from Dr. Manning. It must now be seen that these suspicions wronged the right hon. gentleman. So little was there a compact with the Irish hierarchy that they indignantly denounced and disowned his Bill. He had not even been in communication with the bishops, as his predecessors in 1866 and 1868 were. And though his Bill was founded upon a false principle, it was not of a nature to give the Ultramontanists the advantages they have been long pressing for. So far as it did that at least it did it by clauses which might have been lopped from the measure without destroying it.

In this aspect then Mr. Gladstone may be benefited by the rejected University Bill. He has many reasons to wish that some popular notions and traditions regarding him should be

revised in the light of that measure. Therefore it seems short-
sighted policy for his admirers to wish to withdraw the Bill from
the elements given to the country out of which to form its
opinion regarding the character of his Administration. If it
were otherwise it would be hopeless to expect the memory of
the University Bill to be blotted from the record. The fact
that dissolution is deferred until, it may be, time has been given
to allow the Bill to fall into the background in the popular view
does not affect the matter further than this: that the subject
will not bo so prominently before the public as it would have
been in the event of an immediate dissolution and a direct
appeal to the country on the issues of the Bill itself. It is
impossible that large reference should not be made to it in
order to enable the country to decide upon the merits or demerits
of the Government Irish Education policy. And to leave that out
of account would be, if not the play of *Hamlet* without the part of
the Prince of Denmark, yet the play of *Hamlet* without its Polonius.
We have said that the principle of the Bill, so far as we can
make out after all the repudiations and contradictory statements of the past, was the reconciliation of denominational with
mixed education, though with a strong bias to the former. If it
had been possible to get rid of that bias a measure might have
been passed by which not only the legitimate grievances of the
Irish Catholics might have been allayed, but the pledges of the
Government would have also been fulfilled. The creation of a
new University by separating the University of Dublin from
Trinity College, and endowing it from the funds of the latter
and the remains of the Church property, would have established
an institution which if not gagged and maimed as the
Government Bill sought to provide, would have given degrees
to candidates trained in denominational colleges, and provided the scholarships and fellowships which it is deemed
so necessary to offer for the competition of Irishmen. The
Queen's University as the head of the Queen's Colleges, must
in that case, however, have been permitted to remain a separate
and independent institution, and the Government must have
abandoned their idea of abolishing Galway or interfering
with Belfast and Cork Colleges. If the denominational system
was, out of regard for Catholic scruples, to receive a certain
measure of favour and patronage, it was but fair to require that
that should not be granted at the expense of the mixed system,
which, in spite of all Mr. Gladstone's statistics, has worked well,
and has only not succeeded in solving the problem of Irish
University Education more effectively because of the fanatical
denunciations of the Pope and the Irish Bishops. It might have
been allowed to the Catholics to win influence in the government of the new University, if care were taken by the con-

ditions established to prevent that influence being employed in furtherance of sectarian ends. Of course this University, though open to all candidates from the denominational colleges, must have been of a purely secular character, though not the castrated secularism of an arts examination from which moral and mental philosophy might be excluded. Equally of course such an institution would not have satisfied the priests and the bishops. It would have been complementary of the existing mixed system, not antagonistic to it. And it would have done little more in reality than might be almost as well accomplished, and at a much less cost, by a few changes and reforms on the Queen's University and Trinity College. Still we must pay for our statesmen's blunders, and the cost need not have been grudged if it removed the last shadow of an Irish "grievance," and made future agitation of the subject plainly futile. The Irish University system would have continued a mixed secular system. The denominational element admitted through the colleges and the influence of these on the central University might gradually have diminished in importance as the Catholic laity grew independent enough to defy the Ultramontanism of their Church and send their sons to the Queen's Colleges. If the Government Bill had been converted, as it easily might, into such a measure as we suggest, we should have stood on firm ground—we should have been generous without the sacrifice of principle, and even Mr. Gladstone's exaggerated promises would have been redeemed. All pleas for using the University question for political purposes and party ends would have been done away with, and the Ministerial crisis, of which we are feeling the effects, need never have arisen.

That chance has been lost, and the question is, What must be done now? The country will be called upon to declare in the coming general election—unless, which we can scarcely hope, the Government and Parliament are wise enough to accept and make the best of Mr. Fawcett's new Bill, of which the second reading will be proposed on the 2nd inst.—on what principles the University education problem of Ireland is to be solved and settled. There ought not to be much difficulty, and there must be no uncertainty in giving the answer. It is of course open to the Liberal Government to decline now to reconstruct the Irish University system so as to remove existing "grievances." Mr. Cardwell, in the speech in which he surrendered so many of the main features of the measure to which Protestants objected, intimated that they might feel "compelled" to adopt that course. Having exhausted every effort and made every proposition which their pledges and principles permitted them to make, and all to no purpose—all only to be met with contumelious rejection from those they sought to benefit—why should they make another

attempt ? Why not leave the Catholics to reap the fruits of
their folly, and as they would not take what was offered them
let them try some other plan themselves? This may be what
the Government will do for the present. They must leave the
matter alone till after the country has pronounced on the subject
by declaring whom it wishes to reign over it ; and if we could .
get the question of Irish education removed from the sphere of
political agitation, this would be the best course. Unhappily
the Gladstone Administration has rendered that very difficult.
But the debates and discussions of last month have cleared the
air. We know what the Catholics want and we know that it
cannot be granted. We know that the mixed system has not
been the failure they represent and Mr. Gladstone sought to
prove. Even in the case of Galway we know, from the opportune publication of the President's report, that it has done and
is doing good work. If it had not been for the denunciations
by the Catholic authorities of the mixed system, the Queen's
Colleges would have probably done for Ireland all that was
necessary. The fact that notwithstanding the free use of all
the artillery of Romish curses against them, they are growing in
numbers and importance and gaining a stronger hold on the
Irish people, proves their success. The very magnitude of the
means used by Rome to crush them, shows how much it thinks
it has cause to dread them. If the public mind of Ireland were
hostile to these colleges, we may be sure Rome would not waste
so much ammunition upon them. " Why," as President Berwick
asks in his report, " have rescripts been obtained from Rome to
crush them ?   Why have synods been held under every circumstance of solemnity that can give them importance to overturn
them ? Why do the press, the altars, and the hustings resound
with denunciations against them?' If the Irish Catholic laity
were so inveterately opposed to the system of united education
and so attached to denominational education as has been alleged,
why has the Catholic University—situated in the capital of Ireland and surrounded by more than 200,000 Catholics, with a
staff of professors of eminence, and as large inducements to
students in the shape of scholarships as any of the Queen's
Colleges possess—not been much more successful ? as President
Berwick asks. The total number of students (Episcopalian,
Presbyterian, and Roman Catholics) attending Galway during
session 1868-9 was 150 ; session 1869-70, 138 ; 1870-71, 123 ;
and 1871-72, 141. These figures include students in law,
medicine and engineering, as well as occasional and non-
matriculated students. If we take the numbers of the arts
students alone, which Mr. Gladstone says is the only fair test, we
find that in 1868-69 there were 38, the following year 37, in
1870-71 there were 35; and during the last session, 43. On

tho average the half of these were Roman Catholics. These are not great results, but a University system is not founded in a day or even a few years. It may be taken as demonstrated that the united or mixed system, which by its three colleges has educated upwards of 5000 individual students, of whom a considerable number were Catholics, has not failed. Besides these 5000 who have entered the Queen's Colleges during the twenty-two years of their existence, there have been from six to seven thousand students who have entered Dublin University during the same period. Considering that the population of Ireland has diminished from seven and a quarter to under five and a half millions, we do not think there is reason for despondency if we consider all the circumstances and difficulties of the case.

Statistics are proverbially fallacious, and the use made of them by Mr. Gladstone in his opening speech afforded striking proof of the fact. Without entering into the controversy carried on by Dr. Lyon Playfair on the one hand and the representatives of the Irish Catholics on the other, there is yet clear warrant for affirming that united education in Ireland has been a fair if not a brilliant success, although all the weapons in the armoury of Rome have been sharpened against it. It has had but a brief time of trial, for what are twenty years in the history of a people when a great educational experiment is being tried? To subvert, or greatly to cramp and interfere with it would therefore be a supreme act of national folly. One great principle of Irish educational policy to be maintained must be the continued support of the mixed system. Yet the opposition of the Roman Catholic bishops to that system cannot be wholly ignored. However little we may sympathize with it we must regard it, as Mr. Lowe said, as "a convulsion of nature—such as an earthquake or a famine—as something which cannot be helped, and must be made the best of." The Queen's Colleges and the Queen's University have done much, but (thanks to this opposition) they have not realized all the hopes entertained of them. A portion, whether large or small, of the youth of Ireland are at present unable to obtain degrees because of the condition that, in order to receive a degree, the applicant must have studied either in Trinity College or one of the Queen's Colleges. It is legitimate to seek to remedy this "grievance" by ceasing to require residence in Dublin University or the Queen's University, and merely to require candidates for degrees to pass certain examinations. The establishment of a new University accessible to students applying for degrees wherever they might come from, would have done this. It was not necessary that the new University should be the only source of degrees, or that in order to its success the Queen's University should be abolished. The result then would have virtually been to

establish two mixed Universities instead of one. The reform
of Trinity College, by separating the University from the College,
is reasonable and desirable. The oligarchy which rules there at
present is (we agree with the Chancellor of the Exchequer) a
discredit to the country. The abolition of tests, so as to enable
others than the members of the Episcopalian Church to receive
the benefit of the emoluments of Trinity, is not enough. The
constitution of the governing body requires to be altogether swept
away, and it was a disadvantage of Mr. Fawcett's Bill of last year
that under it the change in the constitution would have been
tardy and protracted over a long period.* The last shadow of
an Irish "grievance," however, would have been taken away if
the University had been separated from Trinity College, Dublin,
and made a degree-bestowing institution, though not necessarily
the only one. And it is because the Government Bill might
have been made to do this, while its other objectionable features
were got rid of, that we think its loss is to be regretted. In the
approaching general election the country will be called upon to
declare its resolution to maintain the system of mixed education
in Ireland. And we have little doubt it will show a disposition
to do all that can be done for the Irish Catholics in harmony
and consistency with that principle. The Irish bishops have
declined the generous offer made them of a richly endowed
University, specially devised so as to give degrees to the students
trained in their denominational colleges. That, however, need
not prevent the renewal of the offer if there were good reason
to believe it would ultimately be successful in overtaking the
wants which the bigotry of the priests and the fanaticism of the
bishops prevent being supplied in other ways. A heavy reckoning ought to be exacted from the Liberal members whose votes
have been the means of destroying the prospect of a settlement
of the question and of paving the way to a Tory Government.
The Government gave up the "gagging clauses," they were evidently prepared to abandon the idea of interfering with the
Queen's Colleges ; they would have consented to the continued
separate existence of the Queen's University, to the appointment
of professors of mental and moral philosophy in the new University ; the collegiate element in the University Council if not
dropped altogether, might have been modified so as to supply
only a deliberative and not a controlling element, and the new
University would have been a teaching as well as an examining institution on the basis of the principles of united education. Of course, this implied the sacrifice of much that was
of the essence of the Government scheme ; but when all that

---

* Since the above was written Mr. Fawcett's new Bill has been issued. It
is on this point a decided improvement upon the last.

remained was the creation of a new mixed University in place of the Dublin University, which at present is the adjunct of and subordinate to Trinity College, it is difficult to understand why the Liberal members should have voted against the second reading. Their votes, though few in number, were sufficient to determine the result. Messrs. Horsman, Bouverie, McCullagh Torrens, Akroyd, and one or two more, have brought us the Ministerial crisis, and prevented further dealing with a Bill which might in Committee have been made all they themselves could have wished it to be.

One great advantage of the fight over Irish University education is that it is at length settled that secularism is the only principle on which the State can deal with the question. Even the Tories are now bound to a secular policy. Mr. Gathorne Hardy, though a rigid denominationalist in England, avows himself a secularist across the Channel ; and, as Mr. Harcourt said in the recent debate, talked "pure League." We cannot expect the Tories will be logical, and having found this principle to be best for Ireland will see that Imperial legislation is bound to apply it to England as well. But it is something to have the truth recognised even to this partial or merely geographical extent. "Concurrent endowment," as Mr. Disraeli said, "is dead," and it is one of the greatest of Mr. Gladstone's services that he has killed it. The Catholics too have helped. By the extravagance of their demands, which would allow them to accept nothing short of open and systematic denominational endowment, they have made it certain that they will not get concurrent endowment in education, even in a covert and underhand manner, as we feared might have been the case. Their refusal of the Government's generous offers, will have the effect which the refusal of the Sibyl's books in ancient Rome is fabled to have had. Successive offers must be of a diminishing amount of concession, as they continue to be refused. If they have, and should again reject another chance, for the removal of their educational "grievances," the result can only be that they will get nothing beyond what they may have at present. And their fate will not deserve either pity or sympathy. The result, however, will perhaps be to give a powerful stimulus to Home Rule in Ireland. Indeed that promises to be the one great legacy which the Gladstone Government will leave to us in the sister island.

In the course of four years and a half Mr. Gladstone has succeeded in getting rid of the most magnificent majority any Liberal Ministry has ever had in England. We have shown before how he has managed to do this by playing fast and loose with principles. He has at last fallen—for his overthrow must date from the vote on his University Bill, whatever the upshot at present may be. The Upas tree of Irish educational grievances has proved the Upas tree of his Government. He has frittered away the enormous influence he had by the uncertainty of his policy and indirectness of his aims, and the vagueness and dubiety of his principles. He might have done all he has succeeded in doing in the past, and avoided the dangers by which he has fallen at last by, a little prudence and the practice of straightforward common sense. He might have completed his Irish policy by "a great and generous" measure of University education had he avoided the tortuous paths he seems to love; and instead of assailing, taken his stand steadfastly upon the principle of united education. By his blunders and shortcomings, which have been often vexatious, because so gratuitous, he has not only shaken confidence in himself, but rendered the prospects of a Liberal Government doubtful. The extravagance of the demands of the Irish Ultramontanists shows how well fitted his language was to encourage expectations sure to prove illusory. And he has thus, by the reaction which their awakening to the truth must occasion, given a powerful stimulus to the demand for Irish Home Rule. A general election will alone exhibit the full extent of the mischief that has been done to the Liberal cause. The Conservatives have long boasted of the Conservative reaction. It is time to ascertain with what warrant they have made the boast. Only an appeal to the country can test the question, and that appeal may be a matter of months. What is likely to be the result? Is the country likely to declare for Mr. Disraeli in preference to Mr. Gladstone, or is there not a prospect of such balanced numbers as will give an impulse to political intrigues, and make power the plaything of unscrupulous factions? The answer to this question is not altogether easy. But the probabilities of the case do not encourage the hope of a strong Government. The Conservatives cannot—at least it is eminently unlikely that they should—overcome the majority against them. They may, and very possibly they will, reduce it considerably. They calculate, it is said, on keeping all the seats they have and gaining thirty from their opponents. This would not turn the tables on their antagonists, as on the smallest computation there must still be a Liberal majority of between twenty to thirty. Even, however, though what is called the Conservative reaction—which so far as it has any meaning simply signifies the weariness produced through the blunders and faithlessness of the Liberal Administration, and the consequent desire to try the experiment of a change of rulers—were more thorough and enduring than Conservatives themselves venture to hope, there is no prospect of such a House of Commons as would secure a working majority for a Tory Ministry. Conservatives are fond of adducing the parallel, as they deem it will be seen to be, of 1841. There was then a powerful Conservative majority returned which gave Sir Robert Peel the ascendancy for five years. The House of Commons, some time before that, had been enthusiastically Liberal, but the mistakes and incapacity of the Liberals had repelled the confidence of the country. It is forgotten, however, that the constituencies are no longer the same now as then, as little as the circumstances are. Weariness and disgust among the middle classes, partly due to the errors of the Ministry and partly in reaction against the era of strikes, do not necessarily involve repulsion on the part of the constituencies which now include so large a working class element, likely to be more and more attracted to follow out schemes and a policy of their own. The Ballot indeed has proved a mistake so far as it was expected to help the Liberal party. Hitherto it seems to have rather operated in favour of the Conservatives. In reality we believe it will not make much practical difference if there be any issue presented for which the constituencies care. If they are in earnest, Englishmen will as a rule vote as they please, with the ballot or without it. In all probability then the new House of Commons will be very much the same as the present, with the exception that the Liberal majority may be a good deal smaller than it has been these last few years. A more balanced state of parties, however, means a time of weak governments. If there were any great question presented to the country on which the feelings of Englishmen were strongly excited, there can be little question that a decided majority would be returned of a Liberal rather than a Conservative character. There is no chance, so far as we can see, of the prevalent national tendency towards a progressive policy being abandoned for a policy of reaction. But it is possible enough there may be an interval in which the country will think more of measures of social than of political reform. Such an interval would be favourable to a Conservative Administration, not of the hybrid and uncertain kind which might be formed by and receive its character from Mr. Disraeli, but an Administration such as would be naturally headed by Lord Derby. The nation has confidence in the sound sense, statesmanly prudence, and shrewd far-sighted capacity of the noble lord. He might be able to form a Government that would attract the confidence of the country and the sympathy of a not inconsiderable section of the Liberals. And for a time such a Government might succeed in governing by the promotion of measures of social reform and by firm and able administrative service. In no other shape is a Conservative Ministry with any prospect of endurance possible. And the advent of such a Ministry might be of good service to the Liberal party themselves. Lord Derby would have fair play in trying his experiment, for there is a widespread idea that the Conservatives ought to have a turn to power, if only to let them have

the opportunity of verifying their long continued and rather
noisy boastings of the last few years. There is a good deal of
work to be done which he might do at least as well as the
Liberals. If an appeal were made to the country to decide
whether it would have Lord Derby or Mr. Gladstone to rule over
it, there is some probability the answer might be in favour
of the former. Mr. Disraeli must himself know that the prospects of his party, so long as he remains its leader, are far from
brilliant. There is no reason why he should not subordinate his
ambition to his party's good, and consent to serve under Lord
Derby as Prime Minister. It is scarcely likely, however, that he
will do that. Mr. Disraeli's ambition is very large. His confidence
in his own capacities as a statesman is boundless. He has long
waited for an opportunity in which he might try his powers.
His refusal to attempt to form a Ministry at the present time
was no doubt dictated by the conviction that his temporary self-
denial would soon receive its reward. He calculates on the next
House of Commons giving him his great chance. Even though
it did not contain a decided Conservative majority, it might yet
be so divided that the defeated and discredited Liberal Administration of Mr. Gladstone would not be able to stand against
their opponents. Mr. Disraeli may even calculate on a majority.
It is well known that he looked for one with some confidence at
the last general election. Though then disappointed, he has not
abandoned the notion of a Conservative majority to be found
among the householders. We deem it probable then that Mr.
Disraeli is possessing his soul in patience, in the firm hope of
seeing himself Prime Minister in the course of a few months.
Should that prospect be realized, we shall have a period of tactical administration fertile in combinations and intrigues.
Nothing is impossible to a Tory Disraeli Ministry, and the old
piscatory efforts to secure the Irish vote would doubtless be
renewed. If so, we cannot anticipate a period of legislation and
administration favourable to the dignified conduct of Parliamentary government. We may yet have more cause than at present
to regret the self-destruction of the Liberal leader, which has
dissipated a splendid majority in four years' time. We do not
say that the Gladstone Administration could have long attracted
national support even if its Irish University Bill had been saved.
The sacrifices necessary in order to pull it through Committee,
the throwing overboard of so much of the ship's cargo in order
to lighten the vessel, could not have failed grievously to injure
and discredit it. But we should have been in a better position had the Bill passed in some form, than we can hope to
be now. The means and instruments of Irish intrigues would
have been largely wanting; there could be no trading in Irish

grievances when the only "grievance" remaining was the legislative union, and the only cure for it Home Rule. The retreat of Mr. Gladstone, when it did come, would have been free from some of the sources of embarrassment which must now attend it. The Conservative Government would have had its day, and during the interval Liberalism would have been reinvigorated by the cold breezes that play along the Opposition benches. As it is, the situation is much less favourable and much more complex. If we should have a period of balanced parties—Governments with doubtful majorities, and consequently continuous intrigues on one side or another, or upon both, for the Irish vote—the result will be largely due to the nine English and Scotch Liberals who deserted their party on the morning of the 12th ult. From Irish Roman Catholics, ungrateful as their conduct proved them, much better was not to be expected; but it was different with the Scotch and English Liberals, whose co-operation with the Opposition and the Ultramontanists brought about the Ministerial crisis.

CONTEMPORARY LITERATURE.

THEOLOGY AND PHILOSOPHY.

THE editor's preface to Mr. Godwin's Essays[1] contains an extract
from a letter which the author meant for his daughter, Mrs.
Shelley, a few days before his death, stating his strong desire that the
work should be published, because its tendency was to free the human
mind from slavery. However we may regret the fact of its remaining
in MS. during her life, it is well that it should appear at length, in fulfilment of last wishes that deserve respect. The title-page, however,
should not have been altered from "the Genius of Christianity un-
veiled, in a Series of Essays," into the indefinite "Essays." It is interesting to read the ideas of a man like Godwin on the contents of
the Bible; for though his works are probably perused by few in the
present day, the author of "Political Justice," "Caleb Williams," and
"St. Leon," possessed remarkable talents. The Essays are scarcely in
the exact state or form which they would have presented had Godwin
himself lived to see them through the press. Some are fragmentary;
all have more or less of repetition. They are written in a plain, per-
spicuous style, without elegance or vigour. The sense is obvious.
Judged by the standard of to-day they do not possess a high value,
because all the questions treated of have received great attention from
critics and theologians. The light of modern science has largely contributed to a true estimate of the momentous topics to which Mr.
Godwin applied his strong common sense. The Bible is now understood far better than it was forty or fifty years ago. Hence the discussions need supplementing, correcting, and modifying, to adapt them
to present thought. Yet it is remarkable to note how far the writer
had emancipated himself from the orthodox notions in which he had
been carefully instructed, and proceeded in the path of freedom
characteristic of our own age. The principal tenet which haunted
the mind of the author and turned him away from Christianity
is that of eternal punishment, whose inconsistency with the benevolence of the Deity it is not difficult to see. Assigning to this an
exaggerated position in the conceptions both of the founder and early
disciples of Christianity, he gives a somewhat distorted view of the
entire teaching of the New Testament. In the absence of a critical
knowledge of the canonical writings, the essayist, unaware of the
way in which the Gospels grew to their present form, making little
allowance for different degrees of knowledge possessed by the authors
of the various books, or for the tendencies with which they wrote
according to the circumstances of the Pauline and Petrine parties at
the time, he often fails to give a correct description. In his judgment

---

[1] "Essays." By the late William Godwin. London: Henry S. King and Co.

of the character of Jesus, he quotes with little discrimination the Gospels as they are; without perceiving that many sayings and acts attributed to Him in those writings represent the views of His disciples thrown back into a prior time, or furnish distorted reports of what He really uttered. All His discourses, for example, in the fourth Gospel are the productions of a writer penetrated to some extent with Alexandrian philosophy. It should also be remembered that both He and His apostles spoke habitually in Aramæan, so that their very *words* are not given in the Greek. Occasionally too Mr. Godwin is incautious and rash, as when he says of Jesus, "No one before Him was ever so emphatical in asserting the doctrine of everlasting torments in a future world. He dwells upon this position ambitiously and eagerly, and is never weary of repeating it. He tells His hearers again and again, as we have seen, that there are few that shall be saved, and that the rest of mankind are doomed to everlasting burnings." This is baseless when the matter is rightly examined. The teachings of apostles should not be identified with those of the Master; and even the latter cannot at the present day be derived from epistles once attributed to them, but now discarded as theirs. The Essays, however, contain many just sentiments derived from reason, though sometimes opposite to apostolic ones. The Christian system, meaning by that all the dogmas inculcated in the New Testament books, cannot be accepted throughout. We must select what is to be approved, laying aside what does not harmonize with pure reason or the known attributes of Deity. This is what Mr. Godwin does; and though he conducts the process in a way not altogether satisfactory, handling texts injudiciously, confounding what are the essentials of Christianity with the unimportant, and lumping together the views of Paul and Jesus as though they were of equal or similar moment, yet his book may be read with profit by sincere inquirers who are indisposed to the perusal of that critical literature which, beginning with Strauss was followed up by Baur, and is still in progress till its settled results establish themselves in the minds of intelligent Englishmen. But the book must be read with discrimination, since it propounds statements opposed to present conclusions respecting the contents of the New Testament.

The lectures delivered under the auspices of the Christian Evidence Society do not improve in quality. A second series has been issued,[1] dealing with important questions, in the preparation of which both laymen and clerics have lent their aid. With the exception of the first two lectures, the volume presents nothing striking or good in the way of argument. On the contrary, the matter is inferior; the knowledge imperfect or incorrect. The "Philosophy of Human Responsibility" is a weak essay, destitute of philosophical ability, acuteness, and strength. The worst lectures are those "On the

---

[1] "Faith and Free Thought. A Second Course of Lectures delivered at the Request of the Christian Evidence Society." With a Preface, by the Right Rev. S. Wilberforce, D.D. London: Hodder and Stoughton. 1872.

Corroborative Evidence of Old Testament History from the Egyptian
and Assyrian Monuments;" "On the Argument for the Supernatural
Character of Christianity from its Existence and Achievements;" and
"On Man a Witness for Christianity." Those by the Dean of Ely,
Mr. Shaw, and Dr. Boultbee are better, but of no mark or value. If
the champions of orthodoxy mean to make breaches in the enemy's
fortress, they must employ weapons of a higher order than the present.
They must not deal in assumptions or vague statements. They must
not adduce opinions which have been set aside long ago, nor display an
ignorance inexcusable in the present day in all who profess to uphold
traditional opinions. Nor must clerics treat their readers to sermons containing the usual platitudes. The lectures of the Rev. Drs. Allon and
Angus are nothing more than discourses which might be addressed to
a Dissenting congregation, full of confident statement and barren of
sober truth. Christianity is spoken of, lauded, assumed to be of supernatural origin, called a system or plan, without a proper description
of its nature or essence. The Old Testament is viewed as typical of
the New, which it is not; intimations of a Messiah to patriarchs and
Moses are imagined; it is falsely stated that most scholars admit the
existence of the Pentateuch before the division of Solomon's kingdom,
and that the conception of God in Genesis is perfectly consistent with
the Christian representation. It is hard to realize the mental state of
one who can gravely assert that "a man's feeling about sin is the
measure of his likeness to God;" and talk of "the grand dogmatic
theology of Paul and John;" men whose theologies are broadly different. It is harder still to account for the extreme ignorance of one
who can assert that "when Jesus speaks of Himself it is to assert
His own faultlessness;" "that there is no indication of growth or
modification in Him;" and that the New Testament has "a marvellous unity;" as if the opposite doctrines of Paul and James about
justification were not patent to all. The whole lecture on the supernatural character of Christianity is a signal failure, consisting of a few
trite ideas current in orthodox circles, conveyed in an artificial style
out of harmony with their poverty. Nor is the last lecture better.
In point of diction indeed it is inferior. The lecturer gives an outline
of Christianity which he resolves into Calvinism, beginning with the
total depravity of human nature, the feeling of universal guilt, that
Christ in dying did homage to law, that evangelical holiness is begun
in the fear of punishment, that the conscience of men demands a Law-
giver and a Judge. As long as such a caricature of Jesus's moral
teachings, or even of the Pauline doctrine in certain aspects, is set
forth, man's best instincts will rebel against it. Mr. Shaw's lecture
on the evidences of Christianity deals with the subject in the old way.
It is feeble and inconclusive. The methods of Paley and Blunt have
ceased to be appropriate or effective since new light has been thrown
upon the canonical books by historic criticism. When he states that
the early era at which the Gospels were promulgated does not leave
time for legendary interpolations to have been made, the opinion is
wholly unfounded, as Tholuck himself admits. None of the Gospels

in their present state appeared till about the beginning of the second
century, so that sufficient time existed for legendary and mythical
elements to form themselves around the person of Christ. Sir Bartle
Frere's essay on the suitability of Christianity to all forms of civilization
contains a number of remarks loosely strung together, all tending to a
different conclusion from that which he seeks to bring out, provided
his assertions be scrutinized and the false separated from the true.
It is not easy to accept his statements in the face of history, of
known facts, and of independent witnesses. For example: "Christianity has in the course of fifty years made its way to every part of the
vast mass of Indian civilized humanity, and is now an active, operative,
aggressive power in every branch of social and political life on that
continent." Is this correct? The lecture on the corroborative evidence
of Old Testament history from the Egyptian and Assyrian monuments
shows more marks of ignorance than any other. Thus we are told,
the "king became *hypostated* into the Deity." The lecturer uses
" this *dicta, idiomatisms, sacrasanct, Apii.*" "The compiler of the Pentateuch was an Egyptian priest." The Ephod of Gideon was " a magnificent collar." " Egyptological study has become as necessary for
the interpretation of the Old Testament as that of Greek philology is
to the New," &c. &c. The volume must disappoint the expectations
even of the friends who are most ready to accept all that comes to
them from orthodox sources; if they will only read it attentively.
Nothing can be more detrimental to the cause of an exploded traditionalism than various phenomena presented in the book, the absence
of adequate learning to interpret the Bible, the misinterpretations of
Scripture, erroneous statements, unphilosophical remarks, unscrupulous
assumptions, grotesque phraseology. The men who undertake to instruct the erring in the interests of faith as opposed to free thought,
should refrain from saying that the word *firmament* in Genesis does
not mean a solid arch; that the writer describes only a partial deluge;
that there is a substantial agreement between Genesis and geology;
that Moses goes by external appearance in making the hare chew the
cud; that Adam is one of the *religious heroes* of Genesis; that metaphysical dogma of the very highest kind is of the very essence of
Christianity (compare the Sermon on the Mount for the contrary);
that water has long been a favourite theme with *natural theologians;*
that the Jews kept themselves untainted throughout with the slightest
trace of devotion to the unhallowed offering of man by man (see
Ghillany); that the figures in Genesis v. have been tampered with in
early days; for this is assuredly to prejudice the cause they support.
As long as they ignore and contradict the ascertained results of criticism, talking about Revelation and the supernatural with complacent
volubility while they neither explain nor defend the terms, they beat
the air.

It has been settled by modern interpreters that the design of
Canticles is to depict the heroism of wedded love in humble life. The
virtue of faithful affection tried by a severe test is commended.
The unity of the poem, as well as its authorship, by a member of the

northern kingdom, not very long after Solomon's reign, are generally admitted. The little work of Reville,[3] containing a good summary of the best observations that have been made upon the book, interspersed with remarks of his own, is excellent in design and execution. The author evinces good judgment, taste, and learning. After a brief history of the interpretation to which the canonical book has been subjected, he gives the fundamental idea of the poem, with some pertinent views of its dramatic and lyrical elements. It is then distributed among the speakers. The time and circumstances in which the song was composed are the last topics discussed. Few will dissent from the leading conclusions of the expositor. The difficult part is the division of the contents, to which we may add the translation. Here we should differ from the author in various particulars, especially in his introducing a chorus of Shulamites. His version, too, is not sufficiently exact. Perhaps, however, the translator has not produced the English of the original French, but in various cases that of our received version. Thus, in the fourth verse of the first chapter, "The upright love thee," should be, "They love thee sincerely." The book will serve as an admirable guide to all who desire to know the genius of the song, and to understand how a secular work has obtained a place in the Old Testament canon among religious productions. But it is not alone in this respect; the 45th Psalm and the Book of Esther having as little claim to a religious character.

A small book by the late Dr. Macleod, on the temptation of Jesus,[4] contains five sermons, which may have been preached in the state they are now presented in. The preacher begins with the personality of Satan, which he upholds on the ground of the literal record in the New Testament, and of a few places in the Old. Assuming the temptation to be historically true and objective, he dwells upon each of the stages in succession, and concludes with practical lessons. Difficulties never disturb the path of the preacher; he reads the Bible as the word of God, takes all its statements as literally correct, and constructs or presupposes a curious system of theology, in which Satan is the chief actor. As long as such views are propounded from the pulpit, or taught by the press, the New Testament will not be much esteemed by those who can separate error from truth. A few books would have taught the author juster ideas, and shaken his confidence in the superstitions he held. But he was not acquainted with Reville nor Roskoff, with Ullmann and De Wette. It is impossible to show the probability of Satan's personal existence. Modern thought has killed the imaginary deity of the multitude, as it has extinguished the belief in ghosts and witches. The Jews got the idea from the nations with whom they came in contact, probably from the Babylonians. The Apostles and New Testament writers were

---

[3] "The Song of Songs, commonly called the Song of Solomon, or the Canticle." From the French of Albert Reville, Doctor in Theology. London: Williams and Norgate.
[4] "The Temptation of Our Lord." By the late N. Macleod, D.D. London: Strahan and Co.

Jews, and entertained the notion naturally enough. Jesus himself
conformed to it. The correct view of the temptation regards it as
a historical myth, which represents in objective form certain ideas
that suggested themselves to the mind of Jesus at the beginning of
his ministry, but were at once repelled. The subject is well handled
by Ullmann in his treatise on the Sinlessness of Jesus; though in the
last edition he adopted a view more incorrect than that of the preceding ones. Insurmountable difficulties lie in the way of the objective and literal. How could the personal appearance of the devil be
a temptation to the Son of God? How did he go with him from
the wilderness to Hermon; and from Hermon to Jerusalem? Did
he fly with him through the air, and set him on a pinnacle of the
temple by superhuman power? How could he show him all the kingdoms of the heathen world and their glory? Dr. Macleod believes
that his temptations have been very prevalent in all ages; and sketches
a history of the Old Testament church in which Satan plays the chief
part. He knows a great deal about him, his plans, his purposes, his
doings. "A man who loves God is his greatest puzzle." "There is
no being who makes more gross mistakes." "The bribe which Satan
offered to our Lord was *life without God.*" Such is the interpretation of the kingdoms of the world and their glory. "The devil's
worship was set up by ten tribes at Samaria for two hundred and
forty years." In connexion with the subject, the record of the temptation of Adam and Eve is explained as if, it were a literal history of
what took place between Satan and the first pair. The opinions set
forth in the volume betray a total misapprehension of the subject; and
their sole tendency is to confirm the orthodox in glowing visions of
dualism dishonouring to a benevolent God.

The object of the anonymous author of "Thoughts on Recent
Scientific Conclusions and their Relation to Religion,"[*] is to suggest
difficulties in the way of scientific conclusions relative to man's abode
on the earth, and to bring the Mosaic cosmogony into harmony with
known facts. He argues against the proofs adduced for the great
antiquity of man, thinking them more conjectural than certain, and
inferring that the probabilities are as great on the one side as the
other. The spirit in which he writes is carping, without generosity
or mental power. His reasonings are disjointed and feeble. The
Darwinian theory and Professor Huxley's observations respecting it,
are criticised in an unscientific manner. The author is singularly
unhappy in his attempts to expound Genesis, so as to make it agree
with science. The record clearly implies a belief in the universality of
the Deluge; and it is doing violence to plain words to force upon
them a limited signification. "All the high hills that were under the
whole heaven were covered." "All flesh died that moved upon the
earth." It is also impossible for sound philology to separate the
second verse of Genesis i. from the first, interposing ages between
them; to resolve the days into periods; or to deny that there is a

---

[*] "Thoughts on Recent Scientific Conclusions and their Relation to Religion."
London : Strahan and Co.

different, and in some particulars a contradictory cosmogony in Genesis ii. from that in Genesis i. The author's reasoning is worthless in relation to the Mosaic account of the creation, as may be gathered from his appeal to "Wordsworth's Holy Bible," for nullifying the arguments which prove two writers in Genesis i. and ii. He should be aware of the fact that Dr. Wordsworth, though a bishop, is not a Hebrew scholar, so that he is incompetent to explain the Old Testament except in ways which modern learning has exploded. Like many others to whom Hebrew is an unknown tongue, he can pronounce an opinion about men and things for which there is no justification. One who characterizes Colenso's able criticisms on the Pentateuch as "mischievous and often childish objections," who talks, moreover, of Kalisch's "ignorance," should modestly refrain from mistranslating Genesis ii. 10, lest he appear presumptuous, while ignorant of Hebrew, in doing violence to the original text for the purpose of harmonizing accounts of the Creation that resist unnatural manipulation. The book is a feeble attempt, however well meant.

Dr. Matthew Arnold does not over-estimate the gravity of the question which he undertakes to help towards a rational settlement.[*] Religion and theology have long been divorced; or rather the latter has been put into the place of the former, and has effectually smothered it. Scientific precision, definiteness, metaphysical subtlety in the domain of the spiritual, are foreign elements that suppress its life; making the Bible a plaything for the acute mind that loves to theorize rather than act, to speculate rather than do hard work. The object of the book before us is to show what religion is, and thus to save the Bible for the people, who are ready to cast it aside because of the orthodox theology with which it is charged as it comes to them from the hands of its professed friends. The theme is of immense importance; and Dr. Arnold can treat it with the freedom of a layman, unshackled by subscription to creeds. Coming to the study of the Bible as a man of wide culture, of literary habits and tastes, outside the theological ring, averse to the tactics of the metaphysical religion current in the Church of England and the sects, though not unacquainted with their jargon and jarrings, he possesses qualifications that belong to few, and claims a candid hearing from all truth-loving readers. It is obvious that the received theology is a hindrance to the Bible; so that he who puts the right construction on the Book, giving it a real, experimental basis, does a thing imperatively needed at the present time. According to Dr. Arnold, the first step towards a right understanding of the Bible is to perceive that the language of it is fluid, passing, and literary; not rigid, fixed, and scientific. He shows that *conduct* is the object of religion; or rather *righteousness*, a word he prefers to the other, and which he takes to be the master word of the Old Testament. We are glad to find that he makes no distinction between morality and religion except one of degree; the latter being *morality touched by emotion.* Israel seized and exhibited the idea that

---

[*] "Literature and Dogma: an Essay towards a Better Apprehension of the Bible." By Matthew Arnold, D.C.L. London: Smith, Elder and Co.

righteousness tendeth to life; and his intuition of God was mainly a consciousness of *the not ourselves which makes for righteousness.* But our author supposes that in process of time an *Aberglaube* or extra-belief came in on the basis of the original one that *righteousness tendeth to life,* amplifying but deteriorating it. Such was the Messianic belief, especially as it became expanded in the books of Daniel and Enoch. Jesus restored the intuition of God through transforming the idea of righteousness, bringing a *method* and a *secret;* the one *inwardness,* the other *self-renouncement,* both working in the element of *sweet reasonableness.* The proofs of Christianity from miracles and prophecy are shown to be useless; because miracles cannot stand the test of examination, and definite predictions are hard to find. The testimony of Jesus to himself is the main thing. Internal evidence is that alone by which Christianity should be tried. Dr. Arnold clearly sees also that both Apostles and other early witnesses were fallible; that they attributed to the Master sentiments he did not entertain; that they misapprehended his meaning, reasoned incorrectly, and misapplied Old Testament prophecies. *Aberglaube* re-invaded the region of religion, so that many notions are found in the New Testament, and many more have been since added, which mar the beauty of Jesus's own teaching. The book breathes a healthy spirit. It carries the reader along with it, and is substantially correct. The author shows an excellent critical faculty, and emancipates himself from the traditional opinions that disfigure the Bible and alienate many from its perusal. He goes through the books of the Old and New Testament with a firm step, extracting the best from them, and assigning the rest to their proper places. His description of the Messianic idea as changed and purified by Jesus is excellent; as are his remarks on the beliefs of the New Testament writers about the second advent of Jesus, his corporeal resurrection and ascension, his summoning all to judgment, &c. The author's effective exposure of the pretentious language used by the Bishops of Winchester and Gloucester, his remarks on the three creeds, his identification of the bishops and dogmatists with the chief priests and elders, of the Dissenters with the Pharisees, of the philosophical liberals with the Sadducees, are in his happiest style. The book is calculated to do more good than the officious Convocation speeches and writings of the entire clergy. It is an excellent antidote to their mischievous identifications of religion with absurd dogmas. As such we recommend it to the thoughtful, the moral, the religious, to whom it will suggest correct ideas of a volume which has still its value, however dishonoured by the praises of advocates who misread its contents. Its tenor and tendency are admirable. In a few details the author is not so exact as is desirable; nor do we think that he has correctly apprehended several expressions put into the mouth of Jesus. His remarks on the Fourth Gospel need correction, for he assigns the discourses it contains to Jesus himself, in a considerable degree. No result of criticism seems to us more certain than that these discourses proceed from an unknown writer. In like manner the first Epistle of Peter cannot be the genuine work of that Apostle. It is too Pauline. Dr. Arnold sees rightly that the Ephesian letter is not

Paul's own; but he does not see the disparities between the Fourth Gospel and the first Epistle of John, which disprove identity of author-ship. Nor is it correct to deny opposition between James and Paul in regard to justification. The Apostle of the Gentiles was more technical in his phraseology than Dr. Arnold perceives. As to the Book of Ecclesiastes, it is by no means so early as the 5th century B.C.; and the chief part of the Proverbs does not date a thousand years B.C. The style of the book cannot he commended. The writer resembles a lecturer who tries to hammer a few leading thoughts into the heads of his audience by repetition and diffuseness. Reiteration and verbo-sity are prominent. Nor can we approve of the ingenious but peculiar method into which the esteemed author loves to put his arguments. Words and phrases are elevated into a sort of talismanic dignity, such as *righteousness: that not of ourselves which makes for righteousness; the method and secret of Jesus; the Eternal.* With respect to the last he ought to know that is neither an exact nor good translation of the Hebrew *Jehorah.* Had Dr. Arnold suppressed his idiosyncrasy towards peculiar methods and phrases which he compels to play a prime part, and been content with commoner, more elegant forms of speech, he would have pleased the reader better.

Mr. Shipley has edited another volume of Ritualistic Essays advo-cating ecclesiastic reform.[7] That such reform is necessary most parties in the Church admit; but how it is to be brought about, or to what extent, is matter of disagreement. The editor of the volume, in a long preface, indicates clearly enough the direction in which he thinks changes should be made; arguing from existing anomalies in the State-appointed final Court of Appeal, from the want of confidence in the bishops, from the constitution of Convocation, &c. But we fear that the causes of dissatisfaction with the Established Church are deeper than organic alterations in her machinery would remove. The connexion with the State is not a main source of grievance, except to a party outside' whose beliefs are probably nar-rower than those of the Establishment; yet a disestablished Church would admit the lay element, with which some hope of amendment might be expected to originate. Organic changes such as would adapt the Church to the intelligence and growth of the age need not be expected from clerics. The essays in this volume discuss the rela-tions between Church and State, Convocation and other Synods, Decay of Discipline, Cathedrals and Chapters, Rights of the Laity, Ecclesiastical Suits, Church Patronage, and Creeds in relation to Re-form. Elaborate in texture, carefully written, with an earnest aim and spirit, these treatises deserve the attention of all who are interested in the future of the Church. It is surprising, however, to observe the extent to which the authors have committed themselves in maintaining antiquated notions and superstitions. How they misunderstand the real essence of Jesus's teachings, or even of the Apostolic doctrines; how patristic theology has taken possession of them, how they are contented

---

[7] " Ecclesiastical Reform. Eight Essays by Various Writers." Edited by Orby Shipley, M. A. London : Longmans and Co.

to be led in the wake of antiquity and traditionalism; and how they are out of all harmony with modern culture and freedom, need not be shown. The bishops as a body seem to be in evil odour with these Ritualists. Contempt for their opinions and doings is often expressed. Vigorous assertion makes up for reasoning; and ignorance appears in dogmatic statements. Thus from the last essay, which is excellent in style, proceeding from a man of wide reading, we learn that the rejection of orthodoxy is a breaking the commandments of God; that the Athanasian Creed is the full development of the early baptismal formula which is given by our Lord himself, who appoints belief in it together with baptism as conditions of salvation, so that disbelief in that creed being in fact disbelief in that formula, involves "damnation" expressed by Christ. Thus words never uttered by Jesus, neither Matthew xxviii. 19, nor Mark xvi. 16, are made a divine basis for the damnation of all who will not accept a metaphysical and untrue creed. In other places the cause of infidelity is the counterpart of rejecting the principle of dogma; if one denies the authority of the Church in imposing the creeds, he is in the region of negative criticism, and must take the consequence; and the "creeds certify us of the meaning attached by the Apostles to their own statements in Scripture," which they assuredly do not, for they are human and unwarranted deductions from Scripture. Again, the Christian Church stands or falls, according as it is settled in what sense Christ is divine. The Universal Church is infallible; and men on low levels of faith doubt the real presence in the Sacrament. These and similar statements attest the measure in which faith or rather credulity has supplanted reason in the minds of a party belonging to the Church. The author of "the Decay of Discipline" laments over the practical disuse of measures which would tend to purify the body; but the time for the Confessional and Penance in a corporation that takes private judgment rather than authority for its motto, is assuredly past. His essay, however, is interspersed with stories of bishops and priests that enliven the pages. As long as civilization progresses and the press is free, we must look to men of letters for a right view of the Bible and its teachings; leaving ecclesiastics and their lay sympathizers in the bog of orthodox theology and superstitious ideas, the machinery of rites and ceremonies, in the thaumaturgy and the magic where they love to abide, till men of sense turn away from their illiberal dogmatism.

Few books have been subjected to a criticism so searching as the so-called Speaker's Commentary on the Pentateuch. Bishop Colenso[*] continues to examine it with minute attention, exposing its shallowness and evasions, with a calm confidence arising from his mastery of all the details. How easily he proves the commentators to be weak apologists for Mosaic authorship, need not be shown. His knowledge of the original, and fairness in dealing with it according to the light

---

[*] "The New Bible Commentary, by Bishops and other Clergy of the Anglican Church critically Examined." By the Right Rev. J. W. Colenso, D.D., Bishop of Natal. Part IV. Numbers. London: Longmans and Co.

he has got, contrast very favourably with the criticisms of men who are fettered beforehand. The fourth part deals with the book of Numbers. The Bishop has good reason to complain that no notice is taken by Mr. Espin of the fact, that the post-captivity origin of more than three-fourths of the book has been pointed out by Colenso and other critics; and that the evidence of composite authorship is never discussed. But historic criticism is not the forte of these orthodox commentators; nor do they wish to exercise it lest it prove troublesome in their hands. It is safer to ignore it, and fill their pages with geographical information. The following note is a fair instance of the Bishop's sound sense. After citing the comment on the trial of jealousy in chapter v. 11–31, he says:—

"This ordinance, which was meant 'to remove the very suspicion of adultery from amongst' the Israelites, was very one-sided, since it only attempts to provide for the detection or punishment of an adulterous *wife*, but says nothing about an adulterous *husband*. If 'the water was endued with extraordinary power by Him that dwelt in the Tabernacle' (p. 669), by having put into it some dust from the floor of the Tabernacle (ver. 17), surely this miraculous drink might have been expected to detect the sin of the man as certainly as that of the woman. But, as Mr. Espin regards this law not as divinely revealed—in spite of 'Jehovah spake unto Moses' (ver. 11)—but as 'adopted by Moses, like several other ordinances, from existing institutions,' he may be able to pass lightly over such an inconsistency and injustice as this."

The Bishop still relegates the greater part of the book of Numbers to his L. L. or later legislation; and divides many chapters in a way that appears to us incorrect. Thus he assigns xiv. 26–38 to the post-captivity time. This needs revision. Whatever be said of other verses, 36–38 are clearly Elohistic. We observe too that he adopts the notion of two *Kadeshes*, and places one of them at Petra, which is exceedingly doubtful. Nor can we approve of chapters xxvi.–xxxii., which are Elohistic, being put into the post-captivity legislation. The strength of the Bishop's criticism lies in detecting and exposing the manipulations of the orthodox commentators who force the records to speak in accordance with an early and Mosaic authorship.

The object of Principal Tulloch in his recent volumes[*] is to sketch one phase in the religious history of the seventeenth century which has not received full or adequate attention; or that middle and moderate party which was neither Laudian nor Puritan, the Latitudinarians of the time. Thinking that the questions discussed by the liberal theologians of that century are mainly those still agitated under the name of Broad Churchism, he has set himself to the task of expounding the views of the men who were most prominent or active in working out the great problems which still occupy the intellect and direct the aspirations of theologians who rise above the dogmatisms and disputes of the times, longing for a comprehensive Church where unity

---

[*] "Rational Theology and Christian Philosophy in England in the Seventeenth Century." By John Tulloch, D.D. London and Edinburgh: Blackwood and Sons.

may prevail in its highest earthly form; the unity of religious life and activity, not of creed or opinion. After two preliminary chapters on the spirit of rational inquiry in Protestantism and the course of religious opinions and parties in England, the author portrays the life and views of Lord Falkland, Hales of Eton, Chillingworth, Jeremy Taylor, Edward Stillingfleet, in the first volume. The second describes the Cambridge School, Whichcote, John Smith, Cudworth, More, with the minor members of the School, such as Culverwel, Glanvill, and others. The work shows the results of extensive and minute research, fair criticism, and comprehensive analysis. The author is discriminating and clear. His spirit is tolerant, liberal, devout. He sympathizes with the men whom he describes in many of their opinions and speculations, especially in their noble aims. Their exaltation of reason, of the divine in man, of the morality of religion and its conformity with right reason, call forth his admiring praises. The resuscitation of those almost forgotten men and their writings, seems to be a study congenial to his mind. Alien in spirit as he is both from the Augustinian dogmas embodied in the Westminster Confession of Faith, and the tenets of a sacerdotal theology; favourable to the idea of a comprehensive Church, national and liberal, embracing varieties of opinion on theological subjects, and insisting on life rather than creed, on true religion not dogma; he is fitted by the cast and colour of his mind for summoning forth these old worthies from their obscurity, and presenting them in their characteristic features of speculative thought to the approval of the reader. He does them full justice. Their merits are copiously illustrated; their defects touched with a gentle hand. Perhaps he overrates their importance and influence. They were certainly men of mark in their century, thinkers, philosophers, theorists, scholars, rational theologians, amiable enthusiasts—men of noble aspirations with a divine ideal of humanity before them; and posterity is indebted to them for nothing more than their inculcation of toleration in religion. In many respects, however, they did not rise above their age in leaning on past authorities and insufficient evidence. Their spirit and aims, though somewhat unpractical, are their chief glory. Principal Tulloch introduces short biographies of them which add to the interest of his narratives. But his chapters are too long. He devotes too much space to his heroes. The work might have been condensed with advantage into one volume had the extensive analyses of works and writings been curtailed. The quotations from these are needlessly numerous. He might have given summaries of their views in his own language, instead of transcribing entire pages in theirs. Even when he presents their opinions in his own way he is too diffuse. Occasionally too he digresses, as in speaking of Whichcote's Sermons having been edited by Wishart, where the latter is introduced and discoursed of. So of Emmanuel College and its founder, Sir Walter Mildmay. Though the author is a good historical critic, with philosophic breadth and discrimination, he puts too much into the men he eulogizes. He infuses at times the clearer notions of the present into words of the past. Their speculations receive an interpretation extraneous to the minds of the thinkers themselves. And in labouring to specify their characteristics he falls into repetition, wordiness, artificiality. Had he tried to depict their intellectual features and speculations in fewer, more exact, and discriminating words, his portraits would have left a clearer image on the reader's memory. As it is they are overdone, and become hazy amid accumulated sentences made up of words all but synonymous. Thus we read of John Smith's discourses:—

"Powerful and massive in argument, they are everywhere informed by a divine insight which transcends argument. Calmly and closely reasoned, they are at the same time inspired. The breath of a higher, diviner reason animates them all. The force of a logic nearly as direct and penetrating as that of Chillingworth directs an imagination as opulent as Jeremy Taylor's."

And of Cudworth:—

"Yet there is often a marvellous expressiveness in special phrases and passages; and the general effect is highly definite and significant. Taken as a whole, it is a marvellous magazine of thought and learning, and reminds one of the most undoubted monuments of the philosophical and theological genius of the seventeenth century."

Passing over some faulty specimens of style in the book as, "such men never have of anything which transcends the bonds of party;" "More's writings largely as they *bulk* in his life," we may remark that the Latin, and especially the Greek, of the volumes is incorrectly printed. One has only to look at p. 421 of vol. i.; p. 94 of vol. ii. and elsewhere, not to regret that the author failed to employ a scholar for revising the sheets. But the facts given in the work are generally correct; the information reliable. Dr. Tulloch is wrong about the Earl of Carbery who was Taylor's patron in Wales. It was not the first but the second Earl who befriended him at Golden-grove. The first Earl, John Vaughan, died in 1634, and did *not* therefore "survive to be rewarded for his loyal service at the Restoration." Richard Vaughan, the second Earl, sheltered the eminent divine. The leanings of the author are anti-Calvinistic and of the liberal Broad Church type of the Anglican Communion. He has less sympathy in the Westminster Confession than in the Articles of the Church of England, as is evident from his statements in p. 42 of the first volume, where the language applied to the Thirty-nine Articles admits of correction; and in p. 200, where we demur to the lauded "rationality of Christian sentiment which has been the peculiar glory of the Church of England."

The purport of sermons is to instruct and persuade. The preacher is supposed to possess a competent knowledge of the Bible, so that he can explain its principles and apply them to practice. It is assumed that he has the capacity of awakening his dull hearers from their spiritual sloth, pointing out to them their duties, temptations, and dangers. Now, however, dogmas are substituted for religion; and the inculcation of them is the main work of those who pronounce their platitudes from the pulpit week by week. Ignoring historical criticism or denouncing its conclusions, they proceed in the beaten paths of tradition. The sermons of Dr. Pulsford[10] are of the orthodox type, but tinged with a wordy mysticism that confuses the reader. No vein of clear or healthy thought runs through them. They are full of assumptions and errors, proving that the author is either ignorant of recent investigations in New Testament literature, or is content with dogmatic assertions which contradict that literature, in the directest manner. We have failed to find any intelligible meaning in a great part of his sermons. That on the Ascension of Christ is a notable example of these remarks. After asserting that the facts of the Gospel are inexplicable and incomprehensible as to their nature, and that we are constituted for the reception of such things, that the history of the Jews contains a complete history of humanity, and that the New Testament centres in the resurrection and ascension of the *body* of Christ (all contrary to fact); we are not surprised to read that "truths concerning Jesus, emasculated of their sacrificial contents, possess no gospel for man." The other sermons are similar in their baseless assumptions and unmeaning wordiness. Thus in the first, Christ is called "the door of creation's ascent and descent." "He carried on his heart, as the Great High Priest, the guilt of the world." "His poverty was vicarious." "He made himself, not only subject to the poverty of man's sinful history but to sin itself, and thereby made an end of it in its ultimate possibilities, &c." Seldom does such grotesque, inane orthodoxy appear in the shape of published sermons.— The volumes selected from the MSS. of the late Mr. Melvill are ushered in by a brief memoir of the preacher, written in an admiring and eulogistic spirit, but creditable to the heart of the unknown author. The sermons are of very various contents, doctrinal and practical. Based on what is usually considered evangelical doctrine and pervaded throughout by its spirit, they are composed in a clear style, full of pertinent illustration and felicitous images. Less ornate than Chalmers's, they resemble them in the reiteration of one or two ideas in each sermon; but the style is neater and more elegant than that of the Scottish divine. We can well conceive of their effectiveness; especially as the preacher was an accomplished elocutionist. Like most of the clergy, Mr. Melvill did not concern himself with modern inquiries into the books of the New Testament and their contents; he worked on the old basis, and thought of little else than persuading his hearers to believe in Christ as Saviour and Mediator. His forte was not the interpretation of Scripture, but the illustration of orthodox doctrine as bearing on the conscience and life. In the sermon on the

---

[10] "Sermons Preached in Trinity Church, Glasgow." By W. Pulsford, D.D. Glasgow: James Maclehose.

"Selection from the Sermons Preached during the Latter Years of his Life." By Henry Melvill, B.D. In Two Volumes. London: Rivingtons.

"The Perfect Life, in Twelve Discourses." By W. E. Channing, D.D. Edited from his MSS. by his Nephew, W. H. Channing. London: Williams and Norgate.

"Life: Conferences delivered at Toulouse." By the Rev. Père Lacordaire. Translated from the French, with the Author's permission, by H. D. Langdon. London: H. S. King and Co.

"Omissions of Scripture" he never thinks of his text (John xxi. 25) as not having been written by St. John; nor does he scruple to assert that Christ never passed a moment without a new work of benevolence and power. That on the "Last Judgment" is fitted to terrify; but he uses Scripture language improperly, and inculcates ideas which can proceed from the imagination alone. That on Trinity Sunday is a specimen of dogmatic theology from which reason and charity alike revolt. He who could assert that "the Athanasian Creed goes no further than Christ himself went," is surely ignorant of the ethics of Jesus; and in venturing to say that "to remove the doctrine of the Trinity is to remove whatsoever is peculiar to Christianity," truth is sacrificed to the rashness of doctrinal prepossession. Where the preacher confines himself to the practical, he may be listened to with profit; in matters of doctrine and in a right acquaintance with the Bible, he is untrustworthy. The majority of the sermons are on topics outside the beaten track of evangelical preachers, and deserve perusal.— Dr. Channing's sermons edited from his MSS. by his nephew, are worthy of his reputation as an enlightened preacher. Breathing a pure spirit of religion and holding forth a high ideal as the standard of humanity, they are fitted to enlarge and purify the heart. Having a conception of man's final destiny and perfectibility more comprehensive than that of most Christians, the distinguished orator of Boston expatiates on the moral side of human nature, its capacity for development, its longings and aspirations for closer union with the Infinite. A lofty moralist, he discourses about the objects of life, the religious element in man, and the means of its improvement. The sermons are pregnant with the enthusiasm of one to whom Christianity was a life instead of a creed, lifting him above the narrow views and rivalries of the sects that disgrace the very name of religion by their mutual jarrings. Whatever may be thought of the preacher's notions about the New Testament and the person of Jesus, he unquestionably caught the spirit of the Master and the essence of his teaching. According to him Christianity reveals the moral perfection of man as the great purpose of God. Its essence lies in raising the soul from the power of moral evil to perfection. The last sermon, on "the Church Universal," finely exemplifies the talents of the orator as he describes the living unity of all true Christians—their sympathies and faith—their interest in one another, and their joy in the progressive emancipation of their fellow-members from lower to higher steps of spiritual advancement. The ties between Christians in heaven and Christians on earth are exhibited in beautiful simplicity. The sermons will be welcomed by the admirers of Channing as fresh specimens of eloquent but thoughtful declamation—the musings of an idealist who did not lose himself in dreamy speculations, but entertained an earnest purpose of the amelioration of mankind. His end was practical; the improvement and perfection of the race. If he sought to accomplish it by exhortations pitched in a high key, or by taking a brighter view of human nature than what it presents—if he attributed more weight to moral suasion than appertains to it in a world of sordid action, he set forth at least a picture of perfection sanctioned by Jesus himself. Here and there, the reader will meet with sentiments hardly to be expected from a Unitarian. But Channing was one of an older class who are rapidly disappearing through the force of historical criticism. Miracles seem to him among the most reasonable as well as important events in human history. When he farther asserts that Christ came not merely to teach a doctrine, but to establish a Church, to organize a spiritual community, the language is incautious. To found a visible organized church seems not to have entered into the benevolent purposes of Jesus.— The conferences of Père Lacordaire delivered at Toulouse have *life* for their subject; one which is sufficiently vague for the impassioned father to dwell upon in figurative language. The main value of the discourses lies in their felicitous language, which is feebly transferred into English by the translator. The descriptions are peculiar, presenting much shadowy beauty enveloping a few common ideas. Man, God, Jesus Christ, are the centres round which the thoughts of the preacher revolve. The tendency of the discourses is to elevate and ennoble man by setting forth the Christian life as the highest, and by showing the source of man's happiness in the Infinite. It would be improper to bring logic to bear upon the sermons, for they are not essays, nor even Protestant effusions; they are rather the earnest, serious, eloquent outpourings of a mind in which feeling predominates— a mind fuller of faith than light, refined yet sensuous, in which religion is a sentiment and conviction devoid of intellectual force. The first discourse, on life in general, is a fair index both of the author's strength and weakness. That on the supernatural life is not so good. Too much is made of *seeing the person and substance of God;* but that resolves itself into seeing him whom he calls the man-God. According to Lacordaire the supernatural life is begun in us by the invisible light and movement of grace, while it is consummated by the vision of divine beauty and under the impulsion of divine love. Such descriptions are misty; but the orator's effectiveness lay in a cloudy atmosphere, where his imagination could play freely, without the pure light of reason streaming in to scatter the floating creations. The translation is capable of improvement. French words should not be retained when they can be rendered into English, as *burin* on page 162.

Dr. Newman is collecting his former writings into volumes[11] that follow each other in rapid succession. Encyclopædias and magazines to which he contributed in former years are pressed to give up their contents, that they may be embodied in a form more accessible to ordinary readers. The past fertility of the author was uncommon. He has discussed very different subjects—historical, classical, ecclesiastical, theological, logical; bringing to them all an acute mind stored with knowledge, applying itself to their exposition with facile tact and a power of lucid arrangement which enlists the reader's interest. His stores of information are unfolded in a manner and style singularly appropriate, having all the naturalness and ease of a practised author.

---

[11] "Historical Sketches. The Turks in their Relation to Europe; Marcus Tullius Cicero; Apollonius of Tyana; Primitive Christianity." By J. H. Newman, of the Oratory. London : B. M. Pickering.

The largest essay in the present volume is that relating to the Turks—the substance of lectures delivered in the Catholic Institute of Liverpool during October, 1853. The sketch in question, written immediately before the Crimean War, is spirited. The Turks are judged unfavourably, as the enemies of Christianity and the obstructives of modern civilization. The value of the essay does not consist in any fresh addition to the knowledge we already possess, but in the selection and arrangement of existing materials, the sagacious remarks interspersed, and the shrewd insight into character and motives which the author evinces. The zeal and hostility of the Romish Church for so many centuries against the Turkish power—especially during the pontificate of Pius V.—give warmth to his description; and the invading Mahometan is painted in dark colours not foreign to his true nature. After "the personal and literary character of Cicero," an article first published in the *Encyclopædia Metropolitana* of 1824, we have Apollonius of Tyana, from the same work. These are slight and popular sketches, reprinted in their original state. Baur's book on Apollonius has not been consulted; the ordinary sources, as Brucker and Olearius in addition to Philostratus's life of the philosopher, suffice. The series of papers entitled "Primitive Christianity" from the *British Magazine* of 1833–1836, were written under the assumption that the Anglican Church has a place in Catholic communion and Apostolic Christianity, which the author now denies. This portion of the volume is full of paradoxes and plausible statements which cannot stand the touch of reason or historic criticism. The author's knowledge of early Church history is defective, erroneous, one-sided. Contempt is poured on Protestantism and its right of private judgment; the Church is all in all. The very idea with which he starts is objectionable—viz., that the Primitive Church is that of Athanasius and Ambrose. Nor is it aught else than a baseless assertion that Christ set up the Church as "a peculiar institution, a visible home and memorial of truth." It is of no importance to us what Ambrose said about Primitive Christianity, or Vincent of Lerins. The history of Apollinaris, or Jovinian and his companions, or the Apostolical canons, speak in vain to our reason as witnesses for pure Christianity. Dr. Newman may adduce his reasons for believing that the skeletons of two martyrs restored his sight to a blind man at Milan; he may point in favour of the miracles to the testimony of Ambrose, Augustine, and Paulinus; it is insufficient to prove the truth of the alleged fact. With regard to the Apostolical canons, on which the author dilates with self-sufficient plausibleness, the reasoning is sophistical. Assumptions make up for evidences. Historical criticism, to which Dr. Newman makes no allusion, has shown that there is no reference to them earlier than in the Acts of the Synod at Constantinople (804), and that there is uncertainty even here. We cannot take the phrases *ecclesiastical canons, apostolic traditions*, &c., whenever they occur, as citations of the present canons, because they had a more general meaning. The existence of the collection at the end of the third century is unproved. Drey, himself a Roman Catholic, whose investigations we recommend to our author, does not date their antiquity so high. And they are incompetent witnesses to the state of Christianity even in the times at which they originated, much less to the state of Christianity in the apostolic period. In no proper sense can they be said to represent the mind of the Apostles, except in so far as they are derived from the New Testament. It is strange that one who reprints this essay on the canons, written almost fifty years ago, should ignore the literature of the subject since that day—the works of Bickell, Drey, and Dunsen.

Mr. Booth has put his name to the book issued anonymously about a year ago, and which now appears in a second edition carefully revised and improved.[11] It is unnecessary to do more than direct attention to a work which was formerly noticed in this Review. The time of its appearance is opportune. The author's views on the Church, on the world as controlled by immutable laws, and the prevailing orthodox system will be generally accepted by thoughtful men. He writes calmly, soberly, rationally, draws his conclusions from proper premises, and cites a variety of authorities in confirmation of his statements. A reflective reader, an enlightened writer, he discusses the great problems which occupy more or less the thoughts of man, as he muses on the world around and the powers within him. The work is highly suggestive, commending itself to all who desire to possess rational conviction instead of passive acquiescence, who are dissatisfied with current notions inculcated by theologians, and long for a purer atmosphere to breathe in, where their religious sentiments may have full exercise in reverencing the Infinite Power who informs the worlds of nature and mind.

Mr. Caswall has republished his volume of Hymns and Poems,[12] one-half of which contains translated pieces, the other half being original. It is not said whether the hymns are intended for public worship: if they be, doctrines should not be incorporated in them, but aspirations after a higher ideal, and petitions for grace to further them, and so to help to practice. Among the original pieces some are good; such as hymn xli., on page 248. The poem on "the temple of nature," page 450, has a measure of poetic beauty; and the two stanzas on "faith," in pp. 406, 407, are pertinent and happy. The majority, however, of the pieces, whether translated or original, are inferior in conception and quality. Tinged throughout with a strong flavour of superstition, and occupied with peculiar themes often unworthy of verse, they present a grotesque appearance. Good taste and refined feeling are alike offended by curious addresses to Mary, to apostles, to saints and their wells, to holy relics, and the plumes of a hearse. What can be more profane than—

"O, by that Almighty Maker,
Whom thyself a Virgin bore!
O, by thy supreme Creator,
Link'd with thee for evermore!"

[11] "The Problem of the World and the Church Reconsidered, in Three Letters to a Friend." By a Septuagenarian. London: Longmans and Co.
[12] "Hymns and Poems, Original and Translated." By Edward Caswall, of the Oratory. London: Burns, Oates, and Co.

What more absurd than—

> " What tongue, illustrious Spear, can duly sound
> Thy praise, in heaven or earth?
> Thou, who didst open that life-giving wound,
> From whence the Church had birth."

When Mr. Caswall describes the beauties of nature, addresses the seasons, or poetizes on the soul, he is natural, expressing his feelings in refined language coloured with beauty; but when he descants on the Church and its concomitants, he becomes sensualistic and mystic. His imagery is mixed with grossness. The idolatry of earth clogs the flight of his muse. It hinders heavenly purity by thrusting in persons and things whom he is unable to clothe with ideal beauty, because his conceptions of them are inadequate or distorted.

Mr. Benham has published a commentary on the lessons prescribed in the Anglican Prayer Book," which bears evidence of laborious industry and selection. His strength does not lie in the department of exposition, and his compilation is an uncritical one. No blame attaches to him for avoiding the apparatus and appearance of learning. A critical commentary would be out of place, unsuited to the purpose in view. But a writer who undertakes to give a brief explanation of the Lectionary should at least be acquainted with the best commentators. He should not confine his view to a few works and authors. Above all, he should look outside and beyond the limits of his own Church, supposing that all knowledge is not shut up within its members as a body. A cursory perusal of the volume, still more a minute examination of it, betrays its perfunctory character and inherent defects. Mr. Benham has neither selected his authorities with due discretion nor estimated their value aright. He is not an exact commentator, but one who is easily satisfied with superficial remarks. His authorities are mainly Bishop Wordsworth, Mr. Plumptre, Mr. Maurice, Dr. Pusey, Dr. Westcott, Smith's "Bible Dictionary," the "Speaker's Commentary," Archbishop Trench, and others, including Dean Stanley. The criticism and interpretation of the Old Testament have advanced considerably beyond these authors. Speaking generally, they cannot be relied upon as guides; and Mr. Benham often cites their opinions when they are wrong. This is especially the case in his introductory notes to books of Scripture. Thus among what he is pleased to call Professor Plumptre's *conclusions* as to the Book of Job, it is stated that "the foreign book came into Hebrew literature in the days of Solomon;" whereas it was neither foreign, nor so early as Solomon by at least two centuries. The "angel of the Lord," in Genesis xii. has for explanation the Bishop of Ely's note—a note containing a wrong view. Bishop Wordsworth's "exhaustive" introduction to the Book of Ruth is largely quoted, though it has no value. In the note on Daniel a long citation from Canon Westcott occurs, which gives an incorrect view both of its author and date.

" " A Companion to the Sanctuary: being a Commentary on the Proper Lessons for the Sundays and Holy Days." By the Rev. W. Benham, B.D. London: Macmillan and Co.

Indeed, all belonging to the Book of Daniel is misinterpreted, especially the prophecy of the seventy weeks in the 9th chapter. The reader is referred to Dr. Pusey's "exhaustive work"—a work which is a huge perversion of all that passes under the title of Daniel. The Messiah is not even mentioned by name in this apocalyptic, Maccabean book. Nor are Mr. Benham's own opinions more trustworthy than his quotations from others. Thus he says, that Genesis i. 1, is a distinct statement unconnected with i. 2; that *borrow* is a wrong translation in Exodus iii. 22; that the Canticles were written by Solomon in his young and holier years; and that the author of Deborah's song was herself. "Who shall declare his generation?" (Isaiah liii. 8), is explained, "Who shall tell the wickedness of the age in which he lives?" contrary to the true sense—viz., "Which of his contemporaries thought of it," &c. Mr. Benham says that God himself made Adam and Eve a covering which clothed them, taken from slain animals, so that the first institution of sacrifice appears in Genesis iii. This idea has been exploded long ago. But the errors of the volume are too numerous to be specified. The idea and plan are good; the execution inferior.

Mr. Thornton is a bold man.[14] He undertakes to refute the doctrine of Utilitarianism, even in the form in which Mr. Mill propounds and defends it. He combats the possibility of constructing a science of history, as Mr. Buckle defines it. He picks holes in David Hume's metaphysical coat, dashes against Huxley's protoplasm and materialism, points out the defects of Descartes, exposes Berkeleyism, demonstrates the weakness and credulity of scientific atheism where he encounters Darwin, Comte, and Lewes, and concludes with an exposition of the limits of theism, not without tilting against Professor Tyndall, Sir H. Thompson, and Mr. Galton as to the efficacy of prayer. He is a knight-errant on behalf of old ethics and metaphysics. Yet his spirit is good. Nor is his thinking power contemptible. Besides the amount of reading shown in his essays, he evinces a kind of analytical talent and dexterity exceedingly plausible. His command of vigorous, homely language is large. He is not very acute, a bluntness usually intervening to clog his perception; neither is his mind comprehensive in the range of its reasoning; but his remarks are direct and straightforward. We cannot say that he has contributed much to the elucidation of the difficult topics discussed, or that he has succeeded in dislodging from their main positions the formidable antagonists he grapples with. His inferiority in argument commonly comes out at the end, if not in some of the reasoning steps he takes. The arguments against Utilitarianism are not so strong as those which have been urged by others. He tries to show that it is both false and practically mischievous, resolving utilitarian law into this—that every man shall be a law unto himself; he avows belief in " natural rights," and uses many words to explain his meaning; but the impression left on the reader is not a conviction of the truth of his strictures. The

---

[14] "Old-Fashioned Ethics and Common-Sense Metaphysics, with some of their Applications." By W. T. Thornton. London : Macmillan and Co.

second essay is more plausible than the first, containing some effective objections to Mr. Buckle's theory, with others beside the mark. That on David Hume is the weakest iu the volume. When the philosopher asserts that "all our ideas or more feeble perceptions are copies of our impressions or more lively ones," Mr. Thornton supposes he has found a remarkable exception—viz., in the idea of an idea, which cannot be a copy of a sensation. But Hume speaks of *compounded* ideas as well as of simple ones; and in the former lies all that is meant by an idea of an idea. The philosopher's doctrines of cause and effect, of association and of miracles, are attacked without success. "No testimony," says Hume, "is sufficient to establish a miracle, unless the testimony be of such a kind that its falsehood would be more miraculous than the fact which it endeavours to establish." The proof from uniform experience against the existence of a miracle can only be destroyed by an opposite proof which is superior. Mr. Thornton argues that the completest uniformity of experience cannot create a certainty, but that it is *possible* for natural laws to be violated; and as miracles are violations of natural laws, it remains *possible* for miracles to happen. Of course many things are possible; but where is the testimony sufficient to establish the fact that the possible has become real in a single instance? The arguments against Huxleyism are sometimes strong, at other times weak. But the refutation of Berkeley is a failure. All the knowledge of matter we have is our perceptions of its qualities. The putting of a *power* or *force* into external bodies, by which they become the *causes* of our sensations, is an unwarrantable and unphilosophical assumption on the part of Mr. Thornton. After various remarks on Darwin and Comte, the author assigns the limits of demonstrable theism; and modestly intimates the efficacy of prayer upon man's spiritual nature. By admitting that the only gifts that can be prayed for unconditionally are spiritual ones, he takes a prudent course, in which divines should follow him. The book, though unsuccessful against some of the leading views it combats, possesses characteristic features. Mr. Thornton takes his stand against modern theories with manly bearing. In trying to upset he does not distort or misrepresent them; nor does he abuse their authors. He is a fair, intelligent antagonist, who gives reasons for his faith and doubts. If we cannot perceive the cogency or force of his arguments in many cases, we can welcome an honest inquirer seeking the solution of high problems in lines of thought different from Darwin and Huxley who are too averse to acknowledge a superior Intelligence, independent of and above matter.

Mr. Graham's object is to show the general meaning of Idealism,[16] and the connexion between the two great conceptions of the universe emanating from Berkeley and Hegel. It is his special purpose to explain the theory of Berkeley regarding matter, and to defend it against its many critics, especially Hamilton and Mansel, not excluding Kant. He is in the main a Berkeleyan and a Hegelian too. Rightly believing

---

[16] "Idealism: an Essay, Metaphysical and Critical." By W. Graham, M.A. London: Longmans, Green, and Co.

that Berkeley was one of the greatest philosophical thinkers, and that justice is only now beginning to be done to him, Mr. Graham undertakes to bring out the main points of his system in all their force, with a clearness sufficient to carry conviction on the part of metaphysicians who are not already wedded to other views. Among those who have apprehended and embraced to a considerable extent the principles of Berkeley, he instances Mr. Mill and Professor Fraser. Nor is our author less cognisant of Hegelianism, or of its best English expositors, Stirling and Hodgson. His sympathies are with it as well as with Berkeleyism, the two being different forms of idealism, the absolute and the subjective, or in other words, the rational and the theological. Berkeley's disproof of matter must be admitted as valid. Apart from our sensations, matter does not exist. The external world we commonly believe in is phenomenal. Hume and Mill adopt this conclusion. There is no evidence for the entity called matter. Whether the farther ideas of Berkeley be correct when he holds that the *ego* is given in consciousness and thence infers Infinite Spirit, is questionable. Hume denies that the ego is in consciousness. The book has four chapters—Historical Development, English and German Idealism, Idealism and Materialism, Berkeley and his Critics. The author has a full comprehension of his great subject. All modern metaphysicians of note pass more or less under his notice. He is acute and logical, going directly into all the points of idealism, and the developments which have arisen from it either by sympathetic progress or determined opposition. Where he objects, he gives a reason ;where he opposes, he does so with full intelligence. If he differs from the sensational idealism of Hume and Mill, or from Mr. Spencer's negative realism, he explains why he does so. For the natural realism of the Scotch school he has no words of commendation. He animadverts severely on Hamilton and Mansel, its best exponents. Some of the terms applied to Reid, Stewart, Beattie, &c. are rather strong, because they border on the contemptuous. We believe, however, that he has shown Hamilton's misapprehension of Berkeley very effectually. The form and style, for which the author offers some apology in the preface, are not good. Had more care and time been given, the book would have presented a more attractive aspect to the reader. The language indeed is vigorous, and the author's meaning not obscure; but repetitions and brief digressions mar the general effect. Short, however, as the treatise is, it has the seeds of promise. One who thinks so well on metaphysical subjects of the profoundest significance, and is able to defend Berkeley so successfully against able assailants, may contribute to the development of philosophical truth, and take his place among the best expositors of a completer idealism than that of Berkeley, or of a less daring but more invulnerable scheme than Hegel's *Thought.*

The author of " Philosophie als Orientirung ueber die Wellt,"[17] a very

---

[17] " Philosophie als Orientirung ueber die Wellt." Von Dr. J. J. Baumann, ord. offentl. Prof. der Philosophie an der Universität zu Göttingen. Leipzig : Hirsel.

readable book, is one of the great army of idealistic philosophers whose minds have been moulded and trained in the school of Fichte, Schelling, Hegel, and their contemporaries. There is this great difference, however, between the masters and the pupil we have now to deal with, that whereas the former remained true to their idealistic theories to the last, and passed away before the realistic reaction of the present day had set in, the latter has been fairly swept away by the current of that reaction, and landed on the terra firma of realism, even in spite of himself. The great purport of the work is to show that whilst the direct logical arguments in favour of a purely idealistic philosophy are irrefragable and intact, yet there is an indirect way, a kind of *back door*, by which we can escape into the broad daylight of natural realism without doing violence to the claims of philosophy itself. In the first two chapters (which run out into more than 200 pages) the author expounds with popular perspicuity the Idea of Philosophy, and demonstrates, something in the style of Berkeley and Hume, that logically speaking the universe can be known and comprehended by us solely in and through our own subjective impressions. Accordingly we are shut up in a logical circle, and there is no intellectual road by which an exit can be found from the world of ideas into that of external reality. This difficulty, as we said, is relieved by the discovery of an indirect route by which there is a safe passage from the one sphere into the other. We will not satisfy the reader's curiosity, or anticipate his emotions by describing what the route is; we advise him to procure the book and find for himself how the route opens before him as he proceeds. We do not *promise* indeed that he will feel himself sensibly wiser, or be more firmly convinced that a chair is a chair and a table a table than he was before. But this, at any rate, may be safely affirmed, that the lucid manner in which Professor Baumann lays down the problems he has to solve, the side glimpses he gives more or less into all the philosophical systems of the day, and the strong common sense which pervades his whole writing, cannot but be appreciated by the English reader who has enough German at command to peruse a philosophical work in that language with ease and fluency. The latter half of the book is devoted to an examination of the bearing which the philosophical principles propounded have upon the foundations of natural philosophy, mathematics, psychology, morals, religion, æsthetics, and life. These subjects are treated with a clearness of expression which is as uncommon as it is welcome in a German philosopher; and many remarks are made in the course of the disquisitions which are valuable in themselves, quite independently of any theory they may be designed to support. Whether the reader would incline to agree with the author, especially in regard to the views he entertains on the bases of morals and natural theology, is very problematical; but none can fail to be pleased with the honesty and lucidity with which the problems are stated, the difficulties solved, and the ultimate conclusions deduced.

Professor Fortlage is not unknown to the philosophical world of Germany. In the exciting period subsequent to the political commotions of 1848 he published a "Genetic History of Philosophy," from

Kant downwards. This sketch of contemporary German philosophy was justly regarded as one of the most successful attempts which had been made to interpret the whole of that very remarkable movement, and show the *logical* affiliation of the various systems springing out of the great Kantian revolution. In the year 1855 Dr. Fortlage published a very elaborate "System of Psychology," in which he attempted, as an admiring pupil, to complete the labours of Beneke, and bring all the resources of physiology to bear upon the elucidation of mental phenomena. The two short series of lectures before us "are somewhat closely related to the works already published. They reproduce many of the thoughts previously stated, only in a more popular form; and present some of the best fruits of philosophical research before the reader in the language of every-day life. The first series is almost wholly *historical.* It narrates the story of Kant's life and labours; shows how his philosophy worked upon the effervescing intellectual activity of Jena, as seen in the productions of Reinhold, Fichte, Schelling, &c.; how it reacted on literature as exhibited in Jean Paul and Schiller; and then led to the rise of of the Romantic school, as exemplified in the personality of Novalis. The other three lectures of this series take us back to the history of philosophy in Greece, and treat in an interesting way of the moral system of the Stoics and the symposium of Plato. The second series of lectures are almost entirely *psychological.* They begin with a disquisition on the nature of the soul, pass on to the most important points to be noticed in the theory of memory and imagination, expound the doctrine of the temperaments, discuss very ably the nature of instinct, and end with a lecture on the present features of materialism and idealism. The lectures are all strictly popular. They do not require for their comprehension any previous knowledge of German philosophy. They are replete with anecdotes and concrete illustrations. Those who remember the treatises of Dr. Abercrombie on the Intellectual Powers and Moral Feelings, have in them a good specimen of the *mode* in which the psychological topics are treated by Fortlage. There is the same felicity of illustration, though accompanied with a far greater reach of philosophical thought. Both series are well worth an attentive perusal.

POLITICS, SOCIOLOGY, VOYAGES AND TRAVELS.

A VERY clear and vigorous statement of the question of Irish University Education from a somewhat higher point of view than one of merely sectarian zeal or party politics is made by Mr. Robert D. Lyons' in an address on the "Supply and Demand

---

18 "Sechs Philosophische Vorträge." Von Dr. C. Fortlage, Prof. an der Universität Jena. "Acht Psychologische Vorträge." Von Dr. C. Fortlage, Jena.

1 "Intellectual Resources of Ireland. Supply and Demand for an Enlarged System of Irish University Education." By Robert D. Lyons, M.B. T.C.D., M.R.I.A. London : Smith, Elder, and Co. 1873.

for an Enlarged System of Irish University Education." Mr. Lyons
is Vice-President of the King and Queen's College of Physicians,
Visiting Physician to Maynooth College, and formerly Pathologist-in-
Chief to the Army in the Crimea. Though his arguments have, as
might be expected, a natural bearing in favour of the Catholic population of Ireland, they are made to rest, as far as possible, on a basis of
purely liberal principles or of irrefragable statistics. Mr. Lyons
argues that the Catholic Universities, and thereby the whole Catholic
population, have an undoubted claim to a large share in the national
endowments for the higher education, and it is obvious that no mere
construction of a new examining body accompanied with a weak and
colourless educational staff can satisfy this crying demand. Mr. Lyons,
speaking no doubt in the names of others besides himself, holds that
a settlement of the question must comprise two main conditions :
First, that any contemplated University Board should be one presiding
over all the Universities of Ireland, and dispensing the honours and
rewards in prizes, scholarships, exhibitions, fellowships, and the like,
through an Examining Board under its control, each University
College preserving its distinct autonomy. Secondly, that the Catholic
University, in its then collegiate capacity, should share in the public
endowments alike with all the other then collegiate bodies. The disabilities under which the Catholic University labours, and which prevent it operating more extensively as an educational institution among
the Catholics of Ireland are that :—(1) It subsists by voluntary contributions, which are wholly inadequate for the due extension and the
full working of its various faculties. (2) It possesses no adequate
funds and no sufficient material structure for collegiate purposes, and
for museums, libraries, and laboratories. (3) It can confer no valid or
legally cognizable status on students graduating in its Faculties of
Arts, Science, Law, or Medicine. The main point is that it is through
the development of this Catholic institution that the higher education
of the majority of Irishmen must be hoped for. Statistical tables
are cited by Mr. Lyons as to this.

The assertion that Nonconformity often entails the loss of citizen
rights is an old one, and just now a very loudly and frequently repeated
one. In pouring wrath on the heads of the three Commissioners
first appointed to expose and remedy the abuses of Endowed Schools,
those who make this assertion find themselves in strange company
with those whose usurpations they denounce. But "Vigilans"[a] shows
that history supplies good grounds for their suspiciousness of any Government officials or parties, and on those grounds he urges, what all
impartial persons most agree to urge, the need that Nonconformists
should exert themselves to the utmost to enforce their claims to equal
treatment. Probably, when the work of these much-abused Commissioners is calmly reviewed, it will be found that in cases where they
have admittedly blundered, it has been in consequence of the great and
often insuperable difficulty they have experienced in finding responsible

---

[a] " Nonconformists and their Rights as Citizens." By " Vigilans." London:
Elliot Stock. 1873.

Nonconformist residents either to be or to nominate members of the governing bodies of schools. With a curious disregard of a whole side of the question, "Vigilans" espouses the cause of the effate and obviously incompetent Governors of Emanuel Hospital against the reforms proposed by the Commissioners in its management.

Mr. Adams[3] publishes some facts necessary in order that persons may be able to make observations and suggestions upon the draft scheme for the future management of Dulwich College, recently published by the Endowed Schools Commissioners. He is anxious to counteract the impression likely to have been produced upon the public mind by certain publications emanating from some authorities in connexion with the College, and which are strongly in favour of such a reorganization of it, if any, as would result in converting it into a highly-paid school for the richer classes. Mr. Adams does not adopt the common "pity the poor" plea so familiar in connexion with the agitation about Emanuel Hospital; he appears desirous to keep closely to the wishes of the founder, and that the fees and general scope of the College should carry out those wishes to the benefit of the four neighbouring parishes most concerned. In securing this end Mr. Adams does not think the Endowed Schools Commissioners' scheme satisfactory, and he criticises both the system under which the College has been governed since 1857, and the new scheme most minutely and severely. Certainly the recent management of the funds and estates seems to require explanation or redress.

The topic of "Local Taxation" is one that owes its repulsiveness not so much to the minute details with which it is conversant, or to the haphazard principles by which those details are practically regulated, as to the impossibility of getting at the facts. Any one who has studied the report of the Select Committee of the House of Commons, presented in 1870, will understand what is meant when it is said, that almost infinite diversity and eccentricity prevails both in the laws governing the collection and imposition of the endless local taxes, and also in the modes in which the existing laws are carried into effect. Mr. Goschen[4] has contributed an extremely important work towards facilitating the discussion of all the matters involved by republishing a report made by himself when President of the Poor Law Board to the Treasury, to which are annexed a series of appendices of the greatest value. The purpose of these appendices is to show (1), the annual receipts and expenditure by the various local authorities in England and Wales; (2), the progress of the annual value and rateable value of real property in England and Wales, and of local rates imposed thereon during the present century; (3), the condition of taxation, local and imperial, of various countries of Europe. A variety of other kindred topics are included.

It is well known that the gradual codification of the laws prevalent in British India, coupled with the general movement in this country

---

[3] "Dulwich College and the Endowed Schools Commissioners." By John B. Adams. London: T. C. Davidson. 1873.

[4] "Reports and Speeches on Local Taxation." By George J. Goschen, M.P. London: Macmillan. 1872.

in the direction of legal reform, have caused increased attention to be
given to the possibility of constructing an English code. Since the
time of Bentham there has never been wanting a school of lawyers
and politicians who have earnestly, and at times eloquently, or rather
indignantly, advocated the necessity of this great measure being proceeded with. The main principles upon which the desirability of a
code rests are indeed now denied by scarcely any one. That "certain"
law is better than "uncertain," compendious better than voluminous,
"cognoscible" than hidden, are axioms or indeed truisms needing no
longer the fervour and rugged rhetoric of Bentham to uphold them.
In his new work on "An English Code,"[a] Professor Sheldon Amos
follows up the theoretical principles elaborated in his "Systematic View
of the Science of Jurisprudence," with a direct practical application of
them to the immediate exigencies of English law. Assuming that all
parties are agreed that a code is to be made sooner or later, it is of
vital consequence (1) to estimate the true nature and extent of the
difficulties which underlie the task ; (2) to ascertain the methods of
distributing the topics, of providing for the consistent interpretation
of language, of introducing the most expeditious system of mutual
references, and of having the code amended at regularly recurring
periods; and (3) to determine what are the true lessons taught by
the existing codes in force in other countries. Professor Amos advocates strongly the importance of proceeding with the whole code at
once, so as to insure the utmost unity and harmony in all its parts,
and in this respect he seems to be somewhat at issue with those who,
enamoured with the Anglo-Indian experiments, recommend fragmentary pieces of the code being made from time to time. The work
contains a careful analysis of the real difficulties in the way of codification of English law, resulting from the twofold system of law and
equity (a difficulty shortly to disappear under the new Chancellor's
hands), from the distinction of real and personal property, and from
the opposite character of common and statute law. A vast number of
contemporary codes are submitted to severe criticism, among which
are the New York codes, the Code Napoleon, the Italian code, the
Prussian Landrecht, and the Anglo-Indian code. The book concludes
with two chapters on the modern study of Roman law and of jurisprudence respectively, as affecting the question of codification.

The persevering efforts which Dr. Stirling has made in various forms
to familiarize English readers with, and to render intelligible to them,
the philosophy of Hegel are deserving of all thanks and commendation.
The lectures on "The Philosophy of Law,"[b] delivered before the
Juridical Society of Edinburgh, are a good specimen both of the merits
and the defects of Dr. Stirling's method. Dr. Stirling is a genuine
enthusiast in regard to philosophy generally and to Hegel in particular.
He looks for a corresponding amount of enthusiasm in his reader, and

---

[a] "An English Code ; its Difficulties and the Modes of Overcoming Them. A
Practical Application of the Science of Jurisprudence." By Sheldon Amos, M.A.
London : Strahan. 1873.

[b] "Lectures on the Philosophy of Law." By James Hutchinson Stirling.
London : Longmans. 1878.

no doubt he does a good deal to communicate it; but he somewhat
underrates the ignorance and obtuseness of even the more cultured
portion of the English public, and consequently hardly succeeds, with
all his labours, in conveying the actual position of the best German
philosophers in a really English garb. It is the purpose of these
lectures to explain the course of thought by which Hegel conceived
the notions of *person, property, contract,* and *penalty,* to travel as
it were into one another, and in fact to involve one another.
Dr. Stirling, in his last lecture, makes some sharp and almost bitter
observations on the writings of the late Mr. Austin, and indeed on
the English utilitarians generally.

Among the various recent works that have appeared purporting to
be modern editions, or amended forms, or improved imitations of
Blackstone's Commentaries, a little book by Mr. David Mitchell Aird,
called "Blackstone Economized,"[1] is entitled to hold a good place.
An immense quantity of most valuable matter is conveniently packed
together, with just as much detail as is needed for the commencing
student or even for purposes of ordinary reference. The typography
also is so managed as to display at a glance the contents of every
page, which is a great assistance to the rapid reader. We notice, by
the way, an inaccuracy in the description of the recent Naturalization
Act of 1870, of which it is said that a "declaration of alienage" is
necessary in order to a natural born subject ceasing to be a British
subject. On consulting the 6th section of the Act it will be found
that the mere fact of naturalization abroad, if undergone voluntarily,
results in the loss of British citizenship.

A "Profitable Book upon Domestic Law,"[2] may be sufficiently characterized by saying it is an attempt to make the study of law palatable to the writer's "fair friends," giving them "such a modicum of
law as may be profitable to them, or they may wish to know." It
contains some useful information and a good many legal stories.

It is perhaps an ungracious mode of criticising a work to say it contains
too much matter, but there are cases where, in view of the complexity
and special character of the matter, the mere quantity and compression
of it may constitute serious drawbacks on its aggregate value. Under
the title, "The Institutes of English Public Law,"[3] Dr. Nasmith con-
denses all the main materials of the Science of Jurisprudence, English
Constitutional History and Constitutional Law, and of a large portion
of English Criminal Law and of International Law. There is no
doubt an apology for this mode of distribution in the vagueness and
shiftiness of the expression "Public Law." Recent criticism, however—especially that handled by Mr. Austin—has pointed out the
worthlessness of this expression for any precise purpose of classification. All codifiers and text-book writers who have resorted to its use

[1] "Blackstone Economized : being a Compendium of the Laws of England to the
Present Time." By David Mitchell Aird. London: Longmans. 1873.
[2] "A Profitable Book upon Domestic Law." By Perkins Junior, M.A.
London : Longmans. 1873.
[3] "The Institutes of English Public Law." By David Nasmith, Esq., LL.B.
London : Butterworths. 1872.

have shown the utmost possible discrepancy with one another as to what they have comprehended under Public and Private Law respectively; and it is further true that in some sense all Law is *Public* as keeping in view solely the public good, and all Law is Private as·directly addressed to the individual persons whose rights and duties it defines. It need not be said that the book contains a vast quantity of varied and interesting, though somewhat cursory and desultory, information.

Mr. Walter Bagehot's well-known work on the English Constitution will have in some way prepared his reader for the general character of his new work on a profounder topic. The present work, entitled " Physics and Politics,"[19] is said to be " thoughts on the application of the principles of natural selection and inheritance to political society." The method of inquiry pursued, by which the processes of physiological science are applied to the more complex facts of political development, will be familiar to students of M. Auguste Comte, and more especially of Mr. Herbert Spencer. We have had occasion ourselves also to invite attention to the important historical speculations in the same direction conducted in the United States by Dr. Draper. The main danger in actually working out theories of this sort is lest the analysis be not fine enough, and therefore that some of the coarsest and most accidental phenomena be referred directly to necessary and permanent as well as sole-sufficient causes, instead of only taking their place as the special and temporary mode of development of a given community. A great part of Mr. Walter Bagehot's work is concerned with examining scientific propositions which now-a-days no one calls in question, and it may be doubted whether much is gained by further dwelling upon them. Everybody knows that it depends upon a vast number of favourable and fortuitous circumstances whether a tribe of barbarians ever becomes a nation, and that it needs a vast quantity of struggling, and physical as well as mental antagonism, both within and without, to bring into active energy the true vital elements out of which a self-conscious nation is finally formed. The mode in which "discussion" contributes to the education of these elements as well as to their culture and final growth is also now recognised with a considerable amount of general acquiescence; and it is also confessed that there is the closest analogy between all these events and the operation of the law of "natural selection" as witnessed in the "struggle for existence" of physical nature. It hardly needs Mr. Walter Bagehot to take the trouble to point out that "a government by discussion, if it can be borne, at once breaks down the yoke of fixed custom. The idea of the two is inconsistent. As far as it goes the mere putting up of a subject to discussion, with the object of being guided by that discussion, is a clear admission that that subject is in no degree settled by established rule, and that men are free to choose in it." It may be said in fact that Mr. Walter Bagehot's habitual excellence is the clearness and even liveliness with which he points out how very true and interesting are truisms.

---

[19] " Physics and Politics." By Walter Bagehot. London: Henry S. King. 1872.

All the social and economic problems to which the existing relations of capital and labour in the countries of modern Europe give birth will be found treated in considerable detail and with a careful balance of judgment between the claims of opposing theories by Dr. H. Maurus" in his work on "Freedom in Economical Relations." Of course, he commences by a philosophical estimate of what freedom truly means, and in his introductory chapters alludes to the various fanatical sections of society which would seek this freedom either in unrestricted anarchy and individualism, or in socialistic and privileged communities relying servilely on the general protection of the State. The problem of the work is to find the true limit of State interference which shall facilitate the attainment of the utmost possible personal freedom. The subject is tracked out through all its windings in the intricate regions of labour, wages, taxation, rights of property, competition, banking, exchanges, credit, and assurance. It is obvious that the actual practice of State interference for all countries is very different for these differing regions; and as the amount of that interference is rather determined by accident, caprice, or political selfishness, than by principle, the occasion for such a work as that of Dr. H. Maurus is great.

If the form of question and answer is to be retained for students who are no longer children, Mr. Nicholson's" work on the "Science of Exchanges" deserves to hold a high place as an educational treatise. Indeed the complex economical topics with which it occasionally deals render it a work which even general readers will find highly serviceable by way of clearing up their views of matters which, while everyone ventures to talk about, few people are accurately informed upon. In fact, it is this very implication of commercial and economical subjects with the dialogue of common life which renders the dress of conversation which Mr. Nicholson has chosen a peculiarly suitable one in his case. Generally speaking, the answers are short and direct, such as to the question—" What is the rate of exchange?" It is answered, " It is the price of the money of any one country reckoned in the money of another country." "Are strikes unjust in principle?" " No; there is no harm in men trying to get the best price for the commodity in which they deal, whether it be labour or money." Some of the answers, however, extend over several pages, and are in fact essays, as to the question—" What is the effect of a mintage or embargo on the manufacture of standard silver?"

Mr. Macleod's " Principles of Economical Philosophy" " will be found a very stimulating book by those who delight in controversy and are not repelled by a desultory and digressive style of composition. One of Mr. Macleod's objects is to shatter the position of a large class

---

11 "Ueber die Freiheit in der Volkswirthshaft." Von Dr. Heinrich Maurus. Heidelberg. 1873.

12 "The Science of Exchanges." By N. A. Nicholson, M.A. Fourth Edition. London: Cassell. 1873.

13 "The Principles of Economical Philosophy." By Henry Dunning Macleod, M.A. Second Edition. Vol. I. London: Longmans. 1872.

of Political Economists who insisted and still insist that the "value" of a thing is simply the quantity of labour embodied in it. Mr. Macleod wishes to substitute the proposition (which he holds is that of Hume, Condillac, and Whately) that demand is the sole general cause of the value of all things, whatever their nature be, and that their value or demand is the cause of, or inducement to, labour. He endeavours to show that the phenomena of value and the changes of value are governed by changes in the intensity of demand or in the limitation of supply. Some part of this controversy might, it would seem, be avoided by calling to mind the useful distinction between "value" and "exchangeable value." The value of a thing in one sense is simply its worth in the eyes of some person or persons contemplated by the speaker, and may depend upon the intrinsic usefulness or rarity of the thing—though as yet there may be no demand for it, as its properties or preciousness are not yet known. There is then a value independent of demand.

The work of Mr. Carey[14] on the unity of law, as exhibited in the relations of physical, social, mental, and moral science, may be described as a reactionary philosophic effort in opposition to what the author conceives to be the narrow and generally false views of the leading English Political Economists. Mr. Carey holds that so far from Mr. Ricardo's theory of rent being universally true, it is universally false. The real law is directly the reverse of that propounded by him; the work of cultivation having, and that invariably, been commenced on the poorer soils, and having passed to those more rich as wealth grew and population increased. When this rather startling proposition is amplified into all its applications to the facts of the material and moral universe, Mr. Carey's theory becomes fully constructed. In a few words this theory may be said to be, that man is constantly pushing his way forward and upward; first satisfying his material wants, then his simpler moral wants, then his higher social wants. At every stage he acquires increased capacity for association with his fellows and develops new and original faculties for perfecting that association. In this way the ulterior goal to which he is tending determines his history rather than the vulgar surroundings amidst which his early lot is cast. It is at this point that Mr. Carey joins issue with the English controversialists, who base the progress of mankind either on laws of population or on a struggle for existence.

The purpose of introducing the "British Metric System"[15] is sufficiently explained in the fact that "although we do an aggregate yearly business of some 380 millions sterling with nations using the metric system, yet not one in a hundred of our merchants, manufacturers, or dealers can quote without the assistance of a 'ready-reckoner,' an equivalent in metric measure and metric money for a

---

[14] "The Unity of Law; as Exhibited in the Relations of Physical, Social, Mental, and Moral Science." By H. C. Carey. Philadelphia and London: Trübner and Co. 1872.

[15] "Gregory's British Metric System: a Complete Non-Decimal Assimilation of the British to the Metric System, its Weights and Measures." By Isaac Gregory. London: Cassell.

foot, yard, gallon, pound, or hundredweight of anything he sells
to, or buys from, his foreign *clientelle.* The British Metric System,
which is fully elucidated and illustrated by copious examples in Mr.
Gregory's treatise, may be briefly described by saying it adopts the
French metric names, metric weights and measures for merchants;
but maintains the existing arithmetical modo of units and their halves
and quarters, under old names, for retail metric measures. "If our
merchants were now quoting in metros, with fractions in thousands,
their method would not disturb the mind or mode of a woman going
shopping for a meter and a half of ribbon, or a pound and a quarter
of meat, or two ounces of tea, or for any other part of a metric
measure."

Pending the much-desired establishment of Technical Schools in
England, and with a view to help forward the efforts of isolated
schools and teachers among us who arc anxious in some measure to
supply the void, Dr. Yeats has published, during the last few years,
several volumes designed to make Englishmen acquainted with the
essence of the technical school books of the Continent." He hopes
that the series he has thus begun will serve not only as text-books for
the use of teachers, but represent a class of books almost unknown in
England, namely—books for young people who have left school. Our
neighbours have an abundance of such books, intended to inculcate
self-support, and to induce to further culture, facilitating the retention
of knowledge already gained, and providing copiously for its increase.
They are calculated enormously to help forward scientific, manufacturing and mechanical invention, inasmuch as they do not fail, while
narrating the history of discovery, to point out still existing
defects, and thus stimulate the minds of the young "business
man." The first of these volumes contains an elaborate account of
the raw produce of the British Empire and of the countries with
which it trades, the relations between geological conditions and
mineral wealth, and between climate and soil on the one hand and
organic form on the other, and the modifications of animal and
vegetable life resulting from the conditions of climate and soil produced by varieties of contour and elevation. This is followed by a
scientific and practical account of the commercial products of the
vegetable, animal, and mineral kingdoms throughout the world, with
slight indications of the modes of manufacture needful to render
them serviceable, and of the purposes for which they are employed.
The amount to which the British Empire exports and imports each
article, either in interchange between its different members or with
other countries, is always approximately given. The second volume of

---

" "The Natural History of the Raw Materials of Commerce." By John
Yeats, LL.D. London : Cassell, Petter, and Galpin. 1871.
" The Technical History of Commerce." By John Yeats, LL.D. London :
Cassell, Petter, and Galpin. 1871.
" The Growth and Vicissitudes of Commerce from B.C. 1500 to A.D. 1789." By
John Yeats, LL.D. London : Virtue and Co. 1872.
"A Manual of Recent and Existing Commerce." By John Yeats, LL.D.
London : Virtue and Co. 1872.

Mr. Yeats' series is a history of skilled labour, as applied to production, from the earliest times until the present day. As the former volume described raw materials and their useful properties so far as these are presented to us spontaneously by nature, the second tells how latent powers and properties have been revealed by interference with nature. As the first was intended to further the study of sciences of observation, the second illustrates observation aided by experiment or labour. It traces the development of the necessaries of life, of comfort, abundance, leisure, and the arts and sciences. The third volume naturally goes one step further, to the history of the interchange of the products of nature and of skill throughout the world, up to the year 1789. Prefixed to it is an Historical Chart, showing the rise, 'progress, culmination and decline of commercial nations up to that date, and is a very useful gift to the student of commercial history. It cannot show the relations between contemporaneous trading peoples, nor the causes of their prosperity and decline; the bulk of the book is therefore devoted to supply information on these points. "For, next to a study of the materials and the means for the acquisition of wealth, an inquiry into the principles and rules for its preservation must be most important." The fourth volume, a history of commerce since the French Revolution up to last year, is necessarily somewhat more political in its structure. It is written in order to serve as a more permanent and satisfactory exponent of national progress than any temporary exhibitions can possibly be; and its aim is to prepare youths for the higher departments of commerce, as well as to assist ordinarily intelligent readers in arriving at sound conclusions with regard to the credit of any single State, and especially in studying the present or prospective position of our own country. Teachers and private students, as well as the whole of our commercial community, are laid under deep obligations to Dr. Yeats, both for the scheme of this series, and for the exhaustive and interesting manner in which he has carried it to its present point of development.

A nameless English adherent[v] of the Buonapartes describes in enthusiastic terms what he believes to be the reasons for what he asserts is the "longing of all France for the return of those to power who can give her peace, order, and prosperity—for the Empress-Regent and her advisers, who will guard the throne of Napoleon the Fourth." France has uninterruptedly held the foremost place in the Christian Commonwealth. Its organizing power has had no limits except the boundaries set by nature to human endeavours. Napoleon the First found France mad, headless, lawless, heartless, and he alone knew how to help her; his supreme love of law was the key to his character; he was the one Frenchman in whose mind the old ideas of organization co-existed as a passion in union with the new-born spirit of liberty; wherever he came there was freedom; he fell as a leader of men should fall, blasted by the calm forces of nature, not by

---

[v] "France, the Empire, and Civilization." London: J. Mosley Stark, 1873.

the energy of puny mortals. All that followed was bad and contemptible till Napoleon the Third appeared; he owed little to his name, but much to his known political opinions, and especially to his adherence to the theory of domestic government of his uncle. He was a man of untainted honour, incapable of treachery; strong and above corruption or any hunger for power. The members of the Assembly did not wish the Constitution to work, and so he fulfilled the solemn duty he had undertaken by sweeping away the useless Assembly. Under the Second Empire France enjoyed unexampled happiness and prosperity; but the Emperor was hurried into war with Prussia, and the wrong headed Liberals and the Paris mob prevented the Empress from treating for peace and saving the Empire. The Commune was a few mad fanatics supported by a horde of unknown ruffians. All men know that his death has taken from us the wisest ruler of our time, "the only one among them all who loved freedom and justice at once so well and so wisely, that he dared during his whole life to face obloquy, danger and death therefor." So says the unknown Buonapartist in our midst.

The English residents in Italy are resolved to redeem their race from the common reputation of luxurious idleness, and are, one after another, rendering great services both to their chosen homes and to the many countrymen who must share their pleasures for so short a time that complete and erudite handbooks can alone enable them to attain any satisfactory knowledge of the art of Italy. Mr. Story led the way with his "Roba di Roma," and the Misses Horner have well performed the work for Florence. They have a more directly benevolent end in view also, inasmuch as their hope is to awaken a more lively interest in the men who, under a free government and plebeian rulers, not only counted among their fellow citizens some of the most eminent poets, philosophers, and artists the world has ever known, but no less eminent patriots, legislators, and reformers in morals and religion. "A people who have produced such fruits, need but higher moral and intellectual culture to yield a still more abundant harvest." Commencing with slight historical and topographical résumés, the authoresses of "Walks in Florence"[18] proceed to describe in the utmost detail the principal buildings and galleries of Florence, with all available artistic, traditional, and historical information about every object of interest in them.

The readers of Mr. Hare's "Walks in Rome,"[19] must not be deterred from his new volume by the possibility that it may partake of its predecessor's guide-book character. It will answer many of the same purposes to a traveller in Spain, but it is also a very pleasant book for keepers at home. Mr. Hare's candid declaration that Spain is not beautiful, together with his frequent descriptions of the bare, treeless, stony wastes, and cold, dreary, tedious railway journeys will deter

[18] "Walks in Florence." By Susan and Johanna Horner. London: Strahan and Co. 1873.
[19] "Wanderings in Spain." By Augustus J. C. Hare. London: Strahan and Co, 1873.

quite as many from ever wishing to set foot in Spain as his enthusiasm
for the cities will attract. That Spain has great charms for artists and
architects is easy to understand, but Mr. Hare brings the extreme
discomfort of attempting to see its beauties into so strong relief that it is
just as easy to understand why those who do not court wretchedness
prefer to see them through the medium of well known illustrated
works.   It is a little astonishing to find with what comparative
oblivion of all that is dark and atrocious, Mr. Hare continually speaks
of the Philips of Spain, and how complete his sympathy appears to
be with the Duchesse de Montpensier and "poor Queen Isabella," while
he can speak with no regret of the contemptuous treatment that
Prince Amadeus met with at the hands of the Spanish Grandees.

M. de Carné was the representative of the French Foreign Office
on a commission sent out in 1865, to explore the river Mekong, and to
ascertain whether it was capable of serving as a highroad between
Cochin China and China.   The complete scientific results of this
mission will be told when the official volumes, delayed by the war,
appear.   Meanwhile the father of M. de Carné has published an
account of the journey, prepared by his son as a last effort before his
death." The Mekong proved to be not navigable, and the French
colonists of Cochin China must moderate their ambition for the future
prosperity of the port of Saigon; but the navigability, to within the
bounds of China, of the Songkoi which flows into the gulf of Tonquin,
is established and is of vital importance to French power in Cochin
China and the adjacent regions.   It may be that Englishmen should
hesitate to remark upon the patriotism which sees only subject of
admiration in the manœuvres or force which compel those parts of
the world to accept the protectorate and encourage the commerce of
France; but it is impossible to forego a smile at M. de Carné's naïve
expression of delight, that this time he and his compatriots have
succeeded where "Anglo-Saxons" have failed.   The practical results
of the mission were of great value to geographers, and may turn out
to be advantageous, as bringing to light the persistent encroachments
on the neighbouring territories made by the Court of Bangkok.   M.
de Carné thinks that by extending the French Protectorate, either by
diplomacy or force, over the smaller states, these encroachments will
be stayed, and that the end will be good.   The details of the journey
are well and interestingly told.

Records of mountaineering are apt to be very dry and unattractive
to any but present or aspirant members of the Alpine Club, and the
small public which enjoys the idea of men perilling their lives for
amusement in very cold blood; but Mr. King," a member of the
corps of the Geological Survey of California, brings unusual literary
ability to the task of describing mountaineering, undertaken neither
for the sake of danger, nor merely for pleasure, but in order to complete

   ⁺⁰ "Travels in Indo-China and the Chinese Empire." By Louis de Carné.
(Translated.) London : Chapman and Hall. 1872.
   ⁺¹ "Mountaineering in the Sierra Nevada." By Clarence King. London :
Sampson Low and Co. 1872.

tho necessary survey of the boundaries to be fixed between the different adjoining States. Mr. King probably is best known as the discoverer of the first fossil in the metamorphic Sierra, which he describes as follows—"The fossil, the object for which science had searched and yearned and despaired . . . . But all this came and went without the longed-for elation. There was no doubt I was not so happy as I thought I should be." Years afterwards his pleasure fully came when he met an aged German palæontologist, who greeted him with "a kindle of enthusiasm," crying "Ach! I have pleasure you to meet, when it is you which the cephalopoda discovered has." But the book is chiefly rendered attractive by the singularly picturesque language in which Mr. King transfers to his pages the very forms and colours of the wonderful scenery, the terrors of the wild Spaniard freebooters, and the squalor of the wandering Indians and perpetual emigrants who inhabit the Nevada and its adjacent plains.

Mr. Hazard,[13] the author of "Cuba with Pen and Pencil," an American newspaper correspondent, publishes the results of his own observations in San Domingo, fortified by laborious study of authorities in the British Museum. His own visit to the island was on the occasion of the United States Government sending out a Commission to report on the question of the admission of San Domingo into the Union, and he had the naturally resulting facilities and special difficulties in obtaining a knowledge of the physical capabilities and political condition of the two island republics, San Domingo and Hayti. Interesting as the first scene of Spanish Colonization in the West, and bearing the palm for antiquity in American History, the starting point whence Cortez and Pizarro set out for their conquests, and the place of Columbus's shameful imprisonment by Bobadilla, the Island is little less interesting now as belonging partially to an independent negro Government. Fortunately this is not the only one in the world; for, ever since Boyer's time, 1843, although the Constitution is well framed and the laws good, the country "has never ceased to be in a state of revolution caused by the ambition of those without occupation;" and as "the laws have never been observed," "their violation is the most natural thing in the world." Of course the old roads and bridges and other traces of civilization left by the French are rapidly disappearing, and the material condition of the people is deplorable. Yet so great is their dread of coming under the domination of "Whites" again that, although Mr. Hazard went among them as a simple sightseer, they doubled the guards in Cape Haytian while he was in the town, and would not permit him to see the partially ruined, though still magnificent palace and fortress of San-Souci, the characterististic memorial of the splendid monster Christophe, because they dreaded lest the United States had really sent him to reconnoitre preparatory to seizing the territory. Mr. Hazard believes much of the idleness of the population to arise from their insecurity of payment for their work; "from

[13] "Santo Domingo, Past and Present, with a Glance at Hayti." By Samuel Hazard. London : Sampson Low and Co. 1873.

experience and tradition the poor ignorant people seem to have a bad opinion of the white man, to whom they still apply in a general sense the term *méchant.*" San Domingo, on the contrary is almost unanimous in its desire for annexation with the United States, while President Grant believes it to be practically only a question between the States and some European power,—possibly Germany, which has already a large trade and a large number of resident merchants in the island. As to the resources of the country, writers new and old concur without exception in extolling its climate, its beauty, and its productiveness in all varieties of wealth. Emigrants easily become accustomed to the climate, and colonists from the Northern States of America say that under certain regulations they can labour there with their own hands as safely as in their old homes. The greater number of the persons engaged in commerce are foreigners, chiefly Germans, who enjoy good health. In the eastern portion of the island, that which is proposed to be annexed, the mountains lie so that the valleys are swept by the tradewinds and kept perfectly fresh and pure. That the towns are frequently preyed upon by yellow fever is owing partially to the sites being in some cases badly chosen, but principally to the utter neglect of sanitary regulations. The European armies sent out there from time to time, in the course of the struggles between Spain, France, and England, which have " watered the whole island with European blood," have had health exactly proportioned to the amount of good sense shown in adapting their clothing, food, and work to the climatic conditions. The American plague of snakes does not exist there, nor are the scorpion and tarantula either so painful as has been represented, nor at all dangerous. Land is likely for some time to come to be obtainable on very easy terms, detailed by Mr. Hazard. Indeed the book may be appealed to with confidence as containing all desirable information as to the past history, present state, and future possibilities or prospects of the island, rendered more attractive by the numerous and graceful illustrations supplied by Mr. Hazard's pencil.

M. Pradez[20] apologizes, as do most travellers, for his unaccustomed pen; but the only way in which it would otherwise have been noticeable is in the numerous fanciful, but well worked out and ingenious human analogies which he finds in the virgin forest life of a plantation in the valley of the Parabyba, and in the domestic manners of the poultry, the rearing of which seems to be an important adjunct to the coffee-planting industry of that region. The value of M. Pradez's book lies in his descriptions of slave life and of the conditions of slave-holding property in Brazil since the suppression of the slave traffic in 1850. He wrote before the Act of Emancipation was passed in 1871, by which all children born of slaves are free, and through the operation of which it is calculated that slavery will be extinct throughout the empire in thirty years. The effect of suppressing the traffic was marvellously to increase all other trades and industries, as well as to increase the

[20] " Nouvelles Etudes sur le Brésil." Par Charles Pradez. Paris. 1872.

exports and the imports. Up to that time the number of slaves annually brought into the country was about 15,000; and so sudden an alteration in the prospects of the labour market of course at once trebled or quadrupled the value of the slaves. The necessary and immediate result was an anxious attention to the health and comfort of the slaves; and the result of that again was a great improvement in the quality and quantity of their labour. The weak point of the late Act of Emancipation is that, not having been drawn up by practical men, it does not provide against the danger lest owners of slave women should henceforward be as careless as ever of their health and comfort, and absolutely negligent of the necessities of the free-born infants. This is, however, so obvious a danger that it is likely to be guarded against by a government so anxious to stock its labour market for the future that it has entered into contracts with agents in Germany and England for immigration on the largest scale and most liberal terms. When so much capital was left suddenly unemployed by the abolition of the slave trade, it was only to be expected that many bubble companies would spring up; but time has sufficed to restore the equilibrium of trade, and judicious railway enterprise promises to open wider and even more fertile fields for the future industry of both old and new inhabitants, and of the prolific race of freed Africans.

To all who are interested in the various questions concerning emigration, and especially to those whose attention has been attracted to the *pros* and *cons* of emigration to the Brazils, Mr. Mulhall's account of the German colonies on the Rio Grande,[14] only twenty days from London by steamer, will be not a little useful and interesting. After a short résumé of the conditions of the Brazilian empire, its finances and completed or projected railways, Mr. Mulhall devotes the rest of the volume to the province of Rio Grande do Sul, or São Pedro, and its natural resources and capabilities. With abundant water communication, great and varied mineral wealth, a climate " what an Englishman would consider rather warm, but mild and agreeable compared to that of India," somewhat like that of Algiers, and exceedingly healthy, and the vegetable productiveness naturally to be looked for under such conditions, it is not surprising to find that the forty-three German colonies which have taken root there since the year 1825 are exceedingly prosperous. Only two of the earliest of these have had a hard battle for success, because of ill-chosen sites, and even they are now thriving. It is difficult to understand how the recent complaints of deception made by English emigrants to Brazil can have had any good ground, unless either some similar blunder was made, or our colonists were not trained enough to work together like the well-disciplined Germans; or, possibly our compatriots were like a futile Irish colony out there twenty years ago, who called the farina provided for their bread making, "sawdust," and would not eat it. Whatever be the difficulties of settlement in Brazil there remain two facts; first, that a liberal and

---

[14] " Rio Grande do Sul, and its German Colonies." By Michael G. Mulhall. London : Longmans. 1873.

constitutional government, having recently passed an Act by which
slavery will be extinct at the end of the century, is anxious to attract
English and German colonists into a vast fertile territory; and
secondly, that Germans have found it possible, in great numbers, not
only to exist, but to get very wealthy there under even less advantageous conditions than are now offered. The earliest German colony
now numbers 60,000 persons, besides having " swarmed " several times,
and nothing could exceed the comfort described by Mr. Mulhall as
prevailing among them. Catholic and Protestant churches and schools,
railways, gas companies, and great business establishments of all sorts
attest the progress that has been made, chiefly during the last twenty
years; for in the earlier days of these colonies a civil war was raging,
and their powers of expansion were of course greatly hampered; and
then, also, the first colonists were not so wisely selected as they are
now. They were taken hap-hazard, and some who came had so little
liking for agriculture, that they sold the allotted share of 150 acres of
uncleared land, farming implements, and a right to a daily subsidy
for two years, for a bottle of brandy.

A resident" in Victoria was a passenger on board the first ship that
in 1839 sailed from Great Britain direct for Port Philip. He has
known the colony ever since the time when curiosity as to what existed
on the shores of Port Philip was baffled by the close growth of the
woods, among which not even a tiny puff of smoke rose to give sign of
life, and the road from Sandridge to Melbourne was a well-defined
track through the wilderness. Squatting about eighty miles from Melbourne, " a resident" succeeded in establishing friendly relations with
the aborigines—partly through having, in joke, fostered their superstition by declaring himself to be the spirit of a departed black man risen
again white;—but the panic of 1842 destroyed his prosperity, and he
had to start in life nearly anew. Through the varying conditions of
land tenure, the" gold-fever," and the more recent and substantial prosperity of Victoria, the writer of this volume has persisted, with an
amount of success and a kindliness of nature which have apparently
made him a very fair judge and critic both of what Australia has been,
is, and may be. He sums up his reflections in the opinion that " a
little more age; more stability in her government; less absenteeism
among her wealthy inhabitants; an increase of population, . . . seem
wanting to establish Victoria in enduring prosperity."

Messrs. Sampson Low and Co. render service to many good causes
by issuing in so compact and attractive a form a little volume" of
selections from Prince Albert's public addresses. Already a younger
generation is taking active part in many works at the first beginning
of which Prince Albert helped, and in connexion with which he gave
far-seeing, large-minded, wise advice, in so unpretending a form that
these, his later followers, are in danger of never hearing it. It is not

* "Glimpses of Life in Victoria." By a Resident. Edinburgh : Edmonston
and Douglas, 1872.
** "Prince Albert's Golden Precepts." London : Sampson Low and Co.
1873.

possible to guage the influence upon the late Elementary Education
Act of such addresses as that given by him at the Conference on
National Education in 1857, or on the usefulness and the progress of
the British Association or the Statistical Society, by various speeches
made by him at their gatherings. One subject is brought into relief
by these "Precepts," the importance of which is so little appreciated
as scarcely to rank as a "topic of the day." It is that of the position
of domestic servants, the largest class in the British population, as well
as the class which contributes most largely to the population of our
workhouses. It would indeed be well if some suggestions could be
carried out in reference to this,—such as the establishment of a Registry
to which servants unjustly deprived of a "character" could appeal, and
some system of payment which would result in protecting servants from
the terrible chances of health and fortune which now so heavily press
upon them.

It may be doubted whether the gift of pamphleteering is common
in our day, and whether we number among us any worthy descendant
of Swift. Certainly in the writings of the class of political satires,
which have become so abundant of late years, the amusement of the
reader is more aimed at than his political instruction, but now and
again one of these productions is worthy of the notice of the reviewer.
The writer of "If I were Dictator,"[v] has succeeded in a very happy, if
broad, burlesque of some of the topics current in the political world of
the day. Mr. Strongways is surprised by a deputation from both
Houses of Parliament and the "International," who inform him that
a revolution having taken place, he has, as a compromise, been
appointed Dictator for six months. Being a bold but wary old sea-
captain, he undertakes the office, only regretting that he had not first
secured the money for a first-class "return" ticket to London. Once
there he first goes to the bank to secure funds, by the advice of
Mr. Billings, the representative of the International, who calls on him
to secure "well-feathered nests" for his friends. He finds Mr. Lowe
at the Bank, and receives some interesting information as to the
difficulty Government has in spending the revenue. They use notes to
light their cigars, because Mr. Lowe cannot bear the sight of a match.
The first object with Mr. Strongways is to reduce the National Debt,
which he proposes to do by buying the reversion of the railways after
a period of seventy-five years, at a cost of 20,000,000*l.*, so that when
the reversion should fall in, England would be more than solvent.
Before nightfall the decree for the purchase was published. He then
abolished sinecures, got a banker to put the accounts in order, and
reorganized the army, so as to have a large force and three reserves,
making a total of 1,500,000 men ready in case of invasion. A hundred
and fifty large landowners followed the example of the Japanese
Daimios, and placed their estates in his hands, so that he could appor-
tion farms among the three classes of army reserves, and in the meanwhile, till all should be adjusted, five large railway contractors engaged,

v "If I were Dictator." London: Henry S. King, and Co. 1873.

in case of war, to supply half a million of well-drilled men. Messrs.
Pickford and Co. undertook the transport, and Messrs. Spiers and
Pond the commissariat departments. Bismark telegraphed that he
was going to take Denmark. Strongways answered that he was
sending thirty ironclads. Bismark telegraphed an apology for the
blunder of his stupid clerk. Then Mr. Billings called to say that the
International was dissatisfied, and was going to depose him. Strongways told him he should order out the military, and took the precau-
tion to promise the troops double pay during his term of office, and to
tell them that the International wished all armies to be disbanded.
At his suggestion all Anglo-Saxon Governments formed themselves
into a confederation, which Germany begged to be allowed to join.
This made him popular, and under the influence of adulation and public
dinners, Mr. Strongways became less severe to mark the faults of his
supporters. But the British Lion, about to emigrate in disgust,
called on him and roused him to a sense of his duty. He therefore
arranged a grand International Exhibition of Adulterations, affixing to
each specimen a description of its composition, and the name and
address of its makers and vendors. This made him so unpopular that
he barely held his place till the hour when his term expired, and then
he escaped with his life by means of a balloon.

Twenty sketches of the political career and position of men chosen,
somewhat at random, from among the more prominent members of
both Houses of Parliament of the present day, are republished by their
anonymous writer in the *Daily News*.[*] They do not in any way
trench on the sphere of biography, but give a vivid impression of the
men as they are known "in the House," and are often particularly
happy in the description of the mental peculiarities of their subjects.
Mr. Gladstone is absolved from all charges of inconsistency and
changeableness by the theory that, born a Tory, and yet necessarily a
Liberal by nature, he has all his life been painfully plodding over the
ground that lies between the two, "thinking out aloud" the whole
and detailed application of his liberal principles. Mr. Disraeli is
treated as, in all respects, a foreigner in England and in English
politics, using parties and questions as mere weapons. His imagination is so vivid as to supply momentary belief, and "the changes
which he has undergone may in part be attributed to the instability of
imaginative impressions which never amounted to intellectual convictions." His consistency is largely to be attributed to "a belief in
his race, in the theocracy to which its sacred books and its history
testify, and in the principle of monarchy through which a theocracy
best exercises itself," ideas by which he has been strongly possessed.
His isolation from English life and ideas has enabled him to become
more successful as a manager of his party, but has made him less
popular among them. Mr. Lowe is not a favourite with the writer,
and is said to have very little human nature in him, "and what there
is is not of the best sort." Mr. Bright has been at "much pains to

conceal real moderation under a form of violence." Lord Salisbury has "the courage to be himself, but is not content with this: he wishes that the Tory peers and squires should be himself too." Lord Derby is his father, "with all the 'go' taken out of him." In speaking of Lord Selborne and his party, it is said, "There is a certain want of robustness about these churchmen out of holy orders. They are demure and self-conscious. The drooping glance, which seems to shun the lust of the eye, and the bowed head, which denotes an oppressive sense of humility, suit the cloister and the hood rather than St. Stephen's and the barrister's wig and gown." Sir John D. Coleridge is said to have come to be popularly recognised as not unequally matched for wit and resource with "the Claimant." "Such, in the transitions of time, is the fate which has overtaken a name once and still symbolic of the highest flights of transcendental philosophy, and the subtlest beauty of a mystic imagination and a delicate and airy fancy." Written by a pronounced Liberal, the portraits are fair enough and life-like enough to supply to many the lack of personal sight and hearing of the men they represent.

SCIENCE.

ENGLISH students of Physics have had for many years good reasons for complaining of the want, in the English literature of science, of a higher text-book on physics, such as those written by Janin, Pouillet, Wüllner, Kuelp, and others on the Continent. When therefore, some years ago, the announcement was made that a larger work was to be produced by the joint labours of two such eminent physicists as Sir William Thomson and Professor P. G. Tait,[1] it was hailed with enthusiasm; for national prejudices, and the sickly self-love of scientific men of our time, have not succeeded in darkening the light that has gone forth from England in the modern progress and development of Physics. And to whom else would it be entrusted to open the temple of the refined physical knowledge of our time to the aspiring student, if not to Thomson and Tait, who are among the foremost of its founders and builders? Of the truly great national work which is now being elaborated by the minds of these two illustrious men, the first volume made its appearance a few years ago, and is in the hands of every man of science all over the world. It is the recognised embodiment and book of statutes of the laws of dynamics. It exhibits moreover applications of nearly every one of the more important modern methods of mathematical analysis to physical inquiries, and it may well be said of this book, that if every other work on the subject were lost at this moment, this one work

[1] "Elements of Natural Philosophy." By Professors Sir W. Thomson and P. G. Tait. Part I. Oxford: At the Clarendon Press. 1873.

would bear to all future generations complete tidings of what has been the
result of the labours of all generations that have passed away before our
time. Of this noble work, or rather its first volume, Professors Thomson
and Tait have published a more elementary form, and no greater boon
could have been conferred on the beginner as well as on those who have
not a very extensive mathematical training. The mathematical methods
employed are almost without exception limited to those of the most
elementary geometry, algebra, and trigonometry; where higher methods
are required for an investigation, the reader is in general referred to
the larger work of the authors. The proofs are in various places
simplified so as to agree with the general plan and aim of the work,
and it is particularly interesting to note how many theorems, even
among those not ordinarily attacked without the help of the differential
calculus, have in the masterly hands of these authors, who both combine the most comprehensive acquaintance with modern mathematics
with a profound knowledge of theoretical and practical physics, been
found to yield easily to geometrical methods of the most elementary
character. There is no surer guarantee of readiness for further progress than such a simplification of modes of proof. The work is,
moreover, full of specimens of genuine philosophical reasoning, and
true attempts to place physical definitions on a logical basis. Thus the
reasons given for adapting Gauss's absolute unit of force, the transition from the meaning of the word *moment* to that of being the
numerical measure of the *importance* of any physical agency (p. 61),
and its consequent application to the evaluation of the effect of forces,
besides many other similar passages, have struck us as being admirable; they prove that the study of physics affords an intellectual
training, such as no other science, even pure mathematics itself, can
give. There is no doubt that a book of this kind will not be understood by every student at a first glance, it requires hard thinking;
but there is undoubtedly in our language no work now in existence
which can be placed side by side with that of Messrs. Thomson and
Tait, whether we look upon it as an excellent student's textbook, or
as an elementary statement of the fundamental notions of modern
physics.

We have already alluded to Wüllner's work on physics.[*] The
fourth volume of the new edition, which has been thoroughly revised,
and in great part re-written, has just made its appearance, and as an
independent work on magnetism and electricity it will be welcomed
by many English students of physics and electricians. Terrestrial
magnetism is in this work again treated with the superficiality which
seems to be its fate in nearly every work on physics. Our English
instruments are now in the hands of magneticians in Germany as well
as everywhere else; but we do not find the slightest allusion to them,
and the student who seeks to inform himself of their peculiarities is
left to search the volumes of Transactions, observatorial reports, &c., at

_____

[*] "Lehrbuch der Experimentalphysik." Bearbeitet von Dr. Adolph Wüllner.
Vierter Band. Die Lehre vom Magnetismus und der Elektricität. Leipzig : Teubner.
1872.

great loss of time. Surely Dr. Wüllner might have condescended to describe in a few pages the construction of an English dipcircle, or a Kew magnetograph; and the space devoted to Morichini's so-called experiments on the influence of light on the development of magnetism in bars, which have long ago. been declared to be mere fable, might entirely have been given to more relevant matters. On tho other hand great praise is due to Dr. Wüllner for the new shape in which the portion on electricity now appears. The very latest researches of importance have been inserted in a condensed yet clear style, and the author has selected with great tact from the vast experimental applications of electricity precisely those which will for ever form portions of the skeleton of the science, whatever its future growth may be.

German men of science produce every year a great number of publications in pamphlet form, which are in many cases similar to the papers which appear in this country in the various Transactions and Proceedings of learned societies. But it is also the form in which public lectures given to larger audiences by eminent savans are finally placed before the whole nation.[3] We have before us two such lectures, which both form parts of a larger collection of lectures, given in various large towns in Germany by university professors. One of these lectures is "On the Effects of Lightning," by Dr. Stricker; the other "On the *Bacteria* considered as the smallest living beings," by Professor Ferdinand Cohn. Both subjects are treated in an exceedingly captivating manner, without losing anything of scientific dignity. Although popular lectures, the pamphlets are full of research and give even the literary resources from which the facts are drawn. Thus Pasteur's investigations on putrefaction and the most recent investigations on the influence of *bacteria* in certain decompositions are faithfully represented, and even Sir William Thomson's famous theory of the cosmical origin of life on this globe is not only recorded but also critically examined. It is certainly to be regretted that similar collections are not published in this country.

Professor Willigk's work on Chemistry[4] is an attempt to treat the pure science of chemistry in combination with its technical applications. Most of these attempts have ended hitherto in failure, and the reason for this lies near. Scientific chemists are rarely trained in the technical detail of the various processes to which chemical truths are ultimately applied, and their descriptions of such processes are therefore in almost all cases unsatisfactory and superficial, while the facts stated are frequently even erroneous, and in direct opposition to those stated in other similar works. Professor Willigk has avoided a great source of failure in other writers. He has condensed as much as possible, and given so little of either the science or the art of chemistry that it is somewhat difficult to say for what class of readers

[3] "Sammlung gemeinverständlicher wissenschaftlicher Vorträge." Von Rud. Virchow and Holtzendorff. Berlin; Lüderitzsche Verlagsbuchhandlung. 1872.
[4] "Lehrbuch der anorganischen Chemie." Von Erwin Willigk. Prag: Tempsky. 1872.

or students his work is really intended. The chemistry of the elements and their more important compounds is certainly very well discussed, but when we look into the technical processes we find the descriptions exceedingly elementary, by no means clear to the mere student, and certainly useless for the manufacturer, or the man who enters upon the pursuit of technical chemistry. The book has, however, one recommendable feature: it gives very accurate, although somewhat rough sketches and woodcuts for illustrating many processes, and although their description is often defective, the diagrams are so clear that the reader can have no trouble to understand the principles employed. Some manufactures seem to have been treated with partiality, at the expense of others. Thus the manufacture of glass and that of china have received prominent attention, while the metallurgical processes are passed over with very meagre descriptions.

M. Schlegel's[a] book on the new geometry of space, founded principally by the researches of Professor Grassmann, is a very remarkable work. It is an elementary introduction to a new branch of mathematics, which may be termed a general theory of lineal extension, and which, by novel operations, establishes a geometrical analysis applicable not only to the actual three dimensions of space, but ultimately to any number of dimensions generally. Common arithmetic and the usual Euclidian geometry are only special cases of this analysis, and two apparently so heterogeneous doctrines, like that of numbers and that of space extensions, hitherto loosely and imperfectly tied together by analytical geometry, are now for ever united as branches of one great conception. Nor is the whole a mere philosophical creation. The new theory has already found numerous applications in statics and mechanics, and even in crystallography and magnetism; and in M. Schlegel's work, which is confined to applications of the theory to three dimensions, the reader will be struck immediately with the conviction that even if such applications to physical inquiries were denied to this new branch of mathematics, it deserves, and must ultimately find, wide-spread study and development. Nothing can be more beautiful than to see the conglomerations of the rules and theorems of our usual text-books done away with, to make room for one grand system, from which those rules and theorems are easily-derived consequences, while the principal axioms and fundamental formulæ are quite a sufficient basis for the most refined outliers of modern geometry. We have read this work with immense pleasure, and we feel certain that the subject can only gain in the hands of English students, to whose attention we recommend M. Schlegel's work most earnestly.

We doubt whether the time has already arrived to write a History of Mechanics.[b] We are just now in a period of transition from obsolete notions, antiquated doctrines, and doubtful conceptions to a purer

science of motion, with a great future before it. Dr. Dübring's critical
history of the general principles of mechanics is, therefore, hardly well-
timed. We are still too much surrounded by clouds, though they are
on the point of moving away, to see so clear as we ought to see for
historical criticism. Nevertheless, a work of this kind has its merits,
and is not without some interest. Dr. Dübring has had the unenviable task of deciding many cases on the rival claims of great men
to have their names associated with the discovery of new principles, or
the novel application, or modification of already established truths. The
vast amount of literary research required for such a task is obvious,
and there is not a page in which the author's immense range of biographical and literary knowledge is not manifested. But the author
has not stopped at a mere recital of discoveries. He has entered with
a philosophical spirit into the question, what there is in each mechanical principle of mere logical consequence; how much there is in
each such principle of real experience or of mathematical derivation;
and, finally, how much of it is only assumption, justified by our
present extent of knowledge. The tact which the author has
brought to this history is truly admirable, and he throws light
not only on men and their deeds, but the whole intellectual character
of a scientific generation is often portrayed with the true poetical and
prophetical insight of a great historian. It is extremely pleasant to
pursue the thread of many portions of this history; how some definite
minor problem gave rise in its treatment to the birth of a new principle, a new theorem, full of fertile consequences, which the author
follows through every ramification. The pleasing impression which
the work makes is, moreover, heightened by a simple, yet happy mode
of expression, by a warm recognition of every merit, by apologetic
explanations of failures, and the gentle touches with which everything
unscientific and erroneous is passed lightly over.

Mr. Kalley Miller's[7] work does not present any novel feature which
deserves special attention. It is light reading on various elementary
facts of astronomy, and may well be recommended to young men or
ladies who wish to obtain some knowledge of astronomy. Some
portions are amusing, especially the chapter on astrology. We doubt,
however, whether short sketches of this kind ought not to be left in
the pages of the magazines in which they appeared originally.

A small pamphlet by Mr. William Upton, B.A.,[8] formerly scholar
of Trinity College, Dublin, is more amusing by its preface than instructive by its subject. The author believes himself to have squared
the circle, and possesses all the modesty characteristic of great minds.
"In commencing his preface, the author deems it fitting to state that
he has never either seen or heard of any attempt similar to that which
he is now making, so that, whatever merits or demerits it shall
possess, they must be exclusively his own." The author then enume-

[7] "The Romance of Astronomy." By R. Kalley Miller. London: Macmillan.
1873.
[8] "The Circle Squared." By William Upton, B.A. London: E. and F. N.
Spon. 1872.

rates the well-known " problems " of geometry, namely, the quadrature
of the circle, &c., and goes on : " Now each and all of these the
author professes to be able, with God's blessing, satisfactorily to solve.
He acknowledges to previous failure with respect to the trisection, but
has it now complete." The obvious question, why the solutions of
these problems have not been found before Mr. Upton discovered
them, he meets with the unanswerable argument—" It is, that all
important discoveries tending to the advancement of human progress
have their appointed time." Mr. Upton concludes his demonstration
with—" Q.E.F.—LAUS DEO."

So much has been already said and written about the explorations
of the depths of the Atlantic during the last few years that we need
do little more than notice the appearance of Professor Wyville
Thomson's volume on the results of these important researches.[*] It is
well known that in consequence of scattered observations made by
various voyagers, and the more systematic investigations of Dr.
Wallich in the *Bulldog*, there was every reason to believe that the
extreme depths of the sea were by no means such barren deserts as had
commonly been supposed, and yielding to the instances of the Council
of the Royal Society, the British Government for three successive
years placed at the disposal of certain scientific naturalists a steam
vessel of sufficient power to enable them to carry on investigations of
the deep sea by means of the dredge and other instruments. In the
volume before us, Professor Wyville Thomson gives an excellent
summary of the valuable results obtained by these investigations of
the Atlantic and Mediterranean,—results which have produced a
complete change in our notions of the conditions of temperature at
great depths, and of the distribution and influence of ocean currents,
and demonstrated positively the fact of the existence of a rich and
varied fauna in those abysses of the ocean which were formerly
imagined to be entirely devoid of life. It is impossible to over-
estimate the importance of these results from a natural history
point of view, and especially in their influence upon geological
speculation, not that in the latter respect we should be inclined
to accept Professor Thomson's extreme view as to the continuity
of the chalk with the deposit now forming at the bottom of the
Atlantic, which seems to us to be founded upon a misconception.
In his book Professor Wyville Thomson gives a historical account
of the three expeditions made by himself and his two colleagues,
Dr. Carpenter and Mr. Gwyn Jeffreys, and this is interspersed with
numerous references to many of the curious and highly interesting
forms of animals which were brought up by the dredges and other contrivances in use,—these creatures are also discussed more in detail in a
chapter specially devoted to the fauna of the deep sea. He further
describes the apparatus used for sounding and dredging and for ascer-

[*] "The Depths of the Sea." By C. Wyville Thomson. 8vo. London :
Macmillan. 1873.

taining the temperature of the water at various depths, the results of
the latter series of investigations being exceedingly important, especially in connexion with the currents of the ocean, and leading
Dr. Carpenter to advocate a peculiar system of oceanic circulation.
The work is, if anything, a little too much spun out, but its subject
is so interesting, and its style in general so good, that a small defect
of this kind may be overlooked. We may add that it is illustrated
with numerous excellent woodcuts and with a considerable number of
charts of various kinds.

Some ten years ago we had to notice the appearance of Professor
Jukes's "School Manual of Geology," and we have now to call attention to a second edition of this little work, which has been prepared,
since the death of the author, by his nephew, Mr. A. J. Jukes-Browne.[10]
In a science like geology the lapse of ten years introduces many
changes, if not in the broad principles of the science, at any rate in
those details which are necessary for the proper comprehension of the
subject, and Mr. Browne, whilst retaining the excellent arrangement
adopted by the author in the first edition, and respecting as far as
possible even his actual written words, seems to have modified very
judiciously those parts of the book which required alteration. This is
especially noticeable in the chapters on rocks and on metamorphism.
The new edition of this "School Manual" is an excellent first book
of geology.

As far as scientific instruction is concerned the rising generation of
the present day are certainly much better off than their fathers. In
place of the wretched "Mangnall's Questions," "Lessons on Objects,"
or "Guides to Useful Knowledge," with which we unfortunates used
to be crammed, our children have placed before them the most admirable treatises on the various branches of science, treatises to which
some of our leading philosophers do not disdain to set their hands.
Messrs. Macmillan have already published several most valuable
manuals of various departments of science, and they have now commenced a series of still more elementary works under the title of
"Science Primers." One of these, Professor Geikie's "Physical Geography,"[11] is now before us, and a better first guide to the knowledge
of terrestrial phenomena it would be difficult to conceive. That the
information communicated is of the most elementary character is a
matter of course; the whole book only occupies one hundred and ten
small pages, which is far too small a space to allow an author room for
anything not absolutely necessary; but it is astonishing to see how
much valuable information upon the ordinary subjects of physical
geography Professor Geikie has been able to compress into so small a
compass. The shape of the earth, the causes of day and night (but,
by a singular omission, which, however, may have been intentional,
not the seasons), the air, and the circulation of water in it, the circu-

[10] "The School Manual of Geology." By J. Beete Jukes. Second edition,
revised and enlarged. Edited by A. J. Jukes-Browne. 12mo. Edinburgh:
Black. 1872.

[11] "Physical Geography." By Archibald Geikie. 12mo. London: Macmillan.
1873.

lation of water on and in the earth, and the sea, and its relation to the land, constitute the chief subjects treated of; the reaction of the interior of the earth upon its surface is more briefly touched upon. The questions connected with the geographical distribution of animals and plants are altogether unnoticed, and their omission seems to be judicious in so elementary a treatise.

We have also to mention a new edition of Miss Youmans' "First Book of Botany,"[15] a little book designed to carry out the practical system of botanical education adopted by Professor Henslow for the children in his parish school. It contains a series of lessons in the descriptive terminology of plants, which will doubtless prove useful in fostering a power of observation in those children who are not frightened from its study by the numerous hard names. Its usefulness would have been increased somewhat if examples of the various structures had been named. The illustrations are good.

This is one of those books which are among the hardest of appreciation by a reviewer.[16] The author is an able man, and he is a man of extensive experience of a certain kind; moreover his work has a certain passing value. On the other hand he is a man who lacks the judicial faculty, and if we may criticise the critic we would say in contradiction of some laudatory sentences appended to the volume that he is anything but philosophic. A vigorous, clever, wrong-headed man often has his useful function in the world of thought; he challenges older beliefs with the nerve of a fanatic, and he forces into the front those other opinions which he himself prefers. In this way old beliefs are tested and new or neglected opinions have that chance which all things require when we are to see what stuff they are made of. Dr. Parkin weighs all present theories of the nature and propagation of epidemic diseases in his scales and finds them wanting; especially is he indignant with the theory of contagion, and attacks "contagionists" with the unsleeping rancour with which teetotallers attack the licensed victuallers. To divide writers on epidemics into "contagionist" and "anti-contagionists" is surely a narrow way of looking at things, and reminds us of the local preacher who referred to Churchmen as non-Dissenters. Dr. Parkin does not seem to have read the work of Dr. Ross, lately noticed in these columns and elsewhere, which is really a philosophic work. Poor Professor Pettenkofer again must wish for a like obscurity, for Dr. Parkin, like "The Chicken" in Dombey and Son, doubles up that "worthy professor," as he calls him, in half a page. We are not of those who are disciples of Professor Pettenkofer, but we scarcely feel ourselves as ready to demolish him offhand as the inspiriting author of "Epidemiology." The reader will find the whole question far better handled from the

15 "The First Book of Botany." Designed to cultivate the observing powers of children. By Eliza A. Youmans. New and enlarged edition, with 300 engravings. 8vo. London: King and Co. 1872.

16 "Epidemiology." By John Parkin, M.D. Part I. London: 1873.

sceptical point of view in Dr. Oesterlen's work noticed in our present section. We may add, that Dr. Parkin unfortunately selects the rinderpest as one of his chief subjects of discussion; we trust that Mr. Gamgee may not come across those particular pages, for if we may judge from his published writings, that "worthy professor" is not unlikely to show fight in a rather embarrassing way, and may resist the doubling up process with unexpected success.

Dr. Oesterlen, like Dr. Parkin, considers that the time has come for submitting the phenomena of epidemic diseases to an entirely new scrutiny.[14] The present volume is very fully and very carefully written, and it gives a more than adequate survey of the causes of these visitations. The last two hundred pages, about one-third of the whole, are devoted to the special consideration of each of these diseases taken alone. Like Dr. Parkin, the author is very jealous of the popular belief in the efficiency of contagion or infection as the cause of epidemics. No doubt the strong stand made by these writers, and the chief importance of it, consists in the great fact of quarantine, which, if contagion be a thing of nought, is a gigantic loss of time and money, a huge sacrifice to folly or error. On the other hand, we should be surprised to hear that any really instructed physicians believe that infection is the sole condition under which propagation of epidemics becomes possible. All men of experience admit that other conditions, as yet unknown to us, regulate their appearance and disappearance. We ourselves could refer to more than one instance of scarlatinal epidemics which broke out time after time in certain localities until some general change in the whole surroundings drove the danger away. In one instance the drainage of a marsh thus banished the tendency to recurring outbreaks of the disease; in a second case the removal of large works in which animal matters lay long and decomposed. But, on the other hand, we must not be so unreasonable as to deny that contagion, or infection, comes into action when the outbreak has once commenced. Even Pettenkofer has recently been compelled to admit this in the case of cholera, and proofs of its agency in other kinds of epidemic are too strong to be easily overlooked.

From the way in which this pamphlet[15] comes to us we presume that, although privately printed, it may be noticed in the journals in the usual way; and of this we are glad, as the pamphlet strikes us as having much merit. We write from an imperfect knowledge of dentistry, and it may well be that its contents are familiar to all informed practitioners, but they are in a measure new to ourselves, at least in a practical point of view, and we hasten to say a few words in reference thereto. What Dr. Coffin states is, that dentists find themselves, as practical men, face to face with a peculiar change in the roof of the mouth and in the alveoli of the jaw which is greatly on the increase, and which, if ill-managed, results in a state of much discomfort and disfigurement, to say nothing of any ulterior consequences

---

[14] "Die Seuchen." Von Dr. Oesterlen. Tubingen : 1873.
[15] "On Alveolar Contraction." By C. R. Coffin. Printed for Private Distribution. London: 1872.

in the health. This change, which Dr. Coffin speaks of in terms of
"consternation," is a tendency to contraction of the sockets, especially
in the upper jaw, with narrow and high vaulted roof or palatine cavity;
alterations in the dimensions of the antrum or maxillary sinus, and
contracted nasal passages. This gives the feature of acute angular, or
"prognathous" facial aspect, and close approximation of the canine,
bicuspid and true molar teeth. Thus mastication, speech and beauty
are interfered with, and dental caries and neuralgia, on the contrary, are
encouraged. We wish that space allowed us to quote from Dr. Coffin's
pamphlet, which is a pilot balloon preceding a larger work. We can only
state our own impressions which, chiefly, are two. We are, in the first
place, full of admiration of the ingenuity of the dentists who, by appropriate apparatus, can prevent the progress of this ugly and injurious
change by the use in the mouth of a delicate frame which opposes
the evil without interfering with comfort or function. Nay, say Dr.
Coffin's patients, the presence of the plate in the mouth is a positive
help and convenience. Secondly, we would say that this change, if
seriously on the increase, may be regarded from two opposite points of
view—viz., as evidence either of progression or of retrogression of the
species. If these changes are of the kind described by Dr. Langdon
Down and others as characteristic of congenital tendencies to idiocy,
then its increased prevalence is very alarming, and supports the opinion
of those who hold that lunacy is sadly on the increase also. On the
other hand, however, it must be remembered that coincidently with
the development of the cranium and increasing complexity of the
hands, we find the recession of such mere animal parts as the jaw, which
is no longer used for prehension or for rending food, and consequently
diminishes in size. The so-called wisdom tooth is no doubt becoming
rudimentary for this reason, and when produced generally dies for lack
of function. We hope that Dr. Coffin will keep this distinction in
view in his forthcoming volume, and will tell us whether he thinks
these changes in the jaw are associated with real refinement or with
the morbidezza of decadent organisms.

Dr. Allbutt has forwarded to us a copy of a paper[18] now in the
archives of the Royal Society, and reprinted in the seventh volume of the
Journal of Anatomy and Physiology, which sets forth the results of a
long series of observations upon the temperature of the body during
muscular work. The paper records observations taken at frequent
intervals during fourteen days of Alpine climbing, which seem to
prove that laborious exertion has no great effect in disturbing the
usual relations between the formation and the liberation of heat in
the body. The daily curve is a little sharper than in health, rising
perhaps one or two-tenths above the normal, and falling a little earlier
and more rapidly in the evening than is usual under ordinary circumstances. The temperature tables of each day are published in the
pages of the pamphlet.

Dr. Ringer reprints the pamphlet on this subject which on its first

---

[18] "The Effects of Exercise on the Bodily Temperature." By Dr. Clifford Allbutt.

appearance was received with a great deal of favour." Dr. Ringer was one of the first in our own country to familiarize us with the invaluable observations of Wunderlich and others upon the variations of the bodily temperature in disease. Perhaps Dr. Ringer might not unfairly claim more than this, for by his own researches if he has not advanced anything substantially new, he has so established and defined the results of others, as to have something more than the position of a mere interpreter. This present essay will tend more and more to prove to the practitioner that practice without the thermometer is very rough and ready practice indeed; that indeed the thermometer is really even more necessary than the stethoscope.

Dr. Herbert Tibbits, the Superintendent of the Hospital for the Epileptic and Paralysed, has brought out a small volume upon medical electricity," which is especially intended for practical men. We have often urged, that if electricity is to be a popular remedy, some really handy books on the subject should be prepared. Busy practitioners are simply bewildered by a book full of details upon physiological points, which after all are, in many cases at least, the subject of dispute among the learned. Still less do they want bulky chapters describing every conceivable form of electric apparatus. They wish to be told categorically what instruments they are to buy, and having bought them, how they are to be applied in common cases. This object Dr. Tibbits has set before himself, and has accomplished it really well. When we say really well, we mean that his writing is that of a man who writes briefly from condensation and from judicious selection, and not from scantiness of information. His brevity is the kind of brevity which costs more than prolixity. Again, he has not hesitated to be dogmatical even on uncertain points, and we think he is right. A hesitating timid style is quite unfit for didactic essays, and it is well known of course that the writer speaks only to the best of his knowledge as obtained from careful thought, reading, and comparison. Personally, we ourselves differ from some of the positions thus taken up by the writer, but he would be the first to admit the whole grounds of our dissent, and to grant that the question may be an open one. In a great number of points, however, we thoroughly agree with him, and we are especially pleased to find ourselves at one with him in discouraging all loose speculative practice. Hence we regard the book as a *sound* one, which those who work in this specialty will know to be a very high distinction. The author is familiar, we may add, with both the galvanic and faradic methods. After all, the serious difficulty which withstands the regular use of electricity is the time it requires, and the costliness therefore of its application by skilled hands.

In this second and greatly improved edition[19] Dr. Waldenburg, who is well known as a masterly writer upon the nature of pulmonary

[17] "On Temperature in Phthisis." By Dr. Sidney Ringer. London: 1873.
[18] "Handbook of Medical Electricity." By Dr. Herbert Tibbits.
[19] "Die locale Behandlung d. Krankheiten d. Athmungsorgane." Von Dr. L. Waldenburg. Zweite Auflage. Berlin: 1872.

diseases, discusses at length their treatment by locally applied medications. The advantages of applying remedies to the very seat of the disease is so evident, that only the difficulty of the application can account for the lack of interest in such methods among English physicians. Of late years more than one amongst us have suggested the capabilities and value of this method of treatment, but the use of it is very far from anything like popularity. Dr. Waldenburg, in the first part of his work, gives us a sketch of the history of the method; in the second part he discusses the theoretic basis of it, and by means of experiments upon animals he illustrates and proves the degree in which such local applications to the lungs are possible; the third section deals with the various kinds of apparatus—those in which fluids are pulverised by forcible impact upon a metal plate, those in which a current of air drives them onward, and those in which the same end is attained by compressed steam—and the remainder of the volume, which contains nearly 800 pages, deals with the inhalation of vapours and gases and with the general and special principles of treatment. The book is written throughout, as the author proposed to himself, in a spirit free from fanaticism or prejudice, and forms a very substantial and systematic tractate on its all-important subject. We would suggest that the book may well be translated for the benefit of English practitioners, to whom the whole subject is as yet a mystery. Dr. Waldenburg appends some well reported cases to his various chapters, and speaks in very high terms of the success which attends the careful practice of the method. Too often disappointment arises from unskilful management.

Dr. Seegen's work[20] has now been some time before the profession but our notice of it has accidentally been postponed. On putting pen to paper we have to confess to a degree of disappointment with it which is somewhat unexpected. Dr. Seegen has obtained so high a reputation as an authority on "Diabetes," and his papers in the *Deutsches Archiv für Klinische Medecin* were so favourably received, that our anticipations were raised somewhat too high. We ought not to say that the volume is written from one point of view, that one being the conviction of the supreme value of the Carlsbad water in the relief of diabetes; to say so would be scarcely fair; but at the same time we find that this is the chief object of the volume as it stands. We need not assure our readers that the monograph is an excellent one and is very creditable to the author, but we looked for more than that, for something new and valuable that we should thankfully receive as a help in practice. Setting aside, as perhaps we ought to do, such an exceptional work as that of Professor Bernard, we looked at least for something as novel and interesting as we find in the essays of such men as Pavy or Dickenson, or as learned as we find in Max Solomon. Dr. Seegen, however, gives us no new lights whatever, he simply writes such a treatise as a cultivated reader and experienced observer would write who aimed merely at a survey of the present state of our knowledge and did not hope to enlarge it. Dr. Seegen lays much stress on the distinction between the two

[20] "Der Diabetes Mellitus." Von Dr. Seegen. Leipzig: 1870.

classes of diabetes, those who rapidly improve upon a restricted diet and those who grow worse in spite of it or in consequence of it. But surely this is a distinction very familiar to all consulting physicians, and we wish now to know something more of the grounds of the difference. We hoped too that Dr. Seegen would have had much more to say as a practical observer of the nervous affections accompanying diabetes which have attracted the attention of Dr. Dickenson and several other writers. As regards treatment, we can only say that Dr. Seegen's results as obtained by the regulated use of Carlsbad water at Carlsbad are very far better than any we obtain by the use of the imported water in England. At the same time he gives us notes of a large number of cases, and writes in a cautious spirit and with all decorum. He is no watering-place quack, but a throughly well instructed observant physician, who has written a monograph on a distressing and fatal disease which cannot fail to interest any reader, and which in its careful arrangement and adequate treatment of all difficulties will be simply invaluable to the student. We are surprised that neither Dr. Seegen nor other recent writers allude to codeia which was recommended in diabetes by Pavy, and which we ourselves have found very useful in many cases.

There are a large number of medical men in Great Britain who could write invaluable treatises on idiocy did they undertake to do so. Somehow or other they shrink from the task. This is not only to be regretted on the special ground of the interests of the idiot himself, but on the general ground of scientific investigation. The "reversions" which betray themselves to a careful student of these imperfect organisms must have a priceless value for the student of the developmental history of man, and how important such observations may and do prove themselves to be is evident from the extensive use of them by Mr. Darwin in his last volume, as they were supplied to him by the able director of the West Riding Asylum, Dr. Crichton Browne. Dr. Ireland's[21] pamphlet is a slight contribution, but we hope it may be a prelude to the publication of more extended researches. One point in it we notice especially, which is that abnormal faculties, or rather faculties in disproportional excess, so far from being common in idiots, as we too often suppose, are really very rare. We ourselves, who have no special knowledge of the matter, had certainly believed that musical and arithmetical ability was often seen in idiots. Being ourselves dull at numbers, we had even hugged the belief that there was some hidden sympathy between " calculating boys" and idiots. But we must be convinced of our error, in spite of our experience of one epileptic boy of congenital deficiency, who is always clever at figures, and who spins the most rapid and elaborate webs of calculation as he recovers from his attacks. His brother, also mentally defective, has that faculty in marvellous excess, which, we believe, is the groundwork of instruction for young thieves, the faculty, that is, of passing quickly through a room or a shop and of afterwards describing its contents. This boy brings away a knowledge of minute detail even down to the intricacies of the patterns on the walls.

---

[21] "The Deficiencies of Idiots." By Dr. W. W. Ireland. Edinburgh : 1873.

000

HISTORY AND BIOGRAPHY.

MR. HAYWARD has done well in bringing together those interesting Essays' from his pen which have, during the last ten or fifteen
years appeared in various quarterly and other reviews. There is indeed
no valid objection to this mode of republication, although it is now
and again reviled by critics who call in each case for some special
reason why the essay which has first seen the light in a fugitive paper,
should make any claim to permanent attention. Of essays which have
a necessarily temporary interest we do not speak. Such an interest
will depend upon the subject. A suspended answer to some public
question, a speculative discussion of some future event, may be subjects
of supreme interest, but the interest will be transitory, for it will
cease when the question is answered, and the event realized. But an
essay which has a value in itself deserves a more lasting life than the
pages of a magazine can guarantee. Nor is there any reason why unity
of subject, or chronological connexion should alone be permitted to
confer the right of separate existence, for there is a unity as actual as
that of subject or connexion, the unity of style and uniform excellence.
And this unity Mr. Hayward's essays possess. They have a literary
individuality, which, though not very striking nor very valuable, is
always pleasing. The biographical portion of these volumes is the
best. It deals with personages as widely separated as Richard III.,
Queen Marie Antoinette, Lady Palmerston, Alexandre Dumas, and
Edward Livingstone, and is full of anecdote and epigram. With the
later subjects of his biographies Mr. Hayward was often personally intimate, and his own recollections enliven the general information which
is open to all. No one can tell an anecdote better than Mr. Hayward,
and few writers have a larger or selecter store of them at command.
Moreover he never tells a poor one. The papers on "The Pearls and
Mock Pearls of History," and the "Varieties of History and Art," are
good examples of his style at its best. The essay on "Dumas" goes
naturally with those, as does likewise the account of Frédéric von
Genz, the eccentric pamphleteer of the Napoleonic era. The literary
estimates in these volumes fall short of the social records. Mr.
Hayward's writings remind us rather of the brilliant conversationalist
than of the sober critic. Anecdote, scraps of curious information,
selected gems from the dining-tables, and the drawing-rooms of the
best society form the staple of his interesting notices. He knows
who has the finest set of buttons à la Watteau, and is acquainted
with the process by which the Venetian ladies produced the golden
tint of their hair. He has the letters of Lord Bulwer to the Princess
of Lichtenstein, and he is able to form a good and generous estimate
of the social excellences of Lord Lansdowne, Lady Palmerston, and
many other members of the aristocracy; from which it will be seen
that Mr. Hayward's two volumes are pleasant reading, and that he did
well, as we said before, to republish his scattered essays.

¹ "Biographical and Critical Essays." Reprinted from Reviews. By A. Hayward, Esq., Q.C. 2 vols. Longmans.

The objection to a republication of essays,' which has indeed been suggested by critics in the case of Mr. Hayward, would, if acted upon, deprive us likewise of Mr. Freeman's second series of historical papers, all of which have appeared before, and in some cases in the magazines which have had Mr. Hayward as a contributor. But the loss in this latter case would be incomparably greater. We can ill miss anything that Mr. Freeman has written; and by the present re-issue, Mr. Freeman has almost another generation for audience, since some of the present articles bear a date twenty years old. We welcomed with pleasure the first series of these papers; this second series, though older, is in most respects even better. It is also entirely different in its range of subjects, which belong to classical times. The essays have been re-written, and Mr. Freeman admits with candour that he found much to improve in the English of the earlier writings. He mentions this for the "encouragement of younger writers, whose common temptation it is to write in an elevated style." Occasionally, too, he comments in an amusing way upon the vehemence of his earlier expressions, as for instance in his essay on "Ancient Greece and Mediæval Italy," and in that on Mommsen's "History of Rome." But generally the purged style which Mr. Freeman adopts is faultless, and the matter is equal to the style. The estimates of Mommsen's History of Rome and Curtius's History of Greece are valuable to students who are apt to swear perpetual allegiance to the newest theorist in history or politics. But even the purged and studied style of Mr. Freeman is sometimes vehement. When he speaks of the two great German historians, he forgets that he has set himself as the model of style to "younger writers" who might have been "discouraged" if he had found his own first style as pure as his present language. Of Mommsen's language he says, "No one can give the honourable name of High-Dutch to the half-Welsh jargon of Mommsen." Again he speaks of his "knock-me-down style" (p. 149), and adds (p. 270) the serious charge that "Mommsen has no notion whatever of right and wrong." Yet this purified English admits the expression, "He does not go in for Catalina" (p. 270), from which we infer that Mr. Freeman intended to encourage a class of very young writers indeed. But, as we have already said, Mr. Freeman's general style is faultless. Moreover, the essays themselves have a value which does not depend upon style. The sketch of "Lucius Cornelius Sulla," which is given in the eighth chapter, is admirable for the justice it does to that great and dazzling character. The review of Mr. Gladstone's work on "Homer," seems to us somewhat too flattering. The book referred to is one that will be read more by students of Mr. Gladstone than by students of Homer; and it is simple exaggeration to say of Mr. Gladstone that "He has done such justice to Homer and his age as Homer has never received out of his own land" (p. 92). But it is an ungrateful task to carp at this admirable republication. The truth is that there is just a tone of some-

---

* "Historical Essays." By E. A. Freeman, M.A. Second Series. London: Macmillan.

thing in the writings of Mr. Freeman, a half-heard note of self-assertion perhaps, which awakens a feeling of opposition. The historian seems to be convincing you against your will. But in every case conviction follows his clear and unanswerable arguments.

Another republication[3] is before us in the brilliant series of short papers upon the leading men of the third French Republic. They are upon the whole just, though sometimes severe. The best perhaps is that upon Victor Hugo. We will quote the concluding words :—

"Poet, artist, novelist, dramatist, orator, statesman, letter-writer, essayist, editor, advocate, and song-maker ! He has done all forms of brain work excellently well. Whatever worth and genius can accomplish is still possible to Victor Hugo, and he may yet take part in the regeneration of his country. If he has suffered something from the misrepresentation of fools, and something from the ingratitude of the people he has loved with such passionate fervour, he must find consolation in his own gallant words, now echoing everywhere through the world like the notes of a clarion with a silver sound, ' God suffers not the precious fruit of sorrow to grow upon a branch too weak to bear it.'"

Three essays by the Rev. Canon Kingsley[4] have been reprinted from the *North British Review,* and make a very handy volume. The first gives its title to the book, wherein Mr. Kingsley makes out a good case for the poetry of the Puritans. It is tinged with that colour of Biblical expression which Mr. Kingsley knows so well how to lay on, and which accounts for no inconsiderable part of the fascination of his style; but his words for Milton are strong with the strength of truth. The second essay is upon Sir Walter Raleigh and his time, and the third is the well-known review of Froude's " History of England." These essays have had the fortune of meeting many readers, and we do not feel called upon to speak of them at any length, for (if we are not mistaken) they have been republished before.

Professor Vámbéry, the extraordinary linguist and traveller, has brought his rare accomplishments to a task[5] which no one less excellently equipped than himself could have achieved. The country beyond the Oxus has hitherto remained almost unknown to history ; even Orientalists have had little opportunity of piercing the darkness which involved Transoxiana. Thus, a series of princes, and even whole dynasties, have passed away, regarding whom, as the Professor says, " scarcely anything has as yet been written in Asia, and not a single word in Europe." With these dynasties the second part of Professor Vámbéry's book deals : it occupies entirely new ground, and has no predecessors. For the earlier part our author has used the historical works edited and translated by Orientalists, or has consulted the original manuscripts; but his

---

³ "Men of the Third Republic." Reprinted with large additions from the *Daily News.* Strahan and Co.
⁴ "Plays and Puritans, and other Historical Essays." By Charles Kingsley. London : Macmillan and Co.
⁵ "History of Bokhara, from the Earliest Period down to the Present." By Arminius Vámbéry, Professor of Oriental Languages in the University of Pesth. London : H. S. King.

chief power has resulted from his acquaintance with new or unknown
manuscripts recently brought back from Central Asia. Some of these
which he enumerates seem very valuable, and are in his possession.
Again, there is the *Sheïbani-nameh*, a MS. unique in Europe, which
contains a picture of the ethical, social, and political condition of
Transoxiana, whose value cannot be overestimated. It is the property
of the Imperial Library at Vienna, and has, it is true, been catalogued
by Flügel; but as it is written in the Tchagataian language, of which
he was ignorant, it is now for the first time available. This manuscript has been largely used by our author in his account of the
Ozbegs, and of Sheïbani Mehemmed Khan. The clear straightforward
style of the book leads us by many unknown ways amongst strange
Oriental people, but it brings us into contact with no more striking
character than the great Emir Timour—better known in Europe as
Tamerlane—the conqueror of Asia. His troubled youth and the
magnificence of his court at Samarkand are ably recorded by Professor
Vámbéry. That court, indeed, when at the zenith of its glory can be
compared to nothing out of the stories of the "Arabian Nights." One
traveller has described the festivities celebrated in the plain of Kanigul
"the mine of flowers." Fifteen thousand bell-like tents, each with
its many-coloured flag, contained the rejoicing people, and the gorgeous
curtain-palaces of the king and nobles gleamed with silken domes and
pinnacles. This airy town was the scene of feasts and merry-making.
The bill of fare is not given of any Tartar feast, but mutton and
horseflesh are mentioned as the favourite dishes, and "boza" and
"kimis," whatever these may be, as the favourite liquors. These
liquors were (we may presume) alcoholic, for the first hero who fell
down dead-drunk was rewarded with a title of distinction. Professor
Vámbéry adds:—

"The æsthetic spirit of the Tartars required everything to be done on a
colossal scale, and no dinner was therefore reckoned perfect at which horses
were not served up roasted whole, and at which the wine flagons were not both
extremely numerous and of an enormous size. These flagons and bowls were
ranged in rows, forming as it were an avenue up to Timour's tents; and in
addition to these, other similar vessels were placed at different points of the
city of tents, protected by umbrellas, and periodically filled either with wine or
cream and sugar for the benefit of the people at large."

But the glory of Tamerlane did not depend upon these incidental
displays of barbaric splendour. In spite of the constant wars and
troubles which attended his reign, there was manifest an unmistakeable
awakening of intellect both in art and religion. Poets and mystics
were not rare, and found favour in the eyes of Tamerlane. Ahmed
Kermani, the poet, lived in familiar intercourse with him, and made
jokes—not very good ones—at his expense. Djezeri, the Arabic lexi-
cographist, lived at his court, and the colleges of Bokhara, Samarkand,
and Keah were filled with a learned professoriate. This history of
Bokhara brings down events to the present day. The once splendid
palace of Tamerlane is now a Russian hospital. Bokhara, "the chief
pillar of Islamism"—whither Turanian pilgrims came to touch the
blue pedestal of Timour's throne with their foreheads—echoes to the

steps of soldiers and merchants of the West, and a dark cloud hangs
over the horizon of Islam.

In some respects the work* of Mr. Rawlinson resembles the work
of Professor Vámbéry. It explores ground which is practically unbroken. Modern historians have failed to recognise the real position
of Parthia, as a rival State to Rome not much inferior to that great
power during three most interesting centuries. Mr. Rawlinson maintains that from the time of Pompey's Eastern conquests to the fall of
the Empire, there was always in the world a second power, civilized
or semi-civilized, which balanced Rome, and acted as a counterpoise
and a check—the power of Parthia. With a view of vindicating this
theory, already set forth in the author's " Manual of Ancient History,"
he has written the present work as supplemental to the Greek and
Roman histories in which those periods are commonly studied. It will be
seen therefore that Mr. Rawlinson takes up his position upon unoccupied
territory. The whole history is well treated, and presents such a
complete view of the State as we should have expected from a historian
of Mr. Rawlinson's calibre. The real significance of Parthian history
begins with the reign of Mithridates I. This monarch in a reign of
thirty-seven years, transformed an insignificant kingdom into a great
and flourishing empire. · We have little means of knowing the real
economy of the Parthian court, for it seems to have been visited by
no author of repute, and it is described in the vaguest manner by
classical writers. Yet we know sufficient of Parthian history to know
that Mithridates was both a successful general and a talented organizer.
And it is the mark of no ordinary greatness even amongst great
conquerors, that he was able to win a character for clemency and
philanthropy whilst he was consolidating an empire that lasted for
nearly four centuries. We cannot now follow Mr. Rawlinson through
his excellent narrative of the Parthian and Roman wars, until the
time when the star of Parthia set, and the arms of Artaxerxes
transferred the empire to Persia. The two chapters which close the
book will do much to bring before the student a clear and vigorous
picture of Parthian civilization. The architectural remains of that
nation are still imposing. The city of Hatra, three miles in circum-
ference, by its fallen columns and sculptured pilasters testifies in its
ruins to the former greatness of its inhabitants, and the woodcuts
which the present volume contains will enable the student to appreciate the position of Parthian art. And the highest praise which
we can give to this volume has been given, when we say that it
is worthy to rank with the other works upon kindred subjects for
which we are indebted to the learned author.

Mr. Lloyd's " History of Sicily to the Athenian War"† is one of
those rare books which at once claim and take the very highest place
which their subject can give them. It is a book which by its style and

* "The Sixth Great Oriental Monarchy ; or, the Geography, History, and
Antiquities of Parthia." By George Rawlinson, M.A., Canon of Canterbury.
London : Longmans.
† " The History of Sicily to the Athenian War, with Elucidations of the Sicilian
Odes of Pindar." By W. Watkiss Lloyd. London : John Murray.

by its method ranks itself with the great historical works that deal
with classical antiquity. It is calm, dispassionate, and learned, and
reads like the work of some well-known historian with whom we are
familiar, and which we have laid aside to read again. Half of it deals
with the early history of Sicily; another half is devoted to the elucidation of those odes of Pindar which are connected with Sicilian victors
in the great games. Upon these subjects, we are mistaken if it is not
henceforth the authority. Nowhere have we seen the tangled threads
of Pindaric song more lightly unravelled, or the artful inversions and
complexities of epinician music more delicately resolved, and rewound
into the strands of history. It is a book which cannot well be quoted,
but which henceforth must be read by the students of Pindar. Our
chief feeling is one of wonder that we have not met Mr. Lloyd upon
this field before, and one of hope that wo may meet him there again.

The unpretending book which Mr. Marsh has written upon Venice[*]
is as fascinating as it is instructive. Mr. Marsh has gone for his information to that as yet nearly unworked mine—the State Papers.
Those which we recently noticed in this *Review* have been of especial
service to him, and facts hitherto unobserved have thrown a light
upon portions of history which would otherwise have been obscure.
Two instances of this occur in the present volume which we may
mention here. From the Venetian State Papers we learn that in 1485
Columbus made a piratical attack upon the Venetian galleys. In most
Lives of the discoverer this year has been left a blank. This act of
piracy is recorded only in the State papers. Again, the visit of Henry
VIII. to the Venetian galleys, when they were lying at Southampton,
is vividly described in the Venetian papers. Of course other authorities have been open to Mr. Marsh, and he has used them with effect.
The description of the departure of the Venetian fleet for the Crusades
(p. 31) is a good instance of his pictorial style, and the history of the
Polo family and of the great traveller Marco (ch. vi.) is well told.
The war with Genoa and the war with the treacherous Duke of Milan
are full of incidents which lose none of their interest in Mr. Marsh's
story. We commend especially the account of Sorbolo the Candian
engineer, who carried six large galleys and twenty-five barques up the
mountain of Peuedo, and brought them in to the Lake Garda, to the
wild amazement of the Milanese, who believed that they saw a mirage
when their eyes fell upon this amphibious flotilla. The story of the
Venetian glass factory is no less interesting, and the description of
the millefiori and lace-work goblets with their diamond threads is
particularly good. It is astonishing to remember with how many
great names in science, literature, and art the single city of Venice
brings us in contact. And no one can more gracefully introduce his
readers to these aristocrats of the Adriatic than Mr. Marsh.

The handbook of mythology[*] which Mr. Murray sends us is based
upon the well-known German work of Petiscus, which has already
reached a seventeenth edition. The older English works upon the

[*] " Venice and the Venetians." By John D. Marsh. Straban and Co.
[*] "Manual of Mythology." By Alexander S. Murray. London: Asher
and Co.

same subject are notoriously faulty. Lemprièro's work, like Goldsmith's histories, has ceased to find acceptance, while the form of Dr.
Smith's excellent works still leaves much to be desired. In this neat
manual we have a general conspectus of the ancient deities, we learn
their histories, and we may gain some knowledge of the method in
which they were conventionally represented. Though most of the
work is based upon that of Petiscus, the introduction has been entirely
rewritten. In this an attempt is made to show how the belief in the
existence of the gods originated, and to point out the influence of such
belief with special reference to the ancient Greeks. The articles themselves are well written or translated; we have had no means of ascertaining how far the English version is original. But we think that a
more evident partition should have been made between the theologies
of Greece and Rome; sufficient confusion has already arisen from the
identification of Greek and Roman deities. We are in fact only beginning to recover a right view in this matter, and it is misleading to see
"Vestal Virgins," "Hephæstos or Vulcan," "Demeter or Ceres,"
"Terminus," "Pan," and "Faunus" following one another in close
succession. We notice, moreover, that the Manual is designed for
"art students" and "general readers," and that it contains plates on
toned paper representing seventy-six mythological subjects. What
the art students will think of these seventy-six toned plates we do
not of course know, but to the general reader they are repulsive in
an extreme degree. The toned paper is of a faint offensive yellow,
and the engravings are feeble and misty. Nothing could be more
miserable than the representation of the "Laokoon" group (opposite
p. 310), unless it be that of the "Diana of Ephesus" (p. 138), and of
the "Pallas-Athene of Pheidias" (p. 112). Against this latter representation we protest most strongly. It is to be hoped that in a
second edition this yellow paper will give way to something more
healthy; at present the plates positively mar the effect of the letterpress.

We will now pass into the region of personal biography.

The life of Mr. Robertson, of Brighton,[10] by Mr. Brooke, is one which
has been before the world for some time. It is not surprising that a
new edition has been called for. To write a volume of sermons which
should win the suffrages of all classes, which should be read by all
sects, which should not be spoken of with contempt by men of
advanced culture, and which should be to many men the basis of their
religious faith, is a work which can be done in these days by very few.
Mr. Robertson did it. It is therefore only natural that his biography
should be frequently called for. Mr. Brooke has executed the task entrusted to him admirably. His introduction contains by implication,
rather than by explicit utterance, an excellent estimate of the loving
and amiable character of Robertson. He belongs himself to that section of the English Church which clings to spiritualism, while it does
not reject progress. He is more tolerant than Robertson, for he thinks
that he showed but scant justice to the Evangelical School, and did

---

[10] "Life and Letters of Frederick W. Robertson." Edited by Stopford A.
Brooke, M.A. New edition. 2 vols. H. S. King and Co.

not allow sufficient merit to their theology. But Mr. Brooke speaks
with no uncertain sound upon some topics. We agree with much that
he says, and we accept many of his conclusions, but we hesitate to
accept them all. He thinks (p. xii.) that the spirit of the *Record*
newspaper is the "very spirit of the devil." He may, indeed, be right,
or he may be wrong, we ourselves cannot decide, since we know too
little of the parties compared; but with regard to the controversy
between Mr. Robertson and the periodical mentioned, we are sure Mr.
Brooke takes the right view. And generally in Mr. Brooke's part of
the work before us, there is visible a healthy effort after toleration
which harmonizes with the subject of his biography. And it would
be strange if the character of Frederick Robertson did not exercise
a strong fascination upon many devout minds. He united high culture
with personal devotion, and a heroic military enthusiasm with a
gracious habit of self-sacrifice. He says of himself :—

"There is something of combativeness in me which prevents the whole
vigour being drawn out, except when I have an antagonist to deal with, a
falsehood to quell, or a wrong to avenge. Never till then does my mind feel
quite alive. Could I have chosen my own period of the world to have lived in,
and my own type of life, it should be the feudal ages, and the life of a Cid, the
redresser of all wrongs."

Mingled with these feelings, there was in his mind what Mr. Brooke
describes as "that slight tinge of noble superstition which made at once
the strength and weakness of ancient religious chivalry." In a letter
from Brighton, Robertson says of himself (p. 47) :—

"I remember when a very, very young boy going out shooting with my
father, and praying, as often as the dog came to a point that he might kill the
bird. As he did not always do this, and as sometimes there would occur
false points, my heart got bewildered. I believe I began to doubt sometimes
the efficacy of prayer, sometimes the lawfulness of field-sports. Once too I
recollect when I was taken up with nine other boys at school to be unjustly
punished, I prayed to escape the shame. The master, previously to flogging
the others, said to me, to the great bewilderment of the whole school, 'Little
boy, I excuse you : I have particular reasons for it,' and in fact I was never
flogged during the three years I was at that school. That incident settled
my mind for a long time."

It was in the autumn of 1847 that Mr. Robertson came to Brighton,
and began the attractive style of preaching which gave him fame.
The French Revolution of 1848 stirred him unusually. Writing that
year, he says :—

"Some outlines of a Kingdom of Christ begin to glimmer, albeit very faintly
and far off, perhaps by many, many centuries. Nevertheless, a few strokes
of the rough sketch by a masterhand are worth the seeing, though no one
knows yet how they shall be filled up. And those bold, free, dashing marks
are made too plainly to be ever done out again. Made in blood as they
always are, and made somewhat rudely ; but the Masterhand is visible
through the great red blotches on the canvas of the universe. I could almost
say sometimes in fulness of heart, 'Now let thy servant depart in peace.'"

A cry was soon raised against him in Brighton, but he attracted
immense numbers of the working men to his sermons, and this seems
to have been the most interesting characteristic of his ministry. A

wider popularity soon became a torture to him, and he was morbidly
sensitive to false admiration. In 1851 he was attacked, together
with Mr. F. D. Maurice and Professor Kingsley, by the *Record*
newspaper, and accused of socialistic opinions. The letters which Mr.
Brooke gives in reference to this period are of considerable interest.
Two years later Frederick Robertson died. We shall not quote much
of Mr. Brooke's concluding chapter, but we will close our notice with
the following testimony to the general popularity of Mr. Robertson's
sermons :—

"Working men and women have spoken of them with delight. Clergymen
of the most opposed views to his keep them in their bookcases and on their
desks. Dissenting preachers speak of them with praise. Men of the business
world have written to say that they have felt in reading them that Christianity
was a power and a life, and that its spirit was that of a sound mind. All
sections of the press, even those of such widely-separated principles as the
Guardian and the *Westminster Review*, have expressed even while they dis-
agreed with their views, sympathy with their Christian feeling and noble
thought. There has, however, been one conspicuous exception: the *Record*
newspaper has been faithful to its nature."

Amongst the lectures and addresses which form part of the works
of Mr. Robertson, there was one[11] which showed how nearly the "In
Memoriam" of Mr. Tennyson had taken hold of the mind of the
Brighton clergyman. He says of it: "It is simply one of the most
victorious songs that ever poet chanted. Readers who never dream
of mastering the plan of a work before they pretend to criticise details
can scarcely be expected to perceive that the wail passes into a solemn
and peaceful beauty before it closes." The present analysis of the
Memorial Poem is designed to make the general reader acquainted
with its design. It consists of little more than a heading or thesis to
each lay; but there are students of the poem to whom this will be
useful. It is executed with perfect taste and sympathy.

Mr. Thomas Hughes is certain of a wide circle of readers whenever
he takes up his pen. He interested us in the school life of a Rugby
boy, and his memoir of his brother,[12] Mr. George Hughes, though containing no sensation or incident is interesting too. It may very well
be connected with the life of Frederick Robertson, for George Hughes
seems to have been a lay Robertson, cultivated, manly, and honourable. Mr. Thomas Hughes thinks this short biography may be
interesting to Englishmen in general, because he believes that its
subject was only " a good specimen of thousands of Englishmen of
high culture, high courage, high principle, who are living their own
quiet lives in every corner of the kingdom from John o' Groats to the
Land's End, bringing up their families in the love of God and their
neighbour, and keeping the atmosphere round them clean and pure and
strong by their example ; men who would come to the front, and
might be relied on in any serious national crisis." A great part of

[11] " Analysis of Mr. Tennyson's ' In Memoriam.' " By the late Rev. F. W.
Robertson of Brighton. 4th edition. London : H. S. King and Co.
[12] " Memoir of a Brother." By Thomas Hughes. London : Macmillan and Co.

this book is occupied with Rugby, and it is the most interesting part. George Hughes when at school received delightful letters from his father, some of which are given here in full, and which diminish our wonder at the success of Dr. Arnold, who had such co-operation. Not that the co-operation was in matters of school-discipline, but in the establishment of a manly honest spirit in the boy himself. Indeed, George Hughes seems to have been more than once in trouble with the Doctor, though his character suffered only temporary eclipse. It is curious to compare the letters which he himself received at Rugby with those which he sent his own sons a quarter of a century later. George gets into trouble with Dr. Arnold on account of some Italian image-vendor, whose wares were put up for "cock-shyes" in the "close," and owing to the accurate aiming of the Rugbeians, broken. His father justly writes: "It would have been more manly and creditable if you had broken the head of—— or some pompous country booby in your back settlement, than smashed the fooleries of this poor Pagan Jew" (videlicet, the Italian), "which were to him both funds and landed estate." Many years afterwards his own son is in trouble for a "towel-fight," and George writes: "Your 'war-dance' amused us excessively, and of course there is no harm in a war-dance; but if it is forbidden, what an old goose you are to risk having impositions and extra lessons for it! But schoolboys are always the same, and I can't expect you to be wiser than the rest." Perhaps it is not always well to give to the world memoirs intended, like the present, for a single family. The author says himself, that he has "a sense of discomfort and annoyance at having the veil even partially lifted from the intimacies of a private family circle." But he has a large audience who will deal tenderly with everything that he writes; and there is no public school where he has not many friends for whom he may as confidently write as for his own sons and nephews.

"Ready, O Ready,"[11] is a book written in the same spirit as that by Mr. Hughes. It is the autobiography of the captain of the *Cumberland* training-ship, and is a thoroughly strong, exciting book for boys. The writer has the chivalrous, religious, military spirit which characterized the heroes of our last two books. Indeed it is curious to see how one tone runs through them all. We will take a paragraph from the present work, and we would ask our readers if it might not have been written by Mr. Robertson, Mr. Hughes, or Mr. Kingsley:—

"If I were a public school commissioner, I should recommend that a professor of manly exercises be attached to every school; he should be a gentleman himself in order to teach manliness and gentleness to others; and in time his profession would come to be recognised as a far higher grade than that of any mere Greek or Latin inculcator. And specially would I have boxing taught, for no other exercise carries with it the priceless and manifold teachings of pain in so satisfactory a manner. Singlesticks are good as an alternative." (p. 43.)

[11] "Ready, O Ready! or, These Forty Years." By the Captain of the *Cumberland*. London: Sampson Low, Marston, and Co.

We had thought that there was a reaction against that special school of Christianity which rejoiced in hard blows for the sake of hard blows; but we learn from the Captain of the *Cumberland* that it is not so. Mr. Robertson had said (vol. i. p. 8), "I was rocked and cradled to the roar of artillery, and the very name of such things sounds to me like home." Mr. Hughes (p. 84,) gives us a picture of a battle between his brother and a baker at Oxford. He enters into details, and relates the ill-success of beefsteak as a curative application, and he attributes to this misadventure his brother's loss of a first class. This belongs to an earlier date. But now comes the Captain of the *Cumberland*, calling upon the name of "noble Charles Kingsley" (p. 247), and placing the professor of boxing above the Greek or Latin "inculcator." What is the real meaning of all this, and of the fascination which such a mixture of religion and singlesticks has over many minds? But "Ready, O Ready!" is a readable book, and we can conscientiously give it the epithet which is so much in favour with the school to which it belongs. It is a thoroughly manly book.

M. Lanfrey's "History of Napoleon the First," [11] which has now reached a second volume in the English translation, is the best history of that extraordinary and mean character. The volume which is before us in an English dress deals with an important part of our history—the peace of Amiens, and the war which ensued between England and France. The history of this renewal of war is fairly told by Lanfrey, who describes the haughty conduct of Napoleon to our ambassador (Lord Whitworth). The mistake that Napoleon made was in imagining that he had Addington alone to deal with, and in forgetting that the Minister's power in England depended upon the will of the people, which had undergone a complete revulsion since the peace was signed. The relation of Napoleon to the press is another curious point in the Emperor's life with which M. Lanfrey deals. The Emperor professed a contempt for men of letters which he by no means felt. No journalist was so obscure but that he could make the Emperor writhe by a telling sentence, or a pointed epigram. The papers which dragged on a precarious existence in Paris were all under his surveillance. As M. Lanfrey says (p. 422), "they were condemned to live by gossip; as for news, whenever they ventured to add any to what was furnished them by the bulletins of the police, they did so at their own risk and peril." If any paper ventured to reprint news from a foreign paper, its editors were "sold to England." The *Citoyen Français* published a history of the Saint Bartholomew. Napoleon writes to Fouché: "This detestable journal appears only to delight in wallowing in blood. Who is the editor of this paper? With what enjoyment the wretch gloats over the misfortunes of the nation! I intend to put a stop to this—change the editor or suppress the journal." Upon another occasion, when he had received some notes on the weakness of Russia, he directed them to be published in

[11] "Lanfrey's History of Napoleon the First." Translated. Vol. ii. London: Macmillan and Co

a newspaper "as translated from an English paper. Choose the name of one that is little known." The present volume brings the history of events down to the battle of Jena.

It is no longer ago than the 6th of last October that Sir George Pollock, the venerable Constable of the Tower, died, and we have already a large volume purporting to contain his Life and Letters.[15] The fact is, that this memoir was commenced in 1869, and completed in the following year. Each chapter as it was written was submitted to Sir George for his perusal and revision. Consequently the book is in some sort an autobiography, for his journals and correspondence were put at the author's disposal. The great services of Sir George Pollock in India are not likely to be underrated. The Indian campaign which he conducted was a conspicuous event in the history of the British Empire. The second campaign in Afghanistan is one to which the service may point with especial pride, and one which may be studied with profit by every Indian officer. Sir George went to India as an officer under the Company, without the aid of aristocratic friends or influential connexions, yet he achieved an undying reputation in our Indian annals. This reputation was indeed made in the April of 1842, when Sir George led his troops through the Khyber Pass. That gallant feat has so often been celebrated that we shall say nothing of it here. Mr. Low well treats the course of events at Jellalabad, and brings it down to the time when a vote of thanks was awarded by the Houses of Parliament. Shortly afterwards Sir George returned to England, where he remained until his death. His character was as irreproachable, Mr. Low says, as his services were eminent. He was buried in Westminster Abbey. Mr. Low's book is generally well written, but the last chapter might have been judiciously abridged. The same remark applies to the letter of Sir John Kaye which begins the book, for Sir John says that he did not personally know Sir George Pollock until after the close of his military career.

Mr. Fitzpatrick has produced a very readable and amusing book.[16] It is, however, probable that few English readers will know much about Dr. Lanigan, whose chief work was an ecclesiastical history, but the plan of the present work includes most of the Irish celebrities who were contemporary with the historian, and the book abounds with anecdotes. Dr. Lanigan himself was not an attractive personage, if the description of him by Dr. Reynolds be a true one, for he says that he was "a great wall-faced, overgrown mass of antiquarian erudition, who moved on his course as if he had fins." Be this as it may, the excessive mental work which Dr. Lanigan had to undergo resulted in a softening of the brain and finally in his death, which occurred in 1828. The present book is written from an exclusively Irish point of view, but it is not an unworthy memorial of a strong and vigorous character.

Mr. Campbell, the chaplain of King's College, London, has published

[15] "The Life and Correspondence of F. M. Sir George Pollock, Bart., G.C.B. G.C.S.L, Constable of the Tower." By Charles Rathbone Low. London : W. H. Allen and Co.

[16] "Irish Wits and Worthies, including Dr. Lanigan, his Life and Times." By W. J. Fitzpatrick, LL.D., J.P. Dublin: James Duffy, Sons and Co.

a selection of the reminiscences and reflections of his father, Dr. Campbell." With these are interwoven an account of Dr. Campbell's ministry at Row. The interest of the biography consists rather in the fact that the boldness of his opinions drew upon him the action of the presbytery and resulted in his deposition, than in the value of his reminiscences, which do not rise very much above the level of the sect to which he belonged. The General Assembly however, in 1830, deprived him of the privilege of preaching in the pulpits of the Scotch Church, but he continued to preach in other places. During the next forty years a considerable change came over the religious mind of Scotland, and in 1871 the degree of Doctor of Divinity was conferred upon him by the University of Glasgow. The last two years of his life he spent in writing an account of his early ministry at Row. These labours form the basis of the present volume, which is not without interest for the general reader.

When Dr. Campbell retired from his work as a clergyman, he recommended his congregation to join that of Dr. Macleod in the Barony Church. Dr. Macleod's liberal opinions were as well known as his large and amiable nature was beloved. Mr. Strahan in a pleasing little pamphlet" bears his testimony to the genial open-hearted Scotchman who became so widely known as the conductor of Mr. Strahan's magazine, *Good Words*. The same pamphlet has also an amusing story from the pen of Dr. Macleod.

Some years ago considerable attention was drawn to the muse of John Clare, a peasant of Northamptonshire, and Mr. Martin's "Life of Clare" seemed to have said all that was to be said of so humble a poet. Mr. Cherry thinks otherwise." Mr. Martin did not consider that the great men who interested themselves in Clare treated the poet with that respect which his genius demanded. Mr. Cherry justifies the conduct of Clare's patrons. The Marquis of Exeter read a great many of his poems, and then asked him to dinner in the servants' hall. So did Earl Fitzwilliam; so did General Heynardson. Indeed it seems that he might have lived in the kitchens of the great if he had chosen to do so. Amongst his friends however, who did not send him to dine in their kitchens, were Charles Lamb, Thomas Hood, H. Cary (the translator of Dante), and Allan Cunningham. The poet however, was for the last five-and-twenty years of his life an inmate of the Northampton Lunatic Asylum, where he wrote harmless poems, some of which are not without notes of beauty. And with regard to the poems which are here collected by Mr. Cherry, we think that they would have been upon the whole more pleasing without the Asylum poems. Many of them have been retouched by the editor, and have thus lost their interest. The earlier poems are simple and

¹⁷ "Reminiscences and Reflections Referring to his early Ministry in the Parish of Row." By the late John McLeod Campbell. Edited by his son, Donald Campbell. London: Macmillan and Co.
¹⁸ "Norman Macleod, D.D." By Alexander Strahan. London: H. S. King.
¹⁹ "Life and Remains of John Clare, the Northamptonshire Peasant Poet." By J. L. Cherry. London: Frederick Warne.

musical, and are worthy of a better fate than to be printed with the
later distractions of less happy years.

Some other books have been sent us, with which we are compelled
to deal summarily. Mr. Yerworth has written a volume of what he
calls poems." They have the faults which are attributed to the
school of Mr. Swinburne, and none of the excellences which are
found in Mr. Swinburne's writings. We will quote one stanza as a
specimen of Mr. Yerworth's more decent mood :—

> "Tra, la, la, la,
> Ye never knew
> A daughter damn her mother?
> Tra, la, la, la,
> Did'st ever have a brother?"

Mr. Yerworth calls this "The Song of the Fool." The language is
not ours.

Mr. Hannay" with some pretty verses for children has mixed a great
deal of dreary rhymes for the critics ; we imagine no one else will
read them. Mr. Hannay is very grateful for the commendation
which he has already won from the "Gentlemen of the Fourth
Estate." He is welcome to ours ; his book is an extremely short one.

"The Iron Strike, and other Poems,"" contains lines that are not
unpleasant reading, but we prefer Mr. Swinburne's own work to these
echoes of his music upon inferior instruments. Yet some of the
shorter poems, such as "Wrong," "A Legend of Peel Castle," have a
note of their own, which the author would do well to cultivate.

Mrs. Campbell's "Snatches of Song"" contains some tender and
amiable verses. We think they may fairly rank with many by
Mrs. Hemans.

The series of Ancient Classics for English readers, which is edited
by Mr. Lucas Collins, has been increased by the Hesiod and Theognis
of Mr. Davies." The present volume does not fall below the high
standard which has been uniformly maintained throughout, and is
interesting even to the reader who is acquainted with the original.
One of the best chapters is that on Hesiod's proverbial philosophy.
There is also an excellent account of the "Shield of Hercules," and
the chapter upon "Imitators of Hesiod" shows the great influence
which the early poet had upon later literature. As a whole Mr.
Davies's book may be taken up by the English reader and read with
profit and pleasure ; and the classical scholar will find here a clearly
arranged account of the "father of didactic poetry."

" "Poems of the Passions." By Horace Yerworth. London : John Campden
Hotten.

" "Rhymes and Sonnets." By Robert C. F. Hannay. London : Samuel
Palmer.

" "The Iron Strike, and other Poems." By a Bohemian. London : Trübner
and Co.

" "Snatches of Song." By Jessie Morison—Mrs. Campbell of Ballochyle.
London : Longmans.

" "Hesiod and Theognis." By Rev. James Davies, M.A. Edinburgh : W.
Blackwood and Sons

Nothing can be more perfect in its kind than the exquisite little edition of Greek plays by Mr. Sidgwick of Rugby." It is delightful to take them up and read them; a task which Mr. Sidgwick's running commentary makes easy even to a poor scholar. The few words which are inserted in the form of stage directions give vivacity and force to the words of the speakers and call up a visible image of the scene. The grammatical notes are as good as the design of the work, and as we should expect from so distinguished a scholar. Indeed, none but a scholar could have written the suggestive grammatical index with which the present number closes.

Dr. W. Smith has edited a small history of England," and his name is a guarantee for good work. It is a successful attempt to exhibit the leading facts and events, and is free from political and sectarian bias.

A very interesting and, as it seems to us, important work is now being issued in numbers, of which there will be twelve. The first" is before us, and we are compelled to speak of it briefly as it reached us late. Its object is to bring together in consecutive order some of the results of recent researches in archaic anthropology, comparative mythology, linguistic science, and historical criticism for the elucidation of the natural history of Christianity. The book opens with the date B.C. 14,000, a date derived from a calculation of the rate at which the Niagara Falls wear away their channel. Other dates of remote antiquity are also given, dates derived from geological and anthropological research, which tend to show that the popular notion derived from an inconsiderate view of Scriptural dates is utterly false. The book is full of the results of learning and is deeply interesting. If there is any fault in it, it is that it seems to lack the calm judicial dignity which gives science its strength, and is rather polemic and controversial in tone. Yet it brings together many and weighty facts which cannot be too widely known.

Three large volumes" by M. Dupeyron fill up a gap in the history of French commerce which has hitherto been left blank. The reign of Louis XIV. was important before all others, no less for its commercial importance than its military successes; but this period has hitherto been without a historian who would deal with it from a commercial point of view. With the history of commerce, M. Dupeyron has combined the history of political and military events, and has brought down the whole through the American war of Independence to the end of the eighteenth century.

▪ "Scenes from Euripides." Rugby edition, Ion. By A. Sidgwick, Late Fellow of Trinity College, Cambridge. Rivingtons.
▪ "A Primary History of Britain." Edited by Dr. W. Smith. London : John Murray.
77 "Dates and Data, Relating to Religious Anthropology and Sacred Ecclesiastical History. London : Trübner and Co.
▪ "Histoire des Négociations Commerciales et Maritimes de la France, aux xviime et xviiime siècles. Par P. de Ségur Dupeyron. Paris : Ernest Thorin.

BELLES LETTRES.

MRS. LUNN'S "Only Eve,"[1] decidedly claims a high place amongst novels this quarter. We do not remember to have met Mrs. Lunn's name before. And there are evidences that this is either a first or a very early work. The apprentice hand is more or less visible in minor matters of detail. There is a certain raggedness about parts, which is the more noticeable because Mrs. Lunn is a thorough artist. Certain chapters seem either to have been written in a great hurry, or else never to have received the last finishing strokes. Yet these short-comings in no way detracts from the very great merits of the work. They are mere surface blemishes, which can easily be removed. The merits are real. The story takes its title from the heroine, to whom we are introduced in a most pathetic scene. Our bald version will of course do great injustice to Mrs. Lunn's touching narrative. Late one night, as Mr. Cameron sat playing the "Messiah" alone, pausing for a moment over one of those more delicate passages in which, every time he played it, he found some new grace, he suddenly heard the tones of a fine rich voice outside in the street. And there in the rain and east wind stood a young girl, her bare feet gleaming on the wet pebbles, and her drenched hair blown about her naked shoulders. This is "Only Eve," and the story is taken up with the development of Eve as an artist. We wish that Mrs. Lunn had strictly confined herself to the growth of Eve's character and art, and not been led astray into sensation scenes about some local bread-riots. Ours we know is not the advice of Paternoster Row. Publishers and publishers' "readers" seem to think that sensation scenes are the one thing necessary for the success of a novel. They may be with a certain class of readers, who also admire blue fire and Bengal lights in a Transpontine melodrama. If we want these things we can buy *The Police News*, or turn to the still more stimulating pages of the *Newgate Calendar*. But Mrs. Lunn is an artist, and art knows nothing of sensation scenes. These are left for the daubers—the "Ouidas" and Braddons of the trade. Art lives in a region pure and serene. We feel sure that Mrs. Lunn will be the first to acknowledge her mistake, however great the applause from the subscribers to Mudie's. We repeat, she is a thorough artist. The story could not have been written but by one who is thoroughly imbued with the spirit and passion of music. She shows a love for art in the most trivial points. She cannot even bear the name of Daniel Serle, and changes it into San Serle. She spends exquisite pains in even dressing her characters. Most women write about dress like milliners, Mrs. Lunn like an artist. In one place she says—"Dress ought to be the efflorescence of the wearer" (vol. i. p. 127). "Efflorescence" is not quite the right word, though at this moment we cannot suggest a better. But we

---

[1] "Only Eve." By Mrs. J. Galbraith Lunn. London: Sampson Low, Marston, Low and Searle. 1879.

know what Mrs. Lunn means. Here is but another version of Shakspeare's "The apparel oft proclaims the man," which he has also enlarged upon in *As You Like It*. But upon music Mrs. Lunn has lavished all her powers. To all those who love music, and those who do not—for this novel will most assuredly help even them—we most strongly recommend "Only Eve." We will make only one quotation. Eve is speaking:—

" We singing women have to cultivate every sense ; we have to make ourselves beautiful by all means, and we must learn how to feel the most intensely what is beautiful and good, and then to put it into our very souls, to kindle and glow till it lives and shines before the world ; and yet the clear crystal urn is not to be stained or even touched by the quickening fire. Every time we sing we are like flowers opening their inmost hearts to the sunshine, and the rays go in and warm and sweeten every little nook till all is colour, and bliss, and glow. . . . . Then all at once we find we are not those calm, receptive flowers, but women with every feeling and hue of life crushed in our hearts or world-shamed." (Vol. iii. p. 220.)

This alone ought to send all artists, whether musicians or not, to the book.

Dr. Mayo's[1] English friends have, we fear, by their excessive laudations done him a positive injury. Such is the perversity of human nature, that when we are told that anything is full of beauties, we then go to it simply to pick out the faults. Dr. Mayo, we readily admit, is very clever, and his book is full of smart things. But cleverness and smart writing do not make a novel. There is plenty of cleverness in the world, rather too much of it. We should describe Dr. Mayo as a sort of polyglott Dickens. And a polyglott Dickens means Dickens spoilt. Fortunately for himself Dickens was not a scholar. Had he been so he would probably have written in Dr. Mayo's piebald style. He would have loaded his pages with Latin, Greek, and Italian, and said, as Dr. Mayo does of a fashionable lady, that she possessed "a certain aura of *bon ton*" (vol. i. p. 15). Dr. Mayo, however, is not always a polyglott Dickens. Sometimes he is simply a transatlantic Dickens, pure and simple. Here, for instance, is a prescription for sleep recommended by one of his characters :—

"Shirts is the thing. Yes, warm shirts. I have a dozen shirts lying by my bedside. When I can't sleep, I hop out of bed and change my shirt, and I do that every half hour, until I either fall asleep or go through the whole dozen" (vol. i. p. 92).

Now this is Dickens in one of his second-rate moods. Take, however, another example—

"A flowing (oil) well of one hundred and forty barrels, with oil even at four dollars a barrel, is not to be despised. And Mr. Ledgeral didn't despise it. He respected it—he admired it—he rejoiced in it with a deep and grateful joy. He watched it by day with a sentiment of profound thankfulness. He listened to it at night in a state of solemn delight" (vol. ii. p. 578).

Now this is Dickens in one of his worst moods. And we might find

[1] "Never Again." By W. S. Mayo, M.D. Author of "Kaloolah," "The Berber." London : Sampson Low, Son & Co. 1873.

every variety and shade of Dickens in "Never Again," except his very highest moods. To do Dr. Mayo justice however, we find also the best criticism on Dickens which we have ever met with. Here are his remarks on the American scenes in "Martin Chuzzlewit:"—

"All Dickens' American work is so daubty, that there is no light of consciousness in which we can hang it that makes it look like a picture. It is a kind of threshing roundabout with a ridiculous old broom-handle rather than a rawhide. He reminds one of a blind teamster; he whirls his whip around his head quite vigorously, and makes a devil of a cracking, but never really touches the raw" (vol. i. p. 207).

As far as our experience allows us to judge, Dickens' Americans are about as much like Americans as they are probably like the inhabitants of the planet Jupiter. And this brings us to the really weak point of Dr. Mayo's book. He is constantly going off at a tangent to answer the sneers of *Blackwood's Magazine* and the *Saturday Review* against America. Dr. Mayo in a slanging match is more than equal to both of these journals put together. But what has art to do with such matters? Here then, we repeat, is the weak point of the book— that a man, who can evidently achieve much higher things, allows himself to stoop to such puerilities. There is also another weak point. We do not mean to say that Dr. Mayo ostentatiously parades his knowledge, but he writes, if we may for once be allowed to use a slang expression, "literary shop." He suddenly stops in his narrative to quote, to tell us how such and such historical personages felt or did not feel under similar circumstances. In a word he is literary, and therefore weak. Lastly, Dr. Mayo indulges in the detestable habit of punning. If Dr. Mayo is ambitious of having his work translated, he should remember that puns, as a rule, are untranslateable. Dr. Mayo may, however, reply that upon this score he is perfectly indifferent, as in fifty years' time the American language will be the only one spoken by the civilized world. Now we readily admit that we have done the worst that we can to Dr. Mayo's novel, but we have been prompted to play the devil's advocate through the indiscreet laudations of our contemporaries. We hasten, however, to show that we are not blind to its really great merits and beauties. The book is not a great novel in the sense that "Romola" is a great novel. But it most clearly proves that the author, if he only is true to himself, can write a really great work which may live. He has a keen insight, and a true feeling for poetry, as the following passage will show.—"His beauty was something like that often seen in the road-side pool—a passing glance, and all is dark, stagnant, and forbidding—a second look, and lo! in the depths are flitting clouds, and leafy trees, and waving grass and flowers" (vol. i. p. 32). Dr. Mayo's humour, too, is good, though flavoured with a distinct American tone. But the Dorians of course have a right to be as Doric as they please. To our insular taste American wit has something of the flavour of Dr. Mayo's own canvas-back duck to the palate of an European epicure—it is "dubiously delightful." Here is one of Dr. Mayo's good things—"Millioneuse! where did you get that word?" "Oh! that's newspaper French. You don't suppose that a fellow, who has all his life been taking liberty with his native

tongue, hasn't a right to do what he pleases with a foreign language"
(vol. ii. p. 583). We have heard of "Continental English," but
"Newspaper French" is new to us. Here is another—"I don't
believe he'll leave a cent over a million." "Well that's enough to leave
behind one. To be sure it don't count for much in this world,
but you have the satisfaction of knowing that it will count for a great
deal less in the next" (vol. ii. p. 653). Dr. Mayo is evidently of a
different opinion to the English humourist, who, when he heard that
some one had died worth thirty thousand pounds, replied—"A nice sum
to begin the next world with." Lastly, Dr. Mayo's book is written in
a thoroughly manly spirit, which is perfectly refreshing after the sickly
sentiment of the generality of novels, whether American or English.

We confess our ignorance. We have never before heard of
"Johannes Olaf,"* nor its author, "The German George Eliot." Some
of our contemporaries, we perceive, speak of her as Madame de Wille,
and we shall venture to follow suit. We certainly, after the advertisement of "a German George Eliot," opened the book with the highest
expectations. Here we hoped to find, if not a new "Romola," at
least a German "Adam Bede." Who first called Madame de Wille
"a German George Eliot" we are also ignorant. But we can safely
say that whoever did so was entirely ignorant of both George Eliot
and Madame de Wille. To call things by names which they are not,
and to add big capitals, was one of the chief devices for originality of
the late Lord Lytton. A statesman was with him an English Pericles
or a British Cleon as the case might be. The principal beauty of this
figure of speech, as Martinus Scriblerus observes, under "The Art of
Confounding," is that it generally gives an idea just opposite to what
it means to describe. Whoever called Madame de Wille "a German
George Eliot" must have acted strictly according to this principle.
With equal justice we might call Mr. Tupper an English Goethe, or
Mr. W. M. Reynolds a British Novalis. We laboured under the
idea that we understood some of the merits of George Eliot. We
were under the impression that her novels revealed, to a degree hitherto
utterly unknown, the most subtle analysis of character, high descriptive power amounting to prose poetry, deep humour, and the very
perfection of literary art. We have looked in vain through "Johannes
Olaf" for any one of these qualities. For that perfect expression of
thought, which so distinguishes George Eliot, so subtle yet so clear
in its meaning, we discover only that vague sort of rant, which, unfortunately, is so often mistaken by the mass of mankind for ideas and
principles. Of the humour of Mrs. Poyser and Bartle Massey, and
the other wonderful creations of George Eliot, we can discover not a
trace. For that moral elevation of thought, which, in our opinion, is
after all the great charm of George Eliot, we are treated to a quantity
of passion and mysticism, which we do not care to describe. But the
curious part of the whole affair is that the writer has chosen a really
fine subject for a novel, but has deliberately thrown away her oppor-

* "Johannes Olaf." By Elizabeth De Wille. Translated from the German, by
F. E. Bunnett. London : Henry S. King & Co. 1872.

tunities. She has for instance the chance of describing the Elbe and the Rhine, but her descriptions are in the merest commonplace guide-book style. In a chapter "The Serpent's Whispers" she has the opportunity of painting one of the strongest of human passions, but she falls into such bathos, that we actually found ourselves laughing at the utter absurdity of the scene. And so all through, opportunity after opportunity she deliberately misuses. Her reflections are so trite and so silly that their only place is some school-girl's album. Here is a specimen—"Three months had elapsed. What are three months in the ordinary course of time?" (vol. i. p. 202). Precisely a quarter of a year, by which time, we should think, "Johannes Olaf" will be quite forgotten.

If any one, however, wishes to read an average German novel, let him turn to "Gold Elsie,"[4] a pleasant one-volume tale. A former work by the same authoress was not long ago translated under the title of "The Old Maid's Secret," but did not attain to any popularity in England. The present story is likely to be more successful. It contains some charming descriptions of the Thuringian Forest, for which we wish we had space. We must, however, make room for the following little touch—"Here and there a slender, green-tinted sun-beam would slip from bough to bough down upon the feathery grass, and the little strawberry blossoms, sprinkled everywhere like snow-flakes" (p. 23). The translation appears to be finely done, but we are somewhat puzzled by the mention of a "king-bird" (p. 24), a bird entirely unknown under that name in England, and by such a phrase as a "trig little blonde" (p. 92).

We hardly know how to deal with such a book as "Compton Friars,"[5] by the author of "Mary Powell." It appears from the dedication that no less a person than his Grace the Archbishop of Canterbury is in the habit of studying with, as it appears, the most beneficial results, works by this authoress. To the Primate of England is the tale dedicated. We repeat, we do not feel ourselves either capable or worthy of the task of reviewing such a book. We gladly, however, seize the opportunity of allowing our readers to see the kind of literature which his Grace the Archbishop of Canterbury is in the habit of reading. Here is an extract from the first chapter—"Bats are curious creatures —useful too—they live entirely on gnats and other night insects" (p. 4). It must be refreshing to the Archbishop, after the fierce controversies upon Darwinism and anthropoid apes to which he must have lately been subjected, to read such a simple statement of natural history. Here is another little extract from the same chapter on the habits of some human bats, which will, we feel sure, touch his Grace's heart if not surprise his intellect—"The Hartlepools were not rich. Nor did they enter into county society, though the best county families visited and valued them for the sake of something intrinsic,

<hr>

[4] "Gold Elsie." From the German of E. Marlitt. Translated by Mrs. A. L. Wister. London: Strahan and Co. 1873.
[5] "Compton Friars." A Tale of English Country Life. By the Author of "Mary Powell." London: Sampson Low, Marston, Low and Searle. 1872.

seemingly, that they could not help recognising" (p. 5). Even the county families are such angels of light that they have no aristocratic pride in " Compton Friars," but recognise humble merit at first sight. If this is correct we may say of them, as of the bats, " curious creatures—useful too." One more extract from the same chapter—" The first evening was spent in frank, unlimited chat, truly refreshing and recreating. It was entirely female talk" (p. 6). And this is precisely the character of the whole book. It is entirely female talk. That the Archbishop of Canterbury should be pleased with such stuff as this need not, however, excite our surprise.

" Grace Tolmar"* is a strong book, but essentially unpleasant, not from any moral, but an artistic defect. There is no repose. We are kept at one high pitch of excitement. This is, we are quite aware, the ideal of a publisher's novel. We have seen too many letters from publishers' " readers," urging sensation and excitement, not to know what a publisher's model novel means. And this is one. The writer can plainly do very much better. He is evidently an accomplished man, who has seen much more of the world, its ways, and its men and women, than falls to the lot of most people. He has evidently thought, too, for himself. But all these qualifications may not only be wasted, but even turned to a bad account in a novel. His characters are all too much alike. They all, if we may use such an expression, talk at about the same level of excellence. There is not sufficient individuality in them. In the scenes themselves light and shadow are wanting. Again, the author is far too much given to tell us "about and about" persons and things. Thus we are in one place told of Count Itehden that he "supported his views with such short axiomatic, incisive arguments as were not easily answerable" (p. 178). Now this sounds very well, and is quite good enough for the generality of Mudie's subscribers, upon whom incisive arguments would perhaps be wasted. But for all that we confess that we should like to have some at least of these unanswerable arguments, and should have had a higher opinion of the author's abilities if he had given them to us. Again, in another place the author writes, "Count Rehden had then but just returned to Albano, and he entertained me with his pointed remarks upon the people on his travels" (p. 182). Now, as pointed remarks worth anything are so uncommonly rare in novels, we feel somewhat disappointed in being put off in this cavalier fashion. The worst of the matter, however, is that when we do meet with a pointed remark, it is not precisely new. "I warn you, Count Rehden," I said, "to wait before you provoke me too far. I am your master in two ways." "How so?" "For one, I am careless of my own life, and therefore master of yours" (p. 220). This is thoroughly melodramatic, and would go at once to a publishers' "reader's" heart. But unfortunately the saying is rather stale. If the author will turn to Mr. Hayward's recently collected Essays, he will find at least two similar passages—Seneca's *Contemptor tuæmet vitæ, dominus alienæ*, and Henry the Fourth's "he

---

* "Grace Tolmar." A Novel. By John Dangerfield. London: Smith, Elder and Co. 1872.

who despises his own life will always be master of mine." But of course, in a novel an author must be sensational at any price. We have dwelt upon these shortcomings because we feel sure that Mr. Dangerfield is capable of very much higher things. He must, however, learn to despise all the arts and tricks which lead to a little fleeting popularity at Mudie's, and give an ephemeral reputation in Paternoster-row. His strong points are analysis of character and a cultivated feeling for art and nature. We must not forget to say that there are two duel scenes, which, though unpleasant, are remarkably powerful. We hope to see this power turned to a better purpose in Mr. Dangerfield's next tale.

With the remaining works on our table we must deal briefly. The idea contained in "Stories in Precious Stones"[7] is good, and prettily worked out. The authoress has set each month in a stone, the green of May in an emerald, and hot July in a ruby. Many of the tales are very pathetic, and we can recommend the book as a present for young ladies before they wear either emeralds or rubies.

Miss Hesba Stretton has done good work before now, and we may therefore take her "Doctor's Dilemma"[8] upon trust. We certainly do not, however, like the opening of the first chapter—"I think I was as nearly mad as I could be." We have almost the same objection to mad people in novels as in real life. But there are better things than this in the book, especially some charming descriptions of the Channel Islands.

Colonel Meadows Taylor requires no recommendation from us. "Seeta"[9] is sure to be popular with all Anglo-Indians. One thing let us, however, note to his especial honour. "I have," he says, speaking of the Indian mutiny, "purposely avoided the sickening details of pitiless massacres and sufferings." When we remember how certain popular English novelists would have made capital out of the massacres, and gloated over human misery, we cannot be too thankful that there are really brave men left among us of the high stamp and nature of Colonel Meadows Taylor.

Mr. Marsh has in his "For Liberty's Sake"[10] considerably increased the difficulties of reviewing him by mixing up history and fiction. His book is written in a clear style, and his facts, we suppose, are correct. It would have been better, we should have thought, to have brought out the work in the orthodox historical form.

"The Favell Children"[11] may be recommended to very young persons for Sunday reading.

---

[7] "Stories in Precious Stones." By Helen Zimmern. London : Henry S. King and Co. 1873.

[8] "The Doctor's Dilemma." By Hesba Stretton. London : Henry S. King and Co. 1872.

[9] "Seeta." By Meadows Taylor, C.S.I., M.R.I.A., M.R.A.S. Author of "Confessions of a Thug," "Tara," "Ralph Darnell." London : Henry S. King and Co. 1872.

[10] "For Liberty's Sake." By John B. Marsh. London : Strahan and Co. 1873.

[11] "The Favell Children." By Ellen L. Brown. London : Sampson Low, Marston, Low and Searle. 1873.

We have somewhere seen a calculation that considerably over two
hundred new works of poetry are published every year in England.
During the last twenty years, therefore, making allowances for those
who venture upon a second work, we have had no less than four thousand poets amongst us.   Now, as at the outside there are only some
ten recognised poets in the United Kingdom, there must consequently
be three thousand nine hundred and ninety blighted beings. Of course
this blight amongst the poets is put down to the envy, malice, and
uncharitableness of critics.   If critics only did their duty there would
be four thousand poets amongst us.   Here for instance is one of them,
a Mr. Kentish, who writes about "Cæsar in Britain."[12] His method
appears to be to describe a tremendous battle with as much verbiage
as possible, and what is left over he converts into skirmishes.

Now and then we come across a book which excites some hope. The
author of "Songs of Early Spring"[13] has evidently sat at the feet of
Wordsworth. He is, however, no servile imitator. He goes straight to
Nature for his inspiration. He has sung of her in all her moods. We,
however, prefer his Spring pieces most. He has caught something of
the spirit of the season when "heavy Saturn leaps and laughs." This
is the characteristic of our early poets. But in these days, following
the example of a certain French school, we have suddenly become
enamoured with the decaying beauties of Autumn. We do not for one
moment deny those beauties, but there is certain danger of an over-
morbid treatment. We prefer, therefore, the healthy freshness of Mr.
Rowland Brown's muse. But if Mr. Brown means to win a place
amongst the immortal few, he must exercise a far more rigid self-
control over himself than he hitherto has done. It is not enough to
write prettily and gracefully, as Mr. Rowland Brown certainly does,
about May and April, and blossoming orchards, and brooks flowing
amongst banks of flowers. A good deal more than this must be done.
We repeat, however, that Mr. Brown's book certainly excites our hopes,
and we shall look forward with real interest to his next poem.

The "Anthologia Anglica"[14] has been compiled, we are informed in
the preface, "with special reference to that very numerous class of
readers who have not the leisure to search out for themselves the most
beautiful and most valuable of the flowers, often almost concealed by the
very luxuriance of the surrounding vegetation in the garden of English
poetry" (p. viii.). We are sorry to say that the work by no means
carries out the promise which is couched in such flowery language.
We think that the editor might have discovered something better in
Carew than the solitary piece entitled "The Advent of Spring," which
contains such lines as these—

---

[12] "Cæsar in Britain." By Thomas Kentish. London : Basil Montagu Pickering.
1873.
[13] "Songs of Early Spring. With Lays of Labour Life." By Rowland Brown.
London : E. Moxon, Son and Co. 1872.
[14] "Anthologia Anglica."   A New Selection from the English Poets, from
Spenser to Shelley. By Howard Williams, M.A. London : Longmans, Green,
and Co. 1873.

" But the warm sun thaws the benumbed earth,
And makes it tender ; gives a sacred birth
To the dead swallow ; wakes in hollow tree
The drowsy cuckoo." (p. 121.)

In the first place, the swallow does not pass the winter in a state of
suspended animation. In the second place, the cuckoo does not sleep
through the winter in the hole of a tree. We think, too, that the
editor might have given us more than one piece from Herrick. The
book cannot for one moment be compared with Mr. Palgrave's
"Golden Treasury."

We are very glad to see an edition of Chapman's "Dramatic
Works."[13] The poet whom poets, both ancient and modern, have
honoured, the friend of Jonson and Browne, the translator of
Homer, whom Keats loved and Shelley reverenced, well deserves
such a tribute of respect, the best that can be paid to his memory—
the present handsome edition of his plays. The editor has done
his work well. In a graceful memoir he has told us all that is
known of the poet's life, and added a selection of the best criticisms,
including those by Hazlitt and Lamb, on his plays. The notes are to
the point, and give in many instances really valuable information.
The edition ought to find a place in every well-selected library.

There is a story told of some Frenchman, who after he had been
three days in London declared that he thoroughly understood the
English character. He luckily remained three years, and then confessed that he did not understand it so well as with three days' study.
A little knowledge is certainly dangerous. We do not accuse Mr.
Francillon[14] of this fault. But we think that if, instead of only giving
some six or seven pages to the characters, or rather characteristics, of
each nation, he had devoted six or seven chapters to them, he would
have found his difficulties very much increased. It is of course impossible to do justice to any nation in the small space to which Mr.
Francillon has restricted himself. Still in that space a writer may say
all that he has to say, and say it well. This is what Mr. Francillon
does. His style, as we noticed in his amusing novel, "Pearl and
Emerald," is bright and epigrammatic. We do not know that he has
actually added anything to our stock of knowledge, but he has done
good service in exposing several of our insular prejudices. His two
best sketches are those of the typical Frenchman and the typical
German. He points out what every one who has ever resided for
even a few months either in Paris or a French provincial town soon
discovers, that the French, and not the English, are a nation of shop-
keepers. If a Frenchman is not an actual shopkeeper, he very commonly has the soul of one. Those who are under the delusion that all

[13] "The Comedies and Tragedies of George Chapman." Now First Collected,
with Illustrated Notes, and a Memoir of the Author, in Three Volumes. London:
John Pearson. 1873.
[14] "National Characteristics, and Flora and Fauna of London." By R. E.
Francillon, Author of "Pearl and Emerald." London: Smith, Elder and Co.
1872.

Frenchmen are humorous and polite should certainly read Mr. Francillon's sketch of Alphonse. There are of course, as Mr. Francillon
willingly allows, exceptions. Equally good is Mr. Francillon's sketch
of the typical German, as seen in Hans. With the average Englishman Hans bleibt immer Hans. As Mr. Francillon observes, of course
we understood him ; he was our own cousin, so we naturally understood
him. We were, however, not very proud of the connexion. He drank
and smoked so. He wrote, too, such queer books. He made us feel
uncomfortable. With the Oxford Don we wished all the German
literature at the bottom of the German Ocean. Mr. Francillon proceeds to show us the bright side of the shield. He carefully points
out how utterly false is the common vulgar estimate of the German
nation, such as still lingers amongst our middle classes, gathered, we
may suppose, from watching the movements of itinerant German bands
and "buy-a-broom" girls. In all the sketches we find shrewd remarks
scattered up and down. In one place Mr. Francillon notices, "there
never was a dark-eyed man yet, of whatever nation he might bo, who
was not open to the charge of insincerity, never a grey-eyed man who
was not held to be cold and reserved" (pp. 10, 20). Mr. Francillon
might have strengthened his case by quoting the French lines upon
the colours of the eyes, beginning "Les yeux bleus vont aux cieux."
The second portion of Mr. Francillon's book is devoted to sketches of
London and its motley crowd—actors, actresses, Free Lances, Bohemians, and Street Arabs. We hardly care for it so much as for the
first part. Still there are good things in it. His sketch of the prima
donna, in the chapter "Among the Stars," is very truthful, though
running quite contrary to popular notions. His conclusion is—"The
true enthusiast, the true artist in song, seldom becomes a star. She,
perhaps, has the reward ascribed to virtue. A star may be glorious in
itself, it is true; but far more often it shines with reflected light, and
fashion is its sun" (pp. 85, 86). The world will probably be sceptical of
the truth of this assertion, but we believe that Mr. Francillon is in
the main quite right. Another very truthful, but more painful,
chapter is "Among the Caterpillars." These caterpillars never de-
velope into butterflies. They have reversed the process of nature.
They have been butterflies, and have changed to grubs. Once they
were brilliant wits, now they are sots. Once a splendid career was
before them, now their refuge is the pot-house. We boast of the
present state of literature and the high position of literary men and
their great rewards, but listen to Mr. Francillon :—"Go into the
libraries of our great museums, and you will see to what a last pass
the drudgery of hack work still brings men—aye, and women too. It
is simply terrible to see there the haggard faces, the wasted frames,
the hopeless aspect. . . . . No, Grub Street is not swept away. It
has but changed its name and widened its area—that is all" (p. 100).
And Mr. Francillon has not told the worst.

Mr. Noble's "Pelican Papers"[v] is essentially feminine in the worst

---

[v] "The Pelican Papers : Reminiscences and Remains of a Dweller in the Wilderness." By James Ashcroft Noble. London : Henry S. King and Co. 1873.

sense of the term. Paul Pelican is only the *altera ego* of Mr. Noble.
There is not a single masculine idea throughout the book. The writer
mistakes looseness of thought for breadth, and flabbiness of style for
earnestness. Paul Pelican's mental powers may easily be judged.
He admires A. K. H. B., but not Shakspeare. He likes Mr. Henry
Kingsley's "Ravenshoe," but cannot read a page of Hudibras. He
loves Dr. George MacDonald, but not Montaigne. Such a person puts
himself out of court. We are at a loss to know how to judge him.
When a man deliberately informs you that he does not admire Shakspeare, Butler, Montaigne, and Miss Austen, we can only regard him
as imperfectly educated, or else of feeble intellect. He moves our compassion rather than indignation. It is well, however, to know what
he does like. For humour he admires the "Noctes" of Christopher
North. We, on the contrary, are of Blanco White's opinion that they
are one prolonged "intellectual row." In philosophy his guide is Dr.
George MacDonald. What Dr. George MacDonald may say to his
pupil we hardly care to inquire. Here is a bright little bit of Pelican's
philosophy:—"I will listen to any man's dogmatism, and love him
for it, if he is trying with all his heart to make me right; but I will
not listen with anything but loathing if he is only trying with all his
skill to show that I am wrong" (p. 137). We cannot say that we
should love any man on account of his dogmatism, though we might
do so in spite of it. And instead of loathing a man for trying to convince us with all his skill, we should feel that he was paying us a
genuine compliment. We should advise Mr. Noble rather to take for
his maxim—"I will be tolerant of everything, even of another man's
intolerance." It has only been by keeping this aphorism steadily in
our mind that we have been able to read through Mr. Noble's book.

"A piece of soap, and I am ready to start," said one of our generals
at the Horse Guards in reply to the question when he should be prepared to conduct a campaign. "Shawl-straps, and I am ready to go
round the world," cries Miss Alcott, "provided my trunks are sent
forward by luggage-train." This is one of the many morals of her
charming little book.[16] But it contains a great deal besides. Miss
Alcott describes the adventures of three American ladies through
Europe. Amanda is the guide through France, Switzerland and
Italy; Lavinia, for her knowledge of the language, through England;
whilst Matilda acts as a general female Murray and Bradshaw combined. We are not surprised to hear of Italian Counts madly falling
in love with them, or of enthusiastic antiquarians dividing their books
and treasures with them. They carry good spirits wherever they go.
In fact the authoress is sometimes obliged to apologize for their
vagaries. She confesses that Lavinia in Italy pursued the romantic in
a style that was a disgrace to her years, whilst Amanda on one occasion
almost compromised her nation, and Matilda defied the power of
European despots by wildly going about, like a free-born American
girl, without a passport. For this, however, she was justly punished.

---

[16] "Shawl-Straps: a Second Series of Aunt Jo's Scrap-bag." By Louisa M.
Alcott. London: Sampson Low, Marston, Low and Searle. 1873.

Not even the freest-born American can be allowed to commit such
high treason. For this offence she had to be humiliated to the post
of ladysmaid, and to go for a time without her jewellery and those
beautiful gloves of which we hear so much. This is surely punishment
enough to satisfy the sternest European official. The adventures which
these three American ladies went through are certainly exciting. At
Lugano they witnessed an opera in bedgowns and bedquilts. At
Florence they enjoyed a little earthquake, whilst at Rome the Tiber,
so to speak, was turned on for their especial benefit, and a flood was
the result. We regret to say that the art-criticisms of these ladies are
very profane. They appear to have seen little in the Italian churches
and galleries but "green saints in whirlwinds of pink angels." But
amidst all their pleasantry we find plenty of sober criticism, acute observation, and charming descriptions. The chapter on Britany is
particularly good. The authoress however, reserves all her prettiest
compliments for England and the English. Modesty alone prevents
us from giving a quotation. But we should advise all our readers to
turn to the book and see for themselves what a really nice set of people
we are.

The late Mr. Power's "Handy Book About Books"[13] stands to other
books in much the same relation as *Notes and Queries* does to other
papers. It possesses the same sort of out-of-the-way erudition, the
same pleasant aroma of black-letter. It is a book for the bookish, for
bookworms and bibliomaniacs. Mr. Power was, however, something
more than a bookworm or a bibliomaniac. The present work testifies
both to his scholarly knowledge and his artistic taste. Mr. Power has
practised what he preached. He was a lover of handsome bindings.
He has therefore enshrined his present work in two covers, one Italian
and the other French, both of the best sixteenth century work. He
advocated toned paper for books, and accordingly his pages are of a
soft, delicate cream-colour, which is a great relief to the eyes. He
was an admirer of the so-called "silver letter," and his book is printed
in a type which may almost equal it for clearness. Lastly, he was
always most urgent that every book should be provided with a good
index, and we accordingly find the best and fullest which we ever met.
His index is indeed a work of itself. Now it is obvious that in these
material, but still very important matters, the publisher should share
the credit and the honour with the author. We certainly congratulate
Mr. Wilson on the handsome style in which he has brought out the
work, whether as regards binding, paper, or type. Its contents are
very varied. One of the most interesting chapters to the student is
that on Bibliography. Nothing is so much wanted, so to speak, as A
Catalogue of Catalogues. Thus, a student of Shakspeare wants to
know all the works which have been written on his especial subject.
The shortness of life will not allow him to go hunting through the
British Museum Catalogue. Mr. Power partly supplies this great
want by giving the titles of various catalogues of Shakspearian works.

13 "A Handy-Book about Books. For Book-lovers, Book-buyers, and Booksellers." Attempted by John Power. London: John Wilson. 1873.

This alone is an enormous boon, and will save the student many a weary day's search. Several we perceive, he has omitted, but completeness in such an undertaking is utterly impossible. It is a great thing that such a good start has been made, and we have no doubt that the work will in a second edition be carried on, and as far as it is possible made exhaustive. The chapter on Chronology is excellent. It is full of that out-of-the-way sort of knowledge, of those odds and ends which one so soon forgets, and which one is always glad to learn again. It begins B.C. 50 with the invention of printing in China, and ends A.D. 1870 with the introduction of halfpenny post-cards in England. We notice a slip of the pen under the year 1010 in the statement that Shakspeare and Cervantes died on the same day (page 37). This error has arisen from forgetting that the Styles in England and Spain were not then the same. One of the most amusing chapters, however, is that entitled Miscellaneous. It is full of that sort of lore about rare books and rare editions, and their prices, which delights the hearts of bibliomaniacs. It contains, too, all kinds of hints about bookbinding and the preservation of books. We learn from Mr. Power that morocco, as it certainly is the handsomest, is also in the long run the most durable of bindings, and we are warned to no longer put our trust in Russian leather as a preservative against moths and bookworms. We notice, however, a singular omission. We ventured to look for the true meaning of that mysterious term "foxed," which we find so often in the catalogues of second-hand booksellers, but Mr. Power is silent, and gives us neither the derivation of the word nor a remedy for the evil. The chapter on the Provincial Booksellers' Directory is necessarily far from complete. Now, as Mr. Power has dedicated his book to the readers of *Notes and Queries*, we think it would be only a graceful compliment on their part if they would send to that journal a note of those towns omitted by Mr. Power, where printing has been carried on, with a list of the most remarkable books published. Every collector of glossaries and local works bearing upon provincialisms knows the enormous difficulty that there is, not in merely procuring them, but in discovering even their existence. In this way a very great evil, which is of course growing greater as the books increase in rarity, would be remedied. Few, except scholars, appreciate the real value of local books. Foreigners often notice the fact that we have very few good local presses in England compared with those in France and Germany. We believe, however, that we could show quite as fine specimens of local printing and of valuable local books, as they can, if the matter was properly investigated. In conclusion, let us most strongly recommend "The Handy Book About Books," not merely to bibliomaniacs, who are too often only "collectors of books for the sake of binding," but to all scholars, students, publishers, and booksellers.

In speaking of an "Introduction to the Study of Dante"[*] it is

---

[*] "An Introduction to the Study of Dante." By John Addington Symonds, M.A., late Fellow of Magdalen College, Oxford. London: Smith, Elder and Co. 1872.

fair to regard it from the point of view of those to whom it is
addressed. Now it is not properly addressed to those who have
already, by long and loving study, familiarized themselves with the
poet's writings. Of course it ought to be such that even these will
read it with pleasure and gain something, too, from reading; but they
are not its proper readers. It speaks necessarily, and in the first
place, to those to whom Dante is as yet a sealed volume; to those
who are looking about for some guide to his history and meaning.
First of all, then, they would desire such a sketch of Italian history,
and of the poet's own life and deeds and opinions as might furnish
what may be called the proper setting of the poem. Then would
follow an outline of the poem itself, and an interpretation of its purpose, with such remarks on the distinguishing genius of the author as
might enable them to know what to look for when they commenced a
fuller study for themselves. Now the first part of these conditions
Mr. Symonds has very well satisfied. His early history of Italy and
his account of Dante's own life and personality leave little that could
be desired in an Introduction. His sketch of Dante's principal work,
" The Divina Commedia," is necessarily less complete and satisfactory.
And yet he has told us a great deal that may assist and stimulate
further reading; and has certainly, on the whole, characterized the
author's genius correctly. To say that he has not done so completely
appears almost ungracious where so much has been done well, and
where complete success must be well nigh impossible. The parts
which have been left most imperfect are the chapters on Dante's
similes, and on the metre and laws of the Terza Rima. The former of
these is singularly imperfect; the latter singularly inaccurate. It
is quite untrue to say that much license is allowed in the Terza
Rima, and that the scansion of the verse is determined less by
feet than by accent and emphasis. The apparent irregularities of
the metre almost entirely disappear if the two vowels i and u
are correctly sounded, that is with the consonant sound of y and w.
We remark, too, throughout the volume, a little excess of rhetorical
language. Many pretty little sentences are obviously introduced for
their prettiness, and had far better be omitted. And this is the more
pity, because they are sometimes very pretty and expressive—if only
we had not quite so many of them, and if they bore less obvious marks
of elaboration. We think, too, that Mr. Symonds need not have told
us that " what Dante fancied " in his vision of the scenes of Paradise,
" need not correspond in detail to the actual truth ;" and that " when
the darkness of this life is dispelled, and the wrestling with the flesh is
past, the purged and disembodied spirit may be destined to behold no
snow-white petals of the everlasting rose expand above it." The
remark may be a true one, and might be extended with equal propriety
to the rest of the poem, but it is difficult to imagine what class of
readers would be likely to fall into the error which it is intended to correct. We think Mr. Symonds' best chapter is that on "The Poetry of
Chivalrous Love." It is a little nonsensical in parts, but not more so
than is in perfect accordance with the subject of which it treats. Joie
and Mania can hardly be described with an excess of rhetoric. His

own translations from the Provençal poets are admirable. On the whole we must thank Mr. Symonds very cordially for his little volume; but must add, whether by way of praise or censure, that we think he would succeed better in an introduction to Petrarch than to Dante.

"Beim Lachen kann man werden
Wohl hundert Jahre alt"

is frequently quoted in Germany by the industrious collectors of jokes. But, as a rule, German jest books do not excite laughter, though by the way it must be confessed, that our best Shakespeare Jest Book has been edited by a German. But then the Germans do everything connected with Shakspeare well. However, we have before us a volume[91] which will help to take away much of the reproach which attaches to German collections of jokes. The illustrations, although rather too much in the Kladderadatsch style, are decidedly above the average. One of the best, perhaps, is that which illustrates Heine's "Der liebenswürdige Jüngling." There is genuine character in every face of the audience. Some of the others are far too broad for our taste. The wit which depends upon coarseness simply disgusts. The collection itself is free from this fault. Good wit, as all good art is, is much the same in all ages. We therefore were not startled to find the Aristophanic Βρεκεκεκὲξ κοὰξ κοὰξ reproduced in German. The frogs of Berlin and Athens, we suppose, croak much in the same note. In another piece, "Hindernisse," there is a complete Noah's Ark of animals. The cock crows, the dog barks, the kitten mews, all upon true onomatopoëtic principles. We plead guilty to liking these popular ballads (Volkslieder), or as some people might call them, Nursery songs, far better than those which make greater pretensions. There is an excellent one, "Der Spielmannsohn," to which the reader can attach a second meaning. But we are afraid that that day is still far off when moral sentiment or art shall have any power to restrain the passion of emperors and kings.

There are three achievements to which every literary knight-errant seems bound to devote his energies—to releasing the Man in the Iron Mask, and the discovery of Junius and Mr. W. H. The Man in the Iron Mask, since Matthioli's claims are now generally admitted, no longer excites the curiosity which he did, although MM. Topin and Iung still continue to write, but public interest is as keen as ever concerning Junius and Mr. W. H. For our own part, we consider these two questions as of very secondary importance. If, however, German thoroughness, and we may add German audacity, can settle the matter, Herr Krauss[92] may rest content. If anybody can believe that Mr. W. H. stands for Henry Wriothesley, Lord Southampton, he can also probably follow Herr Krauss in his other ingenious theories. We

[91] "Deutscher Humor in Possie." Illustrirt von Oskar Pletsch, J. Füllhaas, u. A. Zweite bedeutend vermehrte und verschönerte Auflage. Leipzig: G. F. Amelang. 1872.
[92] "Shakspeare's Southampton-Sonnette." Deutsch von Fritz Krauss. Leipzig: Wilhelm Engelmann. 1872.

have only two or three brief remarks to make. We should always remember that it is not Shakspeare, but his publisher, who writes this extraordinary dedication. What kind of men publishers were in Shakspeare's days, and how, for the purpose of making a dishonourable profit, they treated Shakspeare, we need not here say. Had Shakspeare himself written the dedication, it would have been quite another matter. A publisher's dedication should no more interest us than a publisher's puff. In both cases it is done with the same object, and in both cases it is likely to be equally false. It is no answer to say that Shakspeare did not remonstrate, for we know that he did not remonstrate in other cases, where the most flagrant injustice had been done to him by publishers. The true interest, however, of the Sonnets consists in the fact that they show us the man Shakspeare, and open before us his personal history, his innermost feelings, his sorrows, his joys, his doubts—in a word, reveal the creator of Hamlet and Lear. Of the translation by Herr Krauss we can speak in the highest terms. It is not only faithful, but poetical. The notes are to the point. With regard to what flower Shakspeare means by marigold, which Herr Krauss rightly enough translates by "ringelblume," we should advise him to consult Beisly's "Shakspeare's Garden," a work scarcely known in Germany, and which, in spite of Dyce's strictures, is written with great care and industry.

Some thirty years ago Carlyle complained, in a well-known article, that Richter[a] was completely unknown to the English public. Thanks to Mr. Carlyle and others, no writer is now perhaps so well known in England as "Jean Paul," "der einzige." One of those little volumes which Germans always do so well, giving extracts from his works, will be welcomed by Richter's English admirers. It is compiled on much the same method as Herr Merz's little work, "Goethe als Erzieher." It consists of a selection of those thoughts which the Germans delight to call "Lichtstrahlen" and "Gedankenspäne," and the French "Pensées," and for which we have no other equivalent besides "Aphorisms" or "Apophthegms," neither of which quite conveys the exact shade of meaning. There is no occasion at this time of day to pass any special criticisms on Jean Paul's "Thoughts." Their gauge has been long ago pretty accurately taken. Here, however, is a reflection upon anger —"Der Zorn hat die Farbe und die Bedeutung der Morgenröthe." We will not attempt any explanation of this enigma, the mere mystery of which is so delightful to some minds, and which from its very want of clearness passes at once for wisdom. Nor will we compare it with what Bacon has said on the same subject. We will take a master of English humour, as Jean Paul is of German humour—Swift. This is what that satirist, who after Bacon has uttered some of the most trenchant aphorisms in our language, says—"To be angry is to revenge the faults of others upon ourselves." This we can understand, and apply practically in the daily concerns of life. But about Jean Paul's cloudy simile we know nothing, except that a red sunrise is often the forerunner of a stormy day, which is far too prosaic a doctrine for any true disciple in mysticism. We do not, of course, mean to say that there are not better things in the book. On the contrary, many are very noble and highly poetical. But whenever we have been able to test the value of the purely philosophical sayings with parallel passages in our own Bacon, or the more worldly ones with those of Rochefoucault, their inferiority has been apparent. These sayings of Jean Paul's should be compared with those of Vauvenargues or Joubert or Novalis. A study of this kind, such as Miss Martin has so well performed in another direction for Guicciardini, would be of real value. In the meantime we heartily commend the present interesting little volume to all admirers of Jean Paul. It puts in a small compass and in a convenient shape all the best sayings of their favourite author.

It is, however, as a humorist that Richter is most widely known. He has been placed by universal consent in the very first rank of the world's humorists. Cervantes alone has been thought worthy to be his peer. We must confess to having some doubts on the matter; and the examination of a little volume, " Jean Paul als Grossmeister deutschen Humors,"[24] has by no means helped to weaken our scepticism. What we mean is, that his manner of saying a thing contributes far more to the humorous effect than the actual matter. Take for instance his famous comparison of mankind to a flock of sheep all following the old bell-wether, which has been so highly praised by Carlyle. There is nothing very original in the idea, and certainly nothing very humorous ; precisely the same simile may be found in Charron, in whose pages it does not raise the faintest smile. But told in Jean Paul's grotesque fashion, it is undoubtedly humorous and telling. Form in humour is everything. If Grimaldi merely said "Good morning," people roared with laughter. So with Jean Paul. It is his manner which is humorous, rather than the substance. Often in reading the present volume we have turned to the title-page to make quite sure that we had not taken up some second-rate German jest-book. Here, for instance, is a sample of rather feeble joking, for it loses its point in a translation—" Die Bücher haben die meisten Eselsohren, deren Väter keine haben" (p. 27). Without multiplying quotations we can simply say that many of the examples of Jean Paul's humour given in the present volume appear to us fanciful, many strained, and more affected. The editor's excuse will probably be, *Aliter non fit, Avite, liber*. There are, however, plenty of good things to be found. Here is one which contains a subtle bit of criticism—"Die meisten jetzigen Dichter haben von den Spinnen nur das Talent zu spinnen, nicht zu weben" (p. 80). And here is another which is still more trenchant—"Oft ist die Ehe wie zwei Fettropfen, die auf dem Wasser schwimmen, ohne zusammen zu fliessen" (p. 35). We might easily make a tolerably long list of such sayings. It is only justice to add that Jean Paul appears at his best in the longer extracts, for which we have not space. His humour, in short, wants plenty of page to roll and rollick about in.

---

[24] "Jean Paul als Grossmeister deutschen Humors." Blüten und Perlen aus seinen Werken. Ausgewählt von Eduard Kauffer. Reudnitz : C. Förster.

We prefer the introduction of "Der Grobschmied von Antwerpen"[52] to the actual poem. The writer shows facility of expression, a command of metre, and at times a felicity of language, especially in describing scenery. We would gladly, had space permitted, have given some specimens of his descriptive poems. A short time since we called attention to Auerbach's "Zur guten Stunde,"[54] and the same praise which we then bestowed we can extend to the numbers now before us.

We must briefly acknowledge various new editions and reprints. Conspicuous amongst them are "The Idylls of the King,"[57] containing Mr. Tennyson's colonial views, upon which we may have something to say at another time. Mr. Blackmore's "Cradock Nowell"[58] has been revised. We are glad to see that he has not yielded to some of his critics, and removed those provincialisms which gave such a charming local colouring to his descriptions of the New Forest scenery. New editions of the "Fool of Quality,"[59] and Charlotte Brontë's "Professor,"[60] conclude our list. The last is particularly well got up.

ART.

DR. WOLTMANN'S "Architectural History of Berlin,"[1] has already arrived at a second edition. At first sight the subject does not appear to be very promising, either for scientific or for popular treatment. Berlin is (as indeed the author starts by saying) a thoroughly modern town in character, modern to a degree in which it is resembled but by few other cities in Europe. It is true that Berlin dates its existence from the middle ages, but the existing monuments of that epoch which it possesses are neither many nor important. In its later days it has shown no disposition to respect the past, and whilst much has been left to go to ruin, much has also been destroyed. The historian of Berlin architecture can derive therefore, but scanty elements of interest from the usual sources. Two brief chapters sum up the building activity of the city in the middle ages, and

[52] "Der Grobschmied von Antwerpen in Sieben Historien." Von Gottfried Kinkel. Stuttgart: J. G. Cotta. 1872.

[54] "Zur guten Stunde." Von Berthold Auerbach. Stuttgart: Carl Hoffmann 1872.

[57] "The Works of Tennyson." Vols. v, vi. "Idylls of the King." London: Strahan and Co. 1873.

[58] "Cradock Nowell. A Tale of the New Forest." Diligently Revised and Reshapen. By R. Doddridge Blackmore. London: Sampson Low, Marston, Low, and Searle. 1873.

[59] "The Fool of Quality." By Henry Brooke. Newly Revised by Rev. C. Kingsley, M.A. London: Macmillan and Co. 1872.

[60] "The Professor. With Poems by Charlotte Brontë." London: Smith, Elder and Co. 1873.

[1] "Die Baugeschichte Berlins bis auf die Gegenwart." Von Dr. Alfred Woltmann, Professor der Kunstgeschichte am Polytechnicum zu Carlsruhe. 2nd edition: Berlin. Paetel, 1872.

under the Hohenzollern Kurfürsts. The opening of the third brings us at once to the eighteenth century, to the days of Friederick the first King of Prussia. The method which the author has adopted, and by means of which he manages to infuse spirit and vitality throughout the whole book, is to let us know something of the character of each succeeding chief architect as a man. Thus Dr. Woltmann's narrative ceases to be a purely technical account and criticism of a quantity of more or less unsatisfactory monuments now cumbering the ground, and becomes a living history of human effort, and its imperfect outcome. The interest which he thus makes us feel in each individual architect inclines us to be patient even with the defects and shortcomings of his work, inclines us to regard them only as the monuments of not to be avoided failure, which are inevitable in each struggle of the human intelligence to shape for itself outward expression. It is owing to this treatment that the reader follows the history of the works undertaken by Friederick the First with such active attention. In Andreas Schlüter, the court sculptor, the king possessed an artist of unquestionable ability, to whom eventually he confided the direction of the rebuilding of the royal Schloss. The jealousy of the professional architects was aroused, a successful intrigue skilfully employed against him, the insecure construction of his great tower, which was to have formed the principal feature of the whole group of buildings, thus achieved his downfall and disgrace. With the death of Schlüter, the chapter closes, and the charm of genius fades away from the buildings of Berlin. Under Friederick Wilhelm the First nothing was done that had any artistic pretension; it is not until we come to the work executed by Knobelsdorff during the early part of the reign of Friederick the Great, that we find again even the impress of strong individual character. The gap between the death of Knobelsdorff and the rise of Schinkel, is occupied by the ruling days of French taste (Carl von Gontard), followed by the reaction as personified by Langhaus. On the life and works of Schinkel, the writer dwells with zealous enthusiasm at considerable length, and concludes with a careful notice of contemporary work which shows, he says, a tendency to the study of Greek and Renaissance work. It must not however be supposed that Dr. Woltmann has treated his subject from a purely literary point of view, he has not neglected to give the reader an ample measure of technical criticism and information, and every chapter contains a sufficient number of well-executed illustrations, by the examination of which the author's commentaries and conclusions may be tested.

"Studies in the History of the Renaissance"[1] is the title of a volume of essays (several of which have already appeared in print) recently published by Mr. Walter Pater, Fellow of Brasenose College, Oxford. The title is misleading. The historical element is precisely that which is wanting, and its absence makes the weak place of the whole book. The contents embrace a wide field. The names of Pico della Mirandula,

---

[1] "Studies in the History of the Renaissance." By Walter H. Pater. London: Macmillan and Co., 1872.

of Botticelli, of Michael Angelo, of Joachim du Bellay, standing at the
head of respective chapters, will be a sufficient indication of its variety
as well as extent. But the work is in no'wise a contribution to the
history of the Renaissance. For instead of approaching his subject,
whether in Art or Literature, by the true scientific method, through
the life of the time of which it was an outcome, Mr. Pater prefers in
each instance to detach it wholly from its surroundings, to suspend it
isolated before him, as if it were indeed a kind of air-plant independent
of the ordinary sources of nourishment. The consequence is that he
loses a great deal of the meaning of the very objects which he regards
most intently. This is especially noticeable when he passes from the
examination of fragments to deal with the period as a whole. Take
for instance the passages of general criticism with which the first
essay opens. Mr. Pater writes of the Renaissance as if it were a kind
of sentimental revolution having no relation to the conditions of the
actual world. Whilst he discriminates or characterizes with great
delicacy of touch the sentiment of the Renaissance, he does not let us
know that it was precisely as the expression of vital changes in human
society that this sentiment is so pregnant for us with weighty meaning.
Thus we miss the sense of the connexion subsisting between art and
literature and the other forms of life of which they are the outward
expression, and feel as if we were wandering in a world of unsubstantial
dreams. We do not feel that the writer has that intimate possession
of his subject in its essence and entirety which alone can convey to us
the impression of reality. The hold upon the art of the day becomes
uncertain because the grasp of the life of the day is ill-assured. This
it is which destroys for us much of the charm of a charming book, a
book which shows a touch of real genius. Mr. Pater possesses to a
remarkable degree an unusual power of recognising and finely discriminating delicate differences of sentiment. He can detect with
singular subtlety the shades of tremulous variation which have been
embodied in throbbing pulsations of colour, in doubtful turns of line,
in veiled words ; he can not only do this, but he can match them for
us in words, in the choice of which he is often so brilliantly accurate
that they gleam upon the paper with the radiance of jewels. In this
respect these studies of the sentiment of the Renaissance have a real
critical value. But they are not history, nor are they even to be
relied on for accurate statement of simple matters of fact. For instance,
Mr. Pater tells the old legend of how Leonardo da Vinci, when a boy,
was allowed by his master, Verrochio, to paint an Angel for him in the
left hand corner of a Baptism of Christ which Verrochio was executing
for the brethren of Vallombrosa, and how Verrochio turned away when
it was finished as one stunned, seeing the pupil had surpassed the
master. This story has long been exploded as having no foundation,
nor even verisimilitude, and the angel, which may still be seen at
Florence, shows not a trace of special beauty nor even a sign that it
has been touched by a different hand to that which painted the rest of
the picture. Yet Mr. Pater actually calls the figure "a space of sunlight in the cold laboured old picture." And again, Mr. Pater is quite
mistaken in supposing that "M. Arsène Houssaye, gathering together

all that is known about Leonardo in an easily accessible form, has done for the third of the three great masters what Grimm has done for Michael Angelo, and Passavant, long since, for Raffaelle. Antiquarianism has no more to do." M. Houssaye's book is a mere romance of no scientific pretensions whatever.

The first part of Theodor Simons' " Culturbilder aus altroemischer zeit'" is now before us. It contains pictures of a gladiatorial show and a wild beast fight in the arena at Pompeii, and of a chariot race in the Circus Maximus at Rome. In each instance the notes contain a quantity of valuable antiquarian and archaeological matter, out of which the writer constructs the highly dramatic account given in the text. The descriptions are somewhat in the style in which the foreign correspondent of the *Daily Telegraph* might report, during a dull political period, on the bull fights of Madrid. The incidents thrown in to fill the canvas are of the most sensational character. At the chariot race we hear an awful shriek. It comes from a young Roman lady, who falls down dead. Julia, Caesar's daughter, jealous of a Silvia who has surpassed her in the affections of a good-looking charioteer, had sent by her own slave, in the name of the charioteer, a flask of poisonous odours as a gift to her rival. The slave, in his haste, makes a mistake, and instead of Silvia, the young Roman lady drops down dead. However, every one seems equally well satisfied. It seems to us that the effort to reconstruct the Past in this wise, especially when carried out on so large a scale as in the present book, is but a waste of good work. These pictures of the manners and customs of old Rome aspire to be something more reliable than mere fiction, and yet we cannot accept without large reservations the facts which they marshal before us. A great deal of real knowledge and solid labour is applied to the production of a work which, however amusing, effective, and spirited it may be, remains, after all, but an elaborate *jeu d'esprit*. We cannot criticise it as a romance, nor can we give it a place on our shelves amongst works of historical or archaeological research. In spite of all the serious learning on which it is based, the book remains a kind of literary bubble, neither literature nor art. In Alexander Wagner the author has found a sympathetic illustrator, whose pencil possesses all the dash, the spirit, the graphic sensationalism of the text. The picture of the chariot race, for certain lordly qualities of bold theatricality and brazen effect, is worthy Gustave Doré, to whose school Alexander Wagner evidently belongs.

The January and February numbers of *The Picture Gallery*,[4] published by Messrs. Sampson Low and Marston, contain examples both of ancient and modern art, some of which are of considerable excellence. Each part for this year contains four autotypes, amongst which we may specify that from Hanfstaengl's lithograph after Rembrandt's portrait of his daughter, in the Gallery at Dresden, which is given in

---

[3] "Aus Altroemischer Zeit. Culturbilder." By Theodor Simons. With illustrations by A. Wagner. 1st part. Berlin : Pastel 1872.
[4] "The Picture Gallery." Vol. ii., Nos. 1-2. Sampson Low, Marston, and Co. London : 1873.

the February number, and the hardly less charming reproduction by
the same process of Sir Joshua Reynolds' picture of the Hon. Frances
Ingram, which appeared in January. The January number, too, contained
Sir Edwin Landseer's popular composition, "The Stag at Bay." The
letterpress is, unfortunately, hardly up to the mark of the illustrations.

Mr. Cooke tells us that in the production of his volume of drawings
of "Grotesque Animals"[a] he has aimed at simple amusement. Going
down to the seaside for rest, after the meeting of the British
Association at Manchester in 1864, he spent the day in painting
coast scenes; and the evening in making a series of grotesque combinations, "adapted from his multitudinous sketches of fossils, marine,
and other animals, obtained during long workings with the microscope
from nature and museum collections." The first of the series produced
was a sketch of a crested cockatoo, emerging from the shell of an
ammonite; the shell of the ammonite has a tail on one of the ribs, and
stands on a human leg, which terminates toe and heel in talons. The
fault of this combination, and indeed of all the others, regarded from
an artistic point of view, is that we at once become aware that the
animal before us is a mere thing of bits, which are pieced together so
unskilfully that the joins are everywhere perceptible. The imagination
of the artist has in no single instance attained power and heat sufficient
to run these totally distinct morsels into a whole, consequently not
one object can make upon us any distinct impression. Not one can
reach the charm of grace, or force of terror, or accent of drollery, but
all remain ingenious, and sometimes offensive, pieces of patchwork.
Even if now and then some portion of an animal has a touch of character in it, the effect is quickly lost in its war with the other parts
which go to its composition, and the eye goes on instinctively separating the loosely connected bits, uninformed by any common meaning or intention, which it feels to have been brought together out of
pure caprice. It is to be hoped that, should the volume arrive at a
second edition, Mr. Cooke will get some one to look over the spelling
of the Latin mottoes which occur on several pages, and which is far
from correct.

Any observations on the art of singing which come from the pen of
Manuel Garcia[b] have a value and an authority quite unique. The son
of his father (Manuel Vicente Garcia), and the brother of his sister
(Madame Malibran) enjoys a family right to a hearing when a family
talent is in question, but Señor Garcia need not rest one tittle of his
claim upon the renown of his relatives. He himself is a distinguished
man, and as only some twenty years of his life have been spent in England, it may be worth while to show how far his distinction is honestly
enjoyed. Having first studied harmony under the late M. Fétis, and

---

[a] "Grotesque Animals, Invented, drawn, and described." By E. W. Cooke,
R.A., F.R.S., F.G.S., F.Z.S., &c. Longmans, Green, & Co. London: 1872.
[b] "Garcia's New Treatise on the Art of Singing. A Compendious Method of
Instruction, with Examples and Exercises for the Cultivation of the Voice." By
Manuel Garcia. London: Hutchens & Romer.

singing under his gifted father, Manual Garcia went upon the operatic stage in 1825, and accompanied his family throughout a lengthened American tour. Returning to Paris in 1829, he retired from the position of a public performer, and devoted himself to the work of teaching. But Garcia was no mere formalist, satisfied to act in accordance with the accepted rules of his craft; and he began seriously to study the conformation of the vocal organs, with a view thoroughly to master the phenomena of their mechanism. The result was that, in 1840, he presented to the Science department of the Institute a "Memoire sur la voix humaine," concerning which a report, drawn up by MM. Magendie, Savart, and Dutrochet, was read at the sitting of April 12, 1841. In this work, Garcia scientifically proved certain theses of the highest consequence to vocal art, and was felicitated by the Academicians upon the value of his observations. Having been named Professor of Singing at the Conservatoire, Garcia published in 1847 the work of which an English edition, enlarged and improved, is now before us. The "Traité complet de l'art du Chant" was originally intended for his own pupils, but was subsequently given to the world, and received in a manner which, better than anything else could possibly have done, testified its merits. A German translation has made the book popular in the musical country *par excellence*, and wherever the vocal art is studied with earnest purpose, it is accepted as an authority of the greatest weight. Incidentally we may remark, that Señor Garcia's pursuit of special knowledge laid the whole world under a great and enduring obligation. It is to him that medical science owes the invaluable laryngoscope, by means of which not only the mechanism of a wonderful musical instrument can be inspected, but also the symptoms and operation of diseases otherwise obscure. Señor Garcia's position as one of the benefactors of the human race has had handsome acknowledgment—nowhere more handsome than in the "Physiologische Untersuchungen, mit Garcia's Kehlkopfspiegel," of Professor Czermak—and the fact supplies another illustration of the close relationship existing between Science and Art. Eager for the good of Art, Señor Garcia furnished Science with one of her most potent means. The foregoing particulars are given, simply that it may be known exactly who, and what manner of man is our author, and in view of them, not a word is needed to secure a favourable reception for his work. The opening chapters of Señor Garcia's treatise are devoted to a remarkably clear and able description of the vocal organs, and the means by which sounds are produced. Here the author recapitulates much that was first advanced in his French "Memoire," more especially when discussing the frequently-disputed question of "registers" and "timbres." In these introductory questions the foundation of the whole matter lies, and it is no small thing to know that Señor Garcia does not put himself forward as a mere theorist, but as one whose opinions are based upon a careful study of natural phenomena. In 1840, when he published his "Ecole de Chant," writers on music assigned to the chest register and to that of the falsetto an arbitrary extent, some authors even wholly denying the existence of the former.

At that period he demonstrated the existence of the chest register, and also its extent, which he proved to correspond with that of the falsetto, this extent being of course estimated from a physiological, and not from an artistic point of view. He also described the chief characters of the *timbres*, and demonstrated the mechanism employed in their production—facts of which no one had previously spoken. Subsequently, by the help of the laryngoscope, he showed the action of the glottis during the production of the various registers, this demonstration being also a complete novelty.

Señor Garcia demands that every singer shall share with him his physiological study of the voice, and the knowledge arising from it. "A singer," he observes, "who has no knowledge of the means by which vocal effects are produced, and of the intricacy of the art he professes, is merely the slave of routine, and will never become great in his profession. His talent must be cultivated from youth by a *general* as well as *special* education." This is reasonable enough, and young vocalists may well congratulate themselves upon having so excellent a guide as Señor Garcia through the "devious wilds" that lie before them. Our author's remarks upon the emission and qualities of voices are invaluable for their *connaissance de cause*, and the scientific clearness with which they are expressed. Here, for example, is a paragraph wherein few words lay bare the source of many faults :—" It is generally believed that the more we open our mouth the more easily and powerfully can sounds be emitted, but this is quite a mistake. Too large a separation of the jaws tightens the pharynx, and consequently stops all vibration of the voice, depriving the pharynx of its vault-like resonant form. If the teeth be too nearly closed the voice will assume a grating character, somewhat like the effect produced by singing through a comb. By projecting the lips in a funnel shape the notes become heavy. When the mouth assumes an oval shape, like that of a fish, the voice is rendered dull and gloomy, the vowels are imperfectly articulated and all but indistinguishable ; besides which, the face has a hard, cold, and most unpleasing expression. To open the mouth the lower jaw should be allowed to fall by its own weight, while the corners of the lips retire slightly. This movement, which keeps the lips gently pressed against the teeth, opens the mouth in just proportions, and gives it an agreeable form. The tongue should be loose and motionless, without any attempt to raise it at either extremity ; the muscles of the throat should be relaxed." We have transcribed this passage because it serves not only to show Señor Garcia's teaching style, but also to hold a mirror up to the nature—we can hardly say the art— of a host of amateurs and not a few professionals. The introductory chapters are followed by an elaborate series of exercises, which take up the remainder of the first part of the work, and are accompanied by careful and judicious explanatory or guiding observations. In the second part Señor Garcia discusses the important topic of articulation—a matter in which so many who call themselves vocalists are sadly deficient. His remarks upon the practical connexion between the *timbres* and the vowels are extremely interesting, and we would gladly quote them did space allow. But it must be enough to state that the connexion enables the singer "to determine what *timbre* for each vowel is best suited to the proposed effect, and, at the same time, to maintain a perfect equality throughout his voice." It is obvious that we have here the secret of much that is essential to the highest qualities of a vocalist, because through such mechanical means the more subtle processes involved in what we know as "expression" can be largely aided. The student is next invited to a careful study of consonantal sounds, all of which are classified, with "directions for use," and then our author goes on to the important topics of "fullness and steadiness of voice upon words," and "distribution of words with notes." In this case, also, the source of obvious and common defects is pointed out with the case and perspicacity of a master. Beginning with the section on "Phrasing," Señor Garcia next takes the pupil into the *sanctum* of the vocal art, and enlarges upon pronunciation, formation of the phrase, breath, time, forte-piano, and expression. His remarks may be studied even by the amateur with immense advantage; more especially as they are illustrated by musical quotations from the best known sources. The technical details which necessarily abound, would make a lengthened criticism of this portion of the book somewhat unfitted for the general reader; but the most general of readers can follow our author with interest when he speaks of the *summum bonum* of vocalization— expression. "Expression," says Señor Garcia, "is the great law of all art. Vain would be the efforts of an artist to excite the passions of his audience unless he showed himself powerfully affected by the very feeling he wished to kindle, for emotion is purely sympathetic. It devolves, therefore, upon an artist to rouse and ennoble his feelings, since he can only appeal successfully to those analogous to his own. The human voice deprived of expression is the least interesting of all instruments." This is common sense, and therefore sound philosophy. Acting upon it, Señor Garcia gives a series of directions concerning the "modes in which passion develops itself," the assumption being of course that true passion exists, otherwise his teaching would result only in the mere simulacrum of feeling. Distinguished by unvarying ability and clearness are all the remaining chapters of the book, more especially those wherein the various styles of singing are fully discussed, and with which it ends. General observations upon a subject so technical must perforce be unsatisfactory; but we have done our best to call attention to a remarkable work—the most remarkable of its kind, because most clearly based upon scientific knowledge and permeated by true artistic taste.

INDEX.

. *All Books must be looked for under the Author's name.*

———

ABOUT, Edmond, "Handbook of Social Economy, or the Worker's A B C," translated by W. F. Rae, 280

Adams, W. H., "Life in the Primeval World." Founded on Meunier's "Les Animaux d'Autrefois," 292

——— John R., "Dulwich College, and the Endowed Schools Commissioners," 577

Aird, David Mitchell, "Blackstone Economised; being a Compendium of the Laws of England to the Present Time," 679

"Albert's, Prince, Golden Precepts," 520

Albert, Dr. Clifford, "The Effects of Exercise on Bodily Temperature," 602

Alcott, Louisa, M., "Shawl Straps," 631

Ames, Sheldon, M.A., "An English Code; its Difficulties and the Modes of Overcoming them," 678

Apprentices, Two Idle, "Briefs and Papers. Sketches of the Bar and of the Press," 275

Arnold, Matthew, D.C.L., "The Great Prophecy of Israel's Restoration," 250

——— "Literature and Dogma; An Essay towards a Better Apprehension of the Bible," 558

"Art, the Picture Gallery of Sacred," 841

Auerbach, Berthold, "Zur guten Stunde," 638

BAGEHOT, Walter, "The English Constitution," 278

——— "Physics and Politics," 580

Bain, Alexander, LL.D., "Mental and Moral Science," 261

Balcarres, Earl of, *see* Crawford

Bastian, Prof. Dr., "Die Rechtsverhältnisse bei verschiedenen Völkern der Erde," 276

Baumann, Dr. J. J., "Philosophie als Orientirung ueber die Welt," 573

Bell, Currer, "Jane Eyre," 336

——— Sir Charles, K.H., "The Anatomy and Philosophy of Expression," 339

Benham, Rev. W., B.D., "A Companion to the Sanctuary," 570

Blackmore, R. Doddridge, "Cradock Nowell," 638

Bliss, W. H., B.C.L., *see* Ogle, Rev. O., M.A.

Blumé, William, "The Operations of the German Armies in France, from Sedan to the End of the War," translated by Major E. M. Jones, 263

Boguslawsky, A. V., "Tactical Deductions from the War of 1870-71," translated from the German by Colonel Lumley Graham, 263

Bobemian, "The Iron Strike," 619

Bowles, E., "Fleurange," translated by, 322, *see* Craven, Mrs. Augustus

Bowra, Harrietta, "Una, or the Early Marriage," 822

Braithwaite, Henry Thomas, M.A., "Ease and Pows. A Companion of Divine Eternal Laws and Powers, as Severally Indicated in Fact, Faith, and Record," 244

Bray, Charles, "The Education of the Feelings," 281

Brewer, J. S., M.A., "Letters and Papers, Foreign and Domestic, of the Reign of Henry VIII," 317

Brialmont, A., "Hasty Intrenchments," translated by Charles A. Empson, 264

Brooke, Henry, "The Fool of Quality," 638

Brooke, Stopford A., M.A., see Robertson, F. W.

Brown, Ellen, L., "The Farell Children," 627

—— Rowland, "Songs of Early Spring," 628

Browne, J. Crichton, M.D., "West Riding Asylum Reports," 297

"Buckle, Henry Thomas, Miscellaneous and Posthumous works of," edited by Helen Taylor, 302

Burke, Sir B., "The Rise of Great Families," 308

Burton, Richard F., "Unexplored Syria," and Charles F. Tyrwhitt Drake, 273

Bonnett, F. E., "Memoirs of Leonora Christina, Daughter of Christian IV. of Denmark," translated by, 310, see also Lübke, Dr. Wilhelm

Caluerwood, H., LL.D., "Handbook of Moral Philosophy," 260

Campbell, John M., "Reminiscences and Reflections Referring to his Holy Ministry in the Parish of Row," 618

Cappie, James, M.D., "The Causation of Sleep," 298

Capricornus, "Bush Essays," 269

Carey, H. C., "The Unity of Law; as Exhibited in the Relations of Physical, Social, Mental and Moral Science," 582

Carné, Louis de, "Travels in Indo-China, and the Chinese Empire," 586

Caswall, Edward, "Hymns and Poems. Original and Translated," 569

Channing, W. E., D.D., "The Perfect Life in Twelve Discourses," Edited by his Nephew, W. H. Channing, 565

"Chapman, George, The Comedies and Tragedies of," 629

Charity Schools, 450–472; the Grammar Schools of the Tudor Period, 450; in the reign of Henry VIII., 450; in the reign of Edward VI. 450; in that of Mary, 451; Elizabeth, 451; the object of the founders, 451; change of mind and of feeling in the seventeenth century, 451; the difference between Grammar Schools and Charity Schools, 451, 452; Bishop Butler, on the Intention of Charity Schools, 452; Bishop Kennett on, 453; Dean Stanhope on, 453; Bishop Robinson on, 453; Colston on, 454; the general teaching inculcated at these schools, 455; Mandeville on the establishment of these Charity Schools, 455; his criticism on the founder of the Radcliffe Library at Oxford, 456; on Charity Schools, their supporters, masters, trustees and governors, 456; on the aims of the upper classes, in establishing these schools, 456, 457; Grammar Schools for boys, Charity Schools for both sexes, 457; a liberal education reserved only for boys, 457, 458; results of the School's Inquiry Commission, 458; the "pious founder," 459; theory about him, 459; his intentions held sacred, 459; the proper method of dealing with bequests, 460; Sir Josiah Mason's bequest to found a Science College in Birmingham, 460, 461, (foot note); report of the School's Inquiry Commission on Hospital and Charity Schools, 462, 463; criticisms suggested by, 464; Christ's Hospital, 464, (foot note); quotation from Mr. Lloyd's pamphlet Educational Hospital Reform, 464, 465; day school's of the "charity" class, 465; the system of paying a premium to apprentice a boy, 466; the general testimony of official inspectors, 466; power of the clergy in these charity schools, 467; duty of the Government, 468; public secondary schools both for boys and girls proposed, 468, 469; recommendations of the Schools Inquiry Commission, 469; further recommendations of the Commissioners, 470; the true vindication of the Commissioners, 471; the real aim of the philosopher and teacher, 471; how instruction was regarded by Bacon, 472

Chatrian, Erckmann-, MM., "The Story of the Plébiscite," 306

Cherry, J. L., "Life and Remains of John Clare," 618

Christian Evidence Society, The, 186–207; the gradual decay of the old theological beliefs, 186; in Germany, France, and America, 186; in England, 187; the opinion of Mr. Disraeli, and the Times, 187; opinions, however, of others, Archbishop Thompson, Bishop Wilberforce, Dean Mansel, Dean Goulbourn, &c., &c., 188; the spread of scepticism, 189; change in educated feeling on this point, 189; books bearing on the subject now published by publishers of the highest standing, 190; the tone of the press, 190; the Fortnightly Review, the Contemporary Review, Fraser's Magazine, and the Pall Mall Gazette, 190; extracts from the Pall Mall Gazette, 190, 191; tone of the Scotsman, and

Western Morning News, 191; the general attitude of educated men towards the Bible and Revelation, 191; the extent to which these views are held, 192; the Christianity of the first and second centuries and the Christianity of the nineteenth century, 192; an early Christian's views upon the Christianity of to-day, 193; Henry Martyn, a good type of the early Christian, 193; Protection Societies for the support of Christianity, 194; the "Christian Evidence Society," 194; its chairmen, patrons and lecturers, 194; general character and tone of its publications, 195; Professor Rawlinson on the "Alleged Historical Difficulties of the Old and New Testament," 196; his concessions, 196; Mr. Gladstone on a partial deluge, 196, 197; the Bishop of Carlisle on the first chapter of Genesis, 197; Mr. How on the miracles of the Bible, 197; it is better that Atheism should be true than our present theological system, 198; proof of this, 198, 199; what is the teaching of Revelation? 198, 199; universal oblivion is better than the bell of our theology, 199; the inspiration of Scripture, 200, 201; upon what grounds it must be believed, 201, 202; the precise character of the inspiration of the Bible, 202, 203; Bishop Goodwin on, 203; the dishonesty of his statement, 204; his argument applied to the sacred writings of the Hindoos and Persians, 204; Messrs. Webster and Wilkinson on plenary Inspiration, 205; considerations with regard to the divine character of the Bible, 206; conclusion, 207

Christina, daughter of Christian IV. of Denmark, *see* Bennett, F. E.

Churchill, H. G. "Puttyput's Protégés," 815

Chynoweth, W. Harris, "The Fall of Maximilian, late Emperor of Mexico," 811

Cockayne, Rev. D., *see* Morris, Rev. R.

Coffin, C. R., "On Alveolar Contraction, 661

Colenso, Right Rev. J. W., D.D., (Bishop of Natal). "The New Bible Commentary by Bishops and other Clergy of the Anglican Church. Critically Examined," 246, 561. (Parts III. IV.)

Combe, George, "The Relation between Science and Religion," 247

"Compton Friars," 625

Conington, John, M.A., "The Satires of A. Persius Flaccus," by, and edited by H. O. Nettleship, M.A., 303

Cooke, E. W., R.A., "Grotesque Animals, Invented, Drawn and Described," 642

Cowper, J. M., *see* Morris, Rev. R.

Coxe, Rev. H., (Bodley's Librarian), *see* Ogle, Rev. O., M.A., and Macray, Rev. W. D.

Craven, Mrs. Augustus, "Fleurange," 323

Crawford and Balcarres, Alexander, Earl of, "Etruscan Inscriptions," 840

Cronin, David E., "The Reforms which should Precede, and the Results which must Follow the Equal Distribution of Wealth," 268

Cumberland, Captain of the, "Ready, O Ready! or, These Forty Years," 615

Cusack, F. H., "The Liberator; his Life and Times," 306

DANGERFIELD, John, "Grace Tolmar," 626

Darwin, Charles, M.A., F.R.S., "The Expression of the Emotions in Man and Animals," 289

"Dates and Data, &c.," 620

"Davidson, the True History of Joshua," 332

Davies, Lady Clementina, "Recollections of Society," 308

—— Rev. James, M.A., "Hesiod and Theognis," 619

"Dictator, If I were," 591

Dosalerlein, Julius, "Goethe Dasein bewiesen am Wissen und Sein," 251

Döllinger, John J. I. von, D.D., D.C.L., *see* Oxenham, H. N., M.A.

Doré, Gustave, "London," and Blanchard Jerrold, 310

Drake, Charles F. Tyrwhitt, *see* Burton, Richard F.

Dühring, Dr., "Kritische Geschichte der allgemeinen Principien der Mechanik," 596

Dupeyron, P. de Ségur, "Histoire des Négociations Commerciales et Maritimes de la France," 620

ELIOT, George, "Middlemarch. A Study of English Provincial Life," 325

Empson, Charles A., *see* Brialmont, A.

Everett, Professor, "Deschanel's Natural Philosophy," (Sound and Light, Part IV.), 263

FALCONER, W., M.D., "Dissertations on St. Paul's Voyage from Cæsarea to Potuoli; and on the Apostle's Shipwreck on the Island Melita," with additional Notes by Thomas Falconer, E.q., 254

Farries, R. Spearman E., "Electoral Equality considered in relation to the Recent Returns as affecting England and Wales," 267

Field, Horace, B.A., "Glitter and Gold," 324

Fitzpatrick, W. J., "Irish Wits and Worthies," 417

Flint, Austin, Jun., M.D., "The Physiology of Man," 295

Flower, J. W., "A Layman's Reasons for Discontinuing the Use of the Athanasian Creed," 248

Forbes, Archibald, "Soldiering and Scribbling," 201

Forster, Jonathan L., "Biblical Psychology in Four Parts," edited by his son, Henry L. Forster, 254

Fortlage, Dr. C., "Sechs Philosophische Vorträge," 575

"France, the Empire and Civilization," 584

Freuzillon, R. E., "Pearl and Emerald," 221

———————— "National Characteristics, and Flora and Fauna of London," 629

Freeman, Edward A., D.C.L., "Historical Course for Schools," 279

———————— "Historical Essays," 607

French Monarchy, The Decline of the Old, 70—111; development of royal authority in France, 70; the policy of Charles VII., 70; of Louis XIV., 70, 71; results of the latter, 71; opinions of the Duc de Bourgoyne and Fénélon, 71; Fénélon's political principles and morality, 72; the three estates in France according to Montesquieu at this period, 72; death of Louis XIV., 73; changes, 73; the minority of Louis XV., 74; his early education, 74, 75; the petits soupers of the period, 75; Cardinal Dubois, 76; his character analysed, 76, 77; did he sell himself to England? 78; the Cellamare conspiracy, 79; difficulties which the Government of the Regency had to encounter, 79, 80; the Duc de Noailles and Law, 80; the faults of the Regent, 80; Madame de Prie, 81; Fleury, 81; his policy, 82; his part in the Treaty of Vienna, 83; his policy in the internal affairs of France, 83; towards the Church, 84; his death, 84; how it was regarded in France, 85 (foot note); the character of Louis XV., 85; compared with Charles II. of England, 85, 86; Louis XV. as his own Prime Minister, 87; as the "Well-beloved," 88; his mistresses, 88, 89; the Treaty of Aix-la-Chapelle, 89; general condition of France, 90; Madame de Pompadour, 91; condition of the Government, 91; a new power, that of Philosophers, 92; general inconsistency manifested in every department of Government, 92, 93; the Jesuits, 93; the Monarchy weakened on all sides, 93; Voltaire, 93; analysis of his character, 94; the tendency of the speculative thought of the period, 95; how the "Well-beloved" now fared, 96; the weapons which were being forged against the Monarchy, 97; the conduct of Louis XV. at this period, 98; the punition and conduct of M. de Maleshorbes, 98; of the Duc de Choiseul, 99; Maurepas, 99, 100; Frederick II. on Voltaire, 100; Louis XV. before the coming danger, 101; alliance between the Princes of the House of Bourbon, 102; character of Choiseul, 102; his shortcomings, 103; the Comtesse du Barry, 104, 105; the Contrôleur-Général Terray, 105; Chancellor Maupeou, 106; the condition of the Parliament, 106; conflicts between the Parliament and the regal power, 107; prosecution of the Duc d'Aiguillon, 108; a new Parliament, 108; Seguier's declaration to the King, 108; condition of Louis, 100; his death, 110; the task and difficulties to be encountered by Louis XVI., 111

Froude, James Anthony, "The English in Ireland in the Eighteenth Century," 305

"GALLERY, the Picture," 541

Garcia, Manuel, "New Treatise on the Art of Singing," 612

Gardiner, W. W., "The Chatterbox," 342

Garrod, A. H., "The Law of the Frequency of the Pulse," 295

Geikie, Archibald, "Physical Geography," 599

Gervinus, Georg Gottfried, see Lechmann, Emil

Gladstone Administration, The, 208—241; from what the decay of a ministry proceeds, 208 ; the particular case of Mr. Gladstone's ministry, 208, 209 ; general distrust in, 209 ; the causes for this, 209 ; Mr. Gladstone's accession to power, 210 ; his Lancashire speeches, 211 ; his majority of one hundred to one hundred and twenty on accession to office, 211 ; character of the New Parliament, 211 ; Mr. Bright as a member of the Government, 212 ; Mr. Lowe, 212 ; Irish legislation, 213 : Gladstone's error, 213 ; the disestablishment of the Irish Church, 214 ; the Land Act, 215 ; the benefits wrought by both these measures, 216 ; the Irish difficulty, 217 ; Home Rule, 217 ; the Tenant Right question, 218 ; the Land question, 219 ; causes which have brought discredit on the Gladstone Government, 219 ; the English Education Bill, 220 ; difficulties of, 220 ; Gladstone's compromise, 221 ; The natural result, 221 ; the action of the Dissenters, 221, 222 ; Gladstone's sacerdotal tendencies, 222 ; their effect upon him, 222 ; the Scotch Education Act, 222 ; blunder in, 223 ; Gladstone's educational policy one of shifts and compromises, 224 ; his policies of impulse, 224 ; his whole administration a series of blunders, 225 ; Lord Kimberley on religious endowments, 226 ; Gladstone's levelling-up process in Ireland, 226 ; his method of dealing with Fawcett's Trinity College Bill, 227 ; artifices and tricks to which he had recourse, 228 ; his views with regard to the Irish Catholics in detail, 229 ; the action of the Irish Catholics, 230 ; their demands, 230 ; the true state of the case, 231 ; Gladstone's conduct in the matter, 231 ; how Government intends to extricate itself from the difficulty, 232 ; the Army Bill, 233 ; the Ballot Bill, 233, 234 ; the character of the Opposition, 235 ; general apathy of the country, 236 ; conduct of the Government on the Contagious Diseases Act, 236 ; on the Thames Embankment Bills, 236 ; on the Licensing and Public Health Bills, 236 ; the Government and Colonial affairs, 237 ; its foreign policy, 237 ; the Foreign Office and the United States, 238 ; action of the Government during the Franco-German war, 238 ; the Alabama Arbitration, 239 ; what the Government ought to do, 239 ; what particular questions require to be taken in hand, 239, 240 ; general summary of the blunders and incapacity of the Gladstone Government, 240, 211

Gladstone's, Mr., "Defence of the Faith," 367—386 ; the peculiar circumstances of Mr. Gladstone's address, 367, 368 ; the important movements which have been going on since Mr. Gladstone's own theological views were formed, 369 ; the causes of Mr. Gladstone's annoyance, 369 ; the charge of being a Roman Catholic brought against Gladstone, 370 ; his peculiar position and its effects, 370, 371 ; Mr. Gladstone's objections to professors of the natural sciences arrogating for themselves the names of "science," 372 ; answer to the objection, 372, 373 ; Mr. Gladstone on the denial of a personal God, and its results, 374, 375 ; examination continued, 376, 377 ; is it true that the doctrine of evolution is fatal to religion ? 377, 378 ; quotations from Dr. Carpenter, 379 ; Mr. Gladstone and Dr. Strauss, 380 ; St. Paul and Free Thought, 381 ; Mr. Gladstone on the achievements of the nineteenth century, 382, 383 ; Mr. Gladstone on the divisions of Christians, 383 ; his statement examined, 384 ; what is a true Christian ? 384, 385 ; is man responsible for his belief ? 385, 386 ; crucial instances, 386 ; conclusion of Mr. Gladstone's lectures, 387 ; parting advice to Mr. Gladstone, 388

Gneist, Dr. Rudolf, "Der Rechtsstaat," 277

Godwin, William, "Essays," 552

Göschen, Right Hon. George J., M.P., "Reports and Speeches on Local Taxation," 577

Gottschall, Rudolf, "Die deutsche Nationalliteratur de neunzehnten Jahrhunderts," 314

Graham, Colonel Lumley, see Boguslawski, A.V.

—— W., M.A., "Idealism. An Essay, Metaphysical and Critical," 572

Green, M. A. E., "Calendar of State Papers, Domestic Series of the reigns of Elizabeth and James I." Addenda 1580—1625, 317

Gregory, Isaac, "British Metric System," &c., 582

Grieve, R., M.D., "On Vaccination," 301

Grotefend, Dr. H., "Handbuch der histerischen Chronologie des deutschen Mittelalters und der Neuzeit," 316

Guillemin, Amédée, "The Forces of Nature," 295 (see Lockyer, J. Norman, F.R.S.)

HAGEN, Dr. Fredrich W., "Studien" (Theil: I. und II.), 296

Hannay, R. C. F., "Rhymes and Sonnets," 619

Hare, Augustus J. C., "Memorials of a Quiet Life," 313

———— "Wanderings in Spain," 855

Harrison, Agnes, "Martin's Vineyard," 324

Hayward, A., Q.C., "Biographical and Critical Essays," 606

Hazard, Samuel, "Santo Domingo, Past and Present, with a Glance at Hayti," 587

Henle, Dr. J., "Anatomischer Hand-Atlas," 294

Hensley, Lewis, M.A., "Figures Made Easy. A First Arithmetic Book," 384

"Hera, Doctor Jacob," 316

Higginson, Thomas Wentworth, "Atlantic Essays," 330

Horner, Susan and Johanna, "Walks in Florence," 685

Hughes, Thomas, "Memoirs of a Brother," 614

"Humor, Deutscher, in Poesie," 635

Humphrey, G. M., M.D., F.R.S., "Observations in Myology," 294

IRELAND, S. W. W., "The Deficiencies of Idiots," 805

Irish University Education and the Ministerial Crisis, 529—551: defeat of the Ministry on the Irish University Bill, 529; results of that defeat, 530; Mr. Gladstone's speech, 531; how Irish University Reform had become a Government question, 532; what alone will satisfy the Irish premier, 533; governing Ireland "according to Irish ideas," 533; the Premier's mistake on the second reading of the Bill, 534; Mr. Fawcett's description of the Bill, 534; Mr. Harcourt on the principle of the Bill, 535; the "gagging clauses," 536; what would have been the results of Mr. Gladstone's scheme, 536; 537; the second portion of the Bill, 537; analysis of, 538, 539; difficulties, 539; the Premier's speech at the banquet given to Mr. Locke King, 541; Mr. Gladstone's culo-

gists, 541; considerations regarding the Government Irish Education policy, 542, 543; how the question should have been dealt with, 543; the mixed system, 544; President Berwick's remarks, 544; the success of the mixed system in Ireland, 545; Mr. Fawcett's Bill, 546; its benefits, 546; advantages arising out of the debates on Irish University Education, 547; Mr. Gladstone's fall, 547, 548; present condition of political parties, 548; what we may expect in a new Parliament, 649; Mr. Disraeli, 550; reasons of his refusal to form a ministry, 650; the political future, 650; to whom our thanks will be due, 651

JACOX, F., "Aspects of Authorship," 328

Jacquemyns, G. Rolin- "De la Manière d'apprécier au point de vue du droit International les Faits de la dernière Guerre," 265

Jerrold, Blanchard, "London," and Gustave Doré, 340

Jones, Major E. M., see Blumé, William

Juhos, J. Davis, "The School Manual of Geology," 599

KEATINGE, Mrs. R. H., "Honor Blake. The Story of a Plain Woman," 324

"Kensington (South) Museum, Description of the Ancient and Mediæval Ivories in the," 339

Kettle, Rosa M., "The Mistress of Langdale Hall," 318

Kentish, Thomas, "Cæsar in Britain," 328

King, Clarence, "Mountaineering in the Sierra Nevada," 586

Kingsley, Charles, "Plays and Puritans, and other Historical Essays," 608

Kinkel, Goufried, "Der Grobschmied von Antwerpen," 636

Kohlrausch, F., "Leitfaden der Praktischen Physik," 293

Krauss, Fritz, "Shakspeare's Southampton-Sonnette," 635

Kugler, Franz, "Handbuch der Kunstgeschichte," 338

LACORDAIRE, Rev. Père, "Life: Conferences delivered at Toulouse," translated by H. D. Langdon, 566

Laufrey, M., "History of Napoleon I.," 616

Lehmann, Emil, "Georg Gottfried Gervinus, Versuch einer Charakteristik," 316

Laupoldt, D. I. M., "Ueber Geist und Leben in der Medicin," 296

Lloyd, W. Watkiss, "The History of Sicily to the Athenian War," 610

Lockyer, J. Norman, F.R.S., "The Forces of Nature." By Amédée Guillemin. Translated from the French by Mrs. Norman Lockyer, and edited by, 285

Low, C. R. "The Life and Correspondence of F.M. Sir George Pollock, Bart, G.C.B., 617

Lübke, Dr. Wilhelm, "History of Sculpture," translated by F. E. Bunnett, 328

Lomley, K. J. R., "Polychronicon Ranulphi Higden, Monachi Cestrensis," edited by, 317

Luno, Mrs. Galbraith, "Only Eve," 621

Lyons, R. T., "On Relapsing Fever," 300

—— Robert, D., M.B., T.C.D., "Intellectual Resources of Ireland," 575

MacCarthy, Denis Florence, "Shelley's Early Life," 308

Macleod, N., D.D., "The Temptation of Our Lord," 556

—— H. D., M.A., "The Principles of Economical Philosophy," 581

Macquoid, K. S., "Miriam's Marriage," 320

Macray, Rev. W. D., "Calendar of the Clarendon State Papers Preserved in the Bodleian Library," edited under the direction of Rev. H. Coxe, 317

Mailly, E., "Tableau de l'Astronomie dans l'Hemisphere Austral et dans l' Inde," 283

—— "De l'Astronomie dans l'Académie Royale de Belgique," Rapport Séculaire, 288

Marlitt, E., "Gold Elsie," 625

Marsh, J. B., "Venice and the Venetians," 610

—— For Liberty's Sake," 627

Maurus, Dr. H., "Ueber die Freiheit in der Volkswirthshaft," 581

Mayo, W. S., M.D., "Never Again," 622

Melville, Henry, B.D., "Selections from the Sermons Preached during the Latter Years of his Life," 565

Miller, R. Kalley, "The Romance of Astronomy," 597

Mirus, Major General von, "Cavalry Field Duty," translated by Captain Frank S. Russell, 264

Mocatta, J. L., "Moral Biblical Gleanings and Practical Teachings," 243

Moryan, Augustus de, "A Budget of Paradoxes," 282

Morison, Jeanie, "Snatches of Song," 619

Morris, Rev. R., LL.D., "An Old English Miscellany"(containing Pieces edited by Rev. O. Cockayne, J. M. Cowper, R-v. W. Skeat), 303

—— "Historical Outlines of English Accidence," 333. See also Skeat, Rev. Walter, M.A.

Mounsey, A. H., F.R.G.S., "A Journey through the Caucasus and the Interior of Persia," 274

Mulhall, Michael G., "Rio Grande do Sul, and its German Colonies, 589

Murger, Henry, the Bohemian, 403—449; the causes which lead to "Bohemian life," 404; Murger's birth and parentage, 405; as a child, 405; Pauline Garcia, 405; his cousin, and lines to her, 406, 407; day dreams, 407; ambition to be a poet, 407; M. de Jouy, 408; the brothers Bisson, 408, 409; fathers and poetry, 409; account of Murger in 1838, by Lelioux, 410; Pottier, 411; Murger takes to poetry, 411; his method of proceeding, 411; Bauville's "Cariatides," 411; Murger as secretary to Count Tolstoy, 412; quarrel with his father, 412; joins the Bohemian brotherhood, 412; the true aim and meaning of Bohemians, 412, 413; their aspirations, 413; Murger in the Rue d'Auvergne, 413; his mode of life, 414; Les Amours d' Olivier, 415; M. Duchampy, 415; his wife, Marie, 415, 416; Murger's love with, 416; their separation, 417; effect on Murger, 417; Murger's illness, 418; leaves the hospital, 419; works at night, 419; returns to poetry, 420; Murger's picture of his own hopes and dreams at this time, 420; life in Bohemia, 421; La Jeunesse n'a qu'un temps, 421; the "Buveurs d'Eau," 422; their creed and principles, 422, 423; principal members of this society, 423; the Café Momus, 424; Murger's life at this period, 425, 426, 427, 428; Murger at Champfleury, 429; Champfleury's picture of this joint life, 429, 430; Murger obtains a situation on the Journal de Commerce, 431; his diary, 432; poems, 433; Murger on the Moniteur de la Mode, 431; on the Artiste, 434, 435; Orbauson le Confident, 435; Scènes *de la Vie Bohême*, 436; receives thirty-four pounds for the copyright, 436; extracts from, 437; further extracts and analysis, 438, 439; Mimi, 440; song to Musette, 440, 441; career of the *Buveurs d'Eau*, 442; Murger's fortunes improve, 442; the Vie Bohème on the stage, 443; Murger and Madame Anais, 443; the *Buveurs d'Eau*, 444, 445; Murger retires from the *Revue des Deux Mondes*, 445; he lives at Marlotte, near Fontainbleau, 445; as a sportsman, 446; *Les Nuits d'Hiver*, 447; dies in the hospital, 448; his funeral, 449

Murray, A. G., "Manual of Mythology," 611

NAPOLEON I., *see* Lanfrey, M.

Nasmyth, David, "The Institutes of English Law," 579

Newdigate, Colonel Edward, "The Army of the North German Confederation," translated from the Corrected Edition, 263

Newman, J. H., "Historical Sketches," 597

Nicholson, Henry Alleyne, "A Manual of Palæontology for the Use of Students," 292

——— N.A., M.A., "The Science of Exchanges," 581

Noble, James Ashcroft, "The Pelican Papers," 630

Nomentino, "Nuova Italia," 328

OESTERLEN, Dr., "Die Seuchen," 601

Ogle, Rev. O., "Calendar of the Clarendon State Papers Preserved in the Bodleian Library," edited by, and W. H. Bliss, B.C.L., under the direction of Rev. H. Coxe, M.A., Bodley's Librarian, 317

Owen, Sidney, "India on the Eve of the British Conquest," 317

Oxenham, H. N., M.A., "Lectures on the Reunion of the Churches," by John J. I. Döllinger, D.D., D.C.L., translated, with a Preface, by, 253

PALGRAVE, William Gifford, "Essays on Eastern Questions," 271

Parkin, John, "Epidemiology," 600

Parliamentary Eloquence, 30 – 69; Parliamentary Government on the English model, 36, 37; the origin of our English House of Commons, 37; its present position and power, 37; Bunsen's description of, 37, 38; Macaulay's definition of parliamentary government, 38; lawyers as parliamentary speakers, 39; bishops as, 39; William Johnson Fox as a speaker, 39; authors as speakers, 40; Sir James Mackintosh on parliamentary eloquence, 40; Sir Robert Peel introduced a new style into the House of Commons, 41; Burke, 41; Lord Bacon as a speaker, 42; the elder Pitt, 43; quotations from, 43, 44; the younger Pitt, 44; Fox, 44; quotations from, 45; further quotations from, 46; Fox and Cobden compared, 47; Canning's reply to Mackintosh, 47, 48, 49; oratory in the Reformed House of Commons, 49; Sir Arthur Helps on parliamentary control, 50; Bright's earlier speeches, 50; Earl Russell, 51; Disraeli's criticism on, 51; examples of Earl Russell's oratory, 52; Earl Russell on the ballot, 53; scene between Lords Derby and Russell, 53, 54; Lord Russell on the Liberal Association of the City of London, 54, 55; Mr. Disraeli, 55; characteristics of his style, 56; its bombast, 56; his misuse of words, 56; Dr. Newman's reply to Disraeli, 56; quotation from Disraeli's speech in 1858 against the Borough Franchise Extension Bill, 57, 58; Lord Derby as a speaker, 58, 59; Brougham on, 59; Lord Russell on, 59, 60; scene between Lord Derby and O'Connell, 60, 61; Lord Derby's speech on Roman Catholic Oath Bill, 61; Gladstone, 62; Cobden, 62, 63; Sir Robert Peel on Cobden's eloquence, 63; quotation from Cobden's speech in 1849 on the question of International Arbitration, 63; the secret of Cobden's influence, 63, 64; his own account of the way and care with which his speeches were prepared, 64; Mr. Lowe, 64; quotation from, 64, 65; his peroration on the third reading of the Tory Reform Bill, 65; a parallel between Lowe and Canning, 66; knowledge of the forms and usages of the House and tact required to be a successful speaker, 66; instances, 66, 67; the case of Mr. Milner Gibson, 66, 67; as a tactician, 67; as a speaker, 67; Mr. Henry Berkeley, 67; his speeches, 68; Mr. Carlyle's objections to parliamentary debate, 68, 69; the answers to them, 69

"Parson, Country, Recreations of a," "Sensible Musings and Week Days," by the Author of, 249

Pater, Walter H., "Studies in the History of the Renaissance," 619

" Paul Jean, als Dichter und Prediger,"
644

———— "als Grammeinterdeutschen
Humors," 637

Perkins (Junior), M.A., " A Profitable
Book on Domestic Law," 579

Perowne, J. J. Stewart, B.D., " The
Athanasian Creed." A Sermon, 248

Pettenkofer, Dr. Max von, " Beziehungen der Luft zu Kleidung, Wohnung,
und Boden," 208

Plath, Dr. Wilhelm, " Sternkunde für
Frauen," 283

" Political Portraits," 592

Power, John, " A Handy Book about
Books," 632

Pradez, Charles, " Nouvelles Etudes
sur le Brésil," 588

Prendergast, John, see Russell, Rev. C.
W., D.D.

Prime, S. Ireneus, " Fifteen Years of
Prayer in the Fulton Street Meeting," 256

Procter, Richard A., B.A., " The Orbs
Around Us," 287

Pulsford, W., D.D., " Sermons Preached
in Trinity Church, Glasgow," 565

R——, Baron, " Russian Conspirators
in Siberia," 274

Rae, W. F., see About, Edmond

Ralston, W. R. S., M.A., " The Songs
of the Russian People," 279

Ranking, R. Montgomerie, " Streams
from Hidden Sources," 334

Rawlinson, George, M.A., " The Sixth
Great Oriental Monarchy," 610

Reid, T. W., " Cabinet Portraits:
Sketches of Statesmen," 309

Religion as a subject of National Education, 111—146; the views of the
secularists with regard to religious
teaching, 111; views of the Denominationalists, 111; popular signification of the words "secular" and
"religious," 112; difficulties involved,
113; divisions amongst the Denominationalists, 114; the difficulties in
their case, 115; considerations with
regard to teaching the Bible, 116;
the Bible read without note or comment, 116; the Bible taught with a
commentary, 117; the difficulties to
be encountered, 118, 119; further
difficulties in teaching and explaining
the Bible, 120, 121; the particular
case of Scotland, 121; the morality
of the Bible, 122; teaching of the
Westminster Confession of Faith on
this point, 122; the morality of the
Bible compared with that of other

religions, 123; morality of the Greeks,
123; examples from Æschylus, 123,
124; from Sophokles, 124, 125;
from Euripides, 125; from Socrates,
125; from Isocrates and Plutarch,
126; the morality of the laws of
Sparta, 126; Seneca and St. Paul,
127; examples of agreement between,
127, 128; proposed method of teaching children, 129; facts and opinions,
how they should be discriminated,
130; objections against the proposed
plan, 131; these objections considered,
132; the history of the growth of
Christianity, 132, 133; of Romanism,
133; of Protestantism, 133; laws of
the Puritans in Virginia, 134;
bigotry, in Scotland, 134, 135; the
relationship of science and religion,
135; the law of Progress and the law
of the Church, 135; their antagonism,
136; its results, 136; how the
Church has so far triumphed over
Science, 136; the Church and witchcraft, 137; the Church and reason,
137; their opposition, 137; hostility
of the Church to intellectual influence, 138; intellectual submission
taught by the Church, 139; its view
of human nature, 139; exceptions in
the case of individual clergy, 140;
general results of the teaching of the
Church, 141; the case of the Roman
Catholics considered, 142; difficulties in teaching science, 142, 143;
the present intention of the state as
regards education, 143; what the
results will be, 144; compulsory
education, 145; conclusion, 146

" Republic, Men of the Third," (reprinted from the *Daily News*, 608

Republicans of the Commonwealth, The,
146—186; the despotism of Charles I.
and Cromwell compared, 147; Republican leaders opposed to Cromwell,
148; Mr. Disraeli's " History of the
Commonwealth of England," 148;
extract from, 149; Cromwell's dealings with the Republican party, 149;
his death, 150; appointment of his
son as successor, 150; the character
of Richard Cromwell, 150; the remoos
of his successalou, 151; deputation of
officers to Richard, 151; the distribution of seats, 151; the influence of
the government brought to bear
against the Republican party, 152;
the strength of the Republicans in the
new Parliament, 152; of the Cavaliers, 152, 153; meeting of the new
Parliament, 153; the attack of the

Republican's 153; Haslerig's character of Cromwell, 153; movements of the various parties, 154, 166; Richard and his soldiers, 154; the Government in the hands of the army, 154, 155; restoration of Parliament, 155; Mazarin and Oxenstiern on the formidable power of the Commonwealth party, 156; remarks by M. de Bordeaux, 156; the Council of State, 156; Vane on the financial position of the country, 157; Slingsby Bethell on, (foot note), 157; retrenchments and reforms, 157; Oliver Cromwell and the army, 158; his recruits, 158; M. de Bordeaux on the state of the army, 158; the Wallingford House party, 159; state and feeling of the army, 159; the aims and opinions of the Long Parliament, 160; Harrington, 161; his "Oceana," 162; the MS. of "Oceana" seized by Cromwell's police, 162; the Rota Club, 162; Harrington on the historical character of the Great Revolution, 163; Harrington on the balance of property, 163; his other views, 163; the great danger of a world-wide despotism in those days, 164; the United States of the Netherlands, 164; causes of the failure of the English Republic, 164; the historians of the English Republic, 165; projected insurrection of the Royalists, 165; petition from the officers, 166; Haslerig as described by Ludlow, 166; fall of the Long Parliament, 166; their foreign policy, 167; the Committee of Safety, 167; proceedings of Monk, 168; character of, 169; Vane on Monk's designs, 170; Monk and the army, 170; was the crown offered to Monk? 171; Scot on his share in the execution of Charles I., 171, 172; the great mistake of the Long Parliament, 172, 173; restoration of the King, 173; proceedings of Charles II., 174; the Cavaliers and their losses, 179; the declaration of Breda, 175, 176; punishments inflicted by Charles II., 176; the executions, 177; Milton saved by Sir William Davenant, 177, 178; the fate of the other republicans, 178; the trial of Sir Henry Vane, 179; his character, 180; his execution, 180; a new House of Commons, 182; its proceedings, 182, 183; the boroughs and their charters, 184; Algernon Sydney, 184; his fate, 185; Edmund Ludlow, 185; his death and grave, 186

Resident, A, "Glimpses of Life in Victoria," 590

Réville, Albert, "The Song of Songs, commonly called the Song of Solomon," from the French of, 656

Ringer, Sidney, M.D., "Handbook of Therapeutics," 201

—— on "Temperature in Phthisis," 603

"Robertson, Frederick W., Life and Letters of," Edited by Stopford A. Brooke, 612

—— Analysis of Mr. Tennyson's "In Memoriam," 614

Robinson, Wade, "Songs in God's World," 325

Roscoe, Thomas, "The Pleasant History of Reynard the Fox," translated by, 342

Rush, Richard, "Recollections of the English and French Courts, 1817-1849," edited by his son Benjamin Rush, 312

Ruskin, John, LL.D., "Fors Clavigera," 266

Russell, Frank S. see Mirus, Major-General von, 264

—— Rev. C. W., D.D., "Calendar of State Papers, relating to Ireland, of the Reign of James I. 1603-1604," edited by, and John Prendergast, Esq., Barrister-at-Law, 316

—— Clarke, "Memoirs of Mrs. Letitia Boothby," 325

SALOMON, Dr. Max, "Geschichte der Glykosurie," 209

Sandeau, Jules, "The Seagull Rock," translated by Robert Black, M.A., 325

Sandford, J. Langton, "Estimates of the English Kings. From William the Conqueror to George III., 308

Schasler, Dr. Max, "Aesthetik als Philosophie des Schönen und der Kunst," 336

Schellen, Dr. H., see Secchi, P. A.

Schlegel, Victor, "System der Raumlehre," 696

Scientific Research, the National Importance of, 343-366, who have been the greatest discoverers, 343; how oxygen was discovered, 343; Crooke's discovery of thallium, 344; the difference between discoveries and inventions, 344; the invention of telegraphy through Oersted's experiments, 344; the invention of the mariner's compass, 344, 345; political changes and social results effected by the compass, 345; the invention of gunpowder, 345; of printing, 345; of the telegraph, 345, 446; of electro-plating, 346; photography 346; gun-cotton, 346; chloroform, 346; the spectroscope, 346, 347; steam engine, 347; new knowledge is new power, 347, 348; how manufacturers enjoy a benefit from each new discovery, 349; examples, 349; how landowners receive a pecuniary benefit from each new discovery, 350; general practical benefits, 350; how little money has been bestowed on science, 351; the Smithsonian Institution at Washington, 352; original research more difficult in England than it was, 353; Government and Science, 354; the case of Archibald Smith, LL.D., F.R.S., 354; the case of Dr. J. Stanhouse, F.R.S., 354, 355; what should be the relationship between Government and Scientific bodies, 356; the Universities as schools of Science, 356, 357; contrast between the rewards of scientific men and generals, 357; between them and Bishops, 357, 358; the case of Faraday, 358; the inadequate rewards of scientific men, 358; the causes of this, 359; suggestions for remedying this state of things, 360; difficulties, 360; loss to the nation and to scientific men by the present state of things, 360, 361; how the progress of discovery is stopped, 361, 362; why is scientific research not encouraged in England? 362; Science must result from a search after pure truth, 363; the cause of the ignorance of scientific research in England, 363, 364; the Universities and Scientific research, 364; the Germans and scientific research, 364, 365; remedies proposed, 365; further suggestions, 365; local efforts should be made, 366; local laboratories, 366; the ignorance of the country is the great obstacle to any plan, 366; the future of England in the hands of Scientific men, 366

"Seamen, Our," 504—529; present condition of our merchant shipping, 504; sea assurance, 504; Mr. Bright on free competition, 505; paternal Government, 505; the object of the present paper, 506; table of wrecks, 507; extracts from the Lifeboat, and Board of Trade Report, 507, 508; further table of wrecks and losses, 508; the process of insuring, 509; how it is effected, 509, 510; further

explanations, 510, 511; the demoralisation which attends such a business, 511; proposals for improving the business of underwriters, 512; the risks and liabilities of shipowners, 513; dishonesty in insuring the freight, 513, 514; "Lloyds Register," 515; the "Liverpool Registry," 515; proposed plan of registration, 515, 516; Mr. Plimsoll's propositions considered, 516; further considerations on Mr. Plimsoll's proposals, 516, 517; Mr. Plimsoll's promised Bill, 518; attitude of the Government towards private Committees of Registration, 519; under-manning, 520; bad stowage, 520; deckloading, 520; deficient engine power in steamers, 520; over-insurance, 520; defective construction, 520; Mr. Plimsoll on "devils" or sham bolts, 521; Mr. Plimsoll on over-loading, 521, 522; petition of the Chamber of Commerce of Newcastle-on-Tyne and Gateshead, 523; the assertion of Mr. W. W. Rundell, of Liverpool, 523, 524; adequacy of ground tackle, 524; the morals of the forecastle, 525; government system of registration, 525; the debate on Mr. Plimsoll's motion, March 4th, 526; observations of the Right Hon. the President of the Board of Trade, 527; comments on, 527, 528; the character, ability and completeness of Mr. Plimsoll's work, "Our Seamen," 529

Secchi, P. A., "Die Sonne," herausgegeben durch Dr. H. Schellen, 284
Seegen, Dr., "Der Diabetes Mellitus," 604
Septuagenarian, "The Problem of the World and the Church Reconsidered, in Three Letters to a Friend," 569
Sherring, Rev. M. A., M.A., "Hindu Tribes and Castes as represented in Benares," 317
Shipley, Orby, M.A., "Ecclesiastical Reform. Eight Essays, by Various Writers." Edited by, 560
Sidgwick, A., "Scenes from Euripides," 620
Simcox, Theodor, "Aus Altrömischer Zeit. Culturbilder," 641
Skeat, Rev. Walter, M.A., "Specimens of Early English," by, and the Rev. Richard Morris, LL.D., 338
Smith, Rev. Barnard, M.A., "Easy Lessons in Arithmetic, combining Exercises in Reading, Writing, Spelling, and Dictation," 283

Smith, R. Prowde, B.A., "Latin Prose Exercises," 335
—— Dr. W., "A Primary History of Britain," 620
Sophokles, 1—88; Sophokles and English scholarship, 1; the impression about him, 1, 2; require loving and leisurely attention, 2; his the highest art, 2; Professor Plumptre's version and merits, 2; why the average reader will fail to appreciate Sophokles by it, 2, 3; the standard of the Athenian intellect, 2; other guides and introductions to Sophokles, 3; the first trilogy of Sophokles, 3; general state of Athens at the time, 3; the *Triptolemus*, 3, 4; victory of, 4; Sophokles a favourite actor, 2; the Choragus, 5; parentage and family of Sophokles, 5; his early life 5; the morality and leading ideas of the Æschylean drama, 6; analysis and explanation of, 6, 7; the advance made by Sophokles, 7; separation of author and actor, 7; introduction of the third actor, 7; his mode of treating the subject, 8; events in Greece, 8; the *Antigone*, 8; events at the time of its production, 9; its plot, 9, 10; the character of Antigone, 10, 11; Ismene, Kreon, Hæmon, 11; the chorus in the *Antigone*, 11, 12; Sophokles as statesman and general, 12; the *Œdipus Rex*, 12; its outlines, 13; internal evidence as to its date, 14; the modern tone of the choruses, 15; its failure, and probable reason, 15; the *Œdipus at Kolonus*, 16; its plot, 16; its date, 17; the beauty of its choruses, 18; the *Elektra*, 19; plot of, 19, 20; contrasted with the Æschylean trilogy, 20; character of Elektra, 20; the *Ajax*, 21; sketch of, 22; its Shakspearian qualities, 23; breathes of the sea, 23; the *Philoktetes*, 24; character of Philoktetes, 24, 25; the *Trachiniæ*, 25; plot of, 26; criticisms on the play, 26; its chief beauties, 26, 27; the last years of Sophokles, 27; his wife and son, 28; his religious views, 28; examples from the *Elektra*, 28; the *Œdipus Rex*, 29; the moral views of Sophokles and Æschylus contrasted, 29; examples of their teaching, 30; general summary of the teaching of Sophokles, 30, 31; the spiritual teaching of Sophokles, 31; his views on the immortality of the soul, 31; his idea of duty, 32; his general religious code, 32; Lessing's remarks on, 32;

his private character, 33; Sophokles and Goethe, 33, 34; remarks on Jebb's and Campbell's editions of Sophokles, 34, 35, 36; on the irony of Sophokles, 35, 36; the two editions compared, 36
Statham, Reginald F., "From Old to New. A Sketch of the Present Religious Position," 242
—— "The Social Growths of the Nineteenth Century: an Essay on the Science of Sociology," 267
Stirling, James Hutchinson, "Lectures on the Philosophy of Law," 578
Stockmar, Baron, Irresponsible Ministers, 472—503; character of the *Memoirs of Baron Stockmar*, 472; Stockmar's position in England, 473; the Queen's opinion of Stockmar, 474; King Leopold's, Lord Melbourne's, Lord Palmerston's, Lord Aberdeen's opinions of Stockmar, 473; Stockmar's opinion of Earl Derby, Earl Russell, and Sir Robert Peel, 474, 475; Professor Müller on Stockmar's two political ideals, 475; objections to Stockmar's position, 476; Stockmar's early life, 477; his acquaintance and opinion of the Duke of Wellington, 477, 478; illustrations of Wellington's character, 478, 479; "Wellington and Polignac," 479; Stockmar's estimate of Peel, 480; Peel on socialism, 480; Lord Palmerston on the debts of the King of Belgium, 480, 481; Stockmar and the Whigs immediately after 1832, 481; further intrigues, 482; memorandum by Lord Palmerston, 483; another extract, 483; memorandum by William IV., 484; analysis of, 485; further extracts, 486, 487; the Peel-Wellington Ministry, 487; ministerial responsibility, 488, 489; Stockmar's position on the Queen's accession, 489; his situation at the English Court, 489, 490; Stockmar and Melbourne, 490; Stockmar's anomalous position, 490, 491; Stockmar from 1836 to 1840, 491; Stockmar and the Queen's marriage, 492; subsequent events, position and salary of Prince Albert, 492; Stockmar on Peel in 1844, 493; Stockmar on the position and status of Prince Albert, 494; criticism on, 495; Stockmar's aversion to parliamentary government, 496; further examples of, 497; what would have been the result of his policy, 497, 498; Lowe's opinion as to the improvement of the House of

Commons, since the first Reform Bill, 498 ; Stockmar's great object, 498, 499 ; Stockmar on Palmerston, 499 ; his further comments and criticisms on Palmerston, 500 ; on the Russian war, 500, 501 ; Sir Colin Campbell and Prince Albert, 501 ; general observations on Stockmar's career and policy, 502, 503 ; the contemptible position which Stockmar after all occupied, 503 ; its punishment, 503

"Stockmar, Baron, Memoirs of," by his Son, Baron E. von Stockmar. Edited by F. Max Müller, 307

Stowe, A., "Times and Places ; or, Our History," 325

Stormonth, Rev. James, "The School Etymological Dictionary and Word Book," 338

Strahan, Alexander, "Norman Macleod," 618

Street, Rev. B., B.A., "The Restoration of Paths to Dwell In. Essays on the Re-editing and Interpretation of the Old Testament Scriptures," 256

Stretton, Hesba. "The Doctor's Dilemma," 327

Student, Old, "Leaves from my Writing Desk ; being Tracts on the Question, What do we Know ?" 261

Symmonds, John Addington, "An Introduction to the Study of Dante," 533

Tait, Professor P. G., "Elements of Natural Philosophy," by, and Sir W. Thomson, 593

Taylor, Meadows, Col., "Seeta," 627

Tennyson, Alfred, D.C.L., Poet Laureate, "Gareth and Lynette," 326

———— "The Works of," 338

"Thief, the Insidious. A Tale for Humble Folk," 324

Thom, John Hamilton, "Letters of John James Taylor, B.A., 313

Thompson, C. W., "The Depths of the Sea," 599

Thornton, W. T., "Old Fashioned Ethics and Common Sense Metaphysics," 571

"Thoughts on Recent Scientific Conclusions, and their Relations to Religion," 557

Thudicum, J. L. W., M.D., "A Manual of Chemical Physiology," 298

Tibbits, Dr. Herbert, "Handbook of Medical Electricity," 603

Tiele, C. P., "Vergelijkende Geschiedenis van de Egyptische en Mesopotamische Godsdiensten," 238

Travers, Mar, "The Spinsters of Blatchington," 324

Trench, Richard Chenevix, Archbishop of Dublin, "Gustavus Adolphus in Germany, and other Lectures on the Thirty Years' War," 315

Tulloch, John, D.D., "Rational Theology and Christian Philosophy in England in the Seventeenth Century," 562

Tyndall, John, "Contribution to Molecular Physics in the Domain Heat," 236

———— "The Forms of Water in Clouds and Rivers, Ice and Glaciers," 287

Tytler, C. C. Fraser, "Margaret," 322

Upton, William, B.A., "The Circle Squared," 597

Vámbéry, Arminius, "History of Bokhara, from the Earliest Period down to the Present," 608

Venetian Painting, 389—403 ; in what way Venice was fitted for the complete development of the Renaissance, 389 ; its streets and architecture, 389 ; its material wealth and pomp, 389 ; its situation by the sea, 389, 390 ; Shelley's description of a Venetian sunset in "Julian and Maddalo," 390, 391 ; extract from a letter by Pietro Aretino to Titian describing a Venetian sunset, 391 ; the side of the Renaissance which Venice represented, 392 ; its contrast with Florence, 592 ; the Ducal Palace at Venice, 592 ; description of, 393, 394 ; commencement of the Venetian School of painting, 391 ; Gian Bellini, 395 ; his colouring, 396 ; Giorgione, 597 ; Tintoretto, 597 ; Veronese, 599 ; his style and art described, 339 ; Tintoretto's style, 400 ; his marriage of Bacchus and Ariadne, 401 ; Titian, 402 ; his Assumption of the Madonna, 402 ; art completely emancipated from servile obedience to ecclesiastical tradition at Venice, 403 ; the spirit of Humanity in the Venetian painter, 403

Verne, Jules, "Twenty Thousand Leagues under the Sea," 341

"Victoria, Glimpses of Life In," by A Resident, 590

"Vigilans," "Nonconformists and their Rights as Citizens," 576

Virchow, Rodolph, "Sammlung gemeinverständlicher wissenschaftlicher Vorträge," 595

Waldensvag, Dr. L., "Die locale Behandlung d. Krankheiten d, Ath-mosysorgane," 603

Wallace, Alfred Wallace, "Contributions to the Theory of Natural Selection," 291

Wellington, F. M., the Duke, K.G., "Supplementary Dispatches of, &c., &c." Edited by his son, 317

Wicks, Frederick, "The British Constitution and Government," 279

Wilberforce, Right Rev. S., D.D., "Faith and Free Thought," with a Preface by, 553

Wille, E. de, "Johannes Olaf," 624

Williams, Rowland, D.D., "Psalms and Litanies, Counsels and Collects for Devout Persons," 255

——— Howard, "Æthologia Anglica," 628

Willigk, Erwin, "Lehrbuch der anorganischen Chemie, 595

Wolf, Max, "Das Evangelium Johannes in seiner Bedeutung für Wissenschaft und Glauben," 251

——— Rudolph, "Handbuch der Mathematik,".288

"Women, Married, Fifth Annual Report of the Executive Committee for Amending the Law with respect to the Property of," 268

Wood, Andrew, M.D., F.R.S., "The Epistles and Art of Poetry of Horace." Translated into English Metre, 336

Woltmann, Dr. Alfred, "Die Baugeschichte Berlins bis auf die Gegenwart," 638

Wüllner, Dr. Adolph, "Lehrbuch der Experimentalphysik," 591

"YARNDALE," An Unsensational Story, 320

Yeats, John, LL.D., "The Natural History of the Raw Materials of Commerce," 583

——— "The Technical History of Commerce," 583

——— "The Growth and Vicissitudes of Commerce," &c., 583

——— "A Manual of Recent and Existing Commerce," 583

Yerworth, Horace, "Poems of the Passions," 619

Youmans, Eliza A., "The First Book of Botany," 600

Young, William, "Picturesque Architectural Studies," 842

ZIMMERN, Helen, "Stories in Precious Stones," 627

www.ingramcontent.com/pod-product-compliance
Lightning Source LLC
Chambersburg PA
CBHW021929110726
47901CB00003B/769